John Richard Houlding

Australian Tales, and Sketches From Real Life

John Richard Houlding

Australian Tales, and Sketches From Real Life

ISBN/EAN: 9783337011499

Printed in Europe, USA, Canada, Australia, Japan

Cover: Foto ©Andreas Hilbeck / pixelio.de

More available books at **www.hansebooks.com**

AND

SKETCHES FROM REAL LIFE.

BY

OLD BOOMERANG,

AUTHOR OF

"AUSTRALIAN CAPERS; OR, CHRISTOPHER COCKLE'S COLONIAL
EXPERIENCE," &c., &c.

LONDON:
SAMPSON LOW, SON, AND MARSTON.
SYDNEY: JOHN L. SHERRIFF.
MELBOURNE: GEORGE ROBERTSON.
HOBART TOWN: WALSH AND SONS.
1868.

CONTENTS.

PREFACE.

Most of the following tales and sketches have appeared in the "Sydney Mail;" and I have good reason to believe that they have been favourably received by thousands of subscribers to that influential newspaper. In publishing them in a volume, I am yielding to the persuasion of many kind friends, who have expressed their belief that they will be well received, and be useful.

I have spent much time in altering and improving all the articles; and they will be fresh to my old readers. The fact of the articles having appeared in the columns of the "Sydney Mail," will be a sufficient guarantee to parents, that they need not scruple to place the volume in the hands of their children. I will only add, that there is nothing controversial or sectarian in it; and I have used my utmost efforts to make it both amusing and instructive. English readers will find many phases of Australian life depicted; for which I claim this merit, that their accuracy may be relied on.

The extensive circulation of my recent work, " Australian Capers," (see appendix,) encourages me to hope that this volume will meet with a favourable reception ; not only from my many friends in Australia, but also in Great Britain.

OLD BOOMERANG.

Darlinghurst, Sydney, N.S.W.
    August 31, 1867.

AUSTRALIAN TALES;

OR,

SKETCHES FROM REAL LIFE.

MR. PHIGGS AND HIS CHRISTMAS BREAKFAST.

A SEASONABLE STORY.

"GOODNESS me, Mr. Phiggs, be rational, there's a dear! Only fancy; boiled fowls smothered in rice, currants, and onions; or curried nonsense, fiery as red-hot cinders, for friends coming hungry and squeamish off a steamboat, and on a Christmas morning too! You surely must be joking! But I tell you seriously, I cannot cook an Indian breakfast, so pray do not miscalculate my skill; and I'm sure Sally would as soon consent to cook a horse's head. I dislike such peppery messes at any time; but at this special season for old English cheer, I particularly disapprove of foreign trumperies on my table. Consider again, Jacob, and don't perplex me at this critical time, there's a good man."

"Patience, Dolly," said Mr. Phiggs, with a smile. "It is plain that you know very little about Oriental fare, or you would not speak so disparagingly of it. When I proposed to give our expected guests an Indian breakfast, I did not suppose that you would cook it. Not at all. But if you will tolerate my little whim, for once and away, I shall esteem it a favour. I have a strong desire to try my skill in cookery by way of experiment; and if you will allow me the undisturbed use of the kitchen and the cooking utensils to-morrow morning, I think I shall be able to remove your prejudices against foreign messes, as you call them. I breakfasted with Captain Carraway the last time I was in Sydney, and such a dainty meal (prepared under his own supervision) I never before partook of. I wished you had

1

been there to enjoy it with me, though I know you always advocate simple diet. I procured from the Captain plain written directions for making veal olives, curried kidneys, pillaued chicken, savoury omelettes, milk coffee, cream potatoes, and sundry other exquisite dishes (from recipes furnished to him by Rajah Mulleegrubbee's chief cook); and as some of our oldest friends are coming to spend Christmas with us, I should like to surprise them with something out of the common way, and of my own preparation. Friend Samson will assist me in the kitchen; and, as I do not wish to trouble you, or either of your servants, you can lie in bed an hour later than usual, and the cook can go for a morning walk if she likes. You, of course, can cater for the Christmas dinner, which is the grand social event of the year, but do let me have the pleasure of providing the breakfast, just to see what I can do. Now, don't object, Dolly, there's a duck;" added Mr. Phiggs, coaxingly kissing his loving wife, who during his explanation had sat thoughtfully pondering how she could humour her worthy spouse's odd fancy without upsetting all her domestic arrangements for the day, which were rather more onerous than usual, considering that she was expecting eight or nine friends from Sydney by the next morning's steamer, to spend a merry Christmas with her and her family.

In anticipation of the reader's inquiry, " Who are Mr. and Mrs. Phiggs?" I briefly explain that they were a crummy old couple, brimful of human kindness, who lived in a quiet little sea-side town, not a hundred miles from Sydney, and were well to do in the world. They were decidedly not fashionable folks, but they liked to entertain their friends in a cozy, homely style, which all true lovers of comfort appreciate, and they often welcomed visitors beneath their hospitable roof, and used their utmost efforts to make them feel at home. Although they had been many years in the colony, their early imbibed tastes for old English customs were as fresh as ever. Foremost among the endearing remembrances of their loved native land was Christmas-tide, with its special family reunions, its joyous festivities, and peculiar good fare. Mr. and Mrs. Phiggs loved to keep up Christmas Day's social rites, if they were less zealous of the more hallowed observances of the time, of which, however, they were not wholly unmindful; and while all within their own household were regaled with seasonable good cheer, they took care that the homes of their poor neighbours were supplied with material comforts, for rejoicing the hearts of the inmates; thus testifying their Christian love and good will towards all men, free from narrow prejudices against country, colour, or creed. I trust there are thousands of good souls in this land who will, at this auspicious season, especially remember their duty, and try to gladden the hearts of their needy neighbours around them, by dispensing with an ungrudging heart, a portion of the good things with which kind Providence has entrusted them.

I would not have my reader suppose that Mrs. Phiggs was unreasonably tenacious of her domestic prerogatives, or that she was at all inclined to exercise an arbitrary dominion over her good husband's will. Far from it. She was the most ductile little wife in the district; one who neither snapped nor sulked, and who never encroached beyond her own strict line of duty on her husband's right of rule. But on the present occasion she foresaw a houseful of troubles and vexations attendant on his odd whim; not the least of which was the risk of rousing the fiery spirit of Sally Skewers, who, cook-like, was very jealous of undue interference in her department, and whose services were especially necessary on that day to prepare a suitable dinner for the unusual number of guests who were expected. Mrs. Phiggs also lacked confidence in her husband's skill in culinary matters. She did not really believe him capable of cooking a potato, or a red herring, for he had never manifested the least talent in that way; and as for his plainly-written recipes, on which he placed so much reliance, she well knew that such things are generally of not much more practical use than the written directions of a conjurer, as to the safest method of swallowing a sword, or a bundle of paper-hangings; and she dreaded the failure of his projects at a time when such a mishap would be particularly inconvenient. She urged her objections in her usual out-spoken, though good-tempered manner; but Mr. Phiggs so pertinaciously clung to his crotchet, and pleaded his cause with so much tact, that she at last, like a good pliant wife, withdrew her opposition; though, at the same time, she laughingly predicted that " he would make a pretty mess of it." To that monition Mr. Phiggs nodded his head sagaciously, and replied, " Wait a bit, Dolly; I believe I shall astonish you, and receive the commendations of all our company."

After despatching Samson to various tradesmen in the town for the extra provisions required, and which were to be at the kitchen door at peep of day, Mr. Phiggs sat down to study his chart—as he called it—the plain directions for cooking an Indian breakfast, which he had received from Captain Carraway, and which seemed to Mr. Phiggs as simple as a little boy's " Reading Made Easy."

An hour before daylight next morning, Mr. Phiggs crept quietly out of bed, as he supposed, without awakening his wife ; but had the bedroom lamp burned a little brighter he would have seen the tassels on the curtains dancing in sympathy with the merry mood of Mrs. Phiggs, who was making the bedstead shake with her smothered laughter, at the idea of the " pretty mess " she would have for breakfast.

Friend Samson turned out of bed at the first word of command, and very soon he had kindled a fire in the old-fashioned kitchen range, large enough to roast a calf.

Punctually at the prescribed time came the milkman with a large can of extra milk and a basket of eggs ; other tradesmen speedily followed with various articles ordered on the previous night, and the dresser was soon strewed with a strange collection of crude material for the feast.   The butcher brought the kidneys all correct, but " was very sorry the thunderstorm in the night had spoilt his veal, so he had brought a nice bit of tender beef instead."   That was annoying certainly, for the veal olives were intended to form the leading triumph ; however, Mr. Phiggs promptly decided upon making some savoury sausage-cakes instead ; so Samson set to work with an axe, and soon the house began to vibrate with his vigorous blows as he chopped up the beef into sausage-meat, and at the same time chopped the kitchen-table into corduroy grooves and ridges, the cedar chips nicely mixing with the meat by way of seasoning.

The noise of Samson's axe awoke Sally Skewers, as it might have done if Sally had been sleeping in the house on the opposite side of the street ; and although she had been nervously apprised by her mistress on the previous night of what was to take place in the kitchen the next morning—and notwithstanding she had given her mistress a sort of sulky promise that she would not interfere with her master's whimsies for once, seeing her nice, smooth table greased and cut up in that savage style was too severe a trial for her forbearance ; so out she came, half-dressed, and both Mr. Phiggs and Samson were positively electrified by the fiery torrent of temper which she poured forth. "Molly-coddles" and "fishfags" were the mildest epithets she applied to them, and there they stood gazing at each other, as if deciding whether it was not their safest course to flee from their unexpected assailant. They, however, stood their ground like men, and tried, though in vain, to soothe Sally, by promising to vacate the kitchen in two hours at the farthest. After exhausting her stock of expletives, she flung a chopping board on Samson's toes, and a chopping knife on to the table, then bounced into her bedroom again, from whence she soon afterwards re-issued in her holiday frock, her hat and feather, and dove-coloured boots. With a passing anathema on her dirty pots and kettles, and a glance at her master and Samson, fierce enough to frizzle them both, she flung herself out of the kitchen, and slammed the door with a bang like a great gun.

"I hope she won't come back till we have finished our business," said Mr. Phiggs, with his eyes full of tears, as he handed some chopped onions to Samson to mix with his sausage-meat. "I had no idea that Sally had such a tongue in her head, she fairly frightened me. I'm very glad she is gone out for a walk."

"So am I," said Samson ; "I don't like her. She has nearly knocked my little toe off with this chopping board. I am sorry I have spoilt the table though ; but I didn't see the board and mincing knife before."

"Never mind the table," said Mr. Phiggs, "that can be mended to-morrow. Now then, Sam, if you have done the sausages, just smash up these potatoes ; I think they are boiled enough ; and mix—let me see (consulting his chart)—yes, mix a quart of new milk, and beat all up fine with a fork ; that's the way to make cream potatoes. Now go to work, while I see after the curried kidneys. Stop, hand me another saucepan and a long spoon."

When she heard Sally's violent tirade, and her noisy exit from the house, Mrs. Phiggs thought it was time for her to bestir herself ; so she got up accordingly ; and first of all quietly peeped into the kitchen, when the sight she beheld was anything but exhilarating on a merry Christmas morning. There was Mr. Phiggs, his face as red as the warming pan, against the wall, puffing and perspiring before an enormous fire, stirring a saucepanful of rice, which she judged

by its odour had been allowed to burn. The floor was garnished with grease, onion parings, cinders, egg shells, and a
variety of other refuse, whilst cooking utensils and dishes of
all sorts and sizes littered the place in every direction.
Every saucepan and kettle in the kitchen had been brought
into use, and the range was covered with them. The fryingpan, filled with curried kidneys, was on a chair, the long
handle of the pan protruding through a broken window-pane,
and the sooty coffee-pot, with the spout burnt off, was
placed on the dresser shelf. Samson was sitting on the
floor with a saucepanful of potatoes between his knees,
which he was actively stirring with a toasting fork, and
smoking a cigar at the same time.

"Now, then, Sam, let us consider," said Mr. Phiggs,
again consulting his chart ; "I think those potatoes will do
now. Dear, dear !" he added, after a short pause, "I see
we have made an annoying blunder ; the quart of new milk
should have been boiling hot. What a nuisance ! the cream
potatoes will be as cold as cream ice before they are dished.
However, it can't be helped now ; we must try if we can
warm them up again. Turn them into that pie-dish, and
put them on the hob. Look alive, there's a good fellow !"

" Don't you think they would have looked nicer if they
had been peeled before we made cream of them ?" asked
Sam.

"Peeled, to be sure ! why what a precious gowk you
must be not to have done that without my telling you,"
said Mr. Phiggs, with considerable warmth of temper.
" Who the dickens would have thought of smashing potatoes
with the skins on but a pig with his tusks or a donkey with
his hoofs ?"

Stung by that severe reproof, Samson rose to his feet in
a moment, and sharply retorted upon Mr. Phiggs, in the
attitude of a pugilist. A stormy altercation ensued, and
ended in Samson's donning his coat, and leaving the kitchen
to the sole occupancy of his half-bewildered friend, who had
long since began to wish his Indian breakfast at the bottom
of the Indian Ocean.

Mrs. Phiggs was aware of her husband's dilemma, and
would willingly have gone to his aid, as well for his own
sake as for the good order and credit of her house ; but she
knew his disposition too well to interfere with him at such
an exciting time ; so, like a wise little woman, she kept

aloof, but at the same time actively exerted herself with her other servant in preparing the breakfast-room, as far as she could, for her coming guests, whom she expected very soon, as the steamer had been signalled for some time. She once or twice felt a quizzical disposition to peep into the kitchen, and wish Jacob a merry Christmas, but pity for him would not allow her to tease him at a time when he was almost overwhelmed with perplexity.

"Let me see," soliloquised Mr. Phiggs, putting on his spectacles, "let me see ; one pound of best Mocha coffee, boiled down to a quart, and put into a gallon and a quarter of boiling milk. Yes, that's all right ; there's the milk, and here's the coffee ; I suppose I had better mix them at once." In went the coffee, grounds and all, into the boiling milk, and when too late to remedy it, Mr. Phiggs, to his grief, discovered that he should have strained and fined the coffee first ; for the mixture looked like brown paint, or a road puddle after a heavy shower.

"Everything is going against me this morning," grumbled he, while he turned the curried kidneys into a soup tureen, and put them on the hob to keep warm ; then wiped out the frying-pan and put it over the fire, with the handle poised on the back of a chair. "Now for the omelettes," he muttered, and again referred to his instructions. " Put half a pound of fresh butter into a clean frying-pan, then beat up two dozen eggs, mix an onion chopped fine, and a small bit of sage, fry quickly, and serve up hot." "All right ; that's plain enough any way," he continued, as he put a lump of butter into the red hot pan, which frizzled and sputtered, and slightly scalded his face. "Botheration take the breakfast," he pettishly exclaimed for the tenth time. "Now for the eggs. Well, well ! I declare that stupid fellow Samson has not half beaten them ; I should like to beat his head with this gravy spoon."

"My dear ! our company are coming up the street," said Mrs. Phiggs, peeping into the kitchen. " Is the breakfast ready, Jacob ?"

"Dear me, are they coming so soon ?—that's vexing. I can't get breakfast ready in a minute less than half an hour," said Mr. Phiggs, wiping his heated brow with a smutty towel. "I say, Dolly, send in Jane for a little while, there's a good soul, just to clear the kitchen a bit ; I'm expecting Sally back every minute, and if she catches me here she

will very likely storm my ears off. I am getting on delightfully, only that blundering fellow Samson has — hallo !
ow ! fire ! fire ! Good gracious, Dolly ! send for help —
quick, hoo !" roared Mr. Phiggs, at that instant hopping
about the kitchen with his left foot in his right hand, while
his face expressed terror and torment, and his groans were
heard above the roaring of the fire in the chimney.   In
turning round hastily, with a basinful of eggs in one hand
and a fork in the other, he had trodden on a lump of suet,
slipped down, and spilt the eggs all over him. In falling he
had struck the handle of the frying-pan, and tipped the half
pound of fresh butter into the fire, except a small part,
which had fallen into his left slipper, and set him dancing
like an insane harlequin.

The attempt to describe the uproar and confusion that
ensued would be altogether too much for me.   Just as the
company were walking up to the door, expecting a warm
reception from the Phiggses, as usual, a stream of fire shot up
from the kitchen chimney, high above the roof of the house,
and the screams of Mrs. Phiggs and Jane, the housemaid,
added to the roaring of Mr. Phiggs, were, to say the least,
astounding.   Fortunately it happened that one of their
guests was a member of the Sydney fire brigade, so he at
once mounted to the roof of the house through a dormer
window, and being furnished with buckets of water by some
of the excited neighbours, he poured a copious supply down
the blazing flue, and soon put out the fire ; but at the same
time he put the finishing touch to Mr. Phiggs's Indian
breakfast by smothering everything with soot, making
all the dainty dishes on the hobs as black as an Indian's
woolly head, and turning the kitchen into a mimic Black
Sea.

Mr. Phiggs's guests were all old friends, and jovial ones
too ; and that they were not disposed to desert a brother in
his distress was evident from their all flocking into the kitchen to see their unlucky host, and to cheer him up with
" compliments of the season."   There he sat, covered with
soot, egg sauce, and melted butter, nursing his basted foot,
and surrounded by a confused collection of cooking tools
and little islands of soot, in a sea of grimy water. But
despite his sores and sorrows he could not but join in the
uproarious bursts of laughter, which nearly split the
shingles above his head, as the cause of his mishaps was ex-

plained to the visitors by his waggish little wife, whose eyes were overflowing with fun.

A breakfast was extemporised, to which the guests soon afterwards sat down, headed by Mr. Phiggs, who had cleansed himself, and applied a chalk plaster to his sore foot (which, by the way, is an excellent remedy for scalds or burns), and many were the jokes passed upon his morning's exploits by his fun-loving friends, at which none laughed more heartily than did the good-humoured host himself.

After breakfast Mr. Phiggs put on his hat and went out in search of Samson and Sally, to offer the *amende honorable*, while Jane ran for Mrs. Scrubb, the charwoman, and set her to work to clear the kitchen. Samson was fishing on the wharf, and looking as sullen as a boy in a dunce's cap ; but Mr. Phiggs's frank apology soon restored him to good humour, and he returned to the house laughing immoderately. Sally was sitting in her mother's parlour, crying, and vowing she would never enter old Phiggs's kitchen again, when her humbled master entered. His kind, coaxing words, and peace offering of a new shawl for a Christmas-box, very soon altered her views, and half-an-hour afterwards Sally was stuffing a goose at her damaged table, with her face all over broad grins, while old Mrs. Scrubb was clearing away the wreck like an able seaman.

Mr. Phiggs's dogs, Pincher and Snap, had a dainty Christmas breakfast. They evidently appreciated the pillaued chicken, although it was half raw ; they enjoyed the cream potatoes too, but declined to eat the sausage cakes, possibly because Samson had accidentally put a double quantity of cayenne into them.

And Mr. Phiggs's guests had a dainty Christmas dinner, although it was an hour later than usual. Heartily they enjoyed their good cheer and each other's cheerful society. They were merry and wise, so of course they spent a happy Christmas ; such a happy Christmas as I most cordially wish to all my friends, and my enemies too.

SPEAKING A WORD IN SEASON.

SOME time ago I was told an amusing story about a good old man, who, in his labours of love, occasionally shewed more zeal than discretion. I do not vouch for the authenticity of the incident, but as it may convey a useful moral to other over-zealous workers, I will quote it with a few fanciful variations.

" There once lived a barber, I cannot tell where, but it was in some populous neighbourhood. He was a good, simple-minded man, and feeling in his heart that joy and peace which all true believers feel, he was desirous that his neighbours should share in the happiness he had found ' without money and without price,' and which is as free for the poor as for the greatest personages upon earth. To carry his good desires into operation, the barber resolved upon ' speaking a word in season' to every customer who patronised his ' easy shaving shop'—a praiseworthy resolution certainly—but one requiring much judgment in its execution. One day a crabbed looking old gentleman walked into the shop, and after taking off his hat, coat, and cravat, seated himself in a chair, and gruffly intimated that he wanted to be shaved. The barber bowed politely as usual, placed a napkin under his customer's chin, and began to ply the lather brush about his face in true tonsoric style. Meanwhile, the good barber was mentally debating on the most effective mode of putting the all-important questions to his customer, as to the state of his mind, and whether he had a good hope of heaven. But his visage was so grim, and his demeanour so uninviting, that the barber's courage almost failed him ; so, to sharpen it up, he began to strop his razor, and while doing so, a thought suddenly suggested itself to his mind, that he had better not risk offending a strange customer by abruptly putting questions to him upon so solemn and delicate a subject. ' Ah, that's the devil, but I'll settle him,' muttered the barber to himself, though just loud enough for his lathered customer to overhear ; and not knowing that the zealous shaver's soliloquy had reference to the supposed inward suggestion of Satan to neglect his duty, the old man began to sit uneasily, under the impression that the barber was going mad. Presently, as if he had sufficiently sharpened himself and his razor too, he stood before his palpitating customer, with the blade of the razor at right angles with its handle, and taking hold of his nose, in order to get a fair scrape at the surface beneath the chin, asked in a solemn tone, and with a searching gaze, 'My friend, are you prepared to die ?'

" 'O good lack ! murder ! murder !' roared the old gentleman, starting up, overturning his chair, and rushing out of the shop in the utmost consternation, closely followed by the poor bewildered barber, razor in hand, vainly endeavouring to explain that he was only anxious about the safety of his soul.

" 'Murder ! police ! help !' shrieked the half frantic old gentleman, as he ran down the street, minus his hat and coat, with the napkin about his neck, and his face bedaubed with soap. 'Hoo-o ! for gracious sake, catch him somebody ; he is going to cut my throat.'

" 'I tell you I have no idea of cutting your throat, my good friend,' gasped the barber, close behind his runaway customer ; 'I only wanted to——'

" ' Whoa !' cried a brewer's drayman, putting one of his huge feet before the barber and tripping him up, then sitting upon him kept him down until several policemen arrived, took away his razor, and regardless of his loud attempts to explain his pious motives, hurried him away to the watch-house."

*　　*　　*　　*　　*　　*

As I premised, I am not sure that the foregoing story is veritable, still, it exemplifies the indiscriminate zeal of many good-meaning Christians in the world, who sadly lack tact and judgment to direct their monitory efforts, who—like the barber—are apt to mistake the promptings of common sense for the suggestions of the evil one, and whose commendable desires to do good are often thwarted by the ill-timed or bungling way in which they execute them.

"Shall we try and speak a word in season to any one we see this morning ?" asked a rather eccentric friend, who was riding with me one day towards some of the wharves in Sydney, to go on board of a ship.

"Yes ; certainly," I replied. "That is an everyday

duty; but we must be careful that our words are seasonable, or they may do harm instead of good."

Soon afterwards we ascended the side of a ship, and stood upon the deck. The mate was near the main hatchway, with his cargo book in his hand, superintending the bustling operation of taking in goods of various kinds. He stepped up and politely accosted us, when my zealous little friend held his hand, and looking into his face with a peculiar smile, kindly enquired after the condition of his soul.

The mate looked rather confused, and being anxious to see the mark on a case which was then being lowered into the hold, he returned a hurried but civil answer, and began to make another entry in his cargo book, with something like a curl about his mouth, as if he had just eaten a green gooseberry.

"I don't think that was speaking a word in season," I quietly remarked to my friend, as we seated ourselves on a skylight; "quite the contrary; I think it was decidedly out of season, and may have the effect of making that man think unfavourably of religion, or that those who profess it are troublesome bores. It was very unlikely that he would keep his crew standing idle, while he told you his religious experience before them; but had he been sitting quietly on the booms smoking his after-dinner pipe, your question might not have been inopportune, though even then, I think, it would have been more effective if put in a less direct form. You would be more likely to impress a sailor with a few good words judiciously infused into your cheerful conversation during an hour's walk with him on deck in the middle watch on a quiet night, than you would by preaching to him while he is putting the ship about, or hauling up the main-sail in a squall."

The same principle is applicable to landsmen as well as sailors. Suitable times must be selected for speaking good words, otherwise your good words may be worse than useless, for, like fruit, they are unpalatable, and sometimes positively unwholesome, when "out of season."

I do not think my reasoning convinced my eccentric —though very worthy—little friend, for he had much to say in favour of his system of "sowing beside all waters," notwithstanding his palpable failure to impress the busy mate with a solemn sense of the important question he had just put to him, with the kindest of motives, though with ill-timed precipitancy.

I could give numberless instances, if necessary, of similar lack of judgment, exhibited by well-intentioned persons, which have come under my notice. I have often heard, too, the motives of such persons unjustly impugned, and themselves ridiculed or abused, simply because they failed to make themselves understood by those whom they were kindly endeavouring to benefit. While I have of course deprecated such ingratitude, I have not been surprised at it, and could not but lament that the subjects of it had not, in addition to their other studies, studied human nature a little more.

Few readers will be likely to mistake the meaning of my remarks. It is far, indeed, from my wish to discourage any humble-minded person from endeavouring to comfort or edify his needy fellow creatures around him ; on the contrary, I would encourage him in every way in my power. I simply wish to urge the policy of studying to do good in the most effectual way, and prevent good from being spoken evil of.

WILL HE KICK?

"Will he kick?" nervously enquired Mr. Bradbury Spriggs, a spruce little city friend, who was on a visit to my house, as he prepared to mount my favourite hack.

"Oh dear, no," I replied, "he's quiet as an old cow."

"He'll bear the spurs, then, I suppose."

"Why, yes," I replied, honestly, "he is livelier for a slight touch of the spur now and then. I always let him know that I have them on, though it is very seldom I use them, for I think it is cruelty and ingratitude, drumming a poor beast's ribs with spurred heels, while he is trudging along under me."

"He doesn't shy, does he?" asked Mr. Spriggs again, as he gathered up his reins, and stuck his legs out straight, to show the fashionable cut of his pantaloons.

"Not he," I replied, somewhat impatiently; "he wouldn't shy if he met a gang of gorillas carrying a turnpike-gate."

"All right; good-bye," said Mr. Spriggs. Away he bounded at a brisk canter; and soon I could catch occasional glimpses of his figure, between the distant trees in the bush, riding like Tam O'Shanter.

In a few hours he returned, looking fatigued, while the perspiration was dropping off my steed, and his bleeding sides showed painful evidences that his rider had given him considerably more than a slight touch of the spur *now and then.*

"He's a spendid animal," remarked Bradbury, with the knowing look of a connoisseur in horse-flesh, as he slowly dismounted. "I never rode a beast I liked better. Such paces! and withal so free and gentle; I found, however, that he required the spur occasionally."

"Humph!" I quietly ejaculated, as I led my panting favourite towards the stable—"rather an equivocal appreciation of your merits, my poor old Jack; but I'll sell you to a knacker before I let that hide-rasper mount you again."

*　　*　　*　　*　　*　　*

It was not a rare occurrence for city friends to pay visits

to my house in those halcyon times.   Residing in a pleasant
and accessible part of the country, I had sometimes more
visitors than I could entertain to my own satisfaction.   As
they usually had a *penchant* for riding, I could not ·but try
to gratify them, though frequently to my own inconvenience
and vexation.   I had a strong objection to lend the horse I
usually rode myself—for having drilled him into paces
which best suited my comfort in travelling, I had a dread
lest casual riders should drill him out of those paces again.
Whenever I could hire a nag for a visitor, I did so; but as
that could not always be done, I sometimes found myself
compelled by courtesy to lend my own hack.

About two years after the foregoing incident Mr. Bradbury Spriggs paid me another visit for a day or two : and
one of his early enquiries was for "the splendid animal
which had carried him twenty-five miles in two hours."

"Ah ! I've sold poor Jack," I replied, with a slight sigh :
"he is now drawing a hawker's cart ; an ignoble occupation
for such a handsome beast as he once was.   I lent him one
day to a friend, who unfortunately threw him down and
broke his knees.   But I have another Jack, in the paddock,
a finer horse than the last one, at least he suits me better,
if he is not such a general favourite with my friends."

"Ah ! I should like to see him," replied Mr. Spriggs,
while his face brightened up, like a boy's who is just going
to have the first spin at his new humming-top.   "Could
you let me have a trot on him for an hour or so ; I haven't
had a ride since the last time I was here."

"Hum ! I'll see," I slowly replied, as I tried to see if I
·could find some honourable excuse for declining to let him
have a trot, having an annoying recollection of his two
hours' gallop on the former occasion.

"Yes—you can have him for an hour, Mr. Spriggs," I at
length replied, "but I hope you will not ride very fast, for
I have to take a long journey to-morrow, and I want Jack
to be pretty fresh."

"Oh, certainly not, I'll not ride him hard ; I'll take care
of him, you may depend on it," replied my excited friend ;
and away he went to his dressing-room, to prepare himself
for the jaunt, while I gave orders for the horse to be saddled
and brought to the door.

In a few minutes out came my city friend, armed with a
hammer-headed whip, and glittering spurs at his heels, and

looking as bold as a bushranger. He was preparing to
mount when I quietly asked, "Will you ride with spurs,
Mr. Spriggs?"

"Ye-e-s," he replied, with some hesitation, and an earnest
glance into my face. "Why, sir, will your horse not bear
them?"

"He does not like them," I replied, which was true
enough; indeed, it would be hard to persuade me there is
a horse on earth that does like them.

"Oh, well, perhaps I had better take them off. I am
glad you told me!" and forthwith he began to unbuckle his
spur leathers.

"Who-o-o-o, Jack," I shouted, as I suddenly snatched at
my horse's bridle, and began to pat his neck, while he of
course retreated a pace or two in surprise. This was observed by my friend, who timidly enquired—

"Does he bolt?"

"I never saw him *positively* bolt," I replied carelessly.
"Who-o-o-o, Jack, stand away from his heels there!" I
shouted to my grinning groom.

"Will he kick?" asked Mr. Spriggs with a very nervous
look, as he took a wide circuit to hand his discarded spurs
to the man.

"Well, I *have* seen him lift his legs," I replied, "but I
don't think——"

"Ah, that's a very dangerous habit; perhaps I had better
not ride him to-day," said Bradbury, who had evidently
made up his mind on the subject.

"Oh, by all means ride him," I replied, "but ride carefully, keep a tolerably tight rein on him, and do not give
him too much of that whip, I'll warrant he'll not run away
with you—who-o-o, Jack, who-o-o!"

"Well, I don't care much about riding to-day," said Mr.
Spriggs; "a—a—the fact is, I am not a very good rider,
and this is a strange animal, if it were the other horse I'd
—no thankee, I won't ride to-day. I'll just take a walk
into the bush, it looks beautiful. I shall enjoy that quite
as much as a ride, much obliged to you."

*   *   *   *   *

The horse was turned into the paddock again, and as he
kicked up his heels with delight, at being freed from the
prospect of a tiresome duty, I could see that my timid

little friend mentally congratulated himself upon his prudent determination, in the full conviction that he had narrowly escaped breaking some of his bones by riding such a vicious brute; whereas poor Jack was one of the steadiest old roadsters in the colony.

*   *   *   *   *   *

I have occasionally seen a pompous official metamphorically spurring a patient subordinate; and have been at once reminded of the cowardly little griffin, who mercilessly overrode my faithful old hack, because he knew Jack would not kick.

A MATRIMONIAL JUGGLER;

OR, MR. TEDDINGTON TROUT AND MISS CHARITY GLIMM.

"WELL that has a *bonâ fide* look certainly," simpered Miss Charity Glimm to herself, as she pored with exulting eyes over an advertisement in the *Herald*. "There is an air of candour, and a gentlemanly style about it, that struck me at first sight as being genuine. I would not for the world reply to a thing of the sort, if I had the least idea that it was a hoax, invented by a party of idiots, as is often the case, merely for the sake of laughing at creatures almost as foolish as themselves. No, I really believe that this is no meaningless joke, but the pure breathings of a refined, manly soul, which is longing for sympathy and comfort, which it cannot find in an ordinary way." As Miss Glimm thus soliloquised, she took up the paper again and deliberately read aloud the following stimulating composition :—

"MATRIMONY.

"The advertiser, who is turned forty-one years of age, of pleasing personal appearance, and easy means, is desirous of forming a matrimonial engagement with a lady of suitable age. Money is not an object, and will by no means counterpoise a lack of the main desiderata, viz., agreeable person, amiable disposition, and domestic acquirements. The most honorable secresy may be relied on. Address, in full confidence, B. O. H., Post Office, Sydney."

The honest reality of the foregoing so impressed Miss Charity, that her appetite for mutton chops became quite inert ; so she sipped a cup of tea, then opened her writing desk, and after two hours' perplexing study she had produced the following note, in time for the eleven o'clock iron receiver :—

"To B. O. H., Post Office, Sydney.
"SIR,—The apparent candour and gentlemanly honesty which pervades every line of your advertisement in this day's *Herald*, induces me to reply to it with the feminine

candour which it deserves. In full confidence that I am not mistaken, I send you herewith my *carte de visite*, which was taken on the first of May last. I was then thirty-seven years of age, and a spinster ; which I am still. I was brought up under the eye of a virtuous aunt, whose only aim in life was to see me grow up thoroughly domesticated. At her death she left me ninety pounds a year for life, and her little brick cottage nicely furnished. It would not become me to say anything which might be called self-praise, so I will simply remark that I believe you would find in me all those qualities which you so feelingly express your desire to gain in a wife. If you think this worthy of a reply, please address, in the first place, to Floy, Post Office, Paddington.

" P.S.—I had almost forgotten to mention that the spot on the left side of the nose, in my *carte*, is the accidental mark of a fly, and the slight squint in the right eye is entirely owing to the artist forcing me to look animated."

Next morning the postman's sharp rat-tat at the door made Charity's heart bound like a football. In another minute she was gazing with throbbing admiration at a *carte de visite* which was enclosed in a scented note, written with rather a tremulous hand, as follows :—

" MY DEAR MADAM,—My pen cannot express the happiness I felt on receipt of your truth-breathing epistle this morning, accompanied by your likeness. As I have carefully studied Lavater, you will perhaps allow me to say, without suspecting me of flattery, that yours is a face which indexes a mind—such a mind as I am sure could appreciate the warm overflow of my soul. I will not stay to write more, for I am impatient for an interview, if your kindness will extend itself so far as to grant it. I enclose my *carte*, and beg to subscribe my real name, as your devoted admirer,

" TEDDINGTON TROUT."

Half an hour afterwards, Charity had posted another note, intimating that she should be happy to see Mr. Trout at his earliest convenience, and then she sat down in her easy chair to study his picture. Whether she took a short nap or not is uncertain ; at any rate, she was still sitting in the chair, fondly gazing at the *carte*, when a rat-tat-tat at the door suddenly brought her down from the top story of a lofty aerial castle, and before she had time to go to her dressing-room to adjust herself, that stupid girl Biddy had shown the gentleman into the parlour. Charity blushed, of course, and nervously apologised for her *deshabille ;* but Mr. Trout put her at her ease in an instant, and with a sweet smile, which displayed a perfect set of teeth, he assured her that he was delighted to find her in unstudied attire, and further, " that it was the charming *naïveté* manifested in her portrait, and in her note too, which had given spurs to his desire to see her, and had induced him to trespass upon her at that unfashionable hour of the day."

At her request he took a seat, then took off a tightly-fitting glove, and passed his hand gently over his hair, which was curly and glossy, and as black as a raven's tail ; with most fascinating whiskers and beard to match, but no moustache, as she was happy to remark. He was rather a genteel figure, though very thin, with a peculiar stoop, which, however, was only to be seen at times, when he appeared abstracted. His putting his hand to his back so frequently, Charity thought was a slight eccentricity, but it could by no means be taken as an indication of weakness, for the unusually bright colour in the parts of his face that were bare, clearly showed the ruddy glow of health. That his legs were curved could not be denied, but that was a trifling defect, which she thought even his handsome beard alone would overbalance. His being " all of a shake," indicated a highly sensitive organisation, and a becoming modesty ; indeed, she concluded that the man who would not shake a little under such circumstances must possess an ossified heart, wholly unimpressible by domestic perfection. Omitting the details of their long interview (during which a mutual confidence had been exhibited, and a satisfactory outline of each other's history had been given), I briefly record, that before the clock struck two their engagement had been ratified by a true lover's kiss ; after which—to the surprise of Biddy—the happy pair sat down to a homely dinner.

I must hurry past the succeeding ten days of active courtship, merely noticing that their admiration for each other hourly increased, and as all needless delay was held to be sheer cruelty, and having neither parents nor guardians to consult, they mutually agreed to be married on New Year's Day. In order to save the unnecessary " fuss of inviting a lot of quizzical friends to their wedding," they decided to go to Newcastle, there to get married in a quiet way, then go to Singleton by rail, to revel in honey moon-shine.

Next Monday morning they joined the seven·o'clock steamer, taking as little luggage with them as possible, to save trouble. The weather was fine and clear, though a strong N.E. breeze made the vessel pitch and toss very uncomfortably for a squeamish man. But Charity—who was never sick—said she enjoyed it amazingly. She playfully remarked, " that her dear Teddy had entirely lost his colour," and advised him to go below and lie down, but he manfully protested against leaving her on deck alone ; so he got some cushions from the cabin, and made her a comfortable couch ·on the skylight, then tucked her feet in his railway wrapper and put his travelling shawl tenderly over her hat, to keep the spray from spoiling the blue feather. After handing her a copy of the *Sydney Mail* to amuse and edify her, he walked about in the fore part of the ship in order. to cure his squeamishness.

There were few fore cabin passengers on board that morning, and those few were below, for the spray made the deck very moist forward. Mr. Trout was glad there were no unsympathising eyes to gaze at him, for he felt woefully sick, and wished to ruminate over the side of the ship, and watch the bubbles gaily dancing by. Quietly stepping down to the cabin, unseen by Charity, he got an old tweed coat and vest from his bag, and returned to the fore deck. He then put on a sailor's tarpaulin jacket (which was lying on the fore hatch) to keep himself dry, and got as far as he could in the lee fore sponson. There, unseen by human eyes, he soon began to make the most varied facial contortions and guttural gwarcks that ever aroused expectation in a hungry fish ; and if he were not very bad indeed, his noises and his wry looks terribly belied him. The spray had long before washed away all his rouge, and his bile-tinted face looked like a suet pudding made for paupers. His change of dress, too, had strangely altered his figure, for there was no padding in his old tweed coat, and the crook in his back was as apparent as the curve in a monkey's tail. Loudly he lamented that he had not gone to Richmond by rail, instead of travelling by steamer on such a windy morning. Severe were his denunciations of steamers in general, and of that one in particular. Horribly profane were the curses he invoked on his own weak stomach, on his eyes and limbs, and on his soul too. Presently, as if in direct answer to his invocations, and to convince him how easily his blasphemous breath could be stopped for ever, he was seized with an unusually fierce internal qualm, during which, a tiny morsel of regurgitating breakfast slipped into his windpipe, and provoked a convulsive wheeze. In an instant, to his intense horror, out flew all his teeth, which were bran new only three weeks ago, and more horrifying still, in his frantic efforts to clutch them he jerked off his cap, and with it his span new wig and whiskers. Away they went, all of a heap, "into the tumbling billows of the main."

For an instant he stood aghast and paralyzed; his sunken chops quivering with emotion, and his dirty, bald head covered with beads of cold perspiration, like a gigantic toadstool in a thunder shower. "Ghost of Buonaparte! I'm ruined! I'm ruined! What shall I do now?" he gasped in tones of wild despair. (The escaped steam from the safety valve at that moment went Who-o-o! as though in mockery of his misery.) He had left his old wig and fixings and his other teeth at his lodgings; so what could he do, so remote from barbers and dentists? And it was not possible to quietly scalp a sailor, for there was not one to be seen in the fore part of the ship. How could he explain his dilemma to Charity? And whatever would she say to his wrinkles, and to the palpable fact that he was sixty-two, instead of forty-one ,years of age? These were thoughts which rushed into his mind with distracting force. In the midst of his dismay, however, was a gloomy joy that no eye had witnessed his disaster. So he resolved to get his shawl to cover his head, then to call Charity into the cabin, there to explain his misfortune, and appeal to her tender sympathies. Accordingly he ran aft (without taking off his tarpaulin jacket), and rushing up to his darling, he mumbled out with awful incoherency, "Gip me my shawl; I'm pery bad."

"Ugh! mercy pon us! get away, you nasty old creature! Wha-a?" shrieked Charity, in terror, and in utter ignorance who the crooked old phantom was, who had so rudely attempted to steal her lover's shawl.

"Led go id I dell you!" he cried, tearing the shawl from her head, while she loudly called for Teddington to come to her aid.

"Hallo, daddy, what are you doing aft?" asked the chief

mate, running up to the rescue of Charity, and collaring the stranger, who was making stuttering efforts to convince her that he was her intended husband.

"Do you know this old chap, ma'am?" asked the mate.

"Goodness me, no! certainly not. I never saw him in my life before. O! for pity's sake drag him away, Mr. Mate," said Charity, looking round for her lover to protect her, and calling for the stewardess to help her below, out of sight of the hideous old lunatic.

"The old bloke is cranky, there is no mistake about that," said the mate. "Lay aft here, the watch. Catch hold of him, some of you, and shove him into the paint locker, and block up the door. Don't hurt him, lads, don't hurt him, poor old fellow. He is a runaway from Tarban, I suppose, but I didn't see him come on board."

In another minute Trout was seized, neck and legs, by half-a-dozen sailors, and, despite his violent kicking and cursing, they carried him forward, and put him into a little closet on the fore-sponson, where they left him loudly protesting against their illegal proceedings.

"O dear me! that horrid old man has given me such a fright," said Charity, rubbing her forehead with rose water. "Stewardess, do go on deck, if you please, and ask Mr. Trout to come down. You will see him in the fore part of the ship—a gentleman with black beard and whiskers, and a military cap on."

Away went the stewardess, and in ten minutes she returned with the startling news "that no such gentleman was on board." An awful scene of excitement ensued. A search was made through the ship, from the hawse holes to the rudder trunk, but no Trout was to be found; and the terrible conviction forced itself upon every mind that the mysterious madman had thrown the unfortunate gentleman overboard, which idea was confirmed by a brief examination of the murderer, who persisted in mumbling that he was the identical Mr. Trout himself. Double irons were procured, and he was securely bound, and barricaded in the paint locker. A flag was hoisted half-mast, and general sympathy was manifested for the disconsolate lady who—as the mate remarked—had so tragically been made a widow the day before she was a wife.

When the steamer arrived at Newcastle, Charity was too much grief-stricken to go on shore; so it was arranged that she should stay on board, and return to Sydney next trip, in order to give evidence against the murderer of her lamented lover. The captain generously gave up his cabin to. the mourner, and the stewardess volunteered to extemporise some mourning gear, taking care, of course, to keep the blue feather and all such unseasonable trifles out of sight, in the hope that they would go out of mind too.

*   *   *   *   *   *

Two days afterwards, Charity, covered in crape, entered the police office with her solicitor, amid the sympathy of the full bench and a crowded court. The prisoner in the dock looked more sanguinary than ever, and eyed Charity with maniacal tenderness, which made her dread that he would leap out of the dock and bite her. Ever and anon he mumbled that he was Mr. Trout, and had never been murdered, and that he was going to be married to Miss Glimm. Close confinement, in irons, amongst the paint pots and oil cans for two days and nights, and on low diet too, had sadly damaged his appearance. His bald head was bedaubed with a·variety of colours, like a painter's palette, and his nose and chin—which nearly met—were garnished with engine grease, from his having used an old wad of cotton waste, in lieu of a pocket handkerchief. It was not until the gaoler threatened to gag him that he was induced to keep silent, while Charity gave her evidence.

After a lengthened examination—during which it was pretty generally believed that the prisoner would be hanged —the magistrate asked, "Have you had any previous acquaintance with the prisoner, Miss Glimm?"

"O dear no, your Honour. I never saw him in my life before he attacked me on board the steamer, in the way I have described," said Charity, with an affecting shudder.

"On your oath, madam. Do you say you never saw the prisoner before?" asked the counsel for the defence.

"Certainly I do, Sir," said Charity, with a toss of contempt at the mere assumption that she could be guilty of telling a falsehood. The counsel then requested that the witness might retire, which she was politely ordered to do. He then drew from his blue bag a set of teeth, a black wig with whiskers and beard conjoined, and a black surtout, coat, and vest, and handed them to the prisoner, who forthwith arrayed himself in them with magical alacrity: and the improvement in his appearance caused a buzz of admiration throughout the court, which six constables shouting silence could not smother. He was then told to step out of the dock, and to stand near to the door of the ante-room, and Charity was re-admitted. The moment she saw him, she exclaimed, hysterically, "Good gracious! Is it possible? Yes, yes, it is my own dear, dear Teddington!" then flung herself into his arms and fainted away. She was carried from the court to be rubbed and rinsed into consciousness, and in twenty minutes she re-entered looking much better.

"Do you still assert that you never saw the prisoner at the bar before?" asked the counsel, pointing to Trout, who was again in the dock in all his paint-disfigured baldness. "Look at him carefully, Miss Glimm; don't hurry with your reply."

Charity looked steadily at the prisoner for half a minute, then replied with the fervour of honest conviction, "I solemnly declare that I never saw him until he assaulted me; but I don't accuse him of murdering Mr. Trout, because he is in court somewhere, I'm happy to say."

"Oh, is he?" said the counsel, with a waggish smile. He then handed his blue bag into the dock to the prisoner, who again arrayed himself in his whiskers, wig, and teeth, amidst the loud laughter of the assembled crowd, which no one attempted to check; while Charity covered her face, and "fie'd for shame."

The prisoner was of course acquitted of the charge of murder; but failing to satisfy the Bench how he obtained an honest livelihood, he was committed to gaol for three months, as a rogue and a vagabond. Swifter than a scared sheep, Charity sped out of the court, then got into a cab and drove rapidly homeward, wringing her hands in vexation of spirit. Next week she left the colony, under the *nom de guerre* of Nancy Dunn. Where she is now I do not care to know, but I trust she is growing wiser; and I heartily hope that her humiliating experience may be a warning to her sex in general against the egregious folly of answering matrimonial advertisements, and thereby subjecting themselves to the terrible risk of being made miserable for life.

BRYAN GRADY AND HIS TWIN BROTHER TEDDY.

A PARTY of gentlemen (including Dr. McMerry) in travelling overland from New-South Wales to Victoria, camped one Christmas eve in the bush : and as they sat around their camp fire, they each related an incident from their colonial experience.   The following is the doctor's story :—

"It is thirteen years this Christmas-tide since the events I am about to relate.   I was surgeon of the ship Walrus, on my first voyage to Melbourne.   Amongst the emigrants were Bryan Grady and his wife Bridget, his daughters Nora and Judy, two buxom, blue-eyed girls, and three ragged-headed gossoons, 'with cheeks like thumping red potatoes,' as the old song says.   Pat, Mike, and Denis played more mischievous pranks on board than the boatswain's baboon, and the frequent whacks with the thin end of their father's shillelah were apparently as inoperative as gentle words to deaf bears.   While watching the capers of those youngsters I have sometimes been strongly inclined to Monboddo's whimsical notion, 'that men are monkeys with their tails rubbed off.'   Bryan Grady was an unsophisticated, honest-hearted Irishman, with a merry face, twinkling eyes, and an active tongue strongly tipped with the brogue. His wife was a quiet little woman, without the least pretensions to anything out of the common ; in fact, the whole family were of the humblest class of Irish peasantry.   They had long 'struggled with hard times in the ould country,' as Bryan remarked, 'an shure enough, dochter, everything was dead against us, an it was nigh starvin we wor, though it was hard enough we toiled for the rags on our backs an the bit o' victuals we ate, which wasn't enough to kape us from bein cowld an hungry.'

"'What are you going to do in Australia?' I asked him one evening, as he was sitting on the windlass smoking his little black dudheen.

"'Troth an I can't tell yez that, sir,' he replied, running his fingers through his grizzly locks.   'I don't know what I'll do at all, but it's mighty little I frit meself about that

same, cos we're not half-way there yit.   I'm able an willin'
to work, thank God, an the bhoys and girrls are rale good
workers too, so it ull be hard enough iv we don't pick up a
clane honest crust.   Anyhow we can't be worse off .nor we
wor in the land beyont, unless we are stripped an starved
out an out.   Besides me brother Teddy is in Australy some-
wheres, an iv I can only find him he'll help me on a bit
niver fear—that is iv he's able to do it; and if he isn't,
why dash it all, we can help ourselves and no thanks to
nobody, as the rats sed whin they got into ould Mulligan's
granary.'

   " ' In what part of Australia does your brother reside ?' I
asked.

   " ' Shure an I don't know where he is at all, sir ; I whish
·I did know.   Teddy ran away from home many years agone,
when he was a gossoon not much bigger nor my bhoy Mike.
He sint us a letther soon afterwards, to tell us that he wasn't
drowned on the voyage to Sydney, and that he wos goin'
up the counthry to some outlandish place wid a long whuzzy
buzzy name that I cud niver spake widout coughin', and
which I've clane forgot years agone.   That's all I know
about Teddy ; but maybe I'll find him one of these days, an
he'll be plaised enough to see me, I'll wager, for it's twins
we were whin we were bhoys, and as much alike as two
wild rabbits, only he'd got a dale more gumption nor meself,
which was plain enough from his rinnin' away from poverty,
while I stopped in it till it pritty nigh ate the heart clane
out ov me.   Och hone ! an thire's a mighty lot ov poor
hungry souls in ould Ireland, so there is, wus luck.'

   " Soon after the Walrus's arrival in Melbourne I took
steamer for Sydney, intending to stay there a month or two,
in order to secure the best season of the year for returning
home by way of Cape Horn.   I went to stay with my old
college friend, Grant, who was living in tolerably good style,
in a pleasant part of Sydney.   The day before Christmas I
had been strolling about the city, looking at the numerous
well-stocked provision shops, and the fruit market, and con-
trasting the sultry, dusty atmosphere with Christmas weather
at the antipodes.   I returned in the afternoon, weary, warm,
and dusty to my friend's house, and stretching myself on a
sofa in his sanctum, was watching the pertinacious attempts
of a grey mosquito to tap my nose, when Grant walked in,
with a letter in his hand.   ' I have been' looking for you

Mac. Here is an invitation for you to accompany me to a dinner party to-morrow, at my friend O'Grady's. I hope you are not otherwise engaged,' he said, tossing the letter to me to read.

"'Your friend, O'Grady, is not a scholar,' said I, smiling, as I returned the quaintly worded note of invitation, 'However, he may be a clever fellow for all that, and I am sure he is a respectable man or you would not own his acquaintance. I will go with pleasure.'

"'O'Grady is certainly not a scholar, as you remark,' said Grant, 'still he has a large share of good practical sense, with general information, and a vein of native humour which the most prosy *savant* in the land would appreciate; in short, he is a capital fellow, and you will enjoy his company—for I know you love thorough men, whatever their condition in life may be. His wife is a high-bred lady; perhaps a little too stately beside her uncultured spouse, but withal a kind-hearted woman. O'Grady's history is rather an amusing one. He came to this colony thirty years ago, a mere lad, or a bare-legged gossoon—to use his own words. He went into the bush, and ten years afterwards he won the heart of a rich widow, with his handsome face and his blarneying ways; and now he owns several stations in the interior, and I don't know how many houses in Sydney besides. He is member for Midgyborough; and though he admits that it is mighty little he knows of political science, he has more influence in "the House" than many men of greater pretensions. In his own house he is one of the most hospitable, off-hand, humourous Irishman that I have ever met with; but you shall see him and judge for yourself.'

"Next day my friend Grant and I drove to Derrydown Hall, which was a stylish mansion, charmingly situated in the most fashionable suburb of Sydney. We were met at the door by our host, whose hearty, homely salute assured me that I was welcome, more than the most polished address would have done. I fancied I had seen him before, but could not remember where. His wife received me with stately etiquette, and presented me to her daughters, three tall, handsome girls, whose bearing more resembled that of mamma than papa. There were about a dozen guests in the drawing-room, and the hostess expressed to Grant her regret at the absence of others—who had been invited—through a sudden family bereavement. I need not minutely describe the house and its contents, suffice it to say that the mansion was commodious ; it was furnished in elegant style, and its surroundings showed a rare combination of natural and artistic beauties.

"The company were in that peculiar state of suspense which is often observable a few minutes before the hour for dinner, each one seeming undesirous of beginning a conversation, which might be abruptly terminated by the summons to adjourn to the dining-room, when suddenly the awkward silence was broken by noisy voices in the hall, accompanied with sounds of scuffling. I had a few minutes before observed a spring cart, full of men and women, pass the windows towards the front door of the house.

" 'Och bad manners to yez ! ye pickled pork-faced spalpeen ! what do ye mane by kickin' me down the steps an' spillin' me bist hat ?" uttered an excited voice, which sounded familiarly in my ears. 'Be the hoky iv ye lift yer hoof to me agin, I'll knock yer big head into brawn, so I will. Go an' tell yer masther I want him, an' bad cess to yez.'

" 'Be off I tell you ! you can't see Mister O'Grady to-day,' said the footman.

" 'Be off is it ! Wheugh ! an who are you to tell me I can't see him, when I've come a hundred thousand miles amost on purpose. Och Mike, what next ! I'll bet a penny ye'll see somethin' yerself pretty quick that you won't like above a bit ; ye'll git the dhirty kick out by and bye, an' go howlin' home like a hound wid a bad leg, or maybe ye'll get yer blatherin head put in a sack, an' sarve ye right for yer imperence.'

" 'Get out you saucy ragamuffin ?' said the servant angrily, at the same time we heard a heavy thud outside, and the door was slammed to. It was evident that the intruder had been pushed out of the house, which seemed a clear indication that he was not welcome in it.

" 'Hallo ! hallo ! what's all that whirly burly about, I'd like to know ?' exclaimed the host, walking from the farther end of the drawing-room as though intent upon going into the hall to investigate the cause of the uproar. At that instant a man, covered with dust, presented himself at one of the open French windows, holding a battered hat in his hands.

" 'Be the livin' jingo! iv that isn't Teddy himself !' shouted the man, dropping his hat and springing into the room. 'Savin' yer prisense, ladies and jintlemen, and axin yer pardon for gettin' in at the windee like a thief, I've come to see me brother, an' here he is sure enough, God bless him. He's the ony son ov me mother, barrin' meself an' me sisther Meg. Troth, I'd know him in the middle ov a regiment ov sogers, iv they were all as nakid as skinned weasils—so I wud. Teddy, honey! an' don't ye know yer own darlint brother Bryan?' he added, advancing nearer, with his eyes full of affectionate earnestness.

"The host stood for a moment as if petrified with amazement, while his handsome face twitched with emotion. Then a happy smile began to play round his mouth, but almost simultaneously he burst into tears, and flung himself into the open arms of the dusty man, whom I at once recognised as my humble friend Bryan Grady; at the same time I observed his wife and five children grouped round the window, staring into the room, with faces expressive of wonder and delight at the moving scene. The surprised looks of the guests, and the very natural embarrassment of the hostess and her daughters, at the unexpected arrival of relatives with whom they were wholly unacquainted, would have made a rare picture. Releasing himself from the athletic hugs of his brother, Bryan blundered out an apology to the guests, then turning to the group at the window he exclaimed :—

"'Arrah, come inside here, ivery one ov yez, Nora and Judy darlints! kiss yer uncle tinderly. Bhoys take yer skull caps off an' wipe your noses. Bridget jewel! this is me brother Teddy, as ye've heard me mintion a million o' times. Long life to him, and God bless everybody else.'

"'Wisha! wisha! an' is that Teddy himself now? Shure I'm right glad to see yez, honey!' said Bridget, humbly approaching to take the proffered hand of the host. Then the girls, pushed onward by their father, timidly drew near to kiss their sobbing uncle, while the boys were making a series of bows to the whole company, in a style peculiar to peasant boys in general, and shuffling about on the velvet pile carpet like young bears on hot tiles.

"'Save us iv there isn't Dochter M'Merry here too,' exclaimed Bryan, as he caught sight of me for the first time; then in the same breath he said to his boy Denis, 'rin and tell Barney not to go away wid the cart, we'll be wid him in a jiffy. We mustn't sthop here to bother all these ladies and gintlemen. Och philleloo, whack! good luck to this happy day! who'd ha' thought ov seein' all this fun at onst? Troth an' I'm feard it's ony draming I am afther all.'

"'Stay boy,' cried the host, as Dennis was bounding through the window, 'ye shall all stay an' dine with me, every one ov ye.   It isn't meself that would sind any mortal out ov me house hungry on a blissed Christmas Day, not a bit ov it.   Ye're all honest and clean, I'll be bound, though ye're not rigged out in superior gear; an' anybody prisent who is ashamed ov me for doing what's right and fair to me own flesh and blood may go an' git his dinner somewhere else if he likes.   That's all I've got to say, maning no offince nathir.'

"In order to shorten my story, I pass over the comically expressed objections of Bryan and his wife to 'dine with sich elegant company,' the good-natured way the hostess seconded her husband's hearty invitation to his humble relatives, the cordial manner in which the guests received the strangers, and the thorough enjoyment of the whole amusing scene.   Soon afterwards the whole family were seated at the lower end of the dining-table, in the places of the absent friends before alluded to, and dinner was served up in grand style.   To relieve the embarrassment of the party to some extent, I arranged to sit at the lower end of the table too, and it was only by extraordinary effort that I preserved becoming gravity during that meal, as I witnessed the awkwardness of the boys, and the anxiety of their father 'to make thim behave dacintly before their supariors.'

"'Arrah, Mike! look out that ye don't poke that big fork in yer eye.   Shure an' ye niver ate yer dinner wid sich a tool as that afore,' said Bryan, in a loud whisper; and in the same breath he added—'Pat, where's yer new pocket-hancher what I bought yer yestreen? Be dacint, can't yez? Norah, jewel! it isn't manners to be houldin' that turkey's leg wid both hands; an' don't be shovin' yer elbow into Judy's mouth naythir.   Dash that bhoy Denis! kick him, Bridget. Bad scran to him, look at him now, the greedy spalpeen!   Och, I'm ashamed ov yez outright, so I am,' he vociferated, with a severe look across the table at the culprit, who had taken a tureen of mint sauce—which was before him—and was supping it with the ladle, in utter ignorance that he was transgressing the rules of etiquette.

"'How did you discover your brother's whereabouts,

Bryan ?' I asked, hoping to relieve his chagrin by engaging him in a little conversation.

"'It was mighty curious altogether, sir. I wint about Melbourne every day for a month or more, axing everybody I met wid iv they knowed Teddy Grady; but not a sowl culd tell me a haporth about him, an' I was afeard I'd never find him at all, in this great big counthry. But as good luck wud have it, I wint on board the steamer what had jist come in from Sydney one mornin', an' axed the captain, who was a rale sinsible-lookin' man, an' ses he to me, "I know a jintleman in Sydney, named Edwin O'Grady, Esquire, M.L.A."

"'"Shure that isn't me brother Teddy, sir," ses I, "for he isn't a squire, nor a Malay naythir; he's an Irishman every bit ov him, an' there isn't a single tint ov black blood in his carcass, I'll engage." The captain laughed, an' ses he, "What sort ov a lookin' chap is this brother Teddy ov yours?" "Dear knows what he looks like now, sir," ses I; "but he was a rale broth ov a bhoy thirty years agone; jist like meself, an' not a morsel or difference atween us, only he'd got more sinse in his head nor me." "I know him well enough," ses the captain; "he has often sailed wid me. Hasn't he got a scar jist over his nose?" "To be shure he has, sir," says I, "an' well enough I ought to know it, too, for it was meself as made it for him. We was havin' a bit ov sport one day, in Larry Flynn's barm, an' me sthick slipped an' hit Teddy a little bit too hard, wus luck, an' pretty nigh knocked his nose off altogether. That's him safe enough, sir," ses I, "an' though he's got a little O nailed afore his name, an' a hape ov jinglin' titles afther it, like tin pots to a dog's tail, he's me own brother Teddy, an' all the whizzi-nags in the world won't alter it, soh. I'll go an' see him pritty quick," ses I. So I shouldered me luggage an' took all them crathers wid me on board an empty collier brig, an' the captain gave us a passage chape bekase we found our own victuals an' slept on the stone ballast in the hold; an' here we are all on us safe and sound—thank God—an' there's me brother Teddy too beyant, lookin' as grand as the Lord Mayor ov Dublin—long life to him. Troth it's the merriest Christmas Day I've ever seed in my life, so it is; though that long flunkey there, in the yellow breeches, knocked me spinnin' down the steps, and made this big bump on top ov me head. But niver mind that, good luck to everybody, that's all I've got to say. Ugh ! Pat, what a gorf ye must be to go an' choke yerself wid that red hot what-you-may-call-em ?' added Bryan, with a reproving glance at his son, who was sneezing and coughing immoderately, having eaten a large capsicum, supposing it to be an Australian plum.

" After the cloth was removed, the host—who had been unusually thoughtful during dinner—rose, and in a rich musical voice spoke as follows:

" ' My dear friends, I'm not a man to spake much, and dear knows, some ov the fellows who gabble a mighty dale had better be quiet, there may be fewer folks would know they were sich fools. I'm plaised to see ye all here to-day, and though there are more here than I invited, there's not one that isn't welcome. Frinds, whin I look beyant there (pointing to his brother's family), I feel like a fellow who has just been caught cheating a poor blind man, and that's a fact. It's more nor thirty years since I seen thim crathers ; leastways, I didn't know the young uns at all thin, bekase they wasn't born ; but as I was going to say, I've bin in this counthry living in luxury, rolling in riches, as the saying is, and not a blissed thought did I think about me poor frinds at home, till they all walked in at me windee this morning to ate their Christmas dinner wid me. Troth they might all have bin starved outright for all I knowed, or all I cared either, and I could aisily have sint them a good big Christmas-box ivery year, widout hurting meself the laste bit in life ; but I didn't do it, more shame to me, and it's a wonder to me that God didn't take all me money away from me, for being so greedy. I'm worse nor a haythin, a mighty dale, bekase I knew what was me duty and I didn't do it. Shure many's the time I've read in me Bible, " Whoso hath this world's good and seeth his brother have need, and shutteth up his bowels of compassion from him, how dwelleth the love of God in him ?" Poor Bryan ! you've bin in need bad enough, and I'm rale sorry I didn't help you ; but I'll be a brother to ye from this out, honey, niver fear, and may God forgive my past neglect. You shall niver see hard times agin, Bryan, if I can help it, take my word for that.' Here the host's voice faltered, and his eyes filled with tears, while all the company showed sympathy.

" ' Aisy, darlint !' said Bryan, rising as his brother was

about to say more ; ‘ whisht a bit, Teddy, dear, an’ let me spake a word or two.’

“ Bryan’s address would, doubtless, have been very pathetic, but unluckily at that moment a pet kangaroo bounded across the lawn towards the window. ‘ Ow ! ow ! ow !’ yelled the boys in concert ; ‘ och, what a rum-lookin’ donkey—look at his tail !’ shouted Dan, standing up and pointing to the animal, while his mothers and sisters opened their mouths wide in wonder and consternation.

“ ‘ Ye’re a donkey yourself, and bad manners to yez !’ vociferated Bryan, at the same time giving Dan a cuff on the head for his breach of decorum.

“ A simultaneous burst of laughter from the whole company drowned Dan’s howls, and the balance of Bryan’s speech too.

“ But I must soon end my long story,” said the Doctor. “ I cannot tell you all that took place at Derrydown Hall on that merry Christmas Day, unless I keep you here all night ; but it was certainly one of the pleasantest days I have spent in the colony.

“ O’Grady faithfully kept his promise, and soon afterwards settled his humble relatives on a snug farm at Illawarra. In a few years the boys and girls formed comfortable homes for themselves ; and Bryan has now a score or more of blooming Australian grand-children. He blesses the lucky day that he landed on these shores ; and on every Christmas Day he stands up at the head of his well-filled board, and shouts ‘ long life to his twin-brother Teddy,’ till all the children around him laugh like merry little elves, and his good wife’s eyes overflow with love and gratitude.”

JOEY GOOSGOG AND JASPER SPINDLE'S TRIP TO BONDI BAY IN A PONY CHAISE.

MR. Joseph Goosgog and Mr. Jasper Spindles were a comical looking pair of Cockneys. They had voyaged from London to Sydney together a few years ago, and from those four months of constant intercourse, and the mutual participation of the dangers and disagreeables, inseparable from a long voyage, a close friendship had sprung up. Though in their externals they were the very antipodes of each other, their habits and tastes were strangely identical—their minds seemed to have been cast in the same mould, and were as much alike as two winter mornings.

Mr. Goosgog, in his city shoes, stood exactly five feet three and three-quarter inches, and was what is termed a podgy man, of fourteen stone or thereabouts ; while Mr. Spindles, though three or four stone lighter than his friend, was a trifle over six feet one inch in his slippers, and was lathy, leathery, and angular, with his shoulders peeping into his ears, and his face as long as a gold-digger's boot.

They were confirmed bachelors, and as shy of young ladies as they were of sharp dogs. They lodged in the same house, near Sydney, and boarded together, of course. They were engaged in trade in the city during the day-time, but they invariably spent their spare hours together,—in fact, they were almost as uniform in their movements as the Siamese twins, or a pair of coach wheels. They were plodding men of business, sharp as razors in their own particular department of soft goods, but outside that they were *soft goods* themselves. They knew the value of time, and seldom took a holiday out of the general course, but they invariably commemorated their birthdays by a little merry-making to themselves, and at those times especially they were " jolly good fellows " by their own unanimous verdict.

One evening in January, that pair of odd fellows, and their landlady, Mrs. Cobbrer, might have been seen very carefully packing sundry edibles into a market-basket, together with knives and forks, plates, tumblers, and table-napkins for two. The next day was Mr. Spindle's birthday, and the two friends had decided upon a trip together to Boudi Bay in a pony chaise, which Mrs. Cobbrer's cousin Phil. had agreed to lend them for a moderate consideration.

"It will be a baking day," said Mr. Goosgog, who sat pouring out the coffee at the breakfast-table on the following morning ; " a fiery hot wind, I think."

"Hot enough to cook a salamander," replied Mr. Spindle, with his mouth full of cold mutton and chutney. "I shall wear my grasscloth suit, and my Chinese hat with a white turban. What time was the chaise to be ready, Goosgog?"

"Nine o'clock—oh, here it is, I declare, punctual to a second. I like that," said Mr. Goosgog, rising, and going to the window. "And it's a neat turn out too ; just big enough to seat two, comfortably. The pony pricks his ears rather suspiciously though ; I hope he won't run away with us. By the bye, can you drive, Jasper? I forgot to ask you that before."

"Ye-yes—certainly—I have driven on several occasions, that is to say, I have sat on the box with the driver, which is all the same, you know, for I was very observant. It's a simple operation, very ; you have merely to pull the rein gently, whichever side you wish your horse to incline, and it's as easy as opening oysters when you get the knack of it. Oh, yes, I can drive delightfully."

"I am glad of that," said Mr. Goosgog, "for I could not drive a lame donkey ; and I am always rather nervous in vehicles, unless I am with an experienced driver. I think the sooner we start the better, Jasper ; and we shall get down to the sea beach before the hottest time of the day. We had better take some towels, and our oilskin skull caps, and we can have a delicious bath in the surf, free from dread of sharks and stingerees ; for those disagreeable fish don't like the surf, I have heard sailors say. Bring in the basket, Mrs. Cobbrer."

"Yes sir," said Mrs. Cobbrer, hobbling in with the market basket, which was rather more than half a load for her.

"Have you got the mutton chops from the butcher, Mrs. Cobbrer?"

"Yes, sir, two pounds and a half ; they are in the basket,

with the cold sausages, and sardines, and the peach pie, and
the bananas, and a pineapple, and a big sugar melon."

"And some nice potatoes, Mrs. Cobbrer ?"

"O yes, sir, I forgot—ten beautiful taters ; I washed 'em
all ready for cooking ; and I put in a screw of pepper and
salt too."

"Thank you, Mrs. Cobbrer ; you have managed very
nicely. You may expect us home about seven o'clock this
evening. Good morning, Mrs. Cobbrer."

Very soon afterwards the two friends got into the chaise,
after lashing the basket behind it ; and as the driving seat
was, of course, a few inches higher than the other seat, Mr.
Spindle considerately insisted upon his friend taking it, as
he was decidedly the shortest man.

"But I can't drive," urged Mr. Goosgog, with slight trepidation, " I told you that before, Jasper."

"I don't want you to drive, my good sir," replied Mr.
Spindle, taking the reins and whip in his hands, like an expert Jehu. "It does not matter a tittle to me which side I
sit, I can manage capitally. Now pony, get away, sir ! Hi !
what's his name, boy ?" he asked of the grinning youth who
had been holding the pony's head.

"His name's Jerry, sir."

"Ah ! O yes, thank you. Get along, Jerry," said Mr.
Spindle, giving the reins a jerk, and just stroking him with
the whip-lash.

"Hit him hard, sir," said the youth aforesaid ; "he's as
knowing as an old magpie, that pony is. He won't care no
more for your just tickling him with the whip-cord, than if
a mosquito was kicking him, not a bit."

"He won't run away, boy, will he ?" asked Mr. Goosgog,
in rather an anxious tone.

"Not he, sir," said the boy, grinning as before ; "he's a
plaguey deal too lazy for that. He wouldn't run away if
you'd got a hen-coop full of cockatoos in the chaise all in full
scream, or a fire bell hanging to the axletree, ringing for the
engines. Dash him ! I often wish he *would* run away. Hit
him *very* hard, sir, he won't hurt you."

"Ah ! I'll make him go, I'll warrant, the lazy fellow,"
said Mr. Spindle, giving him a savage slash with the whip,
which Jerry seemed to understand from experience, for he
whisked his tail—rather pettishly though—and started off
at a smart trot, while the two friends smiled and looked as

triumphant as if they had tamed a tiger. The boy grinned again, then went on his way home, whistling "Billy Button."

Away they jogged, behind Jerry, through the turnpike-gate, along the red road to Paddington, without anything very remarkable occurring. They roused up a disagreeable dust, which their white jackets evidenced; but that is not remarkable on that road. The soldiers at the barrack gates, and the idlers at the roadside inns, stared and giggled at them as they trotted by; but it would have been remark-able if they had not done so, for Mr. Spindle was adminis-tering half minute strokes with his whip on the pony's hips and ribs as vigorously as if he were killing snakes, while Mr. Goosgog assisted to stimulate the sluggish brute to go forward, by giving him frequent downward digs, on a con-venient part of his body, with the ferule end of an umbrella, and at the same time peremptorily commanding him to "come up." Round spun the wheels, and soon the city of Sydney was more than three miles behind them, and the spirits of the two liberated tradesmen were as light as gossamer or blond tulle.

"Ah! this scenery beats Richmond Hill all to ribbons; it is richer than our show-room, I declare!" exclaimed Mr. Spindle, with lackadaisical rapture, as he ceased working with the whip for a short time, and let the pony take his own pace when they had got to the top of Waverley heights, to allow time for enjoying the magnificent views of Port Jackson and Botany Bay, with the lovely landscape all around, where nature and art combine to make a picture which is unrivalled in this world of beauty. "Oh, dear, dear," sighed Jasper, "this *is* a charming prospect; eh! Joey?"

"Beautiful, beautiful!" responded Mr. Goosgog, in a sentimental tone, at the same time gazing around, and gasp-ing in the fresh air, like a snapper just taken off the hook. "I should like such an excursion as this once a fortnight, Jasper; my mind being freed from the shrivelling influence of the shop, would expand like a patent mackintosh life preserver. The pure, invigorating air, the balsamic frag-rance from the bush flowers, the thrilling music of the locusts, and the intensely gratifying pros——,Good gracious, Jasper! whatever is the matter with that abominable pony? I'm afraid he's going mad; O dear, dear! look at him!"

" Whoa—whoa—wa—quiet, sir—quiet, pony !" shouted
Mr. Spindle, turning as white as his grasscloth waistcoat.

" Whatever ails the disagreeable beast, I should like to
know ?   I never saw such an extraordinary horse in my life
before.   Oh ! ah ! I see now what's the matter with him ;
the right rein is under his tail ; that's what makes him kick
so dreadfully.   Don't be frightened, Joey ; I'll soon pull it
clear.   Coil your legs up on the seat.   Whoa, Jerry ! whoa,
my boy ! poor old fellow ! whoa, then—whoa !"

But Jerry seemed determined not to whoa, for the harder
Mr. Spindle tugged at the rein, in his violent efforts to disengage it from Jerry's tightly tucked-in-tail, the more he
kicked and jibbed ; knocking the dashboard to tatters, and
putting the poor travellers behind it into intense bodily
fear, and bodily danger too.

" Lift up his tail, Joey, while I pull the rein," cried Spindles, in an imploring tone ; at the same time he doubled his
long legs under him, on the seat, like a tailor or a Turk, to
keep out of the reach of Jerry's active hoofs.   " Make haste,
Joey, lift up his tail."

" Oh, Goblins ! I won't lift his tail ; he'll kick my nose
off, or do me some other horrible damage," groaned poor
Goosgog ; " I'd sooner lift a hot poker.   I never handled
a tail in my life, Jasper ; you lift it ; you are stronger than
I, and you have had experience with horses."

" What's to be done ?   What's to be done ?" gasped Spindles, not noticing what his terrified friend had just advised
him to do, and evidently resolved not to risk *his* brains by
touching Jerry's tail.   " What shall we do to stop him ?
he's running backward, the contrary creature.   Here, hold
the reins, Joey, while I jump out over the back, and run to
the hotel yonder for a hostler."

" No, no, no !" vociferated Joey ; " you shan't jump out,
Jasper ; he'll run away with me while you are gone, and
break my neck.   I won't have anything to do with the
reins.   I know no more about driving than my old Aunt
Becky."

" No more do I ; no more do I ; and I fancied I did,"
howled Spindles, now nearly frantic.   " Oh, Dimity, we
shall be smashed up like old bonnet-boxes directly, for he'll
back us into that quarry. What an ass I was, to say I could
drive a horse.   Something must be done at once.   Whoa,
horse ! whoa ! whoa, I say ; confound the animal ! he

doesn't mind a bit what I say to him. Just hoist up his
tail with the hooky end of your umbrella, Joey; he can't
kick you if you're careful. Try, Joey, pray do, there's a
good fellow."

"Ods bodkins! I'm afraid I can't do it; his tail fits so
close; but I'll try, I'll try," whined Joey, trembling with
terror, as he wriggled his umbrella through a rent in the
dashboard, and, by a powerful lunge, succeeded in forcing
the hooked handle under Jerry's tail, which had the immediate effect of making him dreadfully indignant, and to
kick and plunge twice as hard as before, threatening the
entire demolition of everything within reach of his iron
heels.

"O lawk a mercy! that won't do, Joey—that won't do!
pull your umbrella away again; pull it away, quick,
quick!"

"I can't, I can't! He won't let it go; it's under his tail
as tight as if it grew there. Hoo lud! now it's gone altogether," roared Goosgog, with despair stamped on his tur-
nip-coloured countenance. In his nervous efforts to release
the umbrella he had let it slip from his grasp; when falling
down behind Jerry's legs, and opening out wide, it so
thoroughly roused and scared him that he started off at a
run-away pace, for the first time in his life.

"Stop him! Stop him! Boo-o-o!" bellowed the terrified
friends. But as there was no person within hearing to stop
him if it had been practicable, they thought they had better
try to do it themselves; so they seized the left rein, and
pulled together like sailors at the main-tack, till Jerry's head
was exactly square with his tail; the natural result of which
was that the chaise inclined to the left side of the road.
Presently it came in contact with a thick bush, and the next
instant it was lying on its side, with one wheel spinning
round horizontally, and the pony lying on his side too,
while Goosgog and Spindles were sprawling in the dust,
like gigantic frogs, rather out of their element, surrounded
by knives and forks, cold sausages, raw potatoes, and the
whole contents of the market-basket. Their Chinese hats
were rolling briskly down the hill before a fair wind, and
the sugar melon was rolling down the hill too, closely followed by the basket itself.

"Oh, dear me!" gasped Jasper, who was the first on his
legs, and looked as if he had been peppered all over with

Scotch snuff. " How are you, Joey ? Are you hurt, my friend ?"

" I'm afraid I am," replied Goosgog, in a dismal tone, " I fear so, but I'm not quite sure.   What shall we do now, Jasper ? I'm a good mind to kill that pony now he's down, for he certainly tried to kill us, confound him ! What shall we do now ? that's the first consideration."

Jasper would have been totally unable to tell his friend what to do under the circumstances, but fortunately for them, just at that moment, two working men came up, and in the prospect of a liberal reward they speedily put the pony and chaise upright. Jerry had lain quite still ; no doubt being glad of the temporary rest, and there was nothing broken by the upset ; so in less than an hour they were once more on the road to Bondi ; with their basket lashed up behind, as before.   But Mr. Spindles was particularly careful to keep clear of Jerry's tail, and to that end, he took the driving seat, and held the reins up about level with the top of his hat ; using both hands ; while Mr. Goosgog exerted himself with the whip.

In due course they arrived at Bondi Beach without further mishap.   They drove the chaise into a shady nook ; then took the pony out, unharnessed him, and tethered him by the reins to a green bush, off which he was expected to dine : for Mr. Spindles assured Mr. Goosgog, that he had been informed—upon no less an authority than a squatter—that horses in the interior are very glad to eat bushes sometimes ; but it did not occur to Mr. Spindles that horses generally ate bushes upon the same principle that hungry men have sometimes been glad to eat their boots—when they could get nothing better to eat.   Jerry might have been more satisfied with his scrubby dinner, if he had had a draught of water first ; but his drivers forgot that, in their haste to get into the water themselves.

I do not mean to imply that those gentlemen would have grudged Jerry a shilling's worth of corn and hay had they *thought* of it while they were packing up their own provisions, for they were not niggardly men, far from it.   But with obliviousness which is peculiar to that class of horse-masters, they thought no more about baiting their nag than they did about greasing the wheels of the chaise.   A feed of corn and a bucket of water would probably have induced Jerry to stand quietly, and would thus have saved his drivers much subsequent suffering.   Careless horsemen had better take warning from the mishaps of these two unlucky excursionists.

The market basket was carried down to a convenient place, under an over-hanging part of the cliff, close to which was a deliciously-cool streamlet of fresh water trickling down the rocks above into a little natural basin, for which many thirsty boys have been grateful.

Bondi Bay is one of the many romantic spots around Sydney which often allures and delights the holiday-loving citizens.   But I cannot now attempt a description of its beauties.

Jasper and Joey were enraptured with the place; and were overjoyed, too, at being mutually assured, after a careful inspection, that they were free from all personal marks of their late mishap.   With that important matter decided so cheeringly, of which before they were both in some anxiety, they walked together on to the beach, pleasantly conversing as they went; they stepped into the sea together, and, in another minute were dashing about in the water like dugongs.   Previous to undressing, they had lighted a fire on a rock, and put the potatoes down to roast.

"Halloa, Joey ! look at that confounded pony," said Jasper, about ten minutes afterwards.   "What's the matter with him now, in the name of wonder?   I do believe he's trying to break loose.   He's a perfect torment, that animal ; and I would rather have walked here, and carried the basket, than have been bothered with him, if I had known his vicious disposition before, I believe he is a thoroughly bad horse, Joey, and that's the reason we got him so cheap.   I must run and fasten him up with double reins ; and I'd tie his legs, too, if I thought he wouldn't kick me."

Now whether Jerry had never before seen a tall bony man without his garments, and was, naturally enough scared at the spectacle ; or whether the desire had entered his head to bother his inexperienced drivers as much as he possibly could for the day ; or whether, which is the most likely, he wanted something to eat and drink, and he saw nothing to prevent his getting it, but the clumsily fastened tether, I, of course, am not certain ; but he no sooner saw Mr. Spindles striding towards him, like a "native companion," than he gave a smart tug, and broke his tether, then leisurely jogged off into the bush.

"Hoy! Joey!" shouted Spindles; "here's another nuisance, Jerry's got loose. Come and help me catch him. Make haste, there's a good fellow. Bring the boots with you, for the ground here is covered with prickly things, like pins and needles."

Goosgog emerged from the sea, like some rare amphibious animal, and was soon waddling towards his friend, as fast as his short legs would allow him to travel; with two pairs of Wellington boots in one hand, and a long rough stick in the other, which he thought might be useful to assist him in catching the pony.

After putting on their boots, which was not a very easy operation with wet and naked feet (as most people know who wear Wellingtons), they ran after the fugitive beast, and a most uncomfortable run it was, for the bushes are rather thick about Bondi, and some of them stimulate, very much like furze or gooseberry bushes, which the wincing pursuers soon discovered, and they were reminded every minute that they had omitted to put on their garments as well as their boots. However, they were sanguine of soon catching Jerry, for Spindle had several times stridden within seven yards of him; but, after many experiments, he found that he never could get half a yard closer than that, which was again rather discouraging when weighing the chances of catching him. After spending more than an hour in that doubtful chase, Mr. Goosgog, who had followed up, with his long stick, as fast as he could trot, and who was grunting like a hunted hippopotamus, and perspiring, too, like a gentleman lying on a wooden griddle in the Turkish bath, now declared, with tears in his eyes, he would rather be flogged with a birch broom, than run any further through those horrible bushes in his present vulnerable condition. So it was hastily decided that Jasper should run back to the beach for their clothing, while Joey kept watch over the pony, who had just discovered a small spot of green grass, and was quietly grazing, about one hundred yards distant.

Mr. Goosgog accordingly sat himself down under a tea-tree, and busied himself in the three-fold occupations of picking some of the thorns out of his irritated skin, brushing away the mosquitos, and watching Jerry; while Mr. Spindle endeavoured to make his way back to the beach at a quick march.

Now Mr. Spindle, in his exciting chase after the pony,

had omitted to take notes by the way, so being a bad bush-man, and unskilled in tracking, and withal having to dodge away from the most formidable of the bushes, he wandered about in a circle, or rather in a series of zigzags, for an hour and a half, and at last, when almost ready to lie down in despair, he unexpectedly returned to the spot, where Mr. Goosgog sat under the tree, fast asleep, with myriads of grey mosquitos covering him, like young feathers.

" Halloa," roared Jasper, scratching his head, and gazing at his friend with a woe-stricken visage, which might have forced a sigh from a Cossack. " Halloa, Joey ! why here I am again. Bless my soul ! I'd no idea where I'd got to ; I thought I was lost altogether."

" Hey-day, Jasper !" muttered Joey, rubbing his eyes, having just woke up. " I'm so glad you've come back, for these horrid mosquitos have been poking their horns into me, like five thousand of the ' best drilled-eyed sharps,' and I can't keep them off. I never knew the value of a suit of clothes before, though I have sold hundred of suits. I shall always feel for the poor blackfellows in future. Where are my clothes, Jasper ?'

" Where's the pony, Joey ?" inquired Mr. Spindle.

" Eh ?—there he is—no—yes, he was there a few minutes ago, I'm sure," stammered Joey, rising and gazing around him, and seeing nothing but bushes and sand-hills. " Well, I declare he's gone ! Yes, confound him, he's gone, and I don't know which way no more than this stump that 1 am standing upon. I have been asleep, and that designing beast has taken advantage of my unwatchfulness by running away ; that's all I know about it. Good gracious me ! I wish we had never come out to-day ; or I wish 1 had killed that wretched horse, when he upset us at Waverley, and then gone back to the shop. What shall we do now, Jasper ?"

" Let us go back to the beach as fast as we can, and get our clothes on first of all," said Jasper, " for I'm blistered with the sun, and nearly irritated beyond endurance with these prickly bushes, mosquitos, and soldier-ants. I am getting very hungry, too, and I'm afraid we shall not have fire enough to cook the chops, when we get back. But come along Joey, let's get back, let's get back. The pony may go to the dogs before I look for him any more in this plight ; and if he's lost we must pay for him, that's all.

He isn't worth much.   Ugh ! I shall never like live horses again as long as I live."

It fortunately happened, that Mr. Goosgog had not been able to run so fast as his long-legged friend, so he had had more time for observation as he ran, consequently he knew the track back to the beach, to which they made the best of their way,—walking side by side, like the "babes in the wood".   But when they got there, to their intense horror and grief, they found that some person or persons had taken away every article of their apparel, and their market basket too, and had literally left them "on the strand," hungry, and totally destitute of every article of civilized convenience, with the exception of their bathing caps, their Wellington boots, a few baked potatoes, and the pony chaise.

It would be cruel to picture their unphilosophical endurance of that new and most trying misfortune.   They were not large-brained men, as I before hinted ; but I omitted to say, at the same time, that two more inoffensive creatures never entered Sydney Heads.   Their tempers were sweet and smooth as "Everton toffee," or "golden syrup."   Not a single jar—even of the smallest size—had ever been exchanged by those stanch friends from the first time their eyes met up to that distressing hour.   But now, alas ! that friendship, which ordinary mishaps and the struggles of every day life had tended to rivet as strongly as a high-pressure boiler, was doomed to a temporary fracture, through the accumulated disasters which had on that memorable day descended about their devoted heads, like a cataract of icicles, and, for a time, frozen up the best sympathies of their kind hearts.

I will but cursorily glance at the events of the next hour and a quarter ; how, alas ! their native suavity totally forsook them for a time, and they, first of all gave vent to intemperate outbursts of wrath at the unknown peculators who had so disgracefully wronged them ; while Mr. Goosgog brandished his long stick, like a cannibal chief, and loudly declared that if the thieves were anywhere near, and would come forward at once, he would thrash them into barley straw.   And after that fierce paroxysm was over, how Mr. Spindle gave vent to his feelings, and rashly cursed his birthday ; and afterwards bitterly inveighed against the pony, and the chaise too.   How Mr. Goosgog just then, with unprecedented haste, and in terms of caustic severity, condemned his friend for his bombastic vanity and downright deceit in pretending to drive ; when it had been so miserably evident that he knew no more about a horse than a stupid ass, or the "tailor's dummy" that stood just inside their shop door. How Mr. Spindle, at that unexpected thrust and the degrading comparisons, got madly wrath with his friend ; called him a fat China pig, and knocked him down. How Mr. Goosgog got up again, like a game-cock, and fought three rounds with Mr. Spindle, and got knocked down six times more. How they then simultaneously burst into tears, and embraced each other like brothers, then mutually apologised, shook hands, wished each other many happy returns of the day, and sat down on a rock to devour the half-cooked potatoes, which had been overlooked by their spoilers, and to discuss what it was best to do next.

After a short time they decided upon drawing the chaise and harness to the junction of the South Head Road, there to wait till darkness should partially hide their unfortunate poverty of apparel; then to draw the conveyance and appurtenances aforesaid to the nearest hotel, and wait there until they could send to Mrs. Cobbrer, for fresh suits from their wardrobe.

Fortunately, the apron of the chaise, and the dog skin mat, were not taken away, so Jasper took the former, and Joey the latter, and tied them about their persons with parts of the harness. Then Jasper took the shafts, and Joey pushed behind, and, with many sighs and groans, they slowly moved the chaise along the sandy road towards Sydney. They had not gone far, however, when they heard merry voices just before them, and had barely time to leave the chaise and run into the bush, when a furniture van appeared in sight, containing Mr. and Mrs. Duddle, with their large family of grown-up sons and daughters, and two or three neighbours beside, who were on their way to the beach to spend an hour or two.

Of course they stopped to examine the chaise, and to speculate upon the cause of its being left there, apparently abandoned, in the middle of a wild bush road. . The opinions expressed on the subject were very varied; old Mrs. Duddle, however, was the only one of the party who believed that it was exposed there for sale. The discussion was abruptly closed by Mr. Duddle, who, having caught a glimpse of the remarkable figures of Jasper and Joey dodging through the scrub, and thinking of course that they were escaped lunatics, he, in consideration for his large family, and possibly for himself too, thought he had better drive away from their dangerous vicinity as fast as he could, which he did accordingly.

Goosgog and Spindles wriggled on their way, they knew not whither, in a state of bewilderment and physical suffering only to be imagined ; but before long they came in sight of a large house. Luckily for them—as they then too sanguinely thought—two maid-servants were engaged outside the fence, shaking carpets.

Leaving poor exhausted Goosgog at the foot of a large spreading tree, Mr. Spindle stealthily approached, under cover of the scrub, till he got within hail of the maids aforesaid, and screening himself behind a favouring stump ; he called out in his most insinuating tones, " Young women, young women,' if you please."

" Oh, gemini ! what's that, Jane ?" enquired Jane's fellow servant, turning very pale, and gazing all round and up in the air too.

" Goodness me ! I don't know," replied Jane ; " I heard somebody, but I can't see nobody."

Mr. Spindles, with the most scrupulous delicacy, just then peeped from behind the stump and said with an intensely imploring look, which ought to have had more influence—

" My dear girls, just listen a moment——"

" Ah lud !" screamed the girls in concert ; " there's a nasty great fellow behind the stump. Aaron ! Aaron ! Aaron !"

" For pity's sake, listen to me one moment, dear young women," implored Mr. Spindles ; " do, pray hear me—I've lost my clothes."

" Aaron ! Aaron !" screamed the girls, fairly terrified, while they ran inside the fence as fast as they could, leaving their carpets on the ground. Mr. Spindles sprang forward in desperation, seized a piece of the carpet, wrapped it closely round him, and was going up to make an appeal to the master of the house, when a savage-looking gardener, and a still more savage-looking dog appeared at the gate hastily advancing to welcome him. Mr. Spindles turned round instinctively, and ran away much faster than he had ever ran before ; and he never had such good reason to be thankful for his long legs and his Wellington boots, for he had barely time to get to the tree, up which Goosgog had already climbed, when the dog was at his heels. Fortunately for Jasper, he dropped the carpet in his rapid flight, which the dog stopped for a second or two to smell, and gave him barely time to mount into the tree, and thus save himself from being partially devoured.

"Hoold him ! hoold him ! hoold him ! Growler," cried the savage man, running after Jasper with a garden rake in his hand. "Catch him, boy ; catch him."

But Mr. Spindles had very fortunately got out of catching distance, and when the gardener came up the wretched friends were perched on opposite branches of the tree, looking like two strange species of melancholy monkeys, almost breathless with terror and their violent exertions of climbing to their refuge ; while Growler—an immense mastiff—was sitting at the base of the tree, showing his teeth, with his mind evidently made up to wait there till they found it convenient to come down and be worried.

"Hur yer bushranging ruffians ; I've got yer now safe enough ; I've been looking for you this long time," snarled the man, coming up within pistol shot of them—but no nearer. "Look to them, Growler ! Hoy, Mike," he roared to a stable boy, "Mount black Jack, and ride in for three or four constables ; tell em to bring handcuffs for two, for I've got two desperate rascals—Gardiner and Gilbert I think—bailed up in a gum tree. Look sharp, do yer hear, Mike ?"

"I'll be there an' back agin afore you could ate a hot murphy," said Mike, as he ran to the stable for the horse, and was soon riding off at full gallop towards Sydney.

"Now, my pretty 'Cockatoo Islanders,' you'd better hop down off your perch, and march to the stable yonder," said the gardener, "and then I can keep you under-lock and key. I'm not going to stay here all night looking at your ugly mugs."

"Oh, pray hear us speak ; for mercy's sake do," whined Mr. Goosgog and Mr. Spindles together, " we are not thieves, sir, we are——"

"Not thieves, eh !" sneered the man, "why confound your impudence, what next will you say ? didn't I see you running away with the parlour carpet, with my own eyes, eh ? And haven't you frightened my wife into a fit,. yer great, long, ugly bundle of bamboos. You're the very same fellows as stole the garden roller, and the gig harness, the week before last. I know yer manœuvres, my boys—you came here on a foraging expedition, and yer thought if yer came naked, I shouldn't be able to swear to yer clothes, but that old trick won't do at this shop. I'll write my mark on yer directly, and you won't be able to scratch it out very quickly. Now then, my hobgoblins, are you coming down into the stable or not? that's what I want to know."

"Oh, for goodness sake, hear us! Call away that great dog, there's a dear man, then we'll come down directly—we are—"

"Call away the dog, eh? I dare say, and give you a chance to bolt? No, no, not to-day, daddy-long-legs. I've seen how you can run, and perhaps the fat fellow can run too; I might as well try to catch a kangaroo as catch you, if I let you give me the slip. No, no, I can't do without the dog; but I'll give you a few minutes to consider about it, while I go and get my gun : and if you don't come down I'll tattoo you all over with dust shot ; and then if you do get away from me, I shall know you again. Look to them, Growler, my boy, pin 'em, Growler."

The surly gardener then went into the house for his gun, leaving the dog sitting at the foot of the tree ; looking at his poor shivering prisoners, as stolidly as if he were made of the hardest timber.

The gardener returned from the house in about ten minutes, armed with a double-barrelled gun, and a shot belt round his waist. "Now then; once; twice; thrice; as the soldiers on sentry say. I'll give you fair warning, and if you don't come down from the tree, and walk straight into that stable yonder, I'll pepper you till you do; so mind your eyes. I don't want to kill you, though you don't deserve any mercy (dust shot won't break your bones) but I want to caution you like I do the flying foxes, that steal my peaches. I told master last week I thought I'd catch you fellows soon. Now then ;—once."

"Hoo-o—hoo-o—hoo-o," roared Mr. Goosgog.

"Ay, it's no good making that row, my native bears ; you had better come down. Twice——"

"I protest against your murdering us in this cold-blooded manner," shouted Mr. Spindles, rousing up his courage.

" You shall suffer for this outrage, you cowardly villain. We are gentlemen, and we——"

" Ho-ho-ho !" jeered the gardener. " Gentlemen, are you ? That's just what Dick Turpin and his mate, Tom King, the infamous highwaymen, used to say. You look very genteel, certainly. Now, don't give me any more of your sauce. Time's up—thrice. My name's Aaron Horseradish, and *that's my mark*—I can't write."

Saying which he pulled the trigger, and the charge of dust-shot scattered through the tree, and a proportion of it entered the skins of poor Joey and Jasper, who acknowledged the receipt thereof by a prolonged howl.

" There, that's one ; and as you don't seem to like that, I'll give you another," said Aaron ; but just as he was about to give them another, his attention was drawn to a number of horsemen, who were riding rapidly through the bush towards him.

" Hoy, my man," shouted one of the horsemen, " have you seen anything of two nak——"

" Seen 'em ? ay, to be sure I have," interrupted old Horseradish, dancing and pointing with his gun to the tree with fiendish triumph, while the dog got up and wagged his stumpy tail in delight, as if he were exactly of the same opinion as his master—that the horsemen were detectives, come out in search of two notorious bushrangers.

" Hurrah ! here they are," yelled Horseradish, as the strangers rode rapidly up ; " I've bailed them up in the tree, and I was just going to give 'em some more black pepper. They're an awful looking pair of scoun——"

Before he could finish the libellous sentence he was knocked down, gun and all, by the excited party of horsemen, who crowded round the base of the tree. But the joyful exclamations of Goosgog and Spindles drowned the cries of the unlucky gardener ; with the howls of Growler too, who had his toes trodden on by one of the panting steeds, and had run away to his kennel lest he should get them trodden on again.

Words are inadequate to describe the delight of the two poor sufferers at beholding the welcome faces of about half a score of their intimate acquaintances ; and it would be equally impossible to describe the consternation of Aaron Horseradish, on finding that he had been shooting at two

respectable citizens of Sydney, instead of those terrible
scourges of society, Gardiner and Gilbert.

A rapid explanation followed, which I must give as rapidly. It appears that some boys who had wandered along
the rocks, from Coogee to Bondi, had found, first of all, the
market basket ; and as " boys will be boys," they sat down
and ate everything in it that was eatable. After they had
done so, and while they were perhaps looking about for
another basket to devour, they espied two heaps of clothing
under a cliff, at which they were rather alarmed, for they
naturally concluded that the owners thereof were drowned.
After a hasty look for bodies on the rocks, and along the
beach, without being able to find any, they took the clothing
and the basket, and hurried into Sydney with the alarming
news.

A " hue and cry " was raised immediately, and poor old
Mrs. Cobbrer went into hysterics. When she came out
again, she found her house full of sympathising enquirers of
both sexes, whom she was, of course, unable to enlighten in
the smallest degree, beyond giving them a sight of the empty
basket and the empty clothes, for which they all seemed very
much obliged to her.

A general muster of the friends and acquaintances of the
lost ones took place, and a large muster it was. Without
loss of time, they started out on horseback and in vehicles
of various kinds to Bondi Bay. Their good friend Captain
Codger, had a coil of rope round his horse's neck, with a
small grapnell attached. The crowd increased as it went
forward, and about four o'clock, to the astonishment of Mr.
Duddle and his party, who were just taking tea, a multitude
of persons descended to the beach, and began to search
every hole in the rocks big enough for a large crab to crawl
into, while the captain uncoiled his rope and grappled in the
surf with an energy and anxiety quite touching.

As soon as Mr. Duddle ascertained the object of the excited seekers, he informed them of the two nude figures he
had seen dodging through the bush ; so a party of horsemen immediately started in search of them ; but the
majority of the friends were sceptical of Mr. Duddle's information, and remained behind to examine the rocks, and
assist old Codger to investigate the rollers with his grapnell.

The reader knows the result of the bush expedition, and
my story will soon be ended. It is not necessary to dwell

upon the horror of Aaron Horseradish, who dreaded being tried for " wounding with intent, &c." Nor upon the magnanimous manner in which the truly kind-hearted friends raised the contrite gardener from his knees before them, and how they afterwards accepted his pressing offer of the loan of two suits of his best clothes. How that four policemen rode up, armed with loaded carbines, just as the friends smilingly emerged from Aaron's house, clad in suits of worsted cord and colonial tweed, which could hardly be called " good fits," considering that Aaron was a slim man of only five feet six.

Mr. Goosgog and Mr. Spindles were taken home in triumph in a " Hansom," with the chaise and harness towing behind, and followed by an immense cavalcade, including the constables ; and as they rode along, their honest hearts glowed with pride and amazement at the general affection which was manifested towards them. They had not the least idea before that they had so many friends ; quite forgetting, in their simplicity, that they were *supposed to be dead.* In the excess of their joy that they were not dead, and at being so highly appreciated by such a respectable multitude, they nobly invited everybody to sup with them, to the utter bewilderment of poor Mrs. Cobbrer, whose house was filled to overflowing, and the contents of many cooks' shops were necessary to feed the hungry guests.

Mr. Spindles made his *debût* as a speaker that night ; and in returning thanks for an appropriate toast to his honour, he, among many noteworthy sentiments, remarked emphatically " that he had never spent such an exciting birthday since the day of his birth."

*   *   *   *   *   *

Soon afterwards Jasper and Joey went into partnership ; and in a few years the firm of Spindles and Goosgog was reputed to be wealthy. Wealth and wisdom are often supposed to be associated, and Mr. Spindles was waited on by a deputation, requesting him to represent them as Member of Parliament for East Sydney. They declared their unanimous opinion of his fitness for the work and honour, in such forcible terms, that his doubts began to dissolve. He smirked and tried to look modest, while his long face was flushed with new pride. He was about to express his willingness to exert his talents for the public good, when

Mr. Goosgog stepped quietly up and whispered in his ear, "Remember Bondi Bay, and the pony chaise." Jasper was startled at the salutary hint, but so far from getting cross, he smiled pleasantly at his partner, and manfully confessed to his admiring friends, that he was totally ignorant of political science, for which simple reason, he must decline the honour of representing them in parliament.

There are many eager aspirants for legislative honours, who know as little of political economy as Jasper knew about driving a pony, and if they will follow his prudent example, and leave parliamentary seats for able men to occupy, they will confer a great benefit on the community, and perhaps save themselves from Aaron Horseradish's "black pepper," in the form of public contempt and ridicule.

POOR GIRL!

THERE she stands, under that public-house gas-lamp, with a maudlin smile on her faded face, and an affected, careless air; but her soul is as be-clouded as a winter's night, and her heart within her is seared. She attracts but few libidinous glances from prowling "fast men," for her charms are all blighted by disease, anxiety, and sensual excesses; and, like a tender flower, withered by a hot wind, her beauty is gone. Her draggled finery is faded too, and betokens poverty and neglect, while scarcely a trace of maidenly modesty, or self-respect, is visible.

But she is still young, and her figure retains somewhat of its bygone symmetry; while her long brown tresses—though dishevelled by the rough wind—tell of the time when they fell in flowing ringlets over her fair shoulders, and attracted the admiration of all beholders. Her full blue eyes too, though lustreless as rough pebbles in a rock, are mournfully suggestive of those happy days of girlhood and innocence, when the proudest youth in our city would have felt honoured by a favouring glance from Mary May.

Why stands she there in her scanty attire, on this bleak night? Dark storm-clouds are gathering in the western sky, and the rumbling thunder forewarns that a tempest is approaching. Why stands she there, as if in defiance of the warring elements, while most of the citizens of Sydney are preparing for their beds? Why does she not go home? Alas! poor girl! In all this wide world she has not a roof to shelter her head from the angry winds; she is homeless, cheerless, and penniless. A wreck on the strand, or a waif on life's turbulent ocean. A miserable outcast—a poor lost girl. May God pity her! for no pity does she get from man, and very little from woman either. To the tender sympathy, and kindly offices of her sex, she has long been a stranger; and she is ignorant of God's love and mercy, in providing a way of redemption for even such as she. Spurned and contemned by all but the very lowest dregs of society, she is a sworn foe to mankind, who have severed her from all endearing social ties, blasted her hopes, and

made her young life a dreary waste, and an intolerable burden ; from which she has often been tempted to rid herself
by violent means, and wickedly to rush into the awful presence of her Maker.

Do you ask me, reader, who is this poor girl?   Are you
anxious to know what has so cruelly blighted her happiness ?
Listen then and I will tell you, for I know her history well.
I have known her ever since the time when her prattling
tongue could but imperfectly pronounce my name ; and
when her little hands were often held.out for the "sweeties,"
which my coat-pocket usually contained for my many young
favourites.

Memory—obedient to my will—flies back a dozen years
or more, and presents poor Mary to my mental gaze, as I
knew her, a frolicsome girl of thirteen ; the hope and pride
of indulgent parents, who idolised their only child, and expected for her the admiration of all their friends and neighbours.   Mr. and Mrs. May were a simple-hearted old pair ;
true and just in all their dealings ; unsuspecting and con-
fiding in their nature.   They had seen very little of the
world, and were unacquainted with its sophistries.   Their
beloved daughter was as innocent as a lambkin sporting in
the green meadows beside its dam, and as unconscious of
evil lurking in her pathway.   If she knew that she was
beautiful, she knew not the dangers to which that much
coveted gift would expose her.   Life was full of happiness
to her sanguine view, for she had seen nothing of its dark
obverse.   Trouble had never darkened her happy home, and
real sorrow had never chased the sunshine from her charming face.   The world to her seemed bounded by the meandering river, whose noiseless current—typical of her own
life—flowed before her parents' cottage in peaceful beauty,
and the wild woods beyond, whither she so often rambled
to gather flowers to bedeck their rustic home, or to weave
garlands for her pet kangaroo.

> " Far from the busy world's ignoble strife,
>   Her sober fancies never learned to stray ;
> Along the cool sequestered vale of life,
>   She held the even tenor of her way."

Well do I remember little Mary in those days of innocence ; often have I stroked her sunny ringlets, and gazed
with delight into her merry blue eyes, so full of artless love
and childish fun.   She was indeed as joyous hearted a

maiden as ever made a wilderness vocal with cheerful melody. I can fancy I see her now : and as I contrast her with that draggled, forlorn creature under the gin-shop lamp, my heart within me sickens at the sight, and with difficulty I restrain the rising feeling of wrath, which would tower over my settled loathing for the creature who could deliberately lure to ruin an innocent girl, whom he should feel bound by every manly consideration to shield from impure influences, and be ever ready to guard from injury or insult. While I tearfully gaze at the wreck before me, at the wretched victim of a villain's perfidy, my fervent prayer ascends on her behalf to the mercy seat of the Almighty Judge of all the earth, who alone can comfort her care-worn spirit, and redress her wrongs.

But I have promised to give an outline of poor Mary's history. Very brief it will be, for my pen falters at the task. This is not a solitary case in my experience, I have seen many such, and have been an eye witness to scenes of anguish, which might move the veriest *roué* in the land to pity, if his heart were not wholly burnt up by the lustful fires which his life has been spent in feeding.

Mary's father died when she was about sixteen years of age, and it then became necessary for her to contribute to her mother's support. To that end she bound herself for a term to a respectable woman (who kept a little shop in the country), to be taught the millinery business. Every morning after breakfast Mary hastened away to her work, and returned home in the evening : the distance was but little more than a mile. For a few months all went on smoothly. Mary made good progress in her new occupation, for she was a quick, intelligent girl, and she looked joyfully forward to the time when she would begin to earn a little money and be enabled to add to her mother's comforts, and perhaps to increase her own limited stock of finery and necessaries.

About this time, Lionel Wolfe, the eldest son of a wealthy landed proprietor in the neighbourhood, returned to the colony, after finishing his education and his travels on the continent of Europe. He was a young man of showy exterior, about twenty-five years of age ; and being the heir of the Wolfden estates, his return created no small stir in the usually quiet village of Woollaburra.

If I say that Lionel Wolfe was a " fast young man," almost every one will understand his character, so I need not particularise it. It was not long before his gloating eyes were fixed upon Mary May. Her rare beauties and modest mien smote his heart with love,—stay; what am I writing? A feeling so holy and pure as love never entered the heart of a practised debauchee, never! It was not love, but quite a different kind of passion, which inflamed Wolfe's breast at the first sight of the pretty little country lass, as she tripped along one evening towards her mother's cottage. He saw her, and at once conceived the designs against her virtue, which, alas! he too surely carried into effect.

To describe all the arts employed by that accomplished seducer, would require a more patient pen than mine. He did not effect his purpose by a *coup de main*, he was too wily to attempt anything so bold, with the timid unsophisticated girl, who trembled at the notice of one so much her superior in position. Slowly and deliberately he concocted his schemes; slily he spread his nets, and anxiously he watched them, until the poor little bird was inveigled within their fatal meshes; then very soon her lovely plumage was ruffled, her golden wings broken, and her joyful song of innocence was silenced for ever.

Here I will digress from my story a little. Grieved indeed should I be, to pen one word which would raise a blush on any fair cheek. I do not willingly choose this delicate and distressing subject for my pen; nor do I enter upon my task with a light feeling; but a fatherly love for, and an earnest desire to guard the virtue of the young maidens of this land, constrain me to offer a few words of counsel, which I pray them to ponder over.

'I would speak to you, fair girl, whose bright eyes glance over these sketches! In words of affectionate warning, I would say to you, beware of the first advances of the bold designing man. One repellent look, indicative of the horror with which your pure young mind regards his rude remarks, full of hidden meaning, his sensual leers, the undue pressure of your gentle hand, or any other ungentlemanlike way in which his insidious work is begun. One such look may save you from a repetition of the rude familiarities of those traitors, with whom you are too often thrown into accidental contact. Very few such fellows would have the courage to renew an attack, when thus foiled in the first instance, for they are usually as cowardly as they are treacherous. Poor

Mary May neglected that precaution; perhaps she had never been warned of the danger of encouraging the forward salutations of strangers; howbeit she *did not* repel young Wolfe's first advances; an intimacy sprung up, and in a very short time she fell a victim to the practised arts of the seducer. Pardon me, dear young reader, for naming you in the same lines with that polluted wreck under the gas lamp yonder; and for beseeching you to take warning by her sad fate, and flee from the voice of the flatterer. Pardon me, I ask, and remember that I knew her when she was as lovely and as pure as you are now; and when all about her pathway was sunshine and joy.

I shall never forget the heart-rending scene which my eyes beheld in widow May's cottage, a little more than a year afterwards; a scene which I should like to compel every seducer to witness before receiving a merited flogging. Months before I had heard of the *faux pas* of the village belle; for in small country communities scandal flies swifter than swallows. I had heard of her intimacy and her flirtations with Lionel Wolfe, and had warned both Mary and her mother too of their danger, and advised them at once to sever their connection with the unprincipled rake, who from his antecedents I judged was plotting the young girl's destruction. But my advice was too late to be of real service to them, for Wolfe had completely gained the girl's affections, and had persuaded her mother that he loved her daughter, and intended to make her his wife. I need not enter into painful details; it is the old sad story, which has been told hundreds of times before, which has been the death blow to many aged parents, and "brought down their grey hairs with sorrow to the grave." Poor Mary fell a victim to the plots of Lionel Wolfe: how could it be otherwise after she had once admitted his influence? She was a comparatively easy prey, for her mind was unfortified by religion; she had not been early instructed in divine truth; she had not learned to know and love the Saviour, and to flee to Him at all times for support and guidance; she lacked, too, sound paternal counsel and protection. A resolute sire, or brother, are as effective in scaring prowling villains from the domestic hearth, as sharp dogs are in guarding back-yards from petty thieves. But she had no such trusty guardians, which her deceiver well knew; moreover, she loved him with all the warmth of her young heart's first affections; and for that

love, that self-immolation, he very soon returned coldness,
then closely followed neglect, scorn, and positive brutality.
To her impassioned appeals to him to save her reputation,
to fulfil his oft-repeated promise and make her his wife, he
from time to time returned evasive answers ; and to her last
pathetic appeal to him, on her knees, for the sake of the
infant which she shortly expected to bring into the world,
he spurned her from him, and coarsely applying an epithet,
at which every woman shudders, he left her tearing her hair
in an agony of grief.

  *   *   *   *   *   *

There she lay, with an infant folded to her bosom, when
I entered her cottage, about a week after her accouchement.
I shall ever remember that dreary morning, though I wish I
could forget it, for my heart aches while picturing it, even
now.

Pillowed up in an old arm chair in the front room, sat
Mrs. May, with the marks of death in her countenance.
The anxiety of the last few months had proved too severe
for her impaired strength, and she had sunk beneath the
trial. Her mind, too, was as enfeebled as her body, which
was perhaps a merciful alleviation of her sufferings. At
times she seemed to forget her griefs, and to fancy her Mary
was again a child playing beside her, in the same merry
mood that she used to do in happy days gone by : and then
the poor old soul would hold imaginary conversations in the
fondling style in which she used to talk to her "wee Polly;"
and repeat the nursery rhymes, which in those days delighted her little smiling companion. Suddenly, however,
the recollection of the present forlorn condition of her still
idolized daughter, would burst upon her mind like an overwhelming flood, then her anguish and weeping exclamations
of despair were more than I could bear to witness, and I
was glad to escape from that scene of sorrow, even to one,
scarcely less painful to behold, in the adjoining room, where
lay poor Mary on a clean little stretcher bed, with her infant
pressed to her agitated heart. Her disengaged hand was
held before her eyes, but tears coursed down her face, and
her sobs prevented her from articulating a word. I stood
beside her bed and gazed at her in mournful silence. My
heart was too full to speak, but she knew that I sincerely
pitied her ; she knew that I had not called to upbraid her,
as some of her neighbours had done not an hour before,

while they professed to condole with her. There lay the poor young creature almost destitute of common necessaries, and oppressed with grief indescribable ; and as I gazed at her I could not but contrast her deplorable condition with a scene fresh in my memory—that of a happy young wife, with her first-born on her bosom, and every comfort at her command ; cheered by the caresses of her loving husband, and the congratulations of surrounding friends, and her heart bounding with joy and pride while fondling her precious little new-born treasure, which every one was praising.

But I must hasten on with my dismal story. In a few days Mrs. May died of a broken heart, and before poor Mary could rise from her wearisome couch, she had the anguish of seeing her only parent's body borne away to the grave, and the additional pang of feeling that she had been the cause of her beloved mother's untimely death, and the months of misery that had preceded it.

I should have mentioned before, that directly Mrs. May had. discovered her daughter's critical state, she made a personal appeal to Lionel Wolfe's father and mother to use their influence and induce their son to do justice to her daughter, and marry her, as he had solemnly promised to do. But the arrogant old pair would not listen to the end of her tearful address ; she was moreover told by Wolfe's prudish sisters, that she and her brazen-faced daughter had designedly entrapped their brother to the disgrace of his family. They also refused the smallest assistance, and ignored Mrs. May's claim upon them in any shape ; then peremptorily ordering her not to enter the gates of Wolfden again, they turned from her in disdain, and left the old lady to retrace her weary way home with her heart stricken by a sorrow which can only be comprehended by those whose domestic hearth has been similarly desolated.

How Mary May struggled on for the next two years was often a matter of speculation for those who feast upon scandal, and there were many such moral pests in Woolla-burra. Several respectable residents, however, could testify that Mary lived a virtuous life during that period. She worked to support herself and infant, and her scanty earnings were supplemented by voluntary donations from friends who carefully watched over her. She lodged with a worthy old couple in the outskirts of the town, and kept very secluded; seldom going beyond the garden which surrounded her humble domicile.

Her infant died when about two years old. Doubtless it was a merciful dispensation of Providence in removing it beyond the influence of a frowning world, and taking it to Heaven; but it was a terrible loss to poor Mary. She felt it hard to part with her baby, though it had caused her such crushing trouble. It seemed the only tie she had to life; it was her constant companion, and the only creature in the world that she had to love. She lavished all the affection of her nature upon it, and its innocent prattle helped to lighten her life's dreary burden, and to cheer her blighted heart. Mothers will understand her feelings better than I can describe them, and I need not further dwell upon this fresh trial, which very nearly shattered her reason. Daily she would wander to her baby's grave to moisten the cold sod with her tears, and pour out her sorrows unseen by any eyes but the little birds in the tall sighing oaks around the cemetery, and by that Omniscient eye which watches the little birds, and sees that all their wants are supplied. Poor girl! she was almost broken-hearted; the woods often re-echoed her melancholy lamentations for her lost baby, and throughout long sleepless nights she would bemoan her hapless misery.

About that time, Lionel Wolfe (who had settled in Victoria), paid a visit to Wolfden for a month, and, during that period he had repeated interviews with Mary May, notwithstanding the remonstrances of the honest old folks with whom she lodged. Weakened as her mind was by her various troubles, and especially by her recent bereavement, it is no marvel that he easily obtained a mastering influence over her, and that she became again his willing slave. One morning, shortly after Wolfe had departed for Victoria, Mary was missing at Woollaburra, and for sometime her whereabouts was a mystery; but at length it transpired that she was in Melbourne, in the keeping of the unprincipled author of all her miseries.

Further efforts were made by friends who were interested in her case, to rescue her from her betrayer; but the means they tried were all in vain, she seemed fast bound by a fatal spell which she would not try to break. Drink was resorted to by her to drown reflection, and madly she sped in the race to ruin, as thousands of other miserable girls are rushing at this very hour. She lived but a few months with Wolfe; he soon grew tired of his companion, who was usually either madly hilarious from the effects of drink, or suffering from its reaction, and sorrowing in all the bitterness of ruined hopes and down-crushed love.

Soon she was an inmate of a fashionable brothel in Melbourne. She had been cast off by her paramour (who had gone into the far interior to evade his creditors), and was pounced upon by one of those wicked hags who live by the wages of poor deluded women, to whom a young and still beautiful girl like Mary, was a prize which would for a short time prove a new attraction to her horrible lair, and bring money to her hoard. I dare not trust my pen to express my abhorrence of these rapacious fiends, or those persons who encourage their iniquitous calling.

Down, down, down! whirled poor Mary, like a frail canoe in the rapids. No mind can picture her sufferings during the succeeding five years. Her own sad words were, "My body and mind have been racked with the tortures of hell; and death, in its most painful form would have been a luxury to me. Disease, delirium, madness! have poisoned my blood! have wrecked me!" Poor girl! what a wasted life of misery has yours been! Who can understand the anguish of your blasted heart? Tottering old *roués* look at her! Fast young men look at her! Mothers and sisters look at her! May God look in pity upon her, and may He inspire many Christian hearts to pity her, and others who are like her, dreary wanderers on the world's wide stage.

Mary has recently come from Melbourne in search of Lionel Wolfe; and she harbours wild vengeance in her heart. She will perhaps try to murder him if they meet, and then commit suicide, for she is desperate. There she stands, on the verge of perdition; but she must not be suffered to go over, while she is within the reach of Christian hands. "Haste to the rescue." Her blood will be upon your head if you allow her to perish without attempting to save her.

*　*　*　*　*　*

There is a " Home " in this city for such as she; and polluted as she is, she will be gladly received within its walls, and have all her wants kindly attended to. There she may find a refuge from the cold winds and still colder blasts of the world's scorn. There she will be led to Him who kindly suffered such an one as she to wash his sacred feet with her tears; to her Saviour, who loves her, who will graciously receive her, and fill her poor torn heart with peace, such as she never felt, even in the blithesome days of her childhood; He will gently guide her along life's rugged road, and when she arrives at her journey's end receive her cleansed soul into His glorious rest.

All honour to those benevolent ladies and gentlemen who conduct the Female Refuge. Through their noble efforts many fallen women have been lifted up, almost from the depths of despair, and restored to the path of virtue. The great day alone will declare the sum total of good, which has been wrought by that excellent institution.

Reader! help it with an annual contribution. It will be money well invested, and help to make its freely offered hospitality known to those homeless wanderers, who you so often see staggering in your pathway. Pity the poor creatures, and try to turn them gently round and put them on the road to heaven. And if this should be read by one of those forlorn ones; I beg of her to go at once, knock at the door of the Refuge, and therein find rest for her weary body and mind.

OLD DADDY GUMMY AND KITTY MAYBERRY.

" HA, ha, ha ! I'm so glad !" chuckled Jabez Gummy, as he
sat on the side of his bed, stitching a brace button on his
drab kerseymere small clothes, one Monday morning. " No
more stitching for me after I have fastened this blessed button : this is my last act of molly-coddlery. Hurra ! I'll
throw my thimble out of the window in a minute, and give
my cotton box to old Mrs. Budge—no, no, I won't though,
I forgot, it was a present from my grandmother, forty years
ago last Christmas, so I'll keep it for her sake ; it would be
undutiful to part with it, and Mrs. Budge does not deserve
it, for she has woefully neglected my wardrobe. My best
linen shirts look as yellow as old blankets, and I do believe
she wears my flannel waistcoats, drat her. Ha, ha, ha !
I'm to be married next Friday ! Won't it be funny? If I
had plucked up heart to take the mysterious leap long ago,
I might have made some pretty little maid a happy wife,
and have had—but never mind, I'm just in time. The fact
is, I have been afraid of the feminine gender ever since that
unlucky affair with Ann Spike, in 1840, which split my
heart like a ripe plum. But bother her, I don't care a button for her now ; my dear little Kitty is worth forty old cats
—ha ! ha ! ha ! Bravo, Jabez ! you have not forgotten the
way to wheedle the women, though you have been long out
of practice, but you have got a real jewel at last—or almost
as good as got her. Hurra ! again ; no more domestic discomforts, which I have writhed under for nearly half a
century. No more losing arguments with old Mother Budge
about her omnivorous cat, and her mischievous boy Billy, or
her mystified accounts. No more dull wearisome days, and
lonely nights. No, no ; I shall have a dear little wife to
develope the latent virtues of my disposition ; to love, honour, and cherish me, and make this sombre old house as
shiny as a light-house lantern. Ho, ho, ho ! how nice it
will be !"
The exciting idea made Mr. Gummy chuckle again, till
he began to cough so fiercely, that he owned to himself, as

he sat down to his solitary breakfast-table, a few minutes afterwards, " that he felt quite weak in the knees."

*   *   *   *   *   *

" Zounds ! what next ?   Daddy Gummy is actually going to marry Kitty Mayberry," grumbled Mr. Grouts.   " Did anybody ever hear of such an old gooseberry ?" He is sixty-five years old if he is a fortnight, while the girl has only just done with her dolls, and has no more love for the tooth-less old toddler than I have for Mammy Wombat, the black gin.   Poor little puss, she is bedazzled by the glitter of his money, the idea of a grand wedding, and riding to church in a coach.   I dare say it is rare fun for her to prattle with her playfellows about her fine house, and her dear old fogey who doats upon her, but I doubt if she has bestowed five minutes serious thought on the responsibilities she is taking upon herself; much less has she foreseen the gloomy reality of being tied to a ricketty old man, whose temperament is as opposite to her own as June is to January.   I pity her, poor thing, but as for Jabez—well, perhaps I had better not say all I think of him, or I may be thought uncivil.   I will say though, that he ought to have common sense enough to know that a giddy girl will not make him a good wife.   In his long life he has doubtless seen scores of homes made wretched by want of sympathy and unity of feeling, and he cannot reasonably expect much of those social virtues from a girl young enough to be his grand-daughter.   Pshaw ! I have no patience with the old gander !   But I consider it is positively wrong to sit still and see a silly couple plunge into misery, so I am determined to stop them, if warning words will do it."

" Ugh ! stop them indeed ! you may as well try to stop a train by whistling ' Cockabendy,' " growled Mrs. Grouts. " They will be tied together, as tightly as you and I are, before this day week in spite of all you can say.   The little minx told our Betsy last night, that she will jingle the mil-dew off the old boy's money as soon as she can coax the keys of the cash box from him ; so it is plain enough what she is marrying for, and I'll bet you a penny she will bolt off with young Ben Spry before she is a year older.   As for Jabez he is up to his eyes in love, as the saying is, and all the words in the dictionary won't cure him, so don't bother yourself in trying, master ; that's my advice.   You had better take warning by what your Uncle Dick got for himself when interfering in a similar case.   You know he had to wear a bob wig, all his days, to hide the mark of the hot fire-shovel on his crown."

"I don't care for hot fire-shovels if they are in the way of duty," said Mr. Grouts, bravely.   "I mean to use my influence with Kitty's mother, if Jabez won't listen to reason."

"Poogh ! that's no use neither, for she told me only yesterday she knew Gummy would make her girl a good husband. 'To be sure he is older than Kitty,' said she, 'but that isn't of much account now a days ; you often see such disparities. He is a healthy man, though rather skinny, and he is as merry and frisky as she every bit ; besides, he is not so old as folks say, and is able to provide handsomely for her, so I don't see that it is such a bad match as the times go.   He is doatingly fond of her, there is no doubt of that, and Kitty will like anybody who is kind to her.' Those are the very words widow Mayberry said to me," continued Mrs. Grouts, "so it is pretty clear that what you may say to her will not stop the match, but will very likely make all the family enemies to us ; then woe to our garden, for they will let all their cocks and hens loose again !"

"Humph !   But Jabez is an old crony of mine, and I am really more concerned about him than about the girl," said Mr. Grouts.   "We know that only a week or two ago she was flirting with Ben Spry, and I dare say she is fond of him, for he is a smart young fellow, only he happens to be poor, which is equal to a serious failing with widow Mayberry ; more simpleton she, for I declare if Kitty were my girl, I would rather let her have Ben with only his trade to depend on, than old Gummy if he could load the ship "La Hogue" with Spanish dollars.   I don't like to say anything to Jabez about Kitty's flirtations, for it would look like tattling, and you know I abhor that sort of mischief ; but if I could stop his marriage by some honest means, I am sure he will be much obliged to me when he returns to his senses. At any rate, I'll try what I can do," added Mr. Grouts, taking his hat and stick.   "I'll walk over to his house and have a little quiet chat with him, and if love has not blinded him outright, he will see that he is running into nettles, and stop in time."

His wife exclaimed, "Stuff and nonsense !" Nevertheless, away went Mr. Grouts on his delicate errand, and soon he was welcomed by his old friend Jabez, whom he found very busy overlooking his wearing apparel, and arranging it in a handsome wardrobe, which had been sent from the upholsterer's that afternoon.

"Glad to see you, Grouts," said Jabez, grinning like an ape who had just picked up a soldier's jacket; "I'm in a bit of a muddle, you see, but I know you will excuse it. Take a seat—stay, stay, don't sit on my frilled shirt, or you'll ruin me. That is an important part of my wedding outfit. Blue coat, drab breeches and gaiters, buff waistcoat, and a frilled shirt; shan't I look buckish? ho, ho, ho! Wasn't you tremendously tickled when you heard I was going to tie the knot?"

"No, I wasn't tickled at all, Jabez, but I was very much astonished at your choosing a girl who only a month or two ago was in short petticoats," said Mr. Grouts, drily. "We have always been in the habit of speaking plainly to each other, so I tell you candidly that I wish you had courted her mother instead."

"Ha, ha, ha! I always liked spring lamb," chuckled Jabez; "Kitty is much handsomer than her mother, and she is intensely fond of me. She is always stroking my beard, and calling me her pee-weet. She will make a loving little wife, I'm sure; just the one for me, for I like to be petted. The darling! ho, ho, ho! Don't you wish you were Jabez Gummy, eh, Grouts?"

"Bah!" grunted Mr. Grouts. "I hope you won't get pepper-mint sauce with your spring lamb. Now, seriously, Jabez, do you think it is natural for a lass of seventeen to be very fond of an old chap of seventy."

"Stop, stop, I'm not seventy," said Jabez, with a show of anger, "I am only sixty-six next January, so don't cheat me: and I can't see anything so unnatural in the affair as you wish to make out. You see old chaps, as you call them, marrying young girls often enough, so there is nothing very wonderful in my preferring a young wife to an old one."

"Yes, and you often see those young wives neglecting their homes and their old husbands, and there is nothing wonderful in that neither," replied Mr. Grouts. "I don't intend to say a syllable to the prejudice of Kitty, or to insinuate that she will not make a faithful wife, but in general terms I mean to say that when old men are silly enough to marry young girls, they usually look for more attention from them than they get, or than they can reasonably expect ; thus they are very often tormented with jealous fears and fancies, real or imaginary, and their lives are made miserable. I will give you one sad example, which just occurs to me. A gentleman, more than threescore years old, married his gardener's daughter, a buxom lass of nineteen or thereabouts. She was a good girl, and I believe for several years was as true a wife as any in the land, still her husband suspected her of flirting with every young fellow who presumed to look at her pretty face. In vain did she try to reason him out of his jealous fancies, and give him every proof she could give of her fidelity ; he grew worse as he grew older, until her life was a complete burden. She became reckless and ill-tempered. Horse-whipping did not improve her ; she took to drinking, and a few years ago you might have seen her on any night you chose to look into one of the singing saloons of Sydney ; so you may guess her deplorable end. Mind, I don't say that all such unequal marriages terminate so badly, for I have known cases quite contrary ; but they are rare, and I take the freedom of an old friend, to warn you against the risk you are incurring in marrying a girl so much younger than yourself. That lassie will not make a suitable wife for you, Jabez, I am sure of that, and I advise you for pity's sake to give her up."

"O dear me ! I can't, I can't. Don't say that again, Grouts, it hurts. I love the girl, and if I give her up I shall give up the ghost in less than three weeks ; I am sure of that. Can't you see how my knees are knocking together, at the bare idea of it ? The fact is my heart has been as impenetrable as a fire-proof safe for nearly thirty years, but Kitty has picked the lock at last, and got right inside, and to turn her out would be ten times worse than skinning me. I can't do it, Grouts. Ask me to do anything else that's reasonable, and I'll oblige you in a minute, but I can't give up Kitty, I'd almost as soon give up taking snuff, and that would be the greatest trial in life that I can think of. Besides, look at this house full of feminine knickknacks, what would be the use of them to me if I lost my little doxey ? They were all bought for her, bless her heart !"

"Please, sir, a boy has brought a lot of bottles and things from Mr. Lint, the chemist," interrupted Mrs. Budge, opening the door, without knocking.

"Yes, yes, all right, lots of scent ; I shall smell like a

nosegay on Friday. Bring them in, Mrs. Budge. Let me
see, I think I'll put them on a shelf in my wardrobe for the
present," said Jabez, who forthwith began to stow away
sundry bottles of perfumery, and a large gallipot full of
pomatum, which Mr. Lint had specially prepared and warranted it would make hair grow on Jabez's bald head, and
turn his grey beard dark brown. "Excuse me for neglecting you, Grouts, but you see I am up to my neck in confusion.   I wish you would come and see me this day
fortnight, and stay a long while : I shall be calm as a dish
of cream then, and we can talk over things comfortably.
Say you will come, and bring Mrs. Grouts with you. Hoy,
Mrs. Budge ! stop the boy ! he has left a bottle of soothing
mixture for Mrs. Fitz, over the way." Jabez hobbled out
of the room with the mis-sent bottle, and while he was gone
Mr. Grouts glanced over the perfumery on the shelf,
especially noticing the pomatum pot, which was without a
label.

"I don't want to hinder you," said Mr. Grouts, as Jabez
returned breathless and faint, after his exertion of running
to the front door, " but I was going to remark, when your
housekeeper disturbed us, that if you love Kitty as I believe
you do, you may prove the disinterestedness of your love,
and do a noble action for which she will ever venerate you.
This is the plan I would suggest : Take a cottage for her,
furnish it with some of the superfluous things that you have
recently bought, and give her away to some deserving young
fellow, who will make her happy—in short, adopt her as
your daughter. You have neither kith nor kin in the land,
and you have more money than you can reasonably spend
on yourself. Take my advice, Jabez, and you will rejoice
over it by-and-bye, and the girl will rejoice too. You may
live to have many merry romping games with your adopted
grand-children, and—— "

"Pshaw ! get out Grouts ! what nonsense you talk," said
Jabez, sharply. " The girl would break her heart if I jilted
her in that underhand way, poor little bird ! give her away
to some deserving young fellow, indeed ! poogh, I won't.
Besides, where will I find one more deserving of her than
myself ? I love her, and she loves me ; that's a mutually
admitted fact, and I won't allow anybody but grim Death
himself to separate us—that's the way to say it. Excuse
me for getting warm," added Jabez, relaxing into a grin,

" but you are too late with your advice, my boy.   My honour and happiness are at stake.   I must be married on
Friday : ho, ho, ho !   I must have a wife, for my feet get
very cold on winter nights ; very cold indeed ; but Kitty
will be twice as good as my water bottle, or a hot brick, ho,
ho, ho !"

" Now go home, Grouts, there's a good fellow ; don't
bother me any more, for I want to look to my linen.   Hoy !
Mrs. Budge, bring me a flat iron and the marking ink.
Excuse me, Grouts—good night—much obliged to you.
Give my love to Mrs. G.—Good night."

CHAPTER II.

AFTER Mr. Grouts left his friend Gummy's house, he walked
slowly homeward ; and any one meeting him would have
fancied him under the influence of laughing gas, or something else equally exciting, for he chuckled and poked the
air with his stick in the most facetious manner imaginable.

" Whatever is the matter with you, Grouts," asked his
wife, when he entered his home, still laughing and blinking
both eyes at once.   " You haven't broken your pledge, I
hope ?   Let me smell you.   All right," she added, after a
few satisfactory sniffs at her jovial spouse.   " You are quite
sober, though you look half drunk ; but what is tickling
you so amazingly ?   Tell me this minute, you giggling old
image, or I'll run up to Gummy's house and ask him."

" Sit down, missus, and I'll tell you a secret," said Mr.
Grouts : so Mrs. Grouts sat down, and her husband told her
all about his interview with Jabez, and something besides,
which set her giggling too.   After an hour's merry conference, the old couple went to bed, laughing all the way up
stairs.

*   *   *   *   *   *

" Oh, my dear ! what do you think ?" exclaimed Widow
Mayberry, entering Mrs. Grouts's cottage—in a state of great
excitement—two days after the above recorded events.
" Would you believe it, Gummy is a—a—a deceitful old
cripple ; I have made such a humiliating discovery.   I don't
know when I have felt so staggered, since the night I was
run over by the safety cab."

" What in the world is it, neighbour ?" asked Mrs. Grouts,
with well feigned wonder in her looks.   " Sit down and

compose yourself a bit, then tell me what has happened. Let me get you a cup of tea with an egg in it. Poor thing! You look quite upset. There now, untie your bonnet strings and sip that, while you tell me what is the matter. It is something serious, I'm afraid. I hope it isn't fire or——"

"I'll tell you in a few words. An hour ago I was up at Gumberry Lodge—though I don't mean to call it by that name any more, the old fellow named it after himself and Kitty; for he said that his and Kitty's names looked uncommonly nice together; but he must stick something else to his gum now, or leave it bare, for he shall never have Kitty Mayberry while my name is Ruth. Well, as I was saying, I went there an hour ago to see him about the stuffing for the sucking pig—for I don't think he likes sage and onions—and he had gone into Sydney. So naturally enough I began to look about the house, as it belongs to me in a manner of speaking, and, of course, I was anxious to see what was in it. In peeping into his wardrobe, what do you think I beheld?"

"Patience knows! A lot of old fusty clothes, I suppose."

"No, I didn't look at the clothes, but I dare say they are mere rags. A shelf full of doctor's bottles and pots caught my eye, and my curiosity was excited in an instant; so I began to examine them, and the very first thing I looked at was a big pot, marked in pencil, 'salve for sore legs.' Ugh! fancy how I felt, my dear! I was too much shocked to look any further, for I was afraid of seeing something worse still, so I slammed the wardrobe door to and sat down to stifle my feelings, which kept bubbling up like boiling stew. Presently Mrs. Budge came into the room; so without telling her what I had seen, I said to her as calmly as I could: 'Mrs. Budge, you are a mother and know a mother's feelings, tell me like a good honest soul, what is the matter with your master's legs?' She seemed startled at the solemnity of the question, but after a moment she said, 'Upon my word and honour I don't know, ma'am—leastways, I don't know for *certain*, for I never saw them in my life. I have lately noticed his knees knock together harder than they used to do, and he has worn long worsted stockings all the summer; but I didn't suspect there was much the matter with his legs, till two nights ago I overheard him say—mind this is a secret, Mrs. Mayberry, I would not for the world let him know that I was listening—he said to old

Mr. Grouts, in this very room, that Kitty would nurse him and do him more good than a hot brick.'

"'Ugh! the nasty old fellow!' said I, boiling over with wrath. 'How dare he compare my daughter to a hot brick? How dare he to have the impudence to say that she would nurse him? Bah! she wouldn't touch him with a clothes prop,' said I. 'Oh, the dirty old man! I'll let him see when he comes home; I'll talk to him with a vengeance. He ought to be ashamed of himself!'

"'Oh for goodness sake, ma'am, don't say a word to him,' said Mrs. Budge, beginning to cry. 'I shall lose my place, and my poor boy Billy will be turned out of house and home. I'm sorry I told you, ma'am,' said she; 'but, as you say, I know a mother's feelings, and I shouldn't like for a girl belonging to me to be compared to a lump of dirt—for a brick is nothing more—and be made to nurse a miserable old man all the days of her life. I had no other motive in telling you, I assure you, ma'am—for I have no objection to your daughter as my mistress—and I hope you won't get me into trouble.'

"So I promised I wouldn't say a word about it, and told her not to let her master know that I had called. Then I went straight home and told Kitty."

"Did you though?" exclaimed Mrs. Grouts, "and how did she bear the shock? poor thing! I suppose she was sadly cut up?"

"Cut up, not she indeed! why she would have gone right straight off to the lodge and scratched his face, only I stopped her. She has her mother's spirit in her, and that's not to be trifled with I can tell you. Between you and me Mrs. Grouts, Kitty never cared a threepenny-bit for Gummy, and only that she was anxious to be married before Lotty Jiggs, she is glad enough for an excuse to be rid of him. That shows how much she is cut up. She'll cut *him* up, for she never intends to see him again. A hot brick indeed! a pretty thing to call a young girl, who is worthy of the best man alive."

"But had you not better see Jabez, and come to some understanding, so that he may save the wedding breakfast and stop the company from assembling on Friday?"

"No, I won't see him, that's plain; I have too much pride in me to go near him, after his cruel attempt to kidnap my poor girl. Leave matters to me, Mrs. Grouts; I'll explain all to him at the right time. Promise me you will not say anything about it, or take any notice of what I've told you." ·

"Oh dear me, I don't want to have anything to do with it, I'm sure," said Mrs. Grouts. "Poor Gummy will be dreadfully disappointed. It is a pity he had not made you his confidante; if his legs are so much out of order, perhaps you might have helped to cure them, and then——"

"Faugh! Do you think I would have let him court my girl if he had told me that?" asked Mrs. Mayberry, fiercely. "Not I, indeed! Though I am not rich, I am clean and wholesome, Mrs. Grouts; I have sprung from a sound stock, and there never was a bad leg in my family, I am proud to say. Before I gave my consent to the match I was careful enough to ask him if he was healthy, and he told me he was as sound as a new tub, and never had a serious ailment in his life, those are his very words, the wicked old fellow."

*   *   *   *   *   *

"But I say, Grouts, don't you think you ought to tell Jabez that Kitty will not have him? It is a pity for him to prepare an expensive breakfast for nothing," said Mrs. Grouts to her spouse, after she had told him all that widow Mayberry had said a few hours before.

"Don't disturb your mind about that, Missis; the breakfast shall not be wasted, I'll engage. It's many a long day since Gummy prepared a good meal in his house for guests or himself either, and all his kitchen tools were as rusty as prison bars. If I knew that he could not afford the expense, of course, I should act differently; but he has plenty of money, and it will do him good to spend some of it, and do others good too. Where is Kitty, do you know?"

"She has gone up to her Aunt Sally's at Lane Cove. Her mother said Jabez wont dare to go there to trouble her; but if he does he had better mind his bad legs, for her cousin Phil has come back from the diggings."

"I am glad she is out of the way. Now, don't you say a word to any of the neighbours about this affair. It will all turn out right if you act prudently, and have patience. In the meantime, gossips will be busy enough, but don't let them be able to say that they heard your tongue in the matter. That's my advice to you, Missis."

*   *   *   *   *   *

On Friday morning, Jabez was up at the first streak of

light; in fact, he had lain awake all night, thinking of the bliss that awaited him on the coming day, and picturing himself in his wedding suit.

"Friday isn't a lucky day with me in general," he soliloquized, as he began to fit on his new flannels. "I was wrecked on a Friday, robbed on a Friday, fell down an area coal-hole on a Friday, and—but pooh, pooh! I won't be superstitious."

"Hoy, Mrs. Budge! send Billy up with my shaving water, and a cake of scented soap; and just air those new lambswool stockings for me, will you? Ahem-hem-hem! dear me, my winter cough is not coming on to-day, I hope. I'm afraid my nightcap was damp last night. That old woman is so careless; she thinks I'm made of gutta percha. Ah, never mind, I shall have a young woman in the house presently, and all my own too—ho, ho, ho! all my own for life! how nice! Bless her heart! she'll see that my linen is well aired, I'll be bound. She'll coddle me up, and pat my back when my cough is choking me. She'll rub away my rheumatism, and make me as lively all day long as a Scotch fiddler. Heigho! I wonder how she is this morning? I dare say she is rather mournful at leaving her mother, poor little thing! I'll cheer her up as soon as I get her. I feel uncommonly shivery, but I suppose it is natural for a man to be nervous on his wedding morning. I hope I sha'n't cut my nose off while I'm shaving my upper lip. That would be a bad job indeed—ha, ha! I should look funny going to church to be married without my nose. I wonder if Kitty would love me then as now? or whether the loss of half-an-ounce of gristle would be a serious consideration with her? Pooh! not at all; I won't wrong her by supposing such a thing. She has a soul far above such petty influences, and would love me all the more for my misfortune. The loss of my nose would doubly endear me to her, especially as it was cut off on my wedding day, and in her service I may say, for if it wasn't for her I should not shave at all. Pretty little dear! she does not like moustachios, so I'll mow them down twice a week, as long as I live. Hurrah! I've got over that hazardous operation, and my nose is as sound as a new bugle: now for some of that wonderful pomatum, warranted to make hair grow on a marrow-bone. Ha, ha, ha! won't my bare poll look nice and shiny?" chuckled Jabez, putting away his shaving-tackle, and taking up the pomatum pot. "Eh—hallo! what's this? Botheration take that fellow Lint! if he hasn't sent me a potful of salve for sore legs, in mistake. What a nuisance! Well, never mind, it can't be helped now, and it won't do to get cross this morning. I must sprinkle my head with 'Jockey-club,' and stroke my beard with a wax candle."

Eleven o'clock struck, and Jabez was in the drawing-room receiving his guests, and looking longingly out of the window every minute for his little "robin redbreast," as he called Kitty. Never had his neighbours seen him look so smart before, and compliments were showered upon him till he blushed blue. He was just telling Mr. Grouts that he felt happy enough to fly, when Mrs. Budge placed a note in his hands. He opened it, then turned pale, and with a prolonged groan he hastily left the room, toddled upstairs as fast as he could and jumped into his bridal bed. He was quickly followed by a score of friends, all anxious for an explanation of his mysterious flight, but no clue could they gather from him. To their united entreaties to come out of bed, or merely to show his face, he only replied in smothered yells from beneath the bed clothes, as if his mouth were full of blankets—

"Go home! go home! every one of you. Leave me alone! Leave me alone! I shall never get up any more."

After an excited discussion, which did not enlighten any one in the least degree, all the company—save Mr. Grouts—went home, without breakfast; some declaring that Jabez was drunk, but the majority believing that he was suddenly struck silly. An hour afterwards not less than a hundred boys and girls were seated in a green paddock adjoining Gumberry Lodge, and the wedding breakfast was portioned out to them by Mr. and Mrs. Grouts, to the great satisfaction of the children, but to the marked disgust of old Mrs. Budge, and her ravenous boy Billy.

Mr. Gummy kept to his bridal bed (in full dress) for three days, during which time he doggedly refused to speak or to partake of any refreshment. On the fourth day he felt very hungry, so he got up and ordered a rump steak and fried potatoes. After a hearty meal, he went into Sydney and gave orders to an agent to let Gumberry Lodge, furnished. He then returned home, gave Mrs. Budge and her boy Billy a week's wages and their dismissal, and the next day he started for Melbourne, without saying goodbye to any of his neighbours.

*   *   *   *   *   *

Thirteen months after the above occurrences, Mr. Gummy and Mr. Grouts were sitting by the fireside in a little back parlour at Gumberry Lodge. Mr. Gummy had recently returned from his tour, and regained possession of his house, with a new housekeeper. After hearing various items of local news, he asked his friend, "And what has become of that little rogue that jilted me so mysteriously? Ha, ha, ha! The mischievous young puss! it's a mercy she did not kill me."

"She was married, seven months ago, to a steady young fellow named Spry, a clever mechanic," replied Mr. Grouts.

"I am very glad of that; poor little bird! very glad indeed. I hope she will be happy. She was far too young for me, Grouts, and I ought to have known that; but the fact is, I was struck spoony as they call it, and common sense deserted me. I have often thought of your kindness in trying to dissuade me from the silly step, and I thank you Grouts; though I verily believe that all the friends I have in the world would not have reasoned me out of it at the time; I was so obstinately in love. Ha, ha, ha! What a silly old gander I was to be sure. But tell me why she gave me up so suddenly, Grouts? you see I am sane upon the subject now, so you need not mind telling me all that you know. I received half-a-dozen lines from Mrs. Mayberry, on my wedding morning, telling me 'that she had sent Kitty into the country, and that she would rather bury her in the wild bush, than give her away to a good-for-nothing old cripple, who regarded her as a mere brick.' That's all I know about it, and it's all a mystery to me."

Mr. Grouts then briefly explained to his friend the *ruse* he had invented to prevent a match, which he saw must end in misery, knowing, as he did, that Kitty was a giddy little creature, who could only be managed by a smart young husband; and, moreover, knowing that she was in love with Ben Spry, more than she was, perhaps, aware of herself. "Finding all my logic ineffectual," said Mr. Grouts, "I had recourse to the scheme which I have explained."

"But how and when did you manage it? It seems like a piece of conjuration," said Mr. Gummy, while tears of fun rolled down his merry old face.

"While you went down to the door with Mrs. Fitz's physic, I took out my pencil and wrote 'salve for sore legs' on your pomatum pot, and that is all I did. I intended that Mrs. Mayberry should see it, for I knew it would blister her pride in a minute; but I was saved further trouble by her prying curiosity and Mrs. Budge's tattling tongue together. They managed the rest of the business for me, and that is how you lost your little spring lamb, Jabez. But I have explained the matter to Mrs. Mayberry long ago, and I expect she will call on you, and humbly apologise for her rudeness. For my part, I confess it was a great liberty I took with you, which nothing but the extreme necessity could warrant, and I ask you to forgive me, Gummy."

"Forgive you, my boy! I thank you with all my heart," said Jabez, seizing his friend's hand. "You have not only saved me and that poor girl a life of misery, but you have made a man of me, Grouts. Do you know that while I lay in bed sulking, and trying to starve myself, I overheard the merry voices of the children whom you collected to eat my wedding breakfast, and though it was not welcome music to me at the time, it has since suggested some important considerations to my mind, which I have had ample time to reflect upon. The fact is, I have seen that my life has been a waste; I have been hoarding up money, and living in selfish idleness—burying my talent in a napkin, as it were—and totally neglecting the most important concerns of life; but I hope I am now a wiser, and a better man. If God spares me, you shall see some of my new plans in operation very soon, and I trust that thousands of poor children in this land will be permanently benefited thereby. Forgive you, indeed! ha! ha! ha! You are the best friend I ever had in my life. Ho! ho! ho! Your salve made me smart for a time, but it has doubtless saved me from life-long heartache; at all events it has softened my heart towards my needy fellow-creatures around me, and let me feel the luxury of doing good with my money. Give me your hand, Grouts! God bless you, my boy! This day fortnight is Christmas Day, you know, and you must dine with me, so don't say nay. You shall see such a gathering in my paddock on that day as nobody ever saw there before. I have invited all the poor people I can find to a good dinner, and I am going to give them a Christmas-box beside. Ha! ha!

ha ! won't it be glorious to see hundreds of poverty-stricken mortals filled with joy and gladness ?"

*   *   *   *   *   *

Not long afterwards Mr. Gummy married Widow Mayberry ; and it would be worth while for any old gentleman afflicted with chronic celibacy, to peep into Gumberry Lodge now. Mr. Ben Spry is a master wheelwright. thanks to the timely aid of Mr. Gummy, and his buggies and bullock drays are generally approved of. Kitty makes a devoted wife and a careful mother. Grandfather Gummy may often be seen frolicking with her children, like a sunny old soul as he is ; and when he has done playing, he has always got useful work to do, "to visit the fatherless and widows in their affliction." His home is full of harmony, and his heart is full of love ; but if care-clouds perchance overshadow his brow on rare occasions, his loving wife gently pats his bald head, then coquettishly rattles the lid of the pomatum pot (which is kept as a chimney ornament), when his face brightens up in an instant, and he laughs like a kilted Highlandman trying on a pair of top-boots.

"OLD BOGIES."

NOT long ago I overheard a mother thus address her little daughter, who had strayed from her side, and with childish curiosity was peeping into an open door-way. "Come hither, Minnie! you little monkey! Do you hear me, miss? Old Daddy Longlegs will catch you in a minute, if you don't mind what I say to you. Here he comes! My goodness! he'll catch you!" The dread of Daddy Longlegs had an immediate effect upon Minnie's short legs, and away she ran towards her mother, who seemed much pleased at the manifest alarm of her offspring, and at the success of her own silly expedient.

I do not refer to that occurrence on account of its novelty, for it is not uncommon to hear mothers call their children names, even less complimentary than "little monkeys," and to consign them to powers more terribly real than "daddy Longlegs." I wish to make a few remarks on the folly and danger of exacting obedience from children by operating on their fears ; and I would commend my subject to the consideration of mothers, and of nurses in general.

I was recently conversing with an intelligent lady friend upon various matters connected with the training of children, when she related the following facts, and gave me permission to make what use I pleased of them. She said that when about eight years of age, she was on a visit at the house of a relative ; and during her stay there she shared the bedroom of two adult female cousins. One night she had been rather tardy in disrobing, and her cousins were in bed before her, so the duty of extinguishing the candle devolved upon her. "If you don't make haste and put out the light, Annie," said one of her cousins, " old Bogy will catch hold of you as you are getting into bed."

My friend said that she put out the light instantly, and sprang into bed with a palpitating heart, and there she lay conjuring up a hideous array of images, which scared away sleep, and filled her mind with horror. The next morning she was in an unusually excited state. In the course of the day she went shopping with her cousins, and while in the

city she suddenly left them and ran as fast as she could to
her home, which was some distance off. When she arrived
there, she rushed up to her mother, flung herself into her
arms, and burst into an hysterical fit of weeping.

"Next day," my informant remarked, "I was seized with
an attack of St. Vitus's dance, which baffled all the remedies
of the doctor for several months; indeed, I was subject to
periodical returns of the disorder for years; but by degrees
my nerves recovered their tone, and now—thank God—I
am as free from dread of old bogies as most adults are. But
I have not forgotten the occurrence, and it has made me
very careful to avoid exciting my children in a similar way;
and also to be very watchful over my nursemaids, for I have
good reason to believe that children are sometimes terrified
by servants, as the following tragical incident will prove."

"A lady whom I knew very well," resumed my informant, "was one evening at a party at a friend's house, when
suddenly she was impressed with an unaccountable idea that
some terrible disaster had befallen her child, a little girl
about five years of age, whom she had left in charge of the
nursemaid. The lady hastily departed for her home, and
on reaching it, ran up-stairs to the nursery, when to her
horror, she beheld her darling child lying in its little bed—
dead. Its eyes were wide open, and were directed with a
ghastly stare to a hideous-looking figure at the foot of the
bed, which the lady speedily discovered was a broom, dressed
up with a black shawl and other sombre habiliments, to represent an 'old bogy.' The poor child had actually been
frightened to death; and perhaps it was well for her she
was dead, for it is probable, had she lived, she would have
drivelled out her days in hopeless idiocy. That unpardon-
ably cruel trick had been perpetrated by the nursemaid, to
make the child lie still, and allow her to go to the servants'
hall, and join in the revels, which were there going on in
the absence of the mistress of the house."

I do not mean to insinuate that such barbarity is often
practised by nurse-maids in civilised life. I hope it is a
very rare case, and I further hope that if the foregoing fact
should be read by persons who have the charge of young
children, that it may serve as a warning against the dangerous expedient of quieting them by means of "old bogies,"
tangible or otherwise. Nurses would do well also, to beware
how they instil into young minds frightful tales of ghosts

and goblins, which many children have an eager desire to hear, or the consequences may be very serious ; and if not in many cases so disastrous as in those above related, it may tend to mental imbecility and other evils of a life-long tenacity.

An old friend of mine has assured me, that though grey hairs are frosting his brow, he has not forgotten the ghostly legends which were crowded into his mind when he was a child. Even now, he is obliged—when in certain positions —to keep a vigilant check on his imagination, lest it should overpower his reason for a time, and surround him with a host of self-created phantoms, horrible as the figure of death itself. He further told me, that a schoolfellow had once declared to him, that he had accidentally run up against his Uncle Bill's leg, as he was crossing a country churchyard one dark night. The leg was sticking up perpendicularly, with the toes bare. " That grossly absurd story," added my friend, " had such an effect on my boyish fancy, and created such a dread of straying legs, that rather than even pass the churchyard wall after dark, I have walked two miles round."

I remember stopping—some years ago—at a comfortless bush inn, after a wearisome day's journey on horseback. The weather had been wet, and the roads were boggy. I reached the inn about two hours after sunset ; and a more uninviting reception I never met with in travelling. I was shown into a dreary apartment, and after the lapse of an hour was supplied with a greasy supper.

When I had finished my meal, I rang the bell and asked the landlady if she could accommodate me with a news-paper. She replied, that in consequence of the river being flooded, there had been no postal communication for several days ; but she had last Saturday's ——— *Mercury*. I had read that issue of the paper, so I asked if she could oblige me with a book. She thought she could, and in a short time brought me a tattered volume of Mrs. Crowe's " Night Side of Nature." I sat before the fire and read about ghosts and spectres, until a sort of horrible fascination stole over me ; and it was long after the house had been closed, that I was warned to bed by the flickering candle. But the terrors of that night are still vividly before me, when I allow my mind to dwell on them. A short allowance of bedding, a hard bed, an ill-ventilated room, and a supper of

fat bacon, are quite enough to mar refreshing slumbers ; but
my physical discomforts were nothing compared with the
mental horrors which gradually crept over me, until they
completely got the mastery of my reason, kept sleep from
my eyelids, and filled my chamber with imaginary spectres,
diabolical enough to scare even Mrs. Crowe herself.   I have
not seen that lively book since, nor do I wish to see it again.
I recommend it—with all similar books—to be carefully kept
out of the reach of children, and dismal-minded adults ; as
it is very likely to frighten them out of their wits.

I would advise parents, and all persons entrusted with
the care of children, to be very cautious what story books
they allow them to read, or what stories they allow them to
hear ; for I have good authority in stating, that many poor
children have had their minds shaken to idiocy by ghastly
legends and romances, which only Satan himself could dic-
tate, and which can serve no better end than to please him.

I wish all those persons, who either thoughtlessly or
savagely delight in frightening children, could be made as
thoroughly ashamed of themselves as my literary friend
Grinn was, some time ago.   Mr. Grinn was by no means an
enemy to children ; on the contrary, he was usually a
favourite with them, and few old men studied to please
them more than he did, in general.   But even literary men
are peevish at times, and the event I am about to record,
happened on one of those days when Mr. Grinn's brain was
rather over-taxed, and he was as indisposed for infantile fun
as a giant with a broken jaw.   He was on a visit to a friend
in a neighbouring colony, and was one morning busily engaged preparing a lecture which he had promised to deliver
that evening.   His quiet studies were frequently intruded
upon by the son of his host, a pretty, merry little fellow,
just beginning to chatter ; and though at most times Mr.
Grinn would have been glad to see him, and have a frolic
with him, his private opinion, on that occasion, was that
Jamie was a little nuisance.   At one time he would open
the door to show Mr. Grinn a wooden horse, without head
or tail ; then he would apply for instruction in spinning his
humming-top ; and soon afterwards tease his old friend with
a box of puzzles, or a squeaking cat.   At each visit Mr.
Grinn received his little tormentor as blandly as he could,
and used every legitimate artifice to induce Jamie to stay
outside, but to very little purpose, for at intervals of seven

minutes he would return, in full song, and though Mr. Grinn had fastened the door, it did not avail him in the least degree, for Jamie would kick it until it was opened.

"Here, Jamie, my dear, run and get some lollies; and don't come in here again, there's a good boy. I am very busy this morning, and can't spare time to play with you," said Mr. Grinn, with an appealing look at the boy, on his ninth visit. "Here's a penny for you; run away now, there's a man."

Jamie took the money and ran away to buy his lollies, and probably ran all the way back too, for he was not gone long, and of course he rushed directly into the room, to share his purchase with his generous friend.

"I don't want any lollies, Jamie. Do go away, there's a good boy," groaned Mr. Grinn, who was just finishing a passage which he expected would produce thunder-claps of applause from the body of the hall, and "hear, hear," from all the sedate gentlemen on the platform. "Go away, Jamie; I think mamma wants you. Go and give her a lolly."

Jamie ran away, and Mr. Grinn resumed his work, but in less than five minutes the boy was back again, disarranging the lecturer's papers with his sugary fingers, and singing "diddle daddle, diddle daddle dum," with all his vocal energy. Mr. Grinn's patience forsook him for an instant, and he grew positively savage. Throwing down his pen, and looking straight at the boy, he made a grimace hideous enough to make an old cab-horse bolt, and exclaimed in hissing tones, "If you don't go away this instant, I'll eat you up."

"Hoo-o! hoo-o! hoo-o-o!" roared Jamie, as he ran out of the room in terror, while his mother rushed down-stairs to meet him, and to learn the cause of his unusual outcry. "Hey, Jamie, my darling! what's the matter?" asked his fond mother, in excited tones.

"O mammy, mammy! gent'man going to eat me up," screamed Jamie, while poor Mr. Grinn felt that he would be glad for somebody to eat him up, just then, and save him the shame of confronting his kind hostess, and confessing his folly in thus frightening her boy; which he really did not intend to do.

"No, no, Jamie! Mr. Grinn will not eat you. He is a kind gentleman, and loves nice little boys."

"Yes, mammy, he will eat me. Hoo! hoo-o!" roared Jamie.

"Nonsense, my sonnie! he won't eat you. Come in with me," said the lady, walking into Mr. Grinn's studio, with Jamie in her arms, his little eyes staring with terror.

Mr. Grinn blushed and shivered, as guilty men usually do, while he stammered out an awkward explanation, the effect of which was to incline the lady to the horrible belief that he really had cannibalish designs upon her chubby little son. Few modest men have ever felt more abashed than poor old Grinn did, at the look of contemptuous surprise which over-spread the handsome features of his hostess. She spoke not a word, but, hugging her trembling boy to her breast, walked out of the room with a calm dignity and closed the door, leaving her guest as miserably chapfallen as if he had been publicly exposed as an impostor. His studies were completely upset for that day, and his lecture at night was a failure.

While I feel a good deal of sympathy for my unlucky friend, under the peculiar circumstances, I cannot too strongly denounce the practice of frightening children, either by threatening to eat them, or by invoking "Old Daddy Long-legs," or any other mystical nobody, to catch them. And though I have a thorough contempt for old bogies in general, I think I could countenance a special one, whose office should be to nightly twitch the noses of all disseminators of hideous ghosts and goblin stories; the tendency of which is to spoil promising children, to oppress their young brains with pernicious trash, and terrify them into miserable imbeciles.

DON'T LIE DOWN AND FRET.

ONE afternoon I was sitting on the poop of a fine ship, then on a long voyage, when we were overtaken by a violent squall. The majority of my readers doubtless know what a scene of bustle and commotion a ship's deck presents at such a time, so I need not minutely describe it. The wind roared, the officers shouted, and the sailors sung hoy, hoy ! as they hurriedly clewed up, or hauled down the flapping sails. All hands were on deck, and actively engaged. In the midst of the exciting scene, I particularly noticed the eccentric movements of a pale little man, who was yclept "Jemmy Ducks," the cognomen which is usually given to the individual who has charge of the pigs and poultry on ship-board. The poor fellow was on his first voyage, and had scarcely got what sailors call his sea legs. He was evidently sea sick, and looked as helpless and scared as a black fellow on a runaway omnibus. Presently I saw him fall flat on the deck, having lost his footing in a violent lurch, caused by a sea striking the ship on the broadside. While I was preparing to go to him, to ascertain if he were hurt, I observed a rough-looking old seaman (who was running with some others to the main topsail reef tackles), as he passed the prostrate Jemmy Ducks, gave him a smart kick in the ribs, and at the same time grumbled out, in that dry ironical tone so peculiar to sailors, "don't lie down there, you'll be in the way." The poor poultry man scrambled up, and with a rueful face, staggered to his hen coops under the top-gallant forecastle ; doubtless thinking it was an equivocal sort of sympathy which the old son of Neptune had manifested for his downfall, and his bruises. I confess that while I pitied him, I could not avoid smiling at the sailor's mode of emphasising his advice, by kicking the poor fellow, instead of helping him up ; and the comical expression on the faces of the other sailors, shewed that they viewed his discomfiture with much the same feeling that they would display at shaving an uninitiated shipmate, while crossing the line.

I was at that time comparatively inexperienced in the ways of the world ; and I bestowed but little reflection on the incident ; but—trivial as it was—it has often recurred to my mind, when I have seen the spirit of the old sailor imitated by folks on shore, on their luckless friends who have been knocked down, either by their own folly or by misfortune ; though I have not always felt so disposed to laugh at the exhibition, as I did at the prostrate Jemmy Ducks and his kicking shipmate.

"Don't lie down there : you'll be in the way !" I would address the words of Jack Junk, to such of my readers who may be disposed to lie down and despair, in consequence of present trials and difficulties, which to their troubled minds appear insurmountable. , So far from administering a kick with my caution, I would offer a few words of counsel and friendly encouragement to such downcast ones, and endeavour to lift them up ; lest some of their neighbours stumble over them.

In general, those persons are disappointed who look for much sympathy from the public for their pecuniary reverses, or at all events who expect that feeling to be very lasting ; and it would be unwise to calculate upon much revenue in return for a tale of ruin. Your society is more likely to be shunned than courted, if you are too ready to pour out your troubles. A fire, a shipwreck, an explosion, an inundation, or any other great catastrophe, which had suddenly reduced you to poverty, might create a strong impression, and procure you general condolence for a brief period after its occurrence ; but the emotion would be very transient, and it is marvellous how unsympathisingly the majority of folks would hear you recite the details of the mishap, twelve months afterwards ; and what difficulty you would experience in raising even the price of a dinner, by the most dismal story you could tell. Do not then voluntarily lie down and fret, in the belief that you will gain much by doing so, for you are more likely to be kicked than pitied. Rather try to stand up and face your trials and difficulties, whatever they may be. Put a manly, cheerful courage on, then half your troubles will fly away, and you will probably find help to battle with the other half. It is an old saying, that " a merry-faced fellow could raise a guinea at any time, but a dolorous individual, on the contrary, could not raise ninepence if his life depended on it."

"Do you see that gentleman on the opposite side of the street ?" I enquired of a friend with whom I was walking one day.

"Yes, I see him. He looks very miserable : who is he, and what is the matter with him ?"

"I knew him a few years ago, as a flourishing merchant," I replied ; "but he failed, from some cause of which I am ignorant, and he has never held up his head since. He seems to have lost heart and energy altogether, and looks grief-worn and poverty stricken."

"Poor wretch !" exclaimed my friend, with a momentary glance of sympathy towards the desponding merchant ; then he added, "what a simpleton he must be not to stand up stiff under his burden, if he cannot shake it from his shoulders entirely."

"There are the old sailor's sentiments again, and the kick too," I thought, as I continued my walk beside my friend, who, by the way, was not an unfeeling man. Like scores of other men immersed in business, he had neither time nor inclination to moralize on such apparent trifles ; and he would probably never take the trouble to enquire into the causes of that poor man's dejection, or offer to help him with even ten pounds' worth of goods, to make a fresh start in the world. But were any brisk, energetic-looking individual to present himself at his warehouse, and ask credit for a hundred pounds' worth of goods to help to re-stock his shop, which was burnt out the other day, it is probable my friend would give it cheerfully.

"*Nil desperandum*" is a capital motto ; and "never give up,"—which is almost the same sentiment—has saved many a storm-shattered ship from sinking to the bottom of the sea. Courage and perseverance often overcome extraordinary difficulties ; and a hopeful spirit at such times is as cheering as sunshine in a gale ; while anxiety, and gloomy misgivings, destroy that cool presence of mind, which is so essential in all emergencies ; paralyze the faculties, and hasten on the evils you so much dread.

"The ship is sinking !" raved a terrified man from the fore part of a steamer, which was labouring heavily in a furious gale, on this coast, one memorable night.

"She is not sinking !" shouted the captain from his post on the bridge. "Bale the water out of the fore cabin, and nail tarpaulins over the skylights."

The cool, determined spirit of that commander, inspired his crew with hope and energy, and their efforts saved the vessel. Had he suffered that startling cry to paralyze his judgment, the steamer would doubtless have foundered, and the lives of all her passengers would have ended. The same hopeful energy, put forth in the storms which often threaten our social or commercial prospects, would generally help us to escape them, or at any rate it would help to alleviate their effects; while, on the contrary, a desponding, lie-down-and-die sort of spirit, would be productive of disaster, and perhaps ruin; to say nothing of its panic-raising influence on our neighbours.

"What are you going to do?" I once asked a farmer, who was gazing at the smoking ruins of his barn, which had been burned to the ground.

"Do, sir?" he replied, "why go to work and build a bigger barn: it's not a bit of use crying over those cinders."

"Bravo, Sam! that's plucky," said a good-natured bystander. "I'll lend you my bullocks and dray, to draw in the split stuff from the bush."

"And I'll give you nails for the job," said another friend.

Sam's barn was soon rebuilt, and if he did not altogether forget his mishap, he soon ceased to trouble himself about it. By showing a manly resolution to help himself, he got help from his friends, and his temporary troubles were surmounted. If you have obstacles in your way, reader, push them aside if you can; if not, jump over them, run round them, or do anything but lie down beside them and fret, for by doing so you will increase your troubles, and you will probably be kicked for being in the way, by some of your bustling neighbours.

> "We overstate the ills of life, and take
> Imagination, given us to bring down
> The choirs of singing angels, overshone
> By God's clear glory,—down our earth, to rake
> The dismal snows instead; flake following flake,
> To cover all the corn. We walk upon
> The shadows of hills across a level thrown,
> And pant like climbers."

*   *   *   *   *   *

I do not mean to infer that it is always possible to chase away distressing thoughts, by a mere effort of the will; or as easy to put away our troubles, as to throw off an overcoat ; but as I believe it is possible to increase them by fretting over them—for like produces like—so it is possible to lessen them, by looking hopefully to the probability of their terminating. It is much more comforting to hope for things to mend, than to fear they will be worse ; and it is miserable waste of time to dread evils which may never come near us. Unavoidable troubles, of course, must be borne, and the more patiently we bear them the less are we likely to be galled. A man who has used every honest effort to avert disaster, will feel a degree of satisfaction at having done his duty, and his conduct will doubtless be rightly estimated by thoughtful men around him.

That there is a good deal of distress, at the present time, throughout the colony, is indisputable ; and to trace some of the causes and their effects, would not be difficult. There are few reflecting men, however, who did not expect severe straits to result from the terrible inundations which lately ravaged many of the agricultural districts, and the repeated failure of wheat crops from rust. Droughts, too, have seriously affected some of the pastoral and mining districts. The lawless depredations of bushrangers, and political disruptions, together with many other minor occurrences and calamities, have tended to depress trade, and the influence is easily traceable to individual exchequers. However much these things are to be deprecated, merely deploring will never remedy them, and the truest philosophy is to look at our difficulties boldly, and strive to diminish them if we cannot surmount them altogether. We only double our trouble when we trouble ourselves over it. Though many persons just now join in the cry of bad times, there is plenty of room for hope that times will mend, for this is a great country with boundless resources, and no rational man will fear that general distress can be permanent. Every one knows the beneficial influence the frosts of winter have upon the soils of some parts of our globe, in destroying noxious weeds and vermin ; and may not such seasons of depression as the present have a salutary influence on our commercial and social systems. Uninterrupted prosperity would not be good for us, in a moral, or in any other sense, and occasional reverses may be regarded as wholesome correctives. After cool consideration, I have arrived at the firm conclusion—which is strengthened by many years' colonial experience—that there is no need for an honest, industrious, healthy man to despond in Australia ; so to all to whom it may apply, I repeat the old sailor's injunction, " don't lie down, you'll be in the way."   Try to smile away the gloom from your faces, and the effort will lighten your hearts, and shed a cheering influence around you.

It would seem like trifling with the misfortune of those, who from bodily infirmity, or overwhelming distresses, are incapable of getting up to offer them advice suitable only for the strong and healthy.   To such poor sufferers I would say, lie still, friends, and try to bear with patience the trials which you cannot avert ; while you take comfort in the belief, " that all things work together for good."   Remember that precious gems have to be rubbed and ground a good deal before they are fitted to grace the crown of a monarch. There is doubtless a " needs be " for all your afflictions, which by and bye you will joyfully acknowledge.   There will be an end to them all—perhaps very speedily—and like the polished gems, you will shine brighter for the hard rubs and severe grinding under which you now writhe and groan.

SUNSHINE IN WINTER; OR, THE LOVES OF OLD MR. AND MRS. DOVECOTT.

CHAPTER I.

A BEAMING old pair were Mr. and Mrs. Dovecott, whose loves I am about to depict, in the tenderest manner I can. To see them as they toddled to church on Sundays was as pleasing a sight as that of a tree laden with ripe cherries. Arm in arm they jogged along—which they could comfortably do, for Nanny wore no crinoline to rasp her husband's ancles, or to keep him an arm's length from her side —while love and sympathy were evident by their clinging contact, and by their every act and gesture. The simple little fact, too, of Nanny's goloshes peeping out of David's coat pocket, in doubtful weather, and her warm plaid wrapper hanging over his arm, plainly indicated his thoughtful care for the health and comfort of his darling wifie. ·

Almost any one may write a love story ; that is to say, almost any one may find material enough for the purpose, by merely putting his head out of window on a sunny day, or on a moonlight night either ; but I am sorry to believe that he would have to wander about a long while to find many such specimens of genuine old lovers as the subjects of my story. Perhaps it is worth while for the reader to pause a minute and consider the causes of the comparative lack of mutual warmth in aged wedded hearts. Why so many old folks grow cold, and cross, and negligent of each other. I have thought upon the subject carefully, and am of opinion that in most cases the primary cause of unhappiness and discord, is the absence of that strong abiding love which is founded upon a knowledge of, and an esteem for each other's virtues ; and a secondary cause, is the lack of tact and prudence in studying each other's dispositions, and mutually bearing and forbearing with infirmities and peculiarities, which should have been ascertained before the irrevocable marriage vows were made. The following little sketch of marriage *à la mode* will perhaps help to illustrate the latter proposition better than any abstract reasoning.

A soft-hearted pair, just merging from their teens, meet for the first time at a picnic, a ball, a bazaar, or what not, when the young gentleman is "struck spoony" with the bright eyes, the glossy hair, and fascinating air of Julia Daffodil. Of course he is as killing as he can be, and young love boldly enters her susceptible breast, without meeting with the slightest resistance. She is struck too, and forthwith becomes enamoured of sentimental songs, set to die-away music, begins to study the language of flowers, and to indulge in moonlight reveries and rhapsodies. The stricken pair meet again very soon, for love always manages to effect those little amatory *contretemps* ; when the swimming eyes of Horace Hawthorn softly declare his heart's overladen condition, and the dove-like glances, and rising blushes of Miss Daffodil, plainly evidence that the tender feeling is mutual. Horace's love soon grows violent, and impatient : he boldly sues for the heart and hand of his inamorata, and is accepted at once with appropriate tears, and gushing expressions of never-dying constancy. How can two such fond hearts exist apart? Impossible! With such a fierce flame within them they would soon be burned to death. They are speedily married, and revel for a fortnight on holiday fare and love, in their temporary lodgings at Kissing Point. Oh! What a delightful time that is! Comparable to nothing in every-day-life; and only to be rightly estimated by poets. They have nothing to do but ramble about and listen to the pretty birds, and gather bush flowers; or sit beneath a sweetbrier hedge, and mutually confide all the secrets they have ever had in their hearts, and tell each other everything they know, even to their own follies and foibles—which candour they will possibly regret before they are a month older. But the golden days speed by ; alas ! too swiftly for love and them. Their honeymoon wanes. They sigh over departing joys, and wish that honeymoons were perennial. At length, Horace's leave of absence expires, and they go home to begin married life in earnest; he to earn the necessary funds for bread and sundries and she to the matter-of-fact duty of managing her household economy, and examining for the first time the mysterious depths of his trunks, and discovering the shortcomings of his bachelor's buttons, &c.

I shall not accompany this hastily-matched pair through the short stages of their conjugal progress, up to their first quarrel. By an elaborate computation it has been settled that the average duration of amity and peace in such households is six weeks. The satiated lovers then begin to discover what they should have been careful to find out before the fatal knot was tied, viz., that they are wholly unsuited to each other, in every way; which fact they loudly confess with tears and angry recriminations; and in less than six months Horace Hawthorn may be heard, ten times a day, saying in effect, to his pouting spouse—"I wish we were unmarried."

That is a short but far from an over-wrought sketch of flaring affection and precipitate unions; and though it is drawn from fancy, I have only to give my memory a slight rub, to cause many sadder examples from real life to arise. But I am about to draw a far more pleasing picture of wedded life. Leaving young lovers' downy dreams, and their waking flights, to be chronicled by persons who understand them better; I will try to depict the life-long loves of an affectionate old couple, which delicate task has certainly more of novelty to recommend it, for few persons make old folks the hero and heroine of a romantic tale. Love stories usually end with marriage (though I do not see why they should), but the mutual love of my two worthy old friends will not end with my story, and I hope—indeed I feel sure —it will live for ever.

Dear reader! if you knew David Dovecott and his amiable wife, I am sure you would love them as warmly as I do. The mellow tints of a summer evening's sky are not more pleasing to gaze on than the benevolent faces of that genuine pair, and their faces are true indices of their warm hearts. If you are fortunate enough to know them, and can appreciate a simply told tale of honest, enduring affection, take a favourable opportunity of asking Davey to relate his first love impressions, and his marital experience of forty years, and you will have an entertainment far surpassing the Lancashire bellringers' striking melodies. Those who cannot have the superior pleasure of hearing the story from the old man's lips, may—if they choose—read my account of it, which, as I transcribe, I fancy I see him sitting in his verandah on a pleasant evening, with his devoted wife beside him, her eyes swimming in loving kindness, and her silvery hair braided over a countenance which might have been photographed for the emblem of mortal goodness. Here then I begin his story, which I wish I could give in his own rich racy style.

"It is—let me see—sixty-six years come the fourteenth of next July, since I first saw my own darling Nanny here," began Mr. Dovecott, chuckling his smiling wife under the chin at the same time. "Sixty-six years ago : that is a long time, Mr. Boomerang, but I remember it as distinctly as though it were but last Christmas Day. I was going home from Dame Tingle's school, at the end of our village, and was knocking down butterflies with my empty dinner-bag, when I almost ran up against a little girl, about five years old, dressed in a short blue print frock, and a round straw hat ; but with only one shoe on. She was standing near to the crossing-place of the brook, crying : so I went up to her and said—

" 'What is the matter, little girl ?' 'I have lost my shoe,' she answered, wiping her eyes on her frock. 'Where did you lose it ?' said I. 'I was picking a waterlily, and I slipped 'off that rough stone, and my shoe came off and swam away down the brook. Hoo—o— boo—o—o ! What shall I do ?' 'Don't cry, little girl,' said I, ' I'll try and find your shoe for you. Here, hold my dinner-bag.'

" So I pulled off my shoes and stockings, and rolled up my trousers, and away I paddled into the brook. I soon found the shoe, which had a little hole in the side, so it had not floated far. I wiped it as dry as I could with my pinafore, and gave it to her ; when she sat down on the grass and put it on. She certainly looked pleased, but I don't think she said thankee. I am not sure about that, but never mind, she has very often said thankee since then. That was the first time I ever set eyes on my dear Nanny ; and little did I then think that that wee tiny girl would prove to be the best friend I ever found in the world, and would gladden my life with the genial influence of her love—would prove to me a greater treasure than all my gold, even if it were multiplied ten thousand fold, and worked into filigree jewellery."

" Hush, hush ! Davy my dear," said Mrs. Dovecott, while she gently patted her husband's lips with her hand. " You must not praise me any more, or Mr. Boomerang will think me a vain old creature to sit here and listen to you."

" Well, well, my lass, I won't if it makes you feel uncomfortable, though I have not said half as much as I should like to say about you, bless your little heart !"

" Some folks would say it is all nonsense to talk about a boy of seven years old falling in love ; but I can certify that it is quite natural for all that," continued Mr. Dovecott, addressing me. " You will believe what I say, Boomerang, and I assure you I fell in love with that little girl, who had lost her shoe ; though I did not know I had fallen at all, till I got home ; indeed, I did not even then know the name of the strange feeling which came over me. It was a peculiar sort of sweet sensation, with a tingle in it, more like brimstone and treacle than anything else I could then compare it to ; and I used to feel it strongest when I crossed the brook, or whenever I saw a little shoe with a hole in it : and I sometimes used to dream that I saw a little girl picking a waterlily, and crying ' Hoo—o— boo—o ! I've lost my shoe !'

" About twelve months after that occurrence, the same little girl came to Dame Tingle's school, and I felt so glad, though I scarcely knew why.   Whenever I bought a halfpennyworth of hard-bake or bulls-eyes, I always saved some for little Nanny Roseley.   She used to look so pleased when I gave them to her ; and one day she gave me a young turnip, which I thought was as sweet as a golden-pippin, and it was nice and warm too, through being carried in her pocket. I remember the first wicked act which love tempted me to commit, and I did not soon forget the penalty I paid for it.   One morning I was going to school, and in passing Squire Leveret's garden, I saw a bed of lovely pinks just inside a briar hedge.   I thought how much I should like one of those pinks to give to Nanny ; and without stopping to reflect on the sin I was going to commit, I worked my head and shoulders through the hedge, and was in the act of picking the flower, when I was strikingly conscious that some angry person was behind me, with a stick in his hand ; indeed the evidence of that was plain enough five weeks afterwards.   I withdrew my head and shoulders in a very short time, when to my great dismay there stood Squire Leveret, with a savage look, and the ashen switch in his hand, which had descended so smartly on my tight corduroys. ' O my, sir ! pray don't hit me again ; I'll never do so any more, sir !'   ' What do you mean by robbing my garden ?   You young gaol-bird !' shouted the squire. ' I was only picking a pink for Nanny Roseley, sir,' I sobbed. ' Who is Nanny Roseley ?' he asked. ' She is a little girl who goes to our school, please sir.'   ' You had better take care she does not lead you to the gallows,' he replied gruffly, at the same time giving me another blow with the stick ; whereupon I thought I had enough stick for one pink, so I made use of my young legs, and ran off with two large pink stripes on my person, which of course I kept to myself."

"Ha, ha, ha !" chuckled Mr. Dovecott.   "What an old goose Squire Leveret was to utter such a sentiment as that ! I remember feeling more indignant with him for thus defaming my Nanny, than I did for his striking me with the switch, and I was strongly tempted to throw a stone at his head ; but I am glad that I did not.   Lead me to the gallows indeed ! Why the dear soul has all her lifetime been leading me to Heaven. Her gentle, sympathetic counsel has often chased away the ruffles from my troubled brow, and her honeyed words have sweetened many a bitter sorrow.   Her tender nursing hand has softened many a throb of pain ; and her example of Christian patience, meekness, and love, has had more influence on my soul than all the doctrinal sermons I ever heard preached.   But I must not say any more about her virtues, for I see she is blushing again, and I would not cause her a moment's uneasiness, even to give myself a month of pleasure."

CHAPTER II.

AFTER passing a few good-natured strictures on Squire Leverett's angry prognostications, Mr. Dovecott thus resumed his narrative :—

"A short time afterwards I was taken from Dame Tingle's, and sent to Mr. Wagstaff's school—about five miles off—as a weekly boarder ; so I only saw Nanny on Sundays, in our village church.   I loved to sit and look at her, in her brown beaver bonnet with red ribbons, and her nankeen tippet and sleeves ; and I used to wonder if it were wicked for me to think her ten times prettier than the little mahogany angels that sat on the top of the organ. If it happened to be a wet day, and she was not at church, I always felt something like a dry cork sticking in my throat, and when I attempted to sing I would sometimes burst out crying, which usually gained me a dose of rhubarb when I got home, for my mother used to think I was poorly.

"At fourteen years old I was apprenticed to Mr. Smalts, the grocer, on our village green, and Nanny, who had grown a fine big girl, often came to the shop with her little market basket.   I always tried to serve her, though I began to feel unaccountably shy of speaking to her, much more so than I had been six or seven years before.   I often longed to give her a few plums or a stick of barley-sugar, but I was afraid she had grown far above such things, and would feel offended if I offered them.   She always looked so modest and reserved, that whenever she came into the shop I was struck serious, and as overawed as if she were the parson's wife or a young saint.   Had I any idea that the sly little rogue was, at the same time, over head and ears in love with me, it is very likely I should have summoned courage to have said a soft word or two ; but she never gave me the slightest clue to her real feelings, for which becoming maidenly modesty I afterwards admired her the more of course.   I remember one day after she had gone out of the shop, Tom Bullskin, my fellow apprentice, made some coarse remarks about her, when I immediately fired up and gave him a smart knock on the nose, which made his eyes water.   'Now you had better take that from me,' said I, 'than let me tell her father what you have just said.'   'Oho ! that's it, is it ?' said he, trying to look facetious, 'I didn't know she was your sweetheart.' From that time it was the talk of the gossips in the village that Nanny and I were lovers ; still I never even whispered a word of love to her for years afterwards.   At length my passion got to such a pressure that I felt I must ease my heart, or it would burst like an over-fired steam boiler. Nanny was then a lively lass of fifteen or sixteen.   She was handsome as a satin-bird,—but I need not attempt to describe her charms ; just look at her now, Mr. Boomerang, and I leave you to judge what she was then," said the old man, gazing at his wife, and passing his hand gently over her silvery locks.   "You may imagine how she looked as Queen of the May fifty years ago, sir.   You can fancy, too, how anxious I felt lest some one of the smart lads of the village should pluck my pretty May flower (as they were all looking after her as much as they dared, for her father and her big brother scared them from making any bold advances), and, as I said before, I had not the least idea that the little puss was sighing her heart sore for me, and perhaps fearing that some of the other village lasses would win my heart. ,

"How to declare my love to her puzzled me wonderfully. I knew no one whom I could ask for advice except my mother; and I was half ashamed to speak to her on the subject, for I had often told her that I should never love any one in the world so much as I loved her. However, I thought I might get information from her, enough for my purpose, without exactly letting her know that she had; been supplanted in my affections;—so one evening, as she was sitting at her spinning-wheel (I always went home at night) after a good deal of thought how I should put the question, I said boldly, 'Mother, what did poor father say to you ,when he first came courting?' My stars, sir! you should have seen how the dear old lady stared at my unexpected question. 'Why what on earth do you mean by asking me that, Davy?' she exclaimed, stopping her wheel and gazing into my blushing face. 'Oh, nothing very particular, mother, only I like to know all about everything in the world; and you know you encourage me to acquire useful knowledge.—Do tell me all about it, mother,' said I, in a coaxing tone, and putting my arms round her neck at the same time. I could see the loving old lady's heart was warming at the tender recollections which my question had awakened. She sighed, took off her spectacles, and wiped some tear marks from them, then began to smile, and playfully chide me for my inquisitiveness. After a little more gentle persuasion she sighed again and said, 'Your poor dear father was a man of few words, Davy, still for all that, he was very acute, and a man of good taste too. He found out that I loved him, though I am sure I had not told it to a soul in the world; nor did he say a word to me about it either, but went straight off to my father, and said right out in his blunt way, "Mr. Dobbs, I want your daughter Grace; I love her awfully hard, and I am able and willing to work to keep her. What do you say?" My father, who always liked straightforward people, said to him, "Come inside, Master Dovecott, and have a mug of cider; we will talk the matter over." So in he went, and in a very short time he got father's consent. Then he came into the dairy where I was putting a cheese into the vat, and asked me if I would have him for a husband. You must be aware that I did not say nay, boy, and that's all about it. But what in the name of fortune do you want to know that for?' 'Nothing very particular, mother—I will tell you to-morrow night," said I, kissing her affectionately.

"I then put on my hat, and away I went across the fields to Mr. Roseley's house, repeating my father's successful form of address all the way I went. There sat old Mr. Roseley outside his front door smoking his pipe. 'Good evening, Davy, my lad?' said he ; 'Good evening, Mr. Roseley,' said I. Then I felt all of a twitter inside, as though I had swallowed a nest of young skylarks. But I soon plucked up heart, and speaking as nearly as possible in the bluff style that my father always spoke in, I said, 'Mr. Roseley, I want your daughter Nanny. I love her awfully hard, and am able and willing to work to keep her. What do you say?' Goodness me, sir ! how the old man stared at me. His pipe went out directly, and his nose reddened as if it were going to relight the tobacco. He did not swear, certainly, for he was a sensible man in the main, but he blustered like a black north-easter, and almost upset me. 'Look ye, Davy,' said he, 'I believe you are an honest lad, or else, do you see that whip behind the door there? I'd give you that for your impudence in coming to ask for my girl as carelessly as if you merely wanted to borrow my wheelbarrow. "I want your daughter Nanny." Zounds ! is that the way to ask for such a girl as mine? Besides, do you think I am such a; fool as to let a lass of sixteen get married, unless I wanted to see her an old worn-out woman before she is in her prime? Ugh ! get out, you monkey, or I shall kick you into the duck-pond !'

"'Oh, Mr. Roseley, I beg your pardon,' I timidly stammered, 'you make a mistake, sir. I don't want to marry her——'

"'Eh, what ! Then what the dickens do you want with her?' roared the old man, stopping me before I had half said my say, for I meant I did not want to marry her for five years. 'Confound your impudence ! Let me get hold of you ! Here, Boxer, Boxer, Boxer ! Hool him, boy ! hool him !'

"Boxer was a large mastiff that I had often seen following Nanny, as if to protect her, and as I was always timid of dogs, I did not wait till Boxer arrived from the back of the house, but away I went with my heart in my mouth, as the saying is, and jumped over the garden gate just as the dog was about to spoil my Sunday pantaloons. You can have no idea, sir, what a humble opinion I had of myself as I retraced my steps across the fields. When I got home I told my mother all about my misadventure, and she said I was a young gosling for not telling her what I was going to do, and she would have advised me how to go about it better. I ought to have borne in mind, she said, that my father was nearly thirty years old when he went courting ;—moreover, he had a farm of his own, and a good house to take a wife to, ' little matters which generally counterbalance roughness of address, in a great measure, as the times go.' She further told me, 'that I might have been sure Mr. Roseley would not let an apprentice-boy marry his daughter ; that I ought to have gently told him I loved Nanny, and asked his permission to pay my addresses to her.' Of course, that was all I wanted,—I only wished to secure my pretty bird, lest she should fly away with some other mate ; but I sadly blundered in my way of making known my wishes and purpose, and I had not courage to go to Mr. Roseley again with explanations, for I dreaded Boxer's teeth, and the horsewhip behind the door. Nanny never came to our shop after that, so I thought my chance of caging her was very small indeed, and the mental distress I suffered in consequence I cannot well describe. To add to my torment, too, Tom Bullskin had by some means got hold of the story of my running away from the dog ; and sometimes, when he was out of the range of my fist, he would whistle, and call out ' Boxer, hool him, boy !'

" When I was twenty-one years old my apprenticeship expired, and I accepted an engagement with a London wholesale house which supplied my master with dry-saltery goods. I shall never forget the grief I felt at leaving my native village for the first time in my life. I had a few days' leisure before I went, so I resolved to ramble through every lane, and field, and nook, for miles round—which had been dear to my boyhood's fancy. The woods where I went nutting, the old elm by the roadside leading to the church, which I had so often climbed for birds'-nests, and the brook where I used to catch minnows and bullfrogs, or, more endearing recollection of all, where I fished up little Nanny's leaky shoe. All those scenes and objects were dear to me, and I thought as it might be long before I saw them again, I would indulge my fancy with a good long revel among them.   One lovely afternoon, I remember it well, I was slowly walking along the margin of the brook, thinking of the merry days of childhood, when who should I see under a willow tree by the identical place where fourteen years before I had raised the sunken shoe, who but my darling Nanny.   Yes, there she sat with a water-lily in her hand gazing at the brook, perhaps admiring her own beautiful image.   There never was anything like lackadaisical sentiment about Nanny Roseley; so, strange as it seems, she had not gone there on purpose to meet me; not at all, sir, she had too much modesty for that.   She has since told me with her own truthful lips, that she did not know why she went there on that identical afternoon, but we understand it now, sir; her going there was not mere chance.   However, there she sat, looking as graceful and modest as the lily in her hand; and I must necessarily have passed by the place unless I had turned round and walked back, which would have looked very unmannerly if she had happened to turn her head and see me.   So onward I went—timidly enough you may be sure—and when I came up to the spot where she sat, I felt as though I had been electrified; my heart actually leaped up to my throat, and forced my tongue to say, 'Nanny!' she turned round quickly, and, oh, sir! the sight of that beautiful blushing face would have knocked a cannibal down on his knees, or melted a Turk into tenderness.   Of course I had not premeditated my address, how could I do so, when I had had no idea of seeing her?   I rushed in- -stinctively up to her and seized her lily white hand, and my heart spoke again right plump out, 'Nanny, I love you!' That is all I said, all I could say in fact, but that was enough, and I saw in a moment that Nanny loved me, though she did not speak a word.   Oh, what a rush of rapture coursed all through me at that happy discovery!   Never shall I forget it.   It is a wonder I did not clasp her to my heart and kiss her luscious lips.   It is fortunate too that I did not do it, for it might have frightened her, and—but I see you are getting excited, Mr. Boomerang, and so I will hurry past this touching part of my story.   We sat beneath the willow tree for an hour or more, and Nanny lisped out the innocent confession, 'that she had loved me ever since the day when I restored her lost shoe to her.'   Was not that very wonderful, sir?   Of course I did not commit a second blunder by asking for her hand there and then, for I felt sure she would not give me any promise without the cognizance of her father, and I knew, too, that it would be wrong to press her for it.   I merely asked her to reserve her heart for me, subject to her father's approval, which she promised to do, and then an interchange of lovers' vows took place which I sealed with a kiss; the first kiss I had ever impressed on a maiden's lips, and oh, sir, it was—but I beg pardon, I see I am exciting you again; I am afraid you are losing patience at my soft descriptions.

"Next day I went to London, with my mind fully resolved to work my way up in the world, and to provide a comfortable home for my heart's idol.   I had plenty of up-hill work, sir, but I will not trouble you with the details of that.   An honest, determined spirit can overcome a host of difficulties.   I not only acquired a more thorough knowledge of mercantile usages, but I found time to cultivate my mind, and improve the limited education I had received at school.   Eighteen months afterwards I returned to Beechwood, to spend Christmas.   I was then a man; and Nanny would now tell you, if I only paused a minute to allow her to speak, that I was rather a smart-looking young man too. I no longer feared Boxer, or the horsewhip (in fact, sir, I feared nothing in those days but dishonour), so I called on Mr. Roseley, and after much explanation and negotiation, I was acknowledged as Nanny's betrothed.   I spent a merry Christmas at Mr. Roseley's house; and as I sat by the blazing ingle side, with my mother on one side of me and Nanny on the other, I would not have exchanged lots with the Duke of York. What fun we had that night to be sure! Old Mr. Roseley sat in his easy chair puffing his pipe and looking as benevolent as Father Christmas himself; the company roared with merriment when the old man told the story of my abrupt application for Nanny; of his wrathful rejection of my suit, and my flight over the garden gate just as Boxer was about to take a large bite from my maximus muscle."

The recollection of that comical incident was so vividly presented to the minds of Mr. and Mrs. Dovecott, that they laughed till the tears rolled down their faces.   Of course I laughed to see them so merry, and you would have laughed too, dear reader, had you been with us.

"But soon after that an important change took place in my prospects," continued Mr. Dovecott.   "A trustworthy young man was required to fill a responsible post in this colony, and I was strongly recommended for the office by my employers, who, though loth to part with me, felt a true interest in my welfare.   An offer was made to me, which I had three days to consider, and then, if I accepted it, a week to prepare for my voyage.   It would be hard to convey to you an idea of my conflicting feelings at this critical juncture in my affairs.   On the one hand there was a brilliant offer of an honourable and lucrative post, with almost certain advancement to fortune ; and on the other hand, there were ties of the most tender and sacred nature binding me to England.   I was fairly perplexed, and the more I pondered the matter, the more complicated it seemed.   So I earnestly sought guidance and direction from that unfailing source where I have all through my life found help in time of need ;—and after a time I felt my mind perfectly free from doubt on the subject, and I was thoroughly. convinced that it was my duty to go to Australia.   It has ever been my rule, Mr. Boomerang, when I have clearly ascertained the path of duty, to pursue it, without reference to opposing feelings or interests ; so I accepted the offer, then prepared to go down to Beechwood to break the news to my dear mother and Nanny Roseley ; and to take a last look at my native woods, and the old-fashioned thatched house near the village green, where I first drew.the breath of life."

CHAPTER III.

" My mother was overwhelmed with grief when I tremblingly acquainted her with my new designs and prospects," continued Mr. Dovecott.   "And it is no wonder the poor old soul was cast down, for I was her main stay, and the only earthly object of her heart's strong affections to centre upon.   She had buried my father and my sister years before, and had had a hard struggle to keep a comfortable roof over her head, and to give me a little bit of schooling as she called it.   When I began to earn money of course I supported her, for she had grown too feeble to earn much at her spinning wheel ; indeed, I did not allow her to work for pay after I had the means of supplying all her wants.   It was a proud day for me, sir, when I remitted her my first quarter's salary, and told her in a loving letter that she was henceforward to live like a lady.   The idea then of my going from her to the other side of the world, and over the terrible wide sea, seemed like blasting all her earthly comfort, and cutting off her supplies of daily bread too. She could not see a single ray of light through the thick cloud which had so suddenly darkened her life ; and her piteous appeals to me not to leave her alone in the world, almost shook my resolution to pieces. Any logical efforts to assuage her grief just then would have been vain, I knew, so I deferred reasoning with her until the first heavy burst of her sorrow was past. Depend on it, sir, that is the best plan to adopt in such cases. I have often seen sympathizing friends trying to administer comfort to persons who had been suddenly overtaken by some distressing calamity, and I have fancied that the eloquence of their looks would have been more soothing than their tongues. 'Cheer up ! Don't fret ! pray don't give way to such immoderate grief !' and similar little bits of good advice, tend rather to irritate than to console, under the first heavy pressure of calamity. If a horse tumbles down with a loaded cart behind him, a skilful driver does not immediately shout 'Come up,' in his ears, for he knows that the violent efforts the horse would make to rise, under the excitement caused by his fall, would probably break the harness, and perhaps break his knees or his backbone. So the driver lets the poor panting beast rest for a few minutes to recover the shock, and meanwhile eases the load as much as possible, and after that he may say 'gee up' with effect. You may as well try to extinguish a blazing house with a boy's squirt, as to rally grief out of the heart of a poor mortal crushed down with sudden affliction, by saying 'cheer up; don't cry !' Better to let the tears come if they will, for they often afford more ease than a volume of dry philosophy would do. That is my opinion, sir, and I have seen something of human nature in seventy years or more. I gently embraced my poor weeping parent, and whispered 'Mother, dear ! I will leave you for an hour or two, I must go over to see Nanny. You are a Christian ; and when you have calmed down a bit, I know you will consider whether this is not an essential discipline that you have to pass through, and you will seek for comfort and direction from the source of all blessings.' After kissing her again and again, I left the cottage, and as I crossed some newly mown meadows to Nanny's house, the fragrance of the new hay seemed to revive such a gush of recollections of happy school days, that I threw myself upon a haycock, and actually groaned off some of the pent up emotions in my heart.

"Old Mr. Roseley was violently opposed to my going abroad ; and after insinuating many ungenerous things, he told me in plain terms that if I went I must give up Nanny altogether, for he would never consent to her going to Botany Bay, as this colony was called. Australia was then but imperfectly known in England, and was associated in the minds of most persons with convicts and kangaroos ; and a voyage here in those days was thought as stupendous an undertaking—especially by inland villagers—as an exploring expedition to the Arctic regions would be now-a-days. I had anticipated some opposition from Mr. Roseley, but I did not expect to see him so rough and unreasonable, and you may be sure, sir, I did not feel very happy; still my resolution was unshaken, because—as I said before—I felt sure I was in the highway of duty. I kept calm, and used all the arguments I could to convince Mr. Roseley that it was my interest to accept the offer, and that it would probably lead to my advancing higher in the social scale than I ever should in England, when he dashed his pipe on to the hearthstone and said, 'He did not care a flip for social scales or weights either ; he was not going to sell his girl like a sack of malt or barley-meal.' And after working himself into a rage, he finally declared 'that if Nan ever went to Botany Bay, she would go at the King's expense, with iron bracelets on, as many bright girls had gone ; but she should never go with his consent, or at his cost, even though I were made governor of the land.'

"Nanny was sitting by when her father uttered that cruel ultimatum, and her poor pale face might have moved a savage to pity. She did not speak a word, but as she rose and left the room she turned her swimming eyes upon me, and there was something more than mortal love in her look, sir, it seemed to lift my heart like a powerful lever. I soon followed her into the hall, where she silently put on her hat and tippet at my request, and accompanied me for a ramble across the fields, and beside the rippling brook where we had first met. I need not tell you all that passed in the long twilight of that summer evening. As we stood on the margin of that memorable stream, dear Nanny leaned her glossy head on my breast for a few minutes, and wept as though her heart would break. Suddenly, however, she became calm and composed, which quite puzzled me, till she took my hand within hers, and said in a firm but deliciously soft voice: 'Davy, dear Davy! forgive me for exhibiting so much weakness at a time when you most require comfort from me. But I am better now, the sight of this spot with its tender recollections shook all my firmness for a minute. Go to Australia, love! I am sure it is your Providential path, and I would not stop you for the world. I will not pain you by offering to release you from your engagement with me, for I know how you feel just now, dear. I am sure you love me fondly, and I know your inclination is now struggling with your sense of duty; I would rather strengthen your resolution than induce you to break it. I know not what is in the future, but I feel something within me assuring me that all will be well if we pursue the right path. I believe we shall happily meet again, and that hope will sustain me under the pangs of parting with you, for you know how dearly I love you, Davy. Go, dearest, and ever believe that your Nanny is faithful to her sacred betrothal pledge. I will not promise to act in opposition to my father's wishes, you would not have me do that, I am sure, but I feel that in some way, which I cannot at present see, his decision will be over-ruled. However that may be, I promise I will be your wife, Davy, or I will die Nanny Roseley. Go, dearest! and may the great God of heaven and earth go with you.'

"'Was not that nobly said, Mr. Boomerang?" exclaimed Mr. Dovecott, pausing to stroke his wife's silvery hair again, and to look a volume of love into her glistening eyes.

" Well, sir, I parted with Nanny that night, after we had said many soft things to each other near the romantic spot where I had fished up the little shoe, and I then walked towards my mother's cottage with a heavy heart, for I dreaded her sorrowful pleadings far more than I had Mr. Roseley's wrath. Judge my delight, sir, when I entered the cottage to see the dear old lady smiling sweetly, though her poor thin face bore traces of recent tears. She clasped me in her arms and sobbed out in a peculiar manner, between a laugh and a cry, ' Davy, my son! my darling boy! You may go to Botany Bay; and your poor widowed mother's blessing will go with you. I have been on my knees, Davy, ever since you went away, and I have had such comforting answers to my prayers, that my poor old heart has danced for joy. Though I scarcely dare hope to see you again in this world, Davy, I can give you up, for I feel it will be for your good ; and I stay my heart upon the comforting belief that we shall surely meet again in the life beyond this, where there will be no more sorrowful partings. Go my boy! and may God bless you! I will not wound you by asking you not to forget your poor old mother; I am sure you will never do that cruel thing, never. You have been a dutiful son, Davy ; the pride of my life, and the prop and support of my tottering age. To part with you is more than my poor unassisted nature could do, but I have received strength from above, Davy. My heart trusted in God and I am helped ; and am enabled to bow submissively to what I believe to be God's will.' The dear old soul could not wholly conquer nature though, for she then gave vent to a flood of tears, though she seemed smiling all the while. I struggled manfully against betraying weakness, but it was no use, sir, and presently I burst out crying too, and our sobbing and shouts of 'praise God,' were heard in the village smithy, and would you believe it, sir? the wicked old blacksmith told the tapster next door that I was tipsy, and was giving my poor old mother a good beating before I went to Botany Bay.

"Next morning I was up before the sun, and hastened across the fields to the old churchyard, and dropped a silent tear on the graves of my father and sister. Then I crossed the wood, cut this hazel stick on my way, sir, took a last look at Nanny's house, and at old Dame Tingle's school, stopped at the brook to take a long drink, and to fill my waistcoat pockets with pebbles, which are carefully preserved in yonder cabinet ; then returned home damp with dew, to eat my last breakfast under my mother's thatch. I pass over the tender scene of parting with my mother, sir, for I do not think I can trust myself to tell it. At nine o'clock I mounted the London mail coach, and in ten minutes more my swimming eyes took a last fond glimpse of Beechwood, my native village."

The old gentleman's voice here grew husky, and he paused in his narrative to polish his spectacles ; so I took that opportunity to make a few remarks to his affectionate spouse. She smiled, and with a half coquettish glance at her husband, said, " Ah, poor fellow, he did not know how eagerly I was watching him that morning from my bed-room window, and what I was suffering. As the coach descended the hill out of my sight, such a cloud of sorrow burst upon me that my poor racked mind was almost overwhelmed. I threw myself on my knees, and had such a cry; while I sobbed out prayers to God for comfort. I shall never forget, sir, the help I received in that time of need. I seemed to be directed to my little text book, and on opening it I read the consoling words, ' Let not your heart be troubled, neither let it be afraid.' My heavy load of anguish began to diminish at once, and I cried with happiness. In half an hour I descended to my dairy work with my heart full of hope."

"Ten days after that I was on shipboard bound for Sydney, Mr. Boomerang," continued Mr. Dovecott, who had recovered his natural tone of voice, and lost the ominous tinge from the tip of his nose. "It would not interest you much to give you the particulars of our voyage; to tell how we were dismasted and had to put into Rio, how we ran short of water, then short of provisions, and other mishaps. and miseries which were common enough in those days, when ships trading here were of a much poorer class in every way than the ships of the present day. Suffice it to say, that after seven months' voyage, I reached my destination in safety, and was soon afterwards installed to my office.

" Viewing the enlightened state of the colony at the present time, you could form but a faint conception of what it was nearly half a century ago, sir; but I do not mean to allude to that subject further than my story requires me to do. Of course, you know that there were comparatively few free settlers here in those days, and there was not much free labour to be obtained. I had a large number of convicts, or assigned servants, to superintend, and the duty was not a light one, I assure you. Some of my men were very difficult to manage, in fact were incorrigible rogues; but I could give you many cheering instances of fidelity and good principles which I experienced in others under my charge. I could also tell you some harrowing stories of cruel scenes which I have witnessed, if there were any advantage in recurring to the revolting annals of those penal times, which will surely never be revived in this land.

"I had many disagreeables and privations to bear, and

many dangers to encounter during the first five years of my residence in this colony ; and often as I sat in my lonely cottage in the interior, have I been disposed to doubt the prudence of the step I had taken in thus isolating myself from civilized society, and from those near and dear relatives and friends for whom my heart yearned with a fondness which at times induced melancholy thoughts and purposes. Those seasons of sadness were transient, however, for I usually felt buoyed up with a hope that good would spring from it ; and I was not without occasional little proofs of that which it would perhaps not be modest of me to further mention.

"The postal communication too, in those days was very irregular, and often protracted ; still every ship which arrived from England brought me letters from my mother and Nanny, full of endearing tokens of affection and fidelity. I wrote them by every opportunity, and I need scarcely say that I remitted to my mother ample funds to provide her with every comfort she required. Rather strange to say, sir, I had a man as house servant (a convict transported for poaching) who was born in the next village to Beechwood, and at one time had worked for Mr. Roseley. You have no idea, sir, what pleasure it used to afford me on dreary winter evenings to hear that man talk about the woods and fields around my native home, of old Mr. Roseley's peculiarities, and his pretty daughter Nanny's excellencies, though of course he did not know how warmly I was interested in that young lady. Poor Jem Traps was an honest fellow, though he was a convict ; and his simple stories of rustic life around Beechwood were as entertaining to me as a fiddle is to a sailor. But I soon got more agreeable companions than Jem to cheer my drooping spirits. An important change took place about that time in my position and my prospects."

CHAPTER IV.

" As I before remarked, sir, an important change took place in my affairs, after I had been about six years in the colony," said Mr. Dovecott, while his face began to glow like the rising sun just emerging from a fog bank. " One morning at daybreak, I was lying on my stretcher bed, trying to kick myself cool, and cogitating whether I should turn out and have a shower-bath, or take another nap, for I had passed a very restless night. The weather was excessively warm, and the mosquitos had probably mistaken me for a ' new chum,' for they were unusually vicious; my skin was covered with the marks of their sharp little snouts, and my ears had been annoyed all night long with their satirical songs, after drinking my health. While keeping my involuntary vigil, I was thinking as usual about Nanny and my mother, and roaming in imagination through every lane and leafy nook around my native home; until I actually fancied I would rather be a fox in Beechwood Copse, with a fox's freedom, and the society of other foxes, than be in my isolated position, with all its prospective honours and emoluments. There was I—I thought—pining away my prime in forced celibacy, and yonder was the darling of my heart at the other end of the earth, pining for me like a little jenny-wren with her mate caught in a brick trap. And this waste of love was all caused by the stupidity of old Roseley, who obstinately believed that one of the finest countries in the world was as much to be dreaded as the cells of Old Bailey.

"But those gloomy musings were not very lasting, for I seldom encouraged such thoughts.   Hope was a prominent bump in my cranium; still I suppose the most sanguine of men have occasional seasons of dumpiness, especially in close muggy weather, when their gastric secretions are apt to get disarranged. I was doubtless suffering to some extent from the enervating effects of the sultry weather, and the depression which the sight of ruin and semi-starvation induced, for it had been a season of protracted drought, and I was obliged to put my men upon reduced rations.   However, there I lay, rolling about on my stretcher, and avenging myself upon the gorged mosquitos on the slabs, by tapping them on the head with my slippers, when suddenly Jem Traps entered my room in a state of great excitement, and handed me a letter which a special messenger had just brought from Sydney. The missive informed me of the sudden death of my superior officer, through eating toad-fish, and intimated that I was required to proceed to head quarters at once, and fill the important post which had become vacant by his decease.

" I must avoid details, Mr. Boomerang, or I shall keep you here for a week listening to my story.   By that sudden event I was promoted to a position of influence and honour, with a large income, and a fine commodious house, replete

with every convenience and comfort I could desire, except
one—that first essential in a house—a wife.　That deside-
ratum was wanting ; but as I was now able to offer a home,
with every luxury the colony could afford, I thought the
time was come to send for Nanny.　Then came the next
posing question, how was I to win her father's consent.　I
did not for a moment think of her coming without his sanction ; but how to overcome his obstinate prejudices was the
question which knocked my bump of hope as flat as a florin.
Many sleepless nights I spent considering that difficulty ;
and many times, both by day and night, I sought Divine
direction in the matter, for I felt how essential a wife was
to my happiness, and to my usefulness too.　At length my
mind seemed directed to a certain course just on the eve of
a ship sailing for London.　The vessel was a regular trader,
and I was well acquainted with the captain, so I explained
my plans to him confidentially, and arranged with him for
the accommodation of my darling Nanny, old Mr. Roseley,
his son, and his son's wife and children ; also for my dear
mother, my sister's orphan children, and an uncle and aunt,
with a lot of cousins, who were barely earning a livelihood
in England.　Every kith and kin belonging to the Roseley
and Dovecott families were to be comfortably accommodated
in the ' Dolphin ' at my expense, if they chose to come to
Sydney.　The captain promised to see them personally, and
try his best to induce them to accept my, liberal offer before
he let his cabins to other passengers ; but he would use
special efforts to bring out Nanny and her father, and my
mother.　At the same time I sent home money sufficient to
provide them all with necessary outfits ; and I promised to
do my best to settle them comfortably in the colony, and to
have board and lodging ready for them on their arrival.　No
one will be able to tell me that I was shabby enough to
neglect or scorn my poor relations after I had risen in the
world, Mr. Boomerang ; and though I have not often met
with grateful returns, I am satisfied at having performed my
duty, if some of those I have helped have neglected theirs.

"Now comes a very remarkable part of my story, sir.
About two months before the Dolphin reached England, old
Mr. Roseley's house and barns were burnt to the ground ; so
he and his son Matt were totally ruined, for they were not
insured.　Of course it was a sudden downfall to them, and
they felt it severely, for they were all rather proud in their

way, except Nanny. They had lots of sympathy while their buildings were blazing, in fact a good deal more than they wanted, but it vanished with the smoke ; or the only tangible shape it assumed was in a subscription to buy the old man a razor grinder's barrow, for he was remarkably handy with edge tools, and had never seemed happier than when he was doing odd jobs as an amateur tinker. His simple-hearted friends thought they could not buy him an article more to his taste ; and withal, it was a cheap way of setting him up in the world again, and removing their dread of his borrowing or begging from them. So the barrow was bought, and old farmer Vetch drove off in his cart to deliver it, with as much pride and good will as though he were going to present a new organ to the parish church. His surprise was great when after reading the brief address of the donors, Mr. Roseley, instead of expressing gratitude for the gift, cursed the barrow and all the contributors too. A storm of high words ensued and frightened the horse, which bolted off, upset the cart, and broke the barrow to little bits. Nothing was saved but the grindstone.

"My mother offered a temporary home to Nanny and her father, which they gladly accepted. Soon afterwards, Nanny arranged to go to Squire Leveret's, as nursery governess, though she did not much like the idea, for some of the children were as rough as their father. But on the very morning she was preparing to start for the Squire's, my letter arrived, and caused no small commotion amongst them, you may be sure. Strange to say, old Mr. Roseley was the first to propose that they should all get ready to start as soon as possible. 'Botany Bay, or any other cannibal country was preferable to Beechwood,' he said, 'now he had no other prospect than a tinker's barrow or the workhouse. Feed me on kangaroos and cornstalks, if you like, but deliver me from the neighbours who would mock my misfortunes, and send me about the country grinding scissors ! A fugitive and a vagabond, and a poverty-stricken old tramp tinker ! Come along, Nanny, my girl ! I am ready. I can tie all my traps in a bundle handkerchief, so let us be off as soon as possible.'

"A day or two after that, Captain Luff went down to Beechwood. He had no difficulty in persuading them all to accept my offer, though some of the younger ones shuddered at the mention of Botany Bay, as if it were the favourite watering place of old Bogy and his crew.

" I remained in suspense as to the result of the captain's mission, for we were unusually long without a mail. Several months had elapsed since the arrival of a ship from England, and as the time for the return of the Dolphin drew near, you may imagine how anxiously I watched the signal staff from day to day, and how often my fancy pictured in dreams at night the arrival of my fondly expected ones, but only to teaze me on awakening to a sense of my dreary bachelorhood. Ugh, those days of single misery ! of odd stockings and changed collars, broken buttons and yellow linen. Mr. Boomerang, I assure you, I would not be single again—even for six months—for all the brass bedsteads and other bachelor traps in the world, and a cart-load of bead-work slippers to boot. Not I, sir; ha, ha, ha ! Not I. Give me my wife, and water-gruel diet, if you like, and you will see me happy—jubilant ; but give me the range of an oriental palace, with all Rajah Rumanputtee's diamonds to play with, and a daily fare of curried peacocks, and without my wife I should be as miserable as an old jack tar who had lost his tobacco box."

Mr. Dovecott here arose from his chair, kissed his laughing spouse on both cheeks, and told her that she was sweeter than a ton of barley-sugar. He then made a feint to dance a fandango, but was seized with a twinge in his left leg, whereupon he reseated himself, rubbed his hands in merry ecstacy, and laughed again, then resumed his narrative.

" One morning, directly I had got out of bed, I looked as usual from my window at the flagstaff, and to my great delight there was a black ball on the south yard arm, and a square blue flag at the mast head. Hurrah ! there is a ship to the southward, perhaps it's the Dolphin ! and then I merrily sang as I pulled on my holey stockings :—

" ' Haste, Nanny ! I'm weary of living alone.'

" I dressed myself extra smart that morning, and oiled my bushy beard and whiskers. I dare say my servant was a little doubtful of my taste, in preferring the external air to hot coffee and mutton ham for breakfast, for I would rise from the table every now and then and pop my head out of the window to see if the ship were signalled. Presently I saw an angular red flag run up under the blue one. Hurrah ! I shouted ; a ship from London ! ' Tell Trap to get my

boat ready immediately,' I said to the astonished servant.
'Hurry, Duff, hurry : then you can clear the table. I don't
want any more breakfast.'

"Half an hour afterwards I was dashing down the harbour under all sail, with a strong southerly breeze, and as I
rounded Bradley's Head I could see the Dolphin tacking up
to her anchorage. How can I possibly describe the alter-
nations of hope and fear which filled my breast at that exciting time, Mr. Boomerang? But I see you understand
them, sir, by your sympathizing muscular movements ; you
look as earnest as though you were preparing to spring on
deck to catch Nanny for me. I thank you for the interest
you display in my recital, sir. My well manned boat sped
swiftly over the waves, and in a very short time I was
within hail of the ship, and the first persons I distinguished
on the poop, were my darling Nanny and my devoted
mother, side by side, waving their white handkerchiefs in
token of recognition.

"'Ods, bobs, take hold of the tiller, Trap ! boo—hoo—
whoo !' I blubbered, in spite of all my manly efforts to look
composed and dignified ; then dragging my handkerchief
from my pocket, I buried my face in it ; and, as Paddy
Spudd, the bowman, afterwards explained to his hut mates,
'I cudn't cry for laughin', and I cudn't laugh for cryin', nor
I cudn't spake for kissin' the girls afther I got on boord the
ship.'

"Oh what an ecstatic meeting that was, sir ! I can no
more describe it than I could paint a landscape. I mounted
the gangway, and the first thing I noticed was old Roseley
sitting on the capstan playing a fiddle, which set me laughing ; the next minute I was locked in my mother's arms,
which set me crying. Then I embraced Nanny—very gently,
of course—which set me—but I cannot explain all my
emotions on that blessed morning, you must imagine them,
sir—and I must shorten my story.

*   *   *   *   *   *

"Ten days afterwards, the bell in old St. Philip's round
tower rang out like fire, and almost all the bunting in the
colony was fluttering in the breeze to celebrate my marriage
with Nanny Roseley. Good old Archdeacon Cowper united
us, and after a sumptuous dejeuner at my house (which was
partaken of by numerous guests, including thirty-five of my
relatives and friends, who had just arrived in the Dolphin),

we drove off to Parramatta to spend our honeymoon, and a bright moon it was too.

    *   *   *   *   *   *

"Now tell me what you think of that for a tale of true love," said Mr. Dovecott, who was evidently well pleased with it himself. "Is there not more honest wholesome material in it—though badly dressed—than in those insipid hashed-up love stories of the age, full of broken hearts and hobgoblins, and all that sort of calf's head stuffing, which, I am sorry to believe, sell as readily as ripe gooseberries! What do you think of it, sir?"

"In brief, sir, I think your career has been singularly marked by Providential circumstances, and that it is highly suggestive," I replied. "But pray tell me what became of your friends who came out in the Dolphin; I should like to hear a little more about them."

"I will tell you in a few words, sir. My dear mother lived for fifteen years with us in peace and comfort; and Nanny will certify that her experience belies the cynical report, that mothers-in-law are always very troublesome in a household. My mother was a help and a blessing to my wife, and I can testify that I never heard a note of discord from either of them; on the contrary, thanksgiving and the voice of melody filled my home from morning till night. She is now in her home above. Her tomb is on the Sand-hills, and the memory of her many virtues is embalmed in my heart. Poor Mr. Roseley is gone to heaven too. He lived to a good old age in a nice little cottage on the Rocks, and his time was spent in doing good to every one around him. He often blessed the hour when his house and barns were burnt, as it was that Providential circumstance which had led him to Sydney. He had the happiness of seeing his family all flourishing in temporal things—but best of all, of knowing that they were living in preparation for the better life beyond the grave. His son Matt got a grant of land, and in time grew wealthy and influential. Some of his descendants are now filling positions of honour and usefulness in the colony, as you are aware, sir. My uncle and aunt unfortunately drank themselves to death. My sister's children and my cousin's all prospered amazingly. They are well known in the south, and in the west country, for their hospitality and other sterling virtues. Their descendants are branching off in all directions, and some of them are becoming lights in the land. So you see, Mr. Boomerang, that my coming out here as pioneer, was—through God's blessing—the means of establishing two families in respectability and affluence ; in removing them from poverty to a ' land flowing with milk and honey.' "

I freely expressed my opinion on his interesting narrative, and on the useful lessons it was calculated to teach, to young men especially ; showing the advantage of strictly pursuing the path of duty with manly courage and perseverance, and of acknowledging God in all their ways. I then said, " I should like to hear a little of your marital experience, Mr. Dovecott, if you have no objection to relate it."

" Come in and have some supper, sir," said the old gentleman, with a significant glance at me. As we walked towards the parlour, he added, " I will finish my story by and bye, if you wish to hear it ; but I must first persuade Mrs. Dovecott to go to bed, for there are some subjects which I must allude to that would touch her feelings acutely. She is as tender-hearted as a little ' budgery ghar,' bless her ! It would be improper for me to praise my wife, I know, but I must say that she is a model woman ; in short, the nearest resemblance to an angel that I ever saw. That is a fact, Mr. Boomerang."

CHAPTER V.

" Now, my precious koh-i-noor, you had better go to bed, for Mr. Boomerang and I want to have a chat upon a subject which would not delight you," said Mr. Dovecott, addressing his wife, after we had finished supper. " You will forgive me for staying up an hour later than usual, I am sure, for it is not often that our old friend spends a night with us."

Mrs. Dovecott rose, made a few pleasant remarks on the advantages of retiring early to rest ; then intimated to me that I would find extra bedding behind the door if I needed it, shook hands with me, and retired to her chamber.

" Take the sofa, and make yourself comfortable," said my host, at the same time he threw himself into an easy chair and began to rub his nose, his usual expedient for stimulating his ideas in drowsy seasons. " You wish to hear some of my conjugal experience, sir, but it will be comparatively little that I shall be able to tell you before the midnight dial warns us to bed. To concentrate the product of a forty acre vineyard into one puncheon, would be as feasible a task as to give you in one sitting even the most meagre description of forty years of growing love with that estimable creature who has just gone up-stairs. But I will try, sir ; and as I heard a celebrated lecturer from London say a few years ago, ' I will throw out a few jets of thought for your after consideration.'

" Well, sir, my young wife took charge of her household with as much grace and dignity as if she had been accustomed to control a large establishment for years. Nobody ever heard her fussing and grumbling about trifling troubles, peculiar to the colony, or complaining that she had not been used to this or that inconvenience, as weak-minded women often do, thinking thereby to increase their importance ; whereas such airs are usually to be regarded as signs that they never had half so many conveniences before. Nanny was kind and considerate to her domestics, still she was firm and mistress-like, and they all loved her. We had a dozen assigned servants about the house, and with a few trifling exceptions—scarcely worth mentioning—I never had any trouble with them. Of course there was occasional wrangling among themselves, which I did not pretend to hear. I seldom noticed trifles which did not positively infringe my rules and regulations. Nanny managed her household by the rule of kindness, and, on the whole, things went on with perhaps rather more regularity than our town clock in those days. Several of our servants stayed with us after they had received their tickets-of-leave, and one woman lived with us for ten years after she became free, in fact she lived with us till she died. For obvious reasons I refrain from mentioning real names, sir, but I could give you—if there were any advantage in doing so—the history of several of our servants, who became thoroughly reformed characters, who lived useful lives and died happy deaths, and whose descendants now deservedly rank among the patriots and the benefactors of the country.

" About twelve months after her arrival, my dear Nanny presented me with a darling little boy, which seemed to open a fresh avenue in my heart for love to enter. I know you are fond of little boys and girls, sir, for I have seen you hopping about like a kangaroo with a lot of children after you screaming with fun ; so you will understand how I loved my precious boy, who, as he grew up and began to toddle about, seemed to fill the house with rare music, and my heart with new joy. How dearly Nanny and I prized him ! too much, sir, I fear, for we almost idolized him. By his thousand engaging pranks, and his winning little ways, he wound himself round our hearts so tightly, that other and higher love was almost excluded ; and I believe that is why God saw it would be a mercy to take our idol from us, and to ruffle our too even course of happiness a little.

"Sickness prostrated our darling boy, and day after day, and night after night we watched him with that anxious interest which none but fond parents know. Gradually he sank under the wasting influence of fever, which no human skill could allay. His round rosy cheeks became pale and sunken, his plump little limbs were wasted and shrivelled. The merry laughter, which had sounded like the music of spring birds in our home, gave place to a low piteous whine, and the smiles on his pretty dimpled face were changed to the sharp wince of suffering, which racked our hearts to witness. Our house was silent as a sepulchre, for all the servants were fond of little Charlie, and sadness beclouded each face as the doctor went away day after day without saying a word to encourage a ray of hope of the recovery of our loved one. I need not tell you, sir, that I often prayed to God to spare my boy, and my dear wife prayed too. But I did not ask unreservedly for the life of my child ; to my earnest pleadings for him I always added the condition, 'Lord, Thou knowest what is best : help me to say, Thy will be done.' Still I felt it very, very hard to say, 'Take my boy, Lord, if Thou seest it best to do so.' Oh how difficult it is, sir, to see wisdom and mercy in such a dispensation, while our spirits are crushed down by the afflictive stroke.

"One afternoon there was an apparent improvement in him, and hope revived in our hearts. Our darling's eyes looked brighter, there was a slight colour in his cheeks, and he smiled while he faintly lisped our names. How carefully Nanny and I watched him that evening, and how we cheered each other with the promise of his recovery. How we admired his pretty sleeping form, with the curly locks clustering about his noble brow. How we sat and drew bright pictures of our future happiness in training him up to manhood. But all those hopes were suddenly blighted, and the pride of our eyes faded before us like the ephemeral tints of a rainbow. About midnight an unmistakable change stole

over our beloved child's features, and while we stood beside
his cot gazing on him with streaming eyes, his gentle spirit
soared away home.   Oh, sir ! what a crushing blow that
was to us.   But you have experienced a similar loss, so you
understand it.   May God comfort all those who are now
mourning as Nanny and I mourned on that memorable night
of death.

"The loss of that dear child was an intense grief to us for
several months ; but time softens down our heaviest sorrows,
and we tried our best to bear our trial with resignation.
Dear Nanny gathered up all Charlie's clothes and toys, and
everything that had belonged to him, and locked them in a
separate drawer of her wardrobe.   Nothing that could recall
the memory of the dear little fellow was to be seen, and we
rarely ventured to speak of him for several weeks.   It is
marvellous though how small a thing will suddenly re-open
the springs of sorrow, when we think they are almost dried
up, as the following little incident will show.   One evening
I was searching in my study for a document which I had
mislaid, and in turning over a waste-paper basket I found a
little toy kitten, Charlie's pretty little pussy as he used to
call it, and which he had put to bed in my paper basket, as
I remembered, the very evening before he was taken ill.
The sight of that little simple toy proved to me that I had
not forgotten my darling boy, and that my tears would still
flow in spite of my reason.   In fact, sir, I have not forgotten
him to this day, nor shall I ever do so while memory holds
her seat.   But my sorrow is turned into joy and gratitude,
for I cannot have the shade of a doubt that he is safe in
Heaven, and I shall soon re-unite with him, for the sand in
my life's glass has not long to run.   Yes, he is safe, I know ;
but had he been spared to me when I so earnestly longed to
keep him, how can I tell what sad fate might have befallen
him ?   It is awfully possible that I might now be weeping
in bitterness over his poor wrecked soul.

"Oh, Mr. Boomerang ! depend upon it, it is all right when
God takes our children from us in early life, painful though
it be for us to part with them.   It is all right, sir, and more
a matter for thanksgiving than for sorrowful repining, which
many parents have owned after the keen edge of their grief
has been worn down, and they are able to see through the
cloud that overshadowed their spirits.

"About two years after Charlie's death, we were blessed

with another bright-eyed boy to fill his place, and our hearts again rejoiced. But I must allude very briefly to this subject, sir, for reasons which you will shortly understand. At four years old little David was seized with a dangerous epidemic, which had carried off many children in Sydney. I was almost frantic at the idea of losing him, and I never felt so much opposed to the Almighty's dispensations. I believe I prayed to God unconditionally, to spare my child, to save myself and my wife the bitter pang of losing him as we had lost our first-born. He was spared, sir," continued Mr. Dovecott with increasing emotion. " He grew up to manhood. I will forbear to ' draw his frailties from their dread abode.' He is dead. He died a violent death. Oh, God ! Oh, God ! Would that I had buried him in infancy ! Poor boy ! My poor ruined boy !"

The old gentleman was so overcome by the sad recollections of the untimely death of his son, (who I afterwards learned had committed suicide), that he could not continue his narrative. I refrained from inquiries on the distressing subject, and after a few words of sympathy I bad him good night and went to my chamber, pondering over the mysterious dispensations of Providence, as displayed in the late touching recital.

Next morning—rather to my surprise—Mr. Dovecott was almost merry, but I now ascertained that his cheerfulness was studied, in order to prevent his wife suspecting the gloomy nature of his conversation on the previous night. After breakfast I took a pleasant stroll through the garden with him, when he thus continued his story :—

" My career in this country has not been an unruffled one, far from it, I have had my trials, sir, but I believe I have not had more than was essential to keep me humble ; for uninterrupted prosperity is very dangerous, and is apt to engender pride and self-importance. But whatever troubles I had in my business affairs, I had always peace and comfort at home ; and with the exception of one blighting source of anxiety, which I alluded to last night, my home circle was always a happy one. When reverses overtook me, it was then that I most felt the sympathy and cheering counsel of my dear wife ; and I found that the stormy blasts of adversity only made her cling closer to my side. Twenty-three years ago I was all but ruined, in common with many other wealthy colonists. I had extensive landed possessions certainly, and sheep and cattle too, but, commercially speaking, they were almost valueless, for a monetary panic overspread the country, and there was scarcely a possibility of selling property, either real or personal, except at mere nominal prices. I must tell you that I had retired from my office some years before, an independent man ; in fact, I supposed myself to be wealthy, and had lived in a style proportionate to my means.

"I recollect going home one evening very much cast down with the pressure of my pecuniary embarrassments, and I said to my wife, 'Nanny, my love, I have tried as long as I could to save you from the anxiety of knowing our involved circumstances, but I can't longer conceal from you the fact, that we are on the verge of ruin.' How do you think she bore the news, sir. Did she cry, do you suppose, as some women would have done, and reproach me with want of judgment, or the like? or did she shudder at the approach of poverty and say, that she could not do without this or that luxury or comfort? Nothing of the sort, sir. She clasped her hands round my neck, and with her usual cheering smile, said, 'Davy, dear, I am sorry you did not tell me this before, that I might have shared your burden of anxiety. But cheer up, love ! we both know how to work, and we are not too proud to do anything that is honourable. We have a good reputation left to us, and good health too —let us be thankful for these blessings. Above all, "we know that all things work together for good, to them that love God." And that is a consolation which we may claim, for we both love God, and have hitherto trusted in Him. "Let not your heart be troubled, neither let it be afraid." Listen to some of my plans, dear. We can take a small house, and manage with only one servant, or without a servant at all if needs be; and it will surprise you how little money I shall require to keep house with, for I know how to bake, and to make candles, and butter, and a score of other things which will save outlay of money. Then we can do without new clothes for a year or more, and who knows what may take place in that time? Cheer up, Davy, dear ! "The earth is the Lord's, and the fulness thereof," I am sure he will not let us want.'

"You have no idea how that cheered me, sir. It was like a shower in a season of drought, and my heart was as light as a poppy head in a minute. How I did bless the

day when I first saw her dear face ! Seeing that she could
bear trouble so nobly, I opened my mind freely to her, and
I was really surprised at the solidity and practical character
of her counsel, and her ready plans for retrenchment. We
did retrench, sir—we dismissed all our servants except two,
dispensed with our carriage, and economised in every way
we could ; and though our circle of fashionable visitors was
lessened in consequence (which we found to be an advantage), our real friends did not desert us, and we had the
satisfaction of knowing that we were gradually recovering
ourselves. My wife's inspiriting conduct put new courage
into me, and I went to work like a skilful mariner to save
my shattered bark from foundering. The fortunate expedient of boiling down sheep and cattle, saved me the
necessity of sacrificing my real property, and though it was
a hard struggle with us for several years, we eventually
weathered the storm. Times gradually improved, as you
are aware, sir, and soon after the gold was discovered in
the colony, I found myself in more affluent circumstances
than I had ever been before.

"My children have grown up to comfort me in my old
age—you know the positions they occupy in society, sir.
Poor Davy was the only sad exception, and his case was a
powerful warning to the others. One of these days, I may
tell you in confidence some of the particulars of his deplorable career, and what was the cause of his fine constitution
being ruined, and his intellect shaken to idiocy. Oh, sir, I
often shudder when I see the thoughtless way in which
some parents discharge the responsible duties devolving
upon them, and I long to speak to them and offer some
hints on matters which it is important to study, if they
value their children's souls and bodies. I have had the
pain of seeing many young persons cut off in the bloom of
life, through yielding to certain debasing practices acquired
in childhood. I need not speak plainer to you, sir, for I
think you will understand me, but if not, I refer you for
information to 'Todd's Student's Manual,' chap. 4. The
testimony of an eminent philanthropist, (whose recent death
was a great loss to our community) has proved how deeply
he thought upon that subject to which I allude. Moreover,
I have in my desk a cleverly written treatise, in manuscript,
from the pen of one of the first physicians in the colony,
which not only depicts the terrible consequences of the sin-

ful habit, but proves, alas, that it is sadly prevalent. I heartily wish that I could ensure the perusal of that treatise by every parent in the land. I am sure it would arouse them to watchfulness.

" A short time ago I heard a Rev. Doctor relate an anecdote of a poor widow who lived near a railroad, on some part of the sea coast of England. One winter night, during a violent snow storm, the sea broke over its embankment and made a great chasm in the railway line. The widow knew that a mail train would pass along the line at a certain hour, and that if unwarned it would rush with all its living freight to destruction. So she arose, and facing the pelting storm, waded through the snow to some distance along the railway ; then lighted a fire, and watched beside it till the arrival of the train, which was thereby saved from sudden ruin. That is the spirit which should actuate every heart, sir, when a fellow-creature is in danger. It is that spirit, I trust, which prompts me to caution parents whenever I can, to carefully watch over their children, lest they should unhappily acquire habits which will—apart from the moral aspect—as surely shatter their physical health, as the worm at its root will destroy the vitality of a young tree."

CHAPTER VI.

" I HAVE uttered a good deal of nonsense, Mr. Boomerang, while speaking of my wife, and I daresay you think I am a silly old fellow ; but bear in mind there was fun as well as folly in my remarks, and I did not mean all I said, of course not. I have called my Nanny an angel, and a bird of Paradise, but bless her heart she is only a woman after all, I know that very well. She is as wingless as an emu, and has not even got a feather on her bonnet. My whimsical figures are not intended to be subjected to matter of fact scrutiny, and I don't suppose they would go far with a common jury in establishing my wife's superiority, or my common sense either. Still, for all that, I can and will say in sober earnestness, that she is a superior woman in every way, mentally and materially ; that I can prove by a thousand evidences. But even superior women have little marks of human nature about them, and the man who expects to find a wife without them had much better remain a bachelor all his life.

" As I have said before, sir, Nanny was free from all fussy

whims and fancies, which some young wives think it pretty to exhibit, still she was—she was—well, sir, she was not an angel—that is the best way to express it. She was not perfect, so I began to study her little pecularities or idiosyncrasies, and in a short time I could keep her in tune as mellow as my German flute. She was subject to nervous depressions, poor thing, owing to spinal weakness. Those sufferers who understand what that means, will readily sympathise with her;—but persons with no nerves usually laugh at such disorders, which they call by a variety of ridiculous names, and treat the victims of them with contempt rather than with pity. When at home, her father (who knew no more about nervous disorders than a brewer's horse) used to try to rally her out of her mopishness, as he called it, by blustering at her in his characteristic style, or recommending half-a-dozen rough remedies in a breath, which usually sent her to her room in tears. I took another plan, sir, for I had too high an opinion of her sense to believe that her malady was induced by any whims and fancies as her father said it was. I knew when her nervous attacks were coming on, and I used to contrive to take some little business trip into the country for a week or so, and to take her with me. Change, and cheerful companionship were the best remedies for her complaint, I knew, and after a time she got much better.

"It would take too long, sir, to tell you all the little methods I adopted in order to mould her to my own mind. I had had plenty of time to think over that important subject in my lonely bachelorhood, and I used to reason thus. 'I take a great deal of pains to break in my hack horse to easy paces, and to keep him from buck-jumping, bolting, stumbling, or shying; and I find it necessary to know the dispositions of my servants, in order to manage them efficiently, and shall I neglect to study the characteristics of my wife when I get her? Not I, indeed! that shall be my chief delight.' That's the way I used to argue to myself, sir, as I lay rolling about on my bachelor bed on warm nights; and I carried out my principle when I got married. My wife showed her appreciation of my kindness by studying all my little whims and oddities, in a way that no one had done before; and I became under her gentle treatment, as tractable as a tame lion. Therein lies the grand secret of our life-long happiness, sir, we carefully studied each other's weak points, and tried to strengthen them, while we mutually learned to 'bear and forbear.' There was perfect confidence between us, and we rarely had a thought or a wish concealed. I certainly kept from Nanny for a time, the knowledge of our pecuniary embarrassment, but I regretted it afterwards, and I always found my troubles reduced by acquainting her with them.

"I will not say that we never had a 'tiff,' as it is called, during our forty years intercourse, or you may be disposed to doubt me, but I can truly say, sir, we never 'let the sun go down on our wrath,' if there was any wrath at all in our tiffs. I am rather fidgety at times, sir, as you have doubtless observed, and I dare say if some women had the management of me, I should be known as the 'great bear,' by all the gossips in the colony. But dear Nanny can cure my fidgety fits as cleverly as she can cook a plain dinner. She knows exactly how long to let my ill humours simmer, or ferment, and when to pass her gentle hand over my brow and kiss me into good humour. She can tell at a glance if it would be safe for her to steal up behind me and tickle my ear with a straw, or playfully take hold of my whiskers and say, 'Davy, you rogue! what do you mean by looking so cross? kiss me this minute, sir, and be a good boy!' Of course I never could help smiling under such discipline, and before I had time to recollect my cause of vexation, she would be clinging about my neck and saying all sorts of funny things to me, which would make any man laugh if his house were on fire. Sometimes I have gone into my sanctum to cool down after some vexatious excitement or other, for we are all subject to these sort of trials, sir, and I think it would be a good thing if every one had a sanctum to cool down in. In about half-an-hour my door has been gently opened, and Nanny has just peeped in with her mouth screwed up into kissing shape, and with an arch look such as she well knew how to put on, she has gazed at me for half a minute, then with a roguish toss of her head muttered, 'I don't care for you!' shut the door and ran away before I could throw my slipper at her. In ten minutes more she would slyly open the door again and peep in to find me laughing, of course, how could I help it? That is the way the dear soul would gently chase away little petty vexations from my heart; she took other methods in serious matters, but with invariably the same results.

"Now, sir, I will try to picture for a moment what might have resulted from my impatient temper, had Nanny behaved to me in the teasing spirit which I have seen some very good, but thoughtless wives exhibit when their husbands have been temporarily ruffled. Suppose, when I had gone into my study to cool down my wrath, as I before explained, that Nanny had followed me in and said carelessly, or perhaps sharply, 'What is the matter now?' or 'What makes you look so glumpy?' I should probably have been vexed at her intrusion, and replied hastily, 'I will tell you presently, my dear; leave me just now, if you please.'

"Suppose she had replied, 'I am sure it must be something dreadful to make you look so cross, and I want to know what it is?'

"'I ask you to leave me, Mrs. Dovecott!' I might have said emphatically; perhaps I should have said something much sharper than that, for I confess I am not particularly polite when irritated, and I can easily imagine how a regular storm might have been raised had she retorted in my own pungent style. Had she, too, adopted a popular expedient and ran for her father, or her brother and his wife, or some of her cousins to adjudge our quarrel, their interference would perhaps have provoked me to fighting pitch, and a furious family brawl would have been the result. The parson of the parish would perhaps have been sent for to repair the breach, and seeing faults on both sides he would not have been able conscientiously to decide in favour of either, consequently he would have offended us all, and would probably have lost us from his congregation, for staying from church is the usual silly plan people adopt for evidencing their dislike to their minister, and avenging themselves on his pocket at the same time. The fracas would have been as relishable as hot muffins and eschalots, to the gossips of the neighbourhood, and through their influence the mischief might have spread far and wide like a dust storm. Of course it would have been reported that Mr. and Mrs. Dovecott lived 'a cat and dog life.' Friends would have poured in sympathy and condolence on both sides, and thereby fomented strife; thenceforward family brawls would have been as frequent as the whirls of a weathercock. A deed of separation would have been the *dernier ressort*, as it generally is in such cases, and dear Nanny and I would be perhaps pining apart at this day in solitary sadness, or abusing each other in bitterness of spirit.

"If you think this an over-drawn picture from fancy, Mr. Boomerang, here is an analogous one from real life. I could give you more, but one such specimen is sufficient for you, I'm sure. A young married couple were debating on the tender subject of choosing a name for their first-born. The husband's choice was Peter, but the wife, after sharply condemning his taste, declared she would sooner call the boy Poker or Pitchfork. High words ensued—for they were two simpletons—and grew into a violent quarrel, when the wife, with an hysterical outburst of feeling exclaimed, 'I'll go and tell father!' and ran off to her sire, who lived not far away, and soon he was hastening to the house in a red hot rage with his excited daughter behind him. It is no marvél that the young husband, goaded to fury by his father-in-law's abuse and undue interference, kicked him out of the house. The old man's litigious spirit was aroused, an action for assault and battery—with heavy damages—was begun forthwith, and that trumpery quarrel, which has taken me two minutes to tell of, extended over two years, drove the husband into the Insolvent Court, and forced the wife to earn a separate maintenance. Whether they are reunited I cannot say, but I am half inclined to say—for the sake of posterity—I hope they are not.

"'What God hath joined together, let not man put asunder,' is a solemn injunction, which if more generally observed, would wonderfully add to the peace of many disjointed families, and to society at large. I have known the happiness of a household completely blasted by the interference of relatives or friends, with perhaps the best intention too. When either a husband or a wife begins to even whisper of each other's faults or short-comings to a third person, Ichabod is written on the door of their home. That is my opinion, Mr. Boomerang, and I would affectionately warn married folks—young couples especially—to be very watchful against those rankling sources of discord and hatred, and to bar their doors as carefully against idle gossips and scandal-mongers as they do against midnight robbers.

"I knew a married couple, good old folks they were, too. I believe they loved everybody but themselves—and they would have loved and respected each other, if busybodies had not tampered with them. They had occasional tiffs about trifles not worth a penny cabbage, but instead of going into their sanctums to cool, and to pray at the same time, then to come out and kiss away their contentions, they were in the habit of sending for a neighbour to settle their disputes, and he usually made matters worse, though I dare say he strove to mend them. Mr. Splicem—the said neighbour—was a worthy man in his way, though not overstocked with common sense, or he would have declined the thankless office. Of course he told his wife all about the rupture when he returned home from his unsuccessful missions, and his wife told her grown-up children, so by a natural process, the petty brawlings of Mr. and Mrs. Glumps were soon as public as other sporting intelligence, and the poor old pair were the table-talk of all the vulgar gossips in town.

" I wish I could have the privilege of speaking to the world for even half-an-hour before I die, Mr. Boomerang," said Mr. Dovecott, with earnestness. " Among many important items from my long experience in the world's ways that I could quote, I would say to young folks who are on the look out for partners in life, or rather I would say to their natural guardians, for they are most responsible, ' Be careful that there are no striking disparities between these inexperienced lovers, or they cannot reasonably expect conjugal happiness. Above all, see that virtuous principles are alive in their hearts, for where they are lacking, the consequences may be anything that your imagination can picture that is dreadful.' A moment's sad reflection on passing events is sufficient to convince us of that, Mr. Boomerang. Let your fancy picture a youthful pair tripping jauntily up to the altar in God's house, to be united in holy wedlock, and while the bridegroom is promising to love, honour, and cherish the blooming girl whose hand he clasps, just conceive, sir, that it is awfully possible, that in less than twelve months' time he will go home drunk, beat his wife savagely, and throw her bridal wreath of orange blossoms behind the fire. Ay, more horrible still, that in less than five years hence he will murder her. It is a frightful conception, sir, but true to life. Alas! it is true to life in our very midst. Where virtue is not the guiding principle of the heart, the Devil rules supreme ; and what limit is there to his power for evil ?

" Then I would say to young newly-married folks," continued Mr. Dovecott, " 'You are setting out together on a toilsome journey, friends, and whether it be a long or a short one to you, it is for life; so you had better arrange the cushions in your travelling car so as to prevent bumps and bruises by the way. In other words, you had better begin at once to study each other's tempers and dispositions, and be resolved to mutually yield where principle does not imperatively forbid you. Set up God's altar in your household and take God's word for your guide, and you will be happy.'

"To old folks who are tottering down the hill of life, and throwing glass bottles and sharp pebbles in each other's pathways, I would say, 'Friends, sit down a-bit, and listen to reason. Apart from the sin of your acts, they are irrational, as you must admit if you reflect even for a minute. How much wiser it would be for you to smooth each other's way and jog along comfortably—to be mutual helps instead of hindrances. What cripple is so impolitic as to whittle his crutches, and thus weaken or destroy his only means of moving about? Surely none but an idiot would do that. Wife! what better friend have you in the world than your husband? Husband! what warmer friend have you in the world than your wife? None: certainly not. Cleave to each other then in love; and live in preparation for another world "where they neither marry, nor are given in marriage."'

" Why old folks should not love each other as tenderly as young folks, Mr. Boomerang, I can see no reason at all; but I can see strong reason why they should do so. Surely the recollection of ten thousand acts of kindness and love should foster tender feelings. There are many old pairs in the land who live jarring lives, and I wish it were otherwise. But it is not too late for them to alter their conduct, and henceforward to live in amity and peace. The following little story conveys a useful moral, though it is not so new as some of my stories. An old couple, who had long been notorious for their quarrelsome tempers, suddenly reformed and became loving and gentle. The change excited the curiosity of a kind neighbour, who one day inquired of the old man the cause of the marked change, when he replied, 'that they had lately taken two bears into their house.' The gentleman smiled, while he thought that formerly, when the old man and woman were at home, there certainly were two very savage bears in the house; he then asked the old man for an explanation, when he replied, 'Why, sir, this is it: Sally and I have lately learned to *bear* and *forbear* with each other's failings, and since we have taken those bears into our house, we have lived in peace and happiness.'

"But we have had a long walk, Mr. Boomerang," said Mr. Dovecott, "so come in doors and take a little fruit and rest awhile. It is no use to offer you wine I·know. Nanny! Nanny!" he shouted, as we entered the house. "Come this way, love; I want you. Now, sir, walk into the drawing-room, and I will show you something that I only show to my most intimate friends. Nanny, dear, give me the key of the cabinet."

"Take a careful look at this," continued Mr. Dovecott, walking towards me, after taking from a cabinet in the corner, a little rose-wood box, inlaid with pearl, and placing it in my hands. "Take a good look at it, sir." I did look at it scrutinisingly, and admired the workmanship. "Bother the box! but look inside, sir. Open it." I did open it, and to my surprise, I saw therein a little old leather shoe, with ancle straps and a rusty button. "There, sir," said Mr. Dovecott exultingly, while tears stood in his eyes, "that is the identical little shoe that dear Nanny was crying for when I first saw her sweet face, sixty-nine years ago, on the margin of Beechwood brook. And this, sir," he added, holding up a coarse linen bag, with a tape string in it, "this, sir, was my dinner-bag, that I used to carry to Dame Tingle's school, and these white pebbles I picked from the brook the very last time I set foot on its well-remembered crossing-place."

"At some future time, sir, I should like to philosophise a little on the mysterious influence which even minute circumstances sometimes have on one's whole life," said Mr. Dovecott, handling the little shoe as affectionately as if it was a pet bird stuffed. "Look at that fracture in the upper leather, sir; and reflect that to that lucky little hole I owe the possession of one of the best wives in the world! for it is clear to me that if the shoe had not leaked it would not have sunk, and Nanny would have recovered it without my aid, and would perhaps have gone home singing, instead of standing by the brook crying, for me first to pity her, then to love her, afterwards to marry her, and after living forty years with her, to love her forty times better than ever! Ods, bobs! talk about love stories! where did you hear one to equal mine? Why there is romance enough in it to make a book twice as big as 'Robinson Crusoe.'"

WIDOW GILES'S LITTLE GROCERY SHOP.

A GLANCE at Widow Giles's little shop would suffice to convince an observant person, who knew anything about shop-keeping, that she was a thriving trader. The stock was well selected and nicely kept; there was a display of taste as well as tidiness in the arrangement of the goods on the shelves, and there was no litter anywhere. Her counter was always clean, and the brass scales upon it shone like sovereigns. No one ever saw an unsightly accumulation of scraps of bacon, fragments of cheese, or heads and tails of dried fish wasting on the corner of her counter, for she never allowed "odds and ends," as she called them, to collect, well knowing that they did not improve by keeping, and she usually sold them at a reduction in price, to get quit of them. If you sent to her shop for a pat of fresh butter, you might be sure of having it free from dust, for she always kept a clean damp cloth over her butter dish. If weevils invaded her rice bag, or her pearl barley drawer, she got her boy Billy—when he came home from school—to sift them out into a tub of water, in the back-yard. The mice never had a chance of nibbling at her mould candles, and soiling them at the same time; for she always kept a lid on her candle-box. In fact, there were not many mice to be seen in her house, for there was no garbage to entice them, and food of all sorts was usually kept beyond their reach; besides, the cat kept a sharper look after them than even her mistress did; and mice very soon desert a house where they see such unmistakable signs that they are not welcome in it.

Mrs. Giles had a drawer under her counter for waste paper which she used for wrapping up rough articles. No one ever saw her wastefully tear a piece off a large sheet of new paper, to wrap up a pound of candles, or soap, or a red herring; in short, she was an economical woman, and though she certainly did not make large profits out of her little shop, she made a comfortable living, and was enabled to keep her children decently clad and to give them a suitable education, which was the height of her ambition. She could get credit at more than one wholesale house in Sydney ; but she had a wholesome dread of going far into debt, and usually bought her little stock with ready money ; consequently she often got better bargains than some of the neighbouring shopkeepers, who bought on credit, and were not very punctual in their payments.

Widow Giles was careful, though not parsimonious ; she was fair and just in all her dealings, and her neighbours had confidence in her.   She lost one or two customers soon after she began business, through her firmness in refusing to open her shop door on Sundays ; but she gained many others, who respected her consistency ; and, what was better still, she had the consciousness that she acted uprightly, and she had faith in the promise of the God of the widow and fatherless, that, " He would never leave them nor forsake them."

If my readers have patience to follow my simple story, they may learn how Widow Giles got her nice little grocery shop.

Peter Giles, her late husband, was a joiner, and a very good hand at his trade.   He worked for one of the best masters in Sydney, and always got full wages.   But Peter never saved money, and friends often wondered why he could not do so, for his wife was a very thrifty body, and he was by no means an idler or a drunkard.   The fact of the matter was, Peter had never studied that fundamental principle of domestic economy—viz., " taking care of the pence." He would have shrunk at wasting a pound, but pennies were of little value in his eyes, and he recklessly parted with small sums, which in the aggregate represented a tolerably large sum at the year's end.   For instance—he usually spent three or four " threepenny bits " every day, for beer ; and on Saturday nights he thought he was moderate in allowing himself two shillings or half-a-crown to "stand treat " to his shop-mates.   Still, he never got drunk ; he would have scouted the idea of thus disgracing himself in the eyes of his family and his neighbours.   Then he liked good clothes for Sunday wear, and he would have the best tools ; but he had not an economical way of buying them, for instead of saving his small money until he had sufficient to buy what he needed, he generally bought on credit, and paid by instalments ; thus he doubtless paid a higher price than he otherwise would have done.   To describe his character in the briefest manner, he was not a thoughtful or a provident man, though he was an affectionate husband, and an indulgent father.

On the afternoon of a public holiday some years ago, Peter was sitting on a form in Hyde Park, watching his children, who were sporting about on the green sward, when an old gentleman seated himself on the same form to rest, for he looked weary. Presently little Bobby Giles ran up to the stranger, and, child-like, began to play with his walking-stick, which had rather an attractive top to it.

"Bobby, come here, sir," said his father; "you mustn't be rude."

"Let him alone, sir, if you please," said the gentleman, kindly. At the same time, he produced a few lollipops from his coat pocket, and gave to the curly headed little fellow, who soon proved that he liked lollipops. Then the gentleman asked Peter how many children he had.

"I have five, sir—these four, and a baby at home with its mother."

"May I ask if you have made any provision for the poor little things if it should please God to take you from them?" said the gentleman, after a short pause, and in a tone which plainly evidenced that he was not making the inquiry in an inquisitive or meddling spirit.

"Well, I've never thought much about it, and that's the truth, sir," replied Peter. "I'm a strong healthy man, thank God, I haven't had a day's sickness for the last ten years, and I don't think I am in danger of dying yet awhile. The young ones will grow bigger, and by-and-bye they'll be able to shift for themselves, as thousands of other children have to do."

"That is true to some extent," said the gentleman. "But you look like a sensible man, so you don't want me to remind you of the uncertainty of life, even with the strongest of us; and you know, too, that thousands of poor children make very bad shifts for themselves. You heard of that sad accident to the workmen on the railway line, last week, I dare say."

"Yes, sir, I did. Ah, that was a bad look out for those poor navvies, and for their wives and families too."

"They were men of the strongest class, and yet you see death passed by many weaker men to clutch them. I fear their families will be very badly off."

"Yes, that they will, sir," said Peter, "and these are

hard times for poor lone women to struggle along, and support young families. I pity them, poor things!"

"I hope you will excuse me for putting such a plain question to you," said the gentleman, "but if you were taken off by death, as suddenly as those navvies were, would it not be a hard struggle for your wife to bring up your young family comfortably?"

"Ay, that it certainly would," said Peter, with a sigh, "but I hope she will not have to do it, poor lass, for she is not one of the strongest women in the colony."

"I hope she will not, indeed," said the gentleman, "but as it is awfully possible, would it not be humane of you to provide as far as you can, against such a calamity?"

"There is no doubt about that, sir, and I'd do it too if I knew how; but I can't work harder than I do, and I don't know that I am over extravagant in anything. All the money that I could put in the savings bank wouldn't be much good to them, I'm afraid."

While Peter was speaking, the gentleman took a piece of paper and a pencil from his pocket, and began to jot down a number of figures. Presently he said, "Will you excuse me asking your age?"

"I shall be thirty-six next August," replied Peter, who was rather puzzled to conceive what the old gentleman was doing with his pencil and paper, and had some idea that he was making his will, and was going to leave little Bobby a good legacy. In a few minutes he handed the slip of paper to Peter, remarking as he did so, "You will see by these simple calculations, that for £8 11s. 3d. a year—which is less than sixpence a day—you may insure £300 to be paid to your wife and family at your death, let it happen when it may. If you cannot spare so much you may insure for £100, by paying £2 17s. 1d. a year, which is less than twopence a day. Did you ever think of making a provision for them in that way?"

"Never, sir. I joined a benefit club when I was in England, but I have never thought of anything of the sort since I came here. I have heard tell of assurance societies, but I don't understand them; and I haven't much time to bother my head with such things; for when I have done work I'm generally pretty tired, and don't care to think about things that are troublesome."

"I am a stranger to you," said the gentleman, "but I

assure you I have no other object in offering you advice than your good, 'and the interest of your family. Take that little slip of paper home with you, and think over it to-night, as you will not be tired from hard work to-day. I am sure you can afford to pay the premium on a life assurance policy; and it will afford you great comfort to know that your wife and children will not be left in poverty, as well as sorrow, if it please God to take you from them suddenly. There are profits of the assurance association or bonus additions, which you would share in if you became a member, so that the longer you lived the more valuable your policy would become, if you chose to allow the bonuses to be added to your policy instead of drawing them periodically as they are declared. I have not time to explain all that to you thoroughly, but I advise you to apply at the office of the Mutual Provident Society, in Pitt Street, or to any other assurance office for further information. I will only add my strong recommendation to you, to lose no time in insuring your life, 'For you know not what a day may bring forth.'" The old gentleman then arose, wished Peter good afternoon, and went on his way.

After tea that evening, Peter sat down in his armchair, lighted his pipe, and ;began to look over the paper which the chatty old gentleman had given him. His wife was sitting opposite him darning the children's socks. Presently Peter looked at her seriously and said, "Jenny, do you think we can save sixpence a day?"

"Sixpence a day!" exclaimed Jenny, opening her eyes and dropping her needle. "What do you want it for?"

"Never mind, Jenny: can you spare it? that's the question," said Peter, with a half-comical, half-serious look.

"No, my dear, I am sure I can't spare it. You have no notion how I have to cut and contrive, to keep the children tidy, and to get a good dinner for you every day. I shall want a warm shawl or a cloak for winter; but I don't know how I can get it without going on trust, and I would rather not do that if I can possibly help it. I really cannot save sixpence a day, Peter, and that's the truth."

"Well then, I can," said Peter, starting up like a man who had decided upon doing something noble. "I can spare sixpence a day from my beer money, and if I go without beer altogether, I dare say I shall be none the worse—indeed Tom Bevil is always trying to persuade me that I shall be very much better in every way if I adopt his plan, and drink nothing stronger than tea. He has managed to save money enough to build a snug little house for himself. I can and will spare sixpence a day, Jenny ; and I'll tell you next week what I want it for, but not before then, so don't ask me there's a dear."

*   *   *   *   *   *

About ten days afterwards, Peter Giles handed his wife a large printed paper, in an envelope, and told her to put it away carefully in her drawers. It was a policy of assurance on his life for £300.

*   *   *   *   *   *

Boxing Day of 186— was a sorrowful day for poor Mrs. Giles and her young family. Peter went out that morning, in company with several of his shopmates, to spend the day on the harbour in a boat. That afternoon a furious squall of wind from the south did much mischief to the small vessels in port, and, amongst other distressing casualties, Peter's boat was upset, when he and two of his companions were drowned.

I need not try to depict the grief of poor Widow Giles and her five young children, when the lifeless body of her husband was brought to her home the next day. It was a very sad trial for her ; but, happily, she had not to bear poverty in addition to her intense grief, for Peter had kept his premiums punctually paid to the assurance office, and in a short time she received about £320, being the amount assured for, with bonus additions. That was the capital which enabled Widow Giles to stock her nice little grocery shop.

Instead of speculating on the forlorn condition which Widow Giles would have been placed in, if her late husband had not made that fortunate provision for her, I will close this chapter with the following quotation from a London journal (which I read some years ago), on the " moral duty of Life Assurance." The writer in question, says, " It may be felt by many, that their income is insufficient to enable them to spare even the small sum necessary as an annual premium for life assurance. The necessities of the present can in their case so great, that they do not see how they are afford it. We believe there can be no obstacle which is apt to appear more real than this, when an income is at all limited, and yet it is easy to show that no obstacle is more ideal. It will be readily acknowledged by every one who has an income at all, that there must be some who have smaller incomes. Say, for instance, that any man has £400 per annum ; he cannot doubt that there are some who have only £350. Now if these persons live on £350, why may not he do so too, sparing the odd £50 as a deposit for life assurance ? In like manner, he who has £200 may live as men do who have only £175, and devote the remaining £25 to have a sum assured upon his life ? And so on. It may require an effort to accomplish this, but is not the object worthy of an effort ? And can any man be held as honest, or any way good, who will not make such an effort, rather than always be liable to the risk of leaving in beggary the beings whom he most cherishes on earth, and for whose support he alone is responsible ?"

COMMERCIAL HOBGOBLINS.

In the course of a recent ramble in the city, I called at the counting-house of a mercantile friend, whom I found intently poring over his bill-book. I briefly apologised for intruding upon his studies, and as I had no business to transact, I was about to retire, but the cordial tone in which he said, " I am glad to see you ; take a seat," reassured me, so I took a seat, and silently waited till he had totted up a long column of figures. Presently he raised his eyes from the book, and sat abstractedly gazing at nothing for two minutes. Fearing that he would soon miss his beard, for he was unconsciously pulling the bristles out two at a time, I ventured to ask him " if he found that reading his bill-book was a refreshing mental exercise?" My question aroused him. He shut up the book, pushed it into an iron safe and turned the key, with the grim look of a gaoler who had just locked up a thief, then, rubbing his hands to warm them, he replied, " I would rather read Hervey's ' Meditations among the Tombs.' Still, there are moral lessons to be learned in bill-books, and I believe that if they were studied a little more, it would be beneficial to the world at large, and be especially gratifying to bank managers."

By degrees my friend's face grew solemnly smooth, and with true philosophy, worthy of imitation in these exciting times, he remarked, " Scanning over my bill-book is not an exhilarating pastime just now ; far from it. It is a stern duty, which requires no small amount of courage to perform; still, I dare not neglect it, or I should soon get as bemuddled and panic-stricken as some of my neighbours. There are figures enough in that book to frighten me if I were to yield to despondency ; but I hope for the best, while I prepare to meet reverses with courage, energy, and patience. Most of my bills receivable *may* turn out as good as gold; so I will cling to that comforting hope till I am obliged to relinquish it ; but if they should all prove bad, it would be folly for me to make myself bad too, by fretting over them. Depend upon it, sir, nothing wears a man out sooner than worry of mind.

It impairs his digestion, disturbs his sleep, sours his temper, destroys his vital energy, and makes a coward of him ; aye, and it will soon make a dry skeleton of him too. Bother it all ! I won't yield to it," he added, with a shrug, as though he were dislodging a toad from the nape of his neck. " I'll tell you a tale of the times, Mr. Boomerang, just to divert my thoughts ; then I hope you will tell me something sprightly; and don't be afraid to laugh loudly, for it will cheer up my clerks who are growing dyspeptic for want of work, and if the folks outside hear that we are merry in here, it may help my trade, and do them good too ; for mirth is as contagious as melancholy. It's my belief, sir, that if something could tickle all the business men in Sydney, and make them roar with laughter, even for ten minutes, that the banks would relax their hold upon their hard cash, and be glad to accommodate all their customers, except ' kite-flyers ' and bubblemongers."

My friend reclining in his arm-chair, stroked his beard tenderly, and related the following queer little story (which I have slightly varied), and if it did not tend to encourage his mercantile hope, it evidently helped to make him forget his doubts for a while, and to look as waggishly independent as a man who had neither money nor merchandise to worry him.

He said that a short time ago a merchant was issuing from his store, when he met a doubtful customer from the country. "Good morning, Mr. Linsey ; I am just going in to make up a parcel," said the countryman.

" Humph ! a—a—good morning, Mr. Mopus," stammered the merchant, who was ruminating on the most delicate way of refusing to give him a parcel on credit, for he suspected the man was a schemer, because his competitors in trade said that he sold goods much cheaper than they could buy them.

" I'm going to pay half cash," continued the countryman, without appearing to notice the other's hesitation.

The little word " cash " was as welcome as " whoa " to a jaded cart-horse. At the magical sound the merchant's eyes glistened like pearl buttons, while a tinge of yellow happiness overspread his care-wrinkled face, and he excitedly said, " Pray walk in, sir ; we'll do the thing well for you." Skipping up three steps at a stride, he preceded his rustic customer to the wareroom, and, with a look full of honest earnestness, said to his head salesman, "Mr. Mopus is going to make up a good parcel with us this morning, Mr. Tabb, so put things in to him at the lowest figure, cut everything as fine as you possibly can."

"Yes, sir, certainly," replied the salesman; and forthwith he began to draw his customer's attention to some attractive piles of soft goods in the front warehouse, and to expatiate on the large quantity of scarce articles "they had in the harbour."

Mr. Mopus made line upon line, with a pleasant boldness most cheering to the salesman, for it put him in mind of the golden times, when everybody was independent; and as his ever-watchful ears had caught the glad echo of the word "cash," when it softly floated up the stairway, he naturally thought that Mr. Mopus was a man of *metal*. Mr. Tabb loved his master; so his joy was proportionate, as the countryman bought package after package of well-paying goods, with a child-like confidence in the recommendation of the salesman, which, alas, few good customers display in these distrustful days; and after Mr. Mopus intimated that he had bought enough, and Mr. Tabb's gentle pressure had ceased to be operative, he escorted his customer to the front door as affectionately as a father, and while he grasped his hand at parting, assured him that the invoices should be quite ready and all the goods on the drays by the following day at noon.

The last dray was loading as Mr. Mopus entered the store next day, with cheque-book in hand, and, according to agreement, paid for one-half of his purchase by cheque, and the other half by bill at four months. "Now," said Mr. Mopus to the merchant, "I think you ought to make me a present of something handsome for my wife, considering that I have left you £500 this morning. Times are hard, you know. Money is scarce, and you don't get such a customer as I am every day. Come, now, be liberal, Mr. Linsey: give me something good to take home to Mrs. Mopus; a blessing, as the old ladies say in my part of the country."

"Hum—a—em—I don't see how I can do it. We have put everything in very low, and I can't afford to—a—a—however—I'll see—em—Mr. Tabb, fetch that parcel of shawls from the back store; the lot marked P ses Q, you know," said the merchant, musingly, while he gazed at the cheque with affectionate interest. Soon Mr. Tabb returned with the parcel, when his master selected a shawl worth a few shillings, and handed it to Mr. Mopus, remarking as he did so, "that it was rather against his practice—in fact, he could not afford to be generous these times."

"Woogh! Do you think I would take my wife such a thing as that?" said Mr. Mopus, with excitement. "Blow it all! she hasn't come to that yet. It might suit her servant Biddy, but——"

"Don't be vexed, sir," said the merchant, with a quizzical smile. "I did not mean to slight Mrs. Mopus in the least, and I would rather give five hundred pounds than you should think so. Here is something handsome; suppose I make her a present of this bill which you have just given me; what will you say to that?"

"Give me the cheque," said Mr. Mopus, "and I will say that you have a becoming respect for my good lady."

"I can't spare the cheque; but you had better take this," said the merchant, holding the bill for £500 before his customer's eyes.

"No, no!" said Mr. Mopus, with a roguish wink, which made Mr. Tabb's face turn as blue as book muslin. "Ha, ha, my boy! Walker! Keep the bill; I don't want it; give me the shawl—*that is worth something.*"

*   *   *   *   *   *

I will not further describe my interview with my friend, the philosophical merchant; but after an hour's pleasant chat I left his office, strongly impressed with the idea that if business men in general would face their perplexities as cheerfully as he did, there would be far less commercial depression than there is at present. I had better state that I do not vouch for the accuracy of the foregoing story, though I can solemnly declare that I have both *seen* and *felt* "bills at four months," which were quite as valueless as Mr. Mopus's. Though it be apocryphal, it may help to clear up the mystery which has perplexed many simple ones, and explain how certain traders can afford to undersell their honest neighbours, and live in furious style too.

Soon after leaving my friend's office, I saw a man hurrying down the street towards me, with his head down, his clenched hands swinging rapidly, and his whole mien as fierce as if he were in chase of a rogue who had run away with his wife. I had known the man slightly for a long time. Formerly he was a thriving mechanic, but of late years he had called himself a "wholesale man." It was supposed that the bulk of his merchandise was kept *in bond*, for he displayed very little in his business premises, and the piles of cases near the doorway echoed very suspiciously if struck with a stick.

"What is the matter, Mr. Fluff?" I asked, as he stopped to speak to me.

"Matter, sir? why, everything is going to the dogs, and I am almost bothered out of my wits," he replied.

"That is very likely. Excuse me for speaking plainly, Mr. Fluff, but I am sure it would be better for you to resume your trade ; you will then have less anxiety, and better health than you now have, and you will be doing your part towards remedying the present commercial depression, which is mainly owing to overtrading. The continual excitement of carrying on a business such as yours with insufficient capital is wearing your constitution much faster than the hardest work at your trade would do. But what special trouble have you just now? if it is right for me to ask the question."

"I want to get this bill *done*, to take up another which falls due to-morrow. Do you think you could find a friend who would oblige me, sir? It is drawn by Bladders and Co.—first-rate marks—for £223. I will take £200 for it. It has only sixty-nine days to run, and is perfectly safe."

I told him that I should probably have to run sixty-nine days, or perhaps seventy-nine, before I found any one to *do* his bill ; and my reputation would not be very safe while running on such an errand. I was certain that no person, whom I could call my friend, would lend money at such exorbitant interest, or have any bill transactions with Bladders and Co. Moreover, I said that money jobbing was quite out of my line, and advised him to get his bankers to discount the bill for him, if it represented, as he said it did, an honest business transaction ; but of which I was more than doubtful, having had some experience of Mr. Bladders's financial talents.

"I did put it in my bank yesterday, and they threw it out," said Mr. Fluff, with a dreadfully injured look. Then he belched out a volley of invectives, which would have made the board of directors uneasy, had they heard him. Fearing that I might be supposed by the passers-by to be conspiring with Mr. Fluff to cause a run on the said bank,

I bade him good-bye, and pursued my way homeward, reflecting on the vast amount of misery some men suffer for the sake of keeping up a false appearance.

*　　*　　*　　*　　*　　*

"There is a great depression visible in the city," remarked a nervous neighbour, who soon afterwards overtook me, and who was homeward bound too.

" There is a good deal of excitement," I replied, " but there is more dread than danger. It puts me in mind of the commotion that I once witnessed on board a ship, at a false alarm of fire. The passengers were all running about, looking as scared as a lot of sheep with a dog amongst them ; but not one of them coolly investigated the cause of the smoke, which was merely the cook putting out his galley fire with a bucket of water ; so it was nearly all steam after all."

· " But there is real commercial distress at present, and no doubt about it," said my sombre neighbour.

" It would be unreasonable to dispute that, Mr. Croke," I replied. " In fact, the colony is suffering from a periodical *bill*-ious disorder, accompanied with an extraordinary tightness in the chest. But some of the causes are palpable enough for any one to see, who wants to see them. I have long held the opinion that there are far too many persons engaged in the mere business of exchange, both in town and country ; from merchants down to street hawkers. Sellers multiply much faster than buyers, and trade is too much divided : an unhealthy competition is the result, which honest traders heavily feel. I have just now given a little advice to a pseudo-merchant, which I should like to give to a thousand others who, like him, are struggling to get a living by buying and selling, instead of working at their trades. The man I refer to has no capital beyond some accommodation paper of his friend Bladders, who is in a similar pecuniary position. His bankers have, I suppose, at last discovered the doubtful character of Mr. Fluff's paper capital, and have very properly refused to discount it ; so he is, commercially speaking, 'smashed up,' and I think he is trying his utmost to raise a panic and 'smash up' some of his neighbours, in the hope that his own downfall may be less noticed in the general wreck. Had not poor Fluff been tempted by that accomplished old schemer, Bill Bladders, to throw aside his tools and go into business upon a fictitious capital, he would probably be now, what he was a few years ago, a contented, industrious mechanic, and would be of material benefit to the country as a producer of something tangible, instead of being a drag on our commercial machinery, as all such traders are."

"It's my opinion that the colony is going to ruin," said Mr. Croke, with a grimace, ending in a sigh.

"My opinion is quite different to that, sir," I replied. "This monetary panic, as you call it, will doubtless cause loss and inconvenience to a good many persons, but it will not last long, and it will be as beneficial to our commercial atmosphere as a 'southerly burster' after a hot wind; which, though it makes a great dust, and begrimes a good many of our smartly-dressed citizens, it nevertheless rids the air of an accumulation of noxious vapours, and we all breathe more comfortably after it is past. I could give you more of my views on the causes of the present commercial excitement, but here is your gate; good day, Mr. Croke: keep your spirits up, sir. Though times look bad at present, there is far more reason to hope they will mend, than to anticipate the national ruin which you have just predicted."

*   *   *   *   *   *

It is my deliberate opinion that *bills* are the main-springs of mercantile disasters in general. I do not mean honest trade bills, but kites, windbags, blow-flies, or by whatever other nicknames they are known to the initiated. They are most treacherous things to handle, hazardous as nitro-glycerine, blasting-powder, or any other combustible that is likely to blow your house up, or rather to blow it down, and damage your neighbour's houses too. They are as deceitful as will-o'-the-wisps, and have inveigled many good, simple men into a moral bog, where their reputation has been bedaubed with indelible dirt. They encourage idleness, extravagance, reckless trading, lying, cheating, and a host of other evils too ugly to print. They are the commercial hobgoblins that breed panic and distrust, knock poor men out of work, and make their children go hungry and shoeless. They have caused more sleepless nights than gout, lumbago, painter's colic, and "cats on the tiles" combined; in short, they are a curse to a community, and I heartily wish I could warn everybody against being lured into having anything to do with them.

I do not altogether sympathise with my broken-down friend Stumps, who refused to humour his wife by calling her little son " William," after his maternal grand-sire, lest the boy should by-and-bye be called " Bill." Neither do I go so far as the other over-scrupulous man, whom I heard of, who, " on principle," declines to *accept* even a handbill from a draper's boy in the street, still I have a wholesome dread of bills in general, and if they savour in the least degree of accommodation, I would almost as soon handle a bagful of detonating powder, or anything else that would certainly damage me.

"WHY DON'T YOU SPEAK TO HIM?"

ONE dreary afternoon, I was pacing the quarter-deck of a beautiful little brig, bound to some of the evergreen islands of Polynesia. A fresh south-east gale was blowing, and the white curling billows ran high, while the little stormy petrels, on their rapid wing, whirled about in the wake of our wave-beaten vessel—now lost for a moment in the hollow of the seas, and again mounting to the foaming crests—standing, as it were, on their very summits, and dipping their black bills into the water to pick up some precarious morsel of food.

> "Up and down, up and down ;
> From the base of the wave to the billow's crown ;
> Amidst the flashing and the feathery foam,
> The stormy petrel finds a home."

Pity the luckless passenger who should kill, or in any way maltreat, one of those ominous birds !—he would be sure of the scowling looks and illwill of the sailors for the remainder of the voyage, and would be blamed for every casualty that occurred. I have met with but few seamen who have not had a superstitious regard for stormy petrels, or "Mother Carey's chickens," as they are more commonly called. They are supposed to be the harbingers of bad weather, and may generally be seen, in some latitudes, whirling over the troubled waters with surprising velocity, and apparently in high enjoyment.

Our little vessel was under double-reefed topsails, reefed courses, and storm staysail, and trembled from keel to truck, as she struggled through the heavy seas, which presented formidable barriers to her rapid progress ; while she would occasionally plunge her bows deep into the hissing waves, and send a shower of spray as far aft as the mainmast. The flag at the mainmast head, bearing the figure of a dove with an olive branch, denoted the peaceful character of the vessel, which was then on her way to various mission stations, with annual supplies ; and a hearty welcome awaited her from many anxious ones, who were daily looking for her over the sea with straining eyes.

My sea legs have been pretty well drilled ; and I was never afraid of a little spray ; so I buttoned on my overcoat, and continued my unsteady promenade. As I did so, I could not help noticing the ghastly look of the man at the wheel. Though tall and well-made, he was terribly emaciated, and had scarcely strength enough to steer the ship. There was a peculiar wildness in his manner ; and when the vessel plunged her bowsprit under water, he seemed to lose nerve, and looked actually terrified.

Such an unusual exhibition in a “ Jack Tar ” aroused my curiosity to know the cause of the infirmity which the poor fellow was suffering.

“ Haul up that mainsail and furl it,” cried the captain, as he stepped out of his cabin on deck and addressed the officer of the watch ; then added, while he joined me in my walk : “ It's no use trying to force the ship against this heavy head sea ; we shall only tear and chafe everthing to pieces. I think I'll close reef the topsails before dark, and make all snug for a dirty night. There's mischief in those clouds to windward ; and the glass has fallen two-tenths since eight bells. It will blow blunderbusses before midnight.”

“ Well, captain,” I replied, “ we have a good tight vessel under us, with plenty of sea room, and above all, we know whose Almighty hand can control the winds and waves, so we need not fear. But tell me, if you please, sir, what is the matter with that poor man at the wheel ? He looks as fierce as a heathen Fijian ; and that terrible knife in his belt makes me almost shudder to look at him.”

“ Ha, ha, ha !” laughed the little captain ; “ I'll warrant he won't eat you, while he has got a full allowance of salt junk and yams ; for you don't look very tender ! Why, that fellow is one of the best sailors on board the ship. I'll match him for a day's work against the best man that ever handled a fid, or a palm and needle. He's been ‘ bousing up his jib,’ lately, as sailors say, and now he's suffering from the tail end of the horrors, or *delirium tremens ;* that's what makes him look so shaky and scared, but he'll be all right again in a week or two. He was drunk all the time we lay in Sydney, that is to say, all the time he was out of the watch-house—so it's no wonder he looks wild. I paid three grog scores for him just before we sailed, and I think he left one score unpaid after all. I never came across such a grog-thirsty ragamuffin before, in the whole course of my cruising."

"Poor fellow!" I exclaimed, "but did you never try to persuade him to keep sober, and not run up grog scores, captain?"

"Pooh! what would be the use of doing that," said the captain, with an incredulous curl of his lips. "I might as well try to coax that Samoan pig, under the long-boat there, not to eat cocoa nuts when he can get them! I know too much about drunken sailors to waste my wind in talking to them. That fellow will be sober enough, I dare say, until he gets back to Sydney, for he can't get any liquor to get drunk with; but you watch him as soon as the voyage is ended, and an hour or two after we are at our moorings, and the sails are stowed, if he's not dead drunk come and tell me, and I'll give him a certificate to that effect, or else none of his acquaintance will believe it. Louis has been too long a lushington to be cured by teetotalism, or any other sort of moral suasion, as you call it—take my word for it. He is as incurable as a decayed tooth."

"I am of a different opinion, captain," I replied. "There is something honest and good-natured in that poor fellow's face, now I look at him calmly. I do not think he is so incorrigible as you imagine; and I believe a few kind words would influence him, as I have known them to influence *scores* of persons in his state."

"Why don't you speak to him, then?" asked the captain.

"Your question has suggested itself to my mind several times, captain," I replied; "and I intend to speak to him the first favourable opportunity."

*　　*　　*　　*　　*　　*

One afternoon, Louis was sitting on the spars amid-ships, mending his clothes; it being his "watch below;" so I sat down beside him, and commenced a conversation on some subject, foreign to the one which I intended to introduce. He replied to me in imperfect English (he was a Swede), but in a respectful tone, which contrasted strongly with the wild expression of his emaciated face. He evidently felt that I had a kind motive in speaking to him, and in a short time he voluntarily gave me a few shreds of his history, which were horribly interesting.

He had been educated for a chemist and druggist, but was wild, and had run away to sea. He had passed through many dangers, peculiar to a sea life, and had fallen into many disasters, owing to his fondness for strong drink. On one occasion, he told me he woke up from the effects of a debauch, and found himself in a ship bound for America; he had no recollection how he got on board, but afterwards learned that he had been smuggled on board, as a substitute for one of the crew, who had deserted—but whose name he was obliged to take, as it stood on the ship's articles. He said he had had *delirium tremens*, or horrors, several times; and the last time he was in Sydney, as the vessel lay alongside a wharf in Darling Harbour, " de teevil came on board, and roused him out of his bunk, and chased him on shore." He then went and lay down beside a lime kiln in the vicinity of the wharf, when " de teevil came again, and roused him out of that, and chased him up into George Street," where the constables caught him, as he was running and shouting murder, and put him in the watch-house. " But I vos not drunk then, sir," he said, " I vos mad, that vos it. Oh ! it vos terrible, terrible ! My head vos full of red-hot vorms; my blood was burning with blue fire and brimstone; my heart vos boiling and bubbling like de pitch pot. I could not sleep, I could not eat, I could not be quiet; I could only howl, and shout, and vont to cut my throat; but I had got no razor, nor no knife, dat vos a good job. Oh, my Got ! vot I did suffer, I never can tell. I vould vish to be in de Fijian oven ; or I vould vish de alligators to eat me up altogether, sooner than suffer such dreadful tortures any more."

" I am better now, sir," he added, " but I am very veak, and I cannot vork properly, because I shake like as if I had de palsy : and ven I go aloft I'm afraid I fall off de yard. Ough de grog ! it close up killed me dis time. I did suffer dreadful agonies ! oh ! vot a fool I vos to spend all my money, to buy such teevilish torment."

Poor fellow ! the tears coursed down his rough face, as he finished his horrifying narration. He had nearly wrecked a naturally robust constitution with his excesses, and had brought upon himself remorse and poverty, and, in addition to present suffering, he had laid up in his enfeebled body, the seeds of future pain and misery.

I gave him some advice, and a little medicine, and the

next day, when he was off duty, I had another conversation with him. I endeavoured to cheer him up and stimulate his hope, by showing him that many others who had sunk even lower than himself had been reclaimed, and had risen to positions of eminent usefulness. I gave him my own pocket Bible, also a copy of the thrilling autobiography of the celebrated John Gough, and several useful and entertaining magazines, for which he expressed thankfulness.

On many subsequent occasions, I spoke to Louis, both in private, and also when assembled with all the other sailors on board, and I often had the pleasure of seeing him sitting on the booms, when off duty, reading the books which I had given him.

On New Year's Day, being then on our homeward passage, I was much gratified at seeing Louis in company with every one on board—officers as well as crew—(except two), come aft and voluntarily sign the Temperance pledge! I did not fail to briefly direct them to the Divine source from whence alone they could obtain strength to keep their pledges. I could give some interesting facts from the subsequent history of several of those seamen, but I should too much digress from my present subject.

A little more than six months afterwards, I was sitting one day alone in my study, when a servant informed me "that a gentleman wished to see me;" and in another minute Louis entered the room. He was so much improved in appearance that I did not know him, until he spoke to me; when I recognised his voice. He was really a fine-looking man, and as upright as a soldier. He informed me that he had just come off a voyage, and although there was plenty of spirits on board the ship, he had remained stanch to his pledge of total abstinence, and had tried to induce some of his shipmates to follow his example. He was in good health, and was happy and cheerful. Since I had last seen him, he had bought some good clothes, also a watch and chain, and sent a small sum of money to his mother, in Sweden. He expressed his gratitude to me for speaking to him when he was in such a miserable condition; and assured me that since that time he had daily read his Bible; adding emphatically, while the tears started from his eyes, and he grasped my hand with affectionate warmth, "*I vill never part vid dat Bible!*"

*　　*　　*　　*　　*　　*

A few weeks afterwards, on looking over my newspaper one morning, I was startled by seeing Louis's name in a paragraph, detailing a casualty at sea. While stowing the jib, in a gale of wind, on board a ship bound for New Zealand, poor Louis, in company with another sailor, was washed overboard, and drowned.

*   *   *   *   *   *

Reader, you perhaps know some poor fellow who is groping his miserable way to ruin ! if so, “ *Why don’t you speak to him ?*”

HOW THE KNIPPS FAMILY KEPT "MERRY CHRISTMAS."

"I DON'T see why I should cook our Christmas goose for the Boozems to gobble it all up," remarked Mrs. Knipps to her husband, as they sat at their tea-table, an evening or two before last Christmas Day.

"Well, mother, please yourself," replied Mr. Knipps carelessly. "For my part, I don't care whether we have a goose and plum pudding, or corned beef and doughboys for dinner ; but the young ones will expect something extra, and I should like them to have it too, for custom's sake."

"You need not be afraid that I will neglect the children ; they shall have their Christmas treat," said Mrs. Knipps, "but the idea of having the house full of hungry Boozems, makes me downright cross. I have been thinking, Knipps, how we may get rid of them without telling fibs. It would be easy to say that we were going out for the day ; and we could go out for a picnic somewhere, and save the bother of cooking at home. I am sure we are under no obligation to the Boozems, though we did spend last Christmas at their house ; for they have had favours enough from us since then, in all conscience. They borrowed your bullock team several times, and you broke-in two colts for them for nothing, so I don't think we owe them anything. Their great ravenous boys and girls are enough to breed a famine in the district. I never did see such children to eat in all my born days."

"It's a sign they are healthy," said Mr. Knipps. "There is one thing certain, Missis, if we stay at home on Christmas Day we must entertain them, for they are coming as surely as next winter ; Joe told me so last week, and I said we should be very glad to see them all."

"That's just like you, Knipps," said his spouse pettishly. "You don't consider who has all the work and bother of preparing for a houseful of folks. It is all very fine for you and Joe to sit in the verandah smoking your pipes, and talking about horseflesh—as you call it—but it is no joke for me to stand frizzling before the kitchen fire all the morning cooking dinner for a lot of selfish gormandisers. I won't do it, Knipps, I tell you plump and plain ; I won't do it, so you may get rid of the Boozems the best way you can. Bother the people ! If I could have my way, I would lock up the house, and when they came they would see we were not at home. Then we should get quit of them without a quarrel."

"No, no, Missis, that will never do," said Mr. Knipps. " That ain't manners, you know. If you don't want the people here on Christmas Day, I will ride over this evening and tell them we are going out to spend the day, and ask them to come some other time ; that is the most straight-forward way of doing it. Then, if you like, we will take some provisions with us, and go in the boat down the river to Bandicoot Brush, and dine under the green bushes. What do you say to that, Billy," added Mr. Knipps, addressing his hopeful son of six years old, who sat at the table opposite to him, eating a thick slice of bread and treacle.

"O my ! that will be fun ! won't it, Polly ? May I take my fishing-line, father ?" said Billy, his face brightening up like a new pannikin.

"And may I take my doll's cradle, mother ?" asked Polly, a merry looking little girl, a year younger than her brother.

"Yes, yes, if you are a good girl : and baby shall have his new rattle," said Mrs. Knipps, looking quite pleased at the success of her opposition. "Baby shall have his new pelisse too, bless his heart !" she continued, speaking to a chubby-faced infant, who was lying on his back on the floor, sucking a pewter spoon, and showing his utter contempt for drapery. Yes, and Billy and Polly shall have their new clothes too, if they are good : and we will spend such a merry Christmas, under the shady trees. Yes, we will, so we will, chucky, chucky, chucky ! Hey diddle diddle !" As Mrs. Knipps gave vent to the last expressive sentiments, she seized her baby and tossed and tickled him, until the little fellow crowed with infantile ecstacy, while his brother and sister cut all sorts of merry capers, in the overflowing of their joyful anticipations ; and made father laugh till he dropped his pipe from between his teeth, whereupon they all laughed in chorus.

Mr. Knipps owned a small farm on one of the rivers to the north ; but, somehow or other, as he himself expressed it, he could not get on in the world. To be sure he had had three consecutive seasons of disaster. Once he had been flooded out, and twice his crops were ruined by rust; still, he could see that some of his neighbours, who had been equally unfortunate, and who had rent to pay, were far better off than himself, and he could not comprehend it at all, for he thought he worked as hard as any of them. He had given Mr. Gritts, the storekeeper, an equitable mortgage over his farm, and that circumstance troubled him very much, for he had inherited the homestead from his late father, who, good, honest, old man, had a greater dread of liens and mortgages than he had of floods or droughts.

*　　*　　*　　*　　*　　*

Soon after breakfast, on Christmas morning, Mr. Knipps baled his boat out, and spread some empty corn-sacks in the bottom of it, while Mrs. Knipps packed into a bushel basket, sundry creature comforts, comprising a piece of pickled pork, and some cold cabbage; a boiled chicken and a brown loaf; a plum pudding, a pumpkin pie, a tincan full of new milk, and a bottle of Colonial rum. Half-an-hour afterwards they had all embarked in the boat, and Mr. Knipps was steadily pulling down the river·with the tide, while his wife was singing " hey diddle diddle" to the baby, and Polly and Billy were towing little toy ships from the stern of the boat.

In course of time they arrived at Bandicoot brush, where they landed, and fastened the boat to a mangrove bush. It was a very retired place, and the thick vines overhead formed a pleasant shade from the sun's fierce rays. Mrs. Knipps first of all spread a blanket on the ground, and laid her baby down to amuse himself with his new rattle. She then spread a table-cloth on the ground close by, and placed the contents of the bushel basket upon it. In the meantime Mr. Knipps had uncorked the bottle of rum, and refreshed himself with a strong dram after his long pull. They then all squatted in Turkish style round the table cloth, and made a hearty meal; the young ones paying special court to the plum pudding, and the new milk.

After the feasting was over, Mr. Knipps mixed himself some more rum and water in a pannikin, then lighted his pipe, and seated himself with his back to the trunk of a wild fig-tree, and began, as he said, to make himself happy. Mrs. Knipps sat down on the blanket, and played bo-peep with the baby. Billy went fishing from the boat, and Polly rambled about the brush, picking wild flowers and native gooseberries. The greatest drawbacks to their comfort were the myriads of grey mosquitos, and soldier ants; the latter waggish little insects more than once made Mr. and Mrs. Knipps suddenly jump up and dance, without music; and the former raised innumerable lumps on the baby as large as grey peas. Nevertheless, so far from regretting their position, Mrs. Knipps smilingly observed " that she would rather be tickled by all the insects in the bush, than be bothered with the Boozems," and she ever and anon chuckled out her satisfaction, that she had so cleverly managed to give her hungry neighbours the cut, without appearing to be mean.

Mr. Knipps's eyes twinkled, and his nose glowed with gastric glory, as he sat beneath the fig-tree, puffing his pipe. Under ordinary circumstances, he was a man of few words and slow of action, but rum usually made an alteration in him. On this occasion it wrought an extraordinary change —perhaps it was extra strong—for he grew quite funny, and after his third pannikin he got up and danced the " nervous cure," while his wife (who had some musical talent) played an appropriate air on one of her side combs with a piece of paper over it. In the midst of his comical fandango, which astonished the baby, he was suddenly struck serious by the shrieks of Polly in the adjacent brush. He hurried away, as fast as he could stagger, in the direction of the cries, when he was shocked at seeing his daughter hanging head downwards from a native cherry-tree. The poor girl had been climbing to catch a locust, and had slipped her footing; but a friendly branch 'caught her crinoline, and saved her from bruises or fractures. She was speedily extricated from her unnatural position; and after receiving a good " scatting" from her mother for tearing her new frock, she was told to sit down and not to stir a peg, under certain penalties, which Polly thought were very arbitrary.

Ere they had recovered from that shock, and before Mr. Knipps could stimulate his merry mood to return, their boy Billy came into the camp, covered with mud, and in inconsolable grief at the loss of his new Christmas cap, which was drifting away to sea, with wind and tide in its favour. It appeared from Billy's blubbering explanation, that he had hooked a fine toad-fish, and in his haste to secure the prize, he had fallen head foremost over the stern of the boat into the mud. Billy's wet clothes were stripped off instanter;

and while he was in that favourable condition for appre-
ciating correction, his father administered the rod with an
unsparing hand, then delivered him over to his mother,
who rolled him in the baby's blanket, and seated him
beside his disconsolate sister, remarking, in angry tones as
she did so, " that no woman in the known world was ever so
tried with children as herself;" being quite forgetful at the
time of the great cause she had for rejoicing that one of her
children had escaped a broken neck, and the other a watery
grave. But such anomalies are of common occurrence, and
many a poor child has received a severe beating from an
excited parent, for its good fortune in escaping a fatal
disaster.

The most annoying part of Billy's mishap was, that it
necessitated their returning home at once to get dry clothing
for " the young monkey, lest he should catch his death of
cold." The fragments of the feast were then hastily tied up
in the tablecloth, and the party re-embarked, with disappointment beclouding each face. Those of my readers who
have experienced the peculiar difficulty of launching a boat
from a bed of soft mud, would have readily sympathised
with Mr. Knipps as he pushed first at the bow, then at the
stern, of his stranded boat; and sometimes pushed himself
so deeply into the yielding mud, that he had grave doubts
if he should ever be able to work his way out of it again;
in which case his name would become as unpleasantly familiar in colonial history as the celebrated cockney "Billy
Barlow."

At length the boat was afloat; but navigating it back to
Chickweed Farm was not so easy as gliding down with the
stream to Bandicoot Brush, for two strong reasons, viz., ad-
verse wind and tide, and the weakening influence of strong
rum on Mr. Knipps's powers of sculling. The boat was
heavy, and the oars were not light, still Mr. Knipps worked
with spirit, sometimes standing up and pushing the oars,
sometimes sitting down and pulling them; now and then
lying on his back, after catching a crab, with his heels in
the air, and his hobnails glistening in the sunbeams. After
working in that way for an hour, and finding that he had
scarcely gained half a mile, he naturally enough began to
feel discouraged, so he took some more rum to sustain him,
and tugged away again for another hour with all his might.
Never before had he felt his boat pull so heavily, even when

he had two tons of potatoes in it. Something was the matter for certain, for he had not pulled it a quarter of a mile during the last hour. Her bottom must be dirty, he thought, though Daub, the boatman, had given it a coat of coal tar only a month before. Were the tides always stronger on Christmas Day? he wondered, or what could the matter be? The boat was as hard to move as a brewer's vat.

As he was pushing away at the oars, and pondering over the mysterious cause of his slow progress, he perchance looked round, when he saw that Polly and Billy were towing the empty bushel basket behind—by a long line affixed to the handles—and were enjoying the fun of their mimic water-logged ship, in childish ignorance of the hard labour they were inflicting on their perspiring father. Mr. Knipps dropped his oars, dragged the basket into the boat, and slapped Polly and Billy's heads until their ears were as red as lobsters' legs. He then lighted his pipe, spat on his hands, and resumed the oars; but by the time he had done all that, the boat had drifted back nearly opposite to Bandicoot Brush.

It would make a very long chapter were I to follow that dolorous Christmas party on their tiresome homeward passage, and describe all that they said, did, and suffered. Were I to tell how Mr. Knipps pushed and tugged against wind and tide, and gradually got weary, cross, and drunk. How he profanely cursed his wife, for persisting in hoisting a large gingham umbrella, which, he said, stopped the boat's way more than the bushel basket had done; and, finally, how he threw the umbrella overboard and the basket too. How Mrs. Knipps thereupon got spiteful, and nagged at her husband until he grew uproariously wrath, and threatened to pull the plug out of the boat, and drown them all together. How a fierce recrimination was kept up after they reached their home, until it got to fighting pitch; and after beating his wife with his bridle reins, and receiving in return a stunning knock on the head with the tongs, Mr. Knipps, in a paroxysm of drunken frenzy, smashed every portable article in the house, from the Dutch clock in the corner, to his grandmother's old-fashioned china tea-pot on the mantelpiece.

It would be tedious, too, to record all the minor miseries of Mrs. Knipps and her children, consequent upon their day's pleasure. How the poor baby cried all that night (despite every attempt to soothe him, with rattle and spoon, and every article in the toy way that could be procured), until Mrs. Knipps, in tracing the cause of such unusual grief, discovered two Ticks in a tender part of her infant's person ; and how she soon afterwards found two more Ticks on herself.   How Polly and Billy's faces were blistered by the sun, and all their new clothes were spoiled with salt water and mud.   My readers may reflect, if they choose, over the summary of disagreeables in these last two paragraphs, and draw their own deductions therefrom ; and however much opinions may vary on the merits of the story, there will doubtless be a unanimous conclusion that the Knipps family did not spend a very merry Christmas.

     *   *   *   *   *   *

On New Year's-eve, Mr. and Mrs. Knipps were sitting in their parlour in moody silence ; indeed, they had scarcely exchanged half-a-dozen words since their *fracas* on Christmas-day.   At length Mr. Knipps rose from his seat, and walking over to his wife, kissed her affectionately; and with a look which showed that he felt more than he could express in words, asked her to forgive him for his late unmanly conduct, of which he felt thoroughly ashamed.

" I have been fretting for the last five or six days, Polly ; and I have been thinking very seriously all that time too.   I can see plainly enough that I have been a downright fool for many years past, and I have resolved to mend.   I know the reason why I cannot make my farm pay ; why I am in debt and difficulties, and why I am so often in bad health and in bad temper.   The bills on the file will show that I have had the rum keg filled ten times during this year, which is enough to make any man ashamed of himself.   The cost of that stuff would have kept us all in clothes, or have bought half-a-dozen good cows ; but the actual price of it is not, perhaps, the worst part of the evil ; I have wasted hundreds of hours this year in squandering my strength and my money, and in acquiring pernicious habits.   That is why I'm so much worse off than some of my steady, sober neighbours.   Yes, Polly, the rum keg has been the blighting cause of our unhappiness, and has filled our home with discord ; it is that which has withered the tender love we once felt for each other ; which has mortgaged our farm, and made me miserable.   It is strong drink which has so often made me surly to you and the poor children, and which tempted me to beat you, and smash all our little bits of things on Christmas-day. But it shall do so no more, Polly ; for, with God's help, I am determined to put that curse out of my house entirely. Here, I give you my hand, Polly, and the word of a man who loves you dearly, that I will never taste grog again as long as I live. To-morrow is New Year's-day, and I hope to begin a new life altogether, and to set a Christian example to my children. May God help me to do so, for I am too weak to do it of myself," added Mr. Knipps, bursting into tears.

Polly's tears gushed forth too, as she returned the warm embrace of her repentant husband ; and she sobbed out with a tenderness which she had long forgotten to exhibit :

" It is not all your fault, Bill, my dear ! I feel I am very much to blame for not striving to make your home more happy,—for you always loved your home. I have often given way to a bad temper, and have said sharp things to you, when I ought to have said soothing things, or have been silent altogether, and wore a smiling face. I have often, too, taunted you with running us into difficulties, when I ought to have tried to help you out of them, or to have borne our trials with patience.

" I own how foolish and unkind I was, Bill, in refusing to entertain the Boozems on Christmas-day, after you had invited them ; for I know you are fond of a chat with old Joe, now and then. You have a right to invite who you please to our house, of course ; and I showed great disrespect to you when I objected to your doing so. I am sure I grieved you, for which I am very, very sorry.

" I have done wrong, dear," added Polly, throwing her arms round her husband's neck, " but pray forgive me, and I will promise never to grieve you in a similar way again. It cheers my heart more than I can express to hear you say you mean to make a fresh start, and I intend to start afresh with you. I will begin the new year in a new way of life, and, with God's help, I hope henceforward to see our home the abode of love, peace, and joy."

TWO NOISY BOYS IN A BELFRY.

AN old gentleman, whose varied experience has furnished me with many subjects for my pen, has supplied me with the following authentic incident, which I narrate for the special advantage of my youthful readers. Of course, adults can read my narrative, if they are inclined ; but I trust they will kindly bear in mind that it is written to please and instruct young minds.

"When I was a boy, which is a good many years ago, Mr. Boomerang," said my venerable friend, who was reclining in an old arm-chair in my study. "When I was a curly-headed little boy, nine or ten years of age, I went one Sunday afternoon, as usual, to our village church, in company with my brother, who was about two years younger than myself. The church was a moderate-size building, and was graced with a small bell tower, surmounted by a conical spire, like the extinguisher of a kitchen candlestick.

"On that afternoon, my brother and I seated ourselves in one of the galleries, instead of our accustomed place in the lower part of the church. Soon our attention was attracted to an open doorway, into a narrow space behind the organ, where a tall youth was pulling a bell-rope with great vigour, and with an evident sense of the importance of his work. Instantly I conceived a strong desire to have a pull at the bell—for I had never tested my skill in that kind of music. Upon communicating my longings to my brother, I found that he was anxious for a pull too ; so we left our pew, and introduced ourselves—in boys' unceremonious style—to the youthful bellringer, who condescendingly allowed each of us to have a pull at his bell for a few minutes ; but finding that we did not keep correct time with our ding-dong, and fearing that he might get into disrepute through our imperfect tolling, he declined our eager offers of further assistance at the rope, but consented to our going aloft to see the bell at work. Accordingly we ascended a dusty ladder, which led to a square wooden turret, just above the roof of the church, where a large bell hung on an oaken frame, with a wheel at one end of the axle, and a rope attached thereto, the end of which was in the hands of the lad below, who was apparently using extra exertions just then to astonish us—for the bell was in full swing, or 'sallee,' and shook the steeple so much that we could scarcely stand without holding to the bell-frame or to the bars of the windows.

"The noise was stunning, and at first positively startling; but we soon recovered our senses, and began to make our observations, and to communicate them to each other in unstudied phraseology, plain, though perhaps not polite—for boys are seldom remarkable for strict attention to etiquette.

"'Isn't it a big un, Jack?' remarked my brother, with his eyes full of wonder. I saw his lips move on full stretch, and his countenance express awful admiration, as he nodded at the clanging bell, but I could not hear a word he uttered; so I replied at the top of my voice, 'I can't hear you, Bob! you must squall like an upstairs lodger in a house on fire.'

"'Isn't it a big un, Jack?' repeated Bob, with the utmost emphasis, and with his hands to his mouth in boatswain's fashion, so that I heard him plainly above the deafening din.

"'Yes, a regular whopper,' I replied; and then we commenced a dialogue (which I need not detail) in the same elevated key, and shrieked and hooted like a couple of owls, in order to fully satisfy ourselves that our voices could sound louder than the labouring bell. At the same time, we were innocently unconscious that we were creating a sensation beneath us, or we should have certainly chosen some other occasion and some other place for trying the strength of our lungs. We had no idea of making a disturbance in a church, above all other places—for, though I say it, Mr. Boomerang, we were too well-bred to be wilfully guilty of such ill manners, nay, such gross wickedness, as to desecrate God's Holy Temple.

"In the meantime, however, there was quite a commotion in the church, almost amounting to a panic. The minister had ascended to his pulpit, and the clerk to his 'desk, when our shrill voices startled them and their congregation too. The mysterious question, 'Isn't it a big un, Jack?' and the equally mystical reply, 'Yes, a regular whopper,' sounded through the ventilators in the ceiling, almost as plainly as if we had been shouting in the body of the building itself, while our loud hooting and howling was heard even more distinctly, and which the trembling old sexton believed was a break-out among the ghosts in the vaults.

" Some of the congregation looked at each other in amazement while the extraordinary riot was at its height, and others looked gravely comical. The parson looked at the clerk, and the clerk looked at the beadle, who looked as fierce as a Fijian warrior ; then grasped his club—or rather his cane—as if fairly resolved to wreak vengeance upon the heads of those enemies to peace and concord as soon as he could find them, and waddled down the aisle as fast as he could move his ponderous body. It was some minutes before he could divine from whence the heathenish yells proceeded—for they were unlike the disturbances which he was so frequently called upon to quell. He had, alas ! to his sorrow, and to the disgrace of some of the unruly boys of the parish, often been obliged to exercise his authority to keep order in the church porch, and to flog some of those thoughtless triflers who had so little veneration for the sanctity of God's House, as to create noises and disturbance during Divine Service, to the annoyance of the congregation, as well as to the distraction of the minister in the pulpit.

" When Mr. Budd, the beadle, got outside the church-doors, he soon ascertained that the objectionable sounds came from the bell-turret. So upstairs he hastened, and with difficulty squeezed his big body through the little doorway behind the organ, gave a terrible scowl, in passing, at the tall youth, who was still tolling the bell (which signified that he owed him a caning, and would not forget to pay him when he came down), and began to ascend the dusty ladder, which was not a very easy or dignified job for a bulky parish beadle with his best gold-laced Sunday coat on.

" Just as my brother and I were singing with all our might, ' How doth the little busy bee,' the fat head and shoulders of Mr. Budd appeared through the trap opening of the turret, which put a stop to our music in a moment, and made us shrink into our humblest dimensions—for we had a wholesome dread of beadles, as most little boys have, or had, in those good old times, when beadles were men of more importance than they are now-a-days. In another moment or two my terrified brother Bob and myself were hopping about the shaking turret like scalded frogs, and humbly begging the irate functionary to have mercy upon us ; but he totally disregarded our petitions, or our loud screams (which further astounded the congregation below), and flogged us until he was satisfied he had given us sufficient, or else was thoroughly winded and not able to cane us any more.   While Mr. Budd was taking a rest and wiping the perspiration from his red face, my brother and I descended the ladder faster than lamplighters, and rushed out of the doorway behind the organ, receiving a savage kick each from the bellringer as we departed; then we made the best of our way downstairs, and out of the church, with hundreds of flashing eyes following us, and with more *marks* than we had ever before received in one day, some of which were plainly traceable seven weeks afterwards."

*   *   *   *   *   *

Some readers may be inclined to think that there is nothing in the foregoing incident very creditable to my old friend's young head, or his heart either. So I think; and my old friend is of the same opinion himself. He did not tell the story exultingly—far from it; but he is especially anxious for the welfare of young people; and in his endeavours to instruct, as well as to amuse them, he sometimes refers to his own youthful follies or foibles—not for the imitation of others, but for the purpose of warning them of the treacherous by-paths, from the highway of virtue and wisdom, which he has incautiously taken on his life's journey, and which have invariably led him into a labyrinth of briars and nettles.

This incident could be applied to a good many persons and positions in every-day life, and a useful moral drawn therefrom; many analogous cases are before my mind as I write. I can picture a multitude of thoughtless youths who are now shouting and hooting (like my friend and his brother Bob in the belfry) in the feverish excitement of sensual pleasures, and are unconscious that their riotous revelry is heard above the discord by which they are surrounded. But Mr. Budd will visit them very soon, in the shape of aches and pains, and shattered nerves—for they may be assured they will not transgress Nature's laws with impunity. They had better cease their uproar, and come down from the belfry to their proper seats, like good boys, before the beadle mounts the ladder with his rattan, and makes them smart.

And those two half-tipsy youths, whose fresh, ruddy faces, and wrinkled coats indicate that they have just come on shore from the London ship, which dropped anchor last night in Sydney Cove. They reel along George-street, wildly exulting in their new-found liberty, in being able to indulge their long pent-up propensities without dread of admonitions from parents or guardians. They fancy, too, that as they are far away from home, in a strange place, where no person knows them, their debauchery will not attract attention to their prejudice. But they are egregiously mistaken, poor fellows! Mr. Budd, or his representative, will visit them by-and-by, and sadly they will feel the stripe of his castigatory cane. If they escape the talons of the birds of prey which are constantly on the watch for such green goslings, they will not wholly escape the notice of the respectable portion of our community, which they will, perhaps, soon discover to their great disadvantage. Many a young man has injured his prospects in the colony by indulging in riotous excesses on his first arrival with some of his fellow-passengers, under the foolish idea that he could do so with impunity in a place where he was a complete stranger; whereas, the fact of his being a new arrival had attracted special attention to his intemperance and his swaggering impudence.

Examples—not among young folks only—might be multiplied of persons who are " wasting their substance in riotous living," disturbing their peaceable neighbours, wrecking their health and their reputation too, and, worse than all, perilling their immortal peace ; while they seem—like the boys in the belfry—unconscious of their folly and danger, or else utterly careless about it. Alas! we often see Mr. Budd come to such in the form of grim death, to startle them in their revelry, and to hurry them off to their doom which they have been preparing for throughout their lives.

" The path of duty is the path of safety" for either young or aged travellers. Had my friend and his brother attended to that maxim they would have taken their usual seats in church, like good boys, on the afternoon referred to, and thus saved themselves the subsequent disaster which befel them. In order clearly to perceive the path of duty at all times, it is necessary to ask for Divine light ; and if we ask aright we shall receive plain direction and guidance for every day's journey.

INFLUENZA SEASON.

SCENE: *Sydney, King Street corner, on a drizzling day. Two friends (Minton and Timmins) meet, and shake hands; they are both suffering from the prevailing epedemic.*

Minton: Good bordig, Bister Tibbids ! How are you? I thought you were off to Boretod Bay—ha teoz—ha teez ! (*sneezes.*)

Timmins: How are you, Bidtod? Dasty bordid, this. I've bid laid up with this confounded influedsa, ad bissed the steaber. How is Bissis Bidtod, and Biss Baria? ha teezer? ha teez? (*sneezes violently.*)

Minton: They are all very bad at hobe. By-the-bye, Tibbids, what rebedy do you use for this epedebic?

Timmins: Why, by bedical bad gave be sobe dasty bixture; I dod't dow what it is bade of, but I thik it has dode be good. Whighezm! ha teezum! (*sneezes hysterically.*)

Minton: You bust have bid precious bad, thed, if the bedicine has dode you ady good at all; for you—pardod me —you look just dow like a frost-bitted ghost. But dod't stadd there id the raid, Tibbids. Cobe with be to the Betropolitad Hotel, add have a basid of buttod broth.

*   *   *   *   *   *

If the above brief colloquy has the least resemblance to a joke, it is a very grim one, and thousands of folks in Sydney will confess that the influenza is as foreign to fun as a fly in your eye, or a splinter up your thumb-nail. Its peculiar effect upon the powers of speech of its victims is well understood, though that is the least distressing symptom of the malady, which oppresses both body and mind in a manner which no pen in the world could describe.

I was recently in company with a gentleman, whose brain contains perhaps as extensive a variety of lore as any cranium in the land, and while trying to indite an ordinary letter, he passed his hand across his capacious brow, and confessed " that he had the greatest difficulty in drawing a single rational idea from his bemuddled organs." While afterwards reflecting on that admission of a great mind, I was constrained to sympathise with all those persons whose professions demand the constant exercise of their intellect ; and as I did so I wondered how far that fellow-feeling was general. How many readers of the morning papers would soften their criticisms, in these suffering times, if they missed the usual force, sparkle, and point in the leading columns ; and how many would sigh commiseratingly over the probability of those ideas having flowed from the aching brains of the writers as vapidly as mouldy ink from a rusty pen ? How many persons in that sneezing congregation, yesterday, pitied the poor suffering parson in the pulpit, as he laboured to make his misty syllogisms as clear as sunlight. How many considerate souls sympathised with their worthy pastor's swollen nose, and awed down their smirks when he called " Moses " *Boses*, or when he languidly told them " to udite id siggig the didty-didth psalb." And what proportion of the hearers went home complaining that the sermon was " not up to the mark," compared with those who generously reflected how arduously their dispirited minister had toiled, for the last few days, to urge his flagging brain to its duties, and to *think out* that forty-five minutes sermon.

Then again, I wondered if sympathy was active enough in mercantile circles ? Whether that merchant would pardon his drowsy clerk, for making a few blunders in that complicated account-current ? and whether that master draper, (who was rather cross because customers had been scarce lately,) would debit Influenza with the failure of his shivering shopman to persuade that strong-minded old lady to buy a " shepherd's plaid scarf," instead of a " M‘Gregor tartan shawl," which was not in their stock ? I thought a little too, about milliners' girls, and hard-working girls in general ; many of whom have to please ill and irritable mistresses, and to look pleasantly at troublesome customers, while their interesting little noses look as mottled as blighted mazarine cherries. Then I began to commiserate schoolmasters and mistresses, and to wonder how they preserved their patience, amidst their hosts of little snifflers ; but I suddenly remembered that it was holiday season, and that all those liberated ladies and gentlemen would probably be in bed ; so I began to envy them, until I was seized with a fit of sneezing, which made me forget everything but my own discomfort, and created a mental uneasiness lest I should sneeze my hat off into the muddy street, and have a long chase after it ; for

the wind was gusty, and running after my hat is an exercise
to which I am not at all partial.

During one of the brief intervals of sunshine, last week, I
ventured out of doors again, for an hour—muffled up to the
nose like a Norway skipper—and in that short time I saw
enough to keep my sympathies in exercise to the present
moment. Of course I condoled with the two unlucky ladies,
who slipped down, opposite to the celebrated Doctor's door,
and woefully bedaubed their dresses and their kid gloves
with whity-brown mud. Though I was not near enough to
help them up again, I felt for their discomfiture, but I
could not indorse their ungenerous insinuation, "that the
doctor aforesaid, had pipeclayed his pathway to increase his
surgical practice," for doctors in general have more than
enough legitimate work at the present time.

I took warning by the downfall of the two ladies, however, and picked my way along very warily, for a tumble in
the mud is decidedly unpleasant to my taste. To say nothing of the risk of sprains, broken bones, and bruises, a
person never looks so well, directly after he gets up, as he
did before he fell down, and he always loses dignity, in proportion to the number of spectators around him, and the
quantity of mire which may be sticking to his apparel. Besides, if he were to be unfortunate enough to dislocate his
hip, or break half his ribs, five minutes would at least elapse
before he saw signs of genuine sympathy among the bye-
standers ; for it seems as natural for one person to laugh at
another's downfall, as to laugh under the influence of tickling
fingers. I observed as I went along that pipeclay footpaths
are common in the eastern suburbs of the city ; and if I confess that I wished two aldermen had slipped down, instead
of the two ladies before mentioned, I hope it will not be
supposed that I bear ill-will to the worthy civic dignitaries
of that ward. On the contrary, I have great respect for
them ; but I thought it was probable, if such a mishap occurred to them, that they would take it as a reminder of
neglected duty, and would forthwith send a few Corporation
carts, and labourers, to sprinkle a little sand over those
glycerine pathways. It is not likely that those poor ladies
would have influence enough to effect so much public good ;
besides, I think that either pipeclay or clay pipes are less
distasteful in the hands of the male sex, than in the gloved
hands of delicate females.

As I continued my walk, I noticed an unsavoury steam rising from the damp, mouldy dwellings in several of the narrow lanes of the city, where the sun's rays slanted down on them; and I wished that some Australian "Peabody" would come nobly forward, and erect model-dwellings for the poor, and do his own heart good at the same time. Then I began to speculate whether any of those persons who have lately found the influenza so terrible to bear, even when surrounded by all the comforts which wealth can produce, ever thought of their poor sick neighbours in some of those grimy hovels, who have to suffer amidst poverty and a lack of common necessaries. How acceptable a few old clothes, a few bags of coal, and a little delicate food would be to some of those unhappy ones, I thought; and how easy it would be for those rich folks to spare such trifles.

The wild, murky clouds soon began to wrap up the sun, and to damp my spirits at the same time, so I hastened home again to my snug fireside, thankful indeed that I had those comforts, and heartily wishing that everybody else had a home and a fireside. Anon, the wind began to roar round my chimney-pot again, and the hard rain to patter on my window-pane; the gloom of night gathered around, and the lighthouse-keeper at South Head had lit up his lantern. Ah! a dismal night for poor sailors on the lee shore, I soliloquised, while I gazed through my dormer. I hope all those who have not got a "good offing" have got good tight vessels under them; that they are not overladen, and that their rigging and sails are sound, otherwise we shall hear more sad news of wrecks in a day or two. Then I thought how miserable it must be for poor sailors who have the influenza, to stand shivering at the wheel in such a rough night as that. At the same time I pictured a drenched shepherd, hobbling home to his lonely hut in the far bush, after being out all day in the rain, watching his sheep; and I decided at once that I would rather be a sailor than a shepherd; for I should at any rate have my messmates to speak to, and there would be comfort even in hearing a fellow creature sneeze. But to go home to an empty hut, to make my own fire, and cook my own supper; then to sit moodily nodding at the back log in the chimney, and picturing "old bogies" in the smoke, until drowsiness drove me to my solitary couch; ugh! I shouldn't like that at all. I pity poor shepherds, for they have so few social privileges. Though I don't wish to make them discontented with their lot, I do wish they had a few more civilised comforts and conveniences, and the disposition to prize them; that they had plenty of nice books to beguile their many hours of loneliness. Perhaps some kind master or mistress, who may read this sketch, will be induced to look over their libraries, and send a box of books to their station, for the use of the shepherds, the next time the team goes up.

At length I withdrew from my dreary look out at the window, and stirred my fire into a cheerful blaze; then I began to cogitate on brighter subjects. As my hope became stimulated, I soon perceived that although much mischief, misery, and inconvenience had been caused by the late inclement weather, that those evils are insignificant, compared with the blessings which the timely rain will confer upon this erst thirsty land. Happily the temperature has been genial for the season, and grass has sprung up rapidly where it was much needed. Sharp frosts will doubtless injure it, but only partially, and there will be plenty of fresh feed for the flocks and herds. The sun will acquire additional power each day, and we may reasonably anticipate a thriving spring, a luxuriant summer, and a plentiful harvest. In a few months the whole face of nature will be blooming with flowers, and new verdure; the orchards will be teeming with fruit, and the birds will fill the air with melody. Then this sneezing season of influenza will be forgotten, by most of us, for we shall have warm sunshine around us, and, it is to be hoped, we shall have health in our homes, and "summer in our souls."

> "Be still, sad heart! and cease repining;
> Behind the clouds is the sun still shining;
> Thy fate is the common fate of all,
> Into each life some rain must fall.
> Some days must be dark and dreary."—*Longfellow.*

DON'T FORGET YOUR POOR OLD MOTHER !

ONE afternoon, nearly twenty years ago, a young man was actively engaged behind the counter of a general store, in the interior of New South Wales.   The day was wet, and customers were scarce ; so Mr. Bustle, who was a careful economist of time, as well as of his means, employed himself in dusting and re-arranging the scanty assortment of goods on his shelves—for he wisely endorsed the old adage, " that goods *well* kept are half sold."   If rats and mice were not entirely excluded from his premises, it was not the fault of Benjamin Bustle ; and they had not a very peaceable time therein.   They were not allowed to nestle their mischievous brood among the prints and calicoes on his drapery shelves, nor to burrow undisturbed into the cheeses, packages of starch, or other favourite commodities on the grocery side of his shop.   Mr. Bustle was an industrious man, and, although but a young beginner in business, with a very small capital, at a time of almost general distress and commercial stagnation throughout the colony, he was, nevertheless, a thriving man, because he managed to live below his income.   Thus he gradually increased his stock, which, as I before stated, he took care to keep in good saleable condition.

Mr. Bustle had just given the finishing touch to his haberdashery shelves, on the afternoon referred to, and was standing gazing on his little stock-in-trade (which he knew was all paid for), and wondering whether he would have sufficient cash, by the ensuing week, to enable him to replenish his store from the Sydney market, when in walked Mr. Dubbs, a gentleman who resided in the neighbourhood.

" I have called to asked you, Mr. Bustle, if you will buy a bank draft on London for £25," said Mr. Dubbs.   " I received it a day or two ago, and, commercially speaking, it is of no use to me, for, you know, I am not in business.   I shall be glad if you will cash it for me.   You shall have it for £24."

"If I bought it, I should have to resell it in Sydney," said Mr. Bustle; "and I do not know the present rate of exchange. I have no use for it myself, for I am not in a position to import goods from England, though I hope to do so some day. I am much obliged to you for offering the draft to me, but I must decline purchasing it."

*   *   *   *   *   *

"Is anything troubling you, my dear?" inquired Mrs. Bustle, when her husband sat down to tea, an hour or two afterwards, in an unusually thoughtful mood.

"No, love; nothing is actually troubling me," replied Mr. Bustle, "but I cannot remove an impression from my mind that I ought to buy that bank draft which Mr. Dubbs offered me this afternoon, and send it to my mother. Since the lamented death of several members of my family I have been uncertain as to her pecuniary position; and I feel a strange uneasiness on the subject to-night, nor can I reason it away."

"Well, my dear, buy the draft, and send it by the first ship that sails to England," replied Mrs. Bustle. "If you think your mother wants it, send it by all means; it is a positive duty."

"I do not see that I can afford it," said Mr. Bustle, musingly. "I want to go to Sydney to buy goods next week, and the purchase of that draft would take nearly half my stock of ready money. You know it is useless to ask for credit, now that failures are so frequent, and almost every person is viewed with distrust. No, I cannot afford to be over liberal just now. I will, however, write and ask my mother how she is circumstanced; and if I learn that she requires pecuniary aid from me, I will send it at once. A few months' delay will not matter much to her, and I shall be able to spare money more conveniently by-and-bye. I could turn that £24 twice over in the interim. Yes, that is the best plan," added Mr. Bustle decisively; and then he began to converse upon some other subject, and tried to banish the bank draft from his thoughts altogether.

That night, after he retired to bed, he was unusually restless, and in some unaccountable way his thoughts persistently dwelt upon the purchase of the draft. There he lay, rolling about as restless as if he had a heavy draft to pay, and no money to pay it with. Vainly he tried to woo "Nature's soft nurse;" she would not be wooed by him.

At length he felt so strongly the desire to send the draft home, that he resolved to do it, and very soon after he had thus decided he fell asleep.

The next morning he informed his wife of his resolution, and she kindly commended it. That same day the draft was purchased, and enclosed in a long loving letter to his dear mother, far over the sea; and then Mr. Bustle went about his usual occupations, cheerful and happy, under the sense of having performed an imperative moral obligation.

*   *   *   *   *   *

Reader, please to let your fancy fly forward a few months from the date of my story, and then take a long leap with me over the vast expanse of ocean, which rolls its rugged waves between this great continent and the dear little island almost beneath us, whither our hearts' fond affections so often wander in rapture, tinged with melancholy. Accompany me, in imagination, into a humble, though comfortable cottage, in one of the rural parts of old England. 'Tis a cold winter's day; the leafless hedgerows are white with rime, and the north-east wind is howling through the tree-tops, like the weird voice of famine. Inside that cottage we see an aged widow bowed down with grief. She is sitting all alone, mourning for dear ones recently gone to the grave. She is sighing, too, for an absent son, far away— one whose manly arm she at one time fondly hoped would be the stay of her declining strength; whose youthful energy would be exerted to minister to her wants, when age and infirmity precluded all active efforts on her part. "Ah!" she sighs, "I once had a devoted son beside me, whose fond embrace often cheered my widowed heart, and whose endearing words often lightened my heavy burden of anxiety. Frequently in his boyhood days has he hung about my neck, and whispered in my comforted ears—dear mother!

'When thou art feeble, old, and grey,
My healthful arm shall be thy stay!'

"Yes, he sincerely meant it too; and, were he near me now, he would shield me to the utmost of his power from aught that threatens my comfort and peace. But ah, dear boy! little does he know my present indigence, or, far as he is from me, he would find means to succour me. I will not doubt his affection. How can I? But he is far away from me, and months must elapse before I can let him know my position.   Meantime, I am here alone—bereaved, and overwhelmed with sorrow.   Gaunt poverty is at my door, and my threadbare purse contains my last shilling.   Very soon my little household comforts, and all those treasured mementoes of happier days must be sacrificed to supply my actual necessities.   My lot is hard, and I cannot but weep over it.

"But, praise God! though cast down, I am not in despair," says the widow, as a gleam of heavenly sunshine makes her smile through her tears.   "I am not alone, for the 'God of the widow' hath promised never to leave me, nor forsake me.   'I will trust and not be afraid.'"   She reaches a book from a shelf beside her—the Bible—whose sacred pages her late beloved husband had often bedewed with tears of joy and gratitude during long years of sickness.   "This precious book abounds with comforting promises," says the widow, "and they are all as sure as the glories of Heaven."   She opens the book, and reads a text specially marked by the pencil of her late afflicted husband. "I have been young, and now am old; yet have I not seen the righteous forsaken, nor his seed begging bread."

But look outside the cottage again for a moment, reader! See the village postman hastily approaching with his letter-bag strung before him.   Scarcely has the poor widow read the comforting passage just quoted, when she is startled by the sharp rap-tap of the postman at her door; she hastens to open it, and receives into her trembling hands a registered letter from her absent son, containing the bank draft for £25, and an affectionately worded promise that he will henceforward supply her with the means of procuring every material comfort she needs, as long as she shall live.

*   *   *   *   *   *

That promise was faithfully kept; and so far from growing poorer, Mr. Bustle rapidly grew rich.   I have often heard him say, that it was one of the happiest reflections of his life, that *he did not forget his poor old mother.*

A RUSTIC LOVE STORY.

JONATHAN SPROUTS AND PHŒBE SKIMMER.

CHAPTER I.

JONATHAN Sprouts loved Phœbe Skimmer, as fondly as schoolboy ever loved almond hardbake : and Phœbe loved Jonathan a little bit, but not a soul knew the delicate secret, except her bosom companion Betsy Brown, who lived within call of a shrill cooey.

Jonathan was a roundheaded, honest young rustic, and at the time my story commences, had not been long out from the quiet little village of Dumplyn, in Devonshire. He was hired immediately after his arrival by Mr. Murphy, the market gardener, to drive a horse and cart, and to make himself generally useful. Phœbe was a dairyman's daughter, a buxom lassie of twenty-two, whose principal duties were to help milk her father's cows, polish the milk cans, and ride in a yellow cart with her brother Bob, twice a day, round their milk-walk. In addition thereto, she super-intended the domestic affairs of the household, for her mo-ther had been dead some years.

Jonathan used to blush like a mangel-wurzel whenever he met Phœbe, and Phœbe used to feel as funny as if she had a live mouse in her pocket whenever she met Jonathan ; but not one word had been exchanged by them on any other subject than the state of the weather, although they had passed each other daily for five months or more.

Jonathan was a smart sort of fellow in his way ; he could handle a spade, or a pitchfork, or any other farming tool with any man in his county, and could beat his master in loading a cart for market. He knew how to make the bunches of carrots and turnips look most tempting, and to turn the heads of the cauliflowers and the hearts of the let-tuces to the best advantage : but he was puzzled how to turn the heart of Phœbe Skimmer in his favour ; or to make known to her the tender state of his own heart ; for he knew no more about love making than he did about making air balloons, or steam-engines. Long he had silently admired the pretty dairy-maid, and had spent many sleepless hours on his stretcher, making abstruse calculations on the amount of capital required for a start in the milk line himself, with Phœbe for a partner. I do not say that he had selfishly counted upon any direct advantages, from a union with Phœbe, in the shape of cows, or cow-keeping plant; or that he contemplated taking away her father's customers, as well as his daughter, for he believed the maxim "Better is a portion in a wife, than with a wife; and he who marries for wealth sells his liberty;" but as it is not uncommon for mercenary motives to influence the minds of young wife-seekers, in other grades of society, it is just possible that Jonathan may have encouraged such greedy speculations; though I must, in justice, say, I think the humbler class of mankind are seldom chargeable with meanness of that sort. His castle-building was, however, usually brought to a dead stand—by the puzzling question, how was he to woo and win the fair object of his daily thoughts and nightly dreams, who was almost as shy as himself? He had worn out two new magnum bonum pens in his efforts to compose a love letter, but had never got beyond the first fond sentence; "my dear Feeby;" there his pen stuck fast, like a cart in a bog-hole, and all his ideas were as powerless to help it out as a dead horse. Had he only been scholar enough to add but those two sentences, "I love you! Will you have me for your husband?" his doubts and suspense might have soon given place to the realisation of his tenderest wishes; for Phœbe understood plain English.

I have heard of a similar laconic love letter being sent to a young Cornish lass by a love sick shepherd in the far bush, who sadly wanted a wife to comfort him, as many honest bushmen do at this present time. The girl was delighted with the straightforward declaration "I love you!" and was anxious to reply to the plainly put question, "Will you have me for your husband?" in the affirmative; but how to do it she scarcely knew, for unfortunately she could not write, and she was unwilling to entrust her secret to a hired scribe; so after some consideration, she had recourse to a symbolic correspondence. Having procured an eye from a sheep's head, she carefully cleansed it, and wrapping it in a lock of wool, sent it to her admirer, who of course rightly interpreted it to signify *eye-wool*, or I will. That was enough for him, it was an unmistakable assent to his proposition, and the consummation of his happiness soon followed. I have seen many lengthy and highly elaborated love letters, which did not contain so much honest meaning as the comical correspondence of the shepherd and the Cornish lass : and I may add, for the edification of puzzled lovers like Jonathan, that a frank, common sense avowal of their feelings and wishes is all that is necessary in such circumstances.

Had Jonathan added those two important sentences to " my dear Feeby," although it is not probable that Phœbe would have had recourse to sheep's eyes and fleece, for she could write tolerably well, her reply would doubtless have been the same in effect, " I will," and Jonathan would have been a rejoicing man at once. But the ideas never entered into his round head, so how could he get them out of it ? Though he was a little man he had a big heart, and as it expanded with the increasing force of his pent-up passion, he felt, to use his own expressive words, as if he had a big, boiling hot cabbage inside his breast pocket. It is difficult to conjecture what the consequence would have been, had not the wheel of fortune suddenly turned in his favour, in a way which I shall briefly relate.

One very warm afternoon, Jonathan was returning home from Sydney market, sitting on his cart laden with stable refuse, whistling " The maid with her milking pail," and thinking as usual about pretty Phœbe Skimmer and the probability of her one day being Phœbe Sprouts. When as he rose to the top of a little hill in the road, he saw the well-known yellow cart coming towards him, with his charmer in her straw hat and cream-coloured ribbons, sitting beside her brother Bob, who was beating the old white horse with the butt end of the whipstick, in full assurance that there were no friends of animals near to remind him of " Martin's Cruelty Act," or to give him in charge to a constable, to be punished as all such savages deserve to be. As the milk cart rapidly drew near, Jonathan's practised eye saw in an instant, by the eccentric rotation of the off wheel, that the linchpin was broken ; consequently he judged that the wheel would soon be off altogether, and his beloved Phœbe would probably be upset, and her milk cans too. With a promptness which love alone can stimulate in such an emergency,

Jonathan shouted at the top of his voice: "whoa! stop! Dang it young un! hould hard cant ee? Doan't ee see yer off wheel a wobbling about loike an old grindstone?" at the same time he slid down from his perch on the load of litter, as hastily as if it had suddenly become dangerously hot, or he had just discovered a nest of soldier ants beneath his seat. The boy Bob, however, mistook the meaning of the friendly outcry, and under the impression that Jonathan had some felonious design upon the milk cart and its passengers, instead of stopping or holding hard, he whipped the white horse into a gallop, in order to escape from the supposed bushranger.

"Drat thee emperence! Thee art be-wattled, I do believe!" grumbled Jonathan, as he left his own horse standing in the road and ran after the yellow cart, throwing out his arms to denote danger, like an excited signal master, and shouting "whoa! stop! hould hard!" but with no other effect than to make the terrified Bob beat his horse harder. Presently the off-wheel parted company with the cart, and rolled into a dyke by the roadside, and simultaneously Jonathan saw, to his great dismay, the vehicle itself descend to the ground, and the next moment his charming Phœbe and her savage brother Bob were sprawling in a pool of spilt milk.

With his blushing countenance covered with pity and perspiration, Jonathan ran to the rescue; gently raised the prostrate maiden, and stammeringly inquired whether she had hurt herself.

"Not at all, thank ee," said Phœbe, while her rosy face, bedewed with new milk, looked as glowing as her bashful lover's red plush waistcoat, with pearl buttons. "I'm much obliged to you for helping me up, but I'm sorry to trouble you."

"Doan't ee zay a word about that now," said Jonathan, gallantly. "I wanted to stop en from tumbling down, but that young un there wouldn't whoa when I told en to do it. I be nation glad thee bean't killed, that I be, sure enough. Drabbit it! what a great gorbey thee must be, to ha druv'd along like mad, when I tould en to whoa, as loud as I could yell," he added, with an angry glance at Bob, who was rubbing his grazed head and groaning dismally. "Coom an help un to get the wheel out of the dyke, an put en on again. Doan't ee stand there paking an rubbin all the hair

off yer head. Dang it ! thee beaunt half a man to go wallop-
ing that poor owld bony knacker so mortal hard : thee
moight a smashed thee sister up, loike a basket of eggs, and
it's a marcy thee didn't doot."

After putting on the straying wheel securely, and picking
up the battered milk cans, and again telling Phœbe he was
awfully glad her worn't murdered, Jonathan wished her
good-bye, and returned to his cart, while she and her
brother Bob retraced their way homeward for a fresh supply
of milk for their afternoon customers. As she jolted along
before her empty cans, her heart was quite full of affection
for Jonathan, who had manifested such tender concern for
her personal safety.

Jonathan quickly remounted his elevated seat on the load
of litter, and after gently waking up his horse with the
whip, and telling it to " gee up," he resigned himself to a
delicious contemplation of the late occurrence, and the happy
contingencies which might accrue therefrom. He recollected
a thrilling story, which he had read in his boyhood, of a
gallant young soldier, at great personal risk, stopping four
runaway horses affixed to a carriage, in which was a young
lady as beautiful as Phœbe Skimmer. The terrified steeds
were about to take a flying leap from the top of some lofty
cliffs into the sea, when the young soldier stopped them, by
some means (not very clearly defined), and saved the young
lady's life. The sequel of the story was, that the gallant
young soldier married the grateful young lady, who was the
only daughter of a wealthy baronet.

It was not difficult for Jonathan to draw a pleasing
analogy between that case and the one in which he had
lately taken so conspicuous a part. Phœbe was certainly
not the daughter of a wealthy baronet, but she was the
daughter of an honest dairyman, and was perhaps worth a
carriage full of titled ladies as far as domestic qualities and
working powers were concerned. He regretted of course
that he had not succeeded in stopping the milk cart, before
the wheel wobbled off into the drain : there the analogy
was again interrupted, still his kindly intentions were evidently understood by Phœbe, and he tickled his heart by
believing that she would by and by show her appreciation
of his zeal for the preservation of her life and limbs in a
similar way the rich young lady did to the poor young
soldier. On the whole, he regarded the incident as a

fortunate one for him : the runaway wheel had given a favourable turn to his prospects, for he now had a reasonable pretext for calling upon Mr. Skimmer, to inquire if the graze on the white horse's hip was healing, and whether the hair was beginning to grow over the wound on his boy Bob's head, and to explain to the dairyman his experienced views of linchpins and leather washers for cart wheels. At the same time he intended to keep a keen look out for an opportunity of declaring his love for Phœbe.

Mr. Murphy was one of those good-natured employers who gave their men Saturday afternoon for recreation ; so on the next Saturday after the above recorded event, Jonathan greased his boots and oiled his hair, and put on a clean shirt ; then shouldering a gunny bag, in which he had put a newly-cut water melon, nearly as big as a milking pail—a present for Phœbe—he set off for Mr. Skimmer's farm, which was about two miles distant across the country.

Mr. Skimmer was sitting on the top rail of a pigsty, smoking his pipe, and watching some snubby-nosed pigs at their supper trough, as Jonathan drew near with the bag on his back.

"Good evening, neighbour," was Mr. Skimmer's salute to Jonathan, with whom he had previously a nodding acquaintanceship.

"Good evening, Master Skimmer," said Jonathan. "A foine evening this, ony plaguey warm, and the skeeters are real spiteful across the swamps yonder, they do poke their horns into a fellow loike cranky young steers. How's the old horse's hip ? and how's Bob's head ?"

"Nicely, thank ee," said Mr. Skimmer. "You are the man who picked my girl up the other day, after she got spilt. She told me all about it, and I'm much obliged to you."

"That's naught, measter ; doan't ee speak about it," said Jonathan, modestly ; at the same time he was about to ask if Phœbe was all right, but his heart suddenly seemed to shrivel up like a sunburnt mushroom, so he asked how the cows were getting on ?

"Capitally ! they are as sleek as young rats in a barn," said Mr. Skimmer, with a smirk of professional pride, like an encored fiddler, "there's a nice bit of feed in the paddocks after the last week's rain, and the cows look uncommonly well ; put your bag down and take a look at them."

' "There," said Mr. Skimmer, holding up his hands in admiration as they entered a long shed. " There's as fine a lot of milkers as ever kicked a bucket. Look at their tails ! thin as a stockwhip. There's breed in those cows, I can tell you. Whoa, Daisy ! stand over. Now just look at this ; pretty creature, ain't she ? a regular pet, too. She belongs to Phœbe. Get up, Strawberry ! Here now, take a good look at this one's flank, a perfect picture ! She gives close up three barn gallons of milk a day, a regular gold mine for a poor man, that cow is."

Jonathan made many admiring comments on the cattle, for he was a judge, and knew all their best points better than a butcher. They were a well bred and well-fed lot of cows, so he could honestly say a good deal in their praise : but he was most eloquent on the qualities of Daisy, which was certainly a handsome animal. In thus expressing his opinion, he was not insensible to the fact, that he was on the most direct road to the dairyman's good graces, and before they had finished their survey, Mr. Skimmer thought Jonathan was a nice sort of young fellow, who knew a thing or two about cattle and dairy feeding.

As they emerged from the cow shed, Jonathan's anxious ears caught the sound of cart wheels, accompanied by the jingling of tinware, which was sweeter music to him than the chords of a grand piano, for he knew that Phœbe had returned from her afternoon's milk service, and on turning a corner of the dairy, he saw her descending from the yellow cart, her pretty face blushing beneath her little round hat, like a ripe love-apple in a strawberry basket.

"Hallo ! welcome home, my girl," said Mr. Skimmer, then he added, nodding towards Jonathan, "here's Mr. What's-his-name come to see us. Please to tell us your name, mate."

"Jonathan Sprouts," was the modest reply.

"Thank ee.   Well, Mr. Sprouts will stop and take a cup of tea with us, Phœbe, so get the kettle boiling quickly, there's a good girl."

<h3 style="text-align:center">CHAPTER II.</h3>

"Walk this way, Mr. Sprouts," said Mr. Skimmer, proceeding towards the house. " What have you got in your bag ? Excuse me for asking ; but if it is anything that can run away, bring it inside."

"It's a foine ripe water melon. I carr'd an over from our garden, 'cos I'd a notion Miss Phœbe ud like to have en. I loike em uncommon ; they be rate noice things to eat in warm weathur loike this," replied Jonathan, turning up the bag as he spoke, and rolling the green monster to the feet of his deary, who smiled and said, " thankee, Mr. Sprouts, I am very fond of melons."

"'Take a seat on the sofa," said Mr. Skimmer, when they had entered a snug little parlour, neat as hands could make it. " I'll just go and have a wash, and put on my coat. I'll be with you again in a few minutes ; make yourself happy."

Accordingly Jonathan seated himself, and while his host was at his toilet, and Phœbe was helping the handy little maid-of-all-work in the kitchen, he busied himself in taking stock of the comforts around him. The house, though small, was very convenient, and scrupulously clean in every part. There was not an atom of dust, or cobweb to be seen, and all the furniture shone like a black fellow's face.

" Her be's a tidy wench, sure enough," muttered Jonathan to himself, as he gazed around in smiling admiration on the tokens of good housewifery, which were everywhere apparent, " I believe her do amost bate my dear ould mother, and sister Suke. I wish they could see this room. They wouldn't bother me any more to send for Dolly Daysel, I'll warrant."

Though it is commonly reported that " love is blind," I doubt if it would have blinded Jonathan to the reasonable deduction, that he could have very little domestic comfort with Phœbe for his wife—however comely her person—had he seen evidence of slovenliness, wastefulness, and a lack of cleanliness, which is too often seen in country homes, and in town homes, too. Jonathan, though as shy as a wild turkey, was nevertheless shrewd enough in his quiet way, as most Devonshire boys are—and much as he had admired Phœbe Skimmer's neat appearance out of doors, had he seen anything to indicate that she was a " dolly" indoors, he would have resigned her to some lover less mindful of such important matters, and would have tried to subdue his passion, like a sensible man, while he looked elsewhere for a suitable wife.

An intimate friend of mine—many years ago—fell suddenly in love with a young lady whom he had met at a picnic. She was the belle of the party; and in her flowing riding habit and feathery hat, she looked like Diana, or some other goddess. The first glances of her love-striking eyes went through his susceptible heart, like silver skewers; and her lisping tongue and sonorous laughter tickled his ears like cuckoo's feathers. For nine days his heart was in a simmer of adoration for Miss Birdy; and all the world seemed sad and dreary without her. On the tenth day he called at her mother's villa, in the forenoon, and found his Dulcinea *en deshabille*, lolling on the drawing-room couch, sighing over a sensational novel, entitled the " Blighted Heart, or the Midnight Vow," while everything around her evidenced slovenliness, disorder, and genteel dirt.

"How are you to-day, Miss Birdy?" asked my friend, as he entered the room, with a fluttering heart.

"I'm very poorly," replied the young lady, languidly raising herself into a sitting posture, and hiding the book beneath the sofa cushion; gasping the while with the exertion, like a little gosling trying to swallow a frog: then in a die-away drawl she began to describe the aches and pains which she was doomed to endure, but which my friend— who was rather a sagacious youth—at once saw were whims and fancies, produced by want of proper exercise of body and mind. He felt inclined to recommend her to put on her morning wrapper, and rub the dust and candle spots off her piano, and put the otherwise untidy room to rights: then to go into the kitchen and exercise herself with the rolling-pin and pastry board, while she heated the oven with the " Blighted Heart," and scores of similar books, which littered her boudoir. He was too courteous, how- ever, thus plainly to express his sentiments to the young lady, but he wisely acted upon the judgment of her charac- ter, which that interview afforded, and did not in any way express his feelings. In a short time his hastily-formed attachment succumbed to the sober reasonings of common sense; at a month's end his love for Miss Birdy had flown away, and his heart was again his own. In due course he married a sensible young lady, accomplished and domesti- cated, and has since enjoyed many years of conjugal happi- ness. Miss Birdy married too, and although her husband's income was sufficient for a stylish establishment, her extrava- gance and want of management—in less than seven years —involved him in pecuniary difficulties.

In a short time Mr. Skimmer returned to the parlour and put an end, for a time, to Jonathan's speculations. Soon afterwards, Phœbe—in a neat afternoon dress—took her seat at the tea table, which was garnished with a ham of her own curing, a loaf of her own baking, and some nice fresh butter of her own churning; which interesting facts Jonathan adroitly ascertained in the course of the social meal. Many were the loving glances which stole out of the corners of his eyes towards her, as she sat behind the big tin tea-pot; and when she asked him if his tea was agreeable, he was going to say, "that it would be as sweet as mead, even if she had only looked at it, and had forgotten to sugar it," but he was afraid to attempt such a long speech.

After tea, Mr. Skimmer and Jonathan smoked a pipe together, and chatted about cattle and cart wheels, and many other topics which they mutually understood, while Phœbe sat and listened, and at the same time nimbly plied her needle and thimble in the necessary repairs to some of her father's working shirts. About nine o'clock Jonathan bade farewell to his kind friends, and trudged homeward in the face of the full moon, with his heart full of love and pleasing anticipations, for he had ascertained, in a way unmistakably plain, though difficult to explain, that he had found favour in Phœbe's eyes; and he had also satisfied himself that she was an industrious and domesticated young woman; just the wife for him, and the very identical girl that his mother and sister Suke would have chosen.

Jonathan had been scarcely twelve months in the colony, yet he had saved nearly thirty pounds (out of his pound a week with board and perquisites), besides sending ten pounds to his mother; which is a pretty good proof of his steady habits. As he went on his way, he was busy in forming plans for the future, for he was too wise even to think of rushing into matrimony, before he had the means of providing a comfortable home; he had seen too much misery ensue from such indiscretion. His master had promised him an advance of wages after Christmas, and he estimated that by the end of another year he would be worth seventy pounds, at least. Then he went into a calculation on the cost of a domestic outfit, and by the time he had arrived at his master's gate, he had arrived at the conclusion that he might reasonably hope to marry Phœbe in twelve or fifteen months. How to enter upon the love-making preliminaries was the next subject of his cogitation, which he had not decided before he was fast asleep on his little bachelor bed.

Soon after Jonathan left, Phœbe put on her hat, and skipped across the paddock to Betsy Brown's back gate, and in confidential whispers told her friend the particulars of Jonathan's visit, and all the encouraging things her father had said about him, after he had gone. She furthermore said that "she had made up her mind to take him," for better or worse, if he offered himself; for he was the nicest man she had ever seen, except poor Barney, who had broken his neck on the Homebush Racecourse five years before.

All the ensuing week, Phœbe Skimmer was constantly in Jonathan's thoughts, and no matter how or where he was engaged, her pretty image was ever before his eyes. Day and night he cudgelled his brain to devise some means for making known his love for her; and to get an acknowledgment from her that it was reciprocated. But he was an utter stranger to all conventional forms and phrases. He knew how he felt, but he lacked the power to explain his feelings. He could ride a kicking colt without a saddle, and could do many other things requiring nerve and energy to effect; but he could not even look at Phœbe Skimmer without feeling shaky. It was not fear, however, that made him shake; he was not a coward, but it was an unaccountable sensation which came over him, and which he was powerless to conquer or to control. Many bashful boys will understand his feelings without any further explanation.

One morning, as he was hilling up some young cauliflowers and chipping out the couch-grass between the rows, an idea struck him all at once, and he began to think it out. "Nation hard stuff to get out of the ground, is this couch-grass," thought Jonathan. "It's just like love; when it gets into a fellow's heart, it creeps all over him, with its thousand roots, and burned if he can get it out any how." Then he resolved upon using that familiar figure to convey the state of his mind to Phœbe. She knew what couch-grass was, he was sure, for he had seen lots of it choking the marigolds in her little front garden; and he thought she knew what love was too, so she would readily understand his parabolic addresses. He would go over to her house next Saturday, and trim her garden beds, and then tell her that his heart was overgrown with love, and was in danger of being stifled, like her marigolds, with couch-grass, if she did not promise to be its keeper for life. Pleased with the happy concoction, Jonathan composed a few sentences, embodying the idea in his own vernacular, and rehearsed them as he prosecuted his varied duties day after day, until he felt assured that he had learnt them off, and could say them to Phœbe, without a stammer.

Directly after dinner, on the following Saturday, he trimmed himself up extra smart, and putting (with his master's permission) a large bunch of turnip radishes and some prime young cucumbers into the gunny bag, off he set with hasty steps towards the dairyman's house. As he approached it, he saw his precious Phœbe, with a bucketful of frothing new milk, walking from the stock-yard to the dairy, and looking like a bright star in the "Milky Way."

"Good afternoon, Mr. Sprouts," was Phœbe's cheerful salute as he drew near, ruddy with health and the effect of his quick march across the swamps, with the bag on his back.

"Good afternoon, Miss Phœbe,—I bean't used to be called Mister, and it sounds queer loike. I do wish thee'd call me Jonathan, stead of Mister Sprouts."

"Do you? Very well, then, I'll call you Jonathan," said Phœbe, with a smile and a blush, " it's a very nice name."

Jonathan was just about to begin his prepared address, but checked himself by the recollection that it would be premature : he must trim up her garden-beds before she would see the full force of the grassy figure, with which he hoped to strike her into yielding tenderness, and ease his own breast at the same time. So, after presenting her with the contents of his sugee bag he offered—if she would furnish him with a hoe and a rake—to trim up her bit of garden, while she was gone into town with her milk. After a pleasant interchange of protests, against giving trouble, and taking trouble, Phœbe brought the hoe and rake, and Jonathan went to work with a will, among the marigolds, sunflowers, and other flowers, which were sadly overrun with weeds and couch-grass. Phœbe looked admiringly on for a minute or two, and then went into the dairy to prepare her milk for market ; which process I am not able to explain.

About five o'clock—nearly an hour earlier than usual—

Phœbe returned, with the old white horse covered with lather and bruises, and her brother Bob looking quite fatigued with his exertions. Jonathan had wrought a surprising change in her garden during her absence, and was still busy weeding, when she walked up the centre path, and expressed her satisfaction at his handiwork.

"Now's my time," thought Jonathan, who had been muttering his prepared address all the afternoon. "Now's the time to clinch the nail." "Phœbe, dos't thee see this couch-grass!" he asked, striking his rake vehemently into a heap of weeds just beside him; "dos't thee see this tough wiry stuff, lass?"

"Ye—yes—Jonathan," said Phœbe, rather puzzled at his sudden change of manner, "I see it," of course, she replied, gazing at him, inquiringly. "What is the matter with it?"

"Couch-grass, is—is a—wiry weed—my—stom—no—my breast is chock full of it—no, no, I don't mean that, burn it! It's nation ugly stuff: a—a—choke a pig—a—couch-grass—um—aw. Blained if I know what I was going to say at all. I'm dazed, sure enough!" stammered poor Jonathan, colouring to the tip of his ears, and shaking like a frost-bitten sailor: then added in an excited tone, "Dos't thee loike artichokes, lass?"

"I don't know," replied Phœbe, timidly, shrinking back a few paces, as the idea that her lover was drunk, filled her mind with disgust and surprise; for she had a natural horror of drunkards; and she had previously entertained the belief that Jonathan was a thoroughly sober man; so she replied, rather sharply, "that she did not know anything about artichokes;" then hurriedly withdrew to the house, and whispered her suspicions to her father, while her eyes filled with tears.

"Drunk, girl!" exclaimed Mr. Skimmer with warmth. "Pooh! nonsense! The lad is as sober as old Daisy in the shed yonder. Hasn't he been working away there all the afternoon, as if he were earning double wages, while I have been sitting beside him? Not a drop of anything stronger than skim milk has he tasted since he came here; that I'll warrant. Drunk indeed! what next will you fancy, girl?"

"Well then, I'm afraid he is crazy, father," said poor Phœbe, wiping her eyes with her little white apron.

"Bother you, girl! I shall believe you are downright mad directly," said Mr. Skimmer, pettishly. "The lad is hungry, that's what is the matter with him, I'll be bound; so go and get the supper ready, as soon as you can." Then, putting on his hat, he went into the garden, where Jonathan was busy giving the finishing rake to the flower-beds; and having in a measure recovered from the terrible perturbation which his bungling failure and the sudden flight of Phœbe had caused him, he looked tolerably collected.

"Well, mate, are you pretty nearly knocked up?" asked Mr. Skimmer, at the same time looking very closely at him.

"Not a bit, not a bit, measter. This ground is as easy to work as a sandy flat, only there be's a plaguey lot of weeds and couch-grass in it, and it wants a few barrowfuls of dung."

"Crankey, eh! humph! He's as sensible as a judge's clerk, every bit," muttered Mr. Skimmer to himself. Then, addressing Jonathan, he added, "Come inside, mate, and get a wash before supper. You've done a day's work in four or five hours, that you have. There, that'll do; heave your rake down, and come along; I smell eggs and bacon, and hot scons."

Without farther pressing, Jonathan put away his tools and scraped his boots, and in a few minutes more he was seated at the supper table, with his cleanly-washed face as rubicund as an earthenware flowerpot.

CHAPTER III.

HAD Jonathan been aware of the suspicion which Phœbe entertained to the prejudice of his sobriety, or his sanity, his embarrassment would doubtless have been overwhelming, and instead of appearing at the tea table, he would probably have run away home as fast as he could, and hidden his diminished head in his nightcap. Fortunately, however, he was spared that poignant addition to the self-reproach and confusion, which his late love-making had caused him; still he felt as ill at ease as a dandy who had just slipped down in the mud.

An incident, somewhat analogous, in the experience of an old friend of mine, just occurs to my mind. In his youthful days he had, one summer afternoon, engaged to take a young lady and her mamma for a sail in his smart little yacht; and being very anxious to make an impression on the tender heart of Miss Clara, a fascinating girl of seventeen, he dressed himself with extra taste in a blue blouse and white trowsers

—the *tout ensemble* of a yachtsman of those times. His boat was dancing at her moorings, with sails hoisted and flags gaily flying from both masts, and his crew of merry-faced black-fellows, in blue shirts and red caps, were singing " *Cree-an-dobbria.*" The ladies were waiting on the jetty close by, when my friend—who by the way was rather a retiring youth—walked up in happy consciousness that he was looking rather striking, and that he was exacting the admiration of the groups of spectators—young and old—who were waiting to ·see him get underway, with the fresh breeze which was then blowing. While gracefully lifting his straw hat with one hand, and extending the other to grasp the pretty little gloved fingers which were held out to greet him, he put his foot into an unlucky hole in the jetty, and down he fell flat at the feet of his charmer ; when almost simultaneously, his ears were assailed with the giggles of the grinning crowd, and the loud guffaws of his black crew. Of course he did not lie very long in that undignified position, but when he got up he discovered, to his inexpressible confusion, that he had damaged his apparel to such an extent, that common propriety at once prompted him to run away to the nearest cover, without stopping to look after his straw hat, which had rolled into the river, or to pick up the stray shillings which had rolled out of his waistcoat pocket.

Although twenty-four years have elapsed, my friend still has a vivid recollection of his miserable feelings on that occasion, and of his blushing trepidation, when he re-appeared shortly after he had changed his dress, and limped on his scraped leg towards the ladies to receive their sympathy, while their lips were visibly twitching with suppressed laughter. He never enjoyed a cruise in his boat less than he did that afternoon, although the weather was most favourable, and his fair passengers professed to enjoy themselves very much ; for he fancied that everything they said or did to provoke a smile, was but an excuse for venting their pent-up mirth at his luckless downfall ; and every outburst of merriment amongst his black crew, he regarded with a scowling suspicion that it was at his expense ; like a greedy miser listening to the drawing of corks in his kitchen.

Jonathan felt in a similarly comfortless condition, as he sat, solemnly looking at his plate, or picking up the stray crumbs on the table cloth, like a half-tamed robin ; and scarcely daring once to lift his eyes to Phœbe's face, lest he should see a scowl, or a contemptuous smile. He was not sorry when the meal was ended ; and when Mr. Skimmer asked him to smoke a pipe in the chimney corner, it was a relief as welcome to him, as the lowering of the prop-stick is to a jaded horse in a dray. His embarrassment, however, wore off after his pipe was fairly alight, and he was soon eloquently discoursing upon the comparative merits of English and Colonial systems of farming, and in so doing he displayed so much common sense and practical knowledge of the subject, that long before he left, Phœbe's misgivings had all vanished before the direct evidence of her senses, and Jonathan stood higher than ever in her estimation, while Mr. Skimmer had encouraged serious thoughts of proposing a partnership with him, and taking the adjoining farm to his own ; which was to be had on easy terms, because no tenant had yet been able to make a living off it. About ten o'clock Jonathan said good night and departed, after receiving a pressing invitation from his host to come and see them as often as he could, and after observing at the same time an unmistakable love token in Phœbe's eyes, which plainly meant "I shall be very happy to see you too."

Love lords it over all, and has done so from time immemorial. From the prince to the peasant, from the lofty duchess to the tinker's pretty daughter Polly ; few hearts are untouched by the torch of the ambrosial though inexorable little ruler : few are so crabbed and crusty in their nature as utterly to scare him from their breasts, lest their icy hearts should extinguish his torch and spoil his trade. An old song says : " 'Tis love that makes the world go round." Whether or not the little urchin has that mighty influence, it is certain there would soon be numberless empty houses in the world, if love were less active. But without stopping to analyse that sentiment or any other sentiment contained in the thousand of songs, old and new, on the same touching subject, I may record that love held full sway in Jonathan's heart, and influenced all his thoughts and deeds, whether he was bundling up greens, radishes, and rhubarb, for market, or digging, dunging, raking, or hoeing in the garden ; whether he was greasing his cart wheels, grooming his horse, or oiling his harness, driving to town with a load, or driving home again without a load in his cart, he had always a load of love in his breast, heavier than a bushel of broad beans. Phœbe Skimmer's image was in his eye and in his heart too ; and it would take a waggon load of artists' material and brushes, to paint all the bright pictures which his fancy conjured up, of home and happiness, with groups of little darling appurtenances in the back ground. The magpies, which perched on the swamp oaks at the back of his house, and awoke him at morning dawn with their wild music, whistled Phœbe Skimmer, Phœbe Skimmer ! as plainly as magpies could articulate : the curlews, which sometimes flew high over his dwelling at midnight, when a gale was brewing in the eastern sky, screeched Phœbe Skimmer, Phœbe Skimmer ! The frogs on the flats that skirted her home, croaked the same sweet name, as musically as hurdy-gurdies ; and even the sharp nosed mosquitos, which hovered about his ears just as he was dozing off to sleep, seemed to chant Phœbe, pretty Phœbe !

"Phœbe must be moine," quoth Jonathan, in a positive mood one evening, just as the six o'clock bell began to ring ; at the same time he flung down his spade, and walked towards the house to partake of his solitary meal. "Phœbe must be moine, or my heart wull pretty soon split open loike a ripe apricot ; barn'd if it woarnt. A notion has wriggled into my head whilst I a been diggin up them kidney tatees ; and dash my buttons if I doant think it wull just settle the thing roight off, without any more bother. At all events, there bean't no harm in trying, as the Lancashire chap said when he took a job at mowing beans, and cut his toe big off the first stroke."

Lest I should make my story tedious, I will not detail Jonathan's cogitations in his own provincial dialect, but briefly explain that the plan which he had been pondering in his little spherical skull, was in the first place to ask Phœbe to accompany him on an excursion the following Friday—which was a general holiday—to " Kissing Point." He had never been there, but had heard that it was a romantic place ; indeed, there was something in its very name which suggested enjoyment, such as he sighed for ; and he hoped that when there, he might be inspired with courting ideas, and also with courage to declare them like a man, and thus end his suspense, and set his love-laden heart at ease. After a hasty supper he put off his hobnailed boots, put on his best kangaroo bluchers, and away he went in the cool of the evening towards Syllabub Swamp, which, by-the-bye, was the name of Mr. Skimmer's location.

He met with the usual cordial reception from the dairy-man and his daughter; to the latter he presented a pocket-full of Jerusalem artichokes, and directed her how to cook them. While smoking a pipe in the kitchen half-an-hour afterwards, he asked Mr. Skimmer to allow Phœbe to accompany him on the ensuing Friday for a little bit of a jaunt in the country, as he hadn't had a holiday since the day he first landed in Sydney. Mr. Skimmer offered no objection, and Phœbe was most willing, provided her father would manage her milk properly, and serve her afternoon customers, which he cheerfully promised to do; so the matter was soon settled, and after a little more friendly gossip, Jonathan returned home highly pleased that his happy plan had so far succeeded.

On Friday morning he was up before the magpies began to sing; and after attending to his horse's wants for the day, and sundry other indispensable duties, he began to dress himself with extraordinary care; and when he had completed his toilet, he looked thoroughly satisfied with himself. His worsted cord trousers were faultlessly clean; his red plush vest was as bright as a king parrot's plumage; his velveteen jacket was as sleek as his horse Billy's black coat; and when he stuck his bran new cabbage-tree hat on the back of his head, so as not to hide his honest face, he looked a likely lad to smite the heart of any milk-maid in the world. After breakfast he took another look at himself in the glass, combed his hair down smooth and straight, stuck a flower in his button-hole, then put on his hat again, a trifle inclined to the left side, and off he set for Syllabub Swamp, with a quick step and a hopeful heart.

Phœbe had returned from the early morning calls on her friends in town, and was busy at her toilet, with flushed face and fluttering heart, when Jonathan arrived at her house. Very soon she emerged from her chamber, in her best attire, and shily welcomed her admiring swain, who remarked that it was "a foine morning;" at the same time he mentally remarked, that "she was the finest maid he had ever ventured to look at; as much superior to Dolly Daysel, as a spring cauliflower is to a common curly cabbage."

After giving some final directions to her father, her brother Bob, and to the maid in the kitchen, Phœbe opened her sky-blue parasol and said she was quite ready. Away they went side by side, like Darby and Joan, and half-an-hour afterwards they were on board a smart little steamer, which was fast paddling up the Parramatta River.

"Be's this Kissing Point, Phœbe?" asked Jonathan, when the steamer had moored alongside a jetty, about seven miles from Sydney.

"No, Jonathan," said Phœbe, "this is Bedlam Point. The next one is Kissing Point; a famous place for fruit."

"I'll trouble you for your fare, if you please," said a tall, good-looking man, just then stopping before Jonathan, with a blue ticket-book in his hand. "Are you going to Ryde?"

"Noa, I be going for a walk, as soon as I get ashore at Kissing Point, captain, thank'ee all the same."

A comical smile played about the mouth of the merry looking captain, as he handed a couple of tickets, and at the same time explained to Jonathan that Kissing Point is now generally called Ryde, being a more fashionable name.

"I loike the owld name better than the new 'un, captain, a moighty deal; and I believe the old 'un is more fashionable, after all. I'd a rayther walk to Kissing Point any day, than ride on a thorough-bred racer, to any other point you could tell of," said Jonathan, with a laugh and a shy glance at Phœbe, to see if she understood the point of his joke.

In ten minutes more they had landed at Ryde, in company with a number of genteel residents of the place. After clearing the fruit-boxes and firewood on the jetty, the courting couple walked slowly towards the charming little village on the hill. As they went along, with all their senses active, the warm bright sun shining upon such varied loveliness, had a remarkably mellowing effect on Phœbe's feelings, such as she had never before experienced. Her heart got as soft as a boiled turnip with loving sentiment; her eyes were swimming in tender emotion, and she occasionally glanced at the beaming face of her doting lover beside her, with Kissing Point on her pretty pouting lips.

"Well, well, dash my wig! this is a nation noice place sure enough!" said Jonathan in a transport of admiration, as he suddenly stood still in the middle of a green paddock, and gazed at the rare blending beauties of hill and dale, and meandering stream around him, and sniffed in the salubrious air, rich with scents of orange blossom and sweet brier. "Blaimed if this bea'n't the prettiest place I've seen since I left Devon, an' no mistake! It minds me of the bank of the river Dart, a few miles below Totness, just avore ye come to Dittisham, where the plums grow in galores. Dost thee loike ripe plums, Phœbe?"

Jonathan's tongue was now fairly loosened, and he was waxing warm while he was keeping as cool and collected as a fireman. He knew what he was talking about this time, and was careful not to make another blunder, and thus risk all his hopes; so when Phœbe said she did like ripe plums very much, he said her lips were like plums, and he liked them uncommon; and was just about to say something else equally poetical, when his eloquence was interrupted by Phœbe's calling his attention to the eccentric behaviour of a cow, with a young calf by her side, a short distance from them.

"Drat the beast, what does her mean?" quoth Jonathan, as the cow elevated her tail, and began to bellow in a very ominous manner. "Stand still, Phœbe, and poke the parasol at 'un, whoile I run an' cut a stick; I'll soon settle the cranky owld creetur," saying which he ran towards a tree, about a hundred yards distant, to cut a cudgel, but had scarcely got half-way there, when he heard a shrill cry, and on turning round he beheld Phœbe lying on the ground, and her hat and parasol blowing before the breeze, in the direction of a water-hole, while the cow was making towards him full speed, with head down and tail straight up, like a millet broom.

"Whoa! drat 'ee, what be thee about, nasty toad!" shouted Jonathan, with uplifted hands, trying to strike respect into the cow by waving his cabbage-tree hat, but she paid not the slightest heed to his hat; onward she rushed with fury streaming out of her nostrils, and her glaring eyes looking like railway lanterns denoting danger. When he saw it was hopeless to try to stop her, either with arguments or antics, he promptly decided that it was the wisest plan to run for his life; so he turned and ran very fast, but not quite so fast as the cow, for she overtook him before he got to cover, and tossed him up, ten feet at least, in a direct course towards the noonday sun. After turning a summersault and a half, down he came again head foremost, into a sweet brier bush, and there he stuck as fast as if he had grown up with the bush itself, and all that could be seen of him were his kangaroo boots, his pepper and salt socks, portions of well-developed muscles of his legs, and the bottom hem of his worsted corduroys ; but that he was not dead was soon evidenced by his loud shouts to Phœbe, " to stand clear of that spiteful owld varmin, or she wud toss her into the hedge too."

Phœbe soon picked herself up, then picked up her appurtenances and re-arranged her straggling tresses. She was not at all injured, for the steel bars of her skirt rendered her as invulnerable to cow's horns, as iron-clad frigates are to the attacks of sword-fish. Moreover knock-down butts, or ill-tempered kicks from cows, were regarded by her as professional incidentals, so she was not much terrified by her sudden upset. She had seen Jonathan turning heels over head in the air, and had seen him rapidly descend into the hedge ; but as she had not seen him make a struggle to get out of the hedge again, her anxiety for him was quite natural. It was very brief, though, for his loud words of warning assured her in a moment that his neck was not broken, and that no other vital organ was seriously injured, so she joyfully hastened to his assistance.

<h3 style="text-align:center">CHAPTER IV.</h3>

PHŒBE, though a courageous girl, was not fool-hardy ; so, instead of rushing straight towards her disabled lover, and thus incurring the risk of again being tossed by the surly cow, she trotted across the paddock, crept through a fence, and arrived in a short time at the back of the bush, where Jonathan was stuck fast, with his head where his heels should be. Her proximity was known to him immediately ; for he could see her plainly enough, although she could see no more of him than I have described in the preceding chapter.

" Jonathan, I hope you are not hurt," said Phœbe, in her softest tones of commiseration. " Can't you get out ?"

" Noa, Phœbe, I can't move half an inch, if I try ; these prickly thorns push me amazing sharp. I bean't hurt much, but I be stuck in here as toight as if I wor rammed in with a pile driver. I must be cut out, loike a buzzy in a horse's tail. You can't get me out any other way as I can see ; for if you pull me up by the legs, I shall be scratched all to rags and tatters."

" I'll run and get some help," said Phœbe decisively, " I won't be long away. Poor fellow ! keep your spirits up."

" Stop ; don't ee run away from me, Phœbe," cried Jonathan, " sit thee down beside the hedge, I want to say summat to thee very particular ; and I can say it best now thee can't see my face. Phœbe, I tell thee what it is, I love thee loike a man, an' no mistake about it. If thee wull have me for a husband one of these days, I'll do all that a true heart and honest hands can do to make thee happy, and to keep a good whoam for thee. Say the word, will thee have me, Phœbe ? Dos't thee love me ? Now's the time to own it ; don't ee be ashamed. Speak up, lass ! One word from thee will make me as proud as the governor, though I be standing on my head in a brier bush."

" Oh, Jonathan ! I can't say anything about it just now ; I feel so flurried and tusselled. Don't ask me now, there's a good man," said Phœbe, looking as confused as if the cow was coming again full gallop.

" Then doan't ee try to get me out of this hedge, lass. I doan't want to coom out if thee won't have me. Just go straight whoam, like a good girl, and let the magpies eat me. Give me love to thee feyther and brother Bob. Send my money that's in the Savings' Bank home to my mother, and thee may have all my traps, lass. Don't forget to tell measter that Billy's off hind shoe be's loose ; and that Mr. Nackrum, the omnibus owner, owes for the last load of green barley."

" Oh, Jonathan !" said Phœbe, softening to tears, " how can you talk so strangely. Let me help you out ; I'll soon cut away these sticks. Do for my sake come out of the hedge, there's a dear man ! Don't stand there on your head any longer ; it will curdle your brain like sour milk, and turn your heart upside down."

" Wull thee have me then, Phœbe ?" asked Jonathan, in a more lively tone, " say the word, lass ; yea or nay ; out with it honestly."

" Ye—yes, I will, Jonathan," said Phœbe, tremulously. " I will have you for ever ; for I love you dearly. If father doesn't say nay, I will be your wife by-and-by, and love you as long as I live."

" Bravo, Phœbe ! I'll kiss thee as soon as I get out of this trap. Go to work, lass, and cut away some of this outside wood ; but mind thee doesn't prick thee fingers. Here's my pruning knife close beside my nose, it tumbled out of my pocket ; hook en' out with summat. Thee be'ist a brave girl sure enough ! Codlins ! how I love thee !"

Phœbe hooked out Jonathan's knife from the bush, with the handle of her parasol, and went to work like a skilled hedger, while he plied her with compliments and promises of future payment. In a short time she had cut a great gap in the hedge; then taking hold of her lover's boots, she gently lowered him to the ground, when he wriggled himself out safe and sound except a few scratches on his hands and face, a thorn in his nose, and some trifling damage to his hat.

"Phœbe, thee beest the prettiest maid I ever see'd," said Jonathan, warmly, as soon as he had straightened himself up, "I love thee better than I love my life. Bless thee, lass, give us a buss! Never mind if them folks yonder be looking, it's real honest courting with us; give us a hearty smacker, to bind the bargain, and show that thee bee'st in earnest. Lor love ee lass! thee'st made my heart as light as a yeast dumpling."

Phœbe might have borrowed the language of Shakespere's King Henry the Eighth, and said :—

> "Sweetheart:
> I were unmannerly to take you out,
> And not to kiss you."

But though she did not use such courtly words, her actions were in effect warmly expressive of the sentiment; for she heartily kissed Jonathan, or what amounts to almost the same thing, she allowed him to salute her plummy lips, with a smack like a small stock-whip, without even saying "don't."

Having thus extracted the thorn from his heart, she next volunteered to extract the brier from his nose, with the pin of her gold brooch; and after she had done that cleverly, Jonathan kissed her again for her services; then she dusted his jacket, and straightened his hat, and away they walked towards the hills of Ryde, talking as they went of their future plans and prospects, and looking as happy as the little birds which filled the air with harmony.

It would be tedious to follow them and try to depict their joys; suffice to say it was a delightful day to them, notwithstanding their ups and downs. They rambled about, arm in arm, and talked freely of their future home and happiness, while their hearts were as glad as honest love could make them.

"I tell thee what it is, lass, I'll vind out who owns that cow what tossed me head over heels, and I'll buy 'en. Her is a real likely-looking beast, and got some mettle in her too ; if it hadn't been for her heaving me into the hedge, I'm reared I shouldn't have had the face to tell thee I loved thee to-day ; I was so mortal shy and timid like. What a great gorby I be to be sure, to have been sighing and grizzling so long, and scared to look at such a pretty face as thee has got, Phœbe. Why, making love is as easy as sticking peas, when a man means what he says ; he needn't be ashamed to speak out plump and plain, in his own simple way, when he means to do what is right and straightforward. That's my notion, lass. Those great, lazy, chuckle-headed schemers, who whisper soft lies into the ears of silly maids, on purpose to lead them astray ; those are the fellows who ought to be ashamed of themselves. Egad ! shouldn't I like to leather them all with my horsewhip, or pelt them with swede turnips !"

The blithesome pair returned to Sydney by the afternoon steamer, and at the usual time for tea they were sitting at the table in Syllabub Cottage. Any observer might have seen a marked alteration in Jonathan's looks and demeanour, and Phœbe looked as pleased as if somebody had given her a new bonnet. After tea, as he and Mr. Skimmer smoked their pipes together, Jonathan briefly explained the state of his feelings, and received a cordial recognition from the good-natured milkman, who at the same time looked sadly serious.

"It isn't every young man that I would approve of for my daughter, I can tell you," said Mr. Skimmer, emphasizing his words with his pipe-stem. "I have seen some parents who have thought less about parting with a daughter than they would about selling a favourite horse, or a prime milking cow ; and that's why we so often see miserable homes. Such parents are shamefully neglectful of their duties ; there is no mistake about that. I have been studying your character for some time past, Master Jonathan ; for you know I had a notion what you were coming here so often for, with your water-melons and artichokes. I've had my day at that sort of fun—Ha, ha, ha ! I have satisfied myself that you are a healthy, God-fearing, sober young fellow, and no nonsense about you ; such as you are sure to make headway in the world, and not shame me. If you had not all those good qualities, I would not let you have Phœbe, if you owned a row of houses in the best part of Sydney, for

I should be certain you would not care for your wife and
home very long. Unprincipled men never do. They take
a sudden fancy to a girl (they may usually find some one
soft enough to be caught by their blarney, worse luck), and
a few months after marriage they neglect them for the
billiard table and the bottle, or even worse things still. My
poor old heart aches when I think of the many neglected
young wives that I know, who are at this very time pining
their lives out in poverty and drudgery; while their lazy,
sottish husbands are wasting their time and means without
caring a flip for their wives and children. Excuse me for
getting rather warm; but I can't help giving a little bit of
my mind on that subject. You say you love my girl,
and I believe you, for I have always found you truthful and
straightforward. I know she loves you too, so take her, my
lad, and may God bless you both. Here Phœbe, shake
hands over the bargain."

Phœbe timidly entered from the adjoining room, and tenderly kissed her father. "There she is," said Mr. Skimmer,
with emotion, "and though she is my girl, I will say that
you would not match her every day in the year. Her poor
mother, who is now in Heaven, trained her from childhood
in the right way; that is saying a good deal; and she has
turned out a credit to her teacher. Treat her well, and she
will prove the best friend you ever met in the world."

Jonathan seized her hand, and pressed it warmly, and as
her loving eyes met his, he drew her to his heart, and kissed
her again. How could he help it?

It is not necessary to describe the smooth course of their
courtship for the next few months, or to notice the numerous preparations made by Phœbe and Betsy Brown for the
coming event, so important in the history of Phœbe, and
which most young girls look forward to with peculiar heart
fluttering. Neither is it expedient to record all the preparations which Jonathan made to set himself off to the
best advantage: his injunction to Mr. List, the tailor, about
the cut and quality of his wedding suit; or his cautions to
Mr. Welt, the bootmaker, about the shape of his wedding
cossacks; those are minor matters, still they were all carefully studied. Their household furniture, too, was selected
with taste and judgment; everything was good, serviceable,
and consistent with their means and their station in life;
and when their little cottage was ready for them, it con-

tained everything that was necessary for comfort and convenience, and was quite free from gaudy trumpery—made for show and not for use—which is often seen in cottage homes, to mock the bad taste of the owners, and their extravagance, too, in lavishing money for what is wholly unserviceable, or, at all events, for what they could easily do without.

The long anticipated wedding day at length arrived, and a bright sunshiny day it was. The bride and bridegroom, with brother Bob and Mr. Skimmer, rode to church in the yellow cart (without the milk cans), while Betsy Brown and her sweetheart, Sandy White, with three young lasses and three young lads, dressed in their best, and decorated with nosegays, followed in a furniture van belonging to Sandy. A casual observer might have fancied from their gladsome looks that they were all going to be married that morning except Bob and his father, who were evidently feeling rather sad at parting with Phœbe. When the solemn ceremony was over, they all returned to Syllabub cottage, where a luxurious luncheon awaited them. On the centre of the table, in the midst of some choice bouquets, some one had waggishly placed a miniature sweetbrier bush, the sight of which so excited Jonathan, that as soon as the guests had laid down their knives and forks, he told them all about his courtship at Kissing Point, and his being tossed up " head or woman" like a pieman's penny, and how he made his love declaration to Phœbe, while standing on his head with a thorn sticking in his nose, at which they all laughed long and heartily ; and none more so than Phœbe herself.

" Now just listen to me a minute or two, friends," said Jonathan, as soon as he could control his risibility, " and I'll give ye a little bit of advice for nothing. If either of ye lads loves a young woman, dontee go moping and sighing for months, as I did, aveared to speak up ; or somebody else might pop in and take her from thee, and serve thee right too. But first of all vind out whether her be's a fit wife for ye ; doantie judge by her pretty face merely, but just notice if her be's clean and tidy about her house, as well as about her person ; if her knows how to cook a poor man's dinner, and how to wash and mend his clothes. Ye'll soon vind that out, if ye keep your eyes open ; and ye may tell, too, by the way her treats her parents, and brothers, and sisters, if her be's a good-tempered, sound-principled girl.

If her be's all that, and thee has the favour of feyther and mother, pluck up courage and pop the question at once. Speak out like a man. 'Lass, I love thee,' that's enough, if thee can't say any more ; her will understand thee, I'll engage ; and if her doesn't answer thee all at once—which it is not reasonable to expect—thee will know what her means, by the look of her eyes. Of course I don't advise ye to get married right off ; I know ye have too much good sense, lads, to think of doing that, until you have a comfortable home in prospect ; take my word for it, that sort of love which is in such a hurry, is too hot to last long. Get a good home before thee get yer wife ; but doantee go and spend all yer money in filling yer house with jimcracks that you doant want ; because a little ready money may be handy for extras by and by. Then I advise each one of ye to do as I did last week. Insure your life, so that if ye should die, your wife would not be left destitute. Some pumpkin-headed sawneys choose a wife with as little study and forethought as they would buy a ready-made monkey-jacket. The fit beant of much consequence say they : but they soon find out their mistake, and if they are misfitted with a wife, they are as plaguey uneasy all their days, as a carthorse in chafing harness. Look well, my lads, before you leap into matrimony ; in justice to yourselves, as well as in justice to the lasses of your choice : and if ye all vind such a jewel of a wife as I've got, ye'll be nation lucky fellows : that's all I've got to say." Jonathan then sat down, amid the loud applause and congratulations of the company.

*　　*　　*　　*　　*　　*

Jonathan had taken the neglected farm adjoining Mr. Skimmer's ; and, by dint of hard labour and skill, turned it into a profitable market garden. His home was the abode of health and happiness ; of smiles, and kind words ; not a note of discord was ever heard within its walls. "He and his house served the Lord," humbly and faithfully, and they abode in peace. Twelve months after their marriage, they were blessed with a little daughter, to complete their joys ; and in the overflow of his heart, Jonathan wished to name it Sweet-brier. Phœbe, however, objected to the " brier" in her baby, but by way of compromise, called the little darling Eglantine, and their homestead Sweetbrier Lodge ; in happy remembrance of " Kissing Point."

In a few years Mr. Skimmer died, when Jonathan let his

market garden and took to the dairy, because Bob had turned out wild. Jonathan now owns some of the smartest carts and brightest cans that are to be seen in Sydney, and is a prosperous man ; but he is troubled in mind because his trade necessitates Sunday labour the same as on other days. If his customers would but consent to take their Sunday's supply of milk in the early morning, it would enable him and his servants to attend Divine service, and give his poor horses rest. Phœbe has tried to cheer him up by pointing out how the plan could easily be adopted, for she says, in winter their milk will keep good for more than a day, and in summer time, by scalding what is to be kept till afternoon, it will keep quite sweet and good. She is sure when that is carefully explained, none of their customers will refuse to dispense with their afternoon milk, if they are respectfully solicited.

Jonathan intends to follow his good wife's suggestion, to go hat in hand to his customers, and ask them to grant that great boon, " *a day of rest*," to himself, his servants, and his horses. Reader, if he comes to you, don't refuse him !

SHRUGS.

"Of course you know Mr. Abel Goodenough!" said a merchant in this city, to a trader who had just come from the country to purchase goods.

"I suppose you mean Goodenough the storekeeper, of Midgyborough!"

"Exactly. What sort of man is he?"

"He is a little man with a big nose, a bald head, and a—"

"Yes, yes, I know all about his physical peculiarities; but is he a safe man? or in commercial phraseology, is he a good mark?"

An expressive shrug was the only reply to the questions. "Ah, I see: you would advise me not to trust him. I am much obliged to you for the hint."

"It is not safe to express opinions about one's neighbours; besides, I make it a matter of conscience never to do it," said the countryman, with another grimace more portentous than the last. "Goodenough, you know, is my strongest competitor in the district, and that is a special reason why I decline to say anything about him, for he might hear of it again."

"I understand you. It is well to be cautious," said the merchant. "The fact is, he has written to ask for a renewal of a bill, due on the 4th. Now I know what to say to him."

*　　　*　　　*　　　*　　　*　　　*

A fortnight afterwards, Mr. Goodenough was in the Insolvent Court, and his sinister neighbour was enabled to secure some rare bargains at his clearing-out sale, while he chuckled over his successful *ruse* to get rid of a hated rival in trade. Thus an honest, plodding man was victimised, without knowing who had been the treacherous instrument of his ruin. Two shrugs and a wink had broken up his business, and made his family homeless, for a time.

To record all the mischief and misery that I have known to be caused by such silent scandal—to tell of young maidens stigmatised, of wives made desolate, and husbands driven mad through causeless jealousy, would make a big book, and such a one as I have no desire to make. I notice the foregoing solitary specimen of commercial shruggery, to denounce such contemptible expedients which are especially dangerous in seasons of embarrassment and misgivings.

It will not be thought very remarkable, that in my occasional rambles through the city of late, I have met with many gloomy faces, and have listened to some saddening recitals of real hardship. Passing by certain defaulters (the bare sight of whom makes me cross, and whose deservings cannot be mentioned in *civil* terms), I have had to sympathise with some industrious, honest men, who from sheer misfortune have lost the results of the toil and economy of years. Perhaps harder still, is the helplessness of their employés, who have been suddenly thrown out of work. Scores—or I may safely say hundreds of persons are thus circumstanced, through the mercantile disasters which have lately occurred, and they are now suffering, in many cases, far more severely than their late masters are doing. The failure of a business house, either in town or country, is productive of more misfortune than a mere surface glance will reveal. The more extensive the business ramifications, the wider spread is the mischief, and there are few persons in our community who are not either directly or indirectly affected, to a greater or lesser extent. The downfall of Simon Squash and other great shams have caused me no regret, for their sakes; on the contrary, I am glad to see the reckless career of such men brought to a close ; but it is a real sorrow for me to know that their clerks and porters are thrown out of work, at a time when steady employment is very difficult to obtain. These contingencies are not so often calculated as they should be, but a very little reflection will show their reaction upon a community ; hence self-interest—to say nothing of moral principle—binds every man to use all honourable exertions to counteract the present mistrust, much of which is as groundless as the alarm which is raised by the false cry of "powder !" at a fire.

"But what can I do to quell this popular excitement !" asked a talkative person, to whom I expressed that opinion, a few days ago.

"Though it be merely a negative duty," I replied, "you can keep your tongue quiet. You can avoid raising or propagating mischievous rumours, such as those I have just

heard from you, that certain persons—whom you named—
are ‘shaky.’ ”

“ Well, I only told you what I heard : I know nothing
about their affairs myself.”

“ It would be more prudent to be silent upon such matters,
at any rate,” I answered, “ but it is positively wrong to repeat statements that you do not know to be authentic. If
those persons are really ‘ shaky,’ as you say, prejudicial
reports are likely to make them shake more, and perhaps
to topple them down altogether, and involve others in loss
or embarrassment. The wealthiest firm in the world may
be brought to a stand, if public rumour assails its reputation : in fact it would only have been necessary for a few
persons to shrug at a Bank of England note, some months
ago, to have caused ‘ a run ’ upon that institution ; and had
the Londoners began to run in that direction, urged on by
that powerful stimulus, the dread of losing their money, it
would have taken a good many knowing ones to have
stopped them, and world-wide mischief would have resulted.”

I was in the midst of at least a thousand dupes, on Black-
friars Bridge, one moonlight night many years ago. We
were all intently gazing at the muddy water below, not one
of us knowing what we were looking for. The most absurd
speculations passed from one to another, though nothing
tangible could be seen but the dark river, dotted with coal
barges and dredging machines. I remember I caught cold,
and had my pockets picked ; and I dare say many pockets
were picked besides mine. In a day or two it transpired,
that some practical joker had made a large wager, that he
would collect a crowd on three of the bridges of London
within a given time ; and he won triumphantly. The
scheme he adopted was wonderfully simple, so were the
people who were attracted by it. Stationing himself on a
conspicuous part of the bridge, and looking over the parapet,
he exclaimed in a loud key, “ Hallo ! there it is !” at the
same time pointing to the river. After a minute’s pause, he
shouted with increased gesticulation, “ Look, look ! There
it is again !” The passengers stopped to gaze and wonder,
and a crowd soon gathered, each one eagerly inquiring · of
his neighbour “ what was to be seen,” while all sorts of
rare objects were suggested, from mudlarks to mermaids.
In the meantime the joker slipped away, got into a cab, and
drove to another bridge, to repeat the trick. He succeeded

in attracting three immense crowds within the specified
time—a few hours—thus strikingly exemplifying the old
adage, that "One fool makes many."

Not much wiser than those gaping crowds, were some of
the inhabitants of a certain suburb, who were recently deluded into the belief that one of our local banks was going
to break. The rumour—I am told—was raised by certain
panic-mongers, who hoped to make a little money by buying
up the notes at a discount, regardless of the wide-spread
mischief that might ensue. The growing uneasiness was,
however, quickly allayed, by a tradesman of influence in the
neighbourhood offering to give twenty shillings for every
pound note of the said bank ; for which timely exhibition
of sound sense, and good feeling, he deserves a general vote
of thanks.

A few days ago a nervous gentleman brought me some
startling reports about another banking establishment in this
city. After he had calmed down a little, I ascertained that
his fears had been aroused by overhearing the defamatory
conversation of two persons in an omnibus, one of whom
was drunk.

" Now tell me candidly, Mr. Boomerang, if you had £500
in that bank, what should you do ?" asked my fidgetty friend,
his eyes looking like bad shillings, for want of sleep.

" I should be very glad," I replied.

" But seriously ; in the present unsettled state of affairs,
would you not be anxious to draw it out ?"

" If I had no stronger reason for doing so than you have,
I should certainly not touch it. It is possible that those
persons in the omnibus knew that you have money in that
bank, and they were trying to alarm you, either from love
of mischief or from more selfish motives. My advice to you
is to let your money remain where it is, and avoid expressing anxiety about it, or making suspicious inquiries respecting
the condition of the said bank, or you will soon gather an
excited crowd around you, like the joker on London Bridge.
I have good cause for believing that your bank is perfectly
safe ; in fact I believe that all the banks in Sydney are quite
safe, unless, indeed, everybody should make a sudden rush
at them, as you were inclined to do just now ; which would
indicate a total want of confidence ; and without confidence
all the relations of the civilized world would be paralyzed,
commercial enterprise would be at an end, and general dis-

tress would ensue.   I have no direct interest in any bank, or mercantile firm in the land," I added, "so you may believe that the opinion I have expressed is free from personal bias, whatever else may be said of it."

* * * * * *

It is a pitiable fact, that unprincipled persons are very busy just now, trying to make bad times worse, to serve their own selfish or vindictive purposes: and it behoves right thinking men to use their influence to frustrate the base designs of such persons, and thereby prevent much suffering. Shrugs and winks are commonly used, because they are safer than libellous words, and quite as effective in such times as these.   It is a small consideration to those incendiaries that the downfall of each mercantile house entails loss upon many persons besides the direct creditors, and it would be as vain to appeal to their sense of right, as to try to touch their feelings by pathetic descriptions of the domestic wretchedness which they are creating.

I have been drawn to this subject by my interest in the public weal; and I would warn all my readers against being influenced by shrugs; and also to beware lest they catch the hateful infection, which is as contagious as cholera morbus.

"JOY COMETH IN THE MORNING."

THERE are doubtless many persons in Sydney at the present time who can recal the rage for land jobbing which prevailed about twenty-five years ago ; and many, too, will sorrowfully remember the disastrous reaction which soon followed that unhealthy desire for speculation.   The land mania was not confined to Australia, but extended to neighbouring places, especially to New Zealand, which had not then been formally proclaimed a British colony, and was only partially known to Europeans.   About that time, however, a current of emigration set that way.   Many persons went there from Sydney, in the hope of making good bargains in land from the natives, before the British Government took possession of the islands, and put a stop to the one-sided traffic, while others went with a view of being foremost in the field of enterprise which a new country always offers.   Numbers of young men went in the expectation of being employed as surveyors, or getting appointments, of some kind, under the new Government which was to be shortly established there. The majority, however, were sadly disappointed in their projects ; and if the disclosure would be beneficial in any way, I might adduce some lamentable example of ruin.

It would be difficult for me to offer a satisfactory explanation why I gave up a lucrative position to pursue an indefinite object.   I had heard exciting stories of lucky men buying as much land as they could see from the top of a kauri pine tree for a few muskets, or a keg of tobacco ; and I thought I should like to buy a nice little estate of half a million acres or so, upon some such easy terms.   Perhaps, seeing so many others going to Maori-land, stimulated me to hasten away too, lest I should be too late for the prizes, which the Maori chiefs were distributing so lavishly.   It is certain that many older and more experienced men than myself could give no better reason for going to New Zealand at that time than that they saw many of their neighbours going ; and it is not the only time that I have seen multitudes of men following each other to misery, led away by the force of example.

In the year 1840, I took my passage in a bark of three hundred and fifty tons, for the Bay of Islands, New Zealand. I shared the port stern cabin with a friend, named Archy Weedle, an astute gentleman, much older than myself, with whom I had planned that my future fortunes should in some measure be united. In the hold of the ship were sundry packages of merchandise, our joint property; and in the cabin were several hundred pounds in gold and silver coin, which chiefly belonged to my friend. In those days the rates of insurance to New Zealand were very high, so we sailed from Sydney without effecting an insurance on our shipment.

The first part of the voyage passed pleasantly enough: the captain was an intelligent and sociable young man; our fellow passengers were very agreeable, and our little party at the table was as united as a home circle. On the twelfth day out, we rounded the North cape of New Zealand, and that same night it began to blow hard from the north-east, with thick weather. Sail was reduced from time to time, as the wind increased; but it was necessary to keep a press of canvas on the ship, in order to claw off the shore, which was dead to leeward. The anxiety and discomfort on board the ship that night can only be comprehended by those who have been in similar exciting straits. The vessel plunged, and strained, and half buried herself in the waves, which rose higher and higher, as the wind increased to a strong gale. I was too anxious to sleep, and as I preferred the deck to the close cabin, and the companionship of my sea sick friend, I took my place beneath a tarpaulin in the mizen rigging; and there, throughout the night, I watched the struggles of the weatherly little bark, and also watched the faces of the captain and chief mate, which plainly indicated that their hearts were far from being merry, though they strove, with becoming manliness, to hide their anxiety from their passengers. Still I could tell by their frequent glances at the binnacle, their low-toned conferences, and their endeavours to gaze through the murky darkness to leeward, that they were conscious of danger. Neither the captain nor his officers had been to New Zealand before, and their charts could give them but little reliable information about the coast, which, up to that time, had not been properly surveyed. They were ignorant, too, of the currents, and could only guess the extent of our offing, which was less than five miles.

Some of my readers can perhaps recall to memory a dismal night at sea, when the wind howled through the rigging of their tempest-tossed ship; when wave after wave has rolled on to the deck overhead, and the thunder's roaring has been heard above the noise of the flapping sails. They can recollect how eagerly they scanned the features of their trusty captain, as he entered the well-lighted saloon from the deck, with his oilskin over-clothing dripping with rain and ocean spray; and how much their troubled hearts were re-assured by the composure of his weather-beaten face, or comforted by a few cheerful words from his manly voice, telling them that " he had made all snug for the night," or that " he hoped to see a favourable change soon." And with what pleasure did they see him seat himself at the table, and smile as placidly as if he had just been enjoying a moonlight scene, with a tropical breeze kissing the sparkling wavelets, instead of having been close reefing topsails and setting storm-staysails, exposed all the time to the dangerous forked lightning, and fierce driving rain. Persons who have such recollections can understand why I so often gazed into the faces of the captain and chief mate throughout that anxious season of peril. Who can over-estimate the value of a cheerful look or a hopeful word in such depressing times !

The next day the gale continued with unabated violence, and the sea-sickness of my friend, Weedle, was painful to witness. He had not left his cabin since the commencement of the bad weather, nor could he be prevailed upon to go on deck, even for a minute. He seemed to have given up all hope of our ship weathering the storm; and every time a sea broke on board he thought we were among the breakers. I tried to comfort him, for being quite free from that nauseating malady, sea-sickness, and being full of youthful vigour, my spirits were seldom very depressed from physical causes. Although I really had not much hope that the ship would be saved, the fear of death did not paralyze my efforts to escape from it. We had two Macintosh life preservers in our outfit, and my suffering friend lay in his berth, and eyed me with a ghastly curiosity as I sat on the cabin deck and inflated the belts. I then made the gold and silver coin into two packages, which I lashed together by a strong cord,. and assured Weedle that if the ship went on shore, I would make a desperate effort to. save his money, whether he helped me or not. I advised him to screw up his courage, and if the ship should strike, to put on his life belt and hasten on deck. With a promise that I would give him immediate notice of any fresh danger, I went on deck again, and took my old station under the tarpaulin in the mizen rigging; and there I stood, anxiously watching the bending spars, the loss of one of which would inevitably have sealed the fate of the ship in a very short time.

Night came on again, and a wild-looking night it was. The ship had been wore round four times during the day, and each time we had lost ground (the ship would not stay in such a heavy sea, under the small sail which we could. spread), and we had also drifted to leeward while the crew were replacing a close-reefed foretopsail, which had been blown away. About ten o'clock I overheard the captain say to the chief mate, "We must give her the reefed mainsail, Mr. Blocks."

"She won't stand up to it, sir; and if we spring a spar just now, we are done for, to a dead certainty," replied the mate, who, by the bye, was an older man than the captain.

"We'll try what she will do," said the captain. "It does not blow so hard as it did an hour ago. Lay aft, all hands, and set the main course," he added, in a stentorian voice, to his crew.

The sail was set with difficulty, and the spray flew over the ship from stem to stern, as she plunged into the heavy head seas, under the additional pressure of canvas, and at. the same time heeled over to such an extent, that I had hard work to keep my post in the rigging, and I sometimes feared she would capsize altogether.

"I would advise you to go below and turn in, sir," said the captain, good naturedly addressing me. "You can do no good by stopping on deck, and you may get hurt. I will rouse you out smartly enough if anything happens; but I think the weather is breaking." Just at that moment a heavy sea broke on board, which smashed all the weather bulwarks, and did other damage on deck, besides nearly knocking me overboard. Soon afterwards another green sea tumbled on board, and if I had not previously lashed myself to the rigging I should probably have been lost; so·

I went below, and, without undressing, turned into a berth in a spare cabin near to the companion way, and being wearied out with long watching, I was soon fast asleep notwithstanding the violent pitching of the vessel.

I had had but one nap, and it did not then appear to me to have been a very long one, when I was awakened by a noisy kicking at my cabin door, and the captain, in excited tones, calling upon me to hasten on deck.

“Heave out, Mr. Boomerang; quick, quick,” cried the captain, “bear a hand, sir; jump up on the deck, directly!”

I was out of bed in an instant, and scrambled up the companion ladder, on my hands and knees, urged onward by extreme anxiety, and a resolution to save my life if possible. Never shall I forget the gushing emotions of my heart, as I stood on the quarter-deck and gazed around me, with a bounding joy which language can but feebly express. Of course I had expected to see the ship struggling in the breakers, and I was preparing to battle for dear life, amid the roaring of the surges and the blackness of death. Instead of which, my dazzled eyes beheld the morning sun, rising into a cloudless sky; illumining the rolling ocean, and tinging the wooded shores in the distance with golden light. It was a Sabbath morning, and ever shall I remember the holy calm which reigned around, and seemed to fill my spirit with feelings too deep for utterance; with a solemn sense of mercies experienced from God, for which my tongue could not utter my heart's gratitude. Suddenly the feeling changed to almost a delirium of transport, which tried to vent itself in extravagant outbursts. I rushed up to the smiling captain, seized his hand and uttered a rhapsody of thanks and compliments; then I turned to the mate, who laughed heartily as I shook his hand with true fraternal warmth; and I was almost running forward to hug every Jack tar on the forecastle, for I loved the brave fellows, who had worked so willingly during the late gale. Like a poor felon reprieved under the gallows, I felt rescued from the jaws of death. It was a transition from the darkness of the night of death to the brightness of a sunny, life-breathing morning; and the joyous emotion it wrought cannot be conveyed by ordinary figures.

I was glad, too, for the safety of my friend Weedle's money and merchandise, which I knew were all he possessed in the world, so I hastened below to gladden him; but I thought I would first shock him a little before I over-whelmed him with happiness.

"Weedle! Weedle! Jump up on deck directly," I exclaimed as I entered his cabin, after knocking loudly at the door; but my heart was so full of joy that I could not carry on the little harmless deception which the captain had so successfully practised on me, in order to increase my rapturous surprise. Neither could I bear to see my poor sick friend's woeful face, as he turned round in his berth, and declared that "he had not strength left to save his life, and must just die in his bed;" so I opened the stern windows to let in the sunshine, and the effect on his yellow face was like French-polish on an old stool. Archie Weedle was a living man again in two minutes; and in less than two minutes more he was standing on the deck with me, enjoying the glad prospect, and watching the many native canoes which were paddling off to the ship as she lay becalmed about midway between the outer headlands of the Bay of Islands.

DROPPING IN AT DINNER-TIME.

A BULLOCK'S head suddenly thrust through the side window of a crowded omnibus, could not have caused more commotion amongst the astonished insiders, than did the announcement of a visitor by Mary the maid-of-all-work, just as Mr. and Mrs. Tiddle and the five young Tiddles were sitting down one day to dine off a roasted rabbit, which had been sent to them by a friend in the country, and which they all regarded as an extraordinary treat.

"Please, sir, Mr. Grubb wants to see you," said the maid, "but he says he will wait in the shop till you have done dinner."

"Patience me! that horrid old fellow has come again," exclaimed Mrs. Tiddle, with a sort of farewell glance at the rabbit, and a vicious look at her spouse, as if he had been directly instrumental in bringing the dreadful nuisance into the house; while the children looked as scared as though there was a wolf under the table. "What are you going to do, Tiddle? You will not ask him in, surely! There is barely enough dinner for ourselves, and he usually eats as much as three of us. If he comes in here I shall be mad enough to snap off his legs. It's downright provoking, to think that greedy fellow should poke his nose in here at dinner time two or three times a week; and he always smells when we have anything hot and nice, that's the worst of it, he never comes on cold meat or stew days. What are you going to do, Tiddle? Why don't you speak to me, and not sit there like one of your shop dummies?"

"Hem—I scarcely know what to do, my dear. You see how awkwardly I am situated. Grubb has recommended me to three customers, and he has promised to do all he can for me."

"Yes, indeed! and one of them 'run away in the suit of colonial tweed you made for him, and never paid you sixpence, the shabby cheat. You are much obliged to Mr. Grubb for that customer, certainly! Yes—give him all the rabbit, and let your wife and children go hungry! Ask him in of course!"

"Oh, don't bother me, Becky, pray don't, my head's mithered. I won't ask him in, dear, if I can help it, but I don't want to offend him, I can't afford to lose customers these hard times. O dear, dear, there is so much ruinous cutting, and so many tricky people in trade now a days, that it is a hard matter for an honest man to get along and pay his way. I'm perplexed, Becky, but have patience, there's a dear."

The poor little tailor certainly looked perplexed; the dread of his wife's frown and the fear of offending Mr. Grubb, added to the prospect of a short meal, made him look as dim as a rusty goose.

"Don't stir, Tiddle—don't stir," said his friend Grubb, putting his head in at the doorway, "excuse my intrusion, I am not coming in. How are you, Mrs. Tiddle, I hope the baby's better. Don't move, Tiddle, I've merely called to give you the address of another customer, and I'll wait in the shop till you've done dinner. I'll sit and look at your pattern books."

"Hem—a—won't you pick a bit with us?" asked Mr. Tiddle, in faltering accents, and with a timid glance at his spouse, who was looking knives and forks at him.

"No thank you, no—a—I don't care much about dinner to-day. There is something the matter with me, I ate a hearty supper last night, perhaps that's it. Go on with your dinner, friends, I'll wait till you are done."

"We've just got a little rabbit, which a friend sent us as a rare treat," remarked Mr. Tiddle, in an apologetic tone. "It's a tiny little thing, but—"

"Rabbit, did you say? well, that is a rarity in this country. I haven't tasted rabbit since I left home, and it used to be a favourite dish of mine; I think I will be tempted to pick a bone with you after all," said Mr. Grubb, walking in and putting his hat and stick in a corner. "It smells nice. I see you know how to cook a rabbit, Mrs. Tiddle."

"Ta—ta—take a chair, Mr. Grubb," said the tailor, trembling from head to foot, "Becky, will you tell Mary to bring another hot plate?"

Mrs. Tiddle called "Mary" in such a savage key that her husband turned pale, his appetite forsook him, and he mentally wished he were on Shark Island, dining off raw cockles. He eased off some of his feeling in a quiet sigh, then said to his second boy, "Say grace, Bobby; put your knife down, sir." Bobby said grace, then his father took up the carving tools, and asked Mr. Grubb what part he preferred.

"Ladies first, ladies first, always, sir," said the guest, with a jocose smile at Mrs. Tiddle, who looked as sour as a green lemon.

"I like to serve visitors first," said Mr. Tiddle, helping his guest to a tolerably large portion of rabbit, for the meek little man had determined to dine off potatoes and salt, in order to save his wife and children from short allowance.

Mrs. Tiddle coughed sharply, but her unhappy husband did not look up. He knew it was not a bronchial affection, for it was not the first time that he had heard that telegraphic sound. He knew very well that her cough meant to say "why did you give old Grubb such a big bit of rabbit?" But he was a conscientious tailor and a thorough man, though he was afraid of his wife's frown. He could not bear to ask any one to his table and act niggardly; in fact his heart was much larger than his means, for he would gladly have given everybody in the land a dinner every day.

"I have just a lee-tle bit of pickled pork here, will you take a thin slice, Mr. Grubb?" asked Mrs. Tiddle, with hidden meaning in her words, which touched her husband's feelings like tailor's needles.

"If you please, ma'am; I am very partial to pickled pork and peas-pudding," said Mr. Grubb, passing his plate.

"It is a nice dish," groaned Mr. Tiddle, trying to smile, but looking as ghastly as a pig's cheek overcooked. "We have no peas-pudding, but we have a taste of broad beans, will you take a spoonful, sir?"

"Broad beans? O yes, by all means, they are my favorite vegetable, next to fried onions. My poor wife too was very fond of broad beans and melted butter, though they always made her peevish, poor thing. Thankee, Tiddle—plenty; I can come again, you know, thankee—I really begin to feel I have an appetite after all."

"Mary Ann, how dare you come to table in that dirty pinafore, Miss?" vociferated her mother, at the same moment giving her, what is generally mis-called a good box on the ear, and a peremptory command to go into the kitchen and stay there till she was called or sent for.

"Poor Mary Ann!" sighed Mr. Tiddle, with a sympathising glance at his weeping daughter. "What part do you prefer, Becky?"

"I don't want any," said his wife sharply, "my appetite is clean taken away by that girl's dirty pinafore."

"Nonsense, love! Here's a nice cut with a kidney in it, and a lump of stuffing."

"It's the tenderest rabbit I ever tasted," remarked Mr. Grubb, with his mouth full and his plate half emptied. "I really enjoy it. I wish my poor wife were here, she doted on rabbit dead or alive,—I'll trouble you for another spoonful of gravy, Tiddle."

"Billy, what are you poking your brother with a fork for? I see you, you young monkey. What do you mean?" shouted Mr. Tiddle, whose hungry ire was beginning to master his philosophy. The last fierce question to Billy was accompanied by a thump on the head, hard enough to knock him stupid for life if it had happened to have struck a soft spot. "Go into the kitchen to your sister, this very minute, sir! I'll give it you after dinner, you wicked boy."

The tender-hearted tailor almost immediately repented of his wrath, but the knock on Billy's head could not be rescinded, and that young gentleman was in the kitchen roaring bass to his sister's treble, so he did not hear his recall to his seat at the board. There he sat sobbing, and spitefully wishing that one of the rabbit bones which old Grubb was vulgarly fingering would slip from his grasp and stick in his throat; while his sister was making a variety of ugly faces and menacing gestures in cannibal fashion to mark her contempt for the greedy man who was eating up their nice dinner, and upsetting the peace and comfort of their home, by making mother cross and father miserable.

Angry and hungry boys and girls are in general prone to disagree, so it was not wonderful under the circumstances that Billy and his sister should begin to quarrel. They soon began to fight too, and Mary Ann, who inherited her mother's spirit, being aroused by her rude brother pulling her round the kitchen by her back ringlets, pushed him over a chair with his head in the bread-pan, which was broken to pieces by the collision.

The noise of the affray reached the dining-room, when out rushed Mrs. Tiddle—glad of a chance to vent off her wrath upon some one—and gave her daughter a "good-dressing" with the handle of the hearth-broom. Mary Ann thereupon set up a squall equal in volume and effect to the strains of some amateur singers, while Billy dodged his mother round the kitchen to evade his just share of the broomstick. Stimulated by the sight of the broken bread-pan, Mrs. Tiddle resolutely vowed she would skin him when she caught him. But in order to catch nimble Billy to skin him it was necessary for her to put her best foot foremost; in doing so she put it into a hole in the oilcloth, and down she went in the narrow dark passage with a thud like a falling tower. Out flew Mr. Tiddle to see what all the noise was about, when he innocently tumbled over his prostrate wife, kicking the crown of her head with the toe of his boot, and grinding the tip off his own nose on the rough stone step of the kitchen.

In the meantime Mr. Grubb, who had finished his dinner, rose up and departed, lest he should be called upon to arbitrate upon the complicated quarrel, and he dreaded family brawls worse than cold dinners. Two of the young Tiddle brats, who were left at the table, began to wrangle for the possession of a backbone which they had filched from their father's plate, while little Teddy, the infant, seized the favourable opportunity for helping himself to a red pepper pod from the mixed pickle bottle; but before he had finished eating it, he began to raise his voice in the horrible belief that his head was on fire.

Never was heard a greater hubbub in any quiet tailor's house in this colony or elsewhere; but I must leave my readers to imagine the confusion and to put things to rights again according to their own fancies, while I admit that my fancy has helped me to colour the foregoing picture from every day life.

*   *   *   *   *   *

I venture to think that few, if any, of my old friendly readers will mistake my meaning in the brief comments I am about to make on the foregoing little episode in domestic life. Not one of them, I hope, will believe that I would grudge a meal to a friend let him drop in when he would, or that I would commend such a niggardly spirit in any one. It is those strong-nosed, systematic spongers that I dread at all times, men, who—as Mrs. Tiddle remarked—always smell when there is a good dinner on the table, and slide themselves in uninvited for the mere sake of "getting a good feed" as they vulgarly call it. Men with blarneying lips, but with souls as scrappy as devilled bones. Who invariably praise everything on the table, play with the baby

and talk nonsense to its mother, but who really care more
for the cook than for any other member of the household—
and if your bill of fare is reduced in consequence of a corresponding turn in your circumstances, they will never enter
your door at all.   Those are the creatures to whom I allude
when I say that I dislike such droppers in at my table more
than I do cold potatoes—which by the way is the sole diet
I would prescribe for all such domestic marauders.

Some time ago I went by invitation to dine on board a
ship which was lying at one of the quays in Sydney harbour, when the worthy captain remarked to the mate in
tones of surprise, that there were no "one o'clock boys on
board that day."   On my asking what he meant by "one
o'clock boys," he said there was a host of persons of Mr.
Grubb's class, who made a practice of foraging for a dinner
almost every day, and they were a nuisance to him as well
as to many other skippers in port.   "Ay, and they are a
pest to many good-natured housewives on shore too," I remarked, with a shrug which old reminiscences stirred up.

I would not wantonly annoy any one with my remarks,
but I cannot here resist offering a word or two of friendly
counsel to those who choose to take it.   [In general, those
dinner hunters cannot plead poverty as an excuse for their
sponging habits, indeed a poor man with a manly spirit
would rather dine off a brown biscuit any day than wheedle
himself into a needy household if there was the least risk of
upsetting their little domestic arrangements.]   I would say
to the Grubbs and the "one o'clock boys" of Sydney, go to
some good restaurant, and get ninepenny-worth of dinner,
or more if you want it, and go to your friends' tables only
when you are invited.   Try that manly method for twelve
months or so, and you may probably regain your reputation,
or at any rate lose some of your notoriety as mid-day nuisances.   Then you may occasionally drop in at dinner time
and your friends will not consider you are intruding but
will perhaps be really glad to see you.   But don't go ex-
clusively for what you can get to eat or drink—bah! such
selfishness is only worthy of the big monkey in the Government Gardens and his tribe in general.

"SHOVE IT ON BOARD."

" LET go the bow-line, and haul the stage ashore," shouted the captain of a steamer, on board of which I was a passenger some time ago.

" Hould on a bit, captain dear! Don't lave this little lock of corrn in me carrt, and good luck to yez," said a farmer on the wharf, looking up imploringly at the captain on the paddle-box.

" I can't take it," said the captain, decisively, " my decks are lumbered up already, so that fat passengers can't get aft without climbing over the bridge."

" Arrah, captain, take this small lot; there's a dear man. Shure it won't make much odds to yez ; there's ony tin bags, an' it's mighty light corrn too. I fetched it all the way from the farrm, onst afore, an' shure yer agent here tould me it shud go this trip, anyhow. What'll I do at all if yez lave it behind ? Och captain, do take it, an I'll be everlastingly obliged to yez, I'm going down wid it meself, an me bhoy Teddy for-bye. Shpake the worrd now, honey, an long life to yez."

" Shove it on board," said the captain, " and bear a hand about it, or we shall lose the tide, and be stuck on the flats all day. In with it—in with it."

While that colloquy was going on, I saw two men, in a boat alongside, pushing a coop of fowls on board at the after gangway, unobserved by the captain. In a short time we were paddling down the river, and the crew were busy stowing the deck cargo, and extemporising a pen, or sty, for a score or two of pigs, which would persist in making a noise, although the sailors were using strenuous efforts to soothe them, by beating their greasy backs with ropes' ends. Presently the steamer stopped to take in an old lady from a boat, which had put off from one of the farmsteads on the river bank.

" I can't take any cargo," said the captain, as the boat-man began to hand up sundry packages.

"Bless my heart alive! I have only two small boxes of eggs, and a little pig, and a keg of butter. You surely don't mean to say you won't take them on board, captain? What room will they occupy? Tut, tut, can't take them, that's all nonsense!"

"Shove 'em on board, missis, shove 'em on board," said the second mate, who was rewarded with a grateful glance from the old lady, while at the same time she made some pettish remarks about the captain's ill manners, in wanting to send her pig and her boxes on shore again. Soon the steamer was under weigh once more, and anon we called at another wharf, when the captain had an altercation with a miller, who finally succeeded, by sheer clamour, in shipping the cylinder of his steam-engine, and sundry other heavy pieces of machinery, which he said he was taking to Sydney for repairs, as his mill was standing still, and it was full of grist from bottom to top. We scraped over the flats without sticking, and in due course arrived alongside the old wharf at Newcastle, when the usual scene of bustle ensued, and all the idlers in the City were active, for a season.

"I can't take any cargo this morning," said the captain to the agent's clerk, who was making entries in his manifest.

"You will take my luggage, I suppose?" said a snappish-looking old gentleman, with a barrow full of boxes behind him, and who was evidently determined to have his luggage taken on board, or "know the reason why not."

"Well, I suppose I *must* take that; shove it on board," said the captain; then he shouted to a fisherman with a sugee-bag on his back, "Hey, Mister Squidd, I can't take any oysters this trip."

"They'll stow anywhere, captain; put 'em on the sponson; there are only five bags," said Mr. Squidd, appealingly.

"I'll heave 'em overboard if you put them on my deck, so I give you notice; can't you see that I am loaded down to the port-holes? Confound it all! do you want to sink me at my moorings?"

"The captain ought to be ashamed of himself," said an old grumbler, who was usually to be seen on the wharf when the steamer was alongside, "it's scandalous to take a ship to sea in that trim. Why, she is nearly a foot below her load-line. If anything happens to that steamer, I'll kick up a row about it; mark my words."

"I should like to know what right the captain has to load

his ship in that disgraceful way, and risk valuable lives?” said another bystander, who, like his friend beside him, gloried in grumbling, but very rarely helped to reform evils which he was so quick at discerning. Meanwhile, a consequential-looking gentleman was severely scolding the agent’s clerk for promising to keep room for his horse, and failing to do so.

“Where am I to put your horse, sir?” asked the captain, who had been appealed to. “Just look at my decks, fore and aft; there isn’t standing room for a monkey.”

“He won’t take up more room than a bale of hay, captain,” said the gentleman. “You can tie him to the fore rigging, if you like; he is as quiet as a cat; passengers may rub against his legs, and I’ll warrant he won’t kick. You will much oblige me, captain, if you will take him—in fact I have right to——”

“Shove it on board,” said the captain, who looked thoroughly perplexed, and muttered that he “would rather be drowned than be jawed to death.” After taking in a number of empty beer barrels, a Bath chair, sundry bundles of cabbage-tree, and other “odds and ends,” (which—in the estimation of the owners—“weighed nothing,” the ropes were cast off, and we slowly proceeded to sea. I saw that my luggage was safely stowed, with other passengers’ effects, on the after skylight, then went upon the bridge and sat beside the captain, who had the reputation of being one of the most careful and experienced seamen on the coast.

“You have a large cargo to-day, captain,” I remarked.

“Ugh, cargo! we are smothered with it. They’ll sink us altogether one of these fine days,” replied the captain, with a shrug; then he shouted to the crew forward, to “haul the chain-box over to starboard.”

From my elevated position, I could scan the ship fore and aft, except under the bridge, where I had previously taken stock of four horses, sundry coops of poultry, a stack of wet hides, and some casks of tallow. The quarter deck was crowded with bales of wool and luggage, with a right-of-way left for *thin* passengers. One quarter boat was pretty well filled with dead wild ducks and wallabies, and live cockatoos in cages; the other contained vegetables, sofa-cushions, swabs, and other useful articles. In the forepart of the ship was a travelling carriage, sundry machinery belonging to the pertinacious miller before-mentioned, bales of hay, bags of grain, several fat calves, the pigs, and the horse aforesaid, and an assortment of odds and ends not worth particularising, including the five bags of oysters, which Squidd, the fisherman, had smuggled into the starboard sponson. The steerage passengers were sitting or standing wherever they could find room. Four men were lounging in the travelling carriage, smoking their pipes, and seeming as unapprehensive of danger as if the travelling carriage were on the Paramatta Road. The steamer lurched heavily from time to time, and the crew were obliged to shift the chain-box about, to help to steady her, at which extra work they did not fail to grumble, in sailors' peculiar fashion. Altogether the prospect was enough to frighten any one whose imagination was at all active, whose organs of caution were not concave, and who, moreover, had not a settled belief that he "was born to be hanged." Fortunately the sea was very smooth, and by degrees my qualms subsided into a calm submission to my lot.

"I think we shall have a light north-easter to-day," I remarked to the captain, as he reseated himself, after he had given an order to his mate to send the topgallant yard on deck.

"I don't think the wind will hold long in that quarter," he replied, while his experienced eye scanned the horizon. "We shall have a 'southerly-burster' before long. It will blow like thunder before sundown, or I am very much mistaken."

I thought so too, (notwithstanding I could see a ripple on the water, far away on our port-quarter), for in the south-western sky there were some ominous looking clouds rising, and the air was sultry and oppressive. However, I took a hopeful view of our surroundings, and said I thought we might get to Sydney before the "burster" met us; adding, "we shall be in a dilemma if we are caught in bad weather, with all this deck lumber."

The captain merely shrugged his shoulders, by way of reply, which affected me like a shovelful of snow on my head. One can form an idea in a moment what an Englishman would imply by that kind of movement, though it is not easy to interpret a Frenchman's shrugs. After a few minutes' reflection on my future prospects, I asked the captain what he would do, if we met with a southerly gale.

"Why heave our deck load overboard," he replied. "we

must do that or go down. You see I have a difficulty in keeping the ship upright at the present time; she is rolling about like an old water-butt in a tide-way. I am expecting every minute, too, that some of those passengers forward will get their toes under the wheels of the chain-box, and then there will be a hullabaloo and the doctor to pay. Overboard goes Paddy's corn, and everything else on deck except the live stock, if we fall in with a hard gale—that's certain."

"What troubles me most, is the dread that you will not begin to clear your decks soon enough, captain," I replied; "I have been in bad weather with you several times, and I never saw you throw anything overboard, though you have sometimes been lumbered up almost as much as you are now."

"Well, you see, sir, it isn't a pleasant job to heave away cargo; no seaman likes to do it if he can anyway help it. I always hang on to it as long as I can, for I know there would be a pretty row when I went up the river again, if I were to throw it overboard. All the deck cargo is at the risk of the shippers, and most of them are poor, struggling men, who could very badly bear the loss. But there are lots of fellows who would make more noise about it than the poor shippers; and it is them that I most dread, for their tongues fidget me worse than thunder and lightning. You heard those two old fogies on the wharf at Newcastle abuse me for overloading my ship; and if we met with any mishap, they would exonerate the winds and waves, and blame me for all."

"That would certainly be unfair," I replied, "for I have observed the difficulties you have encountered this morning; and that you had cargo thrust on board, in spite of your appeals, or your emphatic protests."

"Shippers actually force cargo upon us at every stopping-place; and they each think that their 'little lots' can't make any odds to a big steamer; like the old woman with her pig and her butter-tub, and the blustering miller with his iron-work. You saw, too, that I had to stow three bales of hay above the rail, to make room for Mr. Bang's horse."

"It was very unreasonable for him to wish you to take it, captain; and I wonder that you did so."

"Well, you see, sir, he is managing-man for Messrs. Codger and Bloke; and as they are large shippers by our boats, I didn't wish to offend him; besides, he would have stormed my ears, worse than great guns, if I had refused. We are not always so jammed up as we are to-day; but there is a great rise in corn and hay just now, so all the farmers are anxious to get their stuff to market; and our agent up above has not very quiet times, I can tell you, for he can't ship everything and please everbody."

"But the shippers themselves ought to know that they run a great risk in putting their goods on board in this uncon-scionable manner," I remarked.

"Phoo! what do the bulk of them know about loading a ship?" replied the captain, with a faint smile. "Look at happy old Paddy Murphy, sitting on the fore-hatch, smoking his pipe; do you think you could persuade him that his little 'lock ov corrn' made any difference in the trim of the vessel? Not you, indeed; he would tell you it was only like a butterfly on a bullock's back. He is, perhaps, think-ing how lucky he was to get it on board, and of the good price he will get for it to-morrow; but he has never once thought of the probability of its going overboard. And I'll be bound that that miller, who is fast asleep in the bath chair, is not dreaming that his cylinder, and cog-wheels, are in danger of going down to Davy Jones's locker. If I had not taken them on board, he would now be at home bless-ing me for keeping his mill idle, and all his hungry grist customers would have cried shame upon the captain, who wouldn't be so obliging as to take three little bits of iron to Sydney, to save a whole district from a potato diet.

"The captain of a coasting steamer has more anxiety than most persons are aware of, Mr. Boomerang, and the ordinary risks of the sea are not the main cause of it. Do you think I should be so fidgetty about those clouds that are rising yonder, if my ship was in seaworthy trim? Not a bit of it, sir. If I had no deck-load I shouldn't be afraid to face any weather, for this is as good a sea-boat as ever floated; but what can a man do with a whole farm-yard on his deck, and a flour-mill and a cab-stand beside?"

"I don't wonder that you feel anxious, captain; but pray, what remedy would you suggest for this reckless system of overloading vessels, at the imminent risk of life and property?"

"Why, the best remedy that I can see is to take no deck cargo at all; that is a matter for the Legislature to look after, and the sooner they begin about it the better. It would be easy enough for agents and captains, and all concerned, to do their duty, if steamers were not allowed to take cargo except under hatches; for the most unconscionable shipper could be convinced, in a minute, when a ship was full below. *Then* passengers might travel in safety and comfort; but it is plain enough they cannot do that in my ship to-day.”

“But there *is* a law regulating deck cargo in steamers, captain,” I remarked.

“Is there, sir? well, you can see how much it is respected,” replied the captain, with a grim chuckle; then he shouted to the crew, “Haul the chain box over to port: and stop those pigs from crowding up to the hawse holes.”

The dinner bell soon afterwards rang, so I went below and seated myself at the bottom of the table. Next to the advantage of being out of danger altogether, is perhaps the happy unconsciousness of its proximity; that is to say, when one is powerless to avert it. Thus I silently reasoned, as I glanced along the table at the double row of gentlemen eating ox-tail soup. I could not discern the merest tinge of anxiety on a single face; and the extended angles of each mouth were expressive of gastronomic joy, for the soup was rich. It was evident that the fear of death or personal damage, was remote from the minds of those happy diners; and that the pleasures of the present time were not marred by apprehensions of future famine, or any other troublesome contingency. Probably not one of them had even the slightest foreboding, that in a few short hours he would be as helpless and undignified as a swaddling infant; that he would be——but I am anticipating my story.

Soon after the cloth was removed I went on deck, and remounted the bridge. The captain was standing on the starboard paddle-box, gazing alternately at the gathering storm and at his struggling vessel, while his face bore evidence of intense anxiety, though not alarm or trepidation, for he was a thorough sailor. I did not speak to him, though I longed to put a question or two to him, and I wished he would speak to me. I usually try to observe a prudent reticence in seasons of peril on shipboard; and it would be well if all passengers would adopt that course. I have seen a captain perplexed with silly questions at times when his mind was anxiously engaged on some important duty, and I have heard him miscalled "a surly man" for giving sharp answers to the thoughtless querist. Presently the captain stepped down from the paddle-box, and laconically remarked, as he nodded his head towards the southwest, " There's dirt there."

"There is a heavy storm gathering," I replied, "but I hope we may fetch abreast of Broken Bay (which was about twelve miles distant) before it comes on."

"No such luck for us to-day, sir," said the captain. "It will be down upon us in twenty minutes; don't you see how fast that long, bolster-looking cloud is rolling along? That is not scudding before a gentle zephyr, I can tell you." Then he called to the chief mate. "Send that foretopsail-yard on deck, and house the topmast. Bear a hand about it."

In rather less than half an hour I hastened below, to escape the heavy rain which began to descend, accompanied with a violent squall of wind, and thunder and lightning. Some of the passengers were still seated at the table, when I re-entered the saloon, and one of them exclaimed, " Halloa! is there a shift of wind?"

"Yes, sir, there is indeed," I replied, "and I think we shall have a very rough night."

"Dear, oh dear! I'm sorry for that," said Mr. Bang, "I shall be awfully sea-sick. Steward, bring me a couple of pillows."

Before I had equipped myself in my waterproof overalls, for the deck, nearly all the gentlemen had taken up positions on the sofas, and were being supplied with pillows, et cetera. With much difficulty I regained my post on the bridge, and the scene around me was terrifically grand, with a dash of the ridiculous in it too. The sea was white with foam, the lightning played about the masts in dazzling streams; the thunder and the wind seemed to be arguing which could roar loudest, while the thick glots of rain descending on the backs of the pigs, made them squeak loud enough to be heard above the warring elements. The four steerage passengers had discovered a leak in the roof of the travelling carriage, and were hurrying out of it; at the same time the miller woke up from his nap, in the Bath-chair, and ran below faster than any invalid could have done. Poor Paddy Murphy saw his bags of corn covered up with a tarpaulin, then took his little boy Teddy under his arm, and descended to the fore-cabin, where, I imagine, the inmates were rather too closely packed to be comfortable. The sailors, in their oilskin jackets, were wheeling the chain-box about (their sick baby, as they called it), and were deprecating the exercise in solemnly quaint ejaculations. The steamer seemed to have merely steerage-way, still she was kept head to the wind, and nobly she struggled against the contending elements. In about an hour the worst of the storm was past, but a strong gale set in and the sea rose very fast.

The captain stood and watched the curling waves with steady nerve ; and every now and then gave orders to ease the engines, when an unusually heavy sea rose ahead of us. By that precaution the steamer rode over the waves more easily, but her onward progress was considerably retarded ; in fact, at times she scarcely appeared to make any headway. When the tea bell rang I again went below, and a moving scene of noisy misery presented itself. Nearly all the late hearty diners were *hors-de-combat*, and looked almost as despairing as a ward full of patients in a blazing hospital. I pitied Mr. Bang least of all the prostrate ones ; and whenever I heard his " Yaawk" which smothered all the whoops of his neighbours, I called to mind his bilious attack upon the polite clerk on the wharf at Newcastle ; and I mentally muttered, " Ah, Mr. Bang ! it is plain that you wanted a short sea voyage, sir. After this day's extensive delivery you will perhaps be in a better temper for a while. So yaawk away, sir ; your wife and children will be gainers by your present exertions ; and nobody here has life enough to notice the ugly faces you are making. Yaawk away, sir, you will be better to-morrow, if you live till then."

Several of the gentlemen made sombre inquiries of me as to our position, and if I could see Sydney lighthouse ? To which I replied, that I could see nothing but black clouds and white-headed waves ; as to our position, I could only tell them that we were not far from Broken Bay. After partaking of a cup of tea, I again went upon the bridge, and there I stood for some time beside the captain without speaking a word, but longing for him to speak to me. Presently he said, " There is an awful ugly sea on."

" There is, indeed, captain ; may I ask if you have any idea of running back to Newcastle ?"

" Back, eh ?" he replied ; " I dare not put her round ; she would almost certainly capsize with all this load on deck."

"Why don't you begin to throw it overboard?" I muttered rather pettishly, but I did not let him hear me. I cannot depict the anxiety I endured for the next hour as I sat upon that melancholy bridge in silent meditation, and watched the seething waves which tossed and tumbled around like monsters preparing to swallow us; while the wind roaring over the top of the big funnel sounded like grim death playing a funeral dirge. My mental calculations as to the consequences of a heavy sea breaking on board (which I momentarily expected), were by no means encouraging, but I could not school my mind to any more cheerful exercise just then. There were about fifty bales of hay and wool on deck; and assuming that each bale would soak up a quantity of water equal to its weight, and allowing three or four hogsheads for the Bath-chair and the carriage; I inferred that the vessel would founder before we could sufficiently lighten her. My second calculation was as to the result, if the pigs should break down their temporary barrier, and crowd together under the topgallant forecastle, and thus bring the steamer down by the head; but I had not quite completed that sum when I was aroused by the captain calling me. I staggered towards him, and stood holding on by the fore shroud of the funnel. "Do you see land on the starboard beam?" he asked.

I gazed into the darkness till my eyes ached, then replied, "No, captain, I can't see it. Can you?"

"Yes; I see the North Head of Broken Bay."

"Bless me! what extraordinary eyes you must have. I can see nothing but thick darkness, like a wall of pitch built up to the sky. Are you going into the bay, captain?"

"I'll try for it, if I see a chance of putting her round smartly," he replied. "Ease her!"

In about half an hour he gave orders for the chain-box to be wheeled over to port, and lashed there; and soon afterwards he shouted, "Haul the fore sheet aft! Port the helm!"

It was a critical time, and a month's anxiety seemed to be concentrated into those few minutes. The vessel slowly paid off, and floundered into the trough of the sea, where a huge mountain of water rose on our port beam, as if about to fall on us and crush us.

"Hold on, Boomerang! here's a sea coming on board!" cried the captain. I held on instinctively, while I commended my soul to my Maker. The heavy combing wave came hissing towards us, and struck our port paddle-box; the vessel lurched violently over on her beam ends, and some of the cargo rolled overboard. I thought of my loved ones at home; I muttered a prayer for them, and I bade the world good-bye. In another moment I heard the captain shout, "All right! all right!" and I whispered, "Thank God!" The sea *did not* break on board; and soon afterwards we anchored in Pitt Water.

"There you see, I've saved my deck load again, Mr. Boomerang," said the captain, rubbing his hands with glee, after the last of the cable was paid out. "It's a blessed good job we are safe and sound in here, but we had a narrow escape in rounding to, and I made sure that big topper of a sea was going to swamp us altogether." Then he called to his mate, "Hoy! Mr. Keel, get a lantern and see what's the matter with that horse; I think he's griped."

A light was procured, and Mr. Bang's horse was found with his fore legs over the rail and his hind legs stretched apart on the deck. It was supposed that when the vessel had given the heavy lurch, the poor beast had tumbled half-way overboard; and in his struggle to right himself, he had received some serious internal injury, for he was dead. Several of the pigs were dead too, and all the deck cargo was more or less damaged.

*   *   *   *   *   *

"What would have been the probable result if that heavy sea had tumbled broadside on us?" I asked the captain, as he was sitting at the supper table, an hour afterwards, looking as composed as if he had just come from church.

He shut his eyes, drew down his features, and laconically replied, "Down among the dead men."

"That is precisely my opinion, captain," said I, as I instantly interpreted his ominous gesticulation. "It would have been *too late* to throw your deck cargo overboard, and we should have gone to the bottom of the sea. Well, thank God, we are safe," I added, solemnly. "But had we capsized; with my last breath I should have denounced *deck loads*, and it is very likely that my ghost would have henceforward been seen, in the wake of overladen steamers, screaming 'Murder!'"

*   *   *   *   *   *

Some of my readers may impatiently ask, "What is the

use of making a long story about a common-place event, which took place years ago?" In anticipation of such an inquiry I explain, that a sense of duty impels me to help, as far as I can, to remedy a systematic abuse, which I believe is, alas, too common all over the world ; and I have written this sketch to illustrate the discomforts and dangers which passengers are frequently subjected to, in these present times, and on our iron coast. I have no facts to warrant me in stating, that the causes of the late melancholy disasters were other than the act of God ; but I can state as a fact, that the last steamer I voyaged in, not long ago, had not less than from twenty to twenty-five tons of butter and coal on her deck. And I can state, as another fact, that the last sailing vessel I voyaged in, the registered tonnage of which was only 198, had 304 tons of coal on board. By whose authority it was put on board I know not, but certainly it was not the captain's. He took his ship to sea, though he admitted to me that she had at least *forty tons* more cargo than she could carry with safety. He hoped to have had a smooth passage to Melbourne, but had a very rough one, lengthened to twelve days ; and during most of that time the sea broke on board in such a dangerous manner, that to take the hatches off to attempt to lighten her, would have been to sink her in five minutes ; and it is firmly impressed on my mind, that if she had not been a remarkably strong vessel, and well found, and withal very skilfully managed, that she would have foundered with all hands.

Those are two facts which I can vouch for. I could give many more from personal experience, equally striking, but those are sufficient, and I would respectfully commend them to the consideration of our legislators. It might be thought invidious to appeal to them through the strongest law of nature, and remind them that they themselves sometimes travel in our fine coasting steamers, and that their families, and their friends, sometimes travel in them, too ; a sense of their duty, as guardians of the public safety, will surely be sufficient to stimulate their zeal in this important matter, especially as we have lately had so many mournful reminders of the perils which beset " them that go down to the sea in ships."

If any person should say, " there *is* a law regulating the deck lading of steamers," I would reply, that stringent measures are necessary to insure its being obeyed ; for that it is very frequently evaded is a glaring fact, which I challenge anyone to confute.*

I believe that such a measure would be hailed with gladness by the agents and officers of steamships in general; for, from causes which I have glanced at, those gentlemen are not always able to control the eagerness of persons to ship goods, in certain states of our markets; and in these days of active opposition, agents and officers are doubtless anxious to please their customers, the bulk of whom are as unconscious of extra hazard, when sending their shipments, as Paddy Murphy was with his " little lock of corrn," or the old lady with her pig and her butter tub.

With earnestness I repeat my conviction, that if immediate measures are not adopted to insure the safe lading of steamers and sailing vessels out of our port, it will not be very long before more brave seamen are sacrificed, and more broken-hearted widows are seen sorrowing over their helpless children.

* A gentleman has recently been appointed to the important office of Inspector of Steamboats, and I believe that he efficiently discharges his onerous duties.

HOW GOLIAH TRUMP CURED WIDOW BLUNT'S LAZY DONKEY.

MR. GOLIAH TRUMP was a man of his word, and if he promised to do a good turn for a friend, it was not his fault if it were not done in due course. He was not a highly polished man, and at first sight did not always make a favourable impression; still he was a good-natured fellow, and that quality compensated for his minor defects and peculiarities with those who knew him intimately.

Though Goliah moved in a good position, was a thriving merchant, and a good mark in a mercantile sense, his native-born idiosyncrasies did not alter with his improved circumstances. He very lightly esteemed the conventionalities of refined life, and rather prided himself on the provincial idiom, the honest bluntness, and the eccentric manners of his worthy old sire, who was as jovial an old English gentleman as ever enjoyed a mug of sharp cyder or a squab pie, or rode after a pack of fox-hounds.

Goliah was a portly man approaching to middle age, with rather a handsome face, and eyes full of fun and frolic. There was a dash more of the latter in his manner than thoughtful persons would approve of, but he would not try to alter his nature to please the taste or fancy of any one; indeed, I doubt if he could have done so for more than five minutes, had he been promised a prize medal for the exertion. It would take too much space to detail the virtues of Mrs. Trump, so I simply say she was one of the excellent of the earth, "respected most by those who knew her best."

Goliah was a man of impulse. He rarely thought long or deeply on any subject, so when he conceived an idea of going home to see his "dear old daddy," he was not long in deciding to do so, as the "ways and means" were within his compass. In three weeks' time his comfortable establishment was broken up, 'and he was on shipboard with his loving wife and family bound to old England. After enduring the blasts of Cape Horn and other inevitables of the long homeward voyage, he arrived safely in the land of his birth.

Previous to leaving Sydney, Goliah had promised his friend Sam Blunt to go and see his widowed mother, who lived in a rural village less than a hundred miles from London. But an afflictive event prevented his fulfilling his promise for several months. At length he wrote Widow Blunt that she might expect to see him on the following Tuesday.

Some of my readers will easily conceive the widow's joy and gladness at the idea of soon seeing a living person who had so recently conversed with her dear boy Sam. There are fond mothers in Australia too, who would hail such pleasure as the happiest holiday they could have, and would sit and listen to good news from their absent sons or daughters with far more delight than they would listen to a grand concert.

On the appointed day Marigold Cottage looked extra stylish, and the widow's cap was unusually prim and stiff starched. The savoury odour which floated from her little kitchen, and the snow-white table-cloth spread in her front parlour, indicated that some one was coming out of the common circle of her visitors, and the good old lady's face was beaming with happy satisfaction. Many longing glances did she cast up the lane for signs of the approach of her expected guest as the hours dragged lazily on; and many gentle bastings did she bestow upon the poor birds before the fire, which had long since been done brown. It was two hours past dinner-time, and her sharp appetite had given place to the peculiar faintness produced by dinner delayed, while her heart was beginning to grow sick with "hope deferred." The ducks were overcooked, and as dry as stuffed shags in a museum; the green peas were boiled to green paste, and the batter pudding was getting hard as beeswax; in fact, the nice dinner was spoiled and not fit to set before her son's friend, who she imagined was a particularly prim and stately gentleman. The widow was just going to sit down and have a good cry—as she called it—when suddenly she began to laugh, for she saw a gig stop at her gate, and heard a strange, comical voice shout out, "Hallo, there, be's that Mrs. Blunt's cottage?"

"Yes, sir, yes, sir," exclaimed the widow, hastily toddling along the garden path. "Are you Mr. Trump?"

"E'es, sure enough I'm he, come to see thee at last. How be'st thee, then?" said bluff Goliah, shaking hands with the widow till he nearly shook her cap off, and made her sneeze. In another minute he was sitting in the best parlour, telling in his broadest style all the interesting news he could think of about her son Sam, his devoted wife, and their boys, Dick, Tom, and Harry. Oh, what a happy afternoon that was for Widow Blunt! she will never forget it. How she sat and laughed and cried alternately, as her loquacious visitor poured out his budget of news from the far-off land, and told her all the pleasing things he knew concerning the loved ones who were as dear to her as her life. All her late troubles about her shrivelled ducks and waxy pudding were forgotten in the joy she felt at the good tidings which Goliah had brought her, and which his fertile fancy assisted to make highly amusing, while his occasional outbursts of laughter made the cuckoos in the adjacent woods wag their tails.

Oh, ye restless seekers after new sensations, did you ever try the refreshing excitement of raising up a down-crushed spirit? or ever sit and see a poor old widowed mother cry for joy over some little bit of good news which you had communicated from her absent boy or girl? Did you ever try that luxury? If not, look out for an opportunity of doing so, and I promise it will yield you a pleasure immeasurably surpassing the excitement of the most improbable love or ghost story, and a delightsome relish such as M. Soyer and all his fry could no more imitate than they could make a live turtle.

Next morning, after breakfast, Widow Blunt expressed a desire that Goliah should see her dear relatives, the Goodwins, who lived at a farm-house a few miles off, but she added hesitatingly, "I really don't know how you will get there, unless I can send a messenger to cousin Peter to bring his gig for you."

"How be'est thee going, then?" asked Goliah, in his own peculiar tone, and with a comical twinkle in his eye.

"Oh, I'm going in my little donkey chaise; I have a nice quiet beast that I can drive myself, but I should not like to ask you to ride behind an ass, you would not like it, I am sure, for we shall meet a lot of people by the way."

"Bless thee heart, mother, I'm not so grand as thee thinks, though I come from a golden land. Where's the animal? I'll harness 'en up in no time. Not ride behind a donkey, indeed! Why, your son, Sam, wouldn't speak to me if I was too proud to ride with his mother. I don't care a flip who sees me do anything that isn't wicked—that's the way to say it. Where's the moke?"

The donkey was soon put into a two-wheeled gig, which was perhaps a size too small for Goliah and his rather stout companion; however, they wedged themselves in with a little exertion, and off they set, Widow Blunt taking the reins. "Gee up, Jacky! gee up, my boy!" she exclaimed, mildly, and gave the reins a gentle jerk at the same time. Jacky looked round at his extra load, then moved his long ears to and fro, and shuffled along at the rate of four miles an hour, which was the pace the widow usually travelled at, for she was fearful of driving fast; indeed, Jacky would not have moved faster had she tried to persuade him with her kindest words, and she was afraid to whip him lest he should damage the dash-board with his hoofs, and perhaps injure her at the same time.

"Won't he move along faster than that?" asked Goliah, who was probably thinking of the fine paces of his mettlesome prad in the colony.

"No, he won't go faster," said the widow. "He is very obstinate sometimes, and won't mind a word I say to him; still he is a good donkey, he never offers to run away with me, and he only kicks when I begin to beat him."

"Oho, Mister Jacky! a pretty character I hear of thee! That's the way you behave to your kind missis, is it? Now let me tell thee, thee'st got her son, Sam's friend, Goliah Trump, behind thee, so the sooner thee begin'st to mend the better, I can tell thee. Drabbit it, let me drive 'en," added Goliah, taking the reins from the widow. "I'll make 'en jump, I'll warrant. Hallo, there! barn it, what dost thee mean by poking along at this pace, like an old cow with a sore leg? Ods dampers and doughboys! what do'st thee mean, eh? Lazy rogue, come up! Hallaballoo! hobgoblins and blunderbuses! get along, or I'll cut thee into catsmeat!"

Goliah shouted thus in very loud and gruff tones, and at the same time threw his gigantic arms in the air in a manner formidable enough to frighten the stubbornest donkey in the world. The effect upon the poor brute was marvellous, and perhaps it is worth noting for the advantage of those who are fond of assinine studies, or who have to do with other obstinate animals. When Goliah first addressed him,

Jacky laid his ears flat aback in token of astonishment, and looked out of the corners of his eyes, as though he were taking the measure of his strange driver. Then he showed his teeth—as marks of opposition, he also slightly elevated his hind [part, ;evincing contempt, and at the same time a disposition to kick. But as Goliah poured out the torrent of hard-sounding words, Jacky's tail began to twitch in a peculiar manner, then to stand up as straight as a boat's jigger-mast, plainly indicating extreme fear and a desire for peace, by hoisting an apology for a flag of truce. After uttering three heavy sighs and a grunt, his pace improved into a quick trot, hence it was quite clear that Jacky was subdued, his stubborn will was broken, and much as it may have annoyed him to be thus humbled before the good old lady, who had been the victim of his lazy tricks for many years, it was nevertheless a fact, which he could not deny, that he was mastered, thoroughly cowed, as most donkeys are when spoken to by men of spirit.

A good moral lesson may be learned by a consideration of the metaphysical aspect of that sudden surrender of the donkey's will. It [is a striking example of the power of mind over mere animal propensity—but I must go on with my story. The widow was highly delighted, and laughed like a merry maiden. "I do think you have cured his obstinate temper,-Mr. Trump," she remarked; "indeed, there is a surprising change in him all at once; I declare I did not fancy he could trot so fast. Well, well, who'd have thought it? Well done, Jacky, my boy! you shall have some beans by-and-bye."

"I'll show thee what he can do in a minute," said Goliah —then, addressing the donkey, he roared out more furiously than before, "Hallo! get along, thee lazy scamp; dos't think I'll see thee impose on my friend Sam's mother in this way? Barn it all, I'll skin thee in a minute, I will. Hallaballoo! bullseyes, and blowpipes! get away with thee goodfor-nothing rascal! I'll let thee see what's o'clock, I'll warrant. Come up thee sleepy-headed rogue!" at the same time he stamped with his big boots on the bottom of the gig, which shocked the donkey to such an extent, that he trembled while he tore along with the gig at a mad gallop. Never before was a donkey seen to go at such a racing pace by the oldest parishioner. Out ran the astounded villagers from their homes—men, women, and children—to gaze at the passing phenomenon. They shuddered for the fate of widow Blunt, and turned pale as they whispered the name of the person whom they supposed was driving her ; while Goliah continued to roar and shout, and stamp his feet purposely to increase their wonderment, until all the children ran indoors again and hid themselves under their beds from the " terrible old Bogy who was flying away with poor old Mrs. Blunt."

" Oh, for goodness gracious sake, Mr. Trump, stop the donkey ; we shall be upset ! O dear, dear me, do stop him, pray do, sir ! The wheels will come off, I'm sure. Woa, Jacky," said the widow, in a state of intense trepidation.

" Barn him, I'll give it him !" roared Goliah, louder than ever. " Lazy jackass, I'll let thee know thee'st got a Sydney man behind thee, and I'll teach thee to shew better manners to a Sydney man's mother. Hoogh ! Hoogh ! Hoogh ! get along thee lazy rogue ! Blurr—r ! I'll blow thee into beanskins."

The poor donkey was scared into a perspiration, and he had never been known to perspire before. As he had no winkers he could see the furious antics of the burly man beside his mistress, and he flew along at a rate that he had never even dreamt of, and which made all the old superannuated asses that were grazing under the hedges " hee haw " with astonishment. Onward he sped with outstretched head, and his tail as stiff as a crow-bar, and not an effort did he relax till his eccentric driver pulled him up, or rather pulled him down on his hind quarters at the gate of cousin Goodwin's farm, then began to laugh till the joints of the old gig rattled again, and all the little Goodwins ran out to see " what was the matter."

" O lawk a mercy me ! how you have frightened me, Mr. Trump," exclaimed the widow, jumping out of the gig with unusual agility for a lady of seventy-two. " I declare I'm all of a shake. But I'm thankful we are not killed. Dear, deary me ! I shall never forget this terrible ride, never."

" Bless thee dear old heart, mother ! there was no danger. I could have pulled him down in a second. Don't thee believe I'd have risked thee neck, not I, thee son Sam would shoot me when I got back to Sydney, if I had only hurt his darling mother's little finger nail. That dose will do master Jacky more good than a bundle of sticks would do about his back. That's what I call moral suasion.

Thee saw I didn't beat him a bit, I only spoke out like a man, and that's the right way to deal with asses of all sorts, for barn em, they haven't got more courage than goslings."

* * * * * *

Prior to getting into the gig to return home, after spending a merry day at cousin Goodwin's, the widow made Goliah promise not to speak a word to Jacky, and to let her drive. But the donkey evidently knew that his late tormentor was behind him, for he trotted along like a butcher's cob. If he showed the slightest symptom of relaxing his speed, Goliah would merely cough—he did not speak—and Jacky's tail seemed electrified in a moment, and he began to gallop till the widow pulled him into a trot again.

* * * * * *

That extraordinary occurrence served for many an evening's chat around the firesides of the wonder-stricken villagers. Some of the unsophisticated natives still dispute about the human identity of the roaring donkey driver, and others shudder to this day at the bare mention of Australia; for they imagine that Goliah Trump, as he flew through their streets in the widow's gig, is a fair specimen of the inhabitants of this famous continent, consequently they infer that we are an awfully fast and furious nation.

Widow Blunt has not forgotten her exciting ride, and the recollection of it has made her laugh away many a melancholy moment. In her subsequent letters to her son Sam, she has often alluded to the comical affair, and has told over and over again how that funny Mr. Trump frightened her poor old donkey to death; for he died three years afterwards.

But Jacky never forgot the lesson to the last day he dragged the gig; and if it were not a perfect cure for his laziness, it was a wonderful corrective. Ever after that, if he showed symptoms of his old habits returning, it was only necessary for the widow to shout through her ear-trumpet "Ods dampers and doughboys!" when Jacky's tail would begin to work like a pump-handle—for the bare idea of those Australian edibles was as terrifying to him as bombshells. But if his mistress at the same time put on her clogs and made a clatter on the bottom of the gig, his ears would fall flat aback, and his tail would point to the moon, and off he would gallop as though he thought Goliah had come again ; for of course his stupid head did not know that that worthy colonist had returned to the other side of the world.

* * * * * *

I am not quite sure that Goliah's " moral suasion " would be effective on lazy asses of another sort, and I fear he would be impatiently disposed to substitute *material* " dampers and doughboys," and to aim them at the heads of his sub-jects, as boys apply snowballs, which of course would not be commendable. I think, however, that he might make a trial of his system on a small scale, without giving himself much trouble to find fitting subjects, and if he were only moderately successful, there would be plenty of scope for his peculiar gift, which by diligently exercising he might greatly ADVANCE AUSTRALIA.

MR. M'FADDLE'S PIC-NIC PARTY.

THAT Port Jackson is a delightful place for boating excursions, few persons deny who know anything about it. For my part, I cannot think of a more agreeable way of spending a holiday, or a more efficient way of rallying vapours from a wearied brain, than a trip in a carefully handled sailing-boat, with a fresh breeze, in and out of the lovely bays and coves, or round the many green islands, which grace our matchless harbour. Away from the excitement and jostle of city life, with nothing but the smoke in the distance, and the softened din of cart wheels, to remind one that mankind were not all asleep, the mind finds rest and quietude ; while the physical senses are refreshed with the uncontaminated air of heaven. Often have I started from home with mind and body impaired by sedentary duties and cares which increased with indoor nursing, like fungus on the mouldy walls of a vault. Sometimes I have been favoured with the company of a congenial friend, who needed gentle out-of-door exercise as much as myself, and was equally disposed to relish an aquatic trip. After selecting a boat to our mind, from the well-kept fleet at the Subscription Boat Club, we have hoisted our sails to the breeze, and bounded over the billows, as rejoiced at our liberty as a couple of seagulls just released from a week's confinement in a ship's hen coop ; and a few hours afterwards to have seen us seated on a rock, eating hot mutton chops (which we had cooked *al fresco* on a *wooden gridiron)* and roasted potatoes, would have astonished a gourmand, and made him long for such an appetite as we displayed. I have pleasing recollections of many such invigorating trips, and can with confidence recommend an occasional treat of that sort (with such extemporaneous meals) to persons suffering from dyspepsia, a disorder which is frequently laughed at—as an imaginary old bogy, by persons who, fortunately for themselves, do not know what they laugh at, or they would confess that a man with fractured ribs, might with equal reason be made the subject of ridicule. But while I so heartily recommend aquatic pleasures, I would at the same time remark, by way of caution, that there is necessity for using judgment in choosing favourable weather, and securing efficient boats' crews, or your excursion may be anything but enjoyable ; as the following little story will exemplify.

Mr. M'Faddle loved fresh air, and rightly appreciated its invigorating influence ; but he was not able to enjoy so much of it as he wished, for he was only a journeyman tailor, and as he had a large family he was obliged to sit pretty closely to the shopboard, in order to support them comfortably, without running into debt.

Happily for the working classes of Sydney, holidays are numerous during the summer months ; and that they are thoroughly enjoyed—especially in fine weather—is apparent from the rosy-faced folks of all ages, who may be seen thronging the steamboats and railway trains, or lining the rocky shores of the harbour in various parts, with their provisions spread out on grassy tables in holiday profusion. There fathers and mothers, and their adult friends, sit and enjoy a little pleasant social chat beneath the shady trees ; and old grandfather, who is fond of fishing, throws out his long line from the top of a rock, then lights his pipe and sits down patiently to wait till he gets a bite ; and dear old grandmother, in her best bonnet, has a merry romp on the soft sward, with little Beckey and Billy ; while the elder boys and girls frolic about in the sunshine like young Wallabys. Thousands of happy maidens anticipate those periodical treats for weeks or months, and eagerly their half awakened eyes peep through their bedroom windows at the signs of the weather, when the first blushes of their holiday morning tinge the horizon. If the sun is about to rise in a clear blue sky, what gladsome faces are reflected by their dressing-glasses, but how sad they look if a drizzling mist hides the sunshine. I always share in the general sorrowful feeling, if heavy rain clouds appear on such days, to cast a pall over the recreations of so many hopeful ones, and spoil their holiday apparel. May no grudging soul ever try to curtail those seasons of healthful enjoyment to the humbler classes of Sydney ! But I am digressing from my story, with my reflections on homely joys.

Mr. M'Faddle and his family had looked forward to one of those holidays, in the early part of the present year, as a day for a special treat, *i.e.*, a pic-nic to Rose Bay. Mr.

M'Faddle loved boating, and fancied he could pull an oar with anybody; but he seldom enjoyed that pleasure. On the present occasion, Archy Twist, a fellow-workman, had been offered the loan of a boat by his cousin, who was mate of a coasting schooner; so an excursion was arranged for the following Wednesday. Mr. and Mrs. M'Faddle, with their two adult daughters, and two half-grown daughters in short frocks, two big boys in jackets, and one little boy in knickerbockers; Mr. and Mrs. Twist, and their two grown-up girls, with their cousin Jane, made in all fourteen souls; and considering that nine of them were ladies, in holiday skirts, it will be inferred that the boat was not a mere dingy.

On the day fixed, which had been eagerly anticipated, and plentifully provided for in the victualling way, the whole party assembled at a jetty in Darling Harbour, at nine o'clock exactly; and soon afterward they had safely embarked in the boat, taking with them two large baskets of provisions, a keg of water, and sundries. After all the ladies were comfortably seated, and Mr. M'Faddle had scraped his way through a mass of muslin and steel bars to his seat at the helm, the boat was pushed off, and away they went right merrily, though slowly, with the two young M'Faddles at the paddles, and Archy Twist sitting, tailor-fashion, in the head sheets, smoking his pipe, and joking the boys on their pulling.

The morning was warm and sunny, with a light puffy breeze from north-west; and not one of the excited pleasure seekers had the slightest misgivings about the weather, for the sky above them was blue, the rippling water around them was flashing with sun beams, and their hearts were all full of holiday thoughts and hopes. What if they had left empty cupboards at home, had they not two full baskets in the boat? Let care of to-morrow wait till to-morrow, they were going to enjoy themselves to-day. So thought every leaping heart, as away splashed the boat under Pyrmont Bridge, and along the eastern shore, Archy Twist keeping a good look out for ferry steamers and mooring buoys. As the tide was at strong flood, and the boat was bluff bowed and heavy, the young M'Faddles soon began to show symptoms of distress, and by the time they had pulled abreast of Blue's Point, they were purple with over exertion, and perspiring like stokers raking out clinkers.

"That's richt, tak it easy, laddies," said Mr. M'Faddle, as the boys stopped to examine the gathering blisters on their hands. "Take it easy, my sons; we are nae in haste; there's naebody expects us to dinner in any of you big hooses doon the harbour; but I think we maun try to mak' the sail do some wark, for the wind is wi' us if there's nae muckle of it. Rig the mast, Archie, ma freend! rest yersels a wee bit, boys."

The mast was rigged, and the sail set, with some difficulty, for Twist knew less about boats than about broadcloth and buttons, and the boat glided along at the rate of two knots an hour. The sun, as it rose higher in the sky, began to glow fiercely upon their heads, and to tinge their cheeks and noses with crimson. However, they were out for a holiday, and were evidently resolved that minor inconveniences should not put them out of humour; so the ladies opened their parasols and said they were very happy; whereupon M'Faddle said he was very happy to see them happy; and, to give vent to the pressure of his high spirits, he volunteered a Scotch song with a lively chorus, and after that was over, Twist gave an Irish song, with plenty of racy humour in it, which provoked a laughing chorus. Then they all sang "Cheer boys cheer," and "Row, brothers, row," until they re-echoed with a row, which must have astounded the crabs, and made the periwinkles ready to jump out of their shells. After they had finished singing, they chatted, and joked, and laughed and giggled, until the boat's topsides groaned with the shaking of the seats. A happy holiday-group were they! A merrier lot never crammed themselves into a collier's jolly boat.

"Phoo! poo, poo! What on earth is that?" squealed Mrs. Twist, suddenly, and at the same time twisting her face into expressive crinkles, as the boat was passing the red buoy off Fort Macquarie. "Patience me! what a wicked smell. Did you ever!"

"It is only the main sewer," said Twist, who, having been accustomed to work in a London cheap tailoring establishment, was not unacquainted with peculiar odours. "It is a fine place for fishing, just here, only the stench is apt to knock one up, especially on warm days like this."

"Knock one *down*, I should think," said Mrs. Twist, with her nose tightly compressed between her fore-finger and

thumb, " It is enough to kill a currier : and I mean to say
it is shocking bad manners of the sewer makers to empty
out their nuisances directly in front of Government House,
and right into the mouth of the main cove in Sydney harbour. For pity's sake, let us get away from this horrible
fume, or I shall faint."

The wind being now scarcely strong enough to make the
boat stem the tide, the sail was rolled up, and M'Faddle
and Twist began to pull, while one of the boys took charge
of the tiller. A discussion then began, as to where they
should land to spend the day. One of the ladies said her
favourite spot was Rose Bay, another said she liked Milk
Beach, and a third preferred Vaucluse. Mrs. M'Faddle
had tender recollections of the first three days she spent in
the colony, at the Quarantine Station, and proposed to go
to Spring Cove ; but Mr. Twist said it was no joke to pull
that heavy boat nine miles against tide, which opinion Mr.
M'Faddle instantly endorsed, and wanted to land on Garden
Island.

" Ha, ha, ha ! You are tired already, mate," laughed
Twist, " and I have been thinking for the last ten minutes
that the boat would go just as fast if you were fast asleep.
But you can't land on Garden Island, because the Government has taken possession of it, more's the pity, for it was
a nice place for picnic parties, and so near home too."

After a good deal more discussion, it was decided that
they should call at Clark Island, to rest for half an hour,
then cross the harbour to Bradley's Head, there to boil the
kettle, cook the potatoes, and make other preparations for
their feast. The two tailors then threw their full power
into the paddles, and at about half past eleven o'clock, the
boat bumped on the rocks of Clark Island, which stopped
her instantly. The whole party then landed, and leaving
Johnny M'Faddle to look after the boat, the others ascended
to one of the caves at the northern end, where they seated
themselves, and gave voice to their appreciation of the refreshing shadow of the rock above them, and the charming
natural grotto which held them all comfortably.

Had any of them possessed even ordinary powers of
observation, they might, an hour before, have seen a heavy
bank of storm clouds gathering above the south western
horizon ; and had one of the older colonists reflected a
minute, he would have remembered that hot puffs of wind

from north west are usually the precursors of hard squalls from the opposite point of the compass. But neither of them observed, or thought of anything that was disagreeable until a strong blast of wind whirled into the cave, and caused a scramble to secure the bonnets and mantles from being blown into the water.

"Ma goodness ! it's gaen to bloo, I'm thinking," said Mr. M‘Faddle, while the wind roared like thunder among the rocks and caverns, and made the previously glassy surface of the harbour seethe and foam like a boiling fish kettle. "Wha on earth wad he thocht it wad a ben sae rough, all in a minute like? Hey ! deeckins ! luke at the boatie, it's ganging off without us; as true as my name's Mac," he added, pointing to the boat, which was fast drifting away from the island, with the sail flapping, and shaking the mast furiously. "Archie, what's to be done, mon? Why dinna ye speak? Why do ye stand there gaping like a swine?"

"Can't you swim after it?" asked Twist, with a bewildered look.

"Toot mon ! are ye daft althegether? The sharks wad bite the legs aff me, before I had kicked out thrice : besides I could na mair catch the boatie, by swimming, than I could catch a Jew fish. What in the warrald shall I do now?"

As Mr. M‘Faddle asked that unanswerable question, he raced down to the rocks below, and the first thing he did there was to well baste his boy Johnny with the leg of an old Chinese chair—which was unluckily lying close to hand— and at the same time scolded him soundly, in broad Scotch, for being "such a gowk as to let the boat gang adreeft."

Johnny acknowledged the basting with a series of howls, louder than the wind, then hobbled away as fast as he could to a stump, where he was sitting rubbing his bruises, when the rest of the party came down to the shore to learn the facts of the case, which were simply this, the boat having been imperfectly fastened, had broken adrift with the first puff.

"I say, Sally, what part of the harbour does Johnny most resemble just now?" asked Nick M‘Faddle of his sister, as he pointed to his discomfited brother in the distance. "Do you give it up, Sally? Well, I'll tell you ; he is like Sirius cove (*serious* cove). Ha, ha, ha ! that's good, isn't it? I made that out of my own head."

"That's good, too, see what you can make out of that," exclaimed his mother, crossly administering a big box on Nick's ear, which sounded like a cracker. "I heard your impudence, you young monkey. You deserve the leg of the chair as much as your brother every bit. Now what cove do *you* look like ?"

It would lengthen my story into a volume, were I to detail all the misadventures of the unlucky islanders. How Mr. M'Faddle scolded his wife for boxing Nick, and Mrs. M'Faddle abused her husband for basting Johnny. How Mrs. Twist's satin bonnet blew into the water, and Mr. Twist tumbled in head foremost, in his vain attempt to recover it, and at the same time frightened his wife into a fit. How Peggy M'Faddle slipped down on a slimy rock, and went limping the rest of the day, although she declared that she had not even scratched herself. How Miss Twist's parasol was blown inside out and ruined ; and her cousin Jane cut one of her best boots, and one of her big toes with an oyster shell. How the infant M'Faddle swallowed a periwinkle, and grew black in the face, until his mother succeeded in curing him by thumping him on the back. How Nick and Johnny while walking round the island, in search of stray edibles, found a cocoa-nut, and began at once to fight for the ownership ; but after boxing each other until they were winded, they discovered that the nut was rotten, which incident, if they remember it, may teach them a good moral lesson for after life ; it would also be useful—if calmly studied—to older persons than they, who are fighting for rotten nuts, or snarling over matters equally worthless.

I might also describe the vain struggles of the party to " cloy the hungry edge of appetite," with native oysters, of the smallest size and the most obstinate tenacity for their rocky beds. But I pass over all these details, and briefly record that hungry, jaded, cold, and cross, they all reassembled in the cave about three o'clock, there to confer upon the best thing to be done to avert impending starvation. Twist moved the first impromptu resolution (as he sat shivering in his wet garments beside his bonnetless wife), which was, " that Mr. M'Faddle should swim over to Darling Point, with his clothes on his head ; then walk to Rushcutter's Bay, and borrow a boat from somebody." The motion was not seconded, but somebody moved that Twist was a brute for wanting to drown his neighbour.

Numerous other suggestions and objections were made, and ill temper was beginning to show itself in the senior ladies, when, perhaps luckily for their caps and curls, one of the boys suddenly called out, "Oh crikey! here comes a boat! Hoorah!"

Every neck was stretched, and every eye directed towards the welcome boat, which was off Shark Island, plunging her way up the harbour under double-reefed canvas. I may here remark that, in consequence of the tempestuous state of the weather, there were very few boats afloat that afternoon.

"Coom awa, coom awa, doon on the rocks," said Mr. M'Faddle, starting up in exciting haste. "Stand althegether, an when I tell ye to skreel, skreel like bogles every ane of ye."

Down the whole party hastened to the water's edge, and as the boat came abreast of the island, Mr. M'Faddle gave the word of command to skreel.

Never was heard such a chorus on Clark Island since the last corroboree of "Old Gooseberry," and her maids of honour: the caves behind them echoed back the sounds, like the cries of tormented water sprites. In an instant they were answered by loud shouts of the six sailors in the boat (which was a man-of-war's launch), but they did not change their course.

"They hear us plain enoo, but they are na cooming to our help," said Mr. M'Faddle; "skreel again, girls, an wave yer linen."

Another screeching chorus shook the island, accompanied by a fluttering of white handkerchiefs in the wind, when all the sailors stood up in the boat, whirled their hats in the air, and shouted hurrah! hurrah! hurrah! until their cheers died away in the distance. The jolly tars evidently mistook the cries of distress, for an enthusiastic salute to their pennant.

The discomfiture of the hungry excursionists for the next three hours was trying in the extreme. A little before sundown they attracted the notice of a boat bound to Sydney with a cargo of fish. The humane fishermen quickly embarked the shivering party, who huddled together among the schnappers and flathead, which furnished very cool seats, although rather slippery. Soon afterwards they all landed at Soldiers' Point, looking as weather-beaten as shipwrecked sailors. The next day their boat was found on the rocks in

Mossman's Bay, badly damaged, and with sails blown to pieces ; their provisions, also, were damaged by the combined influence of saltwater and sunbeams.

It will probably be long before those sufferers forget that day's *treat*, or before Twist's cousin will again lend his ship's boat. Mr. M'Faddle, however, gained wisdom by the mishap, for he declares he will in future " keep his weather eye open," but especially when he goes into a boat. I heartily commend his resolution to all novices who venture on to the tempting, though somewhat treacherous waters of Port Jackson ; and I also advise them, in sultry, north-west winds to " look out for squalls."

CHANGE OF SCENE, AND FRESH AIR.

MR. MOANS was as difficult to move as a dead elephant, when he had a job in hand, as he called it. He was a busy old man, in his way, though some of his neighbours wondered what trade he followed, for he made no more noise with his tools than an old matron darning stockings. Long after many folks in the city were asleep, a light was usually to be seen in Mr. Moan's laboratory; and if any curious person had mounted to the roof and peeped through his dormer window, they would have seen him setting up specimens of various sorts, and looking as weary and worn as most men do who sit up late at sedentary work.

His friends often advised him to try a change of scene and fresh air, to recruit his diminishing strength, though they seldom persuaded him that he needed a change. "Phoo!" he would exclaim, with a smile, "where in the world can I find fresher air than is wafted through my window, from the north-east? and where can I behold more enlivening scenes than the verdant domain and the sparkling harbour afford, without the trouble of moving from my bamboo chair? Only just peep out of my window, to your right hand, and if you have a poet's or a painter's eye, you must be charmed with the picturesque view of Darling Point, and the villa-crowned hills beyond; with Craig-end windmill in the foreground, and St. Mark's church in the distance, with the light-house far away on the cliffs! Change of scene indeed! Fiddle-dee-dee! 'You'll find no change in me,' as the old song says."

One day—not long ago—Captain Gimble called to see Mr. Moans; and being an intimate friend, he was shown at once into the laboratory.. The captain, (who was a fine, robust specimen of the bracing virtues of fresh air, and salt water,) had been away on foreign voyages for several years, so the pleasure of seeing him was proportionately great, and Mr. Moan's yellow face shone with gladness. After a long and pleasant chat, the captain pressingly invited his debilitated friend to spend a few days on board his ship, before he sailed for Hong-Kong.

"My good friend!" whined Mr. Moans, passing his hand across his brow, "I cannot spare time to go anywhere, for several months to come. Besides, I have not so much faith in changes as some folks, who would try to persuade me that moving about in strange places will put flesh on a wooden leg. But, if I could take my work with me, I should very much like to spend a few days on board the 'Wild Duck,' before you sail, for the pleasure of your society, and to hear more of your interesting accounts of foreign travels."

"Never mind your work when you are going to play," said the hearty skipper. "Heave all your curiosities into the locker, and forget them for a time; you may find some funny specimens to study on board my ship. Come, rouse up, my friend! Let me take you in tow, and I'll engage you shall return to Sydney in a few days, with your nerves braced up as tawt as weather backstays. Now then, get your monkey-jacket, and come away with me at once."

A few days afterwards, Mr. Moans might have been seen walking the deck of a fine rakish-looking bark, which was lying at anchor, in a busy port not far from Sydney; and as he gazed up at the tapering masts, and down again at the graceful hull of the vessel, his old roving desires awoke, and he wished he could take a voyage in her; but his work at home rose before his mental vision, and checked his longings. Just then Captain Gimble came alongside in his boat, and after nimbly stepping on board, he said, "What do you say to a trip to Melbourne, Mr. Moans?"

"Melbourne, Captain!—hem—I thought you were bound for Hong-Kong!"

"Well, you see, sir, we are far too deep for a long voyage. While I have been away in Sydney, some of those folks on shore there have loaded my ship down to the scupper-holes; and I cannot take any coal out of her, without trimming the whole cargo fore-and-aft, which would be expensive, as I am short-handed, so I intend to go to Melbourne with this lot; then to return here and load for China."

"But I imagine, captain, if the ship is too deep to go to Hong-Kong, she is not light enough to go to Melbourne, or elsewhere," said Mr. Moans, with a look of concern for the safety of his friend, and his smart ship.

"That's true enough," replied the captain ; then, after a minute's reflection, he added—" It is only a short run to Melbourne, and it's the fine-weather season, so ' I'll chance it,' as the colonial boys say, and as lots of collier-skippers are obliged to do all the year round, poor fellows ! Let me persuade you to go with me. The trip will rouse up your digestive organs, and make your brains as bright as my anchor buttons."

I need not trouble the reader with all Mr. Moan's arguments, or his kind friend's characteristic replies. He longed for the trip, but all his specimens seemed to speak up together and urge that if he wished to complete them in time, he must work as long hours as a druggist, or journeyman tailor. On the other hand the charms of a cruise in such a smart clipper, with such agreeable captain and officers, presented themselves with irresistible force. He glanced at the cosy little cabin on deck, he thought of the benefit his brain might derive from the rest and relaxation, he thought too of the probability of meeting with some rare specimens in his travels, and finally he resolved to go ; at which decision Captain Gimble smiled complacently, then hastened on shore to clear his ship at the Custom House, and to get a few extra stores for his passenger.

Early next morning, a steam tug was alongside, and before Mrs. Moans, in Sydney, was aware of her erratic husband's movements, he was at sea, rolling along with a fair wind towards Melbourne, and looking as pleased as an Irish piper.

"Well, this is really delightful !" muttered Mr. Moans, as he paced up and down the clean flush deck ; now and then stopping to give the sailors a pull up with a sail—as the ship was short-handed—and fancying what an agreeable promenade he had, and how pleasantly he could walk up and down, and think about nothing ; and thus exercise his legs, rest his head, and at the same time refresh his lungs with pure saline air. The " Wild Duck " dashed along in gallant style, passing every other vessel in company with her, and as the wind increased Mr. Moan's rapture increased, till he began to wish he was a sailor. Suddenly, however, his ardour was damped by an intrusive wave, which dashed in at the waist on one side, and out at the other side, filling his boots in its transit, and convincing him directly that he could not walk the deck dryshod; indeed, he soon discovered that no one on board expected to do so, as was evidenced by " all hands " wearing diggers' long-boots.

" This is rather a moist ship," said Mr. Moans, walking up to Captain Gimble. " I wish I had brought my goloshes, —but, lack-a-day! now I come to remember, I have brought nothing with me but my red nightcap, and a toothbrush. Of course I did not anticipate taking this voyage, or I should have attended to my outfit. What shall I do, captain?"

" Never mind," said the good-natured skipper, smiling at his friend's concern about his scanty wardrobe. " I will lend you a pair of sea-boots, and anything else you want; but you had better get on top of deck-house if you want a walk, for you will find the main-decks all awash, as the sea gets up."

" I have found that already," said Mr. Moans, with a a glance at his wet legs. " As for a walk on that *house*, as you call it,—which is not much bigger than a spring-cart— I think a dance on top of a sentry-box would be almost as rational, and much safer exercise. I am afraid I shall grow giddy and tumble overboard, if I get up there; so I will have a quiet ramble round the cabin table instead. But bless me, captain! I had no idea that your smart-looking ship was so wet. Your main-deck is a regular duck-pond."

" Did you ever see a vessel, deeply laden with coal, that was very dry on deck?" asked the captain, with a comical look.

" No, I cannot say that I ever did, for the fact is I have never sailed in an overladen collier before, though I have been in a good many craft since I first smelt bilge water."

" Then depend on it you have something to learn, Mr. Moans; and I hope you will make a valuable use of your experience on this voyage. Hold on, Sir, here is a sea coming over the quarter."

" Hold on, indeed!" ejaculated Mr. Moans, while he ran away as fast as if the water were boiling, and just escaped into the little deck cabin as the wave curled over the taffrail. " I think I had need to hold on and never let go, if I don't want to be washed overboard amongst the sharks. Well, well, this is something entirely new to me," he added, throwing himself on a couch. " This change is as unsatisfactory as getting twenty bad shillings for a new sovereign ;. or a shocking bad hat for a good one at any evening party. I have change of air now, and plenty of it certainly, but it is too strongly seasoned with salt water to be agreeably fresh. If the ' Wild Duck' ship seas at this rate in fine weather, I am afraid she will duck us under altogether, if we fall in with foul weather."

The moon rose punctually at its appointed time that night, but Mr. Moans could only gaze at it through the cabin window ; for the flying spray precluded his going on deck with a dry skin, so he soon turned into bed, and there he lay thinking of his specimens at home, and thinking too, what a rare specimen of a disappointed man he was ; for instead of the delightful moonlight walks on deck with his friend Captain Gimble, which he had anticipated, the only chance he had of having a dry chat with his friend, was by mounting to the top of the house like a prowling tom cat. About midnight he was aroused from an uneasy doze by the well-known whistle of a " southerly burster" among the cordage ; and then began the most extraordinary night in his sea experience, which he is anxious to have recorded, for the special study of certain shipowners who may never have had the advantage of a night's lodging in one of their over-laden colliers in a southerly gale ; and in the hope of arousing their sympathies for the perils to which their seamen are exposed.

In a short time the sea began to boil and bubble, or to tumble about in a very confused manner, owing to the sudden shift of wind. Wave after wave leaped on the deck of the " Wild Duck ;" and as she wallowed from side to side, they had no chance to escape overboard again, except by the small scupper holes ; so they met amidships, and knocking their heads together, like fighting goats, sent fountains of spray flying upwards, to descend in cooling cataracts on the heads of the shivering crew ; while heavier billows thundered against the ship's side, like breakers on the rocks at Bondi. Mr. Moans had often heard poets warble about " dancing waves ;" but he never before completely realised the pretty idea ; and he thought he would like to see the poet who could make a pleasant song about those waves, which were dancing on the deck of the " Wild Duck." He had never seen or heard such a strange corroborree before. They hissed and seethed like a thousand fryingpans full of eggs and bacon, and seemed madly resolved to tear the tarpaulin off the main hatches, and drown the coals. None but a stone deaf person could sleep amidst such a hurleyburley ; at least so thought Mr. Moans, so he got out of bed, and watched the commotion of the elements through the cabin window, and wished he had a poet's fancy that could be tickled with the scene. But even the grim satisfaction of gazing on that strange "meeting of the waters" was denied him, for a lively little wavelet—as though in playful mockery of his plaintive singing, "What are the wild waves saying"—flew directly at his face, dashed through the cabin window, and deluged the sofa and the cabin floor, while an extra lurch at the same moment caused a select library of books to descend about his ears, from a shelf in the corner ; two weighty volumes of "Good Words" giving him some bad blows on the head. Thankful that the wave had not invaded his berth, Mr. Moans hastily jumped into bed again, and there he lay and tried to calmly contemplate the sublimity of the storm without, to calculate his chances of ever seeing his quiet little dormitory again, and to reason with his doubts about his intellectual faculties ever finding their way back to their proper bumps after being shaken and jostled up with the subordinate organs in his cranium like gingerbread nuts in a tin canister.

Presently he heard a clanking noise like a fire-engine, and he soon ascertained that all hands were at pumps, so he reasonably concluded that the ship had sprung a leak, and he began to estimate how long it would be before she sunk, as she had scarcely more than six inches of a side. But before he had satisfactorily worked that problem out, a thumping sea struck the deck-house, close to his ear, making the ship shudder from stem to stern. His mind was thereby diverted into the fidgetty anticipation of a sudden launch over the lee rail in his berth. He had often read of deck-houses being knocked off the deck, and had seen a cook's galley, full of coppers and saucepans, washed overboard ; and while gloomy recollections of those casualties helped him to draw a mental picture of his deck-house being swept away by the next heavy sea that struck it, the contemplation of the event was even less composing than a view of his next door neighbour's blazing house would be while looking out of his own attic window. The most favourable speculations on such a mishap yielded him no comfort, for even should the deck-house be toppled upside down in its transit over the rail—to say nothing of the bruises he would probably receive by being toppled upside down too —the house would be sure to leak at the doors and windows, and he could scarcely expect to navigate it to Sydney without sails, oars, rudder, or other nautical convenience. But if it should happen to go overboard with its roof uppermost, of course he would be as badly off as a man in a diving bell, without an air-pump. As sea after sea continued to strike the deck-house, he felt his tenure to be peculiarly uncertain, and was wishing that he could spread his blankets below upon the coals, and at the same time haul those gentlemen with him who had put too many coals on board, when Captain Gimble, glistening with spray, entered the cabin, and smilingly asked him "How he was getting on ?"

"I am not happy, Captain," replied Mr. Moans, sitting up in his bed. "The fact is, I am frightened, and fear terribly interferes with a person's enjoyment, either on sea or on shore. I have seldom, if ever before, experienced such a feeling on shipboard, but really this ' dreadful noise of waters in my ears' makes my flesh creep. The clanking of those pumps sounds like a horrible mill, grinding up the bones of drowned sailors to make putty for worm-eaten planks ; and the creaking jaws of the main-gaff seems to me like Satan laughing approvingly at his friends, who, for the sake of a few pounds of freight-money, imperil the lives of all on board. Have you stopped the leak ?"

"Not yet : the spear of one of the pumps is disabled ; but we will soon get it to work again. The carpenter was laid up sea sick ; so I went down to his berth just now, and gently hinted to him that the ship was sinking, and that he had better turn out and mend the pump spear. Ha, ha ! my blocks ! he roused out as smartly as if there was a buck rat in his bunk ! I never before saw such a prompt cure for sea sickness."

"Pray what is your real opinion of our present position, Captain ?" asked Mr. Moans. "Don't scruple to tell me the worst, for after all I am not afraid of death, let it come in whatever shape it may. Thank God I know that before the ship got to the bottom of the sea, if she sank just now, my soul would be far beyond the influence of storms and tossing waves. But it has never been my disposition to lie down and die. ' Never let the ship sink for want of pumping' is an old maxim of mine : so I will turn out and take a turn at the pumps, if you like, Captain."

"There is no necessity for your doing that," said the Captain ; " our present position is not very enviable certainly ; still we might be much worse off, under bad owners. Our ship is only leaking in her top sides, through baking so long in the sun, and her seams will probably take up in a few hours. Then our hull is sound and strong, our rigging and sails are good, and we have plenty of sea room. Our shipping so much water, and making such bad weather of it, is of course owing to our being overloaded ; but we cannot help that now, it would not be safe to take off the hatches, to lighten her. Fortunately she is not straining at all, and though it is certainly disagreeable for you, there is not much danger if we don't lose our masts. That is my candid opinion, as you have asked me for it. But if any of those old leaky coasting colliers have got caught in this breeze," added the Captain with a shrug of horror, " there will be more sailors' orphans, and sorrowing widows and mothers, to remember this night's fatal work ; for a rotten ship could not weather it out."

"Tell me, Captain, why are owners permitted to send rotten vessels to sea ?" asked Mr. Moans, with earnestness.

"Ah, why indeed !" said the Captain, " but there is no law to prevent them, or if there is it is considered obsolete. An unconscionable owner could send any old clumbung to sea ; in fact he might rig out a weatherboard barn, and no one would stop him. There was an old hooker lying abreast of us this morning ; her crew had been pumping her nearly all night ; all her sails were as patched as Paddy's breeches ; and there was scarcely a fathom of her running gear strong enough to hang a monkey ; yet she put out to sea as deep as a sand-barge."

"But how is it that owners find crews for their old clumbungs, as you call them, Captain ? Sailors love their lives, I suppose, as all other mortals do.'"

"Why, sir, sailors don't always know the character of ships before they get to sea, and then it is pump or sink, of course. But there are always men hard up, and glad to earn a crust ; and hunger sometimes blinds men to hazards. Hope is a strong trait in a sailor's character, and he has much need of it, too. I was talking with the skipper of a little schooner the other day ; he was waiting for a change of wind, with his vessel loaded almost to sinking point. I asked him why he loaded so deep? when he told me that his owner insisted on it that his vessel would carry one hundred tons, and if he did not take that quantity on board —though she could only safely carry ninety tons—he would be walked ashore as soon as he got to Sydney, and another master would be put in his place, while he went whistling for another ship; and very likely he would be tauntingly told he was no sailor, simply because he valued his own life and the lives of his crew."

"But is there no remedy for those monstrous evils?" asked Mr. Moans, looking very fierce, and dashing his red nightcap on deck as though he were hurling an imaginary anchor and cable on the toes of the niggardly owner just alluded to.

"Of course there is if it were applied," said the captain, "and that is a nice little job for a philanthropic legislator to take in hand; but I can't stop below any longer, I must go on deck and shorten sail again. Take care of yourself."

"Humph! Take care of yourself indeed! that's what Paddy said to his wife, just before he dropped a sack of potatoes on her head," mumbled Mr. Moans, then he lay down again, and amused himself, considering what he would do to the owners of "old clumbungs" if he were "monarch of all he surveyed."

*　　*　　*　　*　　*　　*

After a stormy passage of twelve days, he arrived safely in Melbourne; and though he had had such an extraordinary tossing about, he was glad of it when the danger was past, for it had wonderfully added to his nautical experience, and opened his eyes to the risks which many of our coasting seamen are mercilessly exposed to.

Mr. Moans derived much benefit from the trip; and can feelingly recommend change of scene and fresh air for all overworked students; though he certainly would not advise delicate men to take a voyage in an overladen collier.

MR. MOANS' VISIT TO MELBOURNE.

In the preceding chapter I have explained how Mr. Moans was induced to go to Melbourne for "change of scene and fresh air." I am not about to chronicle all he did, said, and saw there, or I should far exceed ordinary limits, and it would probably be uninteresting to the general reader; but I purpose taking a cursory glance at a few of his movements, and noting some of his observations in that metropolis, and its populous suburbs.

"Pray what is your opinion of Melbourne compared with Sydney, Mr. Moans?" asked an intelligent friend, who very kindly acted as *cicerone* through that surprisingly busy city.

Mr. Moans was an old Sydney man. All his dearest social interests were centred therein. He venerated even its crooked streets and narrow pathways — for they were crowded with happy recollections of youthful days; in short, his home was there, and he loved it; and he was prepared at all times to maintain the credit of the good old city. Moreover he had, on several occasions, observed a disposition in some "fast" Victorians when in Sydney, to underrate that mother-city, in their enthusiastic desire to extol the magnificence of their own colossal capital; so, (though he well knew he need not expect such an exhibition of bad taste in his friend beside him) he cautiously replied to the question — "Melbourne is undoubtedly a very fine city, sir."

"You will of course admit that it is much larger than Sydney?"

"It would be absurd to deny that, sir," said Mr. Moans. "Your harbour too, is very much larger than ours, and has larger waves in it when the wind blows fresh; as I observed during the two days that I was storm-staid on board the 'Wild Duck,' at the anchorage off Sandridge. Those are facts which I must admit; still, for beauty of scenery, apart from other considerations, your harbour would suffer as much in comparison with Port Jackson, as a large potato-field would beside a choicely-stocked parterre; and the

Yarra Yarra is a mere dyke compared with our romantic Paramatta River."

"Stay, sir," said Mr. Titler (the name of his *cicerone*). "Have you seen the Yarra above Princes Bridge ?"

"Not yet, sir; that is to say, I have not been far up it; but I allude to the lower part of the river, where your bone-boilers, tar-refiners, and other fume-raisers combine to suffocate every little indigenous flower that struggles to open its petals to the sunshine; and where the water is usually as thick as tanner's refuse, or Thames mixture."

"You must see the Upper Yarra before you leave, sir," said Mr. Titler, smiling. "Though I fear it will make poor Paramatta River appear to your fancy, in future, as unromantic as its mud oyster banks at low tide. That is our new General Post Office, or rather a part of it," he added, stopping short and gazing exultingly before a magnificent building in course of erection, large enough—in the opinion of one patriotic old Victorian lady—to hold all the letters in the world. "What do you think of our new Post Office, sir ?"

"It is much finer than our old one ; but how it will compare with our new one I cannot positively say just now," replied Mr. Moans, who could not fail to be struck with the extent and the ornateness of the structure. "Have you a building in Sydney to equal it?" asked Mr. Titler, with -more Victorian pride than he had before exhibited.

"Yes, I think our University excels it. But, as I am not an architect, my judgment may be at fault. When you come to Sydney, I will show you some private buildings which will surprise you."

"Humph !—have you been to our Public Library, Mr. Moans?" said Mr. Titler, looking like a rifleman who had just hit the bull's-eye.

"I have, sir, and was very much pleased with my visit. In all my travels I have not seen a Public Library equal to it, out of London ; and I wish we had one only half as good in Sydney. It is an honour to your colony, as well as an inestimable boon', to the population, and your statesmen have shown wise foresight in thus caring for the moral and intellectual improvement of the people. Vast as must have been the cost of that noble institution, it is money well laid out, and will probably save a hundred times that amount to future rulers in the gaol and police estimates ;

while in a higher point of view, the blessings it may confer on this young nation are incalculable."

"You have not such fine wide streets in Sydney as these, Mr. Moans," said Mr. Titler, who was evidently pleased at the last observations of his friend.

"We have not, sir; nor yet such wide gutters to cross in wet weather, and to crack our carriage springs at the street junctions. I suppose it to be on account of the low level of your city that you have these gaping drains in every street. But I cannot say that the sewerage of our City of Sydney is as perfect as it might be made, considering our natural facilities for drainage."

"If we had such facilities in Melbourne," said Mr. Titler, "we should have had underground sewers in every street long ago. But we have plenty of Yan Yean water to flush our gutters in dry weather, so we are not much inconvenienced by foul odours."

"I wish I could say the same of our Sydney gutters," said Mr. Moans. "In many parts the citizens are very much annoyed by the effluvium from stagnant drains, in warm weather especially; and I state on the authority of a clever medical neighbour, that the public health is periodically affected thereby. Pray, what is that new building?" added Mr. Moans, as they suddenly sighted a stylish-looking edifice, near the foot of Prince's Bridge.

"That is our new Fish Market," said Mr. Titler. "It belongs to the City Corporation."

"Fish Market!" exclaimed Mr. Moans, with as much surprise as though the whole tribe of peripatetic fish venders of Sydney had suddenly shouted 'all alive O' in his right ear. "That a fish market! why it is handsome enough for a town hall. I must take a good look at it to-morrow. We sadly want such an establishment in Sydney; for though our coasts and harbours abound with fish, the supply to the citizens is scanty and precarious; and, in general, it is too high in price for poor persons to luxuriate in. Such a market in Sydney would do away with the monopoly which has long been enjoyed by a score or two of barrow-men, and certain middlemen or agents, who, I am told, make large profits by giving the public small quantities of fish, while the poor fishermen, who have all the perils and certainly the largest share of the labour, have but a minimum portion of the gains. Fish market! Hail Victoria! I feel quite enthusiastic, and inclined to shout out the matutinal song of our Sydney piscators, 'Here's your fine fresh fish!' A slice of Murray River cod, fresh from the slate tables of your model Billingsgate, would be a treat."

"I think you mentioned the Town Hall, just now, sir," said Mr. Titler; "I will show it you, presently; you had better take a look at the Town Hall at Prahran, too, before you leave."

"And you had better come and take a look at our new Town Hall at Sydney, when it is finished," drily remarked Mr. Moans.

"That is a fine church, sir," said Mr. Titler, pointing to a tall handsome spire in the distance; "I doubt if you have an ecclesiastical edifice in Sydney to equal that."

"Then it is plain to me that you have not seen our Anglican Cathedral in George Street," said Mr. Moans, in a pleasant mood.

"Oh! yes, beg pardon—that unfinished building near the old burial ground. I forgot that—by-the-bye, have you seen the Melbourne General Cemetery?"

"I have, sir, and a beautiful place it is too. There is much taste displayed in laying out the grounds, and they are kept in admirable condition. Among many good rules for the management of the cemetery, I remarked one in particular, which is worthy of being adopted elsewhere. It is that no inscription shall be made on a tomb or headstone, that has not been submitted for the approval of two of the trustees. That is an admirable way of preventing the exhibition of questionable taste or eccentricities which often interfere with our serious reflections when rambling through grave-yards. You are perhaps not aware, Mr. Titler, that we have a general cemetery now, situate off the line of railway, between Sydney and Paramatta."

"I am glad to hear it, sir," said Mr. Titler, "for crowding the dead among the living is an evil which cannot be too carefully guarded against. You have not yet seen our public parks and gardens, I suppose, Mr. Moans? I should like to hear what you will say to them."

"I have visited some of them, sir; and while I honestly tell you I have not seen anything to equal our picturesque domain in Sydney, I must say your government is very liberal in granting land for public purposes. You Melbourne folks are admirably provided with recreation grounds; and you apparently spare no labour in improving them. I very much approve of your taste in rearing trees wherever there is room for them. The advantages of their refreshing shade and fragrance in this warm climate are inestimable, and grateful pedestrians will doubtless often bless the men who planted those trees, which I have observed growing on the sides of some of your suburban roads. We Sydneyites are certainly behind you in exhibitions of taste in that way, though we are improving, as anyone may observe, who will make an inspection of our public grounds."

*   *   *   *   *   *

I shall not further follow Mr. Moans and his communicative friend, Mr. Titler, or detail his dialogues with other Victorian friends, upon moral, social, sanitary, and political subjects; as the foregoing specimen will show, that while candidly admitting the excellences and the grandeur of the precocious city of Melbourne, he was not slow in defending his own honoured capital from invidious comparisons or ungenerous depreciation.

During his stay he enjoyed some pleasant rural drives in Mr. Titler's carriage; and though he could not be persuaded that any scenery he saw was comparable to that between Sydney and South Head, there was much that was undoubtedly beautiful, and evidenced the highest artistic skill and taste. While driving through some of the suburban towns, he noted many things which he thought might with advantage be imitated by the suburbanites of Sydney, more especially the wide streets and roads, the extensive public reserves, and the prevailing disposition for planting shrubs therein. Mr. Moans had also many agreeable saunters through Melbourne proper, and noted many more things than I have space to enumerate. Among other striking objects, he observed more men walking about with their hands in their pockets, than he expected to have seen, with the numerous avenues for steady labour in that busy metropolis; and considering, too, the facilities for getting into the interior, and the liberality of the Victorian land law: moreover, where there was such a splendid free library, accessible to the humblest classes, at all hours of the day, and till a late hour at night. But it was explained by a lively friend, that hands in pockets was not regarded as an idle symptom; for since "peg-top pantaloons" had become fashionable, the practice was general; indeed it was considered the "correct thing" by all grades and ages of Melbourne males. At the same time he admitted that there were many men who had unfortunately no remunerative employment for their hands; but he thought, in a majority of instances, the causes might be traced to their own indiscretion, or incapacity; and notwithstanding all that had been said and written by interested persons and grumblers to the contrary, he believed there was still ample room in the land for tens of thousands of honest industrious men and women, for the resources of the country—apart from its gold—are almost unlimited.

*　　*　　*　　*　　*　　*

"If any man, who had the free range of a choice flower-garden, chose to go sniffing among the African marigolds in preference to inhaling the balmy fragrance of moss roses and violets, his taste might be justly questioned." Thus reasoned Mr. Moans to himself, as he quietly rambled through some of the well - paved streets of Melbourne. "And instead of choosing to look at the many beautiful objects around me," he soliloquised, "if I preferred to turn into some of the back lanes for the express purpose of finding disagreeable subjects to talk about when I returned home, I should be lacking in taste." Mr. Moans preferred the moss roses and violets, or, in other words, he chose to employ his limited time in observing matters and things which are most pleasant and profitable to contemplate, and to converse with men of corresponding minds. Still he was not wholly unobservant of other things; and the sombre walls of the Gaol, the Refuge, the Hospital, and other receptacles for crime and suffering, and the haggard looks of many poor besotted loungers at public-house doors, often reminded him that all was not *coleur de rose* around him.

He met with much hospitality and kindness from old friends, and from new friends too; and he left the monumental city of Melbourne, strongly impressed with the indomitable spirit of advancement displayed by its inhabitants in general. He had remarked, however, that there was rather more commercial steam or gas introduced into private life than is observable in Sydney society. He noticed, too, that a few of the mercantile men looked fidgety on Sundays, and while they gazed round at the clock in sermon time, he fancied they were longing for Monday to come again, that they might be looking out " for lucky specs."   He met with two or three light-hearted men too, (who were as inflated with civic pride, as smoke-dried cockneys showing their country-cousins the wonders of London from the top of St. Paul's), and he felt constrained to reduce their jubilant boasting by gently reminding them that " after all, it was a Sydney man who planned their grand city—except the sewerage," and he added " that if the Victorians were richer and more influential than some of their neighbours, they should be thankful, and remember that it would be very discreditable to them if it were otherwise with their enormous revenue, and the million of spirited men and women, whom the Victorian gold mines had attracted from all parts of the world."

On the whole, Mr. Moans is of opinion that Victoria is a great land, and that it is destined to become still greater ; and as modesty is a concomitant of true greatness, he expects that quality to increase.   While congratulating that sister colony on her good fortune, and recognising her claim to the respect of the world, he does not yield a jot of the honour due to his own part of the continent ; nor does his admiration for his neighbour's excellences lessen his fealty to his own adopted colony, or wean his affection from its old associations.   Friendly emulation is commendable, and he thinks a better acquaintance with each other will tend to foster that feeling, and at the same time uproot or retard the growth of envy, from which would eventually spring hatred and all uncharitableness.   With that desirable end in view, Mr. Moans would recommend all the good folks in Melbourne to visit Sydney now and then ; the well-bred citizens of Sydney will return the calls, of course ; and if they all enjoy their visits as much as Mr. Moans enjoyed his, they will heartily join him in the glad shout, " Advance, Victoria !" while the Melbournites will stroke their beards, and smilingly reply, in their Columbianized phraseology, " Go ahead, Sydney."

"STONE BLIND."

SOME years ago, a fine vessel owned by my friend Simon Guldman, was stranded, in a gale of wind, within a hundred miles of Sydney. She was laden with flour and maize, and was uninsured. Though much strained, the vessel held together; and when the weather had sufficiently moderated, my friend succeeded, with much labour and expense, in hauling a considerable portion of the cargo through the surf on to the sea-beach, and eventually in getting the vessel afloat and safely moored in an adjacent harbour.

Mr. Guldman had camped near to the wreck for several nights and had undergone no small amount of hardship, as well as annoyance from volunteer helpers, some of whom were most anxious to spare him the pain of ever again beholding such mementos of his misfortune as were not too heavy for them to carry away. He therefore resolved upon offering the vessel and salvage of cargo for sale, while any salvage remained; so he employed a respectable auctioneer; and, at the time appointed, a crowd assembled on the Queen's Wharf, where samples of the damaged cargo were exhibited, and opposite to which the battered ship lay moored, with the crew on board singing cheerily, as they worked at the pumps.

Mr. Guldman soon discovered that the majority of those present were neither bidders nor buyers, but were perhaps attracted to the spot by the craving desire, which is almost everywhere manifested by a certain class of persons, to investigate disasters; generally with a keen eye to contingent personal advantages.

"Now, gentlemen," said the auctioneer, "you have heard the terms and conditions of sale, and you must admit they are very liberal; favour me with an offer to commence with, at per bushel, for all the maize now spread on the ship's sails, on Misery Beach. At per bushel, favour me with a bid, gentlemen. Don't delay now; what shall I say? Start me a bid, gentlemen, at per bushel."

"If you please, sir, do you warrant it sound corn?" enquired a lisping little man in spectacles, whose occasional waggish winks and whisperings to his neighbours, made my jaded friend doubt if the little oddity were really as simple as he appeared to be. " I'm very particular about my pig's diet. Is it sound, sir, do you think ?"

" There it is, Mr. Spikes," replied the auctioneer. " *You* ought to be able to *see* if it is sound ; look at it and judge for yourself ; taste it if you like. Now, gentlemen, with all faults, favour me with a bid, at per bushel ; don't wait. At per bushel, what shall I say ; favour me with a bid. Mr. Phungus, what do you say ? it would suit you as a speculation ; corn is worth five and ninepence in Sydney just now ; come, gentlemen, fav——"

" If you please, sir," interrupted the little lisping man again, speaking with his mouth half-full of maize, " it tastes like bad nuts, soaked in sour beer. I don't think my pigs would like it."

" If you give your pigs that corn, Spikes, it will give 'em the measles," said a greedy-looking man, who was afterwards observed to be the only person who really made a bid for the cargo, which was not badly damaged. " You had better be careful, or you won't save your bacon, Spikes, that musty corn would physic your swine, and make 'em squeak like bagpipes."

" Ah, I think I'll take your advice," replied Mr. Spikes ; " I shouldn't like to make my pigs unhealthy. You had better send it to Sydney to make coffee, sir," he added, addressing the auctioneer, " it would make very good *corffee*, sir, I think."

Numerous sallies of wit, about equal to the above samples, were indulged in by one or other of the grinning group, to the prejudice of the salvage, and to the discomfiture of my crest-fallen friend, who felt as fidgety as an old lady in a menagerie, with all the monkeys loose ; and, notwithstanding the auctioneer exerted his lungs to the utmost, and flourished his hammer most peruasively, only the man, before-mentioned, bid for the cargo, a less sum than it had cost to get it on shore. Feeling certain that there was a combination among some of the bystanders to cheapen his corn, Mr. Guldman, much to their disappointment, withdrew the sale of it, and instructed the auctioneer to offer the vessel.

" Ay, put up the ship," roared a burly sea captain, with a head like a rock-cod ; " put up the ship ; she'll do for a coal hulk, if her back isn't broken, and if it is, she'll make a mud punt ; I'll bid fifty pounds to start yer, I sha'n't lose much, if I am forced to break her up ; though she's an old craft, with iron fastenings."

"You are mistaken, sir," cried Mr. Guldman, excitedly, "she is only a five-year-old ship, and is copper-fastened throughout ; she is well found, and is one of the fastest vessels on the coast."

"Yes, I'm sure she's a very nice ship, Captain Swob," lisped little Mr. Spikes, with a look of virtuous reproach at the burly sailor for his depreciatory remarks. "She'd be a very pretty ship, indeed, if she was mended ; I only wish my old uncle Bartimeus could see her, he'd give a thousand pounds, ready money, and be glad of the chance."

Amidst the depressing jibes and banter, the least exhibition of rational feeling was to some extent comforting. Mr. Guldman felt half-grateful to the little goblin in spectacles, despite his dubious remarks about the maize. After a minute or two's cudgelling of his excited brain, Mr. Guldman decided to ask Mr. Spikes whether his uncle lived in the neighbourhood, and if so, to invite him to go on board the ship and inspect her. He thought possibly Uncle Bartimeus was a capitalist, desirous of being a ship-owner, and might be glad to buy a smart vessel cheap. In fact, my friend was very anxious to sell, and like vendors in general in such cases, he eagerly hailed the prospect of a buyer.

"Will you oblige me by informing me where your uncle lives, sir?" politely asked Mr. Guldman of Mr. Spikes, who was in the middle of the crowd, looking as sedate as a parson sitting on a hearse.

"Oh, yes, sir, certainly," said the little man ; "look there, sir, you see that long white thing, on top of the hill yonder, like a little lighthouse without a lantern. Well, sir, if you go just behind that, and look down, you'll see a great big gully ; uncle's house is right at the bottom. He calls it Bat's Hole. He'd be precious glad to *see* you."

"Do you think he would like to come and see the vessel?" asked Mr. Guldman ; while the auctioneer ceased his vociferous appeals to his company, to listen to the result of the private negotiations, which every one present seemed interested in.

"Ah, he just would like it, and no mistake, sir," replied

Mr. Spikes; he'd give a thousand pounds if he could *see* her; for he's been *stone blind* for five years."

A loud burst of laughter from the assembled company followed the little man's rejoinder; while his face at once altered to an expression of shrewdness and waggery, at which my friend could not help laughing, despite his chagrin at having been so befooled. After whispering to the auctioneer to stop the sale altogether, Mr. Guldman quietly withdrew from the spot, and was half-way towards his dilapidated ship before the noisy crowd had finished laughing at Mr. Spike's wit.

GONE TO HEAVEN.

A BELOVED friend of mine, was sitting near the couch of his dying infant, about midnight. It was the second night of his painful vigil, and he was weary and depressed in body and mind. He had listlessly opened an illustrated volume of Longfellow's poems, which lay on a table: and just above an engraving, representing an angel soaring to Heaven with an infant, were these lines—

> " She is not dead—the child of our affection—
> 　　But gone unto that school,
> 　Where she no longer needs our poor protection,
> 　　And Christ Himself doth rule."

*　　*　　*　　*　　*　　*

At that moment the nurse exclaimed "baby is gone !"

"CALL AGAIN."

"HERE, Jerry," said a decent, hard-working tradesman in Sydney, to his son, one Saturday morning, "put on your best hat and coat, and try if you can collect a few accounts, for I must have some money to pay the man's wages to-night. You know I have been working early and late since Monday, binding those music books and manuscripts for Madam Twangit, of Woolloomooloo, and when I took them home just now, she told me that she would call and settle with me in a few days. I was afraid to be too pressing lest I should lose her future custom; though she might have seen, by my disappointed looks, that I wanted the money. O dear, dear! what a terrible inconvenience this credit system is to poor, struggling tradesfolk. Some persons do not know it though, or I think they would be more considerate. Now, Madam Twangit has plenty of money, and could just as well pay me to-day as a few days hence; and I dare say, too, she would be sorry if she knew the worry and trouble which will accrue to many persons to-day for the lack of those few pounds, for she is really a kind-hearted lady. In the first place, there will be the loss of your time, Jerry, in running about collecting, or trying to collect money. Then our butcher's, baker's, and grocer's weekly bills will not be paid to-night, and our credit may suffer, and they, too, in their turn, may be inconvenienced, for they have their payments to make to the wholesale traders. Then I heard your mother promise Betsy a new bonnet for Sunday. Poor girl! she will be disappointed, and perhaps will not be able to go to church to-morrow; and I intended to have given you a new waistcoat to-night, Jerry. But it's no use grumbling; I must have some money, however, to pay our man, for he had only half his wages last Saturday night; and the poor fellow wants his money, so go away, my boy, as fast as you can, and try your best to collect some. Here's a long list, and some of the accounts have been a long time owing. Tell the parties they will oblige me very much by paying you to-day, for I really want the money."

Poor Jerry took the list, and sallied out as moodily as if he were going to a funeral. He had good cause for not being over sanguine, for many a long trudge had he had before in his unsuccessful endeavours to collect the numerous small accounts, few of which exceeded ten shillings; and he felt that he would rather turn a grindstone in the back yard all day, than go collecting. However, there was no help for it, so away he went, and summoning up his good-tempered looks, he gently tapped at the office door of Mr. Putemoff, whose name stood first on the list. "Come in," said a voice as soft as a flageolet. Jerry's hope revived a little as he walked in, and making a low bow, began to state the object of his visit. "If you please, sir, I've called——" "Oh, ah, yes," ejaculated Mr. Putemoff, interrupting him. "You've come again for that little account, of course. Bless me! hasn't it been settled yet! It ought to have been paid before, but I quite forgot it. Yes, ah! I have the account somewhere amongst my papers," he continued, musingly, as he opened a drawer, and began to rummage among a host of small documents. "Um, dear me; I'm sorry I can't find it, my lad; I must trouble you to 'call again,' when my clerk is in. Yes; just look in again, if you please." "Very good, sir," replied Jerry, as he bowed his way out of the office, pleased that the stinging words, "call again," had been uttered in a civil tone.

"What do *you* want?" enquired Mr. Bluff, the butcher, as Jerry stepped into his shop with a timid air, as if he owed the butcher a long bill and could not pay a penny. "If you please, sir, I've called for that little account for binding your old books—seven and sixpence. My father says he'll be very much obliged——" "You must call again; can't you see I'm too busy to attend to you?" said Mr. Bluff, as he chopped away at a bullock's tail. "If you please, sir," urged Jerry, meekly, "father is——" "Call again, I tell you. Don't bother me now!" roared Mr. Bluff, grinning the while like a shark who is just going to swallow a sailor, which frightened Jerry out of the shop in a minute.

With a heart as heavy as a bag of shot, he next entered the shop of Mr. Mull, the mercer, and civilly asked for the payment of nine shillings, which had been owing for some time. "Where's the account?" asked Mr. Mull, hastily, as he lifted up the flap of his desk and looked inside, remarking at the same time that those petty little bills bothered him twice as much as all his big ones. "I've never seen your account," said Mr. Mull, after an apparent fruitless search in his desk for it. "I have left it twice, sir," said poor Jerry, with an imploring look. "Ah, then it's been mislaid. You must call again with it, and don't come here again on Saturday, d'ye hear?"

"Master's gone to lunch," said a small boy, who was seated on a butter tub, eating a saveloy, as Jerry stepped into the store of Mr. Baggs, the commission agent, in the hope of collecting five shillings and sixpence; so Jerry stepped out of the store again, wishing that he could go to lunch too.

His next essay was at Messrs. Braceup, Sharp, and Co.'s, the ship chandlers. "You've called on the wrong day," said a little old gentleman, as stiff as a ship's figure-head. "It's only eight shillings, sir," said Jerry with half a dash of warmth, as he reflected upon his previous non-success. "Yes, yes, that's right enough, my lad," said the stolid old gentleman, "it would be all the same to us if it were forty times as much; but Tuesday's our pay day, so you must call again."

"Well, well," muttered Jerry, as he looked over his list again, "I've had bad luck thus far. I almost wish it were punishable by a fine, to say 'call again.' I'd rather have a tooth pulled out any day than have a job like this; at least, I think so just now, for I am tired and hungry, and I have not collected the price of a mutton pie. I'll call upon Dr. Dosem; he knows the difficulty of collecting small accounts, I'll be bound, and he'll pay me out of sympathy." Jerry was again disappointed, however, for the doctor had gone out to visit a patient.

Obedient to his father's instructions, Jerry went through his list, and at each place of call got more pathetic in his appeals; but, with two trifling exceptions, he met with no success. Various were the excuses, most of them ending with the tormenting words "call again." Mrs. Phubbs' husband was not at home; Mr. M'Muffin's wife had gone out, and had taken the keys with her; Mr. Steddy had no change; and Mr. Screwdup, whom Jerry met in the street, had unfortunately brought no money out with him, and had left none at home either. Mr. Gruntall would call and see his father, as there was an overcharge of ninepence in his bill. Mr. Doutt was almost sure he had paid the bill before, but would search through his papers for the receipt ; and Mr. Bull couldn't be bothered with such paltry accounts, they must be taken to his private house at Balmain.

Jerry returned home late in the afternoon, with a sad heart, and with pockets nearly as light as when he had set out in the morning.

"I am sorry to say I have had plenty of excuses, father, and rather more scolding than I liked," said Jerry, "but I've got very little money. Here's five and sixpence from old Mrs. Rackem, the teacher ; and half-a-crown from Mr. Scrapard, the currier : that's all I've got ; and I could have earned nearly as much if I had been in the workshop all day."

"Well, it's a hard case, Jerry," said his father, passing his hand across his brow. "There is a matter of twenty pounds owing me, in small sums, and if I had them, I could pay all my debts and be an independent man. As it is, I see no alternative but to pawn the tools again, so take the basket to Mr. Balls, Jerry ; ask him to lend me £5. The man must have four pounds to-night, and we must make the best shifts we can at home. But what we are to do for the tools on Monday morning I don't know. However, there is no use thinking about that just now ; and I hope I shall be kept from thinking about it to-morrow. Well, well, it's downright cruel of folks to be so thoughtless. Most of those whom you have called on could pay their little accounts easily enough, if they chose, for they are mere trifles [to them individually, but in the aggregate a most important sum to me. 'The labourer is worthy of his hire ;' but it is pretty plain that he does not always get it. Oh ! Jerry, Jerry," added the poor man with a sigh, "this is a hard, cold world ; or there are too many hard, cold folks in it, that's what I mean. But cheer up, my boy, I'm sorry I've made you cry : it's sinful to repine. I have yet the means of paying the man's wages to-night, and we shall have a trifle to take home besides, so dry up your tears, Jerry, and don't let mother know we've been obliged to pawn the tools."

WOES AND WORRIES OF MRS. LEMONPIP.

CHAPTER I.

"DRAT the door!" grumbled Mrs. Lemonpip, as she bustled along the passage from the kitchen ; her hands and arms bespattered with pancake paste, and the tip of her strawberry nose garnished with saucepan soot. "Drat that door, I say! I wish I could make the knocker red hot, and keep it so, then I'll warrant those cadgers, and costermongers, and other nuisances, would not be so fond of playing rat-tat-tat, to worrit me till I'm savage enough to bite everybody. What do you want?" she asked sharply, as she opened the door just wide enough to show her face, but not her figure, which was the most comely part of her person. "What do you want?"

"Con you help a poor mon, missis?" said a poverty-stricken individual, with a basket before him, filled with boxes of matches. "I coom'd out from whoam a week or two agone, wi me wife and three young uns, and they be all zick."

"Go and nurse them then," said Mrs. Lemonpip. "You ought to be ashamed of yourself for leaving them if they are sick. There now be off, be off: I don't want to hear any more of your grievances, which I dare say are half sham, I have nothing to give away, and if I had I would not give it to you for your impudence, in rapping rat-tat at my door as if you were an alderman. Be off, or I'll call my bull dog."

"Will you buy a dozen o' matches, missis? you shall have them for ninepence. Do, mar'm, and God bless you."

"No, I won't buy a farthingsworth," shrieked Mrs. Lemonpip, with a look at the poor fellow almost fierce enough to set fire to his basket. "Go and work, you lazy lump, and don't come here any more with your matches or your miserable stories either : I won't encourage hawking, which is very often a mere blind for begging, and begging means stealing. I believe it was somebody like you that stole my door scraper last Monday morning. Be off, I say again!" She then slammed the door in the poor hungry fellow's face, and bustled back to the kitchen, to peel the potatoes, and make other preparations for her gude man's dinner ; and to vent from time to time little accumulations of ill-humour upon the head of the cat, in the absence of any other animate creature, that she could make uncomfortable.

Mrs. Lemonpip had seated herself on a kitchen stool, and began to operate on the eyes and skins of the potatoes in her lap, and to knock the cat's nose now and then with the handle of her knife, when rat-tat-tat rattled the brass knocker again, in a sort of imperative mood.

"If this is another hawker, or beggar," exclaimed the little woman, rising and taking off her kitchen apron, at the same time looking wrathfully round, as if for some deadly weapon, "I declare, if this is another of those pests of my life, I'll knock him down with—with this bar of soap ; (which happened to be the most formidable instrument of torture within her view at the moment,) or kick his basket into the gutter. Eleven times this blessed morning have I danced along the hall to the tune of that tormenting knocker, and that's quite enough to wrinkle the smoothest temper in the world. Confound the knocker, I say, I've a great mind to unscrew it and throw it down the well, for its clatter annoys me more than the three pianos in the boarding-school next door." Thus grumbled little Mrs. Lemonpip, as she again trotted to the front door, her puckered face red with the combined influence of wrath, kitchen fire, and " old tom."

" Hey day, Betsy, my little pigeon !" shouted a fat, merry-faced old man, stepping into the passage when the door was opened wide enough to receive him. " Why what's the matter, ducky ? have you scalded your foot again, or knocked your bad knee, or has the soot choked up the kitchen stove and spoiled your cookery and your temper too. What ails my little popgun ! cheer up and tell your Jacky all about it," continued the merry old man ; at the same time lovingly attempting to kiss his wife. But she looked as combative as a live lobster, and snappishly told him to have done with his nonsense, and monkey tricks, or she should lose her temper and perhaps slap his face and then be sorry for it. " I'm fairly mithered to death with kitchen work and that noisy knocker," whined Mrs. Lemonpip, making her way into the kitchen again, closely followed by Mr. Lemonpip, who was trying his utmost to comfort her, but with scarcely any perceptible effect, for she was inconsolably cross, and instead of cheering up, as her hopeful husband advised her to do, she sat down and rubbed her tearful eyes with a rough roller towel, until they looked like pickled onions in red cabbage liquor, and as she rubbed, she vociferously declared that there was not a woman in Sydney so wofully troubled as she.

"Come, come, Betty, my bird! don't fret, don't fret," said Mr. Lemonpip, soothingly, " some of your troubles will soon be over, deary, and I'll take good care you shall never have this scullery maid's work to do again, for it spoils your natural amiability, sours your complexion, as well as be-smuts it, and makes me as downhearted as an old buttonless bachelor, or a bear chained to a post. When is our new maid to be here, Betsy?"

" To-night, I hope and trust," said Mrs. Lemonpip, in a very desponding tone, while she wiped out the frying-pan and put it over the fire ; then wiped the perspiration from her soot-begrimed face, and sighed like a strong breeze. " She is to come to-night, and 1 wish I had made her pro-mise to come this morning, if only to save me from that plaguey door."

Rat-tat-tat-tat, went the knocker just then, which made little Mrs. Lemonpip jump up five inches at least, and at the same moment drop a pork sausage off the fork among the cinders. " There's that goblin of a knocker again," she muttered with closely set teeth. " It has nearly hunted me to death this morning ; rap, tap, tap, like an undertaker's hammer. I shall do mischief if I go to the door ; I am sure I shall. I could skewer a knocker maker this very minute," she added, while she made a violent probe at some imagi-nary enemy with the carving fork.

" Hush ! calm yourself, my pop," said Mr. Lemonpip, " Go on frying the sausages, and I'll open the door. Folks must use the knocker you know, dear, else how should we know that they are at the door ? Do you want a little round table, Betsy ?" shouted that complaisant old gentle-man, after he had opened the door.

" Round table, no ! What on earth will they hawk about the streets next ? They ought to be punished."

" Or a step ladder, my dear ?" asked Mr. Lemonpip, with something like a comical curl at the left corner of his mouth.

"No!" vociferated Mrs. Lemonpip, "what the plague do you think I want with a step ladder? slam the door in that fellow's impudent face; he was here the day before yesterday with his nuisances. I'll ladder him, if I catch him here again. These hawkers are ten times worse pests than the rats and cockroaches in the kitchen."

Mr. Lemonpip dismissed the ladder merchant, rather more gently than his wrathy little wife had recommended —and returned to the kitchen, with a happy smile on his face, and the desire in his heart to make himself agreeable and useful to the utmost of his ability.

"Now, Betty, my love! only tell me how I can lighten your load, and it will do me good," said Mr. Lemonpip, "I'm your humble and most obedient servant, for any little light job; such as cleaning the knives and forks, filling the coal scuttle, trimming the moderator, or anything else within the compass of moderate powers. What can I do for you, my blackbird? just tell me and I'll jump to do it, as nimbly as a Jack tar in a squall."

"Just get out of the kitchen and don't worrit me—that's all I ask you to do," snapped Mrs. Lemonpip; "I wonder what in the world has brought you home an hour before your usual time. I hope you have not been turned away from Tubbs and Co.'s, I shouldn't wonder if you have though, for they have treated you lately as if you were of no more consequence than an old barrow with a broken wheel—something's the matter, I'm sure, and I should like to know what it is."

"I will tell you all about it, my pet, if you will let me sit down quietly and hold the frying-pan while you look on and rest a bit. I like to see pork sausages frizzle in the frying-pan, and I like to smell them, too, so long as I can keep my imagination within wholesome bounds. I fancy too they have such a pathetic look, after you have pricked them with a fork, just like fat lovers fretting."

"Stuff and nonsense! now be off out of the kitchen, Lemonpip, unless you want to get your best coat splashed all over with pork fat and pancake. I hate to see men making mollies of themselves. I'd as soon see a woman drive an omnibus or a railway engine. If you will fetch me a little drop of old tom out of the black bottle in the chiffonier, you will do me more good than by interfering with my cookery. Get me just a thimblefull, neat, before I begin to fry the pancakes; I feel my troublesome spasms coming on again."

"Oh, Betty, Betty! a thimbleful of gin will do you harm instead of good—it will increase your irritability, and perhaps increase your spasms too. However, I won't begin an unpleasant argument, although I feel that I am paying an awfully dear price for peace." Away trudged Mr. Lemonpip to the cupboard for the gin, with as much shrinking reluctance as if he were going to handle a live badger.

For the purpose of my story, it is not necessary to enter upon lengthy biographical details; still it would be interesting to the reader to know a little more of the characters just introduced: so I will briefly describe them, in order that the subsequent part of my story may be better comprehended.

Mr. Lemonpip was clerk to an old established mercantile firm in Sydney; in which employ he had been for many years; and had been several times stepped over, or superseded, by younger men in the same employ. He was what is commonly called "a slow coach," or a "steady going old stager;" still he was faithful as a mirror, and the personification of cheerfulness and good nature. He might have risen to a higher position in the world, or even have become wealthy, had he exercised worldly wisdom, and studied his own immediate interest a little more, and his neighbour's a little less. But he did not covet high position nor patronage. He had in his heart "Godliness with contentment," and that he proved to be "great gain." He knew that he had made "free selection" of an estate of inestimable value —redundant of "green pastures and still waters," in the region of light itself; where the shades of night, and the gloom of sorrow, are alike unknown; where he would by and by enjoy peaceful possession, free from the encroachments of litigious neighbours, bushrangers, floods, droughts, diseases, or ought else that could mar his immortal joy. He knew, too, that the purchase of his inheritance had been paid—for he had a receipt in full, and he carried his title in his breast—a title perfectly free from flaws, clearer than sunlight. He expected the ancient messenger to call for him, and convoy him to his new possession very soon; indeed, he lived in daily anticipation of the signal to shuffle off his mortal clogs, and soar away home. Why then should he let his heart be troubled because he did not possess a superabundance of the world's goods, seeing that he could carry no luggage with him to his new settlement?   He saw occasionally some wealthy neighbour pass away from commercial scenes as suddenly as if he did not possess a pound note ; one day worth tons of gold, and perhaps toiling with all his might to make another ton, the next day in his coffin—and not personally worth one of the brass-headed nails which studded the top of his narrow tenement.   Why then should he overstrain his nerves in the race for riches, which after all yielded comparatively little solid comfort, and were held with a very uncertain tenure?

Thus reasoned Mr. Lemonpip whenever he reflected upon money, which was not often, for he had generally more sterling subjects for reflection.   Still I hope it will not be supposed that he was one of those moody mortals who are always groaning about worldly vanities (which are out of their reach), condemning rational appropriation of wealth, with short-sighted envious policy, expressing contempt for riches, honours or distinction, and a lugubrious disapproval of innocent recreations ! Far from it ; Mr. Lemonpip had a goodly share of common sense in his head, as well as philanthropy in his heart ; and one glance at his honest face would have sufficed to assure the intelligent beholder that he did not belong to that mischievous corps of misery-mongers and impostors.   He did not affect to spurn money, for he knew its value, and would gladly have possessed a little more of it, if he could have got it honestly—for the sake of helping those who were in need.   He properly viewed money, and the influence it commands, as talents which are bestowed upon certain honoured individuals, to be appropriated by them to God's glory, and the welfare of the world ; and he pitied those persons whom he sometimes saw rolling in wealth, and selfishly clutching it as if it all belonged to them, forgetting that " the silver and the gold are the Lord's, and also the cattle upon a thousand hills."

Such was Mr. Lemonpip—or, to give the substance of the foregoing delineation in a few words, he was a Christian.   I wish I could say as much of his wife, of whom I must give a brief description : it will not be necessary to say a great deal, however, for the reader has doubtless formed an opinion of her from the few colloquial extracts I have already given. The old nursery rhyme is a tolerably apt portraiture of Mrs. Lemonpip,

> "There was an old woman, and what do you think,
> She lived upon nothing but victuals and drink.
> And victuals and drink were the chief of her diet,
> But yet this old woman could never be quiet."

Mrs. Lemonpip lived upon victuals and drink, and not very small quantities either; but as it is not gallant to refer to a lady's gustatory affairs, I will touch as delicately on that subject as possible. In person she was short and stout, with a round, batter freckly face, like a pudding sprinkled with allspice. Her nose was the most cheerful looking feature belonging to her, for it was always more or less rubicund, and had a comical turn up at the extreme tip, as if it were trying to provoke the sharp grey eyes just above, to cut it off—or pertly challenging the clamorous mouth below to storm it from its snug position, between two wrinkles, or rolls of fat face.

Mrs. Lemonpip was forty-six years of age, though she might have been mistaken for fifty. Her temper was seldom sweet, or even quiet, except when she was asleep. Her manner was rarely, or never inviting, and at times she was as unapproachable as a prickly pear tree. Poor old Lemonpip was always patient under the petticoat despotism of his better half, and quietly bore nagging and threatening, which would have provoked many less prudent men to acts of violence, or to run away to California.

I once heard of a burly Yorkshire farmer who always stood still and grinned while his choleric little dot of a wife thumped his hips and ribs (she could reach no higher) with all her might. On being asked one day by a wondering looker-on, why he did not stop her fierce pugilistic attacks on his person, the farmer good naturedly replied, "whoy she loikes it, and it doan't hurt me."

Mr. Lemonpip, perhaps, made similar generous allowance for his wife's unamiable weaknesses, but he did not imitate the tantalising indifference of the Yorkshire farmer. Mrs. Lemonpip was often cross and disagreeable, but her good husband did not taunt or tease her, on the contrary, he tried all he could to soothe her. He loved her, as all good husbands love their wives, and he could not bear the idea of death separating them for ever, so he earnestly prayed for her reformation; and at the same time he set her an example of meekness, temperance, charity, and other Christian virtues (which her every day acts proved that she sadly lacked), for he endorsed the maxim "that those are the best instructors whose lives speak for them."

CHAPTER II.

THE preceding chapter introduced Mr. and Mrs. Lemonpip, but I may further inform the reader, that they lived in the centre of a row of three smart-looking houses, situate within a mile or two of Sydney post-office ; and to help them to pay their rent, they boarded Mr. Dugald McSkilly, a Caledonian dentist (about nine months out from Dundee), and lodged him in the back attic.

Mr. and Mrs. Lemonpip had sat down to their dinner-table. The pork sausages were steaming in a dish before Mr. Lemonpip, and the mashed potatoes were steaming in another dish before his spouse, whose nose, by-the-bye, had deepened in colour a shade since she had taken the thimbleful of gin from the black bottle in the cupboard ; and though the little woman was really anxious to know what had brought her husband home so unusually early that morning, and what made him look so mysteriously waggish, she was too much ruffled in spirit to ask any questions on the subject, but sat and ate her sausages in silence. Presently Mr. Lemonpip arose, and dipping his hand into his breast-pocket, produced a small parcel, which he untied, and exultingly held before his wife's little gooseberry eyes a very chaste gold brooch, with his own photograph in it, and kissing her most affectionately, he presented the glittering gem, while his face looked the picture of gladness in a frost-covered frame.

"Now I'll tell you what has brought me home so early to-day," said Mr. Lemonpip, smiling and nodding his head sideways, in the most facetious style, " I've got a half-holiday, and I'm going to treat you to a trip to Manly Beach ; for don't you know, ducky, this is our wedding-day. The twenty-fifth anniversary of our happy nuptial morn, when we drove to church in your father's tilted waggon, with bells on the horses' hames, and old Godfrey Walloper the waggoner, in his best white smock-frock, and a bunch of marigolds pinned to his breast. Ha ! ha ! ha ! don't you remember that delightful day, Betty, my bird ? Mr. Docket, our head wharfinger, with his wife and children, are going to Manly Beach too ; and I have promised to meet them on board the two o'clock boat, at Woolloomooloo Bay. We will have a nice pleasant afternoon together on the sea-beach, 'jolly companions every one,' as the old song says."

"Pooh! sea-beach, indeed," snapped Mrs. Lemonpip, "I shall see no sea-beach to-day; I've got to clean the kitchen out, and get things straight for the new girl who is coming to-night. The place is like a pig-sty from bottom to top."

"Never mind the kitchen, ducky," said Mr. Lemonpip, "let the new girl clean it when she comes, or send for old Mrs. Dudds, round the corner, and let her do it, she will be glad of the job, poor thing!"

"Ah, poor thing, indeed! you are always thinking of some poor thing or other, to empty your pockets, and keep you poor. If I wasn't to look out a little sharper after the main thing than you do, we should have been out of house and home long ago. Send for Mrs. Dudds, indeed! I shall do no such thing, Lemonpip. If I help all your poor things, I shall soon be a poor thing too."

"Well, well, my dear, don't be vexed; I'm sorry I named it; let us lock up the house, then, and be off. Come, come, make haste, love, put on your best bonnet and tippet, and lock up the house—that's the best plan—nobody will run away with it."

"Lock up the house, eh? I dare say. Pray, who's to take in the milk, and open the door for Mr. McSkilly when he comes home to tea at six o'clock? How thoughtless you are, Lemonpip; I never saw anybody like you in all my life. Manly Beach, indeed! I'm as jaded as a butcher's horse, and more fit to go to bed than to go trapesing about a sandy beach. I won't go outside this blessed door to-day, and you know I mean what I say, when I speak plainly; but you can go if you like; you are fond of gadding about, with a tribe of noisy children at your heels, like a Jack-in-the-green."

"I don't like to go without you, my pop," said Mr. Lemonpip, with a sweet glance at his sour little spouse, and then he added, "but you have not told me how you like your new brooch, nor you haven't admired my picture, deary: you have surely forgotten that."

"The brooch is very good, if it is real gold, but I daresay you have been taken in again, as you were with that brass chain and the gingerbread watch, which you bought for me seventeen years ago. I think you had better have saved your money, than fool it away for things we don't want, or

that we can do very well without. As for your photograph,
I wouldn't give fourpence for it, for I don't like it at all,
that's speaking the plain truth. You are too fat to look
well in a brooch, and so I should have told you if you had
asked my opinion before you went and wasted your money.
There is far too much waistcoat to look commonly decent.
I wonder that you will persist in going out and doing things
without consulting me."

Mr. Lemonpip was too well accustomed to that sort of
rating to be very much pained by his wife's ungracious remarks ; and he was too patient and peace-loving to reply to
her in her own nagging style, for he well knew that it
would speedily raise a storm, before which he would have to
scud away, like a ship in light ballast trim. Besides, from
experience, he knew that it would be useless to reason with
her, when her red-hot nose and fierce little eyes indicated
that her temper was as acrid as gin and weariness could
make it ; so after another gentle, though fruitless attempt
to induce her to accompany him, he put on his best hat,
and hurried away to join his friends on board the Phantom
steamer. In due course he arrived at Manly Beach, and
there with Mr. and Mrs. Docket, and their seven children,
he enjoyed himself in that thorough style, which only such
simple, honest souls as Mr. Lemonpip can understand. He
was a complete boy among the boys and girls, and entered
into their sports with a genuine zest, which quite delighted
Mr. and Mrs. Docket, who sat under a shady tree, beside
their pic-nic basket, and laughed till they almost cried at
the antics of the merry group before them, the merriest
amongst which was their respected friend, Mr. Lemonpip

In the meantime little Mrs. Lemonpip was as joyless as a
pelican with a broken bill. Never was a woman so teazed
and tormented as she, that is to say, she thought so. Nine
times during the afternoon did she answer that clamorous
brass knocker, at the summons of two beggars, four hawkers,
the postman, the milkwoman, and Mr. McSkilly ; and as
each time the self-persecuted little body had to apply to the
black bottle for a thimbleful of comfort, by the time the
last-named knocker arrived, Mrs. Lemonpip was, as she herself admitted, as cross as two sticks ; or, as Mr. McSkilly
whispered, in his own ears, "The auld body was mair than
half fou."

"It is half-past six," exclaimed the wrathy little woman,

as she filled up the tea-pot from the hissing kettle on the hob. "It's half-past six, and Lemonpip ought to have been home long ago; he very well knows our tea-time, and I shall not wait another minute, nor yet half a minute," so down she sat to the table, with her lodger, and began to pour out the tea, and to pour into his unwilling ears a dolorous report of her woes and worries during the day, to which he listened with as much display of sympathy as she might have expected from a wooden highlander outside a snuff-shop. After tea, which was hastily partaken of, Mr. McSkilly went out for a walk, leaving his landlady "to nurse her wrath, and keep it warm," until the return of her hen-pecked husband.

Rat-tat went the knocker again, soon after eight o'clock. Mrs. Lemonpip thought it was her late-staying spouse, so she hastened to the door, hissing as she went, like a squib just before it goes bang; but, lo! to her relief it was her new maid of all-work, with a band-box and bundle. The next hour was occupied in showing Jemima the holes and corners of the kitchen, and in explaining to her the routine of her duties, to which Jemima every minute briefly replied, "Yes, mum."

About nine o'clock Mr. Lemonpip returned home, very tired, but pleased with the way he had spent his half-holiday; the only drawback to his enjoyment was, he said, the absence of his little pop-gun. He soon saw, however, from unmistakable signs, that the less he said to his pop-gun that evening, the less probability there would be of an explosion; so after explaining that he had taken tea with Mr. and Mrs. Docket, he took a book and quietly sat down to study it, until Mr. McSkilly returned home, when they had family prayer, and a little bit of supper, then they all retired to rest, Mrs. Lemonpip having previously taken another little drop of Old Tom, as usual, by way of a night-cap.

In a very short time Mr. Lemonpip was performing a sleeping voluntary on his nasal organ, with open diapason, for he, happy old soul, had no cares or anxieties to keep him awake, and all his organ pipes were as sound as new saucepans. He was strictly temperate in his habits, and had never trifled with his naturally strong constitution; and as he always lay down in peace with God, and at peace with all the world, he passed very few sleepless hours in his bed. His wife, on the contrary, seldom slept throughout the night, and very often her sleepy spouse was aroused, and pestered with her fidgety "night thoughts," or her interminable "curtain lectures."   On the night in question, Mrs. Lemonpip lay rolling about as comfortless as a seal in a warm bath, and every stray mosquito's note sounded like a bugle in her excited ears.   Her favourite Old Tom, instead of soothing her and sending her to sleep, helped to increase her irritability, and keep her awake.   Poor soul! she had been bubbling over with ill-humour all day, and had not had the satisfaction of pouring the usual measure of wrath upon her docile partner ; moreover, she had had no servant to scold, which was an additional trial to her patience.   She was by no means pleased that Mr. Lemonpip had spent an agreeable holiday, and spent a good many shillings too, while she had been so bothered and overworked at home ; and she knew that it would be vain to try to compose herself to sleep, until she had fully unburdened her mind of that matter.   In fact, she had made up her mind to give him a long lecture ; and having thus resolved, she was not long in framing a pretext for awakening him from his peaceful slumber ; so she administered a preliminary · nudge in his ribs with her elbow (which made him cough), and exclaimed sharply, "How you do snore, Lemonpip ! I should like to know who can sleep, while you make that noise ?"

"Bless me ! was I snoring ? I beg your pardon, my duck," said Mr. Lemonpip, half awaking and turning over.   "I'm very sorry I disturbed you.   I suppose I was lying on my back, and I believe I do breathe hard when lying in that position."

"Humph ! lying on your back, or lying in any other way, it is all the same with you, after you have been holiday-keeping, for you always make a noise like an over-fed calf."

Mr. Lemonpip was dosily conscious that a storm was brewing inside his wife's breast, so he pulled his nightcap over his ears in silence, and tried to go to sleep again.

"I smell fire !   Are you sure you put that kerosene lamp out, Lemonpip ?" said the little mischief-maker, who was well aware that nothing would so soon arouse her husband as an alarm, or even a suspicion of fire.

"Eh, what, fire ?" exclaimed Mr. Lemonpip, who was thoroughly awake in a moment, and sitting up in the bed he began sniffing and trying his utmost to smell the element he most dreaded.

" Lie down, Lemonpip," said his wife pettishly, " you are letting the wind into the bed, and making me shiver.   Lie down I say, directly."

" Well, my dear, I don't like to lie down if the house is on fire.   I can't smell anything to be sure, but I've got a slight cold in my head.   I'll go down stairs and see if all is safe, though I think I put that lamp out all right."

" *Think !* that's just like you : you ought to be *sure* about such a dangerous thing as fire.   You are the most careless man I ever saw, Lemonpip ; you have no more gumption than a donkey."

" Where are the matches, my dear ?" asked Mr. Lemonpip, who had got out of bed, and knocked his toe against the towel horse.

" Matches !   You don't want a light to see if the house is on fire, surely ! if you do, it will be all the same, for we haven't a single match in the house : I forgot to send Jemima for a box before she went to bed.   You had better get into bed again, and don't be pottering about there in the dark.   I think the fire has gone out, for I can't smell it now."

But Mr. Lemonpip thought as he was out of bed, he might as well assure himself that the house was quite safe ; (for he was not certain that he had put out the lamp ; though he could not recollect that he had ever failed to do so one single night since he first owned a lamp,) so he began to descend the stairs, while his wicked little wife lay still, and further plotted against his peace.   She knew that on his return to bed he would be as wide awake as an owl, and she resolved to tell him a considerable bit of her mind before he slumbered again, by way of easing off a heavy load of ill humour, and at the same time punishing her spouse for being happy out of her society.

Thump, thump, thump, went Mr. Lemonpip's heavy heels on the carpetted stairs, until he got to the bottom ; when lo ! on a sudden, the house was filled with the most horrible sounds that ever distracted human ears.

" Waa ! Wa-er ! Wounds ! Woes !" shrieked a terrific unknown tongue, in the hall (at least so Mrs. Lemonpip interpreted the awful yells, which nearly drove her frantic,) followed immediately by a frightful cry from Mr. Lemonp l who felt himself in the clutches of some evil spirit, which was clawing his flesh with demoniacal fury. Almost at the same moment a crash, like the downfall of a brewer's chimney, filled the whole house, from the coal cellar upwards, with an uproar and clatter alarming in the extreme. A few low moans followed, then all was silent as an empty church.

Mrs. Lemonpip sprang out of bed in a moment, though she was rather stout,—and ardently did she wish for a box of those matches, which she had abused the poor Lancashire man for offering to sell her that very morning. She was afraid to go below, lest the evil spirit, or whatever it was, should catch her too; so she rushed to the head of the stairs, and cried Lemonpip, in her most authoritative tone; but the only reply was a rasping guttural sound, which made her flesh creep, and her teeth chatter with terror. She rang the bell for Jemima, but she might as well have rang it for Jemima's mother, who lived at Coogee, for the girl was stone deaf in her right ear, and she was lying on her left side in peaceful unconsciousness of her mistress's distress, and her master's disaster, or of the active bell in the kitchen lobby.

To describe the perturbed state of Mrs. Lemonpip's mind at that trying juncture is too much for my pen : all her cruel persecution of her poor old man, rushed like a turbid torrent upon her distracted senses, and she howled with terror-mingled grief—"Lemonpip! my own Lemonpip! Dear Jacky! speak to your pigeon : only one word, say you are not dead, and I shall be happy!" But not a single word did her dear Jacky utter, a stifled death-like groan was the only response, which ascended through the darkness, and penetrated Mrs. Lemonpip's awakened conscience like a rusty spike.

CHAPTER III.

IN a terrible state of excitement, Mrs. Lemonpip hastened up stairs to the back attic, and called loudly upon Mr. McSkilly for help and counsel, in the extraordinary trial which had visited her. She had previously shouted fire! in order to arouse her lodger. Receiving no answer to her verbal application, she drummed at his door with her knees and knuckles, loud enough to stun the thickest head in Sydney; and when that appeal failed to elicit a response, she boldly opened the door and entered the room, when, to her further bewilderment, she discovered that her lodger was *non est.* The window was wide open, and the full moon was shining into the empty bed, from which Mr. McSkilly had most unaccountably vanished, she knew not whither. Various articles of wearing apparel were lying in confusion on the floor, but not even the shadow of the owner could be seen ; and all sorts of supernatural notions flitted through Mrs. Lemonpip's excited brain, as to the aërial flight of her lodger, and also as to the horrifying fate of her poor husband ; while she intimately connected Satan himself with the mystery and the mischief, both upstairs and down.

Alarmed beyond measure, and apprehensive of personal damage by remaining, Mrs Lemonpip rushed into the front attic, threw up the sash, and, arrayed merely in her night robe and cap, she slid down the dewy slates into the leaden gutter, and made the best of her way to the front attic window of the adjoining house, or number one, which was a young ladies school, kept by Mrs. Backboard. In that attic were three young lady boarders, and a pupil teacher. The latter young lady was just about to put the extinguisher on her candle, preparatory to jumping into bed, when she heard a tapping at the window, and at the same time saw the purple nose, and white frilled nightcap of Mrs. Lemonpip, which was all that could be seen of her, for the window was five feet from the leaden gutter. But even that was evidently more than the pupil teacher rejoiced to see ; for she uttered a shrill scream, which awakened the three young lady boarders, and they all screamed too ; while they tumbled out of bed as nimbly as sailors in a sinking ship, rushed out of the attic to the floor below, and aroused all the other boarders and Mrs. Backboard, with the startling report that a ghost was in the gutter on the roof, and knocking at their bedroom window.

An indescribable commotion filled the house, and the utmost efforts of Mrs. Backboard to restore order and discipline, failed altogether. Threats of long lessons, and " bad marks," on the morrow, had no perceptible effect in quelling the panic, which possessed every fluttering young heart, and blanched every fair face. The housemaid positively refused to go for a policeman, and received a week's warning there and then ; and the cook, with insubordination in her eyes, declared that she would not stir a peg at that time of night, for the best place in the colony. The pupil teacher suggested that they should all shout together from the drawing-room windows, and she was sure they would be heard at all the police stations in Sydney ; but she was peremptorily ordered to be silent, and to go and look for the wooden rattle in the lumber room, which orders she very reluctantly obeyed.

Mrs. Backboard was a strong-minded woman, and had always professed a thorough contempt for spirits of all sorts : so she took a candlestick, and requesting six of the senior boarders to follow her, boldly ascended to the front attic ; but had no sooner entered it, than she turned round and hastened out again, with her face as white as the wax candle in her hand ; for she had beheld Mrs. Lemompip's night-capped head at the window, and had heard her bony knuckles knocking against the glass. The startled school mistress did not wait an instant to see or hear more, but descended to the second floor, almost as quickly as the six senior boarders, who had skipped down the stairs in double quick time, each one believing that the ghost was close behind her.

Meantime Mrs. Lemonpip was shivering on the wet slates, in a state of mind bordering on despair. She had failed to gain ingress to Mrs. Backboard's, and was unable to regain her own house, for she could not reach the window un-assisted. She was afraid to apply for admission at number three, as they kept young men lodgers ; so in her help-less misery she squatted down in the leaden gutter, and there indulged in reflections, bitter as the soot which tat-tooed her scanty attire. Reverses had befallen her, sudden and severe, and withal shrouded in a horrible mystery, which her reason vainly tried to unfold. But a brief hour before she was the most important member of the house, upon the roof of which she now sat shivering, like a robin in a hard frost. She was now learning the sternly practical lesson of the instability and the uncertainty of human positions. An hour before, she had a superfluity of comforts at her com-mand, and was in her warm bed, beside her live husband. She was a reverenced wife, and a respected landlady, in fact, the head of a household ; now she was a poor miserably wet widow, apparently shut out from society altogether, bereft of her husband, deserted by her lodger, slighted by her next-door neighbour, scared out of her house by Satan, or some of his emissaries, and left all alone beneath the treacherous full moon, in that cold comfortless gutter to bemoan her unprecedented misfortunes, and to unbosom her woes before those frowning chimney-pots, and creaking cowls.

But the smallest grains, by attentive culture, sometimes produce a rich harvest. Adversity often teaches a wholesome lesson, and "he is the man of power, who controls the storms and tempests of his mind, and turns to good account the worst accidents of fortune." It would perhaps be wrong to give Mrs. Lemonpip credit for much philosophy, but she was not devoid of feeling. She had a woman's heart in her breast, although unfortunately it had · become rather callous and sour, through long feeding on imaginary woes and worries, petty grievances and old tom; and in brooding over her self-made troubles, she had overlooked the many mercies and comforts with which her lot was crowned. A sensible scribe says, " Women sometimes do not prize their husbands as they ought. They sometimes learn the value of a good husband for the first time by the loss of him. Yet the husband is the very roof-tree of the house—the corner stone of the edifice, the key-stone of that arch called home. He is the bread-winner of the family, its defence and its glory ; the beginning and ending of the golden chain of life which surrounds it, its consoler, its lawgiver, and its king. And yet we see how frail is that life on which so much depends. How frail is the life of the husband and the father ! When he is taken away, who shall fill his place ? When he is sick, what a gloomy cloud hovers over the house ! When he is dead, what darkness and weeping agony."

Little Mrs. Lemonpip felt all the loneliness of sudden widowhood ; and, added to her grief for the loss of a kind devoted husband, was the bitter regret that she had been the indirect cause of his fatal disaster—whatever it was— and the regret too, that she had so very often grieved his loving heart by her pettishness, or positive cruelty. Recollections of the thousand fond acts of her dear lost one rushed into her mind, and tears simultaneously gushed into her eyes—those eyes, which for years had never been suffused except by tears of vexation, began to overflow with genuine contrition. She remembered all his kindness, and solicitude for her comfort and pleasure, as evidenced even that very morning—but which kindnesses she had so often slighted, or indignantly spurned. Then she called to mind his constant example of gentleness, meekness, patience,—his wonderful forbearance with her bad manners, and his frequent prayers for her reformation ; and her conscience condemned her, whichever way she viewed her conduct.

As she sat in searching judgment upon herself, she became clearly convinced of the cause of her irritability and furious temper, which had not only made her life miserable, but had made her dreaded and disliked by all her acquaintance—by every one in fact, but the dear, kind, charitable soul which she had cruelly hunted out of his body. She became bitterly conscious of the way she had been befooled by the tippling tempter for years past; and she fancied she saw at the same time the evil one before her eyes, sitting in the gutter, mocking her misery. Yes, there sat old tom (the arch fiend, whom she had daily hugged to her bosom, for many years) in the shape of an immense goggled-eyed toad, croaking and spitting fire at her. There he sat, with all the malignity of Satan himself; and as she gazed she hated him, and hated herself too for allowing that deceitful enemy to tempt her into such shameful neglect of her sacred conjugal duties; and she there and then resolved, that as soon as she got her boots on again she would crunch old tom beneath her heels. Never more should he enter her household, to breed disorder therein, and to ruin her body, and soul too.

*   *   *   *   *   *

The pupil teacher at number one having found the watchman's rattle in the lumber room, Mrs. Backboard seized it, and entering the front balcony as bravely as a fireman, she rattled a rattle, louder than a sackful of Chinese crackers all alight, which soon brought a posse of policemen before the house, and a large concourse of excited spectators too. Considering it imprudent to admit policemen, or any other men, inside her doors at that hour, Mrs. Backboard explained to the inspector, from the balcony, that a mysterious white figure was on the top of her house.

"Perhaps it is a white cat, madam," suggested the inspector politely, while some of his men were observed to wink.

"It is neither a cat nor a dog, sir," replied Mrs. Backboard, with stately emphasis, "I saw it with my own eyes, and I request that you will get a ladder and catch it, whatever it may be. It has no right to trespass on my roof, and disturb the peace of my household. I give it in charge."

A ladder was procured, when a policeman mounted and peeped cautiously over the parapet, just as Mrs. Lemonpip was vowing total abstinence for life. As she caught sight of the man's head and shoulders, she uttered a shriek, which made the multitude in the street shudder, and made the man on the top of the ladder hasten to the bottom again faster than he went up.

"What is it? What is it?" asked a hundred voices, as the terrified policeman regained the roadway.

"It's a great big ghost, sitting on the slates," said the man, wiping the cold perspiration from his brow.

"Pooh! a great big goose!" sneered the inspector, with an angry glance at his shaking subordinate.—"I'm ashamed of you, Wilkins."

"There's the ghost! There he is, hooray!" roared the excited crowd, pointing to the roof, where, sure enough, Mrs. Lemonpip was leaning over the parapet, and with out-stretched hands was calling loudly for help.

"Get out of the way," said the inspector, as he pushed through the throng to the ladder, with laudable determination in his looks, and nimbly mounted to the roof just as Mrs. Lemonpip had fainted away, fairly overcome with terror and fatigue. The inspector summoned two or three of his men to his assistance, and with their united strength they lifted the insensible little woman through the window into her own front attic.

*　　*　　*　　*　　*　　*

I must now try to explain the cause of the sudden flight of Mr. McSkilly, which the reader doubtless is anxious to learn. When he was first awakened by the unearthly yells which had so alarmed Mrs. Lemonpip, and after he had heard his landlady's loud cries of fire, he sprang out of bed, scrambled out of the window, and hastened to the back attic window of number three. But with characteristic caution he dragged a hair trunk after him, which contained all that he owned in the house, except the scattered garments on the floor, which he would not stay to put on his person.

In the back attic of number three lay a little Celtic doctor, who had recently arrived in Sydney as surgeon of an emigrant ship. He had taken up temporary lodgings in the house of Monsieur Blowitt, a professor of music, and on the night in question, there he lay on a curtainless stretcher, blessing the mosquitos, and other triflers with nocturnal repose, which are not scarce in Sydney in the summer season, as most new comers are aware. The doctor had, a short time before, made a vigorous attack on the mosquitos with his waiscoat, and fancying that he had driven them all out of the window, he had put his head beneath the top sheet and began to dose off. He was dreaming that he was crossing the Line again in the good ship Diver; and that his 340 emigrants were dancing with Neptune's crew on the deck over his cabin, just as Mr. McSkilly was dragging his hair trunk along the roof over the doctor's dormitory.

On arriving at the open window, Mr. McSkilly unhesitatingly inserted one half of his tall bony body into the attic, without asking permission, or indeed without knowing whether there was any person there to consult on the subject; and having thus secured an entry for himself, he was leaning forward with his long arms trying to drag in his hair trunk from the leaden gutter below the window, for, next to his life, he valued his trunk. At that moment Dr. O'Flaherty opened his eyes to behold an undefinable apparition darkening his chamber window and making a rumbling noise on the roof, like a barrowful of bricks, so that in far less time than it takes me to record it, the fiery little Celt decided upon a course of prompt-action to punish the bold invader of the sanctity of his chamber, and the noisy disturber of his slumbers.

It is said that an Hibernian sire once gave this parting advice to his son, who was starting out on his travels in foreign lands. "Phelim, me bhoy! whiniver yez hear of a row hurry to it; an whiniver yez see a head, hit it wid yer sthick." Dr. O'Flaherty probably held similar views respecting the policy of hitting heads; at any rate he was not disposed to allow heads or bodies either to intrude upon his privacy unmolested, so he sprang out of bed in a twinkling, seized his shillelah, which was always handy, and dealt Mr. McSkilly a mighty crack—or rather thud—not on his head exactly, because his head was outside the window. He hit him very hard, however, and his head very soon came inside the window to see what was the matter behind him, and to ascertain who it was that had behaved so inhospitably; and then commenced an awful fight between the doctor and the dentist, which I must describe in my next chapter, where I will also explain the primary cause of all these extraordinary occurrences.

CHAPTER IV.

DOCTOR O'FLAHERTY was not deterred from hitting Mr. McSkilly on the head, in the first instance, by any particular respect for that member, but merely because the head was outside the attic looking after the trunk. The correctness of that assumption is very clear; for no sooner had the astounded Scotchman drawn his head inside, than the choleric little doctor began to rap at it like a volunteer bandsman beating a kettle drum.

"Hook toot mon !" cried McSkilly. " Dinna be fechtin me, I'll gang out of yer hoose agen, if I'm na welcome intil it. I wadna fecht for ony money, I'd rather rin awa ony day."

" What do you mane by poking your ugly carcase inside my window ? You cat-a-walling thief !" With that the doctor made his stick rattle again on McSkilly's head, while the poor bewildered fellow stood for a moment, uncertain whether to fight or flee.

" Don't you know better manners than to come into a gintleman's apartment in that haythinish fashion ? And is this the way you trate your supariors, in this part of the worrld ?" saying which the little Celt moistened his hand to grip his shillelah again, and hopping round the astonished Scot, alternately attacked his head and his shins, until his peaceable spirit was aroused to fighting pitch, in pure self-defence. With a rapid outpouring of Caledonian compliments, he rushed upon his unknown assailant, like a kangaroo dog attacking a terrier, and the little doctor was *hors de combat* in an instant, being unable to stand against the resistless force of his tall sinewy antagonist. With a crash, which nearly shook the house down, the two combatants fell to the floor, and there they lay rolling about, pommelling each other without mercy ; and anathematising in their own peculiar style, until everybody in the house was aroused by the extraordinary riot, and jarring medley of epithets.

In the bedroom beneath the combatants lay Monsieur and Madam Blowitt, the landlord and his lady, quietly enjoying their first nap ; until the grand crash just described, which knocked down half the plaster of the ceiling on to their bed, which soon awakened them. Monsieur Blowitt hastily scrambled from beneath the *debris* of fallen mortar, and with a revolver in one hand, and a bedroom lantern in the other, he rushed up stairs to the back attic, with mischief in his flashing eyes, and murder in his violent gesticulation.

"*Morbleu! qu'est ce que c'est donc!*" roared the infuriate Frenchman. "Vat you kick up dis von great big row, you beggers! Vat for you knock my house down, eh? *Morbleu!* Vat for you do it : vill you tell me dat? I vill shoot you dead, and kill you both vid dis *fusil.*"

A scene of confusion and uproar ensued, equalled only by a sea fight among a forecastle full of tipsy sailors. Fortunately there were no caps on the revolver, or it is probable murder would have been committed. Monsieur Blowitt soon perceived that there was a stránger in the room ; when he, without any formality, allied himself to the doctor, and poor McSkilly got a woeful beating between them. In vain did he try to explain the cause of his nocturnal intrusion, and beg for mercy or fair play ; they evidently mistook him for a burglar, and although he warmly appealed to his trunk on the roof, to attest his honest intentions, and emphatically asked them, "if they ever kenned a thief to tak his box o'claes wi him, when he broke intil a hoose?" his furious assailants disregarded all his appeals, and would not listen to his reasoning, nor look out of the window to investigate his box, but dragged him down stairs, and handed him over to the policemen, whom the uproar had attracted to the spot. Followed by the usual noisy street rabble, the bruised and bleeding dentist was escorted to the station house, vainly protesting all the way there against the illegal seizure of his person, and imploring somebody to look after his trunk.

I must leave Mr. McSkilly to his ruminations in the lockup, (and his self-congratulations on his escape from the "deil himsel,") and return to Mrs. Lemonpip. I would here remark, that these thrilling incidents occurred rather quicker than I have been able to record them ; for they occupied but little more than three hours, from the first outbreak to the *dénouement.*

Mrs. Lemonpip soon recovered from her swoon, and after borrowing a bull's-eye lantern from one of the policemen, she hastened to her chamber to put herself into more becoming attire ; while the inspector and his men, at her request, went down stairs to investigate the cause of such varied disasters. In a few minutes Mrs. Lemonpip descended the stairs too, with a palpitating heart, and the first object her gratified eyes gazed upon was her much prized husband—all alive—sitting upon the hall mat, replying to the numerous questions of the inspector.

"My dear, dear Jacky!" exclaimed Mrs. Lemonpip, rushing up and throwing her arms about his neck with a warmth of affection which she had long disowned. "My own dear Lemonpip; I am so glad you are not dead! Forgive me, pray forgive me, Jacky, my love! It was all my fault that you got into this terrible trouble, but I will faithfully promise and vow, never to grieve you again as long as I live." The little woman was here fairly overcome with emotion and gave vent to a flood of tears, which slightly affected the inspector and all his men. "Oh! I am so glad you are alive, Jacky! You can't think, and I can't tell you all I have felt about you; I have had an awful time, I can assure you, I never was so frightened in all my life before. But do tell me, dear, what has been the matter with you; you needn't mind these gentlemen, they are all friends. Tell us all about it, dear, what it was that knocked you down and hurt you? Where all this blood came from? What it was that made that frightful noise?"

Thus entreated, Mr. Lemonpip began to explain all he could recollect of the tragical occurrences of the last three hours. In descending to the hall in the dark, he had unfortunately trodden upon something soft, which was coiled up on a dogskin mat at the foot of the stairs. The goblin, or whatever it was, had very reasonably shrieked out, under the pressure of Mr. Lemonpip's fifteen stone person, and had at the same time made violent efforts to claw and bite off the leg which had crushed it; as witnessed the marks on the limb itself. The unexpected attack of some unknown, though formidable teeth and talons, and the startling shrieks too, had naturally enough made Mr. Lemonpip jump—as the saying is—and in doing so he had knocked his head against the ponderous umbrella-stand in the hall, and overturned it; then falling down upon it he so stunned himself, that he had lain for an hour or more, totally unconscious of what was going on around him. When his reason returned his nervous system was so shaken, that he had been afraid to move hand or foot, or his tongue either, lest he should again step upon or otherwise arouse the dreaded fury of the mysterious enemy, which had so painfully lacerated his left leg, and so terribly frightened him besides. There he had lain upon the cold oil-cloth, silently watching for daylight, and wondering what all the riot was about outside his house, and inside his neighbour's houses on either side of him. There he lay surmising all sorts of unpleasant reasons for his cruel desertion, in this time of trial, by his wife and his attic lodger, until the welcome arrival of the policeman, and the still more welcome smiles and embraces of his precious little pigeon, had restored gladness into his looks, notwithstanding his wounds and bruises.

That was all Mr. Lemonpip could tell them about his mishaps. In making a search, however, in order further to elucidate the mystery, they discovered Mrs. Lemonpip's favourite old tom cat, lying on the dogskin mat, pressed as flat as a volume of acts of parliament. He was quite dead, of course, but his mouth was wide open, as if he had died in the act of making that awful noise, which had so terrified Mrs. Lemonpip and her lodger too, and which she afterwards regarded as the friendly outcry of the animal against that dangerous rival in his mistress's house, and in her heart too ; as if he with his last outtrodden breath had exalted his voice to a supernatural pitch, to warn her of the diabolical character of that other " old tom" in the black bottle ; her overweening fondness for which, had caused the untimely death of one of the best rat-catching cats in the colony ; it being quite clear that it was the mischief-making gin which had incited her to send her husband down stairs on that disastrous occasion.

It did not fail to strike Mrs. Lemonpip as a remarkable coincidence, that at the very time her poor old tom cat was giving his last kick at the bottom of the house, beside her prostrate spouse, she was sitting on the top of the house in solitary sorrow, resolving upon the total abandonment of the old tom in the cupboard, or in figuratively crunching him beneath her heel. Although she could not but lament the painful end of her faithful old cat, she was ever afterwards consoled when looking at his stuffed skin in the glass case on the side board, that tom's dying cries had been instrumental in arousing her to a sense of her danger of becoming a downright drunkard, and had led to her totally forsaking the pernicious and expensive habit of tippling, or taking a " little drop of comfort" (every hour of the day—a habit which had long since sapped the foundations of all her

domestic comfort, had chilled the natural warmth of her
heart's affections, and made her a misery to herself; a
dreaded nuisance to her friends—and, what is infinitely
worse than all, had destroyed her hope of the life to come.

The inspector soon comprehended the whole affair, and
smilingly withdrew with his men to explain as much as was
expedient to the excited populace outside, in order to induce
them to disperse. He then went to the watch-house and
liberated Mr. McSkilly, and although it was some time before that honest Scot would accept of his "free pardon,"
and talked loudly of bringing actions for damages against
Dr. O'Flaherty, Monsieur Blowitt, and the whole police
corps; after a while, his good nature prevailed over his
litigious disposition, and he laughed heartily at the serio-
comical events, then shook hands with the inspector, said
"gude nicht, freends," to all the constables, and hastened
home to look after his hair trunk. As he limped along on
his bruised legs, he could not fail to remember Dr. O'Flaherty's shillelah, and, doubtless, he reflected at the same
time that had he but displayed manly courage, and a true
friendly spirit, he would have saved his host and hostess the
disagreeable *exposé;* and his next door neighbour on either
side the annoying disturbance of that eventful night, and
would have saved himself too the beating, and the igno-
minious association with the usual nightly denizens of the
watch-house.

*   *   *   *   *   *

"The world rings with answering echoes:" writes a popular authoress, "they come not alone from braes and hills,
but from hearts and lives. Some are soft and low as the
sound of the wind among the leaves; some wild as the
eagle's scream, or sullen as the ocean's roar. Like produces
like is the law. Storm clouds blacken the earth, sunshine
brightens it. Thunder is answered by thunder; bird song
by bird song; petulance and distrust by petulance and distrust; kindness by kindness."

Mr. Lemonpip understood that law, for he was a philosopher in his way. He knew "that as a cross word begets a
cross word, so will a kind one beget its likeness;" and that
it is by little acts of watchful kindness that affection is won;
the comfort of social life is preserved, and a softening influence is secured over hearts which an opposite conduct would
repel, or overload with acerbity."

Mr. Lemonpip had long grieved over his dear wife's infirmities of temper and habit, and had tried with affectionate solicitude, and by every means which kindness could suggest, to restore her mind to that serenity which she once enjoyed, and which had in former days filled his house with happiness. The accursed thing in his household—the blight of his domestic comfort, was his wife's fondness for stimulants, which had gradually increased to a dangerous excess. It was yielding to that debasing passion which had soured her temper and turned her into a shrew. Mr. Lemonpip had tried every means, and had used every effort, both of example and precept, to induce her to abandon that slavish besetment, but apparently without effect. His kind words and tender solicitude, however, were not unappreciated by her, and they were gradually producing their softening effects. That memorable night was the turning point in her life, for she had resolved to banish "Old Tom"—or the gin-bottle—from her house for ever. The resolution was partially carried out next morning, when the black bottle was smashed, and she solemnly promised that she would never again taste strong drink.

The joy of Mr. Lemonpip may be imagined at observing from day to day the thorough change in his wife's habits and temper. The old happy smiles of bygone days returned to her face, and the silvery gentleness to her voice. With her head free from the bewildering excitement of strong drink, she could calmly review her actions for many years past ; and the result was a thorough self-renunciation. She saw with abhorrence the cruelty and ingratitude of her conduct to her over indulgent husband, and the disgrace she was bringing upon his fair reputation. Above all, she saw that she had been sinning against God, and madly rushing to eternal ruin. She sincerely repented of her sins, and humbly sought pardon through the merits of Jesus Christ ; and as no one ever earnestly sought for peace in that way without finding it, Mrs. Lemonpip found it, and from that happy time to the day of her death, a more earnest, zealous Christian could not be found in the colony. Nor could a happier man be found than Mr. Lemonpip : indeed they were a blithe old pair, whose hearts were full of love. Not a jarring word was ever heard in their house from that time forward, except on one occasion, Mrs. Lemonpip forgot herself for a minute and began to scold her Jacky, when he

looked at the glass-case on the sideboard with a merry
twinkle in his eye, and quietly ejaculated "poor old tom."
The cloud on Mrs. Lemonpip's brow disappeared instantly,
and she burst into a hearty laugh, in which her light-
hearted husband joined, and declared, while he kissed her
affectionately, that "there was not a man in Sydney who
was blessed with such a loving little pop of a wife as his
own darling Betty, who was worth her weight in diamond
rings."

SAILORS' YARNS!

" Did you ever sail from port on a Friday, Mr. Boomerang?"
asked a weather-beaten old skipper, who was walking the
deck of his vessel, smoking his pipe.   It is not necessary to
mention either the name of the vessel, or the latitude and
longitude of her position.

" Yes, captain, I have often sailed on short coasting trips
on Friday ; and I can recollect on two occasions putting to
sea on a long voyage on a Friday."

" Humph ! and did you not get into some unlucky scrape
or other before the voyage ended ?"

" We certainly did, sir," I replied ; " for each time we put
back disabled."

The captain chuckled, as though he rather enjoyed mischief, then gave me a catalogue of disasters which were reported to have been caused by certain captains recklessly
persisting in sailing on that ill-famed day.

" But I should be more disposed to think that the disasters, which I alluded to, captain, resulted from a desecration
of Sabbath days, if I believed that special days had any influence at all on the events of a voyage : for on one occasion
the ship was coaled on a Sunday, and the second time we
put back, the various congregations of worshipping Christians in the town, off which we were anchored, were disturbed by the ringing of blacksmiths' hammers, as they re-
paired certain machinery, the breakage of which had obliged
us to return to port."

" Well, sir, there is a smacking of sound sense in your
remarks," said the captain.   " I have seen so many disasters
happen to ships after sailing on Sundays, that I have given
up the practice entirely ; for I believe ill-luck attends it.   I
don't think I would trip my anchor, on that day, to oblige
my father, unless it were to get my ship out of danger, or
some such emergency.   I will tell you what happened to me
the very last time that I got under way on a Sunday, I could
give you plenty more examples of the same sort, but one
fact is as good as forty to elucidate the point I am arguing ;

and I don't want to spin you too many of these dry yarns,
lest you should scud away below, and leave me to talk to
the moon.

"I was once upon a time lying in a certain port to the
northward of Sydney, with a fleet of other vessels, waiting
for a fair wind.　There were not so many steam-tugs in those
days as there are now, and vessels of heavy draught of water
usually waited for a leading wind out of the harbour.　One
Sunday morning I roused out of my berth unusually early,
and went on deck to take a look at the weather.　There was a
light air from the north-west, with a clear sky overhead ; so I
said to the mate, 'If the breeze freshens at all, after the tide
has slackened a bit, Mr. Shackles, we'll up stick and be off ;
so see all clear for a start.'

" 'Ay, ay, sir,' said the mate, but he looked rather dismal
at me, for his wife and children lived in a little house on the
hill, just abreast of us, and I think they were expecting him
on shore for the day.　However, he didn't grumble, poor
fellow ! and I was sorry after a bit, that I had not let him
go on shore to say good-bye to them.　Well, away he went
forward and turned the hands to, to hoist up the boats, and
secure the deck lumber.　About ten o'clock I saw a lot of
other vessels getting ready for sea, so I gave the orders to
heave the cable short, and cast the gaskets off the yards.
Just at that time I saw a boat put off from a rakish-looking
schooner, lying at anchor about a cable's length to windward of me ; and as the boat passed close under the stern
of my ship, I hailed the captain, with whom I was slightly
acquainted.

" 'Halloa, friend ; where are you bound to ?' said I. 'Arn't
you going to get under way, with this fine leading wind ? or
are you going for a day's fishing ?'

" 'No, sir,' said he, 'I'm going to church.　I never sail
out of harbour on Sundays, for there is nothing gained by
it, and it is not fair play to my men to deprive them of their
lawful day's rest.　Besides, my owner wouldn't allow it.'

" 'My blocks and sheaves ! that's a superfine yarn, too,'
said I.　'It's no wonder you did not stay long in Messrs.
Bousem, Tawt, and Co.'s employ.　Now I understand why
they so soon unshipped you ; for I recollect hearing old
Bousem himself arguing that very point, like a sea lawyer,
with one of his skippers ; and proving, to his own satisfaction, that it was right and proper to sail on Sunday ; in-

deed, he showed very clearly, that in some cases it was a sin not to do so. For instance, if the wind was fair, he argued that it would be a contempt of God's providential favours not to make use of it; consequently, the captain who would not top his boom and be off to sea, if his ship was ready, was a wicked sinner. It's a lucky thing for you, my friend,' said I, 'that old Bousem is not your owner now, or you'd nap it pretty smartly for going to church, and letting this fine fair wind blow to waste.'

" ' I have listened to old Bousem's logic,' replied the little skipper, smiling, ' but it never induced me to ignore the Divine command, to keep holy the sabbath day. My principle is to obey that law, even if I offend owners. You had better pay out your chain again, captain, and come ashore with me ; and let your hands enjoy a day's rest, which is their due, and you have neither legal nor moral right to deprive them of it.'

" ' Hoist the fore top-sail, Mr. Shackles,' said I to the mate. My friend in the boat took that for an answer, I suppose, for he shook his head and pulled away to church, singing ' O be joyful.' In a short time I was dashing along ten knots an hour, with a fresh breeze and smooth water, and a regular fleet of coasters astern of me. But I soon met with bad luck ; for just before sundown it came on to blow one of those hard southerly bursters, which are' so frequent on your coast in the summer months ; and before I could get sail off the ship, I carried away the fore-top gallant-mast and jib-boom, and sprung the main-yard, besides splitting some of the sails. It blew hard from the southward for three days, and an ugly sea got up, which strained the ship a good deal, for we were coal-laden, and as deep as a barge. On the fourth day the wind hawled round to the eastward, and we lay our course, with fresh breezes and fine weather, which we carried all the way up to Melbourne heads ; so we did not make such a bad passage after all. On the eighth morning, soon after daybreak I espied—about three miles ahead—a smart-looking schooner, going through the ' Rip ' without a pilot ; and sure enough it was my little church-going friend. In he went, with his colours flying, as if he were crowing over me ; and by the time I got up to the anchorage off Williamstown, there lay the schooner alongside the jetty, all ready for discharging cargo. I felt a bit nettled, though I didn't say anything to

my mate, for I could see he was mightily pleased at it.
Next day I met the little skipper, in Sandridge, looking as
happy as a boy in his first breeches. He told me that he
had spent a very comfortable Sunday on shore, and had
allowed his officers and crew to go to church too ; that he
had lain in port, setting up his rigging and titivating his
ship off, (and she really looked as smart as a new fiddle),
until the gale had broken ; and as soon as the sea had
gone down a bit, he up anchor and away. He had beaten
every vessel bound to Melbourne, which sailed on the Sunday ; and while several of those he had passed had lost
spars and bulwarks, he did not carry away a ropeyarn, or
strain a stick ; in fact, he scarcely shifted a sail throughout
the run, but carried a fair wind and fine weather right up
to his moorings.

"That yarn is as true as my chronometer, Mr. Boomerang," continued the captain, laying down his pipe. "And
when you come to think of it, sir, it is only reasonable to
expect good luck when you are doing what is right. I
mean to say it is not acting fair and square to the sailors, if
you don't give them a day's spell once a week. Poor fellows ! they get extra work enough, in all conscience, especially on board some of those old leaky colliers, or in the
coasting steamers. It is a positive injustice to your officers
and men to make them do unnecessary work on Sundays,
to say nothing of the sin and folly of setting at open defiance the laws of God, who could blow us all to the bottom
of the sea in a minute. As for the risk of putting to sea on
Fridays, that is all moonshine, and I was only joking when
I appeared to be talking seriously on that subject just now.
I would as soon set sail on Friday as on Saturday, every bit ;
but I verily believe there is no luck in sailing on a Sunday,
—nay, I maintain it is sinful to do it—except in cases of
necessity ;—and if sinful, it is dangerous, and he is a f—
a—is not a sensible man, who wilfully runs into danger.
That's a little bit of my logic, sir, and I don't think you
can find many rotten strands in it ; at all events, you
wouldn't convince me that it isn't sound and honest, if
you wished to try. I have firmly resolved that I never will
again put to sea on a Sunday, to please the best owners in
the world—but avast, that is stupid talk, for the best owners
would not ask me to do it, in fact, they would very soon unship a master who would have the conscience to do it ; ex-

cept, as I said before, in case of necessity ; and such owners are by no means scarce.

"I am afraid I have wearied you with that long prosy story," said the captain, "but don't go below yet, sir. I'll tell you a very lively yarn about Captain Lindley and the monkey, if you would like to hear it."

"I should like to hear it, captain," I replied ; "but please to tell me first about the poor carpenter, to whom you alluded at dinner-time."

"Ah ! that is an awfully tragical story, and always makes me shudder. You had better let me tell you about the monkey while I am in the humour. I never can spin a lively yarn just after talking about poor Tom Gouge."

"Up goes the monkey, then, but I am sorry you don't know Captain Lindley, because you will not half appreciate my yarn unless you can fancy Lindley is spinning it, for none but he can tell his stories with effect. It was as pleasant to me as a good dinner, any day, to sit and listen to him for an hour or two, for his coil of yarns was like paddy's rope, there was no end to it. But it topped all, to hear him tell about Jacko and the roast beef. There was more fun in his honest face then, than in a cage full of monkeys ; and he would actually thump the table, or hammer away at the bulk-head with his fists, in his excess of mirth, while he described Jacko scudding up aloft with a hot carrot in his mouth ; and when he wiped his eyes, after his ecstacy was over, you would almost fancy he was fretting because he could not laugh any longer. Yes, 'a merry old soul was he,' as scores of his passengers will smilingly testify ; and any man who could sit and look at him while he was enjoying his roast monkey—I mean his yarn of the monkey and the roast beef—any man who could even look at him then without laughing till he cried, would have no more tickle in him than my figure-head yonder. But let us sit down on the hen-coops, sir, if you please, for it is hard work to walk and spin a tough yarn while the ship is knocking about in this chopping sea ; it tumbles all my ideas together, like prize-tickets in a lucky bag."

"When my friend Lindley was third mate of the 'Billy Button,' he was on the watch one afternoon, and was waiting for the steward to bring his dinner on deck, for the captain and passengers had gone below to dine. Being always ready for a bit of fun when it did not interfere with duty, Lindley began to play with a monkey, which was made fast by a chain to the mizen mast. The poor brute was half killed with the coddling and petting of his owner, a whimsical old bachelor, who was a passenger on board ; and Lindley, thinking that an hour's run would be a treat to Jacko, cast off his moorings, when he began to dance about the deck like a dandy in a ball-room.

"Presently Lindley went aft to heave the log, and after he had finished, and had made the entry on his log slate, he looked round for his frolicsome friend, but he was gone from the poop. Fearing he would get into trouble with the old fogy below, who was as particular about his pet as if he were his son and heir, Lindley began to hunt for the fugitive ; but he had not to hunt long, for on looking over the break of the poop, there he was, actually perched on a prime joint of roast beef, which the cook had a minute before placed on the deck, ready to be put on the cabin table, after the steward had cleared away the soup-plates. Yes, sure enough there sat Jacko on the nice savoury roast, with his long tail floating in the gravy, and evidently pleased with his warm seat, as well as with the flavour of the carrots, which garnished the sides of the dish.

" ' Confound your carcase !' shouted Lindley, at the same time throwing a cringle at him, which would have spoilt his appetite, if it had hit him, but Jacko was off in an instant. Stuffing a long piece of carrot into his mouth, he bolted up to the mizen top, and there he sat munching and licking his fingers, like a regular gourmand. Of course Lindley was up after him pretty smartly, but it was not an easy job to catch him, for he climbed right up to the mizen truck. Lindley did catch him, though, and brought him down to his old quarters, and gave him a handsome tickling with the end of the signal halliards. Then looking over the break of the poop, Lindley saw that the dish was gone. ' Why, blow my buttons off !' said he to himself, ' the steward has never taken that foul joint into the cabin !' As he said that, he hurried down the ladder and peeped through the cuddy window, and sure enough there was the beef on the table, and the company were evidently enjoying it too, for it was very tender and juicy, and they did not get roast beef and carrots every day. The old bachelor had the outside cut, which he always preferred, because he liked his meat done brown. Of course, you know, Lindley had much better have said nothing about the monkey sauce, seeing that the meat was half eaten, and the gravy had been equally divided amongst them ; for I daresay, sir, we all eat worse tack than that sometimes, without knowing it. But Lindley was always square and honest, so without thinking twice on the subject, into the cabin he goes, and began to overhaul the steward for presuming to carry a joint of meat into the captain's table, after that mangy monkey had been sitting astride of it, and had bathed his ugly tail in the gravy.

"My blocks ! wasn't there a sudden stir in the cuddy at that instant ?" said the captain, laughing till his eyes watered, " they all jumped up as though they were poisoned, and ran in various directions. The old bachelor darted on deck, and after bowing his head humbly over the side of the ship for a minute, saying his grace, I suppose, he rushed up and kicked the monkey twice in one place. But you must fancy the rest, Mr. Boomerang, I cannot spin the yarn as Lindley does, and it spoils a good thing when it is badly dished."

*   *   *   *   *   *

" Now you shall hear the story of the drunken carpenter," said the captain, after he had ceased laughing at the foregoing yarn. " His name was Tom Gouge, and he was with me two voyages when I commanded a barque in the sugar trade ; he was a smart tradesman, but an awful fellow to curse and swear. By-the-way, sir, that is a habit which many lads acquire when they first go to sea, and, like other vices, it grows upon them by degrees, till at length it becomes almost as natural to them to curse as to eat their rations. No doubt they think it makes them look manly, and sailor-like ; but it is a very great mistake, for coarseness and profanity never can be indications of true manhood, or good seamanship. Pooh ! it would be quite as rational to say that wens and ulcers on a horse's back are marks of high breeding. I wish all swearers—and young ones especially— knew how contemptible they look in the eyes of sensible people, and I'm sure they would set about mastering the bad habit immediately. I think Tom Gouge must have studied the awful art of cursing very diligently, for he was the most inveterate swearer that I ever heard, either on sea or on shore. He could scarcely speak on ordinary occasions without an oath, and if at any time he were roused out of his berth to shorten sail, or put the ship about, it was hor-

rible to hear his blasphemies. He has been heard to say,
like a fool, that there was no God at all ; and at other times,
in his fits of passion, he has defied all the powers of light,
and darkness too.   He got a cutting reproof one day from
a young fellow—a steerage passenger—who had been drying
some of his clothes on the booms, when Gouge came up in
a surly humour to pick out a spar for a new fore-royal yard,
to replace one which had been carried away the night before.
'Move your duds off the spars,' said Gouge, with an oath,
of course.   'Where shall I move them to ?' asked the
young man mildly, at the same time he seemed shocked at
Tom's awful language. 'Move them to hell, if there is such
a place,' said Tom, with another curse.   The young fellow
took up his clothes, and gently said, 'If I were to move
them to heaven they would be more out of your way.'
Gouge looked rather abashed for a minute, but he was too
tough to be seriously affected, even by such a reproof as
that ; long persistence in evil courses had made his heart as
hard as a snatch-block.

   " Well, sir, we had come home from Jamaica, and were
lying off the West India Docks, ready to go in the next tide.
Gouge had been on shore for an hour or two that morning
without leave ; and when he came on board again, I could
see he was half drunk.   Knowing his foul tongue, I did not
say anything to him, until I saw him take the axe on his
shoulder and prepare to go up the main rigging ; when,
thinking it was unsafe for him to go aloft in liquor, I said
to him, 'What are you going aloft for, Chips ?'

   " ' To knock the stun sail boom irons off the yard arm,'
said he, surlily.

   " ' You had better find a job on deck,' said I, ' for you
are not fit to go aloft just now.'   With that he began to
curse and swear like Satan himself, and vowed ' he had not
drank a sup that day.'

   " ' That's right, my man,' said I, ' out with all the dirty
language that's fouling your heart ; you will never be sweet
till you get that nasty stuff out of your limbers.   That's
right, Chips, bouse it all out at once ; it's horrible rubbish.'

   " At that he began to swear worse than ever, and up he
went, in the spirit of defiance, on to the main yard, and
began to knock the boom iron off the starboard yard arm.
The iron was rusted on, and was rather hard to move, so
Gouge kept striking with his axe, and cursing at every blow,

on purpose to annoy me. I had logged down a few of his sayings, and intended to have had a reckoning with him the next day, when he was sober; but I was spared that duty in an awfully sudden manner. After many hard knocks Gouge had started the iron, and was slipping it over the end of the yard, when I called out to him, 'Make a rope's end fast to that boom iron, Chips, or it will capsize you.' Whether he understood my order or not I am not quite sure, but I heard him utter a fearful oath, and at the same time he slipped the iron off the yard, when its sudden weight overbalanced his tipsy brain, and down he fell like a shot seagull. The yards were braced sharp up, so he fell with his back across the poop rail. I heard the horrible crunching of his bones, then overboard he went, and the thick waters closed over his miserable body. Of course I gave the alarm, and all hands were aft in a minute, but it was impossible to save poor Gouge. A few bubbles rose to the surface of the turbid stream, and as I looked at them, I shudderingly wondered whether they were curses. A few days afterwards his body was picked up in the mud off Greenwich; and upon examination it was found that his back was broken. This was the wretched end of the poor swearing carpenter."

FIRE! FIRE! FIRE!

I HAVE vivid recollections of the cry of fire arousing me on one occasion from my midnight slumbers, the lurid glare which illumined my chamber, at the same time alarming me with the belief that the rooms beneath were in a blaze. After hastily dressing, I rushed into the street—thankful that I was not roasted—and joined the excited citizens, who were running to the scene of disaster.

The fire-bells were sending forth their clamorous dingle, dingle, dingle, through the night air ; and the fire engines, with their glaring lamps and galloping horses, and loaded with brave, helmeted men, were racing towards the scene of their hazardous labours, with the impetuosity of war steeds, or express trains.

Soon I arrived at the spot where the fiery element was doing its work of destruction ; and getting, as far as I could, from the jostling noisy crowd, and the mounted policeman's horses, I stood and gazed upon the exciting scene before me.

The flames leaped from floor to floor of the devoted building, and belched out of each door-way and window with the fury of volcanoes ; crackling, hissing, roaring, and sending myriads of bright sparks into the air, amidst dense volumes of smoke ; while the crash of falling beams and rafters, the clanking of the engines, the loud shouts of the leaders of the fire brigade, added to the hubbub of the assembled multitude of gazers, created a din which was awfully distracting.

The firemen, with an intrepidity which I cannot too highly extol, at the risk of their lives and limbs, mounted to giddy parapets ; and there, with hose in hand, stood and combated with the greedy flames. The policemen, too, were exerting themselves bravely to keep the crowd from dangerous proximity to tottering walls ; and the rabble, as usual, were pouring forth indignant protests against the arbitrary encroachments on their rights and liberties, and loading the persevering officers with slangy abuse.

Meanwhile, the tenants of houses adjacent to the burning building were hurriedly removing their stocks and furniture n to the street, aided by willing volunteers, and further *aided* by a horde of nimble thieves, to whom the catastrophe was a joyful "harvest home." In a short time the roof of the doomed house tumbled in, and, soon afterwards, floor after floor tumbled in also. All danger of the extension of the fire being then over, I hastened home to bed.

For an hour or two next morning. there was a stir in the city among commercial men ; and the enquiry, "*Is he insured ?*" was made by many anxious creditors—some hoping, others fearing, and perhaps vainly reflecting upon their want of prudent foresight, in omitting to ask that important question before allowing Mr. Keen to get so far into their books, and wisely resolving thenceforward to make that special enquiry before opening an account with a new customer. Before the day was over, however, all doubts were dissolved : Mr. Keen *was* insured to the value of his stock ; and a day or two afterwards it was announced in the advertising sheets that he had taken temporary premises in —— street until his old stores were rebuilt. Mr. Keen's creditors were relieved from anxiety, and his new offices were thronged, from day to day, with brokers and vendors of various classes, offering tempting bargains to re-stock his new stores, and all having a wistful eye to the ready money —for the insurance offices, in such undisputed cases, always · paid claims in prompt cash ; so they inferred that Mr. Keen was pretty flush of money. Doubtless he was inconvenienced by the disaster ; his business arrangements were unsettled for a time, and he suffered personal disquietude ; but those were very trifling matters in comparison with the ruin which would have overwhelmed him, if he had not been insured.

A case, of an opposite character to the foregoing, just occurs to my mind ; and I will give a brief outline of it to illustrate the disastrous consequences of neglecting the common-sense precaution of insuring against loss by fire. An industrious tradesman was suddenly reduced to poverty by the destruction of his dwelling house and shop. He was wholly uninsured, and had the misery of seeing the results of many years destroyed in a few hours.

For a day or two after the event, and while the recollection of it was fresh in the minds of his friends and neighbours, the poor man received much sympathy in the form of soothing words and sombre looks. There was, too, a spasmodic attempt made by a few friends to afford him more substantial comfort, by means of a public subscription ; but it was a failure—they could not gather twenty pounds after an active canvass throughout the district.

" Poor fellow ! I am very sorry for his loss ; but I really cannot help him at present," said one in reply to the pathetic appeals of the collectors.

" He was a fool for not insuring his property," said another, with more candour than politeness, significantly buttoning his pockets at the same time.

" It serves him right," exclaimed a third. " He might have insured his property for less than ten pounds a year ; and if he was such a dolt as to risk beggary for the sake of a paltry sum like that, which he could well afford to pay, he has no right to call upon me, or the like of me, to make good his loss. Pooh ! what next ?"

*   *   *   *   *   *

Life has been a severe struggle with the poor man ever since that disaster. He was unable to re-establish himself in business from want of capital, and he is now in very straitened circumstances. Through omitting to insure against a calamity (to which every person, however careful, is to some extent liable), he lost the fruits of past years' exertions, and a position of comparative affluence, which he has ever since been vainly striving to regain ; and he has the additional discomfort of feeling that his present poverty is the result of his want of business-like forethought.

These illustrations are, I think, sufficient to demonstrate the advantage of insuring against loss by fire, and the folly of neglecting to do so. I believe it is a positive duty, incumbent upon every person engaged in business, in common justice to his creditors ; and it is equally incumbent upon every head of a household, whether in business or not, in justice to his family. I have frequently heard persons say, " They do not see the necessity of insuring, as they are very careful ;" in proof of which they urge, that " they never had a mishap from fire." Their carefulness is commendable certainly, and their freedom from accidents by fire is a matter for gratulation ; still, it is unquestionable that fire has often destroyed the houses of very careful persons ; and none can effectually guard against the carelessness of their neighbours.

A fire is at all times a deplorable mishap, but, perhaps, never so serious as when it occurs amongst the dwellings of poor persons, for they are generally uninsured. At such

occurrences there is invariably much excitement and confusion. A panic seizes the poor occupants of neighbouring
tenements, and they often hurriedly remove their little
household effects into the streets for security, and frequently,
by so doing, suffer severe losses by breakages, but, worse
still, from the peculations of dishonest persons, who at such
times are specially busy, as they then have good chances of
plying their nefarious calling undetected. A thief can rush
into a house in the immediate vicinity of a fire, and his
wicked designs may be mistaken for good-natured zeal for
the safety of the goods which he is seeking to steal. In
general, the person or family who are burnt out of house
and home are not the only sufferers; and fire is not the only
enemy to be dreaded at such times.

Were persons belonging to the labouring class to insure
their household effects, such losses would be avoided; for if
their houses unfortunately took fire they would be reim-
bursed for the damage they sustained. If a fire occurred in
the immediate vicinity of their dwelling, the knowledge
that they were thus protected from loss would deter them
from rashly removing their effects into the street for thieves
to prey upon; they would most likely coolly lock their
doors, and not allow the contents of their dwellings to be
disturbed, unless ordered to do otherwise by some person in
authority. Thus they would be spared a vast amount of
worry—to say nothing of the comfort which they would at
all times naturally feel in knowing that they were not exposed to the risk of being ruined in a few hours by the carelessness or wilfulness of neighbours, which it was impossible
for them to guard against or control.

All classes of the community *can* insure; and I should be
glad if I could convince even a few poor persons that it is
their duty, and their interest too, to avail themselves of the
privilege. There are not many tenements, I imagine, in
Sydney, on which the insurance offices would refuse to take
a risk. The rates of premiums for risks in the city are very
low too; for instance—a friend of mine, residing in one of
the suburbs of Sydney, has his household furniture insured
for £300, at an annual cost of *ten shillings*. The rate would
be somewhat more for houses of a lower class than the one
which the friend referred to occupies; still, I think, the
average of mechanics, labourers, &c., could insure to the
value of their household effects for ten shillings a year.

What careful housewife could not manage to save twopence halfpenny per week (or rather less than that) for such a purpose ?—perhaps to save herself and children from becoming homeless outcasts.

Fires are less frequent in Sydney than might reasonably be expected, considering the crowded state of some parts of the city, the combustible nature of the materials with which many of the houses are built and roofed, and the heat of the climate ; still such mishaps do occur, alas ! too often, as many persons know to their sorrow. A catastrophe—entailing the ruin of a striving family—is sometimes recorded in a dozen lines, and attracts but little attention from the community on account of its apparent insignificance. The conflagration of a poor man's little cottage would not entice a large concourse of persons from their beds, though it will make the late unfortunate owner toss restlessly upon *his* bed for many nights ; calling to mind that, in a fatal half-hour, all he possessed in the world was reduced to ashes.

Such sad disasters are too frequent ; and, as I read the sentence appended to the usual brief report of them in the newspapers—"*the tenant was*" *uninsured*—my sympathy with the poor houseless sufferers has to struggle against a feeling of vexation with them, for foolishly omitting a precaution which common-sense ought to have insisted upon, and which is within the reach of the humblest householder.

Reader ! I have not the slightest personal interest in any insurance society in the world, beyond being a policy holder for a small sum. The foregoing remarks are written in a disinterested spirit ; and if you will take my deliberate advice, you will *insure your property at once.*

LITTLE STRANGERS.

LIVES there an honest old patriarch in Christendom, whose memory—though dead to ordinary bygone events—has not occasional, softening recollections of the joyful hour, when his tiny first-born, the beloved child of his blossoming manhood, announced its *entrée* to his household by a lamb-like cry, which vibrated through his bounding heart, like strains of music from the better land?

I would not venture—if I were not at leisure—to put that question to a young benedict, the owner of a tender heart as well as a tender infant, because he would almost certainly bother me with a minute description of the " precious poppet," with eyes like jewels, and hair silk, together with all the funny ways of his precocious offspring, which, though not much bigger than a quart pot, he believes to be the finest child in the parish, because the experienced old nurse told him so. Not that I would condemn him for exhibiting feeling, which, as his heart is tender, he cannot avoid doing; quite the contrary. I am always prepared for the excited partiality which every honest young father feels for his offspring, because it is so natural; indeed, I would rather see it verge on the absurd than towards the stony stoicism which some affect, under the contemptible notion that it is unmanly to talk about little babies. I should not condemn him, even if he talked positive nonsense—I generally try to keep in mind my own bygone weaknesses—still I should not care to hear much of his extravagant dilation on his new-gotten treasure; because it soon becomes tiresome.

But I dearly love to hear an *old* man talk about the days of yore, when his children were young, even though he should be over garrulous. I am fond of old *boys* and *girls*, especially when they can be merry and wise too. It titillates my fancy as much as the pages of *Punch*, to see a grey-headed old grandsire initiating his merry young sprouts in the art of " knuckling down" at " shoot in the ring," or peg-top; or to see his venerable spouse playing a game of innocent romps with a lot of laughing little grand-daughters, while her time-wrinkled countenance glistens like a ginger-bread queen, showing that her heart is full of good humour and love. I would rather have a romp with them any day than go to a review.

I have before my mind's eye at this moment a frosty-browed old boy, whom I know well. Though some folks think he is a moody old fellow, they would change their opinion if they could have seen his excited phiz the other evening, when I put the following question to him :—

"May I ask you, Mr. Wobble, if you have a distinct re-collection of your feelings when you heard the introductory little chirping cry of your first-born child?"

The old man's alley marble eyes blazed up like police-men's lanterns at the question, and he replied with a volu-bility almost startling.

"Recollect it, sir? Pooh! Ask a boy if he recollects his first pair of knickerbockers. Ask a young parson if he recollects preaching his first sermon. Ask a young lady if—but never mind that. Recollect it, sir? Humph! pap pots and puff boxes! Do you really suppose I could forget such a thrilling event as that?

"And what a mistake to call that a *cry* which was the softest, sweetest music I ever heard in my life; and I have heard a variety; more than was charming too. I have sat in wrapt enjoyment whilst listening to soprano voices, enchanting as the melody of a grove full of blackbirds. I have also heard deep, bass voices, full and grand as the chords of St. Paul's organ.

"I have heard a disciple of the great Paganini fiddle a sonata on one little string. I have been astounded at hear-ing Herr von Joel (in a saloon near Covent Garden) draw syren-like strains from my blackthorn walking-stick, which was as mute as a pitchfork handle to all my after attempts to make it emit even a single note. Yes, sir, I have heard music of all sorts, natural and artificial, from the most pathetic strains, gentle enough to melt a miser's heart, to the horri-fying opposite; as displayed in the surprisingly elongated howls of the well-known Sydney Tinker, and the dismal chanter of cows' heels.

"But if it were possible to concentrate the sweetness of all the music I have ever heard—throwing away the tin-wa-a-a-a-are, of course—into one grand symphony, it could not produce such an enrapturing tickle on my tympanum as did that first silvery treble which assured me that I was the fortunate father of a living child, and filled my heart with gratitude and pride.   Aye, sir, that was music, indeed, which I can no more forget than adequately describe."

The old gentleman here paused to recover breath after his excited rhapsody, when seeing that I had broached a subject upon which he could be amusingly eloquent, I by degrees led him fairly on to it, and listened to his animated narration till he had run himself down.

" You see, I am now like an old man kangaroo with his tail chopped off, not much spring in me," said Mr. Wobble, " but I was an active young man at one time, Mr. Boomerang, many years ago though, as these grey hairs and wrinkles will signify.   It was in those green, young days, when I first got a delicate hint that I might expect to see a " little stranger" in my home, before I was half a year older. I really fancied that this news had a stimulating influence on my whiskers, which were then only just about as long and as strong as the down on a young duck ; but they took a start from that very time.   Months rolled on, apparently slower than usual, for like young men in general, I was impatient.   At length my dear Ruth began to——h'm——yes, began to be very busy with her needlework.   She kept a big basket under an out-of-the-way table, full of all sorts of mysterious small-wares, including garments scarcely short enough for a very thin body five feet high, and other garments, scarcely long enough for a comparatively thick body. fifteen inches high, which I thought was rather a wide allowance for the uncertain measure of the expected wearer.   But I didn't know anything about rigging out babies then.   There was a variety of other things besides, which of course, you would not wish me to describe ; so we will throw a veil over the basket.

" Well, sir, there my Ruth would sit and stitch, stitch, stitch, till her fingers must have ached ; and sometimes her poor heart ached too, I fear, for I recollect suddenly popping into her room very late one night, and found tears trembling in her weary eyes, and I could also see several little moist spots, where other tears had fallen upon a long white muslin robe, tucked up to the waist, which she had spent many hours over, and of which she seemed very proud.

" ' My dear Ruth,' said I, ' you must come to bed.   I am afraid you'll injure yourself by sitting up so late, night after night, working at those long robes, and short what-do-ye-call-'ems. Come, come, put your stitchery basket under the table till to-morrow ; you'll hurt your bright eyes, and then the house will be as gloomy as a cellar. Why, I declare there is something the matter with them now,' said I, kissing her, and gently drawing her glossy head on to my breast. 'Yes, you are crying, that you are, you little gosling,' said I, kissing her again. 'What is the matter, wifie, dear? Tell me all your troubles, and let me share some of them ; that's only fair you know, for you always insist upon sharing mine.' Well, sir, after a good deal of coaxing, I found that she had been stitching, and thinking, and fretting at the same time, over that fine long robe, which her nimble fingers had worked so neatly, with so many pretty tucks in the skirt, and such lovely embroidery in the bosom and sleeves, until she got weary and sad. Then she began to fear lest her hands should never tie those tiny tape strings, and her eyes never see her darling infant in the robe which she had taken such pride and pains to work. And she wondered too, what would become of me if she should die ; who would air my linen, and look to my buttons ; or smooth my sad brow as I gazed on her vacant chair ; and who would nurse her little one, if it should live ; and whether they would be kind to it and love it. As she finished her sobbing disclosure, she burst into a real flood of tears, and nestled her pale face on my breast, like a poor little weary bird.

" 'Hush, now, Ruth, my ducky,' I said, as softly as I could ; ' don't give way to such gloomy forebodings, or you'll make me cry too. Dry up those tears, Ruth dear, and don't cry any more.' Then I would kiss her again, and try to soothe her. But she did cry more though ; so I thought it best to leave her alone for a little, as she was not one for giving way to sentimental whims and fancies, and I knew she would soon brighten up again, like an April day between the showers. Depend upon it, sir, that is the best way to manage such cases. You can never stop such tears as those with dry reasoning, so you needn't try. Let the floods come if they will, for those ducts are nature's safety valves to the heart, when surcharged with tender emotions, and tears often give immediate ease, like taking off tight boots.

" But I begin to feel as low-spirited as if I had just shot somebody," said the old gentleman, his face brightening up, while he applied a red hot cinder to his pipe. " I shall make you gloomy too, Mr. Boomerang, if I don't alter my strain, which is too dirge-like for such a lively subject as I am going to introduce you to.

"Well, sir, time went on slowly, and the preparations went on nimbly. Mrs. Follidodd, the monthly nurse, came to lodge with us; and a fine, chatty old body she was, too. I felt my responsibilities very much decreased as soon as she took charge of her department in the household; and her ceaseless tongue was wonderfully stimulating to my flagging courage. My dear Ruth, too, kept up her spirits as long as she could keep herself up. I used to try to put on a merry face, when in her company, but I fancy it looked as forced as the polite Frenchman's smile of apology to the stout English lady who had run against him in turning a London corner, and knocked his front teeth out.

"'Mr. Wobble,' said Mrs. Follidodd, as she entered my sanctum a few evenings afterwards, 'I think I shall have to trouble you to go for Dr. Dollop, bye—'

"'Oh yes, certainly,' I exclaimed, starting up as excitedly as if a black rat were running up my leg. 'I'll fetch him in two minutes.'

"'Stop, stop, sir, don't be so alarmed, there's no hurry. I don't want the doctor just yet; only I thought I'd better tell you not to be out of the way. Pray compose yourself, Mr. Wobble, everything is going on very nicely, and there's not the least cause for anxiety. You must not be so excited, sir.'

"'No, I won't, Mrs. Follidodd,' I replied, humbly, 'only tell me what to do, there's a good creature. I'll do anything in the world you tell me; and every thing you want I'll get for you. Never mind the price.'

"'Thank you, sir, I have all that I want at present. Now I advise you to lie down on the dining-room sofa, and take a nap; I'll call you when I want you. There now, be calm, sir; lie down and go to sleep, for you are looking quite fagged.'

"Accordingly, I lay down with my clothes and boots on, and my hat under my arm. But I felt as fidgety as if the sofa and cushions were stuffed with horse-nails instead of horse-hair; and I was as indisposed to nap as the anxious captain of a ship on a lee shore, or an invalid next door to a house on fire. There I lay, wondering whatever I should do if I lost my dear Ruth, and only getting more perplexed

and distressed, the further I ventured on such gloomy calculations.

"Soon after midnight, the nurse crept softly into the room
in her nightcap, and said very composedly, 'Now, Mr.
Wobble, I'll trouble you to go for—'

"'Yes, Mrs. Follidodd,' I exclaimed, jumping up, and without waiting for further instructions, I ran off for the doctor.
In most towns there are, as you are aware, a multitude of
dogs prowling the streets at night, and intolerable nuisances
they are. It is the morbid nature of mongrels in general to
run after everybody that will run away from them. So I
had not run far before I had some of the yelping brutes at
my heels ; and the number increased as I went. Still I was
unwilling to waste time by stopping to kick them. I knew
from experience that curs are more noisy and troublesome
if you take notice of them, and they seldom have courage
to bite. So I kept running, and trying to comfort myself
with the latter reflection, and they ran after me, of course,
until, as I was turning an unlucky corner near a butcher's
shop, a surly mastiff woke up, and like all bull-headed animals, he did not stop to consider why he should join in the
melee, but rushed after me, seized a large mouthful from my
apparel, and dispossessed me of kerseymere enough to make a
pair of gaiters, in less time than the smartest tailor in Sydney could have cut them out. Of course I roared out, for
I thought I had lost flesh as well as cloth, still I did not
stop to argue with the brute. Onward I sped, till I arrived
almost breathless at Dr. Dollop's door, and began to ring
his night-bell a regular "bob major," while the congregation
of curs kept up an irregular bow-wow chorus.

"'Hilloa !' cried the doctor, putting his head out of his
top window, 'Hilloa ! what the dickens are you making all
this noise for ? Is the town on fire ?'

"'Doct—or, doc—tor !' I panted.

"'What's the matter with you ?' shouted the doctor, (confound those horrible dogs.) 'What do you want with me ?'

"'Doc—tor, ma—make haste, co—come with me direct—ly,' I gasped, as plainly as I could speak with my
short supply of breath.

"'Be off you drunken sot. How dare you bring your
filthy dogs before my house at this time of night ?' roared
the doctor, in a very angry tone, being under the impression

that I was some tipsy rat-catcher, and had mistaken his house for an inn.

"'They are not my dogs, Doctor Dollop,' I replied, rather tartly, 'my name is Wobble. I don't breed noisy curs to annoy my neighbours; nor do I get drunk very often.'

"'Oh dear me, I beg your pardon, Mr. Wobble. I had no idea it was you. Wait a minute, sir,' said the doctor, who then hastily drew his head inside, and pulled down the window.

"That seemed the longest minute I ever waited, for I was picturing the while some dreadful results of the delay.

"Presently the door opened, and the doctor appeared, when I stopped him in his apologies, and hurriedly explained the nature of my errand. To my chagrin he did not evince extreme haste, nor even the least surprise, at my wife's sudden demand for his services, but politely asked me to take a chair for a few minutes, until he was ready to return with me.

"In due course the doctor arrived with me at my house. My repeated hints on the way there upon the urgency of the case, did not incite him to run; consequently, the dogs had no more sport that night. After he had had a little quiet conversation with Mrs. Follidodd, they both disappeared from my view.

"Scarcely knowing what to do for the best, after I had exchanged my damaged garments, I walked into the kitchen, and solemnly exhorted the servant maid to exert herself to the utmost, and promised I would remember her at Christmas. The girl said she would do 'all that lay in her power,' then put another shovel full of coal on the roaring fire, and quietly sat down before it, looking very sleepy. I next put the door knocker in an old stocking, and not being able to think of anything else to do that was useful or necessary, I lighted a cigar, and began to pace up and down the verandah in a marvellous state of mental and physical shiver.

"I endured two hours—as long as two days—of that extraordinary admixture of tickle and torment, which must be felt to be comprehended. At length Dr. Dollop came out to me and smilingly said, 'it's all right, Mr. Wobble. I congratulate you on the birth of a fine daughter.' About the same time I heard that delicious music which I have so imperfectly described to you. After almost hugging the doctor, I sat down in my easy chair, and gushed over with fatherly feeling.

"Those dulcet sounds continued, and I sat and listened in silent admiration and with thankfulness for the indications of strength in those infantile lungs. I can recollect the lively ba—a—a, as clearly as if it were only last night; and I can recall most of those nice soothing things kind old Mrs. Follidodd was saying to the little darling, in simple baby dialect, for which I there and then resolved to give her a new bonnet to-morrow.

"By-and-bye the bed-room door suddenly opened, and, ah, thrilling recollection! dear Mrs. Folly, (as I used to call her,) held before my devouring eyes my precious little first-born child. Ah! Mr. Boomerang, I'm not surprised to see you open your mouth wide with ecstacy, even at my meagre description of that happy moment. But had you been there, sir, you would have beheld with your own eyes what no painter or poet in the world has ever yet succeeded in depicting, the fruition of a doating young father's hopes, and realization of his fondest dreams.

"I held out my hands very nervously, and took the 'little stranger.' To describe my feelings as I did so, I must use extravagant figures, and you perhaps think I have been rather flighty already, so I will leave you to imagine them. I kissed it again and again, but very, very gently, lest I should kill it. Then I gazed on its calm slumbering face for some minutes—rapt in sublime cogitations, which soon voiced themselves in a spontaneous burst of original poetry, (you know I have a gift that way), while Mrs. Follidodd and Jemima stood by in solemn silence, with wonder and admiration visible in their open mouths.

"'Darling little daisy! it smiles,' I gently ejaculated, as I gazed on its ruddy features with my heart and eyes overflowing with poetic fire and water. 'Can't you see, nurse?'

"'It's only just the wind in its little inside, that's all. Let me take it, sir.'

"I felt vexed with the stupid old woman, and as I handed the infant back to her I replied sharply, 'It's no such thing as wind, Mrs. Follidodd.'

"The old lady did not reply to me, but sat down in a rocking chair and began patting the little dear on its back, and talking at me in a very provoking manner. 'Did de nasty windy pindy dit on its 'ittle tummack, and pain my 'ittle wicksy picksy, an make its 'ittle lips curl up, did it den?

Hoosh sh-sh !   Hark !   There, Jemima, did you hear that ? Didn't I say so ?'

"The old lady then rose from her seat, and trotted into the bedroom with her little charge, and evidently piqued at my rash dissent from her judgment, founded on long professional experience, the correctness of which had been so soundly demonstrated.

"I felt as grieved as if I had wickedly mocked my mother ; and was most anxious to express sorrow ; but Mrs. Follidodd was then too busy to be approached on ordinary errands.   I was terribly disappointed too, for I had scarcely seen my babe, much less had time for the observations which I was desirous to make on its phrenological development.   Fulsome pride at my new dignity of father had blinded me to the respect which was due to one whom I had a few hours before felt under such weighty obligations for her unremitting care for my dear Ruth, and upon whose watchful skill my happiness so much depended.   I felt humbled, even in that season of exultation ; and as I resumed my promenade in the verandah, I was led to reflect on the power of truth, and how the simplest little thing will sometimes force conviction on the mind as sensibly as a broadside from a frigate.

"The next morning Mrs. Follidodd looked rather cross, but my well-timed allusion to the new bonnet completely cured her, and removed a load from my conscience at the same time.   I was soon afterwards invited inside to see my dear Ruth and my darling babe, who were looking so pretty in their nice white caps, et cetera.   How pleased and proud I felt to be sure, as I stood and gazed at them, and kissed them alternately, while I fancied that I never before felt my heart so brimfull of love.

"In a fortnight my dear Ruth was able to get on to the parlour sofa ; and you can fancy how delighted I was to see her there, dressed in a chaste print robe, with bows down the front ; a white cashmere shawl over her shoulders, and her long dark hair falling in negligé bands over her delicate face.   I often stood and gazed at her as she sat with her baby in arms, till I felt my breast swelling with fatherly pride and affection.

"Soon afterwards, Mrs. Follidodd took her departure, with her bonnet-box and carpet-bag, and, to tell the truth, I did not grieve after her ; although she was a nice old lady,

and as merry as a magpie. I am fond of music, Mr. Boomerang, as I have before stated; still I got very weary of
nurse's standard melodies before her month expired.
Those ancient rhymes commencing with

> ' Hey diddle diddle,
> The cat and the fiddle,'

are not lacking in startling incident, and in their moral
aspect, are preferable to some of the popular songs of modern times; still, I doubt if any person would like to hear
' a cat and a fiddle' all day long, unless he were music-mad.
That was a favourite song with Mrs. Follidodd, and she believed it had a soothing influence on my infant, though I
think she must have observed that it had a contrary effect
on me.

"My darling's vocal performances, too, began to be less
interesting to me than they were when I first heard them;
not that they were diminished in power—quite the contrary
—but they were rather too frequent, and they occasionally
interfered with my nocturnal repose.

"'Do pat that dear child's back, my love,' I said to Ruth
one night, as I sat up in bed and rubbed my sleepy eyes with
my nightcap. 'I cannot think whatever ails it. Are you
quite sure there are no pins irritating its little person, my
dear?'

"Ruth answered me in a quicker tone than usual, that
' it had neither pins nor needles to worry it.'

"'Well, then it must be ill,' I replied, ' and I will consult
Doctor Dollop about it to-morrow.'

"Accordingly, the next morning, I called at his surgery,
and explained to him very carefully all the distressing symptoms I had observed in my infant, especially dwelling on its
frequent fits of grief.

"The doctor smiled blandly, as if I were joking with him,
which rather vexed me, for I thought it no joke to lose two
hours' sleep on the previous night'; and perhaps that had
given a slight acerbity to my temper that morning, for I
tartly remarked, ' You do not seem to want patients, Doctor
Dollop.'

"'That is quite a mistake, my dear Mr. Wobble,' replied
the doctor with another bland smile. 'I assure you I want
patients much more frequently than patients really want me.
But pray sit down, sir, and let us have a little quiet chat.

Your infant is in no immediate want of my services, so make you mind easy about that ; and if you can spare half-an-hour I will give you a few hints which may be useful to you as a father, and perhaps spare you and your good wife much unnecessary anxiety in future, and your infant much discomfort too.   Will you take the arm-chair, sir ?'

"So I sat down, and the doctor gave me some advice, which certainly saved me a vast deal of worry afterwards, and perhaps saved my infant from having unlimited doses of physic poured down its little throat, to half poison it, and make it grow up as sour as native currants.   Some of his hints may be useful to you, Mr. Boomerang, if you should ever have any 'little strangers' in your establishment.

" After advising me to accustom my child to a cold bath morning and evening ; to abstain from administering narcotics, or medicines of any kind except under professional advice ; to avoid coddling in its multitudinous forms ; and to allow it plenty of pure fresh air, Doctor Dollop further remarked—

" 'With regard to the frequent cries of your child, Mr. Wobble, it is not right for you to draw an unfavourable inference from them ; for in most instances their cries imply the effort which children make to exercise the organs of respiration.   Nature has wisely ordained that by these very efforts the power and utility of functions so essential to life should be developed.   Hence it follows, that those over-anxious parents who always endeavour to prevent infants from crying, do them a material injury ; for by such imprudent management their children seldom acquire a perfect form of the breast, while the foundation is laid in the pectoral vessels for obstructions and other diseases.   In the first period of life such exertions are almost the only exercise of the infant ; hence it is improper to consider every noise that it makes as a claim upon our assistance, and to intrude either food or drink with a view to satisfy its supposed wants.   There are instances, however, in which the loud complaints of infants deserve our attention.   Thus, if their cries be unusually violent and long continued, we may conclude that they are troubled with colic pains.   If on such occasions they move their arms and hands repeatedly towards the face, painful teething may account for the cause.   In such, and in many other symptoms, remedial measures may be called for.   But, depend upon it, Mr.

Wobble, that in general, the less you try to assist nature the better; for we learn from daily experience that children who have been the least indulged thrive much better, unfold all their faculties quicker, and acquire more muscular strength and vigour of mind, than those who have been constantly favoured, and treated by their parents with the most scrupulous attention; or in other words who have been coddled and spoiled.'

"I thanked Dr. Dollop for his kind and candid advice, which had sensibly shaken my confidence in flannel bed-gowns and nightcaps, as well as in soothing syrups and other compounds, which I had had a sort of traditionary belief were as indispensable to the nursery as life-buoys were to a fleet. I went home with my mind much relieved, and at once began to enlighten my dear Ruth, and to confer with her upon the most judicious course to mark out for the future physical and moral training of our darling, having in mind what somebody has sagely remarked, 'That children are like jellies, as they are moulded so they turn out.'

"Our numerous friends now began to make their formal calls, to see Ruth and the baby. I cannot tell you all the extravagant eulogiums they bestowed upon the latter; but I may say, that the generally expressed opinion was that it was a perfect beauty, the very image of its mamma, with a remarkable resemblance to its papa.

"Time rolled on, and of course, trouble rolled on with it. Measles and mumps, and other incidental ailments, came to prove to us that our little treasure was not exempt from the common inheritance of mankind. Still it suffered far less than some poor infants do, who are half suffocated with physic and flannel by over-anxious nurses. Like a tight little bark, it weathered all those waves of trouble; though the squalls were sometimes very long and strong, and our hearts were often anxious. There were many seasons of joy for us too, when the sunshine of hope chased away the mists of gloomy fears. There was the joy of welcoming our darling's first 'ittle toosy,' as it cut through its soft rubicund bed; and of beholding the first capering signs of recognition of its doting parents; of its first attempts to creep, and of its precocious efforts to talk. I shall never forget the bright evening when my delighted wife assured me immediately on my return home, that she had distinctly heard our poppet call, 'dad, dad, dad!' How eagerly I listened and longed to hear it repeat that infantile abbreviation of its father's name. Nor shall I forget my joy when the next week I heard it say, 'mam, mam, mam!' Those early efforts to talk were considered remarkable by all our friends, some of whom appeared to take a peculiar interest in the budding wisdom which we from day to day observed in our offspring, and coincided in our opinion that it was not a common child.

"It had a hard fight with its eye teeth, and symptoms of convulsions more than once appeared; but a tepid bath wrought wonders in relieving them, and a sixpenny rattle was a hundred fold more efficacious in restoring quiescence than a gallon of soothing syrup would have been.

"At ten months old my little tiddledum trots began to toddle. Ah, sir! you should have seen the animated faces of my wife and myself while squatted in opposite corners of the room, and with outstretched arms, we alternately stimulated our wee tiny legs to 'tum to its mammy,' or 'dow to its daddy;' while the fun of seeing it tumble down two or three times on each short journey, was richer than 'blind man's buff.'

"But I must get on a little faster with my story," said Mr. Wobble, "for I'm afraid you'll get sleepy, Mr. Boomerang. Years rolled on, and my happy home resounded with juvenile fun and frolic, for I have been blessed with more little strangers in the meantime, all of whom sprung up healthy and strong except one, who was nipped down like a young rose-bud. But I will not tell you about that darling one just now, sir," said the old man, as he dashed a tear from his eye-lid. "She is not lost; and anon I shall see her again; not as a child, perhaps, but as a lovely maiden, fairer than the flowers of paradise, arrayed in dazzling immortal robes, 'brighter than brightness.'"

Old Mr. Wobble was here seized with a troublesome spasm in his windpipe, but he soon recovered, and thus began again—

"Habit in a child is at first like a spider's web, neglected it becomes like a thread or twine, next a cord or rope, finally a cable; then who can break it? Those thoughts are not my own, Mr. Boomerang, but I can attest their truth; and I ever tried to keep them in mind in the early training of my young ones. Without curtailing their childish amusements, I have been careful in seeing that they were of an innocent character, and have frequently joined in their romping games, in order to observe if there were anything objectionable in them or in their playmates, and though I was sometimes as merry and frolicsome as a schoolboy in their midst, I was guarding them against vulgar or pernicious actions, or slangy expressions, with the vigilance of a schoolmaster.

" 'I'll slap your head,' said Ruth, one day to little Joe, who had accidentally thrown his boot into a saucepan full of beef-tea. Ruth would get rather excited sometimes, poor thing, about trifles; but her anger usually subsided quicker than the effervescence on a bottle of ginger pop. She was as good a mother as ever rocked a cradle, only she now and then got impatient, and would say cross things which she didn't really mean, and which she would cry over afterwards, and then be foolishly indulgent to the little object of her wrath. 'Drat that boy,' said Ruth, 'he's spoiled every drop of that nice beef broth with his dirty boot, I'll slap your head for you, I will, you young rattletrap.'

" 'Slap it gently then, my dear,' I whispered, 'as you have promised to do it, but don't promise to slap it again; for the head, though it looks pretty hard externally, contains some exquisitely delicate material, as physiologists explain to us; and they in general agree, too, that the brain is the seat of the reasoning faculties. Now, my dear, suppose you were to slap the bump of conscientiousness, which is in a very handy position, and were to depress it, and at the same time elevate the bump of combativeness, or destructiveness, that would be a very serious matter, no doubt; but what would be your feelings as long as you lived, if your hasty slap on the head were to disorganise those wonderful faculties of the brain altogether, and cause poor Joe to drivel out his days a moping idiot, or a raving maniac?'

" Ruth looked horrified at my question, as well she might. 'Oh! Peter,' she said, with tears in her eyes, 'I have never thought of that dreadful risk. I will promise never to slap a child on its head again—never.'

" 'That's right, my dear,' said I, 'for it's a dangerous mode of inflicting punishment, although a very common one. 'I'll box your ears!' is the last expression which many a poor child's reason has comprehended; and I dare say there are wretched beings this day in our lunatic asylums, whose incurable maladies are really chargeable to unlucky slaps on the head in childhood ; and many other poor creatures are wriggling through life with crooked spines, or otherwise distorted limbs, caused by hasty blows of heavy-handed parents. Whenever I hear folks pettishly talk of giving their children a good thumping, I shudder worse than if I were in danger of being kicked by an elephant.'

"I disapprove of corporal punishment as a rule, Mr. Boomerang, still I do not dispute the correctness of the proverb about sparing the rod and spoiling the child, by no means. A rod in a household of young children is perhaps as essential for the preservation. of peace and decorum as policemen are in a city ; but if proper judgment be used, the rod need only be kept to look at. That is my opinion, founded upon experience. I used to keep a short switch, a little thicker than a lark's leg, hanging over the clock ; and on rare occasions I have taken it down and administered two or three smart strokes to . a refractory youngster, on a part where there. was no risk of bruising bones. It tingled unpleasantly, no doubt, but it did no physical injury ; and it is surprising how durable its moral effects were. I had only to look up at the clock if Master Joe were uproarious, and perhaps, quietly remark that a small piece of stick liquorice might do him good, when he would be as quiet as a dead mouse in a minute. Joe knew what was the time of day when I looked at the clock, if he were naughty ; and he knew too, that if he did not immediately mend his manners if would soon strike one. But the rod over the clock was something like my grandmother's warming-pan, which hangs up in my kitchen, more for show than for use ; and I don't think I have used it four times in forty years.

"I have heard it remarked, ' that the most uncomfortable house to live in, is a house full of pets ; such as pet dogs, pet canaries, pet parrots, cats, and cockatoos, but worse than all pet children.' I subscribe to that opinion, though not so much from personal experience, as from casual observations. I believe it is a positive sin for parents to pamper their children, by giving them everything they ask for, or by allowing them to do anything they like, to keep them from fretting. Such pet children are not much less than little nuisances ; and I feel almost malicious enough to make faces at them, and frighten them away, whenever they come near me. If such spoiled ones do not grow up mischievous, and immensely troublesome to their parents, and to society at large, it will only be through the merciful interposition of Divine grace.

"I could give you a score of illustrations on the subject, but you are nodding, Mr. Boomerang, which shews that you have had enough of it, and I must beg pardon for keeping you so late. I declare it is past midnight."

"You have not far to walk home, however," continued Mr. Wobble, as I buttoned on my overcoat, and walked to the door. "But stay, sir, take my knobby stick, to keep the street dogs from picking your bones on the way. By the by, I wish you 'could add to the present Dog Act a little clause, making it compulsory on owners of curs to chain them up, or hang them. Then equestrians would run less risk of having their necks broken, and pedestrians of having their legs bitten, and everybody's ears would be relieved of an intolerable nocturnal discord, equalled only by the screams of the prowling cats that infest this locality, and so frequently spoil my repose.

"I have often thought of extemporising a cataract of scalding hot water from my bedroom window on to the screeching toms and tabbies beneath ; but it would probably damage the fur of the animals, and if they happened to be pets their owners might be pettish, and sue me for damages."

"Good night, Mr. Wobble," said I as I shook my old friend's hand. "Don't stand any longer in the open doorway talking about cats, or you'll catch catarrh."

THE WAG, AND THE WAGER.

THERE once lived a tippler, I need not tell where,
The genus is lucklessly not very rare.
If you doubt it, just walk through our streets for an hour,
And doubts will flee, faster than pigs in a shower.

The veteran toper of whom I now write
Would tipple strong liquor from morning till night;
His nose was as red as an over-ripe plum,
Surcharged with the essence of brandy and rum.

He one day agreed a large bet to decide,
And prove his *good taste*, all his glory and pride :
With eyes closely bandaged, by taste or by smell,
The names of all liquids he'd instantly tell.

The stakes were paid down, and the bandage was tied,
Then Nosey with spirits and wine was supplied.
Each sample presented, he named with a grin,
Which shook his fat sides, for he thought he would win.

And said, as he chuckled, " why who would suppose
I'd not know the stuff that has painted my nose ?
My every day diet for forty-five years !
Pooh ! none but sheer ninnies could have such ideas."

" Come take off the bandage—the wager is won."
" Hold ! hold !" cried a wag, " wait a bit, I've not done."
He then of pure water, poured out a full glass,
And grinned like a blackfellow riding an ass.

Old Tom took the glass, and sipped and then smelt it,
Then close to his ear he attentively held it.
Quoth he, " it's not grog ; to that fact I would swear ;
But what stuff it is, I don't know, I declare."

" It ain't got no flavor ; it won't hiss nor fizz—"
" Time's up," cried the wag, " Can you tell what it is ?"
" I can't," said old Tom, (with a grunt like a boar),
" For I never have tasted such liquor before."

JACK TARS, AHOY !

HEAVE to, my hearties ! while I spin you a yarn, which
may serve you for a life-line, if you will coil it away in your
memory's locker. But hold on a bit, let me hoist my number, lest you mistake me for some hungry cruiser, wanting
to board you for your dunnage. I am as true a Briton as
ever loved roast beef, or sung " God save the Queen ;" and
the Union Jack is flying at my mizen peak, which is a sign
that I am not a pirate, or a privateer. I claim to be a
friend of seamen, and though I am not a professional sailor
(as the cockney said, when he voyaged round the London
Tower ditch in a baker's trough), I know all the ropes on
board a ship, from the spanker sheet to the flying-jib down-
haul. I can hand, reef, and steer—or I could when I was
young and able—I could also splice a rope, strop a block,
or do an odd job with a palm and needle; though only in
amateur's style. I have been shaved by Neptune's barber,
with a razor like a saw, and shaving paste *à la tar* tub ; and
have been bled and blistered by the same amphibious functionary, though I cannot recommend him either as an easy
shaver or a satisfactory surgeon. I have doubled Cape Horn
in winter, and was nearly doubled up myself with cold, I
have scudded round Cape of Good Hope under bare poles,
but have not the slightest wish to scud round it again in
similar weather, I have made several long voyages, and
scores of short voyages to sea, and have had many sailors in
my service, at sea and on shore too ; so I may without pre-
sumption say I know something about sea life, and seamen.
I have always felt a strong interest in their welfare ; and it
is that friendly feeling which prompts me now to take up
my pen.

Yes, I recollect, feeling a strong affection for seamen, long
before I ever stepped on a deck, or knew the flavour of salt
junk, or the colour of sea water. Many a time have I sat,
when a boy, under a tree in Greenwich Park, and listened
to a tough yarn from some old weather beaten tar, in a
quaintly cut blue coat and cocked hat, a timber leg, and his
face the colour of a cedar chest ; and as he has stumped to

and fro, with his telescope under his arm, as if he were pacing the deck of the forecastle ; narrating in his sea lingo, the exciting particulars of the action, in which he received that slash on the cheek, or that smash on the nose ; where his starboard arm was disabled by a splinter, and his larboard leg carried away by a chain shot ; I have felt, as he touchingly described his sufferings, my soft young heart move, and almost melt, like a lump of pitch in a hot ladle.

I can call to mind too, my tender emotion, when for the first time, I visited Greenwich College, and the Dreadnought Hospital-ship, and saw many poor old veterans on their "beam-ends," total wrecks ; and others "hove down in their bunks for repairs."   I ever afterwards felt a virtuous disposition to thrash the vulgar street boys, who cruelly delighted to tease some of those poor old pensioners, as they hobbled through the streets, by shouting "timber toes, or goose."

I recollect too, when I was a schoolboy, how I used to admire, and envy, the natty little midshipmen, whom I occasionally saw on shore, dressed in their gold-laced caps, blue jackets with gold buttons, and "white ducks."   I used to think they were all embryo heroes, and that no profession was so full of adventure, and *éclat* as theirs.   I longed to be a middy, for I fancied they *always* wore "white ducks" and faces as bright as their buttons ; and I knew that they rejoiced in the favour of the pretty girls and fond old matrons all the world over.   Of course, I had *then* never seen middies as I have since seen them in a gale of wind, huddled under the lee of the long-boat, like half-drowned chickens, or dancing beneath the break of the poop, on a cold stormy night, to keep their toes from freezing, dressed in rough monkey-jackets, sou'wester hats, and tarpaulin trousers. There was very little romance about them or their rig, at such time : and no more shine in their buttons then than in rusty rivets ; while "white ducks" were as scarce on deck as white swans.

Poor Jack tars !   I have often lain in my cot on a dark stormy night, and listened to your shouts and songs, sounding in dismal concert with the howling of the wind through the ratlines.   I have often, too, had troublesome fears, while you were aloft on the top-sail yards, lest the rigging should be chafed or rotten in any part, and, during a heavy lurch, the masts should carry away, and I should see you no more. Aye, and I have frequently gone on deck to lend you a hand when the sails were wet and heavy, and the ropes ran stiffly through the blocks ; and you were glad of my little voluntary help. The officer of the middle watch, too, was often glad of my company when on his dreary duty.

I can call to mind many dismal nights, far in the icy south ; when running under small sail, and the sea like a cliff high above the taff-rail, threatening every minute to overwhelm us. And one night especially, when the decks were white with snow, and the wind roared through the shrouds like thunder : scarcely a stitch of canvas could be spread on the groaning ship, which was rushing through the foaming waters like some mad monster of the deep, and the officer of the watch stood by the steersmen, anxiously engaged in conning the course. Two men, as white as millers, were lashed to the helm, and skilfully they performed their arduous duty. " Steer steadily, my brave men," I shiveringly ejaculated as I hurried below to my comfortable cabin ; " but one false turn of the wheel, in this frightfully heavy sea, might broach us to, and send this stately ship and her gallant crew, with her tons of gold, and her forty sleeping passengers, to the rocky caves below ;" and as I turned into my warm cot, how much I sympathized with those poor fellows on deck !—how much I felt indebted to sailors ! Doubtless many of my readers have felt in a similar way.

I have also seen a ship trembling like a terrified steed, as she rushed before the fury of a tornado, and while some of the sails, which had been blown from the gaskets, were flying in ribbons, and making a noise like a hundred stockwhips ; and while the strong masts bent before the blast, like bulrushes ; I have seen a sailor, with an axe in his hand, lay out on the main yardarm, and cut away the *chain* topsailsheet, which had got foul, while other equally brave men, at the imminent risk of their lives and limbs, cut the flapping sails from the yards. Such feats of daring deserved something more than coarse fare and four pounds a month.

And I have been on board a steamer, off the Australian coast, when I would have gladly given a year's income to have been safe on shore. When the green seas were tumbling over the vessel, and carrying away chain boxes, and everything moveable, from the decks—when blue lightning played dangerously about the masts and funnel, and the pealing thunder was heard above the roaring of the wind and waves—when the captain and his officers were eagerly looking for Sydney lighthouse through the thick rain and darkness—and when many of the sea-sick passengers below were fearing they would never see that welcome light again. How much I felt indebted to sailors then !

By the way, I remember on one occasion, while lying wind-bound in a northern port, hearing several wealthy colonists—at a dinner table—describe a fearful night they had passed in a favourite coasting steamer, during an easterly gale. They stated that the captain kept on the bridge during the whole of that protracted passage, exposed to the full force of the storm ; and on their arrival at Sydney the next day, he had to be carried below, and put to bed, being completely exhausted. I heard those gentlemen confess that they owed their lives, on that awful night, to the watchfulness and skilful seamanship of the captain, aided, of course, by his officers and crew. But whether those wealthy colonists ever acknowledged their obligations in any more tangible shape, I am not aware.

As I write, I have harrowing reminiscences of my visit to the ill-fated Orpheus, at the invitation of a beloved friend, a promising young officer (and a true Christian), who perished at his post, in the sad wreck on Manakau Bar, on the 7th February, 1863.

I inspected nearly every part of that noble steamship, which then lay at anchor in Farm Cove—and as I walked round her decks, I could not but be struck with the healthy and cheerful appearance of her crew. A finer lot of young seaman I never beheld.

Poor fellows ! it is sad, indeed ! to reflect upon their untimely fate, so soon afterwards. That melancholy wreck engaged my thoughts by day, and my dreams by night, for weeks after its occurrence. Often I have imagined the heart-piercing cries of those *one hundred and ninety noble fellows*, as my fancy has pictured the terrible scene, at the moment when the masts fell crashing over the side, and hurled them through the boiling surf, into the jaws of death.

Yes, I sympathise with sailors most cordially. I love them as a class, and feel glad to observe any movement for their benefit.

Of course I do not mean to say that they are all honest hearted, though rough and rollicksome. I have occasionally sailed with intolerable nuisances, yclept " sea lawyers," with tongues as lively as seals' flippers, though not so harmless ;

I have also met with lazy, drunken, and dangerous fellows, who would do anything Old Mischief prompted to annoy their captain or officers ; and I have also seen captains and officers who would do anything to annoy their crew.   Still, such characters, though by no means rare, are not plentiful ; and I have met with honest and true men in an overwhelming majority, and I believe that most unprejudiced travellers could make a similar report.

But I fancy I hear some impatient son of Neptune exclaim, as he hitches up his nether garments, " Odds ! blow me through a bunghole, shipmate.   This yarn of yours arn't no use to us for a ' stand-by !' Belay that lady's bobbin, and pay out something handy for us, as you promised to do, when you first hailed us to heave-to.   We don't want any more wordy sympathy, and that sort of music, because, though it sounds as sweetly as a jew's-harp, it isn't very satisfying—as the hungry sailor said when he swallowed a snowball.   We are nice, handy men in a squall, as everybody knows who has been to sea ; and most people believe that they would be very short of sugar and tea, and one or two other things, if it were not for sailors.   Oh, yes, sir ; all the world knows our wonderful virtues, and *sometimes* we are appreciated too—by timid passengers, in very bad weather especially.

" Please to bear a hand, Mr. Boomerang, and spin something worth our while to coil away in our sea chests."

" Ay, ay, my hearties !" I reply.   " Stand by for it now. You know that old age overtakes seamen as well as landsmen, and the former are peculiarly liable to infirmities, besides those which are usually incidental to old age.   You active young A.B.'s (able seamen) can now shin up to the maintruck, and slide down again by the backstay, or lay out on the yard-arm in a gale, as nimbly as squirrels, and you can do a hard day's work and laugh all the while, for your supple limbs are as strong as capstan bars.   The winter winds may howl along our iron coast and lash the sea into foam, but they are harmless to your hardy frames.   So long as you have a good ship and a good offing, you care no more for the equinoctial gales than an albatross.   But hold on a small bit, mates !   I am sorry to prognosticate bad cheer, but I must be faithful, or I should not be your true friend. By-and-by old Time will make most of you shiver in the wind.   Old age comes prematurely to the sailor, and is frequently attended with an unwelcome train of disorders, especially induced by hardship and exposure, and sometimes by culpable neglect, and excesses of various kinds. Rheumatism, and other painful affections of that class, will probably coil round you, and disqualify you for able seamen's duty. At the call of the boatswain—'all hands reef topsails' you could no more take your old place at the weather earing, than you could dance a hornpipe on your head. Perhaps all your bones will ache as if you had been under a coal shoot for twenty minutes, or been caught in a hurricane in a cocoa-nut plantation. As a sailor, you will not be worth your beef and biscuit ; and if you are not fortunate enough to get a berth in the galley as cook or cook's mate, you will be roused ashore like an old rust-eaten cable, or a sprung spar that can't be fished. Then if you have not friends, who are able and willing to give you daily rations, and a place to sling your hammock for the rest of your life, you must steer for the Benevolent Asylum ; or else wander about the streets, without home or habitation, picking up a precarious meal where you can ; sleeping under gateways, or doorways, or under the trees in the Domain, with the dark clouds for your blanket ; varied only by a night's lodging, now and then, in the watchhouse, by way of a luxury.

Shipmates ! this is no overdrawn picture from imagination ; and if you doubt it, just pay a visit to the Benevolent Asylum any day in the week, or get up early on any Sunday morning in the year, and go to the Temperance Hall, to the breakfast for destitute outcasts. You would see many poor old sailors, jury-rigged, stagger into those places, the latter place in particular, deplorable looking objects, without a shot in the locker, without a cover from the storm by night or by day ; ill-clad, hungry, diseased, and friendless. Poor old tars, whose best years have been spent in hard service ; but now, disabled and unfit for sea, they are cast ashore like drift wood, or sea-weed, to be tossed about on the rocky strand of poverty, by the surges of misfortune, till death terminates their earthly sufferings, and they are rattled away to a pauper's grave.

I repeat it ; this is no flight of fancy, but a sadly accurate, every-day picture from real life, of which any of my readers, be they seamen or landsmen, may satisfy themselves, without much trouble.

Messmates, help a brother sailor ! All you able seamen

can lend a hand to some of these poor old disabled brother tars, if you have the will, and many of them would be very grateful if you would throw them a tow-line or a cork fender. But my present object is not so much to appeal to you on their behalf as it is to warn you to look out for yourselves, and make a provision for *your old age*, when *you* will be unseaworthy, and I am going to tell you of a good plan for doing so. *Now carefully log down what follows.*

I will assume that I am addressing an active young man of twenty-one years of age. ' Well, brother, you may make a comfortable provision for your wants in old age by means of a *deferred annuity*. I will simply explain to you what that means. By paying yearly, the sum of seven pounds two shillings and sixpence, which is about two shillings and ninepence a week, or about fourpence-halfpenny a day, you may insure fifty pounds a year (with bonus additions), to be paid to you as long as you live, after you have arrived at fifty-five years of age ; at which age, I dare say you will begin to feel you have had enough of sea service. You can insure for a larger or smaller amount, than fifty pounds, at the same rate ; and a man of any age may make a similar provision ; only, of course, the older he is, the higher rate of premium he will have to pay.

You would have no difficulty in making the above provision, if you were so disposed, either in Sydney or elsewhere, for you will find assurance offices in almost every sea port. There are many other advantages offered to the careful man, besides a deferred annuity, by those excellent institutions, of which you could acquaint yourselves, by getting printed rules, or by applying for information to any of the Life Assurance agents.

The expense cannot be a real obstacle to you, for even at the present rather low rate of wages, I believe it would be possible for any steady seaman to save enough to pay an annuity premium, and put something in the Savings' Bank too. I would strenuously urge seamen in particular, but landsmen also, to lose no time in making that easy provision for their life's winter.

Shipmates ! my yarn is nearly spun out ; but before I whip the end of it, I want to ask you to read the story—in another part of this volume—about my poor friend Louis, the sailor, who was washed overboard on his voyage to New Zealand, and let me urge you to do as I trust poor Louis did, viz., live in preparation for the awful call, which death will make upon you, at some time, and you know not the day nor the hour. You are peculiarly exposed to danger, and like Louis, *you* may be washed overboard without warning.

And now, my hearties, fill your sails and go on your voyage; I hope you may have fair winds and fine weather. But hold—luff up a bit; listen attentively to these few words before we part company; get such a *chart* as I gave to poor Louis (if you have not one) a Holy Bible—study it carefully, and frequently; steer by its directions; and if you do so, when the stormy seas of life are passed, you shall enter with flowing sheets the placid haven of Rest above, and there let go your anchors for ever.

A CRIPPLED SHIP WITH A WRANGLING CREW.

MANY years ago, when our fleet of coasting steamers was far less extensive than it is at the present time, and when perhaps the discipline on ship board was less perfect, I left Sydney one night for a northern port not far away. I was accompanied by a young gentleman (now occupying an influential position in the colony), who was about to pay a visit to my house, for a little relaxation from hard college studies. Strange to say, although a native of the colony, my friend had never before been on the sea, and when the steamer first felt the ocean roll as she passed the light ship, he began to anticipate that awful sensation, of which he had heard and read such moving descriptions, *i. e.*, sea sickness ; and the bare idea of it turned his complexion a blighted lemon colour. To counteract his squeamishness if possible, I led him under the bridge between the paddle-boxes, where the motion of the ship was less perceptible ; and there he stood trying to analyze his peculiar feelings, and philosophising thereupon, much to my edification and amusement, for I had never experienced sea sickness, and had never before seen a sea-sick man merry, or heard one make a joke that was not of a dismal cast.

There were many passengers on board, but they were all below, for there was a strong head wind and a drizzling rain, though the sea was not so heavy as I had often seen it at the same spot. Soon after the steamer had shaved round North Head, she began to pitch and toss and to duck her head under water, after the playful style of fast steamers in general, which astonished my inexperienced friend, who, by-the-bye, asked me in rather a quavering voice, "If there was any danger of our going to the bottom?"

"Oh, dear, no !" I replied, "we are safe enough. This is the best sea-boat in the colony, and the captain knows the coast as well as you know Church Hill. I then explained that the vessel was in troubled waters, caused by the rebound of the waves after striking the base of the cliffs, but that she would be steadier when we got further to sea. As I was ending my comforting explanation, I saw an immense breaking wave rise on our starboard bow, and I had just time to direct my half paralyzed friend to hold fast to the handle of a pump, affixed to the paddle-box, when a green sea broke over the bows and filled the decks with water, knocking a number of barrels of beer down to leeward, turning a carriage on deck upside down, and nearly throwing the vessel on her beam ends. Simultaneously I heard the well-known voice of the captain, shouting loudly for help; so I ran aft, and found him at the helm, and the late steersman (who was thrown over the wheel and had his jaw broken), lying in the lee scuppers groaning with pain. I was about to lift the poor fellow, when the captain called to me " to let him lie, and to run forward and rouse the hands out."   My allusion to the improved discipline in coasting steamers in the present day, will be appreciated when I state that the captain, the second mate, and the steersman, were the only persons belonging to the ship on deck at the time of the mishap.   I ran forward, but found that the crew were "rousing out" without being called, for the forecastle was nearly half filled with water, and the sailors were hurrying up like drowning rats, and grumbling after their usual custom under such circumstances. while the second mate was violently kicking at the chief mate's cabin door, accompanying each kick with a curse, or something equivalent to it.   Presently the door was opened, and the chief in a furious tone demanded what the other meant by knocking at his door in that sledge-hammer style.

" Can't you see the ship is on her beam ends ? Heave out and rouse some of this deck load up to windward, if you are not too drunk to stand.   Bear a hand, or the ship will go down under us !" roared the second mate.

" Bless the ship !" vociferated the savage chief. " How dare you talk to me in that manner? Bless your impudence ! what do you mean by it ? I'll punch your head in a minute," he added, as he hastily drew on a necessary garment.

" Will you ?" exclaimed the second mate, squaring up like a professional boxer ; " come on, I'm your man. I'll knock marlinspikes out of you !"

While that angry dialogue was going on, the captain was shouting loudly from his post at the wheel, but no one heard what he said, or heeded his orders in the excitement of the affray, for the crew seemed all more interested in the sea fight than for the safety of the ship, which was plunging about in the trough of the sea, with one paddle-wheel submerged, and the other one high out of the water; while scarcely more than a quarter of a mile to leeward were the dark cliffs, looming upon us like the jaws of death. In the meantime my terrified friend was clinging to the pump-handle, in awful dread of tumbling into the engine-room, or being washed overboard, if he relaxed his hold for an instant, and wondering at the same time if that were an extraordinary occurrence in sea-life, or a mere nothing if he were used to it.

I rushed in between the sparring mates, and in a tone of anthority, which the emergency of the case warranted, I asked, "If they were mad, to waste time in quarrelling and fighting, when the lives of all on board were in peril?" adding, " get the ship upright, gentlemen, 'for mercy's sake! and fight afterwards if you choose. Be reasonable, gentlemen, I pray : leave off wrangling, and get the ship in trim, or we shall soon be knocked to pieces on the rocks."

My appeal was effectual, for after promising to pay each other by-and-bye, they set to work in earnest, and aided by the crew, soon got the drifted cargo up to windward, and afterwards shifted some of it aft, for it had been ascertained that the ship was seriously out of trim; being fourteen inches by the head, which accounted for her shipping seas over the bows in such an unusual manner. After the vessel was properly trimmed, and a skilful man sent to the helm, she went along comfortably, and without further mishap, for she was a fine lively sea boat, and sufficiently powerful to make headway against a hard gale, if properly managed. But she had a narrow escape from total wreck that night, through clumsy stowage in the first place, and afterwards through the insane disposition of her officers, to wrangle and fight, when they should have been using their utmost efforts to remedy their previous blunders, and to rescue the ship from the critical position in which their mismanagement had involved her.

After the sailors had fairly got to work, and I saw that my aid was not further required, I assisted my friend down to the cabin ; and as I changed my wet clothing, I quietly chuckled at the various remarks of the scared passengers around me, few of whom really understood the nature of the disaster. While some blamed the captain, the ship, or the steersman, others included everybody and everything on board in a general grumble ; but I remarked that only two or three of the more sensible sort went on deck to see what was the actual state of affairs, or to offer a helping hand.

*   *   *   *   *   *

As I before remarked, many years have passed since that occurrence, but analogous circumstances have often recalled it to my mind. In trying to draw a parallel between that crippled steamer and the political condition of the colony, I do not indulge a cynical spirit. I would rather burn my pen than merely use it for the purpose of exposing the faults and follies around me, with no better motive than to provoke a sneer at them. Though I seldom trouble any one with my political opinions, I am far from indifferent to subjects which it is the imperative duty of every man to gain an intelligent insight into ; and saying that, is virtually admitting that I have been often pained at the waste of time and talent in our Legislative Assembly, which I could not fail to observe.

Often as I have glanced over reports of stormy debates in the House, have I thought of the two belligerent mates, with the careless crew watching them sparring, while the poor captain was at the helm shouting himself hoarse, to no purpose, and have wished that I could step on to the floor of the House, between the contending parties, and say earnestly, but politely, " Gentlemen, for mercy's sake attend to the important business you are entrusted with, and which you have sworn to perform to the best of your ability ! Why waste time in needless debates and factious opposition, when the interests of your constituents are in peril. Would you not censure the directors of a joint-stock company, if, when they met to discuss important measures for the benefit of their association, they showed the spirit of antagonism which I observe in this Assembly? And would you not expect to see their business soon go to wreck, and the poor ruined shareholders looking woe-begone at their unsaleable scrip? Pray don't let personal feelings or petty interests mar the general good of this great land ; but be reasonable, gentlemen, ' leave off wrangling, and put the ship in trim.' "

I would scarcely have hoped to arouse every one to a sense of the value of my semi-nautical suggestions, for some of the honourable members might have been obtuse, and others sleepy ; but if a majority had seen the common sense application of my remarks, my object would perhaps have been gained. What a few irascible members would have said to such an uncommon message is, of course, uncertain, but the reasonable deduction is not flattering to myself, so I had better not speculate farther.

But I wish to deal seriously with this subject—to say my little say, and thus ease my conscience, and to some extent fulfil my duty as a colonist, deeply interested in the moral and social welfare of this land and its people, and I would express myself with all due respect to our rulers, and without the slightest intention either to offend or to flatter one of them, on either side of the House. It is useless to lament over irretrievable errors, either public or private; but past experience should help us to regulate our future course. Happy for the colony if all our legislators have profited by the lessons which a careful review of past misapplied time is calculated to teach them.

As I pen this rustic expression of my sentiments, "the House" is re-opening for business, under—to some extent—a new Ministry; and from a careful survey of the list of honourable members, and a personal acquaintance with some of them, I cannot but believe that there are the essential elements for a good and wise government in the Assembly. If they would but waive all minor differences of opinion—which, after all, are not very distinguishable—and bring their collective wisdom to bear upon the various matters which imperatively call for prompt legislation, the effect of the past unskilful seamanship, and bad stowage (to continue my nautical figures), may be soon remedied, and the crippled ship put in good sailing trim. And notwithstanding the shaking she has had, with the heavy seas which have broken on board, she is still staunch and strong, and will soon begin to gather headway again; confidence in her officers and crew will be restored, and the passengers will all be happy and hopeful: while friends afar off will shake off their distrust, and heartily join in the glad shout, "Advance Australia."

That is a pleasing picture; but as I look complacently at it, grave doubts arise in my mind if it will meet the eyes of our rulers, so I cannot hope it will effect all the reform I desire; and I fancy I hear some of my kind country friends say, "Ah! Old Boomerang is off his beaten track, and will soon be lost in the bush if he does not look out. Political economy is evidently not his favourite theme, for he handles it as nervously as a black fellow would a lighted sky-rocket. He had better stick to his story-telling, and leave politics for bolder pens." I reply, "I don't often touch upon politics, for I have many other matters in hand; and as Hudibras says, ' A man can do no more than he can do.' But I ask you—my friends—to kindly bear with me while I offer you a word or two of counsel on this subject; and please to excuse me for comparing you to the passengers in the crippled steamer's cabin. Some of you, I am sure, are ready and willing to spring up on the deck of our colonial vessel, and lend a hand to trim it upright; but there are too many who choose to stay below and grumble, and frequently those persons talk loudest who cannot consistently say a word ; I mean, those who were too apathetic to record their votes at the last general election, and those who voted without due discrimination.

Many of you old men are fond of talking of politics by your evening firesides, which is very right and proper, and I should like to have a chat with you, now and then ; and perhaps some of you have occasionally lost patience (at which I do not wonder), and have freely expressed disapprobation of doings or misdoings, while your young sons or grandsons have sat by with open ears. It is no marvel, then, if they, when out of your sight, should talk politics too ; and in order to show that they are as witty as their sires, they ridicule certain members whom, perhaps, you have nicknamed, which is certainly not polite, to say the least of it, nor is it at all encouraging to a legislator to know that it is the popular sport to roast him behind his back, and joke about all that he says and does. In the name of fair play, I say, friends, remedy that as far as you can, and be as ready to award a meed of praise where it is due, as you are to censure ; for after all, you know, legislators are only men. And depend upon it, if the ship is to be put in good trim, you must help to do it, either positively or negatively, according to your ability and influence ; so calmly consider how you can best lend your aid, and then do it heartily.

If these remarks, written with an honest motive, on the first day of a new session, should in any way help to right our lop-sided ship, I shall be much more pleased than I should be if I were triumphantly elected to the vacant seat for West Sydney, and further honoured with the Speaker's chair

"DRIVING A HARD BARGAIN."

WHEN on a visit to England, I went one day to the far-famed gardens at Kew, where I saw, amongst many other things worthy of admiration, a variety of Australian shrubs, &c., which carried my gratified feelings away for a time to my loved adopted land far over the sea.

Returning to London by railway, the train stopped for a few minutes at the Vauxhall station, when my attention was attracted to a placard, announcing that a "monster balloon" would ascend from some celebrated gardens in that vicinity, at seven o'clock, and would have accommodation for four passengers.

Having travelled by almost every other mode of convey-ance, I was seized with a strong desire to try a sail in a balloon, and get a bird's-eye view of London at the same time. ·So I alighted from the train, and walked straightway to the gardens before mentioned, whither crowds of people were wending their way. On paying the fee for admission, I was presented with a ticket, which entitled me to an equal chance with the other visitors, to a seat in the balloon car.

The process of filling the balloon with gas now com-menced ; and for a small additional fee I was permitted to go within an enclosure and witness the manipulations. In a comparatively short time the enormous sphere of silk and network was sufficiently inflated, when that veteran aëro-naut, Mr. Green, got into the car, and another man—his chief mate, I supposed—seated himself upon a sort of hoop above the car, and began to overhaul the valve lines ; while Mr. Green arranged the ballast bags, coiled away sundry ropes, and secured his grapnels, with the carefulness and coolness of an expert yachtsman, when seeing his tacks and sheets all clear. In the meantime, a large black board was elevated in a conspicuous part of the garden, with four numbers chalked upon it; and the fortunate holders of tickets corresponding to those numbers were invited to show themselves. I was not one of the fortunate ones, so I saw that my chance of a ride in the air was gone, unless

I could purchase a seat, as other persons, ambitious of lofty position, have done.

In a short time four men hurried into the enclosure to claim their privileges as holders of the lucky numbers; so selecting the most nervous-looking man, I asked him if he would sell his ticket.

"Yes, sir," said the man, while his face underwent a rapid change for the better, "you shall have it for a pound."

I drew out my purse, but found that it contained only fifteen shillings, which I offered to the man, who shook his head, and scornfully declared "he wouldn't take nineteen and sixpence—that it was dirt cheap at a pound."

"Jump in, gentlemen," cried the captain of the balloon; "look sharp! look sharp! take your seats."

"Are you going to give me the pound, mister?" asked the nervous little man, as he scrambled into the wicker car.

"I tell you again, I have but fifteen shillings with me," I replied, "so I cannot give you more; and you had better take my offer. I don't believe the change of air will do *you* any good."

"Now I tell you what I'll do with you," said the man, "I will take fifteen shillings and your umbrella—what do you say?"

At that moment, the men who were holding the ropes, which secured the balloon to the earth, slackened them, when the machine ascended a few yards, and swayed to and fro, as if impatient to be off among the clouds.

The little man began to look sea-sick as he shouted out with a considerable display of trepidation, "Well, here you are, sir; hand me the fifteen shillings and take my place, we won't fall out about an old umbrella."

But it was not an easy matter to hand him anything, considering that he was eight or ten yards above my head: so I replied, as I held up my purse, "Here is the money; come down one of the ropes, and I'll climb up by the same means."

"Oh, I'm afraid to go down the rope—pull the concern down, can't you," shrieked the little man. And then, turning to the captain of the balloon, he said, "Hoy, master, tell those fellows to pull the thing down again; I want to get out—I'm not well, and I've sold my ticket."

The captain made some testy reply, and called to the men below to get ready to let go at the word of command.

"I want to get out, I tell you," roared the little man, who was now as pale as a white cat. "Hoy, you sirs; pull the concern down, and I'll give you sixpence.

"Ha! ha! ha! ho! ho! ho!" laughed the unsympathising crowd, as the poor excited fellow stood up in the car, and was rather roughly pushed into his seat again by the irate aëronaut.

"Yah! You'll never come down again on this side of the world, unless the balloon blows up," roared one of the mob. "This is a fair wind for the East Indies; you'll land in a jungle, and be bolted by a boa constrictor."

"I wouldn't care if my wife knew where I am," groaned the little man, scarcely knowing what he said. "I say, you sir; just go and tell her, will you? There she is yonder; that young woman in a red bonnet, with a baby in her arms."

"Ha, ha, ha!" laughed the mob again, in a tumultuous chorus louder than before.

"You'll never see that red bonnet, nor that baby any more," shouted another of the comforters in the crowd. "Your wife is as good as a widow now; but don't cry, Joby; I'll take care of her—I'm a single man."

"Hoy! hoy, mister! You shall have my ticket for nothing!" shrieked the little man in the car. "Pull this confounded thing down, and let me get out. I don't want to go in your balloon at all, governor; I want to go home; I'm very ill, I tell you," he continued, frantically addressing the obdurate old captain, who gruffly promised to throw him out "if he didn't sit down and make less noise."

"Good-bye, Joby," cried a previous speaker. "I'll look after your missis; tat-ta—give my love to the Great Bear."

"I'd smash you, if I could get out of this basket," roared the little man, in a great passion, shaking his fist at his tormentor.

"Let go!" shouted the captain to the men below. The men let go, when, amidst the shouting, the loud laughter, and varied compliments of the assembled multitude, the balloon rose above the trees in the gardens, and was soon high in the air, looking not much bigger than a water-butt. I have no doubt that my haggling friend's enjoyment of the panorama beneath him was sadly marred by his extreme terror, and his self-reproach for refusing my reasonable offer for his ticket, combined with his anxiety for his wife and baby.

Although I felt vexed at missing so favourable an opportunity for a ride above the world, I enjoyed a hearty laugh at the farcical discomfiture of the miserable little mortal, who had been so promptly punished for his cupidity in trying to extort from me more for his ticket than I was able to give him, and certainly more than he really thought it was worth.

The foregoing little incident—although it taught me nothing new in principle—has often recurred to my memory, when I have seen the same covetous spirit exhibited in various ways, in my everyday intercourse with the world; and I have on other occasions seen speedy retribution follow similar acts of greediness, or attempts at driving hard bargains.

I have repeatedly seen servants lose good situations, through obstinately demanding higher wages than they are worth, or than their employers were able to give them; and afterwards I have seen those same servants soliciting employment, of less desirable kind, and at much lower wages, when compelled by their exhausted finances to obtain work at any price. I have seen combinations of men striving to exact a little more pay for their labour than their employers could reasonably give; and invariably such attempts have been disastrous to the men and their families.

I have seen, too, an industrious tenantry forced off an estate, by the landlord or his agent, demanding a little more rent than they could possibly make off the farms; and the same farms have remained unoccupied for years afterwards. I have also seen the shelves of a trader's warehouse filled with old-fashioned, or shop-worn goods, which he might have sold long before, at a moderate profit, but he chose to hold out for higher prices until his goods were almost unsaleable. Stores filled with grain and breadstuffs have often been over-run by devouring rats and weevils, while the owners have been waiting for famine prices, though they ultimately had to sell out at a ruinous loss.

Covetousness, and the passion for driving hard bargains, or, in other words, extortion, is sadly prevalent the wide world over; and it would perhaps be unfair to particularise itinerant fishmongers, cabmen, or any other special class in the community, as the most incorrigible. I am prepared to demonstrate that such policy is a most unwise one ; but I think I need not trouble myself to do so, as most persons who have tried it, have proved it so by their own experience ; and some even more disagreeably than did the nervous little man who coveted my umbrella ; besides, I have no faith in the power of mere human efforts, or dictums, to effectually cure that or any other extensive evil. I will, however, venture to offer a few words of advice, to newly-arrived immigrants especially ; many of whom I have seen in our city of late, and to whom I tender my congratulations and hearty welcome. Doubtless some of them have brought their strength and skill to labour, as their only capital, to this new land ; and they will generally find that they have not brought it to a bad market. You have an undoubted right, friends, to make the most you can of your capital, in common with every one else in the community ; but I would kindly caution you not to be too extravagant in your expectations of immediate returns. At the present time there is a depression in the labour market, which perhaps most of you have discovered. That can be but temporary, still it is the case, and not many employers of labour are in a position to pay extreme wages just now. Beware, then, how you refuse steady employment, from good masters, at fair remuneration ; and if you should be tempted to do so, think for a moment of my poor scared friend in the balloon. The same reflection I would recommend to any other person who is prone to driving hard bargains. I may just add my opinion, that employers will not act wisely if they take advantage of the present temporary depression, to drive too hard bargains with their employés ; for by doing so they may drive away useful servants, and perhaps create a prejudice against themselves, which, to say the least, must be undesirable.

If some folks do not really think the " Proverbs of Solomon " are obsolete, they sometimes act as if they thought so ; or, indeed, as if they never thought of them at all. There are many men in this land—and elsewhere too—who have cause to regret that they did not allow those inestimable precepts to regulate their daily transaction in the busy world of bargain - making, and thereby save themselves many sorrows.

MICKY MAHONY'S MISHAPS.

CHAPTER I.

" Joe, my jewel ! whisht a minit, while I spake a little bit
iv common sinse ; an that's a sort of music you don't hear
every day uv yer life, so it will be a trate to yez.   There's
no mishtake but it's mighty aisy worrk, squatting under a
tea-tree all day long smoking me dudheen or darning me
duds, and singing 'Molly Bawn ;' while the sheep are nibbling away at the green grass, or capering about like young
haythins, and my ould dog Nip is kitchin the flies on his
stumpy tail, or scratching them other teazing things out uv
he's curly coat.   It's a rale jintleman's life, to be shure, and
not bad pay for it naythir ; still an all, I'm gittin as rusty
as an ould pickaxe, for want of a little dacint society—that's
a fact ; an I'm afeard I'll forgit all me manners if I don't go
into the worrld and exercise 'em a bit.   I've bin thinkin'
that as my agreement wid the masther is up to-morrow, an
I'll thin be free to go anywhere my two legs 'ill carry me,
I'll be off to the diggins, at daylight ; and if I can pick up a
few nuggets, only as big as a lamb's tail, me fortune is made
intirely ; an I'll have nothing to do the rest uv me life, but
smoke me pipe an ate me rations, which delicate imploy-
ment, 'ill shute my wake constitution illegantly.   Yes, Joe,
me bhoy ! I'll be off to-morrow morning, and your new chum,
Sawney M'Grim, can take out my flock ; an good luck to
him.   I'll lave him my poor dog Nip, for I dare say rations
are dear on the diggins, an Nip wull be no sarvice to me in
my new perfession.   Maybe, too, some of them yellow
Johnnies wud ate him, poor cratur, and that wud grieve me
mortally, for poor Nip is the only relation I've got in the
colony."

These remarks were addressed to Joe Griddle, the hut-
keeper on a sheep-station—in the interior of New South
Wales—by Micky Mahony, the shepherd, as they sat down
to a hot dish of " bubble and squeak," one evening, after
Micky's flock had been counted in and hurdled.

" To the diggings, eh ?" quoth Joe, with a sombre grin.
" You'll soon be glad to come back again, Micky, I'll bet
you tuppence. Hard work in a deep claim won't suit your

rusty joints, I'm thinkin'; and you'll miss old Joe Griddle to prepare your supper, after you've bin working all day long, up to your middle in mud. You'll get no nice hot dishes of Irish stew on cold days; no roaring fire in your hut when you come home; and maybe you'll have no hut at all to put your head in. You'll be roaring all day long with the rheumatiz, like an old bull stuck in a bog; and have no friend near to rub you as I do sometimes. You couldn't rough it in a tent, Micky, like a born digger, not a bit of it, so don't try it, mate. Stay where you are getting good wages and good rations, under a good master; with easy work that you have been used to the best part of your life, or you'll very likely live to be sorry you didn't take my advice. The diggins arn't fit for the like of you or me, Micky, for we are both as stiff as old stock horses. One might just as well set a couple of blackfellows to split slabs or build a woolshed, as expect worn out old tools such as you or I to dig gold enough even to find us a ration of rice and treacle, let alone anything else to make our miserable lives happy.—You dig! pooh, nonsense!"

"Be the piper," cried Mick, "an haven't I dug acres of praties in owld Ireland, an oceans of turf in the bargain? Whew! not know how to dig, eh! What next will yez be after telling me? Why, I'd bate any perfessional digger in the colony, wid the long shovel or pratie fork; aye, or the pick either, though I nivèr tried that tool. An. maybe I'll pick up goold enough widout any tools at all but my fingers; faix, I'll be a match for anybody on airth at that game. Then agin, I've got purty nigh twinty pounds saved up, an what wull I do wid it here, I'd like to know? I might dale a little bit at the diggins wid my capital, for I'm thinkin I've got as much sinse in my head as many swells who have made their fortins at daling. Shure an didn't we hear Denis Whackduffy the daler say tother night that a wide-awake fellow can allers make more wid his head than his hands? Besides, I'm dying for a little gintale company. I haven't had a fight for four years, an I haven't seen a reglar shindy since I've bin on the station. I'm getting as mouldy as an old boot for want of a shine now and agin, that's a fact. Bedad, I'll be off to-morrow, Joe me bhoy! I'll try my luck at some more lively money-making game nor shepparding, so don't try to coax me to stay; for you may jist as well try if your argiments will stop that tom cat from licking out the camp oven in the chimney yonder. Maybe you'll see me come back agin a gintleman one of these days, Joe, an thin you shall be my chief cook, so you shall, for you're a broth of a bhoy to make doughboys, an a reglar tigar at rubbin away the rheumaticks."

The next morning Micky was up before the "laughing jackasses," and was busily engaged packing up all his personal effects into a compact bundle, while his friend Joe prepared breakfast.

"Suppose you should meet any of those bushranging cossacks that are prowling about everywhere now-a-days, Micky? What will you do if they take away your swag, and murder you, or else leave you as naked as a pickaninny?" asked Joe, with a very sober face. "An honest man's life and property are hardly worth owning these times."

"Niver fear," said Micky, his merry eyes twinkling as if it were a good joke to be robbed of his all. "Niver fear, Joe, they won't rob me I'll warrant, unless they murther me firsht; an thin I'll have the playsure of knowing they'll be hanged, the vagabins."

"Have yez got sich a thing as an owld pill box to give me, to put me money intil? You may kape the pills yerself; the box will do me more good."

"Put your money into your boot, Micky;" urged Joe. "Don't trust it in pill boxes, nor pockets neither. Your boot is the safest place—take my word,—inside the lining. Howsomever, if you want a pill box, here is one which I got from Doctor Dux tother day! a timber-box half as big as a pannikin."

"Hand it here, Joe, my jewel, you're the bist frind I've got. That's jist the identical thing; it wud hold pills enough to comfort a hape of poor miserable mortals or scare starvation out of a little village, so it wud. Ho, ho, ho! them's univarsal pills," chuckled Mick as he counted nineteen new sovereigns into the pill box, which he then put into the centre of his bundle, rolled all up tightly in a blue blanket and affixed straps thereto for the convenience of carrying it on his back.

"Now I call that a jintale little swag," said Mick, tossing it on a rough bedstead in the corner of the hut, and then sitting down to his breakfast. "A rig out that Prince Alfred would be glad to own if he hadn't got a betther one. It's all my own, every bit of it, an it's all I've got in the wide worrld to bother me, barrin the clothes I stand up in, an the old boots under the bed, which I will lave to you, Joe, as a kapesake. And now my darlin't, I'll wager me fortin there to your long-handled frying-pan that no bushrangers will ;rob me, unless they knock me spacheless firsht and foremost; and I won't fight wid em naythir. Bedad, what ud be the good of my shallaley aginst the involving pistols of thim savages ?—not a bit in the worrld, I might as well try to bate em wid a German sassage. No, no, I won't fight wid em anyhow, nor I won't rin away naythir, and yet I tell you agin Joe, there isn't a bushranger in the bush as 'll rob me of a haporth; that is if I can ony make him jist understand plain English, mixed wid a trifling taste of ginuine Irish brogue."

Soon afterwards Micky arose from his meal, took an affectionate leave of his friend Joe, and his dog Nip, then shouldered his bundle, and went on his way laughing as if somebody were tickling him.

Onward he trudged, whistling "The Wanderer from Clare," and other fancy tunes; stopping now and then to wet his whistle at a waterhole, and to have a few whiffs from his little black pipe, which he carried in his hat-band; and then onward he would trudge again, twirling his shillelah over his head, and making the bush musical with his joyful exclamation, and merry Irish airs.

About two hours before sunset, as Micky was calculating whether he should be able to reach a neighbouring sheep station before night, or be obliged to bush it, he heard the tramp of a horse's heels behind him, and on looking round, to his surprise and terror, he beheld a great rough looking fellow, well mounted, and armed, who, in a gruff voice called upon him to "bail up," at the same time presenting a revolver. "Bail up there, paddy from Cork; or you'll be as dead as dog's meat in another minute."

"I'll bail up fast enough," cried Micky; "so don't be after shooting me, if you plaze, sir."

"Hand up your swag, and turn out your pockets," said the bushranger; "and don't stand there staring at me and taking my measure."

"Och hone !" whined poor Micky, "an is it me swag you mane? Shure, thin, ye'll not be afther stripping a poor mortial intirely ! Don't do that same, good luck to yez ! This bundle is all I've got belonging to me, an that's not

23

much to the likes uv you. An me pockets—be the same token—are as impty as a pair of ould left-off stockings—there isn't the price of a ha'penny pipe——"

"Stop that beggar's yarn, and roll up your swag inside mine," said the thief, at the same time he unbuckled a large bundle from his saddle before him and threw it on the ground. "Look sharp now, do you hear? or I'll give you a dose that will send you hopping like a French fiddler all the days of your life."

"Och, musha, musha!" cried Micky, writhing and twisting like a scalded eel. "Don't, there's a good sowl; I don't want a dose of that sort of physic. I'll give you me swag, ivery bit uv it, an' I wish yez luck wid it; but don't murther me, whatever you do." He then began to unroll the bushranger's bundle, while his eyes glistened at its valuable contents.

"Troth, an' you've got a mighty fine swag uv yer own, so you have. Two pairs of blankets, half-a-dozen bran new shirts, wid a rale gintleman's turn out of broadcloth, an' a hape of other things besides. Now, what for do yez want to take away my poor little swag from me, when you've got goods enough here to start a store wid? Arrah! lave me my swag, there's a good thief; don't rob a poor ould beggar like me. Good luck to yez, lave me me swag."

"Roll it up inside mine, I tell you," roared the ruffian, "and don't give me any more of your brogue."

"O, crikey! what 'll I do at all, whin I'm ruined intirely?" cried poor Mick, as he began very carefully to make up the bundle again, after he had placed his own swag inside it. "Ye'll be laving me as miserable as a blackfellow's dingo, so you will; and be dash'd if I know what I'll do afther that, at all at all. I'm fear'd I'll lose all me frinds, whin I've lost me swag."

"Roll it up tight, and put those straps round it," shouted the thief; "and look sharp about it, I say, or I'll shoot you as dead as a mutton chop."

"Och! don't do that, sir. I don't like to be shot; 'an I'm not worth the bullet ye'd murther me wid, that's a fact. I'm ruined outright, like a frost-bitten murphy, so I am. But maybe ye'll be so ginerous as to give me a fig of tobaky, ye'rve got plenty inside yer swag. Do if you plaze honey! jist one fig, to keep me from starving intirely."

"Not enough to choke a cockatoo," roared the thief.

" Be smart, I tell you again : the troopers are on my track."

" Are they ? Shure then I'll make haste, for fear they'd catch you," said Mick, apparently working hard to make the straps meet round the bulky bundle, which having done, he handed it up to the horseman, with difficulty, remarking, as he did so, that " he feared it was too big for him to carry convaniently."

" Never you mind that," said the bushranger, surlily, as he began to strap the bundle before him, while Micky walked up to a stringy bark sapling, and rubbed his back against it, like a scabby sheep.

" Misther What's-yer-name," whined Mick. " Aisy a bit afore you fasten the saddle straps. For pity's sake be afther giving me the box o' pills out of me swag, and I'll be iverlastingly obliged to yez ; bekase don't you see I'm dying wid the itch ; and nothing but mint pills will aise me."

" The what ?" roared the ruffian, at the same time throwing the bundle off his saddle, as if it were scalding hot. " What ; you've got that horrible nuisance, have you ? Confound you ! what did you put your mangy swag inside mine for ? Do you want to infect me and all my mates too, and ruin my horse into the bargain, eh ? Bad manners to you !"

" Sorra a bit iv it sir," cried Mick. " I wouldn't give such an ugly plague to ' ould scratch' himself, not if I could help it ; that would be a rale unjentlemanly trick, soh. You towld me to give ye me swag, sir, and I've give it yez, every bit."

" Hur you dirty ragamuffin ; I've a great mind to blow your brains out, if you've got any, for spoiling all my traps, with your confounded bundle of filth. I'll shoot you as dead as——"

" Och musha ! Good gentleman don't do that," roared Micky. " Take me swag althgether, but spare me brains."

" Take your swag, eh !" sneered the thief. " I wouldn't touch it with a shovel, if it were full of bank notes, nor my own traps neither, now they have been bundled up with your leprous kit. They'll want fumigating with a barrowful of brimstone before any body could touch them, but a dirty scavenger like yourself. Why didn't you tell me you'd got the plague ? Confound you !"

" Shure an didn't I tell you so plain enough, sir, when I axed yez to give me the box iv pills out ov me swag ?"

"Bah! For threepence I'd give you a *barrel* of pills," growled the ruffian, as he gathered up his reins, and held a revolver to Micky's head. "Don't let me catch you again, mind that."

"Faith ye'll not catch me again, if I can any how rin away from you," whined Micky; "and I hope you won't catch anything else belonging to me, or you'll wish yourself scratched to death wid a bush-full of native cats, I'm thinking."

"Hold your blatherin' tongue," vociferated the bush-ranger, as he fired two shots over Micky's head, and then rode off at full gallop, leaving his bundle lying on the road.

CHAPTER II.

MICKY fell flat on his back with affright, and there he lay for some time, wondering whether he was dead, and hoping if he were so, that the troopers would soon be up to bury him dacintly, and to catch the murtherin thief who had shot him. Bye and bye he began to feel his head for bullet-holes, then his body and legs; but finding no wounds or fractures, he by degrees felt assured that he was not kilt at all; but that he was Micky Mahoney still, with his skin as sound as a pair of new saddle-bags, and his swag twice as heavy, and thrice as valuable as it was when he left the station in the morning.

"Och philleloo!" shouted Micky, jumping up and dancing a little corroborree round the bushranger's bundle. "This is a whacking day's work to begin wid and no mishtake. There's the work of twelve month's wages in that fellow's swag, anyhow, an it's all mine, as honest as if I'd bought it an paid ready money for it, every bit, for shure I arnt it wid me brains. Denis Whacduffy, its thrue for ye, that a man can make more by his wits thin by his work, for haven't I proved it this lucky day? Sorra a bit av the diggins 'll I dig; I'll set up shop and make a fortin; thin I'll go back to owld Ireland and buy a whisky-still, a hogshead av tobaky, and a cart-load av pipes, and I'll spind the rist av me days in pace and quietness. Yes, that's jist what I'll do, an may be I'll git a wife too. Ha! ha! ha! he! he! he! whack row de dow!" roared Mick, while he capered about as nimbly as if a fiddler were sitting on the stump beside him, playing "Donnybrook Fair," or "St. Patrick's Day in the Morning."

"Och, I'm delighted, so I am! Long life to yez, Doctor Dux!

yer pill-box has done me more good nor all the physic I've swallowed iver since I was a bald-headed babby. An this swag's mortal heavy too," continued Mick, lifting it on his back, then throwing it off again, and dancing round it until he was almost out of breath. "Ho! ho! ho! what a lark! I wish Joe Griddle could see me jist now; he'd grin like an owld monkey cracking a hot nut. Ha! ha! ha! he! he! he! Be dash'd if I ain't a lucky dog to-day."

"Bail up there!" roared a terrible voice just then, close behind him, which stopped Micky's merriment in a moment; and on turning round, with his face as pale as a white bullock's, he beheld the bushranger again, with a revolver in his hand.

"Hilloa, old scurvy bones! I've been watching your heathenish fandangoes from the tea-tree scrub just behind you," said the thief, "and now I mean to make you cut capers to quite another tune. You first spoil all my traps with your filthy kit, and then you have the impudence to laugh at me, till you frighten my horse. Now I'll see how you laugh under my particular tickle."

"Arrah! laugh did ye mane? shure thin isn't it crying I've bin, honey, till I'm nigh broken hearted?"

"Give me no more of your blarney," roared the bushranger. "Didn't I see you hopping about my swag, like a cannibal round his cookery?"

"Troth thin, you'd hop too, I'm thinking, sir," said Micky, "if ye'd git Saint Vitus's dance as bad as I have."

"Oh, you've got that lively disorder too, have you? You must be shocking bad; but I'll see if I can cure you."

"Thankee, sir," said Mick, trembling. "I shall always owe you somethin. You're a good gintleman, an I shall niver forget yez."

"Shoulder the bundle," shouted the bushranger.

"That's jist what I was goin to do sir, whin ye come back agin," said Micky, hoisting the bundle on his back. "Troth it's mighty heavy, so it is. I'm afeard your horse wouldn't ha run away from the troopers wid this load on his back, sir."

"Now march along before me—double quick time," said the thief; "and if you speak another word I'll blow your head off, so take warning."

"Sorra anither worrd will I spake, sir, good or bad," whined Micky. "But pray don't hurt me head; it aches awful jist now. Mine's a very bad head, so it is."

After a short march through the bush they came to a creek, the waters of which were running bank high, and foaming and bubbling as if they were boiling hot.

" Now," said the ruffian, " pitch those mangy swags into the creek ; they want washing."

" I'd rayther carry em home an wash em wid soft soap if you plaze, sir," said poor Mick, trembling with terror.

" Would you though ?" sneered the thief. " I'll save your soft soap. In with them. I can't bear the smell of them any longer."

" Och hone ! pity a poor old cripple, and jist let me take out me pills. I'm gettin very bad agin, sir. Wud ye be ginerous enough to let me save me pills, yer honour."

" No, not if they'd save you from scratching your hide off ; pitch them in, pills and all, or in you go yourself." As the ruffian thundered out this alternative he fired off another shot, which blew the top of Micky's hat to tatters.

" Ow, ow, ow ! murther !" groaned Micky. " There they go, sir, there they go ;" and away went the swags, rolling over and over in the turbid waters of the creek.

" Now, off with your coat, waistcoat, and boots," shouted the bushranger, cocking his pistol again.

" I will, I will, sir ! Och, mercy, don't slaughter me outright, as well as frighten me to death ! Pray don't, sir," shrieked Micky, hurriedly disrobing himself as directed.

" Pitch your dirty duds into the creek," roared the bushranger. " They want washing too."

With a yell of anguish Micky obeyed ; and away floated his garments, while his boots sank at once, like water-logged colliers.

" Now you can dance as long as you like, Mr. Paddywhack, and the more you caper the less likely you are to catch cold. Think yourself lucky you've got a whole skin to dance in. You are the most troublesome customer I ever traded with ; and mark me, if I meet with you again, I'll bore a hole through you, as shure as my name isn't Dick Turpin ;" saying which, the ruffian rode away through the bush, and left Micky to his solitary meditations.

" Well, well ! this is a suparior situation for a poor crater bothered wid rheumatiz, and no mishtake," muttered Micky, after he had somewhat recovered from the effects of the terror which the foregoing incidents had naturally caused him. " Here I am—bedash'd if I know where—but I'm here shure enough, half-naked, half-murdered, and frightened to death, in the bargain. Dear knows what I'll do at all at all, for I'm afeard me sinces are clane gone, as well as me swag. Well, well! I've heered tell of revarses av fortin, but I never seed any afore, cos I never had any fortin till to-day, au shure it's turned out misfortin afther all. Ugh! what for did I lave the station, where I could get all I wanted to make meself comfortable, and put by a dacint little bit av money every year for a rainy day—as the saying is—if I had a mind? What a donkey I was to think of going to the diggings. My own gumption might ha told me, that an owld crawler like me ud do no good there; and mayhap, have me toes trodden off by gettin in the way av the hapes av great busy fellows who are diggin and delving and staring their eyes out in search for big nuggets, and some av them as savage as sharks bekase they can't find any. Joe Griddle, you were right me bhoy! an I wish I'd a tuk yer advice. Denis Whackduffy, you're a blatherin guffy, and maybe, ye're a roguo to boot. Ye may say what you like about working wid yer wits, but it's my exparienced opinion that a man can make more by the honest work of his hands than by schaming, anyhow, he'll get more pace an comfort through his life. But it's no good me stoppin here, howlin over me troubles; I'll get no pity out av these iron-bark trees. I'd betther find me way back agin to me owld berth as fast as I can crawl widout boots; an then if any of these bush tigers catch me on another such a cruise as this, I'll give em lave to skin me out an out."

Micky then began to retrace his way towards the high road, stepping very carefully, for he was not accustomed to walking in the bush barefooted; and many were the wishes —not very cordial ones—which he sent after the unmerciful thief, who had compelled him to "drown his brogues, like a pair of blind puppies." He had not travelled far when he saw an old rusty, single-barrelled pistol lying on the ground, and close beside it a long grey cloak which the bushranger had either dropped from his saddle-bags or thrown away as useless to him.

"Hilloa, what's this thing?" quoth Micky, as he picked up the cloak and examined it with as much joy and amazement as a wild Figian, who had just found a barber's poll in a bamboo brake. "It's big enough to kiver me an Joe Griddle together; how-an-iver, I'll make it fit me soh! an it'll be handy to hide me nakedness, though there ain't much heat in it." He then put it on, and gathered its folds closely about him, with a strip of stringy bark by way of a girdle. "An this concarn may be handy too, in case I shall mate any more bushrangers," continued Mick, picking up the pistol, and peeping down the barrel with one eye to see if it were loaded. "Shure it wud be a convanient way of settlin all me sorrows if I was to put this pisthle into me mouth, and fire aisily down me throat. But it is not loaded, so I suppose it won't go off."

The shades of evening were fast closing around when Mick regained the road; but a full moon was rising, and the sky was clear and bright; so onward he trudged in the direction of Joe Griddle's hut; very often his clamorous appetite helped him to picture his old friend Joe, with his new friend Sandy McGrim and his dog, Nip, sitting down to their substantial suppers, and much he longed to be sitting with them.

Micky had not travelled far, when on turning an abrupt angle of the road, he met a colporteur, carrying a valise in one hand and a bushman's outfit in the other. In a moment Micky conceived the idea of stealing the latter, and before his better judgment could influence him he had called upon the stranger to stand and deliver up his swag, under divers horrible pains and penalties. "Bail up, honey?" shouted Micky in as gruff a voice as he could assume, at the same time flourishing his pistol about his head as if it were a shillelah. "Bail up I say, and hand up yer swag, or you'll catch it, an no mishtake."

"You surely don't intend to rob me, friend?" said the gentleman, in a tolerably composed tone of voice. "I fear you will not value the contents of my valise very much if I give it to you; if you did you would not make this wicked demand."

"Troth thin I've been robbed meself to-day of eviry haporth I have in the worrld," cried Mick; "an shure you can't grumble if I just take a little trifle from yerself. I don't care what you've got in yer leather box, ye can kape that: but I want yer blankets an quart pot and yer vittles, for I'm gettin cowld and hungry, and savage to boot; so hand up yer swag, misther, or by the piper I'll shoot off this pisthle, and blow ye into the middle av next Friday."

"Well, you shall have my bundle," said the traveller,

quietly. "Here it is ; but don't commit murder, there's a good fellow. You had better be careful too, with that pistol, or you may shoot yourself. I think it would be safer in my hands than in yours ; and you can have no farther use for it at present. Will you sell it ?"

" Yes, honey ; I'll sell it chape as dirt, for I don't want it ; give me the price of a new pair of boots and the pishtle's yours so long as you live. It's a raal good un, I think, ony it's a little bit rusty."

The gentleman handed over some silver, and took the weapon ; then suddenly turning upon Micky, he said, in a firm tone, "Now, Mr. Bushranger, you bail up, and hand me back my blankets, and my money, or I'll fire at you."

" Ho ! ho ! ho ! blaze away, me bhoy !" said Mick, laughing heartily ; "there isn't a tint av powther or shot in it, ho ! ho ! ho ! It's as innocent as the marrow-bone of a little sucking-pig, so it is."

" That's it, is it ?" said the gentleman, smiling goodnaturedly ; " well, I thought at first sight of you that you were not a practised footpad, and that you didn't intend to shoot me, although you flourished your pistol so formidably. Now suppose we come to terms. You say you are hungry and tired ; so am I ; and I was just thinking of camping for the night when I met you ; shall we camp together, and share our provisions and bedding ? What do you say to that ?"

" Wid all me heart," said Micky. " Give us yer hand, jewel ; long life to yez ! Here, take back yer money ; sorra a sixpence will I kape ; and ye may kape the pishtle too if you like, for I don't know how to use such tools as that, nor don't want to know nayther."

They turned off into the bush for a short distance ; and very soon a cheerful fire was blazing, and the quart pot was simmering over the embers. The gentleman then opened his bundle, and produced some tea and sugar, cold meat and damper, and helped his thankful guest to a plentiful share, also to a share of the boiling tea when it was prepared.

" I always ask God's blessing on my meals before I begin to eat," said the traveller, lifting his hat reverently. Micky sighed, and lifted his hat too, while his neighbour uttered a few devotional sentences.

"I allers used to say grace meself whin I was a bhoy," said Micky with another long sigh, and then he fell to work upon the viands before him, and was apparently absorbed in his reflection until the repast was over.

"Ho! ho! ho!" laughed Micky, after he had been fumbling in his pocket for a minute or two. "That murtherin thief has jist lift me a pipe or two av tobaky afther all. If he'd only a known I'd got that morsel av comfort in me fob, he'd a made me pull off me breeches and pitch em into the creek, wid me other clothes, that he wud, the spalpeen, for he's got no more feelin nor a dead cow—not a bit. Bedad an it's lucky he didn't break me pipe whin he blow'd me brains out, leastwise whin he blow'd the top of me old hat all to smithereens. Och, I thought I was sittled jist thin; I'd have sowld my head for a peck av green peaches, so I wud." Micky then filled his pipe, and as he sat puffing away by the blazing fireside, he gave a detail of his day's adventures with an occasional allusion to parts of his previous history, while his companion sat and listened with deep interest.

CHAPTER III.

"WHAT thumpin whacks an cracks a poor mortial catches during a day's tramp sometimes," said Micky, as he laid aside his pipe after he had finished his smoke, and the narration of his day's mishaps at the same time. "This is a terrible worrld av thrubble, Misther Mefriend," he added, after a short pause, and with a very grave air, which contrasted strangely with the grotesque appearance of his tattered and long cloak, with its stringy-bark girdle, "a worrld of botheration an bad luck, sure enough; an I've had my allowance av it if I niver git any more after this blessid night. Jist fancy, Misther Thingummeebob——"

"My name is Hopewell," interrupted the traveller, mildly. "Will you tell me your name, if you please?"

"I ax yer pardin forty times, Mr. Hopewell; my name's Micky Mahony, at yer sarvice. But I was going to say, I lift my home this lovely summer's mornin wid a swag fit for a mimber of parlimint, an nineteen bran new suvverins in me midcine chest, for-bye a rispectable suit on me back, and a lovely pair av kangaroo cossacks on me feet, an here I sit to-night—savin yer presence—as poor as a blind beggar, wid nothin to cover me nakidness but this long, comical cloak, an me owld hat, which looks as if it had bin in a sassage machine. Blow'd if I iver heerd tell av the like run av bad luck, niver since I've bin on the frosty side av the Blue Mountains. It bates all my bush exparience out an out, so it does."

"Yes; you have certainly met with some strange disasters to-day, Mr. Mahony, but I must tell you, I think some of them were the results of your own improper conduct. You coveted that thief's plunder, and to obtain it, you were untruthful in many particulars. Although punishment does not always follow similar acts so soon as it has done in your case to-day, it is certain that, sooner or later, all acts of deceit, and falsehood receive their due; and you may depend upon it, my friend, that truthfulness at all times, and under all circumstances, is the only safe course you can adopt; and whether you work with your hands or your head, *honest* work is the only work you can expect to prosper. I am, however, far from thinking that this is the worst day in your history, after all, for I have hope concerning you, which I cannot explain just now. You are here, alive and well, and you have been mercifully preserved from bodily injury; you should thank God for that. You have had food enough for the day, and you have had strength given you to bear all your troubles: be thankful for that also. This day's trials are past, and you will not see them again; so as you cannot remedy them by fretting over them, your wisest plan is to look hopefully to the future, while you strive to profit by your past mishaps."

"Yes, sir," replied Micky; "that's thrue for yez—what's done's done, and it's not a bit av good grumblin. If I was to howl for a fortnight it wouldn't rise my brogans from the bottom of the creek, nor sthop me swag from swimming out to sea; so the best plan I can think av is not to think av them at all, but to hurry back to my owld berth as fast as I can, an earn money to buy another rig out, and thin afther I've got it, thry to take betther care av it. This day's disasters will help to make me more continted in time to come, an make me thry to kape a good berth when I've got one, an not be thryin me hand at things I don't know nothin about."

"I see, you are a philosopher," said Mr. Hopewell, smiling.

"Police officer! not a bit av it, sir, nor niver was in my life; I niver had the good luck to dhrop into sich an aisy billet. I've bin a shepherd more nor twenty years; an afore that I tried me hand at almost ivery sort av bush work, barrin bushrangin, an I niver thried that game afore to-day ; nor I'll niver thry it agin naythir, for it's a villainous trade, that's purty shure to lead to Jack Ketch's castle at last. I should jist like to tell all the bhoys in the bush my honest opinion av that cowardly way of getting a livin."

" How many years have you been in this colony, Mr. Mahony ?" asked Mr. Hopewell.

" Will ye be afther callin me Micky, sir, if ye plaze ? I'm downright scared when ye call me Misther Mahony, bekase it makes me think av me poor owld dad, who's dead an gone. Folks used to call him Misther Mahony on Sundays ; and well he desarved it too, poor sowl, for he was as honest a man as iver peeled a pratee, so he was. Well, sir, I've bin in this counthry two and thirty year come next March. Ye naydn't axe me who paid me passage out here ; it wasn't me poor owld dad though. I'd a free passage give me, by order of a larned owld frind av mine at home, and Governor Darling was recommended to take great care av me, an mind I didn't catch cowld by being out at night. Whin I got to Sydney, I was pressed to stay and help to build a large house of accommodation for other visitors like meself ; an there was a good lot in thim days—more's the pity. Afther a time a frind av the Governor's invited me to go into the bush wid him ; an I was glad enough to go, bekase the *cats* in Sydney used to throuble me a good deal. Faith an I soon found there were *cats* (wid nine tails) in the bush too ; but they didn't bother me quite so often as they did in Sydney. Well, sir, I've bin in the bush pritty nigh iver since ; and though I says it meself, there isn't a cove this side av the counthry as knows more nor I do about bush-work av all sorts, from shepherdin to shingle-splittin, an from plaitin cabbage-tree sinnet to makin whishky on the sly."

" You must have been a very young man when you first came here, Micky," remarked Mr. Hopewell.

" I was, sir ; an able young fella too ; as sthrong as a cart-horse. Troth I'm not very wake now for an old man, though I didn't allers take the best care av meself. Still an all, I've seen many fellers put under ground who were as able an as hearty as meself : be the same token, some av thim didn't come to their end through fair play, worse luck. I've had no end av 'scapes from death afore to-day ; but I'm as hard to kill as a native-dog. Twice I was speared by the blacks ; onst I was nigh drownded in a flood, an another

time close up roasted in a bush-fire; onst I was tossed by
a wild bullock; onst I was bitten by a shnake; an onst I
tried to hang meself wid me belt; but the sthrap broke
just as I wor giving my last kick."

"Dear me!" exclaimed Mr. Hopewell, with a shudder;
"and had you died then where would you be now?"

"Dear knows," said Micky; "I niver thought much about
it, sir. It would a bin a settler wid me, that's all I know. I
shouldn't ha drawn any more rations, nor slops nayther,
that's sartain. But bless yer heart, sir, I've know'd lots av
poor craters who have killed themselves to get out av their
misery; an ye wouldn't wonder at it nayther, if ye know'd
all the misery they'd got to bear, in one shape or another,
that you wouldn't. Troth, I could tell you yarns as wud
make all yer hair stand up as stiff as spike nails."

"To get out of their misery, indeed!" exclaimed Mr.
Hopewell, solemnly. "Micky, hear me, my friend, and
pray remember what I say, for you told me just now, that
you thought of shooting yourself to-day when you picked
up that pistol. I fear that fatal sin is sadly frequent in the
bush as well as in our cities. By such a frightful act a man
certainly plunges into the gulf of eternal misery. Of all
sins self-murder is the most horrible. It is utterly hopeless,
for repentance is impossible. By such an act man rushes
unbidden into the awful presence of his offended Maker.
Oh, Micky! be thankful that you were spared from such a
terrible crime, and pray that you may be kept from another
such attempt. But will you tell me why you were led to
such a sad act?"

"I will, sir," said Micky; "though when I think av it it
makes me shiver an shake like a black-fellow on a frosty
morning. Well, sir, it's many years agone: I'd had a long
job splittin posts an rails, an puttin up stockyards, an other
rough work, on a new station, far away backwards. My
mate, Jem Wedges, an I, had a pritty good sum av money
comin to us, an we wanted a bit av a spree, jist to knock
some av it down; so we goes to the Super one day, an axes
him for an order for forty pounds, and thin away we goes
straight to the grog-shop at Guzzleton, which was about
five-and-twenty miles off. Whin we got there in course we
handed our order to Misther Tapps, the landlord, and thin
began knockin it down, like jolly bushmen allers does. We
know'd old Tapp wud pritty soon tell us whin the order had

all run out, so we didn't bother ourselves about nothin but dhrinkin an playin ' all fours,' and singin a bit now an thin, av course. Our order lasted eight days, for there were not many fellers about the place at that time to help us knock it down quicker; an it was rayther a dull time altogether, for we only had three little bits av fights—but niver a reglar shindy at all. On the ninth mornin Mr. Tapps sings out,— ' Hilloa me hearties, yer order's all knocked into nothin, ivery hapeny, and thirty shillings to the new.' My mate was knocked down too; he was very bad in his head; I don't know whether it was from the bad rum, or from a crack he got wid the leg av a stool the night afore. Well, I kno'd it wor no good stoppin there any longer after old Tapps had tipped us the wink to be off, so I coaxed a quart av rum out av him on the new score, an away I goes towards the station agin, all alone; for my mate couldn't walk at all, an I hadn't got sinse enough in me to sthop and look after him, so I lift him at the shanty, fast asleep and spacheless. Well, I reeled along about seven miles suckin out av the bottle ivery now and agin, till at last I tumbled down head over heels, and wint to sleep. When I awoke agin it was dark night, so I finished the rum in the bottle, an soon wint to sleep agin. The next mornin whin I roused up I was as stiff as a skeleton, an awfully miserable soh; I wud almost hav given me sowl for a gill av rum; but there wasn't a tasthe in the bottle; so I got up and hobbled along a little further towards home. Och ! what I suffered thin ye couldn't picture if ye tried for a month; nor I couldn't tell ye if I'd got twenty tongues. It frightens me to think av it.

" By an bye I heerd a horrible noise behind me, an whin I looked round I seed the divil on a black horse ridin afther me as hard as he could gallop, an roaring like a tiger. Off I scampered through the bush, straight towards a runnin creek. Whin I got to it I dashed down the steep bank and jumped into the wather; but it wasn't deep enough to smother me, so I groped through it to the other side. The divil followed me to the top of the creek, thin got off his horse, tied him to a saplin, and looked at me wid his great big red-hot eyes, like doctor's door lamps; an he roared out, ' Micky Mahony, I've got ye now, anyhow; you can't git away from me, so ye naydn't thry.' He thin began to wade through the creek to git at me; wid that I pulls off me belt

and made one end fast round the limb av a tree, and put
the other end round me neck ; but jist as I was turnin meself off I seed me poor owld mother right afore me, which
scared me worse still, for I know'd she wor dead long agone.
I don't recollect anythin more, till I awoke lyin under the
tree, wid the broken strap round my neck.   How long I'd
laid there, whether a day or a week, I never could tell ;
but I was awful bad for many a day after that ; an the firsht
bit ov news I heard, when I got back to the station, was
that Jem Wedges wos dead an buried, poor fellow ! I niver
tried to hang meself agin, nor I niver will if I kape me sinses.
I allers think my poor owld mother hud somethin to do wid
the breakin ov that strap ; an nobody 'ill make me think she
hadn't.   I was mighty sober for a long time after that
sheavo ; still I wasn't meself at all, for a very, little noise at
night used to set me tremblin like an owld lady in a cellar
full of rats."

"O Micky, that is indeed a dreadful tale," said Mr. Hopewell.   "You were providentially saved from an awful doom,
for which you should thank God with all your heart.   Was
your mother a good woman ?"

"Indeed she was, sir," replied Micky, while the tears
coursed down his rugged face.   "She was a dear lovin owld
sowl ; an shure enough she's gone to heaven.   I can call to
mind, as plain as if it were but a week agone, how plazed
she wor whin she could coax me to go to church wid her,
which wasn't very often, more shame for me.   An how she
wad pray be me bed after she thought I was fast asleep.
Ah, many times I've heard her sighin' and sobbin, an
prayin God to bless me, wicked haythin as I wor.   I can
remember, too, the prayer she tached me to say whin I wor
a gossoon, not taller nor my shtick, an the hymns she used
to sing—for she could sing like a bird, ay, sweeter nor all
the birds in the bush.   Ah, poor sowl ! I'll never hear her
darlin voice agin."

"Can you repeat one of the prayers your good old mother taught you, Micky ?" asked Mr. Hopewell kindly.

"I don't think I can, sir ; for somethin sticks in me
throat, an nearly chokes me, wheniver I think ov anythin
me mother tached me ; but I'll thry to say one, or a bit ov
one, if it will plaze yez, sir."   Poor Micky thus began to repeat a simple little form of prayer ; but before he had uttered
three sentences, he burst into an immoderate fit of weeping,

and sobbed as if his heart would burst. "Och, mercy, mercy! I can't spake it if I was to be killed outright. I havn't said that prayer for nigh forty years. Och me darlint owld mother! it smashes me intirely to think on yez, so it does; an I'm feard I broke your tinder lovin heart too, wid my wickedness. Och hone! och hone! The darlint owld cratur; I shall niver see her agin, niver, niver, niver!" Poor Micky then put his head on his knees, and cried aloud; while his prudent companion sat quietly by, until his paroxysm of grief was over.

"I am pleased to see these signs of affectionate remembrance of your dear mother, Micky," said Mr. Hopewell, at length breaking a long silence. "But you need not sorrow without hope, friend; you may meet her again in Heaven, and share with her the joys of that happy home of rest and peace for ever."

"Och, sir! Ye don't know what a wicked wretch I've bin, or yez wouldn't be after saying that, I'm sartin. Whisht, sir, an I'll tell yez truthfully, as ye've bin sich a kind friend to me. I onst robbed a church, so I did, an that's what brought me to this counthry. You can't say I'll go to Heaven afther that, I'm thinkin."

"Well, Micky, that is a very grievous sin; but had you killed all the congregation belonging to the church, too— nay, had you committed ten thousand other crimes equally bad, if you truly repented of your sins, resolved to forsake them entirely, and humbly asked God for the sake of His Son Jesus Christ, to pardon you, God would surely forgive you freely, restore you to his favour, and receive your soul to Heaven at last. Here is God's own word pledged to do it."

Mr. Hopewell then opened his pocket Bible, and read a few encouraging passages therefrom, and afterwards briefly explained the simple plan of salvation through faith in our Lord Jesus Christ while Micky sat by and listened, with overflowing eyes and a throbbing heart.

CHAPTER IV.

"Yer'll be afther thinkin I'm as soft as a great big batter puddin, I'm afear'd, sir," said Micky, when he had succeeded in restraining his sobs and tears. "I haven't had such a bout ov cryin for many long years before; though, dear knows, I've had throble enough to break me heart if it wasn't too hard to break. I've bin close up cut to pieces on the triangles; but sorra a tear did I drop at all. I howled an roared purty swately, to be shure, but that's nothin; a man can't help doin that, when his flesh is minced in that cannibal style, but they might hav cut me heart out ov me, before I would uv *cried* a single squeak, or shed a tear as big as a mosketer's eye; that's a fact, sir. An yit, whin yez begin to talk to me, as gently as a woman, it makes me cry like a babby in long clothes. It's mighty queer, so it is, but be dash'd if I could help it—if ye clipped me ears off for it. I axe yer pardon, sir, for——"

"Don't mention it, my good friend," said Mr. Hopewell smiling. "I am delighted to see it; and there are other eyes too, that we cannot see, which are rejoicing over your tears. Look up Micky, and ask God to give you pardon, and peace, and He will surely answer you; for He has said in this Holy Book—which I have just read to you, 'Ask and ye shall receive.' Ask then, just as you used to ask your kind old mother to give you bread, when you were a hungry boy. You always believed that she would give it to you, did you not?"

"Troth I did, sir," said Micky, with earnestness. "She niver said nay to anythin I axed her for, poor soul; barrin it wor something that she know'd wouldn't do me no good."

"Just so," said Mr. Hopewell, "and your Father who is in Heaven will not refuse you anything that you ask Him for, if He sees that it is needful, or that it will not be hurtful to you; for He has promised to 'withhold no good thing from them that walk uprightly.' Ask God to forgive you all your sins, and give you grace to walk uprightly, in time to come, to help you to love Him, and to strive to serve Him. Jesus Christ died to atone for your sins and mine, and for the sins of the whole world. 'Believe on the Lord Jesus Christ, and thou shalt be saved.' These words are written in this Book. Kneel down, Micky, and I'll pray for you, and you pray too. Pray with all your heart."

They knelt, and Mr. Hopewell offered up a short, appropriate prayer to God, and at its conclusion Micky said Amen, in a tone which plainly evidenced that it was sincere.

For some time after they arose from their knees they sat without speaking, each one being absorbed in his own reflections. At length the silence was broken by Micky, who had resumed his roofless hat, and was preparing to relight his pipe.

"I've bin thinkin, sir, while I was fillin me pipe, that if I could be sartain I'd go to heaven and see me dear owld mother, when I die, I'd be happier than if I'd got the whole world full of tobaky."

"Well, Micky," said Mr. Hopewell, with a smile, "and what prevents your being certain of going to heaven? Search the Scriptures, and you will there find your title, as clear as the light of heaven itself. You say you believe that the Bible is the word of God."

"I do that, sir, most cartinly, for me darlint mother teached me to believe that as soon as I could spake; an she, poor dear ould sowl, believed every word of it, and so did me fayther too. They used to say it wor the greatest help they'd got in life. Whatever mishaps befel them, they'd go to that book, an they allers said they found comfit and direction there."

"So have millions of poor heart-weary persons beside them, and so may you, Micky," said Mr. Hopewell. "If you take God's word and read it carefully, you will find plain direction in every difficulty, and comfort under every trial of life. You may learn the way to live happily, to die peacefully, and after death to share everlasting happiness in heaven. There is not a poor shepherd in the bush, who is able to read, but may find his title to those blessings, by 'searching the Scriptures.' What books have you got at home?"

"Sorra a book have I got at home at all, sir," said Micky; "an barrin a pair ov ould boots, an me poor dog Nip, I haven't a haporth in me hut belongin to me name. Joe Griddle has got the 'Newgate Calender,' an the 'Mysteries of London,' the 'Bottle Imp,' the 'Black Dwarf,' an a few other story books ov that sort; forbye a 'Joe Miller,' an a fortune tellin book; that's all Joe's libery."

"Have you not a Bible in your hut, Micky?"

"No, sir, nor niver have had, iver since I've been in the bush; but it will not be long afore I git one afther this, if I have to travel a hundred miles to buy it; I'll get one pretty quick whatever I pay for it."

"Dear, dear me!" apostrophised Mr. Hopewell. "There is certainly great need for the 'Bush Mission,' and I trust it will be supported. Have you not divine service, of some kind, on your station on Sundays, Micky?"

"Sometimes we have, sir, at the head station," replied Micky, " a minister calls there now an agin ; an then all the men as likes to go are axed into the house ; or if its shearin time, they muster in the wool shed. But at most of the out-stations there is no Sunday to be seen,—Sunday and Saturday are all alike there ; an we don't know no difference, bekase some of us have lost connt of the days intirely. I've often thought the masthers an supers might take jist a trifle ov care about their men's manners, an it wud be all the better for iverybody. Most ov em take a mortial sight ov pains about the breed ov their sheep ; in trainin their kan-garoo dogs, or breakin in their saddle horses ; but sorra a bit do they care for the sowls of their servants, and not much for their bodies ayther, forbye kapin them in workin trim."

" Stay, my friend," said Mr. Hopewell, gently. " It would be unfair to say that such selfishness is general ; for I have met with several squatters, and superintendents, who have a kind regard for the welfare of their servants ; for their bodies and souls too."

" Have you so, sir ?" replied Micky. " Troth then I'm glad enough to hear that same ; still-an-all, I haven't had the good luck to fall in wid the like, all the time I've bin in the bush. I will spake me own exparience, an its ivery worrd thrue. Nayther masther nor mishtress, nor super, nor any body else belongin to em, iver said a single worrd to me about me sowl, if they thought I'd got one at all. I've niver heerd so much of the Scripture (so that I could understand it, I mane), as yez have tould me this blessed night, niver since I wer born into the worrld ; an that's a fact, sir. I niver knowed that I could git forgiveness from God for robbin that church, and for doing no end ov wickèd things beside. I'd have bin afraid to ax for it. If I'd a know'd as much as that I should huv jumped for joy hun-dreds ov times, when I've been wretched enough to hang meself, wid the remembrance ov me blagger'd tricks, soh. I allers thought I was damn'd, for sartain ; an that it wor no good frettin about what couldn't be cured at all. ' Och ! happy go lucky : I'll live till I die !' I used to shout, when I was half drunk, an then I used to say the divil was me best friend, bekase I'd heerd tell that he firsht invinted rum. But, forbye all me blather an bounce, and me haythenish schaymes for drivin away ugly thoughts ov me past wicked life, I used to feel as miserable as a murtherer sometimes ;

an many's the time I've wished meself a bullock, or a bandicoot, or anythin else that I know'd had nothin at all to do
wid any other worrld, but this one. Och musha musha!
many's the melancholy day I've spent in the bush, sittin
under a gum tree, thinkin upon nothin but me own miseries;
while me sheep have been bitin away at their green feed,
or jumpin with joy, like young wallabies, till I've felt quite
savage that I wasn't a sheep too. But, praise God," added
Micky, while his face brightened up like the moon, which
was just emerging from a dark cloud, "I feel forty times
better already. I'm downright glad I've seen yez to-night,
sir, so I am; an I mane to turn over a new leaf intirely,
with the help ov God. I know lots ov poor fellows in the
bush who are terribly unaisy in their minds whinever they
think about death; they wud be plazed enough to know what
ye've bin telling me to-night, sir; that they had a chance of
being forgiven for all their thievish tricks, an in sich a
beautiful, aisy way too. Gorra! I wish I could rin an tell
em all, just now, so I do."

"That is a very proper spirit, Micky, and I trust you'll
encourage it all you can," said Mr. Hopewell; "I also
strongly feel for those poor men in the bush who are far
away from any religious and social means of instruction;
and I heartily wish I could see more done to improve their
condition. I should like to see more efforts used by influential residents and employers in the bush. It is sad indeed
to be obliged to believe that some settlers care more for the
improvement of their cattle, or the condition of their crops,
than they do for the moral culture of their servants or their
tenantry. I think, however, that few would be so careless
of their duties, if they but reflected on their positive moral
responsibilities with regard to those who are dependent upon
them; and also upon the easy way in which they might add
to the comfort and happiness of those who serve them, by
furnishing every station, out-station, or hamlet, with a small
collection of books; and by occasionally speaking to such of
their servants, or others, who are, perhaps, as ignorant of
the Gospel plan of salvation, as you were, Micky, a few hours
ago. I think, also, that it could be easily shown that the
social comfort and security of our rural communities (apart
from higher considerations), would be increased, if all those
persons who have the time to spare, and the talent requisite
for the work, were to assist in establishing Sunday schools

(where there are none) for the religious instruction of the many poor children who, alas! I fear, are now growing up in ignorance of their important duties to their Maker and to their fellow-creatures. The grounds of *economy* might also be urged in favour of religious teaching, for it is terribly probable that some of those spirited boys, who are now allowed to run as wild and untaught as the aborigines, will, by and by, follow the sad example of those misguided youths who, some little time since, filled certain parts of the bush with excitement and alarm, causing much pecuniary loss, and in some instances loss of life, to unfortunate individuals, and an enormous drain upon the public funds.

"But it's getting late, Micky," said Mr. Hopewell, looking at his watch, and rising from his lowly seat. "I think we had better prepare for rest. You take one blanket, and I'll take the other."

"Not a bit ov it, sir, axing yer pardon," exclaimed Micky, "I'll not take yer blanket, ye'll be catching cowld. I'd rayther sit by the fire all night, an injoy meself; for I've got plinty ov plisant thoughts to think about jist now, so I have. I'm as happy as a bhoy that's jist found a honey pot."

With much difficulty Mr. Hopewell at length prevailed upon Micky to take one of the blankets; and, after replenishing the fire, they prepared for their repose.

"Can you sing, Micky?" asked Mr. Hopewell, as he rolled his blanket around him.

"Yes, sir, a little bit," said Micky. "I can sing 'Rory O'More,' an 'Groves ov Blarney,' an—"

"No, no, I don't mean that sort of music," interrupted Mr. Hopewell, with a smile, "though I don't object to harmless songs occasionally. Can you sing hymns, or psalms?"

"Not a bit, sir," said Mick, with a sigh. "I don't know half a one. I've clane forgot all I know'd years agone."

"I am sorry for that," said Mr. Hopewell. "You must try and learn some. Singing praises to God often helps to cheer me on my weary way through the bush, and makes the time fly lightly and pleasantly." He then sang, "Praise God, from whom all blessings flow" in a clear, ringing voice, which seemed to awaken a hundred echoes among the giant forest-trees around; then, wishing Micky "Good night," he lay down before the fire and was soon fast asleep.

Just as the sun was rising in the morning, they were

awakened by the loud cachinations of those well-known punctual bush birds commonly called "the settlers' clocks ;" and after a short devotional exercise, a bath in a neighbouring lagoon, and a hearty breakfast, they prepared to go on their separate journeys.

"Now Micky, my friend," said Mr. Hopewell, opening his valise, and producing two books (a pocket Bible, and a small illustrated edition of Bunyan's "Pilgrim's Progress,") "I trust you will not forget my advice to you last night. Take these books as keepsakes, to remind you of our meeting in the bush. Study that Bible, and pray to God to help you to understand it. Keep your eye of faith steadily fixed on Christ, who is ' the way, the truth, and the life ;' and by-and-bye, when we have done with this world, and all its anxieties, we shall surely meet again in that eternal home of rest, joy, and peace, where pains and sorrow are unknown, and where thieves cannot molest us. Give me your hand, Micky ; farewell ! may God bless you ! farewell !"

Poor Micky was completely overwhelmed. He could not speak a word, but after wringing his kind friend's hand affectionately, he sat down, placed his head on his knees, and sobbed like a child.

CHAPTER V.

"THAT'S a raal jintleman, God bless him !" exclaimed Micky, after he had in some degree recovered from the emotion which had overcome him on the departure of his kind friend Mr. Hopewell. "A raal, out-and-out jintleman, every bit ov him ; an I'll niver forgit him, so long as I've got sinse enough in me to think of anythin at all. An sure I'll take his advice, an maybe this 'll turn out the luckiest cruize I iver took in me life. I feel a mortial sight aisier in me mind than I iver felt since I crossed over the sea from owld Ireland. Troth, an I don't think I iver felt so plazed, like, even in that same darlint little green isle, which bates the other green isles in the world, all to pebbles an brick-dust. Me heart feels rale glad, so it does ; an I could hop about wid delight—if I'd got me boots on—an if it wasn't for the sorrow I feel at partin wid me bist frind : I'm afear'd I shall niver see the dear cratur any more. Oh, yis, I shall, though ; I'm forgettin what he tould me already. Yes, I shall see him agin in heaven, so I shall ; an wid the help ov God I mane to get there, soh. I know the way there now, an that's worth more nor all the other knowledge I iver had in me head, iver since I owned a head at all; be the same token—I believe a head isn't worth ownin, if it hasn't got that same knowledge in it."

Micky then arose from his seat on the ground, picked up the old pistol which was lying near, and put it into the pocket of his cloak, remarking, as he did so, that he might swop it for a pair of new boots, or a new hat. He then tied his books carefully up in his neckerchief, and with his precious little bundle in one hand, and his shillelah in the other, he resumed his journey homewards.

He trudged along for several hours, pleasingly engaged with his reflections on the last night's conversation with his kind instructor, and occasionally expressing his grateful feelings in loud exclamations, and pithy encomiums, on the "Good frind who had helped to make him feel as happy as a parson." As the sun rose higher in the cloudless sky, its fierce beams began to attack poor Micky's head through its dilapidated covering; and, withal, being rather footsore and weary, he seated himself, about noon, at the foot of a large tree to rest, and at the same time opened his little bundle to gaze again at the treasures therein, which he was so proud of possessing. He had sat for some time pondering over the passages in his Bible, which Mr. Hopewell had specially directed him to study, and was unconscious of the proximity of any human being, until he heard a shuffling noise close to him, and on looking round, saw a stout old man, genteelly dressed, lying in the road, and his horse galloping away through the bush. Micky immediately arose and ran to the assistance of the fallen man, when his ears were assailed with a volley of oaths and curses.

"What do you mean by squatting your ugly carcase right in the road, to frighten people's horses, and break their necks, you blundering baboon," roared the old man, with another torrent of oaths, and at the same time rising, and rubbing his left hip and elbow.

"I'm mortially sorry," said Micky, in a commiserating tone; "very sorry indeed, but I hope ye haven't hurt yourself."

"Hold your tongue, you thief, or I'll kick your ribs into bone dust," howled the old man, foaming with rage.

"It's well for yer own ribs, and yer cobbera too, that I've larned better manners since yesterday mornin," said

Micky, firmly, " or I should be afther giving ye a tashte ov me sthick, for callin me them ugly names : I should so. I was just sittin down under that tree, wishin no harm to nobody, an not thinkin a bit about your comin up—harf drunk—on a shyin horse. Sorry enugh I am that ye got upset ; how an ever, if ye'll just sit down for a bit, like a raysonable man, I'll go an thry to track yer horse, an bring him back to yez. Yez can take care ov me books while I'm gone, and if ye'll study that beautiful sarmont which I was a reading when you came up, it 'll do yer good, I'm thinkin. It wull tache yez to ' swear not all,' an a hape ov other things that you ought to larn, unless yer want to be miserable all yer life, and afther yer dead too." Micky then handed his books to the old man, and started after the runaway horse as fast as he could limp. It proved a much more difficult and tedious job, however, than he had calculated upon. He was two hours on the tracks before he could sight the horse, and two hours more elapsed before he could catch the timid brute. (He had picked up the saddlebags lying in the bush, but did not examine their contents). Weary work it was, too, and the blood was trickling from Micky's naked feet when he mounted into the saddle, and made the best of his way back to the spot where he had left the infuriate swearer ; but when he got there, to his great dismay, the old man was gone and the books too.

Poor Micky was well nigh distracted at this fresh mishap. To lose his books so soon after receiving them " as keepsakes," was more than he could calmly think of. In utter uncertainty of the direction the old man had taken, he continued to ride up and down the immediate spot, cooeying and shouting at the top of his voice, while his long grey cloak was fluttering in the breeze. Presently he observed, on a rocky ridge a short distance from him, two gentlemen on horseback, apparently watching his proceedings. In a moment his horse's head was turned, and he was galloping in the direction of the strangers.

" Ye haven't seen anything ov an ould gintleman, have ye ?" asked Micky, in an excited, hurried manner.

" What old gentleman ?" asked the strangers, eyeing Micky very closely, and with evident symptoms of distrust and trepidation.

" A fat ould gintleman, shure, all over dust, wid a red

face, an a bald head, sitting under a turpentine-tree, reading
a Bible."

The strangers smiled, and whispered together for a minute,
then one of them asked Micky what he wanted with the old
gentleman.

"Why, I want to give him his horse, and git back me
Bible and Pilgrim's Progress; that's what I want wid him.
I don't know where he's gone, an I don't know what I'll do
at all, no more nor a fellar wid a wooden head. I want
me property; I don't want his horse, no more nor I want
an ould catsmeat cart. Och, bother! where's he got to, I
wonder? I want me property, so I do."

"What property do you want?" asked one of the strangers.

"Why, I tould you what property jist a minute agone,
didn't I?" replied Micky, hastily. "An shure it's property
worth all the sheep an cattle in the colony, soh,—aye, an all
the goold nuggets intil the bargain."

"Come along with us, and we will take you to the old man's
house," said one of the strangers, after a little more private
conference with his companion. "You must ride fast, my
man; but keep a few rods away from us, do you hear?"

"I hear, yer honours," said Micky; "I'll follow yer like a
red-hot cannon-ball. Hurry now, jintlemen, if yer plaze;
ride as if yez was huntin kangaroos, an good luck to yez."

Away they rode at a hand-gallop, up hill and down hill,
through the bush, and across the plains, for many miles.
At length, just as it was getting dark, they arrived at a
sheep station. The strangers cooeyed, when a hairy-faced
man made his appearance, and on receiving some hurried
instructions from one of the gentlemen, he ran off towards
some huts a short distance away. In about five minutes he
returned, in company of five or six other men, who surrounded Micky, and before he had time to surmise what
they were going to do, they seized and pulled him from his
horse, pinioned his arms behind him, tied his legs, and carried him into a large wool-shed, where they threw him upon
a heap of sheepskins.

"Murther! murther! robbery!" shouted Micky, with all
his might. "Bad cess to yez! what on airth are ye afther
traitin a poor crater in this cannibal style for? What
harrm have I done to any ov yez, that you want to kill me
in this cowardly way? Och! rob me if ye like—ov course
you'll do that pretty quick, an faix ye won't have much to

share betwixt yez, when ye've done it ; strip me stark naked if yer a mind [to, but spare me life, good luck to ye—me owld carcase isn't worth a dead parrot to any of yez."

" Where's Hopping Sam ?" asked one of the gentlemen. " Oh, here he is. Sam, mount the bay mare, and gallop to Gallipot Station ; ask Dr. Strapping if he can ride over the first thing in the morning to see this poor fellow. If the doctor can't come, ask him what we shall do with the patient."

" Is he clean cranky, do you think, sir ?" asked Sam as he prepared to mount the mare's back.

" Clean cranky, eh ! why, he's raving mad," replied the gentleman. " When we found him, he was riding about the bush, looking for an old man reading his Bible."

" It's a clear case, sir, I'm afraid," said Sam, with a shrug, and a shake of his head ; then, putting spurs to the mare, he galloped out of sight in a few minutes.

In the meantime, the entire population of the station, young and old, had assembled in the wool-shed, to gaze at Micky, who was lying on the sheep-skins, sometimes whining about the loss of his Bible and Pilgrim's Progress,—sometimes demanding what for they sarved him in that cruel cowardly way. Why they tied his legs and arms like a fat pig going to market ; and now and then entering into detached portions of his recent adventures ; commenting upon the same, in his characteristic style. To the whole of his remarks, inquiries, arguments, or entreaties, his adult audience merely laughed ; while the swarm of juveniles positively howled with delight, at the comical sayings of the " cranky man."

" Troth an is it cranky ye think I am ?" asked Micky, as the true cause of his incarceration suddenly dawned upon his mind. " Och blathereens ! What nixt ? ho, ho, ho ! Be dash'd if I could help larfin at that notion, if a dray wheel was on my toes. Cranky, eh !—ho, ho, ho ! Hear me spake raysonable, friends. It's a mistake altogether, as thruc as me name's Micky Mahony. I'm no more cranky nor the masther there, and maybe not nigh so much. It's this ould coat as spoils the look uv me, and me ragged hat beside. But me brogans are drownded, and me swag's gone to sea, an I shall niver see them no more ; so I can't wear me best clothes. Arrah, niver mind, I'm as rich as a king's son, after all, so I am. Jest let me loose, honies ! if yez plaze, an I'll show yez I am as sane as the 'torney-jineral. I'll forgive yez all, for all ye've done to me, if ye'll only let me loose, an let me go and look afther me property."

"Ha, ha, ha!" laughed the obdurate assembly, which so aroused poor Micky's outraged feelings that he poured out a cataract of threats, of legal penalties, which he would visit upon the heads of them all, when he regained his liberty, and finally he began to make strenuous efforts to disengage himself from the fastenings on his hands and legs; but to no purpose, for the green hide with which he was bound was too strong to be broken by him.

About midnight Hopping Sam returned on the bay mare, with a message from Dr. Strapping that he would be over early the next morning, and in the interim, if the patient got worse, they were to shave his head, and keep wet cloths upon it, and give him a little sedative medicine.

Micky was in the midst of a vehement declamation against cowardice and cold-blooded murther, when Sam returned; so, after a short consultation, it was agreed to shave his head at once, as he was decidedly worse. Micky's emphatic protestations against their proceedings were utterly disregarded, while his resistance was overruled by the main strength of numbers, and in about half-an-hour his long grizzly beard, his shaggy locks, and his bushy whiskers, were lying on the dungheap, and his face and head were as bald as a bladder of putty. A wet cloth was then wrapped about his head, and a couple of shepherds, armed with pokers, were left to keep watch over him till morning.

Soon after daylight the doctor arrived at the station. I need not enter into particulars of what took place then; but merely state that Micky was speedily released from durance, and was overloaded with apologies from the gentlemen who had, unwittingly, been the cause of his new mishaps. Micky listened gravely to all they had to say, but declined their invitation to stay at the station until his hair grew to a becoming length; and also declined every other offer they made to him, but the offer of a breakfast; and not feeling very comfortable in a place where he was conscious that he was a laughing-stock for the whole community, he as soon as possible mounted his horse, taking with him the saddle-bags, and then took the shortest course across the bush to his old station.

The sun was just setting when he came up to Joe Griddle's

hut; and, in order to give his friend a sudden surprise, Micky fastened his horse to a tree some distance off, then crept stealthily up to the hut and peeped through a crack in the slabs. There was Joe, presiding over the long-handled fryingpan, which was full of beefsteaks and onions, the steaming savour of which was most stimulating to Micky's hungry senses.

"Ha, ha, ha!" chuckled Micky. "How plazed the jolly ould sowl 'll be to see me, to be shure! An there's poor Nip, too, sittin beside the kettle; may be he's thinkin about me this very minute. Ha, ha, ha! he'll be fit to devour me wid delight, so he will. I'll jist creep in an astonish 'em both." Micky then stole into the hut, unseen by either Joe or the dog, and seated himself on his old bedstead in the corner. There he sat for a few minutes, delightfully antici- pating Joe's surprise, and his friendly greeting. Presently Joe lifted the fryingpan off the fire, and was about to turn its contents into a tin dish on the table, when he caught sight of Micky sitting in the corner, with his bald face and head, and his long wizard-looking grey cloak.

"Hoo! hoo! hoo! Goblins!" roared Joe Griddle, drop- ping the fryingpan, and rushing out of the hut in terror, which was increased tenfold by Micky's rising and holding out his arms in the futile attempt to stop him, while Nip tucked in his tail and ran away, howling as if he had all the hot onions on his back.

Micky ran out of the hut, and called as loudly as he could, Joe, Joe Griddle, me jewel! and Nip, Nip, Nip! but neither of them regarded his call, nor stopped to look behind them, away they ran into the bush, as fast as their legs could carry them; Joe Griddle shouting for Sandy M'Grim, and Nip howling a dismal accompaniment, until the sound of their voices died away in the distant bush.

Micky slowly returned to the hut, then gathered up a part of the late contents of the fryingpan, off the earthen floor, and sat down to his solitary supper.

CHAPTER VI.

"Well, well! dear knows I've had cracks enuf, the last two days, to kill a crocodile," muttered Micky, as he sat down on a log stool inside the chimney, after he had finished his supper; "and it isn't the smallest bit ov me thruble naythir, to see me owld frinds runnin away from me, as if

I was a churchyard ghost. If iver any innocint crater was sarved worse nor me, in two days, I should jist like to see him, that's all. I've bin robbed an murthered, an shaved, an straight-jacketed, till I'm got so ugly that all me frinds are scared outright; an here I am, forsaken by all me kin, like a buck rat that's tumbled into a tar-but. Och, blarney! what'll come nixt, I wonder? I naydn't frit much about what's coming, anyhow—nor yit about what's gone naythir; I shall have strength given till me to bear the next thruble, whatever it may be. I feel that, shure enuf, an that's a blissed comfort, that I niver felt in this hut afore. I've had pirplexity in galores, since I left this tother morning, still an all, the pace I feel in me heart now, would help to make me smile if I met wid forty times as much. I'm not afeard of thruble, not a bit. But, ah, Musha! I wisht I'd got me books, so I do; I could read sich a lot ov thim, now I'm all alone an quiet. I wonder where that owld bloke has gone to wid em? but I hope he'll be readin em till I git em agin, an they'll do him good, soh; for he was a terrible owld Turk to swear. Well, plase God, I'll git up in the mornin an ride his horse till I find him, if he's in this part ov the worrld at all. Be the same token, I must go an look afther the poor baste; for he'll not like to be standin gnawin a gum saplin all night. I'm forgettin him clane, for I'm not used to the convanience of a horse to ride; I think I'm the firsht ov me family that iver sat in a raal pigskin saddle."

Accordingly, Micky went out, took off the saddle and saddle-bags, and after rubbing down his horse, led him away to a waterhole to drink; then tethered him on a nice fresh piece of feed, and slowly returned towards the hut. As he approached it, he heard voices inside, and, to his great joy, beheld through the open window Joe Griddle and Sawney M'Grim, apparently holding a consultation. Fearful of again frightening Joe, Micky paused awhile, and as he did so he overheard part of the conversation.

"I dinna believe a word aboot ghaists," said Sawney M'Grim, in a positive tone. "There are bogles and kelpies in Scotland as plenty as thistles; but I never heerd tell o' ony o' them crossing the ocean to this unco hot coontry— they're nae sich fules. It wasna a ghaist at all ye seed, Joe; it was a muckle thief, that's my fancy; and ye should have knocket him doon with your frying-pan. Hoot mon; ye've

nae mair pluck than an auld wife, not you. If ye saw a
wallaby or a white coo in the bush on a dark night, ye'd rin
daft wi' frigcht, and ca' it a ghaist or a bogle. It wasna
Micky Mahony's ghaist ye seed at all, I tell yer, ye great
gowk, so dinna fash me wi' yer hobgoblin stories; an if it
was, it wadna harm ye, nae mair thon a moonbeem, or a
whiff o' smoke fra a cutty pipe."

"Be Jabers, ye're right, Sawney!" shouted Micky, springing forward into the hut, with his right hand extended to
greet him; "an suppose I was a ghost wid iron claws, I
wouldn't scratch a——"

But neither Sawney nor Joe stopped to hear the conclusion of Micky's animated address. Away they both scampered out by the back door, faster than if the hut were on
fire, closely followed by Nip, and despite Micky's loud shouts
and cries, in his earnest endeavours to recal them, they
bolted through the bush like wild cattle, and Micky saw
them no more. After enjoying a smoke by the fireside, and
an hour's quiet meditation, he turned into Joe Griddle's bed.

In the morning, before sunrise, Micky got up, and after
praying a few words on his knees, he put the kettle over the
fire, then went out and watered his horse, and returned to
the hut to breakfast. When he had finished his meal, he
saddled his horse and rode away, with the intention of finding the owner of the beast, and the possessor of his much
prized books. He had provided himself with a little tea
and sugar, some tobacco, and part of a damper, from Joe
Griddle's stock; also with a blanket and a quart pot; for
he was of course uncertain how far he would have to travel.
Away rode Micky at a jog-trot, for he knew that that was
the best pace for a long journey; and as he jogged along he
tried to refresh his mind with the recollection of some of
the important truths he had recently learnt. About the
middle of the day he stopped, and tethered his horse, then
made a fire, and put on his quart pot with a handful of tea
in it. He was quietly enjoying his reflections and his pipe,
while the tea was brewing, when he was suddenly startled
by the well-remembered cry, "Bail up there!" and on looking round he beheld two horsemen, well armed, within shot-
range of him. Instantly Micky's hand was in his side pocket,
and pulling out his pistol he flourished it in a most threatening manner, at the same time hopping and dancing about
to strike terror into his assailants with a display of his

ferocity, as well as to baulk their aim if they attempted to shoot him.

"Ye'd betther take care how you come a-nigh this pishtle. Be the hoky, it's a rum un whin it goes off, so I jist caution you, me bhoys. Mind what yer afther, I tell you, for I won't be robbed agin, so long as I've got a gun to shoot wid. Be off wid yez, yer murtherin thieves ! go and arn yer livin honestly, an not be afther stalein from the likes ov me. Be the livin jingo, if this pishtle shu'd go off wid a bang, yer'd both of yez be blow'd into bits, not bigger nor gum leaves."

"I call upon you in the Queen's name to surrender," said one of the horsemen. "I arrest you for horse-stealing ; and if you don't drop your arms this instant I'll shoot you dead."

"Wheugh !" whistled Micky, dropping his pistol, "that's it, is it, me jewell ? Ho, ho, ho ! I beg yer pardons, soh. I thought ye were thieves, ye look just like em. It's all right frinds ; I'll pritty soon explain iverythin to yez. It's a mishtake altogether, an if ye'll jist git off an take a pot of tay wid me, I'll tell yez all about it ; then you can trot home agin, an save yourselves a hape of thruble and bo-theration."

The troopers dismounted, but instead of accepting Micky's kind invitation to tea, they seized and handcuffed him, then commanded him to sit down while they caught his horse.

"Och murther !" groaned Micky, "what for do yez put these bracelets on to me ? I won't rin away, nivir fear. I didn't stale the horse at all, not I faith ; an if ye'll jist sit down, as I axed ye before, I'll tell ye all about it, an ye'll see in a jiffy that I'm as innicent as the horse himself, every bit."

"It's my duty to caution you, that anything you say will be produced in evidence against you," said the trooper, kindly.

"To be shure, honey ! that's jist what I want, produce every haporth ov it, that's a good sowl." He then began a rambling version of the way he got the horse, and expressed his anxiety to see the owner of it, to confirm his story, and return him his books, which were worth a stud of horses.

"You'll see him to-morrow safe enough," said the trooper. "Now then, here's your horse, mount and come with us."

Micky mounted, and away they rode at a moderate pace, and a long weary ride it was. For some time Mick employed all his eloquence in defence of his honesty, but finding that it was entirely wasted upon the troopers, that they were as stolid as dead stumps to all his appeals to their "common sinse," he concluded that they had got no sinse at all ; so he rode the rest of the journey in silence. Some hours after dark they entered a small straggling township, and stopped at the door of the lock-up ; therein they incarcerated poor Micky, and fastened him to a chain. After one or two attempts to enlist the sympathies of the lock-up keeper, but finding him as iron-hearted as the troopers, Micky ate his allowance of victuals, then lay down upon some straw, and thought of his kind friend Mr. Hopewell, and upon all the good words he had spoken to him, until his heart grew as cheerful as if he had all he wanted in the world at his command.

The next day, about noon, he was unchained and escorted to the Court-house, followed by a concourse of idlers and newsmongers. The Court waited some time in vain for the arrival of a second J.P., when the magistrate present, after a consultation with the prosecutor (who had been accommodated with a seat on the bench), decided to hear the case prior to remanding it to a future day.

The prosecutor was then sworn in the usual form, and gave his evidence substantially correct. He described his disastrous meeting with Micky, and the latter volunteering to catch the runaway horse. He further stated that he had sat for three hours under a tree, reading the two books—produced—which prisoner had recommended him to read, till he returned with the horse. That a traveller had passed who informed him that he had met a man riding a horse, which, from the description, he concluded was his own beast ; and also concluded, that he had been duped out of his horse and saddle-bags. He then started on foot towards the nearest station, but was benighted in the bush : finally he reached that township, and a warrant for the apprehension of the prisoner was immediately issued on his application.

" You swear positively to the identity of the prisoner, do you ?" asked the magistrate.

" I do, your worship," said the prosecutor, " though he has attempted to disguise himself by shaving all his hair from his head and face, since I last saw him. Still, I clearly identify him by his peculiar idiom, his long cloak, and his ragged hat."

"I don't deny anythin in the worrld, yer honor," interrupted Micky; "leastways, I do deny—"

"Silence, sir," said the magistrate, with a severe frown: "you don't deny, and you do deny; what do you mean by such impudence?"

At that moment the unpunctual J.P. walked into Court and took his seat on the bench.

"Arrah, be jingo! that's the jintleman what shaved me, as clane as little Judy Fagan," shouted Micky, while he danced with delight and pointed to the bench.

The barefaced assertion that a magistrate had acted barber to a bushranger was a severe shock to the sensitive feelings of the two constables in court, and far more than their patience could quietly put up with. They both shouted silence, and at the same time shook poor Micky, till all his joints cracked like dry sticks.

"Leave the man alone, constables," said the gentleman just alluded to, sternly. "How dare you illuse a prisoner in that way?"

"He's an incorrigible miscreant," said the other J.P., with a defiant look at his colleague, and an approving glance at the constables, who straightened their shirt collars, and coughed.

"What is the charge against the prisoner?" asked the rational J.P.

With some *sotte voce* insinuations, that if the inquirer had not been absent from his duties, as usual, he would have heard the charge,—the testy J.P. ordered the evidence to be read over by the clerk of the court.

"It is clear to me thât I shall be a material witness in this case," said the gentleman, rising, after the evidence had been read. "I have seen that poor man before."

"Hurrah!" roared Micky, "didn't I tell ye so? I'm as innicint as a little duck inside a hen's egg, so I am."

"Silence!" shouted; the senior J.P., and his *posse comitatus* echoed the order, making ten times more noise than Micky.

The gentleman then briefly but lucidly, explained his meeting with Micky, and the subsequent events; especially commenting upon his extreme anxiety to find the old gentleman, with whom he had left two valuable books. The deponent also expressed his regret that he had, through the novelty of the prisoner's anxiety, mistaken him for, and treated him as, a dangerous lunatic; and finally stated his belief that he was an honest man, whom he would be very glad to have in his employ.

A wonderful reaction in Micky's favour commenced from that moment. The frowns of the prosecutor's face relaxed into bland smiles. The testy J.P. began to look good-tempered, and the constables seemed sorry for having rattled Micky's bones so roughly. The saddle-bags were next examined, and proved that Micky had not extracted an article from them. The saddle was examined too, and its evidence was also favourable; the examination of the horse was dispensed with. After a few minutes' conference between the magistrates, Micky received an honourable acquittal; and what pleased him still more, he received back his precious books from the hands of the prosecutor, who remarked, "that he had read them with pleasure and profit; and intended to buy copies of them as soon as he could."

As Micky took the books into his hands, his honest face glowed with happiness which seemed to illumine the gloomy court-house, and make everbody smile. Making a feint to touch his forelock to the bench and the prosecutor, Micky exclaimed in a hearty tone, "Long life to yer honors! May God bless every sowl of yez—constables an all," and then he hurried out of the building.

He was quickly followed out by a dilapidated looking personage, with a purple nose, who tapped him on the shoulder.

"Mr. Mahony," said the phenomenon, "allow me to offer you a little advice, for I see you are an ill-used man. You have grounds for two good actions for damages; and your fortune is as good as made, if you go the sharp way to work. You have a first-rate action against old Nobbles, for false imprisonment. He is as rich as a copper mine, and you may knock a handsome sum out of him. Mr. Phinewoll, the J.P., is rich too, you have a stunning action for assault and battery there, and are sure to get heavy damages. Will you step with me to my office?"

"Not a bit of it, Mr. What's-yer-name. I've got no grudge aginst ayther of them gintlemen. They shaved me head an face as bald as a hatter's block; but that's all the damage they've done me. I don't want to go to law wid em for such a trifle as that. Beside, I'v got betther law nor yourn to go to, here," said Micky, laying his hand on his Bible. "An I'm thinkin, if ye was to study them laws abit, every day ov your life, yez would learn better manners than to be setting yer neighbours a squabblin an fightin ; an ye'd larn to make pace, instead of kickin up rows." He then turned on his heel and walked away.

He had not gone far, before he heard some person calling him, and on looking round he saw Mr. Nobbles hobbling after him as fast as his short legs could carry his fat body. " Hoy, Mr. Mahony," said Mr. Nobbles, " don't be in such a hurry, I want to speak with you. Give me your hand," he added, as he came up to Micky, " You are one of the right sort, I can see, and I respect an honest man, whether he be rich or poor. I am very sorry, indeed, that I caused you so much trouble, and I hope you'll try to forget it. I've been under the impression that you were one of those mischievous hypocrites, who make a trade of their piety ; I suspected you were one of that dangerous fry ; and that you had recommended me to sit and study your Bible, while you stole my horse and saddle-bags. I have heard of similar tricks before to-day. I see, however, that I have made a mistake in your character, Mr. Mahony. I think you really believe in that good book which you have under your arm, and which I am very glad I have seen, for I intend to turn over a new leaf from to-day. Now, I'm a man of few words, and I'll make a bargain with you on the spot if you like. I want an overseer for my head-station, and you are just the man for me. What do you say—will you engage with me at once ?"

" Wid all me heart," said Micky, " for I'm out of a berth, unless I unship Sawny M'Grim agin, and I won't do that anyhow, bekase it wouldn't be fair play."

" That's settled then," said Mr. Nobbles, " and now I'll treat you to a new outfit, for the annoyance I have caused you ; come along with me to the store."

So Micky went with his good friend to a store near at hand, and although he modestly demurred at taking so many articles as the storekeeper forced upon him—his new employer, who stood by, insisted upon his having a thorough rig out ; and when Micky left the store, he had a larger stock of necessaries than he had ever before possessed in his life-time ; and was, as he himself humorously expressed it, " dressed better nor his masther."

" Don't say a word," said Mr. Nobbles, interrupting Micky's torrent of thanks. " Let's get home as fast as we can. Go and mount the old horse again ; there, there, no more thanks ; go and mount Ginger, and follow me." Micky obeyed, and soon afterwards he and his new master were trotting along the road towards Dingobones Station.

*   *   *   *   *   *

I should have much pleasure in continuing Micky's history at length, but could scarcely do so under the title of our present chapters ; for "Micky's mishaps" were over. He had begun an entirely new era in his life, and in a short time he was, to use his own words, " a new man altogether." He daily rose in the estimation of his kind master, and also in the good graces of all the employés on the establishment. Micky was a true believer in God's word, and strove to walk humbly and truly by its Divine precepts, which were his daily study, and he earnestly strove to give evidence of his firm faith in it, by his upright walk and conversation ; and never did he omit a seasonable opportunity of directing a poor un-instructed neighbour to the plain simple way in which he found peace with God, and the hope of Heaven. He was untiring in his unobtrusive, though cheerful efforts to do good, in his homely way, and his influence was felt, not only in his master's household, but on that and the neighbouring stations.

Joe Griddle was in course of time installed as *Mr. Mahony's* house-servant ; and the Bible, the " Sunday at Home," the " Leisure Hour," and other good books replaced the trashy pernicious volumes in Joe's library. Very soon he, too, could feel that his old tormenting fears of death had been driven away by the light of Divine truth, and that he had a comforting hope of " life beyond life."

*   *   *   *   *   *

Reader ! whether you live in the bush, or in the city, whether you be rich or poor, old or young, gentle or simple, if you want to be happy and useful through life, peaceful in the hour of death, and glorified throughout eternity, the simple plan to obtain those blessings, is to do as poor Micky Mahony did, viz.,—" Repent, and believe the Gospel."

"LIGHT WEIGHTS" AND "SHORT LENGTHS."

I REMEMBER my scepticism, on being told (when I was a little boy) that a " pound of feathers was equal to a pound of lead," and when good old dame Birch, who taught me the rudiments of my " mother tongue," reiterated that fact, and, with a grave look declared that " a pound was a pound all the world over," my childish mind still doubted. Poor honest old soul ! she has gone out of the world long ago ; and here am I, her dull pupil, still acquiring rudimental knowledge, but no longer doubting about her last-named theory ; for my experience in travelling the world over has fully convinced me that a pound is *not* always a pound, of which fact I have had many expensive reminders. I will give one example of recent occurrence, which, though insignificant compared with other parts of my experience, will help to illustrate certain very common tricks of trade. that unconscionable persons have invented, and on which I purpose making a few comments.

The other evening, my servant brought two miserably thin composite candles into my study ; and being too small to fit the sockets of the candlesticks, they were leaning over, like the wonderful tower of Pisa ; while the grease dropped on to my table cover, and soiled some of my manuscripts. On questioning the girl, I learned that she had bought the candles at a shop in the city ; and on examining a *pound* packet, I judged it weighed not more than thirteen ounces, possibly not so much. " Ghost of old dame Birch," I exclaimed, holding the packet up at arm's length. " Look at this for a pound ! and if you still love fair play, go and pinch that swindling candlemaker's nose. You will probably find him in Russia ; unless—and you must be very careful to ascertain that fact—some rogue elsewhere, has *borrowed* the candlemaker's brand. Pinch the real culprit till he roars, for greasing my papers—stay, I forgive him for that ; but please to punish him for cheating thousands of poor people who *must* work for their bread by candle light, out of three ounces of matter in every packet of his skeleton composites that they buy. Pinch him for dimming the prospects of a host of honest diggers, who are hard at work in the bowels of the earth, far below the reach of a ray of sunlight. And pinch him very hard for tempting many an honest trader to sell short weight wares, in the erroneous belief that it is necessary for him to do so, to save his trade from suffering from the competition of unscrupulous neighbours. But nip all these 'honest traders' at the same time, for they must know that it is not right to countenance wrong, in any shape, or under any circumstances."

The servant looked startled at my ghostly invocation, and explained, "that the candles had not been sold to her as full weights, but were merely recommended as 'very cheap.' She was certain sure the shopkeeper was a fair dealing man, and would not tell a lie for a cargo of candles." But when I asked her how I could possibly believe that, with the palpable fact before my eyes, that he had given her but "thirteen ounces for a pound ;" she fumbled at her apron strings, and said "she didn't know she was sure ; but she fancied it was only for want of thought ; and nobody would believe it was anything more than an error of the head, who knew Mr. Brown." After cautioning the girl not to buy any more cheap candles, or short weight articles of any sort, I sat down in the dim glimmer of the thin tapers and began to ruminate on the light weight, and short length system, which is at the present day so glaringly tolerated in these colonies, and which sometimes bears the sanction of trade marks, either genuine or forgeries.

But first of all, I tried to unravel the mystical legal distinction between the open sin of Mr. Brown, in selling pounds of candles weighing only thirteen ounces, and that of his neighbour, Mr. Doughnut, in owning sundry two pound loaves, each being about an ounce short of the standard weight ; and I called to mind a case which was investigated at the Police Office the other day. I mention it for the sake of the analogy, rather than to enlist sympathy for the mulcted tradesmen. A baker pleaded guilty of having thirteen loaves in his cart, which in the aggregate, were fourteen ounces less than their proper weight ; but his feasible explanation of the accidental cause of the short-comings of his bread, was not received in extenuation of his crime, and he was mulcted in the full penalty by law made and provided. *Why* Mr. Brown should not be fined for his short-weighted candles, or anything else short weight in his shop, I failed to find a satisfactory reason, after half an hour's study, so I gave it up; but would beg respectfully to commend the puzzling subject to some of our active legislators, in order to get the consideration of "the House" upon it, and if possible to remove the seeming antagonism between justice and common sense.

But composite candles are not the only articles deficient in weight and measure, and of inferior quality, which find their way to our colonial markets, to prey upon the health and pockets of the humble classes especially. It is not easy for me to enumerate the deceptive goods, nor is it necessary to do so. I can adduce facts enough to draw attention to the evil, and I wish I could hope to cure it.

There are many articles of daily demand in which the judgment of the purchaser is less likely to detect fraud than in the consumptive-looking candles just alluded to. For instance, in haberdashery wares, where short lengths, and forged marks, are as common as the goods they represent. Take "short lengths" reel cotton for example, with the borrowed name of some well known maker, "warranted 200 yards." The retail buyer has no guarantee of the quantity specified, save the honour of the shopkeeper; for the most careful old lady in the land would hardly stay to check the measure before paying for her reel of cotton; and it would be only when too late for a remedy that she would discover she had been cheated, and that she had far more wood than cotton for her money. Some good folks may, perhaps, exclaim impatiently, "Pooh! that is a mere trifle to write about." But I would earnestly remind them that it is only a solitary example of a system of fraud which is too palpable to be mistaken; and I am sure they will not call that a trifle, especially if they bear in mind that it generally affects a class of persons who are least able to bear such a raid upon their pockets, and to whom these multiplied peculations swell to a serious aggregate in the course of the year.

I know a respectable old widow who is too proud to beg or to run in debt, but not too proud to earn her livelihood by plain needlework; and since sewing machines have become as fashionable as pianos in gentlefolk's houses, this honest old lady finds it a difficult matter to earn full diet by finger stitching, for the price of her work is reduced far below a remunerative standard. Of course, she has to find her own cotton; and if her " 200 yard reels" only turn out 100 or 120 yards each, is it not a severe inroad upon her hardly earned income? Is not 80 or 100 per cent a serious sum for her poor pocket to be plundered of?

Some persons may reply to that question, "Let the old lady buy her cotton from respectable tradesmen, then she is not likely to be cheated." That is certainly the best remedy within her reach, but I wish that her humble protest could reach the ears of manufacturers far away. There is the source of the wrong; for it is clear that if they honestly refused to " make up" short length, or short weight wares, there would be no wholesale or retail vendors of them, nor duped purchasers either.

I don't wish to make a long chapter on this unpleasant subject, lest I should not be able to restrain my pen from expressing strong feeling; but I would like to gently remind those factors and dealers in deceptive goods, that though— humanly speaking they may carry on their nefarious traffic with impunity, and perhaps grow rich upon their spoils; yet they will not escape [the penalty, which sooner or later is visited upon bad actions, as certainly as effects follow causes in material affairs; and a careful consideration of passing events from day to day, even within this city, might instil that belief into the most sceptical mind. Who of my readers has not seen ill-gotten wealth melt from the grasp of its possessors, and " leave not a wrack behind?" I have seen it, and expect again to see it; and I emphatically declare that I would rather be a corporation stone cracker, than I would luxuriate in the profits which those factors and vendors make by false weights and measures, by selling *timber*, instead of cotton to poor old widows, for my conscience would not fail to warn me in the night watches that the God of the widow would assuredly visit my unjust dealing with His awful judgment.

"DON'T MENTION IT."

" I WOULD not tell another being in the world beside yourself, for I don't want it to be said that I tried to ruin the
poor wretches.   You won't mention it, will you?"

" Not I, indeed, if I were chained to a hot griddle ; you
may safely trust me with anything.   But it is very disgraceful.   When did you hear of it?"

" On Tuesday evening, and I have been dying to see you
ever since.   Bear in mind, dear, I don't vouch for the correctness of the report, but I give it you just as I got it from
Sukey Sleigh, who overheard the servants next door whispering it over the back fence.   It is likely enough to be
true, though, and I am not surprised at it, for these shabby-
genteel folks are often great schemers.   I have always said
those Campbells were haughty, stuck-up people, and I shall
be pleased to see them pulled down from their stilts and
rolled in the dirt."

" So shall I, for I hate them.   They are proud as peacocks,
and as poor as caged owls, too.   Mrs. Campbell has worn that
everlasting blue silk dress three summers, and her grey horse-
hair bonnet has been cleaned twice, to my certain knowledge.
The old man, too, looks as dismally seedy as an undertaker's coachman ; and as for the girls—ugh ! I've no patience with them.   The butcher's boy told our servant, Mag,
the other day, that they never order anything but shins of
beef and sheeps' heads, or now and then a neck of mutton
for Sunday.   Pooh ! I should like to know what they have
to be proud of, the nasty, disagreeable, unsociable creatures.
I should like to see them obliged to leave the neighbourhood altogether."

     *   *   *   *   *   *

Thus, Mrs. Gabb, and her spinster cousin Miss Pryer (a
precious pair, of the backbiting genus), scandalized a respectable family over the way, who have unconsciously incurred the envy and hatred of their detractors for no other
cause than their having prudently kept aloof from the society
of such ill-bred, dangerous characters.   Miss Pryer tells
Mrs. Gabb, as a profound secret, that Mr. Campbell is me-

ditating a moonlight flitting from his house, to defraud his landlord, which report is without the slightest foundation. Mrs. Gabb of course tells Mr. Gabb while she is preparing for bed that night, and at the same time adds a little to the story, from her own private stock of spite. The next morning Mr. Gabb whispers it confidentially to a fellow toper, over a nobbler, at the Nag's Head, and with a roguish wink declares his belief that the Campbells are going to bolt to New Caledonia. The scandal flies, of course ("for lies have wings and can fly, though they cannot stand for want of legs,") and a few hours afterwards, to the consternation of the maligned family, their landlord distrains for a quarter's rent only due last week, and which they were anxiously struggling to raise, in total ignorance of the plots of their neighbours, or the legal process of their too credulous landlord. Their troubles do not end with the sacrifice of their household goods, for the rumours have affected Mr. Campbell's business in the City. Excited creditors rush into his office, and demand payment of their claims, or satisfactory security. Vainly does the astounded man try to explain his solvent position, and plead for a little time, and he will pay them all; the majority of them will not wait—"they are not going to be duped while they are wide awake." To meet their claims immediately would be impossible—(almost everybody knows the difficulty of realising suddenly upon assets, however safe they may be)—so, to protect his few reasonable creditors, and in justice to all, Mr. Campbell sequestrates his estate, which is his only alternative. Very soon his name appears in the insolvent list, and he may be seen any day walking about the city with his head bowed down. Thus, a striving, inoffensive family are suddenly overwhelmed with sorrow and inextricable pecuniary difficulties through the idle whisperings of a couple of scandal-mongers.

    *   *   *   *   *   *

I will give another instance of the disastrous effects of gossiping, and it is as substantially true as the preceding one.

"Have you heard the rumour which is afloat about Emily Green?" asked Widow Wen of her bosom friend Mrs. Cackle, as they sat at a little tea-table, munching hot muffins, and scrutinizing the failings of their friends and neighbours. "Have you heard about the impudent hussey?"

"No, my dear," replied Mrs. Cackle, with eagerness; "what is it? Tell me all about it."

"I'll take a little more sugar," said Mrs. Wen, handing her cup. "You shall hear the story word for word, as I heard it from ——, but I mustn't tell you who told me. You won't mention it again?"

"Oh, dear, no; you ought to know me better than to ask it : mum is my motto."

"Well, then, you must know that my informant has been watching Miss Green's movements for some time past, never feeling satisfied that she was getting her living honestly; indeed, it has puzzled many persons how that girl managed to hold up her head so loftily, for she has only her salary as assistant governess at Mrs. Blank's school, and the fees of a few drawing pupils of an evening. Her old mother lives with her too, and she is too lazy to earn a penny a month, so it is plain they must have some way of getting money that all the world does not know of. Well, the secret is out at last, as you shall hear. For five consecutive evenings last week, my friend, who was on the look out, saw a dashing looking gentleman get out of a hooded buggy at Miss Green's door just after dark. She saw Emily open the door for him each time, and invite him in, and——"

"Oho ! that's it, is it?" croaked Mrs. Cackle, with her mouth full of muffin, and her heart full of envy. "I see, I see, the brazen-faced minx. That's the way she gets her finery, is it? That's why she tosses her handsome head about like a soldier's horse ! I understand it now ; and, to tell you the truth, I suspected as much. Well ! well ! well !"

"Now, pray don't mention it," reiterated Mrs. Wen, "because I might get into trouble. We had need be careful what we say about that sort of people, for I dare say they have friends."

"I tell you again I'll keep it quiet, though she deserves to be exposed, the good for nothing slut," said Mrs. Cackle, looking as fierce as a hawk tearing a young pigeon to pieces.

Somebody *did* mention it, however, for it soon reached Mrs. Blank's ears. She did not trouble herself to investigate the truth of the rumour, but summarily dismissed poor Emily without a word of explanation. The scandal rapidly spread, and her drawing pupils one by one left her, when she was obliged to sell, from time to time, first all her little trinkets and articles of luxury, and afterwards her household furniture, for the support of herself and invalid mother.

It was some time before Emily learned the cause of her sudden dismissal from Mrs. Blank's, and the removal of her drawing pupils, but when the cruel reality burst upon her, it proved too much for her weakened body and mind to bear. Her attempts at explanation were coolly repulsed by Mrs. Blank and others, and on every hand she met with insults and scorn, which crushed her sensitive spirit, and overwhelmed her with sorrow. Anxiety brought on sickness and rapid decline, which was accelerated by her constant attention to her bedridden mother, and want of necessary comforts. The melancholy sequel is soon told : her sufferings, though severe, were mercifully shortened by that kind Providence which specially watches over the helpless. She was not left long in lonely indigence to mourn the loss of her mother. Death soon came to Emily, with the welcome passport to a better world, and her weary soul soared away to its rest, "where the wicked cease from troubling."

Under the sandhills yonder, lie the remains of mother and daughter, in one grave, hapless victims to the tongues of their maligners, which proved fatal as the teeth of black snakes. But a great day is approaching when they will know that the helpless girl whose character they so cruelly assailed was as chaste as an infant, and that their wicked insinuations were utterly groundless. Emily Green was a noble-spirited girl, well educated, and piously trained. Her disposition was too refined for Mrs. Wen and Mrs. Cackle, and their gossiping connections. She treated them with neighbourly courtesy, but avoided a closer intimacy. Hence their dislike to her, and their plots against her reputation. The gentleman whose visits to her house had given rise to the innuendoes which had so fatally injured her, was an eminent physician, who had kindly called to see her sick mother, at the recommendation of a friend of the afflicted. Poor Emily ! slanderers will by-and-bye see her "righteousness as clear as the light," but in the meantime they had better "take heed to their ways," or a totally opposite judgment will at that day be passed upon their lives.

*   *   *   *   *   *

Open rebuke is sometimes seasonable, and friendly warning or reproof — judiciously given — is often useful ; but

nothing can be said in favour of covert fault-finding and
backbiting. It is cowardly, mischievous, and sinful. "He
that winketh with the eye causeth sorrow." Sorrowfully
true has that been proved by a host of unfortunate victims
of malice and uncharitableness. Many a worthy man and
woman's good reputation has been ruined by a wink, or a
significant shrug ; perhaps accompanied with a hypocritical
expression of pity. Many noble actions, offsprings of true
philanthropy, have been condemned by a sinister look, or
belied by a mysterious elevation of the eyebrows, or some
other facial contortion, slyly meant to impute selfish and
other unworthy motives too base to be expressed in words.
Many pure-minded young girls have had their fair fame
blasted by the breath of envious prudes, who, at the same
time, have appeared to commiserate the failings of their
victims, well knowing, too, that the charges against their
virtue were malicious falsehoods.

"I am very sorry for the poor thing," whispers Mrs.
Gabb, across her counter, to a twopenny customer. "She
has had heavy trials certainly, but that's not an excuse for
acting as she does. She will never be able to pay her way,
I'm sure. It is a thousand pities to see a widow, with three
young children, setting them such a sad example. Drink is
a great evil, and, of course, leads to everything else that is
bad. Those friends who subscribed money to start her,
don't know of her doings, that's plain ; and I shouldn't like
to tell them. Don't mention it again, will you ? At any
rate, don't say that I told you."

Ugh ! you old sinner ! I should like to make you eat
a bottle of mustard ! Are you not ashamed of launching
such gross fabrications, to ruin that poor widow, who is
striving to train up her little children in the fear of God,
and to lead a 'sober, righteous, and godly life,' herself ? Is
it not fiendish of you to try and crush her, and starve her
little ones, simply because she has opened a lollipop-shop in
the same street in which you trade ?

Cheer up, poor widow ! Be not afraid : you have an
Almighty Friend above, whose unchangeable word is pledged
to protect and provide for you and your fatherless children.
"Commit your way unto Him ; trust also in Him ;" and the
malignant whisperings of your foes shall be as powerless to
injure you as the hissings of a toothless viper.

That burly trader, too, whose purse is heavier than a sack

of potatoes, might well afford to spare his abuse of the striving young man, who has opened a shop next door but one to him ; in the hope of earning an honest living, with "Live and let live" for his motto. Be assured, Mr. Bigbody, that your grudgery will recoil upon yourself. Your policy will be unprofitable, in a pecuniary sense, to say nothing of a far higher sense in which you will be a sad loser, if you encourage such evil passions in your heart. You know it is unjust to injure your neighbour in the opinion of his creditors and his customers ; and if your bulky purse tempts you to laugh at the law of libel, let me remind you that there are infinitely higher laws, which you cannot break with impunity. I have seen the boasted hoards of purse-proud men leak away like wild honey from a cracked calabash, and leave them more miserable than a starving blackfellow. But whether your money is taken from you, or you keep it until you are taken from it, is a matter of small moment, compared with the judgment which awaits you, where ready cash cannot bribe. You need not be offended with me, Mr. Bigbody, for my straightforward comments. I do not dislike *you*, but I cannot like your unprincipled doings. Take my advice, like a sensible man, mind your own business in future, and let your struggling neighbour earn an honest loaf if he can : there is room enough in the city for you both.

＊　　＊　　＊　　＊　　＊　　＊

A wise man has remarked, that "envy is the most inexorable of all passions. Other sins have some pleasure attached to them, or seemingly admit of an excuse : envy wants both. Other sins last but for a while : the appetite may be satisfied ; anger remits, hatred has an end—but envy never ceases." A far wiser man has declared that "wrath is cruel, and anger is outrageous ;" and he adds the enquiry, "but who is able to stand against envy?" The same high authority says that "a sound heart is the life of the flesh, but envy the rottenness of the bones." Verily there are thousands of tons of such rotten bones in the world (carrying living souls, too), which taint the moral atmosphere, and breed "plague, pestilence, and famine ; battle and murder, and sudden death," from which we pray to be delivered.

DOWN IN THE PIT.

"I FEAR that the hearts of those dusky-looking hills yonder, will soon be torn out of them; and then what will become of this rising city? and what will its busy population do when they have no coal to sell?"

Thus I soliloquised, whilst seated in a friend's house, which overlooks a considerable portion of the harbour and city of Newcastle. I had just before counted nearly forty square-rigged vessels, besides smaller ones, in the port, all loading or preparing to load coal; while long coal trains whirled past me at brief intervals, shaking the roof over my head, and suggesting unpleasant ideas of a sudden downfall, if the props in the old coal workings beneath the city should give way.

"In former years," I continued, "when they used to load vessels with a wheelbarrow, or cane baskets, there was but little cause to fear that the coal supply would run short; but now they ship it by steam; and more than a thousand miners are at work supplying those ponderous trains, which seem to be always screaming for more. I was told, that 1048 tons of coal were shipped yesterday, from the A. A. Company's shoots alone. What a gap they must have left somewhere! At that rate the very hills themselves would soon be cleared away, if they were all saleable matter. I feel uneasy upon the subject, for it is of vital importance to our national advancement. But yonder comes a gentleman who can see further into a coal seam than most men; I will ask his opinion. He certainly has not a desponding mien. Perhaps he will enlighten me a little, and allay my apprehensions of a famine in fuel."

In a few minutes I was accosted by the manager of the principal mines, of whose courtesy I cannot speak too highly. When I mentioned my foreboding, his eyes twinkled like "Davy lamps," and he remarked, that my grandchildren might depend upon an abundant supply of firstclass coal, from the mine which he had the honour of superintending; and which I was told he had incurred the hazard of opening. Perhaps observing that I was still dubious, he kindly invited me to view the mine, and judge for myself as to the probability of its being soon exhausted, even by an increased demand upon it.

A short time afterwards I was on a locomotive engine, driven by a shrewd-looking little man, who I was informed, had driven the celebrated George Stephenson's first "puffing Billy." With one hand on the steam valve, and the other on the break, he seemed to manage the machine as easily as I could handle a child's cock-horse, and pulled or pushed the loaded coal waggons about, at will, as though they were mere bonnet boxes. In company with the manager and another friend, I in a few minutes arrived at the mine, which is rather more than a mile from Newcastle.

I cannot minutely describe the gigantic works either above or below ground, which are triumphs of perseverance and engineering skill, perhaps unparalleled in this part of the world.

I gazed with wondering admiration at the machinery about the pit's mouth, and marked the order and system that prevailed, in the midst of noise and activity, which made my brain simmer like a stewed cabbage. I noted the waggish looks of some of the smutty-faced boys, (who were wheeling little coal skips about,) at my nervous care to keep my toes clear of their iron wheels, and to keep a look-out for my head and my other important members at the same time ; while I mentally admitted that the smallest boy there was wiser than myself, or at any rate possessed more useful knowledge, adapted to that particular locality. The various modes of raising, weighing, inspecting, and screening the coal, were briefly explained to me in terms comprehensible to my uninitiated mind, which was dark as coal itself on such subjects. I was shown a huge box-full of "nuts," without longing to crack one ; and another box full of "duff," which even a starving sailor would despise as a ration, though the engine furnaces daily devoured a large quantity, with greedy gusto.

I next arrayed myself in a borrowed coat and cap—neither of which fitted me nicely—and with a little tallow lamp in my hand, took my stand in an iron cage between my two guides, and down, down, down, I went two hundred feet into the bowels of the earth. On stepping out of the cage, at the bottom of the shaft, I found myself surrounded by coal-begrimed men and boys, with little lamps stuck in their caps ; whilst the clanking of chains, the rumble of coal skips on the rails in long dark lanes, the shouts of the horse drivers, and other sights and sounds altogether strange to me, helped my imagination to conceive many startling things.

The overman of the mine lighted his lamp, and formed a rear guard ; so away I went, with difficulty keeping up with my active friends in front, and sadly knocking my toes now and then against obstructions in my pathway, which my lamp but dimly revealed, but which my practised companions stepped over, as briskly as rabbits in a warren. Away we went, up a long black passage, which I called Ebony Highway—I forgot to enquire its proper name. On either side of us was a wall of solid coal, which sparkled in the glare of our lamps, like patent leather. The roof varied from ten to twelve feet in height ; but occasionally it was much lower, as I discovered by my bump of firmness coming in contact with some stimulating substance, but whether it was rock or coal, I did not stay to examine.

Turning round a rugged corner into Nobbley Nook, my nose suggested that horses had recently slept in that neighbourhood ; and presently my eyes assured me that my nose was quite right, for I beheld stabling for fourteen beasts, with the name of each written in chalk, on his appointed stall. Many ill-kept horses above ground, might envy Tommy and Jerry, and the rest of the sleek coated stud, their snug lodgings below. Onward we went again, and by and by the manager turned up Smut Court, to examine a newly discovered dip in the seam : meanwhile I sat on a lump of coal and chatted with some men, who were eating their dinner with an enviable zest, which even " Lea and Perrin" could not create. A little farther on, I saw a man on a very moist seat, and in Adamic simplicity of attire, picking with all his might beneath a block of coal, which I thought was dangerously liable to fall on his head. As I noticed the rapid movements of his powerful muscles, I reflected how hard some men work for their bread, compared with others, and how richly they deserve the compensating advantages of real enjoyment of their humble diet and sound sleep. I further speculated, on the probable social influence on some of those creatures of the " Dundreary" class (who would almost shudder to touch a knob of coal with a pair of tongs) if they could be persuaded to spend half a day, now and then, in a coal mine. If the bare idea of such a task did not shock them to death, I am sure the reality would in some degree help to make men of them.

On we went again, in another direction, up a grimy alley, half a mile in length, which I was informed was an old worked out passage, leading to the ventilating shaft ; and I began to fear that I should be worked out too before I got to the end of it. Masses of rock had, in several places, fallen from the roof, and as I hastened past those suspicious parts, I sincerely hoped that no more rock would fall for the present. The sides of the passage and the rotting props were thickly covered with a strange variety of fungi, while long filmy festoons of the same hung waving from the roof, as though a thousand fairies had been having a grand washing day, in the gaseous pool which I had just passed, and had hung up their " cutty sarks" to dry in that draughty alley. In vain did I hint to my foremost guide that I had seen enough ; that my scepticism on the subject of the coal supply was perfectly cured, and that I wanted my dinner. He evidently had but little consideration for diners at that hour of the day, and was desirous of showing me the admirable arrangements for ventilating the pit. I was obliged to submit, for to be left in that mouldy locality would have been, to say the least, very unsatisfactory, especially if my lamp had gone out ; and it is extremely doubtful if I could have groped my way back to the shaft, in thorough darkness.

Presently I fancied I smelt day-light dashed with soot ; and on looking up an old chimney, or shaft, I saw a patch of blue sky a little larger than the roof of a coach. I was glad to see even that small bit, but was not allowed to look at it very long. Following my leaders round a mass of hot brickwork, I beheld an enormous fiery furnace, many times larger than the stoke hole under Messrs. Tooth's big brewery copper, and the air rushed towards it with the force of a brisk gale. While I stood silently sympathising with the half-roasted man, who was stirring the fire with a long poker, I decided, that if I were forced to select one of two trying services, I should prefer his red hot post, to that of the lookout man, of the middle watch, rounding Cape Horn, with a double reef breeze blowing icicles from the South Pole. -

I rested but a short time in the melting vicinity of the furnace, for my friend the manager is perpetual motion personified. Off he started again through Fungus Alley, and anon, after a ramble of several miles in sum total, we returned to the foot of the main shaft; a sort of "Charing Cross," or grand junction, for all the tramways which branch off in every direction. Here my friends paused to draw breath, which they had scarcely given me time to draw before; and as I fancied they were beginning to consider which way they should go next, I plaintively assured them, " that I was more than satisfied with what I had already experienced, and would willingly take their joint testimony for all the rest. I had seen sufficient coal for the present generation, gluttons though they be, and my mind was at rest on the subject. At any rate, I positively could not walk any further, if it were to save the next generation from being driven to charcoal, or faggots. Finally I remarked, " that if my friends were fully bent upon showing me through any more long passages, they must carry me a pig-a-back."

The latter proposition seemed to have more weight than all the others; and being evidently indisposed to take such a troublesome burden on their shoulders, they smilingly accompanied me to the cage. The telegraphic hammer then struck two, and in another minute I was hoisted up into the sunshine, very weary, but somewhat wiser than I was when I descended the shaft, four hours before.

"SEE, papa," cried Minnie Maybud, one doubtful looking afternoon. "See, papa, the smiling sun is peeping out at last, from behind those cross looking clouds; there is a bit of blue sky too, as big as my parasol, and it's getting bigger every minute. Yes, the rain is all over, I do believe; so we can have our drive to Coogee beach after all. I'm so glad," said little Minnie, clapping her hands with joy, as she bounded inside from the balcony, bringing sunshine with her.

"I have been quite vexed with the weather all the morning," continued little Minnie, "though I know it was silly of me, and perhaps sinful too; for as you have explained to me, papa, all the clever men in the colony could not have saved the thirsty vegetation, if the rain had kept away much longer. I am sure the poor cows, and horses, and sheep, will be glad. I will be more patient in future, during wet weather; yes, that I will. Now, papa dear, please tell Simon to get the carriage ready, and come along, Anna," she added, as she caught her sister round the waist, "come away, dear; let us get on our hats and mantles; and find our shell baskets. We will have a merry afternoon on the nice white sandy beach, and play at catch-me-if-you-can, with the big waves which come toppling over and over each other, with their white curly heads looking like cart loads of cauliflowers." Away skipped the happy girls to their room; humming "shells of ocean."

Half an hour afterwards, the carriage containing Minnie and her sister with their mamma and their governess, was rolling briskly along the road towards Coogee. The morning showers had imparted new life and loveliness to the vegetable world, and everything looked refreshed. The pretty bush flowers, which bloomed in profuse variety on either side of the road, seemed to vie with the smiling faces of the blooming maidens in the carriage. The sun shone out bright and warm; making the drops of moisture on the bushes sparkle like diamonds, and the mimic rain pools in the road to look as if they were full of new sovereigns;

while the air was far more fragrant than the shops of Rowland, Rimmell, or any other great perfumer.

"Stop, if you please, Simon," said Mrs. Maybud to the coachman, when he had driven to the end of the smooth road. The road was not then made quite down to the beach, as it is at the present time. "Stop, Simon, I think you had better not make Jacky draw the carriage through this heavy sand ; the poor old fellow has trotted along very nicely, so now he may rest. We will walk down to the beach."

"Come, sister dear," said lively little Minnie, after they had alighted. "Let us have a run to yonder rock that looks so like a nice couch, with a green velvet cover to it. We can leave our mantles with mamma and Miss Prosody while we gather sea-weed, and shells, to make a wreath for dear grandmamma in England."

Away ran the light-hearted girls, and soon they were skipping about the beach, while the sea breeze blew their clustering curls about their rosy faces, and their bright eyes beamed with enjoyment.

It cannot, with strict correctness, be said that there is not a *variety* of conchological specimens on Coogee beach. Indeed, that can scarcely be said of any sea beach ; still the sea shores of Australia—the eastern coasts at least—are not so remarkable for rare or beautiful specimens of shells as other parts of this hemisphere ; and especially some of the coral islands of Western Polynesia, which I have visited.

The girls amused themselves for more than an hour, and gathered what appeared to them a choice assortment of univalves, and bivalves, together with seaweed, pebbles and sea-eggs. At length, feeling rather tired, they proceeded to where mamma and governess were seated, on the green rock before alluded to, there they spread out their little baskets of treasures, and amused themselves in sorting and arranging them, for another hour or more.

"Now, my dears," said Mrs. Maybud, rising from her seat, "I think it is time to return home. The sun is beginning to make long shadows, and the air from the sea is getting rather chilly, so put on your mantles, and we will walk to the carriage."

"Oh mamma, mamma," shrieked one of the girls, at that instant in an agony of terror, "a snake, a snake, close to your feet."

Mrs. Maybud cast her eyes downwards, and, with indescribable loathing, beheld a brown snake within a few inches of her feet; with its fearfully fascinating eyes gleaming upon her. With more haste than elegance, the whole party sprang from the rock; fortunately without the least injury; but as may be imagined, with feelings of intense alarm. During the whole of the time they had sat on the rock, there is no doubt that the deadly reptile had lain coiled up in a crevice, at their feet, and had probably been asleep until awakened by the slight noise they made in rising; or possibly by some part of their dress touching it. They hurried to the carriage with hearts full of gratitude to God, for their providential escape.

About a fortnight afterwards, Mr. Maybud, with Anna, and Minnie, drove to Coogee beach, during a south east gale, when a scene of awful grandeur was before them, worth going thrice the distance to behold. While the gigantic waves were breaking in rapid succession upon the long shelly beach like avalanches, far away seaward, confused tumbling masses of foaming waters were warring with the howling winds, and black, angry looking clouds above, seemed to frown on the strife of the turbulent elements.

After enjoying the sublime spectacle for some time, Mr. Maybud allowed his daughters to lead him to the rock, where they received the terrible fright above described.

"That's the spot, papa," said Minnie, pulling Mr. Maybud towards it. I know it by its nice, soft green surface; and that's the crevice where the snake was. Mamma's and Miss Prosody's feet were right over the spot for more than two hours. How very providential that the dreadful thing was asleep all the time. There, that's the hole, papa," said Minnie, pointing to it with her parasol.

"Hush, my dear," said Mr. Maybud, excitedly, "there is the snake now; I saw it move. Stand back, stand back!" As he spoke, he thrust his walking-stick into the crevice, and by a dexterous movement forced the reptile from its hiding place. In another minute it was writhing on the sand with its back broken. It was a brown snake, about three feet in length, and of a very deadly species.

*   *   *   *   *   *

Coogee is now much less infested by snakes than it was at the time the above incidents occurred. Much of the land has been cleared and cultivated, or built upon; and a great many snakes have shuffled away to more secluded haunts, for they generally prefer the solitude of the thick bush, or reedy swamp. They do not, however, always object to the society of mankind, or to share his domestic conveniencies; as some of the following examples will attest.

A married pair—intimate friends of mine—were sitting on a sofa in their little bush cottage, one Sunday afternoon, when to their dismay, they beheld a black snake, about five feet in length, leisurely wriggle from beneath the sofa, into an adjoining bedroom. My male friend immediately ran out of the room for some weapon, to despatch the unwelcome intruder : leaving his wife to watch its movements ; but before he returned, the snake had disappeared. It was, however, killed that same evening, by a neighbour ; who kept watch outside the cottage, until he saw the snake emerge from beneath it, when he chopped its head off with a spade. My friend after that occurrence lost no time in plastering his cottage, and in carefully stopping every hole in the flooring, or fireplace, large enough to afford ingress to such loathsome visitors. Persons living in bush houses, will do well to follow my friend's example and stop every hole in their walls, or floors ; which can easily be done with a little management even in the most rudely constructed habitations.

*   *   *   *   *   *

A young gentleman, (with whom I was well acquainted), one morning, took up his cap, from the place where he had left it the previous night, when to his surprise, he found a small snake coiled up inside it. I am not quite sure whether he had put the cap on his head *before* he saw the snake inside it ; but I do feel sure, that he did not put it on his head, *after* he saw its ugly tenant, until he had given it summary notice to quit ; and had assured himself, more certainly than by bonds and covenants, that it would never get into his cap again.

*   *   *   *   *   *

I was travelling on horseback, one sultry day, through a part of the bush to the north, that I had never travelled before, when I overtook a man on foot, who offered to put me upon what he called "a short cut" to the place to which I was going. As the man walked beside me, he treated me to the horrifying details of a murder which had been committed sometime before, in a deep creek, into which we had just began to descend. "Here you are, sir, this is the very spot where the murdered man was found," continued my garrulous informant, as I reined up my horse and got off his back, to allow him to drink from the pure cool stream. The banks of the creeks were precipitous ; and the dense umbrageous foliage above and around totally excluded the sunshine. Not a solitary stray beam could pierce through the tangled masses of vines and creepers ; and even dull daylight itself could scarcely find its way to the bottom. " Well," I remarked, " this is the sort of place I should expect a murderer to select for his dreadful work ; where he would not be very liable to be intruded upon."

" It has been called ' Dead-man's Creek' ever since that murder ;" said my informant, as a wind-up to the sanguinary tale, which he had told with such scrupulous regard to minute particulars, that I almost feared he would want to give me a practical illustration of the exact way in which the poor victim's head was cut off.

I was very glad when he had finished his story, for I never was fond of tales of murder ; and that awful recital by a strange man, in such a gloomy spot, was particularly uninteresting.

My horse had finished drinking, and I was about to sit down on the gnarled roots of a tree, which was close beside me ; when to my horror I saw, what appeared to me to be a cluster of snakes coiled up, on the very spot where I had intended to seat myself. I hastened up the opposite bank of the creek, tied my horse to a tree, and aided by the man, broke a small sapling short off by the roots, then descended the bank of the creek again, and forced the jagged end of the sapling down on the reptile, when it slowly uncoiled itself, and dropped into the pool of water beneath, from which, after some difficulty, I dragged it ashore, and killed it. It was a diamond snake, rather more than twelve feet in length, and was in a state of repletion ; having but a short time before, swallowed a kangaroo rat. The details of that cruel murder, and my escape from sitting on that formidable reptile, have impressed "Dead-man's creek" vividly on my memory.

I could write a long chapter, horrible enough to scare a soldier, about wonderful escapes from " tremendous snakes" of which I have been told. By-the-bye, most of the snakes *that escape* and that, of course, are never measured are of *enormous dimensions ;* and the same remark applies to sharks, and many other terrible things, that travellers frequently talk about. I have heard too, some hair-raising stories of snakes being found in beds, and *under* beds ; in bonnet boxes, in flour bags, in chests with Sunday clothes, or coiled up in a stockman's empty boots, or in the pocket of a farmer's great coat, which hung against the wall of his slab hut. Although many of those stories are quite authentic, I shall not relate them in detail; for I do not wish to intimidate my young readers. It is very far from my desire to create bugbears, or to encourage pusillanimity in any form. I only wish in giving a few examples, to induce ordinary prudence in guarding against accidents from those deadly reptiles.

I once met with a gentleman in the interior, (a new arrival,) who had such a horror of snakes, that he would scarcely stir out of his house, on foot, after dark ; and even in daylight he walked through the bush in nervous trepidation. He had heard " travellers tell strange tales," of the dangers of the bush from the prevalence of deadly reptiles, until he had got a settled dread on his mind, which was excessively painful to him, but which he could not reason away. He seemed surprised and somewhat relieved, when I told him, that although I had been more than twenty years in the colony, and had lived much of that time in the interior, that I had not seen a hundred snakes. I owned that I probably might have seen many more if I had specially searched for them, for on one occasion, I went out with my gun and my pointer dogs, on a sultry afternoon, to the margin of a small lagoon, not more than a mile from a country town, and there shot seven or eight black snakes, in about two hours. But that locality was notoriously infested with those reptiles.

Pedestrians should look carefully to their feet, when travelling on a hot day in the vicinity of swamps, lagoons, or drains, as snakes particularly inhabit such localities, and they often come out of their hiding places, and lie in the footpaths, for like cats they are fond of basking in the sunshine. They will, however, generally wriggle away as fast as they can, on the approach of a human being, although on several occasions, a snake has reared its head, and glared on me with its basilisk-like eyes, and has not attempted to flee, while I kept my eyes upon it, but the instant I have turned for the purpose of picking up a stick, it has attempted to escape at its utmost speed.

I have seen a bold bushman go close up to a snake, and strike its head with the hammer head of his riding whip, but that was certainly running an unnecessary risk, and I have always preferred a tolerably long stick as my weapon in such encounters. Snakes are easily disabled, one or two smart blows are sufficient, but they are as tenacious of life as silver eels, and bushmen have a tradition, that "snakes never die till sundown."

It is best to approach them in front, as they are apt to spring backwards upon an assailant, though they cannot spring forward, and in general they cannot creep so fast but even a lazy man might easily get out of their way. I have heard of snakes attacking persons, but I never saw one do so, and those that I have seen, have seemed glad to get away from me. Vicious animals in general have a fear of man which deters them from assailing him, unless they are incited to it by provocation or in self-defence, and the most noxious species of reptiles have generally some distinguishing characteristics by which their hurtful properties may be known, and counteracted. In that we see a mark of God's providential care for us.

I repeat my declaration. I have not seen one hundred live snakes during over a quarter of a century; and I have not known of *one* fatal case of snake poisoning, within my own circle of friends and acquaintances. That may be rather surprising to those persons who fancy our fine continent is dangerously overrun with those loathsome reptiles.

But there is, alas ! a *black snake*, terribly prevalent, which is caressed by thousands of persons in this land; though many of them know from personal or family experience that it is far more dangerous than the deaf adder. I mean the " dram bottle." That is the snake which has desolated hundreds of homes, and sent thousands of poor souls to ruin ; that has done infinitely more mischief in this fine country than all the snakes in the bush.

I have seen the serpent — intemperance — writhe its treacherous way into many happy households, and first fascinate, then crush within its powerful folds the most promising members of the family. I have seen the hope of a respectable house—a fine, broad browed youth—his father's pride, and his mother's idol ; upon whose education the fond old pair had lavished their hardly earned little hoard ; I have seen that beloved boy's fine intellect vitiated, his once athletic frame palsied and wasted, and with sorrow I add, that I have stood upon the graves of the suicide son and his broken-hearted parents.

I have seen a sunny-hearted little child grow up to girl-hood, and fall a victim to the fascinating influence of intemperance. With aching heart I have marked her rapid decline from the paths of innocence and virtue, to vice, poverty, disease, and an agonising death; long before she had reached life's meridian.

I have seen a decrepit, grey-headed widow groping her way through life in penury and grief. I knew her in former days, when she was rich in this world's goods, and blessed with an industrious husband, who walked with her to the house of God. But, alas! in an evil hour he fell a victim to the world's great curse; and now he fills a drunkard's grave, while his poor old helpless widow is left to mourn in hopeless sorrow.

I have seen——But ah! I dare not write more on this harrowing subject; for well-remembered faces rise up from the dead before my mental gaze; and my heart sickens at the dreadful contemplation.

Boys and girls! beware of snakes! beware of snakes! But especially beware of the last one I have alluded to, of which I lack words sufficiently strong to express my horror.

THE END.

* * * "It is moral in its tone. There is not a bitter line in it, and we trust the warnings it contains will answer the benevolent intentions of its author." * * *—BATHURST FREE PRESS.

* * * "The book is really of much merit."—FREEMAN'S JOURNAL, SYDNEY.

* * * "We feel assured that this little work is calculated to effect much good." * * *—MAITLAND MERCURY.

* * * "The object of the book is good, and we wish it every success. It is admirably printed, and got up in a style, a credit to the publishers." * *—WESTERN POST, MUDGEE.

* * * "Full of incident, life and truths, for none of the incidents are in the slightest degree improbable. * * * A deep and good purpose shines throughout the volume." * * —NEWCASTLE CHRONICLE.

* * * "Written in such an amusing and instructive style as cannot fail to command a large circulation." * * * *— SYDNEY ILLUSTRATED NEWS.

* * * "It is well written, and embraces many scenes which are rich and racy." * * *—SYDNEY TIMES.

* * * "There are lessons in the work which old and young in the mother country, and in the colonies, need to be taught. * * The book ought to be—we hope it will be —circulated by tens of thousands." * * *—P. M. MESSENGER.

"Old Boomerang needs no introduction to our readers. His sketches are familiar to most Australian homes. They have found their way into cosy city parlours; they have circulated among scattered hamlets; they have broken the monotony of the squatter's home, and beguiled the loneliness of the shepherd's hut. * * * Quaint, humorous, full of grotesque fancies, and full, too, of wit and wisdom, with here and there touches of pathos and tones of warning; the sketches of this fertile old scribe have gone forth far and wide over the land, and made the name of Old Boomerang a household word."—CHRISTIAN ADVOCATE.

"This book—albeit its somewhat peculiar title—will be found to repay perusal. It has both wit and wisdom to commend it. The characters are well drawn, and the descriptions of scenery very picturesque. * * * We commend it to our young men."—CHRISTIAN REVIEW, MELBOURNE.

' * * * "Our author has managed to produce a volume which in a remarkable degree unites amusement and instruction. We cannot imagine any one reading it through who does not laugh and cry, and almost in the same breath." * * —MELBOURNE WESLEYAN CHRONICLE.

"We can assure our readers that they who buy the book will not regret the small outlay of capital necessary." * * * —SOUTH AUSTRALIAN WESLEYAN MAGAZINE.

* * "A noteworthy addition to works of fiction of Australian production." * * *—AUSTRALASIAN.

* * * "It reminds us of some of Albert Smith's works. * * We are thankful for Tim Rafferty. He is a funny dog." * * *—MELBOURNE AGE.

* * * "It is well able to stand on its own merits, as a book of its peculiar class." * *—HOBART TOWN MERCURY.

* * * "We can commend it to the perusal of readers who admire and appreciate a combination of wit and wisdom artistically put together." * * *—LAUNCESTON EXAMINER.

* * * "Possessing literary merits such as will give it permanent value."—LAUNCESTON TIMES.

* * * "Old Boomerang will be found in every emigrant ship, and in many an Australian home ; dispelling sorrow by his quaint humour, and teaching the weary and desponding to cheer up, and profit by his colonial experience."—ROCKHAMPTON BULLETIN.

* * * "We feel assured that those who will devote a few hours of the coming winter evenings in perusing the adventures of Christopher Cockle, will find much to amuse and instruct." * * *—ILLAWARRA MERCURY.

* * "The work abounds with wit, humour, and cogent observations on men and manners, and cannot fail to interest readers of all kinds." * * *—BATHURST TIMES.

* * * " The dialogue is animated, and the descriptions are true to nature. The moral tone of the work is admirable, and it is calculated to impart to home readers much useful information on Australia." * * *—MAITLAND ENSIGN.

* * * " It is a thoroughly readable book, and deserves extensive patronage. * * * The entire work is pervaded by a spirit of purest morality, without one scintillation of cant enthusiasm, moroseness, or bigotry." * * *—SINGLETON TIMES.

BILLING, PRINTER, GUILDFORD.

Crown Buildings, 188, Fleet Street,
London, October, 1874.

SAMPSON LOW, MARSTON & CO.'S
NEW BOOKS FOR THE
SEASON, 1874-5.

∗※∗

BIDA'S FOUR GOSPELS, WITH THE WHOLE OF THE ORIGINAL ETCHINGS.

As promised last year, the Publishers beg to announce

THE GOSPEL OF ST. MATTHEW,
CONTAINING FORTY-ONE ETCHINGS.

Price to Purchasers of the FOUR VOLUMES, *when published, £3 3s., and also to Non-Subscribers until the 1st of February next; after which date the price of this Volume, in consequence of the extra number of Engravings, will be raised to £4 4s.*

∗∗∗ THE GOSPEL OF ST. JOHN, *containing* 27 *Etchings, price* £3 3s., can also now be had.

Now Ready, in One Volume atlas quarto, handsomely bound in cloth extra gilt edges, £3 13s. 6d.

MASTERPIECES OF THE
PITTI PALACE,
AND OTHER PICTURE GALLERIES OF FLORENCE,
WITH SOME ACCOUNT OF THE ARTISTS AND THEIR PAINTINGS.

TO those who have had the good fortune to visit the Picture Galleries of Florence, it is unnecessary to speak of the glories of painting that hang on those wonderful walls. They have, for many centuries, attracted the homage of all men possessing a knowledge of art, and among the thousands who have annually crowded those galleries, there must be many to whom this volume will be very welcome; first, as a memento of the pleasure they experienced while looking at the triumphs of the great painters of Italy; and secondly, as the most perfect record which can be obtained of these celebrated works.

The twenty pictures now presènted were photographed direct from the Original Paintings, by the well-known artists, Alinar Brothers of Florence, *expressly for this work.* The impressions are untouched, showing, it is true, the blemishes which time has made, but rendering faithfully the beauty and charm of the originals in every particular save colour.

In One Volume, Royal 8vo., cloth extra, numerous Woodcuts, Maps, and Chromolithographs, 35s.

THE SECOND NORTH GERMAN POLAR EX-
PEDITION IN THE YEAR 1869-70
Of the Ships "Germania" and "Hansa," under command of Captain Koldeway,

Edited and condensed by H. W. BATES, ESQ., of the Royal Geographical Society, and translated by LOUIS MERCIER, M. A. (Oxon.)

The narrative portion of this important work is full of interest and extraordinary adventure in the ice-fields; and, in addition to much matter of great scientific value, gives a graphic account of the hardships and sufferings of the crew of the "Hansa" after the crushing of that ship in the ice.

*This Collection of Reproductions from Choice and Rare proofs represents,
in perfect facsimile, Engravings, the aggregate value of which
is certainly not less than Twelve Hundred Guineas.
Imperial folio, cloth extra, price £3 13s. 6d.*

OLD MASTERS.

DA VINCI, BARTOLOMEO, MICHAEL ANGELO, ROMAGNA,
DEL SARTO, CORREGGIO, PARMIGIANO, CARACCI,
GUIDO, DOMENICHINO, GUERCINO, BAROCCIO,
VOLTERRA, ALLORI, MARATTI, AND
CARLO DOLCI.

REPRODUCED IN PHOTOGRAPHY FROM THE CELEBRATED ENGRAVINGS BY
LONGHI, ANDERLONI, GARAVAGLIA, TOSCHI, AND RAIMONDI, IN
THE COLLECTION OF PRINTS AND DRAWINGS IN THE
BRITISH MUSEUM, WITH BIOGRAPHICAL NOTICES.

BY STEPHEN THOMPSON.

FLEMISH AND FRENCH PICTURES.

WITH NOTES CONCERNING THE PAINTERS AND THEIR
WORKS BY F. G. STEPHENS,

AUTHOR OF "FLEMISH RELICS," "MEMOIRS OF SIR EDWIN LANDSEER," ETC.

Small 4to. cloth extra, bevelled boards, gilt sides, back, and edges, 28s.

This Volume contains twenty Etchings by famous modern French en-
gravers, taken from well-known pictures, most of which are in the private
galleries of amateurs distinguished by their love of art.
The names of Rembrandt, Frank Hals, Watteau, and Greuze, of past
time, and of Troyon, Baron Leys, Meissonier, and Madame Henriette
Browne, of the present century, are household words in England; though it
is seldom that on this side of the Channel we meet with good transcripts of
their work. The exhibition of the magnificent collection of Sir Richard
Wallace has done more than anything else to popularize the best French Art
among us; and two annual exhibitions of French pictures in London—one of
which has flourished for nearly twenty years—have familiarized Englishmen
with the rich genius and diverse styles of modern celebrated French and ·
Belgian painters. The older schools of the Low Countries are better known
through their masterpieces in the National Gallery.

THE PICTURE GALLERY.

CONTAINING THIRTY-EIGHT PERMANENT PHOTOGRAPHS
AFTER THE WORKS OF THE MOST POPULAR ARTISTS.

The New Volume is now ready. Large 4to. cloth extra, gilt edges, 18s.

WARBURTON'S JOURNEY ACROSS
AUSTRALIA.

An Account of the Exploring Expedition sent out by Messrs. Elder and
Hughes, under the command of Colonel Egerton Warburton; giving a full
Account of his perilous Journey from the centre to Roebourne, Western
Australia. With Illustrations and a Map. Edited, with an Introductory
Chapter, by H. W. BATES, ESQ., of the Royal Geographical Society.
[In the Press.

Demy 8vo. numerous Illustrations, cloth extra.

TURKISTAN.

NOTES OF A JOURNEY IN THE RUSSIAN PROVINCES OF CENTRAL ASIA AND THE KHANATES OF BOKHARA AND KOKAND.

BY EUGENE SCHUYLER, Secretary of American Legation, St. Petersburg.

A MANUAL OF PRECIOUS STONES AND ANTIQUE GEMS.

BY HODDER M. WESTROPP, Author of "The Traveller's Art Companion," "Pre-Historic Phases," &c.

Small post 8vo., numerous Illustrations, cloth extra, 6s.

The Death of the Great Historian will not affect the Completion of this Important Work.

**** *Volumes I. to III. are now ready, and it would be difficult to select any more useful or appropriate work for a Christmas Present.*

A POPULAR HISTORY OF FRANCE, FROM THE EARLIEST TIMES.

By M. GUIZOT, Author of "The History of Civilization in Europe," &c.

WITH NUMEROUS ILLUSTRATIONS BY A. DE NEUVILLE.

Translated by ROBERT BLACK, M.A.

Volumes I. to III., royal 8vo., cloth extra, each 24s., now ready.
(Volume IV. is in progress.)

The *Times* says:—"M. Guizot possesses pre-eminently the historic faculty. For the past there are few guides so trustworthy, and none who interpret history more faithfully than the illustrious author of 'The History of Civilization.' He lifts the mind to heights of history. He unfolds it as a drama, which interests young and old. The careful study of such a work as Guizot's 'France' is an important element in culture and training. It is impossible to over-estimate the importance of a history where facts are chosen to illustrate principles and enforce great truths; where there is a continuous protest in favour of liberty, whether political, intellectual, or religious, and where good and evil are not tampered with to suit party purposes, but the historian is as impartial and open to the reception of truth as he hopes to make the students who follow his pages. The work supplies a want which has long been felt, and it ought to be in the hands of all students of history. We cannot doubt that it will meet with the same favourable reception in England which has already attended its publication in France."

CRUSTS. A SETTLER'S FARE DUE SOUTH; OR, LIFE IN NEW ZEALAND.

BY LAURENCE J. KENNAWAY.

Crown 8vo., Illustrations by the Author, cloth extra, 5s.

BRYANT'S POPULAR HISTORY OF THE UNITED STATES.
A POPULAR HISTORY OF THE UNITED STATES.

By WILLIAM CULLEN BRYANT, ASSISTED BY SYDNEY HOWARD GAY.

To be profusely Illustrated with numerous Engravings on Steel and Wood, after designs by the best artists.

Messrs. SAMPSON LOW and Co. beg to announce that they have arranged with the American publishers for the simultaneous publication of a Popular History of the United States by William Cullen Bryant, assisted by Sydney Howard Gay. The work is to begin with the earliest authentic history of the Western Continent—though not ignoring the earlier mythical period—and to come down to the close of the first century of American Independence. It will occupy four or five volumes, and is to be profusely and largely illustrated from original designs.

The aim of the publishers and authors is to supply a want which has long been felt by the reading public, and is well understood by booksellers. Admirable histories of America, of the United States, of different portions of both, and of many distinguished men whose lives at one time or another have helped to make those histories, have been written, and are familiar to scholars. Some of them cover one period and some another ; and some are more, some less, full and exhaustive. But a popular history, in the true sense of that term, one that shall be instructive through the sense of sight as well as through the labour of perusal ; one which is sought for by that immense number of readers with whom literature is not a profession, but who choose to be well informed in the history of their own and other countries, however much their lives may be absorbed in other pursuits—a popular history of this sort, compendious and not appalling from its size, accurate without being tedious, and one that at the same time shall be attractive by its appeal to the love of the picturesque and the artistic, has as yet no existence. Such it is meant Bryant's "History" shall be, and the name of that distinguished author is an assurance of its success.

LAOCOON;
AN ESSAY UPON THE LIMITS OF PAINTING AND POETRY, WITH REMARKS ILLUSTRATIVE OF VARIOUS POINTS IN THE HISTORY OF ANCIENT ART.

By GOTTHOLD EPHRAIM LESSING.

A new translation by ELLEN FROTHINGHAM, crown 8vo., cloth extra, 5s.

Crown 8vo., cloth extra, price 10s. 6d.
TE ROU; OR, THE MAORI AT HOME.

A TALE. Exhibiting the Social Life, Manners, Habits, and Customs of the Maori Race in New Zealand prior to the introduction of civilization amongst them.

By JOHN WHITE, *Native Interpreter, Auckland; formerly Resident Magistrate at Wanganui, and Native Land Purchase Commissioner.*

New Work by REV. EDWARD BICKERSTETH.
THE SHADOWED HOME,
AND THE LIGHT BEYOND.

NOTICE.—*An entirely New Edition at a lower price.*
PLUTARCH'S LIVES.

An entirely new and Library Edition, Edited by A. H. CLOUGH, ESQ. 5 vols. 8vo., £2 10s. ; half morocco, top gilt, £3.

NOVEL BINDING.

Printed in colours and enamelled, quite smooth, and free from finger-marks and adhesiveness.

THE ROSE LIBRARY.

POPULAR LITERATURE OF ALL COUNTRIES.

HIS Series has been commenced with the view of presenting to English readers *in the cheapest possible form*, works by the best writers in *English, American, French, and German* popular literature. The works chosen being intended for family reading, and for readers of all ages, it is almost needless to say that the greatest care will be taken in the selection, so that nothing shall be introduced which is not calculated to amuse innocently, to interest, and to instruct. Owing to the doubtful reputation which French literature has (in many instances quite deservedly) obtained in this country, it has become a fashion to exclude it wholly from the family library. In so doing, we hope to prove by our selection that many English readers have thus been shut out from a source of amusement and instruction quite as innocent and pure as is to be found in the literature of any country.

One of the special features of this series, which, it is hoped, will commend itself to all readers, is its price, which will rarely exceed

ONE SHILLING EACH VOLUME.

Another special and attractive feature is that many of the volumes will contain

NUMEROUS FULL-PAGE AND SMALLER ILLUSTRATIONS.

The following Volumes are now ready.

I. SEAGULL ROCK.

By JULES SANDEAU, of the French Academy. Translated by Robert Black, M.A.

**** *This little volume contains many of the Illustrations which are in the handsome Edition published two years ago.*

"A story more fascinating, more replete with the most frolicing fun, the most harrowing scenes of suspense, distress, and hair-breadth escapes from danger, was seldom before written, published, or read."—*Athenæum.*

"It deserves to please the new nation of boys to whom it is presented."—*Times.*

"The very best French story for children we have ever seen."—*Standard.*

"A delightful treat."—*Illustrated London News.*

"Admirable, full of life, pathos, and fun. . . . . . It is a striking and attractive book."—*Guardian.*

N.B.—A few copies of the best Edition, printed on toned large paper and in large type, beautifully bound, 7s. 6d., still on hand.

II. LITTLE WOMEN.

By LOUISA M. ALCOTT.

The Rose Library—*continued.*

III. LITTLE WOMEN WEDDED.

(Forming a Sequel to the above.)

NOTICE.—The immense popularity which immediately followed the first introduction of this work (originally published as one consecutive story) by the present publishers, led other publishers to appropriate it, divide into *two* shilling volumes under titles quite unauthorized by the author, and then puff them off as a marvel of cheapness. The present volumes, and others which the present publishers propose to issue, will certainly compete with any such surreptitious issues, not only in quality, but in price. On this subject we beg to add a quotation from the *Spectator :—*

"We may be allowed to add that Messrs. Low's is the 'Author's edition.' We do not commonly make these announcements, but everyone is bound to defeat, as far as he can, the efforts of those enterprising persons who proclaim with much unction the sacred duty of *not* letting an American author get his proper share of profits."

IV. THE HOUSE ON WHEELS; OR, FAR FROM HOME.

By MADAME DE STOLZ.
With numerous very graphic Full-Page Illustrations.

V. LITTLE MEN.
By LOUISA M. ALCOTT.

VI. THE OLD-FASHIONED GIRL.
By LOUISA M. ALCOTT.

NOTICE.—These two volumes, being copyright, cannot be reproduced, as "Little Women," has been, by any other house. The public and the trade will therefore see the advantage of purchasing Miss Alcott's four volumes in one uniform series.

‡ *New copyright work by the Author of "Arthur Bonnycastle."*
VII. THE MISTRESS OF THE MANSE.

By J. G. HOLLAND ("Timothy Titcomb"), Author of "Arthur Bonny-castle," &c.   [*This work is copyright.*

VIII. TIMOTHY TITCOMB'S LETTERS TO YOUNG PEOPLE, SINGLE AND MARRIED.

NOTICE.—The Volumes in this Series are also published in a more expensive form on fine-toned paper, cloth extra, gilt edges, at 2*s.* 6*d.* or 3*s.* 6*d.* each, according to size, &c.

In Two Volumes, crown 8vo., cloth extra, 21*s.*
AN HISTORICAL AND STATISTICAL ACCOUNT OF NEW SOUTH WALES.

Fourth Edition, thoroughly revised, bringing the history and condition of the colony down to the year 1874, with an Account of the recent remarkable Mineral Discoveries of Gold, Copper, and Tin in its Territories.

By JOHN DUNMORE LANG, D. D., A. M., *recently one of the Representatives of the City of Sydney, in the Parliament of New South Wales, &c.*

New Work, uniform with the 7s. 6d. Edition of Verne's Works.

THE FANTASTIC HISTORY OF THE CELEBRATED PIERROT;

Written by the Magician Alcofribas, and translated from the Sogdien by ALFRED ASSOLLANT, with upwards of One Hundred humorous Illustrations by YAN' DARGENT. Square crown 8vo., cloth extra, gilt edges, 7s. 6d.

"Terribly thrilling and absolutely harmless."—*Times.*

JULES VERNE'S WONDERFUL BOOKS,

"M. Verne exaggerates scientific possibilities into romance in a way so natural and charming that even sober men and women are fascinated by his extravagance."—*British Quarterly Review.*

"These tales are very popular in France, and as the love of the marvellous is no stronger in French than in English boys, they will, no doubt, be well appreciated by the latter, especially as they are full of pictures."—*Times.*

Two new books by Jules Verne.

A FLOATING CITY AND THE BLOCKADE RUNNERS.

Containing Fifty very fine Full-Page Illustrations. Square crown 8vo., cloth, gilt edges, 7s. 6d.

DR. OX'S EXPERIMENT; MASTER ZACHARIUS; A DRAMA IN THE AIR; A WINTER AMID THE ICE, &c.

Numerous Full-Page Illustrations. Cloth, gilt edges, 7s. 6d.
See Alphabetical List for rest of Verne's Works.

NEW NOVELS.

HARRY HEATHCOTE OF GANGOIL.

A Story of Bush Life in Australia. By ANTHONY TROLLOPE. In one Volume, with graphic Illustrations, crown 8vo., cloth extra, 10s. 6d.

THE VILLAGE SURGEON.

A Fragment of Autobiography. By ARTHUR LOCKER, Author of "Sweet Seventeen," "Stephen Scudamore," "On a Coral Reef," &c. One Volume crown 8vo., cloth, 10s. 6d.

OVER THE HILLS AND FAR AWAY.

By C. EVANS, Author of "A Strange Friendship." One Volume, crown 8vo., cloth extra, 10s. 6d.

THE MASTERS OF CLAYTHORPE.

By the Author of "Only Eve." Three Volumes, crown 8vo., cloth, 31s. 6d.

OUT OF THE WORLD. A Novel.

By MARY HEALY, Author of "Lake Ville," "A Summer's Romance," &c. Three Volumes, crown 8vo., cloth extra, 31s. 6d.

A ROMANCE OF ACADIA TWO CENTURIES AGO.

From a Sketch by the late CHARLES KNIGHT. In Three Volumes, crown 8vo., 31s. 6d.

Crown Buildings, 188, *Fleet Street*,
London, October, 1874.

A List of Books

PUBLISHING BY

SAMPSON LOW, MARSTON, LOW, & SEARLE.

ALPHABETICAL LIST.

**BBOTT (J. S. C.) History of Frederick the Great,** with numerous Illustrations. 8vo. 1*l*. 1*s*.

About in the World, by the author of "The Gentle Life." Crown 8vo. bevelled cloth, 4th edition. 6*s*.

Adamson (Rev. T. H.) The Gospel according to St. Matthew, expounded. 8vo. 12*s*.

Adventures of a Young Naturalist. By LUCIEN BIART, with 117 beautiful Illustrations on Wood. Edited and adapted by PARKER GILLMORE. Post 8vo. cloth extra, gilt edges, new edition, 7*s*. 6*d*.

Adventures of a Brownie. See Craik, Mrs.

Adventures on the Great Hunting Grounds of the World, translated from the French of Victor Meunier, with engravings, 2nd edition. 5*s*.

"The book for all boys in whom the love of travel and adventure is strong. They will find here plenty to amuse them and much to instruct them besides."—*Times*.

Aikin-Kortright (Fanny.) A Little Lower than the Angels. Small post 8vo., cloth extra. 3*s*. 6*d*.

Alcott, (Louisa M.) Aunt Jo's Scrap-Bag. Square 16mo, 3*s*. 6*d*.

———— **Cupid and Chow-Chow.** Small post 8vo. 3*s*. 6*d*.

———— **Little Men : Life at Plumfield with Jo's Boys.** By the author of " Little Women." Small post 8vo. cloth, gilt edges, 3*s*. 6*d*. Cheap edition, cloth, 2*s*. ; fancy boards, 1*s*. 6*d*.

———— **Little Women. Complete in 1 vol. fcap. 3*s*. 6*d*.** Cheap edition, 2 vols. cloth, 2*s*. ; boards, 1*s*. 6*d*. each.

———— **Old Fashioned Girl,** best edition, small post 8vo. cloth extra, gilt edges, 3*s*. 6*d*. ; Low's Copyright Series, 1*s*. 6*d*. ; cloth, 2*s*.

Alcott, (Louisa M.) Work. A Story of Experience. New Edition. In One volume, small post 8vo., cloth extra. 6*s.* Several Illustrations.

—— **Shawl Straps.** Small post 8vo. Cl. extra, gilt, 3*s. 6d.*

Alexander (Sir James E.) Bush Fighting. Illustrated by Remarkable Actions and Incidents of the Maori War. With a Map, Plans, and Woodcuts. 1 vol. demy 8vo. pp. 328, cloth extra, 16*s.*

Alexander (W. D. S.) The Lonely Guiding Star. A Legend of the Pyrenean Mountains and other Poems. Fcap. 8vo. cloth. 5*s.*

Amphlett (John.) Under a Tropical Sky: a Holiday Trip to the West Indies. Small post 8vo., cloth extra. 7*s. 6d.*

Andersen (Hans Christian) The Story of My Life. 8vo. 10*s. 6d.*

—— **Fairy Tales,** with Illustrations in Colours by E. V. B. Royal 4to. cloth. 1*l.* 5*s.*

Andrews (Dr.) Latin-English Lexicon. 13th edition. Royal 8vo. pp. 1,670, cloth extra. Price 18*s.*

"The best Latin Dictionary, whether for the scholar or advanced student."—*Spectator.*
" Every page bears the impress of industry and care."—*Athenæum.*

Anecdotes of the Queen and Royal Family, collected and edited by J. G. Hodgins, with Illustrations. New edition, revised by John Timbs. 5*s.*

Angell (J. K.) A Treatise on the Law of Highways. 8vo. Second Edition. 1*l.* 5*s.*

Anglo-Scottish Year Book, The, for 1874. By Robert Kempt. A Handbook of the Patriotic Institutions, Learned and Social Societies, Clubs, &c., in London, connected with Scotland, number of Members, place and date of Meeting. Fcap. 8vo. 1*s.*

Arctic Regions (The). Illustrated. *See* **Bradford.**

—— **German Polar Expedition.** *See* **Koldeway.**

—— **Explorations.** *See* **Markham.**

Art, Pictorial and Industrial, Vol. 1, 1*l.* 11*s.* 6*d.* Vols. and 3, 18*s.* each.

Ashton (Frederick T.) The Theory and Practice of the Art of Designing Fancy Cotton and Woollen Cloths from Sample. With fifty-two Illustrations. Folio. 2*l.* 10*s.*

Atmosphere (The). *See* Flammarion.

Auerbach (Berthold). Waldfried. Translated from the German. 3 vols. crown 8vo. 31*s.* 6*d.*

Australian Tales, by the " Old Boomerang." Post 8vo. 5*s.*

 " an Autobiography. By E. DYNE FENTON, Author of " Sorties from ' Gib ' in Quest of Sensation and Sentiment," " Eve's Daughters," &c. 3 vols. crown 8vo. 31*s.* 6*d.*

BACK-LOG Studies. *See* Warner.

Backward Glances. Edited by the Author of " Episodes in an Obscure Life." Small post 8vo., cloth extra. 5*s.*

Baldwin (J. D.) Prehistoric Nations. 12mo. 4*s.* 6*d.*

———— Ancient America, in notes of American Archæology. Crown 8vo. 10*s.* 6*d.*

Bancroft's History of America. Library edition, vols. 1 to 9, 8vo. 5*l.* 8*s.*

———— History of America, Vol. X. (completing the Work.) 8vo. 12*s.* [*In the press.*

Barber (E. C.) The Crack Shot. Post 8vo. 8*s.* 6*d.*

Barnes's (Rev. A.) Lectures on the Evidences of Christianity in the 19th Century. 12mo. 7*s.* 6*d.*

Barnum (P. T.) Struggles and Triumphs. Crown 8vo. Fancy boards. 2*s.* 6*d.*

Barrington (Hon. and Rev. L. J.) From Ur to Macpelah ; the Story of Abraham. Crown 8vo., cloth, 5*s.*

THE BAYARD SERIES. Comprising Pleasure Books of Literature produced in the Choicest Style as Companionable Volumes at Home and Abroad.

Price 2s. 6d. each Volume, complete in itself, printed at the Chiswick Press. bound by Burn, flexible cloth extra, gilt leaves, with silk Headbands and Registers.

The Story of the Chevalier Bayard. By M. DE·BERVILLE.

De Joinville's St. Louis, King of France.

The Essays of Abraham Cowley, including all his Prose Works.

Abdallah; or, the Four Leaves. By EDOUARD LABOULLAYE.

Table-Talk and Opinions of Napoleon Buonaparte.

Vathek: An Oriental Romance. By WILLIAM BECKFORD.

The King and the Commons: a Selection of Cavalier and Puritan Song. Edited by Prof. MORLEY.

Words of Wellington: Maxims and Opinions of the Great Duke.

Dr. Johnson's Rasselas, Prince of Abyssinia. With Notes.

Hazlitt's Round Table. With Biographical Introduction.

The Religio Medici, Hydriotaphia, and the Letter to a Friend. By Sir THOMAS BROWNE, Knt.

Ballad Poetry of the Affections. By ROBERT BUCHANAN.

Coleridge's Christabel, and other Imaginative Poems. With Preface by ALGERNON C. SWINBURNE.

Lord Chesterfield's Letters, Sentences and Maxims. With Introduction by the Editor, and Essay on Chesterfield by M. De Ste. Beuve, of the French Academy.

Essays in Mosaic. By THOS. BALLANTYNE.

My Uncle Toby; his Story and his Friends. Edited by P. FITZGERALD.

Reflections; or, Moral Sentences and Maxims of the Duke de la Rochefoucauld.

Socrates, Memoirs for English Readers from Xenophon's Memorabilia. By EDW. LEVIEN.

Prince Albert's Golden Precepts.

A suitable Case containing 12 volumes, price 31s. 6d.; or the Case separate, price 3s. 6d.

"We can hardly imagine a better book for boys to read or for men to ponder over."—*Times.*

Beecher (Henry Ward, D. D.) Life Thoughts. 12mo. 2s. 6d.

——— Sermons Selected. 12mo. 8s. 6d.

——— Norwood. Crown 8vo. 6s.

———(Dr. Lyman) Life and Correspondence of. 2 vols. post 8vo. 1l. 1s.

Bees and Beekeeping. By the Times' Beemaster. Illustrated. Crown 8vo. New Edition, with additions. 2s. 6d.

Bell (Rev. C. D.) Faith in Earnest. 18mo. 1*s.* 6*d.*

———— **Blanche Nevile.** Fcap. 8vo. 6*s.*

Bellows (A. J.) The Philosophy of Eating. Post 8vo. 7*s.* 6*d.*

———— **How not to be Sick, a Sequel to Philosophy of Eating.** Post 8vo. 7*s.* 6*d.*

Better than Gold. By Mrs. ARNOLD, Author of "His by Right," &c. In 3 volumes, crown 8vo., 31*s.* 6*d.*

Benedict (F. L.) Miss Dorothy's Charge. 3 vols. 31*s.* 6*d.*

Biart (L.) Adventures of a Young Naturalist. (See *Adventures.*)

Bickersteth's Hymnal Companion to Book of Common Prayer.

The following Editions are now ready :—

			s.	d.
No. 1. A Small-type Edition, medium 32mo. cloth limp			0	6
No. 1. B	ditto	roan limp, red edges ..	1	0
No. 1. C	ditto	morocco limp, gilt edges ..	2	0
No. 2. Second-size type, super-royal 32mo. cloth limp ..			1	0
No. 2. A	ditto	roan limp, red edges ..	2	0
No. 2. B	ditto	morocco limp, gilt edges ..	3	0
No. 3. Large-type Edition, crown 8vo. cloth, red edges ..			2	6
No. 3. A	ditto	roan limp, red edges ..	3	6
No. 3. B	ditto	morocco limp, gilt edges ..	5	6
No. 4. Large-type Edition, crown 8vo. with Introduction and Notes, cloth, red edges			3	6
No. 4. A	ditto	roan limp, red edges ..	4	6
No. 4. B	ditto	morocco, gilt edges ..	6	6
No. 5. Crown 8vo. with accompanying Tunes to every Hymn, New Edition			3	0
No. 5. A	ditto	with Chants	4	0
No. 5. B The Chants separately			1	6

No. 6. Penny Edition.
Fcap. 4to. Organists' edition. Cloth, 7*s.* 6*d.*

₊ *A liberal allowance is made to Clergymen introducing the Hymnal.*

☞ THE BOOK OF COMMON PRAYER, bound with THE HYMNAL COMPANION. 32mo. cloth, 9*d.* And in various superior bindings.

Bickersteth (Rev. E. H., M.A.) The Reef, and other Parables. One Volume square 8vo., with numerous very beautiful Engravings, uniform in character with the Illustrated Edition of Heber's Hymns, &c., price 7*s.* 6*d.*

Bickersteth (Rev. E. H., M.A.) The Master's Home-Call; Or, Brief Memorials of Alice Frances Bickersteth. 3rd Edition. 32mo. cloth gilt. 1s.

"They recall in a touching manner a character of which the religious beauty has a warmth and grace almost too tender to be definite."—*The Guardian.*

—— **The Shadow of the Rock. A Selection of Religious Poetry.** 18mo. Cloth extra. 2s. 6d.

Bida, The Authorized Version of the Four Gospels. With the whole of the magnificent etchings on steel, after the drawings by M. Bida.

It is intended to publish each Gospel separately, and at intervals of from six to twelve months ; and in order to preserve uniformity, the price will in the first instance be fixed at £3 3s. each volume, large imperial quarto. The Gospels of St. Matthew and St. Luke contain more etchings and more letterpress than St. Mark and St. John ; it must be understood that at the expiration of three months from the first issue of each of these two volumes, the price (if purchased separately) will be raised to four guineas. This extra charge will, however, be allowed at any time to all bonâ fide purchasers of the four volumes.

The Gospel of St. John, appropriately bound in cloth extra, price £3 3s., is now ready ; the first volume issued.

Bishop (J. L.) History of American Manufacture. 3 vols. 8vo. 2l. 5s.

—— **(J. P.) First Book of the Law.** 8vo. 1l. 1s.

Bits of Talk about Home Matters. By H. H. Fcap. 8vo. cloth gilt edges. 3s.

Black (Wm.) Uniform Editions :

—— **Kilmeny : a Novel.** Small Post 8vo. cloth. 6s.

—— **In Silk Attire.** 3rd and cheaper edition, small post 8vo. 6s.

"A work which deserves a hearty welcome for its skill and power in delineation of character."—*Saturday Review.*

——— **A Daughter of Heth.** 11th and cheaper edition, crown 8vo., cloth extra. 6s. With Frontispiece by F. Walker, A.R.A.

"If humour, sweetness, and pathos, and a story told with simplicity and vigour, ought to insure success, 'A Daughter of Heth' is of the kind to deserve it."—*Saturday Review.*

Black (C. B.) New Continental Route Guides.

—— **Guide to the North of France,** including Normandy, Brittany, Touraine, Picardy, Champagne, Burgundy, Lorraine, Alsace, and the Valley of the Loire ; Belgium and Holland ; the Valley of the Rhine to Switzerland ; and the South-West of Germany, to Italy by the Brenner Pass. Illustrated with numerous Maps and Plans. Crown 8vo., cloth limp. 9s. 6d.

Black (C. B.) New Continental Route Guides.

—— Guide to Normandy and Brittany, their Celtic Monuments, Ancient Churches, and Pleasant Watering-Places. Illustrated with Maps and Plans. Crown 8vo., cloth limp, 2*s.* 6*d.*

—— Guide to Belgium and Holland, the North-East of France, including Picardy, Champagne, Burgundy, Lorraine, and Alsace ; the Valley of the Rhine, to Switzerland ; and the South-West of Germany, to Italy, by the Brenner Pass, with Description of Vienna. Illustrated with Maps and Plans. Crown 8vo., cloth limp, 5*s.*

—— Paris, and Excursions from Paris. Illustrated with numerous Maps, Plans, and Views. Small post 8vo., cloth limp, price 3*s.*

—— Guide to the South of France and to the North of Italy : including the Pyrenees and their Watering-Places ; the Health Resorts on the Mediterranean from Perpignan to Genoa ; and the towns of Turin, Milan, and Venice. Illustrated with Maps and Plans. Small post 8vo., cloth limp, 5*s.*

—— Switzerland and the Italian Lakes. Small post 8vo. price 3*s.* 6*d.*

—— Guide to France, Corsica, Belgium, Holland, the Rhine, the Moselle, the South-West of Germany, and the North of Italy. With numerous Maps and Plans. Complete in One Volume. Limp cloth, price 15*s.*

—— Railway and Road Map of Switzerland, West Tyrol, and the Italian Lake Country. Boards, price 1*s.*

Blackburn (H.) Art in the Mountains : the Story of the Passion Play, with upwards of Fifty Illustrations. 8vo. 12*s.*

—— Artists and Arabs. With numerous Illustrations. 8vo. 7*s.* 6*d.*

—— Harz Mountains : a Tour in the Toy Country. With numerous Illustrations. 12s.

—— Normandy Picturesque. Numerous Illustrations. 8vo. 16*s.*

—— Travelling in Spain. With numerous Illustrations. 8vo. 16*s.*

—— Travelling in Spain. Guide Book Edition. 12mo. 2*s.* 6*d.*

—— The Pyrenees. Summer Life at French Watering-Places. 100 Illustrations by GUSTAVE DORÉ. Royal 8vo. 18*s.*

Blackmore (R. D.) Lorna Doone. New edition. Crown, 8vo. 6*s.*

"The reader at times holds his breath, so graphically yet so simply does John Ridd tell his tale . . . . 'Lorna Doone' is a work of real excellence, and as such we heartily commend it to the public."—*Saturday Review.*

Blackmore (R. D.) Cradock Nowell. 2nd and cheaper edition. 6*s*.

———— Clara Vaughan. Revised edition. 6*s*.

———— Georgics of Virgil. Small 4to. 4*s*. 6*d*.

Blackwell (E.) Laws of Life. New edition. Fcp. 3*s*. 6*d*.

Boardman's Higher Christian Life. Fcp. 1*s*. 6*d*.

Bonwick (J.) Last of the Tasmanians. 8vo. 16*s*.

———— Daily Life of the Tasmanians. 8vo. 12*s*. 6*d*.

———— Curious Facts of Old Colonial Days. 12mo. cloth. 5*s*.

Book of Common Prayer with the Hymnal Companion. 32mo. cloth. 9*d*. And in various bindings.

Books suitable for School Prizes and Presents. (Fuller description of each book will be found in the alphabet.)

Adventures of a Young Naturalist. 7*s*. 6*d*.
———— on Great Hunting Grounds. 5*s*.
Allcott's Aunt Jo's Scrap-bag. 3*s*. 6*d*.
———— Cupid and Chow Chow. 3*s*. 6*d*.
———— Old Fashioned Girl. 3*s*. 6*d*.
———— Little Women. 3*s*. 6*d*.
———— Little Men. 3*s*. 6*d*.
———— Shawl Straps. 3*s*. 6*d*.
Anecdotes of the Queen. 5*s*.
Atmosphere (The). By FLAMMARION. 30*s*.
Backward Glances. 5*s*.
Bickersteth (Rev. E. H.) Shadow of the Rock 2*s*. 6*d*.
Black (Wm.) Kilmeny. 6*s*.
———— In Silk Attire. 6*s*.
———— A Daughter of Heth. 6*s*.
Blackmore (R. D.) Cradock Nowell.
———— Clara Vaughan. 6*s*.
———— Lorna Doone. 6*s*. "
Burritt's Ten Minute Talk on all sorts of Topics. Sm. 8vo. 6*s*.
Butler's Great Lone Land. 7*s*. 6*d*.
Bayard Series (See Bayard.)
Changed Cross (The). 2*s*. 6*d*.
Child's Play. 7*s*. 6*d*.
Christ in Song. 5*s*.
Craik (Mrs.) Adventures of a Brownie. 5*s*.

Books for School Prizes and Presents, *continued—*

Craik (Mrs.) Little Sunshine's Holiday. 4*s.*
Craik (Miss) The Cousin from India. 4*s.*
—— Miss Moore. 4*s.*
Dana's Corals and Coral Islands. 21*s.*
—— Two Years before the Mast. 6*s.*
Davies's Pilgrimage of the Tiber. 18*s.*
De Witt (Mad.) An Only Sister. 4*s.*
Erkmann-Chatrian's, The Forest House. 3*s.* 6*d.*
Faith Gartney. 3*s.* 6*d.* cloth; boards, 1*s.* 6*d.*
Favell Children (The). 4*s.*
Favourite English Poems. 300 Illustration. 21*s.*
Forbes (J. G.) Africa: Geographical Exploration and Christian Enterprise. Crown 8vo. cloth. 7*s.* 6*d.*
Franc's Emily's Choice. 5*s.*
—— John's Wife. 4*s.*
—— Marian. 5*s.*
—— Silken Cord. 5*s.*
—— Vermont Vale 5*s*
—— Minnie's Mission.
Friswell (Laura) The Gingerbread Maiden. 3*s.* 6*d*
Gayworthys (The). 3*s.* 6*d.*
Gentle Life, (Queen Edition). 10*s.* 6*d.*
Gentle Life Series. (*See* Alphabet).
Getting on in the World. 6*s.*
Glover's Light of the Word. 2*s.* 6*d.*
Hayes (Dr.) Cast Away in the Cold. 6*s.*
Healy (Miss) The Home Theatre. 3*s.* 6*d.*
Henderson's Latin Proverbs. 10*s.* 6*d.*
Hugo's Toilers of the Sea. 10*s.* 6*d.*
   „   „   „   6*s.*
Jack Hazard, by Trowbridge. 3*s.* 6*d.*
Kingston's Ben Burton. 3*s.* 6*d.*
Kennan's Tent Life. 6*s.*
King's Mountaineering in the Sierra Nevada.
Low's Edition of American Authors. 1*s.* 6*d.* and 2*s.* each. 23 Vols. published. *See* Alphabet under Low.
Lyra Sacra Americana. 4*s.* 6*d.*
Macgregor (John) Rob Roy Books. (*See* Alphabet.)
Marigold Manor, by Miss Waring. 4*s.*
Maury's Physical Geography of the Sea 6*s.*
Parisian Family. 5*s.*
Phelps (Miss) The Silent Partner. 5*s.*
Picture Gallery British Art. 12*s.*

Books for School Prizes and Presents, *continued*—

    Picture Gallery Sacred Art. 12s.
    Ready, O Ready. By Captain Allston, R.N. 3s. 6d.
    Reynard the Fox. 100 Exquisite Illustrations. 7s. 6d.
    Sea-Gull Rock. 79 Beautiful Woodcuts. 7s. 6d.
    Stanley's How I Found Livingstone. 21s.
    Stowe (Mrs.) Pink and White Tyranny. 3s. 6d.
    ———— Old Town Folks. Cloth extra 6s. and 2s. 6d.
    ———— Minister's Wooing. 5s. ; boards, 1s. 6d.
    ———— Pearl of Orr's Island. 5s.
    ———— My Wife and I. 6s.
    Tauchnitz's German Authors. *See* Tauchnitz.
    Tayler (C. B.) Sacred Records. 2s. 6d.
    Titcomb's Letters to Young People. 1s. 6d. and 2s.
    Twenty Years Ago. 4s.
    Under the Blue Sky. 7s. 6d.
    Verne's Meridiana. 7s. 6d.
    ———— Twenty Thousand Leagues Under the Sea. 10s. 6d.
    Whitney's (Mrs.) Books. *See* Alphabet.

Bowles (T. G.) The Defence of Paris, narrated as it was Seen. 8vo. 14s.

Bowker (G.) St. Mark's Gospel. With Explanatory Notes. For the Use of Schools and Colleges. By GEORGE BOWKER, late Second Master of the Newport Grammar School, Isle of Wight. 1 vol. foolscap, cloth.

Boynton (Charles B., D.D.) Navy of the United States, with Illustrations of the Ironclad Vessels. 8vo. 2 vols. 2l.

Bradford (Wm.) The Arctic Regions. Illustrated with Photographs, taken on an Art Expedition to Greenland. With Descriptive Narrative by the Artist. In One Volume, royal broadside, 25 inches by 20, beautifully bound in morocco extra, price Twenty-five Guineas.

Bremer (Fredrika) Life, Letters, and Posthumous Works. Crown 8vo. 10s. 6d.

Brett (E.) Notes on Yachts. Fcp. 6s.

Bristed (C. A.) Five Years in an English University. Fourth Edition, Revised and Amended by the Author. Post 8vo. 10s. 6d.

Broke (Admiral Sir B. V. P., Bart., K.C.B.) Biography of. 1l.

Brothers Rantzau. *See* Erckmann Chatrian.

Browning (Mrs. E. B.) The Rhyme of the Duchess May. Demy 4to. Illustrated with Eight Photographs, after Drawings by Charlotte M. B. Morrell. 21s.

Burritt (E.) The Black Country and its Green Border Land. Second edition. Post 8vo. 6*s*.

———— **A Walk from London to Land's End.** Cr. 8vo. 6*s*.

———— **Lectures and Speeches.** Fcap. 8vo. cloth, 6*s*.

———— **Ten-Minute Talk on all sorts of Topics.** With Autobiography of the Author. Small post 8vo., cloth extra. 6*s*.

Bush (R. J.) Reindeer, Dogs, and Snow Shoes. 8vo. 12*s*. 6*d*.

Bushnell's (Dr.) The Vicarious Sacrifice. Post 8vo. 7*s*. 6*d*.

———— **Sermons on Living Subjects.** Crown 8vo. cloth. 7*s*. 6*d*.

———— **Nature and the Supernatural.** Post 8vo. 3*s*. 6*d*.

———— **Christian Nurture.** 3*s*. 6*d*.

———— **Character of Jesus.** 6*d*.

———— **The New Life.** Crown 8vo. 3*s*. 6*d*

Butler (W. F.) The Great Lone Land; an Account of the Red River Expedition, 1869-1870, and Subsequent Travels and Adventures in the Manitoba Country, and a Winter Journey across the Saskatchewan Valley to the Rocky Mountains. With Illustrations and Map. Fifth and Cheaper Edition. Crown 8vo. cloth extra. 7*s*. 6*d*. (The first 3 Editions were in 8vo. cloth. 16*s*.) •

———— **The Wild North Land:** the Story of a Winter Journey with Dogs across Northern North America. Demy 8vo. cloth, with numerous Woodcuts and a Map. Fourth Edition. 18*s*.

ADOGAN (Lady A.) Illustrated Games of Patience. By the LADY ADELAIDE CADOGAN. Twenty-four Diagrams in Colours, with Descriptive Text. Foolscap 4to., cloth extra, gilt edges, 12*s*. 6*d*.

California. *See* **Nordhoff.**

Canada on the Pacific: being an account of a journey from Edmonton to the Pacific, by the Peace River Valley. By Charles Horetzky. Cloth. 5*s*.

Carlisle (Thos.) The Unprofessional Vagabond. Fcap. 8vo. Fancy boards. 1*s*.

Ceramic Art. *See* **Jacquemart.**

Changed Cross (The) and other Religious Poems. 2*s*. 6*d*.

Child's Play, with 16 coloured drawings by E. V. B. An entirely new edition, printed on thick paper, with tints, 7*s*. 6*d*.

Chefs-d'œuvre of Art and Master-pieces of Engraving, selected from the celebrated Collection of Prints and Drawings in the British Museum. Reproduced in Photography by STEPHEN THOMPSON. Imperial folio, Thirty-eight Photographs, cloth gilt. 4*l.* 14*s.* 6*d.*

China. *See* Illustrations of.

Christ in Song. Hymns of Immanuel, selected from all Ages, with Notes. By PHILIP SCHAFF, D.D. Crown 8vo. toned paper, beautifully printed at the Chiswick Press. With Initial Letters and Ornaments and handsomely bound. New Edition. 5*s.*

Christabel. *See* **Bayard Series.**

Christmas Presents. *See* Illustrated Books.

Chronicles of Castle of Amelroy. 4to. With Photographic Illustrations. 2*l.* 2*s.*

Clara Vaughan. *See* **Blackmore.**

Coffin (G. C.) Our New Way Round the World. 8vo. 12*s.*

Commons Preservation (Prize Essays on), written in competition for Prizes offered by HENRY W. PEEK, Esq. 8vo. 14*s.*

Conquered at Last; from Records of Dhu Hall and its Inmates; A Novel. 3 vols. Crown ; cloth. 31*s.* 6*d.*

Cook (D.) Young Mr. Nightingale. A Novel. 3 vols. Crown 8vo., cloth. 31*s.* 6*d.*

Courtship and a Campaign; a Story of the Milanese Volunteers of 1866, under Garibaldi. By M. DALIN. 2 vols. cr. 8vo. 21*s.*

Cradock Nowell. *See* **Blackmore.**

Craik (Mrs.) The Adventures of a Brownie, by the Author of " John Halifax, Gentleman." With numerous Illustrations by Miss PATERSON. Square cloth, extra gilt edges. 5*s.*
A Capital Book for a School Prize for Children from Seven to Fourteen.

—— **Little Sunshine's Holiday** (forming Vol. 1. of the John Halifax Series of Girls' Books). Small post 8vo. 4*s.*

—— **John Halifax Series.** *See* **Girls' Books.**

—— **Poems.** Crown, cloth, 5*s.*

—— **(Georgiana M.) The Cousin from India,** forming Vol. 2. of John Halifax Series. Small post 8vo. 4*s.*

—— **Only a Butterfly.** One Volume, crown 8vo., cloth, 10*s.* 6*d.*

—— **Miss Moore.** Small post 8vo., with Illustrations, gilt edges. 4*s.*

—— **Without Kith or Kin.** 3 vols. crown 8vo., 31*s.* 6*d.*

—— **Hero Trevelyan.** 2 Vols. Post 8vo. 21*s.*

Craik's American Millwright and Miller. With numerous Illustrations. 8vo. 1*l*. 1*s*.

Cruise of "The Rosario. *See* Markham (A. H.)

Cummins (Maria S.) Haunted Hearts (Low's Copyright Series). 16mo. boards. 1*s*. 6*d*. ; cloth, 2*s*.

Curtis's History of the Constitution of the United States. 2 vols. 8vo. 24*s*.

DALTON (J. C.) A Treatise on Physiology and Hygiene for Schools, Families, and Colleges, with numerous Illustrations. 7*s*. 6*d*.

Dana (R. H.) Two Years before the Mast and Twenty-four years After. New Edition, with Notes and Revisions. 12mo. 6*s*.

Dana (Jas. D.) Corals and Coral Islands. Numerous Illustrations, charts, &c. Royal 8vo. cloth extra. 21*s*.

"Professed geologists and zoologists, as well as general readers, will find Professor Dana's book in every way worthy of their attention." —*The Athenæum*, October 12, 1872.

Darley (Felix O. C.) Sketches Abroad with Pen and Pencil, with 84 Illustrations on Wood. Small 4to. 7*s*. 6*d*.

Daughter (A) of Heth, by WM. BLACK. Eleventh and Cheaper edition. 1 vol. crown 8vo. 6*s*.

Davies (Wm.) The Pilgrimage of the Tiber, from its Mouth to its Source ; with some account of its Tributaries. 8vo., with many very fine Woodcuts and a Map, cloth extra. 18*s*.

Devonshire Hamlets ; Hamlet 1603, Hamlet 1604. 1 Vol. 8vo. 7*s*. 6*d*.

De Witt (Madame Guizot). An Only Sister. Vol. V. of the "John Halifax" Series of Girls' Books. With Six Illustrations. Small post 8vo. cloth. 4*s*.

Dhow-Chasing. *See* Sulivan.

Draper (John W.) Human Physiology. Illustrated with more than 300 Woodcuts from Photographs, &c. Royal 8vo. cloth extra. 1*l*. 5*s*.

Dream Book (The) with 12 Drawings in facsimile by E. V. B. Med. 4to. 1*l*. 11*s*. 6*d*.

Duer's Marine Insurance. 2 vols. 3*l*. 3*s*.

Duplais and McKennie, Treatise on the Manufacture and Distillation of Alcoholic Liquors. With numerous Engravings. 8vo. 2*l*. 2*s*.

Duplessis (G.) Wonders of Engraving. With numerous Illustrations and Photographs. 8vo. 12*s*. 6*d*.

Dussauce (Professor H.) A New and Complete Treatise on the Art of Tanning. Royal 8vo. 2*l*. 10*s*.

—————— **General Treatise on the Manufacture of Vinegar.** 8vo. 1*l*. 1*s*.

**NGLISH Catalogue of Books (The) Published** during 1863 to 1871 inclusive, comprising also the Important American Publications.

This Volume, occupying over 450 Pages, shows the Titles of 32,000 New Books and New Editions issued during Nine Years, with the Size, Price, and Publisher's Name, the Lists of Learned Societies, Printing Clubs, and other Literary Associations, and the Books issued by them ; as also the Publisher's Series and Collections—altogether forming an indispensable adjunct to the Bookseller's Establishment, as well as to every Learned and Literary Club and Association. 30*s*. half-bound.

*** The previous Volume, 1835 to 1862, of which a very few remain on sale, price 2*l*. 5*s*.; as also the Index Volume, 1837 to 1857, price 1*l*. 6*s*.

—————— **Supplements,** 1863, 1864, 1865, 3*s*. 6*d*. each ; 1866, 1867 to 1872, 5*s*. each.

—————— **Writers, Chapters for Self-improvement in English** Literature ; by the author of "The Gentle Life." 6*s*.

—————— **Matrons and their Profession;** With some Considerations as to its Various Branches, its National Value, and the Education it requires. By M. L. F., Writer of " My Life, and what shall I do with it." " Battle of the Two Philosophies," and " Strong and Free." Crown 8vo., cloth, extra, 7*s*. 6*d*. [*Now ready*.

Erckmann - Chatrian. Forest House and Catherine's Lovers. Crown 8vo 3*s*. 6*d*.

—————— **The Brothers Rantzau: A Story of the Vosges.** 2 vols. crown 8vo. cloth. 21*s*. New Edition. 1 vol., profusely illustrated. Cloth Extra. 5*s*.

Evans (T. W.) History of the American Ambulance, Established in Paris during the Siege of 1870-71. Together with the Details of its Method and its Work. By THOMAS W. EVANS, M.D., D. D. S. Imperial 8vo., with numerous illustrations, cloth extra, price 35*s*.

AITH GARTNEY'S Girlhood, by the Author of "The Gayworthys." Fcap. with Coloured Frontispiece. 3*s*. 6*d*.

Favourite English Poems. New and Extended Edition, with 300 illustrations. Small 4to. 21*s*.

Favell (The) Children. Three Little Portraits. Crown 12mo. Four Illustrations. Cloth gilt. 4*s*.

" A very useful and clever story."—*John Bull*.

Few (A) Hints on Proving Wills. Enlarged Edition, sewed. 1*s*.

Field (M. B.) Memories of Many Men and of some Women. Post 8vo., cloth. 10s. 6d.

Fields (J. T.) Yesterdays with Authors. Crown 8vo. 10s. 6d.

Fleming's (Sandford) Expedition. *See* Ocean to Ocean.

Flammarion (C.) The Atmosphere. Translated from the French of CAMILLE FLAMMARION. Edited by JAMES GLAISHER, F.R.S., Superintendent of the Magnetical and Meteorological Department of the Royal Observatory at Greenwich. With 10 beautiful Chromo-Lithographs and 81 woodcuts. Royal 8vo. cloth extra, bevelled boards. 30s.

Forbes (J. G.) Africa: Geographical Exploration and Christian Enterprise, from the Earliest Times to the Present. By J. GRUAR FORBES. Crown 8vo., cloth extra, 7s. 6d.

Franc (Maude Jeane) Emily's Choice, an Australian Tale. 1 vol. small post 8vo. With a Frontispiece by G. F. ANGAS. 5s.

—— **John's Wife. A Story of Life in South Australia.** Small post 8vo., cloth extra. 4s.

—— **Marian, or the Light of Some One's Home.** Fcp. 3rd Edition, with Frontispiece. 5s.

—— **Silken Cords and Iron Fetters.** 5s.

—— **Vermont Vale.** Small post 4to., with Frontispiece. 5s.

—— **Minnie's Mission.** Small post 8vo., with Frontispiece. 4s.

Friswell (J. H.) *See* Gentle Life Series.

—— **One of Two.** 3 vols. 1l. 11s. 6d.

Friswell (Laura.) The Gingerbread Maiden; and other Stories. With Illustration. Square cloth. 3s. 6d.

GAYWORTHYS (The), a Story of New England Life. Small post 8vo. 3s. 6d.

Gems of Dutch Art. Twelve Photographs from finest Engravings in British Museum. Sup. royal 4to. cloth extra. 25s.

Gentle Life (Queen Edition). 2 vols. in 1. Small 4to. 10s. 6d.

THE GENTLE LIFE SERIES. Printed in Elzevir, on Toned Paper, handsomely bound, forming suitable Volumes for Presents. Price 6*s.* each; or in calf extra, price 10*s.* 6*d.*

The Gentle Life. Essays in aid of the Formation of Character of Gentlemen and Gentlewomen. Tenth Edition.

"Deserves to be printed in letters of gold, and circulated in every house."—*Chambers Journal.*

About in the World. Essays by the Author of "The Gentle Life."

"It is not easy to open it at any page without finding some handy idea."—*Morning Post.*

Like unto Christ. A New Translation of the "De Imitatione Christi" usually ascribed to Thomas à Kempis. With a Vignette from an Original Drawing by Sir Thomas Lawrence. Second Edition.

"Could not be presented in a more exquisite form, for a more sightly volume was never seen."—*Illustrated London News.*

Familiar Words. An Index Verborum, or Quotation Handbook. Affording an immediate Reference to Phrases and Sentences that have become embedded in the English language. Second and enlarged Edition.

"The most extensive dictionary of quotation we have met with."—*Notes and Queries.*

Essays by Montaigne. Edited, Compared, Revised, and Annotated by the Author of "The Gentle Life." With Vignette Portrait. Second Edition.

"We should be glad if any words of ours could help to bespeak a large circulation for this handsome attractive book."—*Illustrated Times.*

The Countess of Pembroke's Arcadia. Written by Sir PHILIP SIDNEY. Edited, with Notes, by the Author of "The Gentle Life." Dedicated, by permission, to the Earl of Derby. 7*s.* 6*d.*

"All the best things in the Arcadia are retained intact in Mr. Friswell's edition.—*Examiner.*

The Gentle Life. Second Series. Third Edition.

"There is not a single thought in the volume that does not contribute in some measure to the formation of a true gentleman."—*Daily News.*

Varia: Readings from Rare Books. Reprinted, by permission, from the *Saturday Review, Spectator,* &c.

"The books discussed in this volume are no less valuable than they are rare, and the compiler is entitled to the gratitude of the public. *Observer.*

The Silent Hour: Essays, Original and Selected. By the Author of "The Gentle Life." Second Edition.

"All who possess the 'Gentle Life' should own this volume."—*Standard.*

Essays on English writers, for the Self-improvement of Students in English Literature.

"To all (both men and women) who have neglected to read and study their native literature we would certainly suggest the volume before us as a fitting introduction."—*Examiner*.

Other People's Windows. By J. HAIN FRISWELL. Second Edition.

"The chapters are so lively in themselves, so mingled with shrewd views of human nature, so full of illustrative anecdotes, that the reader cannot fail to be amused."—*Morning Post*.

A Man's Thoughts. By J. HAIN FRISWELL.

German Primer; being an Introduction to First Steps in German. By M. T. PREU. 2s. 6d.

Getting On in the World; or, Hints on Success in Life. By WILLIAM MATHEWS, LL.D. Small post 8vo., cloth extra, bevelled edges. 6s.

Girdlestone (C.) Christendom. 12mo. 3s.

—————— **Family Prayers.** 12mo. 1s. 6d.

Glover (Rev. R.) The Light of the Word. Third Edition. 18mo. 2s. 6d.

Goethe's Faust. With Illustrations by Konewka. Small 4to. Price 10s. 6d.

Gouffé: The Royal Cookery Book. By JULES GOUFF , Chef-de-Cuisine of the Paris Jockey Club; translated and adapted for English use by ALPHONSE GOUFFÉ, head pastrycook to Her Majesty the Queen. Illustrated with large plates, beautifully printed in colours, together with 161 woodcuts. 8vo. Coth extra, gilt edges. 2l. 2s.

—————— Domestic Edition, half-bound. 10s. 6d.

"By far the ablest and most complete work on cookery that has ever been submitted to the gastronomical world."—*Pall Mall Gazette*.

—————— **The Book of Preserves;** or, Receipts for Preparing and Preserving Meat, Fish salt and smoked, Terrines, Gelatines, Vegetables, Fruits, Confitures, Syrups, Liqueurs de Famille, Petits Fours, Bonbons, &c. &c. By JULES GOUFFÉ, Head Cook of the Paris Jockey Club, and translated and adapted by his brother ALPHONSE GOUFFÉ, Head Pastrycook to her Majesty the Queen, translator and editor of "The Royal Cookery Book." 1 vol. royal 8vo., containing upwards of 500 Receipts and 34 Illustrations. 10s. 6d.

—————— **Royal Book of Pastry and Confectionery.** By JULES GOUFFÉ, Chef-de-Cuisine of the Paris Jockey Club. Translated from the French by ALPHONSE GOUFFÉ, Head Pastrycook to Her Majesty the Queen. Royal 8vo., illustrated with 10 Chromo-lithographs and 137 Woodcuts, from Drawings from Nature by E. Monjat, cloth extra, gilt edges, 35s.

Girls' Books. A Series written, edited, or translated by the
Author of "John Halifax." Small post 8vo., cloth extra, 4*s*. each.

    1. Little Sunshine's Holiday.
    2. The Cousin from India.
    3. Twenty Years Ago.
    4. Is it True.
    5. An Only Sister. By Madame GUIZOT DE WITT.
    6. Miss Moore.

Gospels (Four), with Bida's Illustrations. *See* Bida.

Gray (Robertson) Brave Hearts. Small post 8vo. 3*s*. 6*d*

Great Lone-Land. *See* Butler.

Grant (Rev. G. M.). *See* Ocean to Ocean.

Greenleaf's Law of Evidence. 13th Edition. 3 vols. 84*s*.

Guizot's History of France. Translated by ROBERT BLACK.
Royal 8vo. Numerous Illustrations. Vols. I., II. and III., cloth extra,
each 24*s*. ; in Parts, 2*s*. each (to be completed in two more volumes).

Guyon (Mad.) Life. By Upham. Third Edition. Crown
8vo. 6*s*.

———— Method of Prayer. Foolscap. 1*s*.

Guyot (A.) Physical Geography. By ARNOLD GUYOT,
Author of "Earth and Man." In 1 volume, large 4to., 128 pp., numerous coloured Diagrams, Maps and Woodcuts, price 10*s*. 6*d*., strong
boards.

HALE (E. E.) In His Name; a Story of the Dark
Ages. Small post 8vo., cloth, 3*s*. 6*d*.

Hacklander (F. W.) Military Life in Prussia.
First Series. The Soldier in Time of Peace. Translated (by
permission of the Author) from the German of F. W. Hācklander. By
F. E. R. and H. E. R. Crown 8vo., cloth extra, 9*s*.

Harrington (J.) Pictures of Saint George's Chapel, Windsor. Photographs. 4to. 63*s*.

Harrington's Abbey and Palace of Westminster. Photographs. 5*l*. 5*s*.

Harper's Handbook for Travellers in Europe and the
East. New Edition, 1874. Post 8vo. Morocco tuck, 1*l*. 11*s*. 6*d*.

Haswell (Chas. H.) The Engineers' and Mechanics'
Pocket-Book. 30th Edition, revised and enlarged. 12mo, morocco
tuck, 14*s*.

Harz Mountains. *See* Blackburn.

Hawthorne (Mrs. N.) Notes in England and Italy. Crown 8vo. 10*s*. 6*d*.

Hayes (Dr.) Cast Away in the Cold; an Old Man's Story of a Young Man's Adventures. By Dr. I. Isaac Hayes, Author of "The Open Polar Sea." With numerous Illustrations. Gilt edges, 6*s*.

—— The Land of Desolation; Personal Narrative of Adventures in Greenland. Numerous Illustrations. Demy 8vo., cloth extra. 14*s*.

Hazard (S.) Santo Domingo, Past and Present; With a Glance at Hayti. With upwards of One Hundred and Fifty beautiful Woodcuts and Maps, chiefly from Designs and Sketches by the Author. Demy 8vo. cloth extra. 18*s*.

Hazard (S.) Cuba with Pen and Pencil. Over 300 Fine Woodcut Engravings. New edition, 8vo. cloth extra. 15*s*.

Hazlitt (William) The Round Table; the Best Essays of William Hazlitt, with Biographical Introduction (Bayard Series). 2*s*. 6*d*.

Healy (M.) Lakeville. 3 vols. 1*l*. 11*s*. 6*d*.

—— A Summer's Romance. Crown 8vo., cloth. 10*s*. 6*d*.

—— The Home Theatre. Small post 8vo. 3*s*. 6*d*.

Henderson (A.) Latin Proverbs and Quotations; with Translations and Parallel Passages, and a copious English Index. By Alfred Henderson. Fcap. 4to., 530 pp. 10*s*. 6*d*.

Hearth Ghosts. By the Author of 'Gilbert Rugge.' 3 Vols. 1*l*. 11*s*. 6*d*.

Heber's (Bishop) Illustrated Edition of Hymns. With upwards of 100 Designs engraved in the first style of art under the superintendence of J. D. Cooper. Small 4to. Handsomely bound, 7*s*. 6*d*.

Higginson (T. W.) Atlantic Essays. Small post 8vo. 6*s*.

Hitherto. By the Author of "The Gayworthys." New Edition. cloth extra. 3*s*. 6*d*. Also in Low's American Series. Double Vol. 2*s*. 6*d*.

Hofmann (Carl) A Practical Treatise on the Manufacture of Paper in all its Branches. Illustrated by One Hundred and Ten Wood Engravings, and Five large Folding Plates. In One Volume, 4to, cloth ; about 400 pages. 3*l*. 13*s*. 6*d*.

Hoge—Blind Bartimæus. Popular edition. 1*s*.

Holland (Dr.) Kathrina and Titcomb's Letters. *See* Low's American Series.

Holmes (Oliver W.) The Guardian Angel; a Romance. 2 vols. 16*s.*

—————— (Low's Copyright Series.) Boards, 1*s.* 6*d.* ; cloth, 2*s.*

—————— **Autocrat of the Breakfast Table.** 12mo. 1*s.* ; Illustrated edition, 3*s.* 6*d.*

—————— **The Professor at the Breakfast Table.** 3*s.* 6*d.*

—————— **Songs in Many Keys.** Post 8vo. 7*s.* 6*d.*

—————— **Mechanism in Thought and Morals.** 12mo. 1*s.* 6*d.*

Homespun, or Twenty Five Years Ago in America, by Thomas Lackland. Fcap. 8vo. 7*s.* 6*d.*

Hoppin (Jas. M.) Old Country, its Scenery, Art, and People. Post 8vo. 7*s.* 6*d.*

Howell (W. D.) Italian Journeys. 12mo. cloth. 8*s.* 6*d.*

Hugo (Victor) "Ninety-Three." Translated by Frank Lee Benedict and J. Hain Friswell. In 3 vols., crown 8vo., cloth, 31*s.* 6*d.*

—————— **Toilers of the Sea.** Crown 8vo. 6*s.*; fancy boards, 2*s.* ; cloth, 2*s.* 6*d.* ; Illustrated Edition, 10*s.* 6*d.*

Hunt (Leigh) and S. A. Lee, Elegant Sonnets, with Essay on Sonneteers. 2 vols. 8vo. 18*s.*

—————— **Day by the Fire.** Fcap. 6*s.* 6*d.*

Huntington (J.D., D.D.) Christian Believing. Crown 8vo. 3*s.* 6*d.*

Hutchinson (T. J.) Two Years in Peru; with Exploration of its Antiquities. By Thomas J. Hutchinson. Map by Daniel Barrera, and numerous Illustrations. In 2 vols., demy 8vo., cloth extra. 28*s.*

Hymnal Companion to Book of Common Prayer. *See* Bickersteth.

ICE, a Midsummer Night's Dream. Small Post 8vo. 3*s.* 6*d.*

Illustrations of China and its People. By J. Thomson, F.R.G.S. Being Photographs from the Author's Negatives, printed in permanent Pigments by the Autotype Process, and Notes from Personal Observation.

*** The complete work embraces 200 Photographs, with Letter-press Descriptions of the Places and People represented. Four Volumes, imperial 4to., each £3 3*s.*

The Fourth Volume, completing the Work, ready this day.

N.B.—Her Majesty the Queen has been pleased to acknowledge her appreciation of this book by presenting the Author with a handsome Gold Medal as a memorial.

Illustrated Books, suitable for Christmas, Birthday, or Wedding Presents. (The full titles of which will be found in the Alphabet.)

Adventures of a Young Naturalist. 7s. 6d.
Alexander's Bush Fighting. 16s.
Anderson's Fairy Tales. 25s.
Arctic Regions. Illustrated. 25 guineas.
Art, Pictorial and Industrial. Vol. I. 31s. 6d.
Blackburn's Art in the Mountains. 12s.
—— Artists and Arabs. 7s. 6d.
—— Harz Mountains. 12s.
—— Normandy Picturesque. 16s.
—— Travelling in Spain. 16s.
—— The Pyrenees. 18s.
Bush's Reindeer, Dogs, &c. 12s. 6d.
Butler's Great Lone Land. 7s. 6d.
Chefs d'Œuvre of Art. 4l. 14s. 6d.
China. Illustrated. 4 vols. 3l. 3s. each vol.
Christian Lyrics.
Davies's Pilgrimage of the Tiber. 18s.
Dream Book, by E. V. B. 21s. 6d.
Duplessis' Wonders of Engraving. 12s. 6d.
Favourite English Poems. 21s.
Flammarion's The Atmosphere. 30s.
Fletcher and Kidder's Brazil. 18s.
Gœthe's Faust, illustrations by P. KONEWKA. 10s. 6d.
Gouffe's Royal Cookery Book. Coloured plates. 42s.
—— Ditto. Popular edition. 10s. 6d.
—— Book of Preserves. 10s. 6d.
Hazard's Santa Domingo. 18s.
—— Cuba. 15s.
Heber (Bishop) Hymns. Illustrated edition. 7s. 6d.
Jacquemart's History of the Ceramic Art. 42s.
Markham's Cruise of the Rosario. 16s.
Milton's Paradise Lost. (Martin's plates). 3l. 13s. 6d.
My Lady's Cabinet. 21s.
Ocean to Ocean. 10s. 6d.
Palliser (Mrs.) History of Lace. 21s.
—— Historic Devices, &c. 21s.
Peaks and Valleys of the Alps. 6l. 6s.
Pike's Sub-Tropical Rambles. 18s.
Red Cross Knight (The). 25s.
Sauzay's Wonders of Glass Making. 12s. 6d
Schiller's Lay of the Bell. 14s.
St. George's Chapel, Windsor.
Sulivan's Dhow Chasing. 16s.
The Abbey and Palace of Westminster. 5l. 5s.
Viardot, Wonders of Sculpture. 12s. 6d.
—— Wonders of Italian Art. 12s. 6d.
—— Wonders of European Art. 12s. 6d.
Werner (Carl) Nile Sketches. 2 Series, each 3l. 10s.

Index to the Subjects of Books published in the United Kingdom during the last 20 years. 8vo. Half-morocco. 1l. 6s.

Innocent. By Mrs. OLIPHANT. 3 Vols. Crown 8vo. cloth. 31s. 6d. Cheap Edition, 1 vol., 6s.

In the Isle of Wight. Two volumes, crown 8vo., cloth. 21*s.*

In Silk Attire. *See* Black, Wm.

Is it True? Being Tales Curious and Wonderful. Small post 8vo., cloth extra. 4*s.*

(Forming vol. 4 of the "John Halifax" Series of Girls' Books.)

ACK HAZARD, a Story of Adventure by J. T. TROWBRIDGE. Numerous illustrations, small post. 3*s.* 6*d.*

John Halifax Series of Girls' Books. *See* Girls' Books.

Jackson (H.) Argus Fairbairne; or, a Wrong Never Righted. By HENRY JACKSON, Author of "Hearth Ghosts," &c. Three volumes, crown 8vo., cloth, 31*s.* 6*d.*

Jacquemart (J.) History of the Ceramic Art: Descriptive and Analytical Study of the Potteries of all Times and of all Nations. By ALBERT JACQUEMART. 200 Woodcuts by H. Catenacci and J. Jacquemart. 12 Steel-plate Engravings, and 1,000 Marks and Monograms. Translated by Mrs. BURY PALLISER. In 1 vol., super royal 8vo., of about 700 pp., cloth extra, gilt edges, 42*s.*   [*Ready.*
"Altogether we think this is likely to be one of the most popular books of the season. It affords a happy instance of the union of taste and science, of learning and refinement, with a very distinct leaning towards the elegant aspect of the subject."—*Athenæum.*
"This is one of those few gift books which, while they can certainly lie on a table and look beautiful, can also be read through with real pleasure and profit."—*Times,* December 13.

Jessup (H. H.) The Women of the Arabs. With a Chapter for Children. By the Rev. HENRY HARRIS JESSUP, D.D., seventeen years American Missionary in Syria. Crown 8vo., cloth extra, 10*s.* 6*d.*

Johnson (R. B.) Very Far West Indeed. A few rough Experiences on the North-West Pacific Coast. Cr. 8vo. cloth. 10*s.* 6*d.* New Edition—the Fourth, fancy boards. 2*s.*

AVANAGH'S Origin of Language. 2 vols. crown 8vo. 1*l.* 1*s.*

Kedge Anchor, or Young Sailor's Assistant, by WM. BRADY. 8vo. 18*s.*

Kennan (G.) Tent Life in Siberia. 3rd edition. 6*s.*

Kent (Chancellor) Commentaries on American Law. 12th edition. 4 vols. 8vo. 5*l.*

Kilmeny. *See* Black (Wm.)

King (Clarence) Mountaineering in the Sierra Nevada.
crown 8vo. Third and Cheaper Edition, cloth extra. 6s.
> The *Times* of Oct. 20th says :—"If we judge his descriptions by
> the vivid impressions they leave, we feel inclined to give them very high
> praise."

**Kingston (W. H. G.) Ben Burton, or Born and Bred at
Sea.** Fcap. with Illustrations. 3s. 6d.

Kortright. See Aikin.

AKEVILLE. *See* Healy.

Land of the White Elephant. *See* Vincent.

Lang (J. D.) The Coming Event. 8vo. 12s.

Lascelles (Arthur) The Coffee Grower's Guide. Post 8vo.
2s. 6d.

**L'Estrange (Sir G. B.) Recollections of Sir George
B. L'Estrange,** late of the 31st Regiment, and afterwards in
the Scots Fusilier Guards. With Heliotype reproductions of
Drawings by Officers of the Royal Artillery—the Peninsula War. 8vo.,
cloth extra. 14s.

**Lee (G. R.) Memoirs of the American Revolutionary
War.** 8vo. 16s.

Little Men. *See* Alcott.

Little Preacher. 32mo. 1s.

Little Women. See Alcott.

Little Sunshine's Holiday. *See* Craik (Mrs.)

Log of my Leisure Hours. By an Old Sailor. Cheaper
Edition. Fancy boards. 2s.

Longfellow (H. W.) The Poets and Poetry of Europe.
New Edition. 8vo. cloth. 1l. 1s.

Loomis (Elias). Recent Progress of Astronomy. Post 8vo.
7s. 6d.

—————— **Practical Astronomy.** 8vo. 10s.

Low's Minion Series of Popular Books. 1s. each :—
The Gates Ajar. (The original English Edition.)
Who is He?
The Little Preacher.
The Boy Missionary.

Low's Copyright and Cheap Editions of American Authors, comprising Popular Works, reprinted by arrangement with their Authors :—

1. Haunted Hearts. By the Author of " The Lamplighter."
2. The Guardian Angel. By " The Autocrat of the Breakfast Table."
3. The Minister's Wooing. By the Author of " Uncle Tom's Cabin.
4. Views Afoot. By BAYARD TAYLOR.
5. Kathrina, Her Life and Mine. By J. G. HOLLAND.
6. Hans Brinker: or, Life in Holland. By Mrs. DODGE.
7. Men, Women, and Ghosts. By Miss PHELPS.
8. Society and Solitude. By RALPH WALDO EMERSON.
9. Hedged In. By ELIZABETH PHELPS.
10. An Old-Fashioned Girl. By LOUISA M. ALCOTT.
11. Faith Gartney.
12. Stowe's Old Town Folks. 2s. 6d.; cloth, 3s.
13. Lowell's Study Windows.
14. My Summer in a Garden. By CHARLES DUDLEY WARNER.
15. Pink and White Tyranny. By Mrs. STOWE.
16. We Girls. By Mrs. WHITNEY.
17. Little Men. By Miss ALCOTT.
18. Little Women. By Miss ALCOTT.
19. Little Women Wedded. (Forming the Sequel to " Little Women.")
20. Back-Log Studies. By CHARLES DUDLEY WARNER, Author of " My Summer in a Garden."

  " This is a delightful book."—*Atlantic Monthly*.

21. Timothy Titcomb's Letters to Young People, Single and Married.

*** Of this famous little work upwards of 50,000 have been sold in America alone at four times the present price, viz. 1s. 6d. flexible fancy boards ; 2s. cloth extra.

22. Hitherto. By Mrs. T. D. WHITNEY. Double Volume, 2s. 6d. fancy flexible boards.

*** This Copyright work was first published in this country in 3 vols. at 31s. 6d. ; afterwards in 1 vol. at 6s. It is now issued in the above popular Series.

23. Farm Ballads. by Will. Carleton, price ONE SHILLING.

The *Guardian* says of " Little Women," that it is " a bright, cheerful, healthy story—with a tinge of thoughtful gravity about it which reminds one of John Bunyan. Meg going to Vanity Fair is a chapter written with great cleverness and a pleasant humour."

The *Athenæum* says of " Old-Fashioned Girl" : " Let whoever wishes to read a bright, spirited, wholesome story get the ' Old-Fashioned Girl' at once."

*** " We may be allowed to add, that Messrs. Low's is the ' Author's edition.' We do not commonly make these announcements, but every one is bound to defeat, as far as he can, the efforts of those enterprising persons who proclaim with much unction the sacred duty of *not* letting an American author get his proper share of profits."—*Spectator*, Jan. 4, 1873.

Each volume complete in itself, price 1s. 6d. enamelled flexible cover, 2s. cloth.

Low's Monthly Bulletin of American and Foreign Publications, forwarded regularly. Subscription 2s. 6d. per annum.

LOW'S STANDARD NOVELS.

Six Shillings Each.

 DAUGHTER of Heth. By W. BLACK. Eleventh and Cheaper Edition, crown 8vo., cloth extra, 6s. With Frontispiece by F. WALKER, A. R. A.

By the Same Author,

Kilmeny: a Novel. Small post 8vo., cloth, 6s.

In Silk Attire. Third and Cheaper Edition. Small post 8vo., 6s.

Lorna Doone. By R. D. BLACKMORE. New Edition. Crown 8vo., 6s.

By Same Author,

Cradock Nowell. Second and Cheaper Edition. Revised, 6s.

By Same Author,

Clara Vaughan. Revised Edition, 6s.

Innocent : a Tale of Modern Life. By Mrs. OLIPHANT. Eight full-page illustrations. Small post 8vo., cloth extra, 6s. [*Now ready.*

Work: a Story of Experience. By LOUISA M. ALCOTT. New Edition, small post 8vo., cloth, 6s. Illustrations.

Mistress Judith : a Cambridgeshire Story. By C. C. FRASER-TYTLER, Author of "Jasmine Leigh." A New and Cheaper Edition, small post 8vo., cloth extra, 6s. [*This day.*
"We do not remember ever to have read a story more perfect of its kind than 'Mistress Judith.'"—*Athenæum.*

Low's Handbook to the Charities of London for 1874. Edited and Revised to February, 1874, by CHARLES MACKESON, F.S.S., Editor of "A Guide to the Churches of London and its Suburbs," &c. Price 1s.

Ludlow (FitzHugh). The Heart of the Continent. 8vo. cloth. 14s.

Lunn (J. C.) Only Eve. 3 vols. 31s. 6d.

Lyne (A. A.) The Midshipman's Trip to Jerusalem. With illustration. Third Edition. Crown 8vo., cloth. 10s. 6d.

Lyra Sacra Americana. Gems of American Poetry, selected and arranged, with Notes and Biographical Sketches, by C. D. CLEVELAND, D. D., author of the "Milton Concordance." 18mo. 4s. 6d.

 AC GAHAN (J. A.) Campaigning on the Oxus and the Fall of Khiva. With Map and numerous Illustrations. Demy 8vo., cloth extra, 16s.

Macgregor (John,) "Rob Roy" on the Baltic. Third Edition, small post 8vo. 2s. 6d.

Macgregor (John). A Thousand Miles in the "Rob Roy" Canoe. Eleventh Edition. Small post, 8vo. 2s. 6d.

—— Description of the "Rob Roy" Canoe, with plans, &c. 1s.

—— The Voyage Alone in the Yawl "Rob Roy." Second Edition. Small post, 8vo. 5s.

Mahony (M. F.) A Chronicle of the Fermors; Horace Walpole in Love. By M. F. MAHONY, (Matthew Stradling), Author of "The Misadventures of Mr. Catlyn," &c. In 2 volumes, demy 8vo., with steel portrait. 24s.

Manigault, The Maid of Florence; or, a Woman's Vengeance. 3s. 6d.

March (A.) Anglo-Saxon Reader. 8vo. 7s. 6d.

—— Comparative Grammar of the Anglo-Saxon Language. 8vo. 12s.

Marcy (R. B.) Thirty Years of Army Life. Royal 8vo. 12s.

—— Prairie and Overland Traveller. 2s. 6d.

Marigold Manor. By Miss WARING. With Introduction by Rev. A. SEWELL. With Illustrations. Small Post 8vo. 4s.

Markham (A. H.) The Cruise of the "Rosario" amongst the New Hebrides and Santa Cruz Islands, exposing the Recent Atrocities connected with the Kidnapping of Natives in the South Seas. By A. H. MARKHAM, Commander, R.N. 8vo. cloth extra, with Map and Illustrations. 16s.

—— A Whaling Cruise to Baffin's Bay and the Gulf of Boothia. With an Account of the Rescue, by his Ship, of the Survivors of the Crew of the "Polaris;" and a Description of Modern Whale Fishing. Together with numerous Adventures with Bears, &c. With Introduction by Admiral SHERARD OSBORN. Demy 8vo., cloth extra, 2 Maps and several Illustrations, 18s.

Markham (C. R.) The Threshold of the Unknown Region. Demy 8vo. with Maps and Illustrations. 16s.

⁂ The object of this Work is to give the public a correct knowledge of the whole line of frontier separating the known from the unknown region round the North Pole.

Marlitt (Miss) The Princess of the Moor. Tauchnitz Translations.

—— Origin and History of the English Language. 8vo. 16s.

—— Lectures on the English Language. 8vo. 15s.

Martin's Vineyard. By Agnes Harrison. Crown 8vo. cloth. 10s. 6d.

Matthews (Wm.) *See* Getting on in the World.

Maury (Commander) Physical Geography of the Sea and its Meteorology. Being a Reconstruction and Enlargement of his former Work; with illustrative Charts and Diagrams. New Edition. Crown 8vo. 6s.

May (J. W.) A Treatise on the Law of Insurance. Third Edition. 8vo. 38s.

Mayo (Dr.) *See* **Never Again.**

McMullen's History of Canada. 8vo. 16s.

Mercier (Rev. L.) Outlines of the Life of the Lord Jesus Christ. 2 vols. crown 8vo. 15s.

Meridiana. *See* **Verne.**

Michell (N.) The Heart's Great Rulers, a Poem, and Wanderings from the Rhine to the South Sea Islands. Fcap. 8vo. 3s. 6d.

Milton's Complete Poetical Works; with Concordance by W. D. CLEVELAND. New Edition. 8vo. 12s.; morocco 1l. 1s.

———— Paradise Lost, with the original Steel Engravings of JOHN MARTIN. Printed on large paper, royal 4to. handsomely bound. 3l. 13s. 6d.

Miss Dorothy's Charge. By FRANK LEE BENEDICT, Author of "My Cousin Elenor." 3 vols. crown 8vo. 31s. 6d.

Missionary Geography (The); a Manual of Missionary Operations in all parts of the World, with Map and Illustrations. Fcap. 3s. 6d.

Mistress Judith. A Cambridgeshire Story. By C. C. FRASER-TYTLER, Author of "Jasmine Leigh." A New and Cheaper Edition. In one volume, small post 8vo., cloth extra. 6s.

"We do not remember ever to have read a story more perfect of its kind than ' Mistress Judith.' "—*Athenæum.*

" We can only simply say it is admirable."—*Morning Post.*

" We will not spoil the reader's interest in such a simple and touching tale as this, by setting before him a bare statement of its course and ending."—*Graphic.*

Monk of Monk's Own. 3 vols. 31s. 6d.

Montaigne's Essays. *See* **Gentle Life Series.**

Morgan's Macaronic Poetry. 16mo. 12s.

Mother Goose's Melodies for Children. Square 8vo., cloth extra. 7s. 6d.

Mountain (Bishop) Life of. By his Son. 8vo. 10s. 6d.

My Summer in a Garden. See **Warner.**

My Cousin Maurice. A Novel. 3 vols. Cloth, 31s. 6d.

My Lady's Cabinet. Charmingly Decorated with Lovely Drawings and Exquisite Miniatures. Contains Seventy-five Pictures. Royal 4to., and very handsomely bound in cloth. 1l. 1s.

"'The fittest ornament for a Lady's Cabinet which this season has produced."—*Athenæum.*

" Forms an excellent pretty book for the drawing-room table."—*Pall Mall Gazette.*

" A very pretty idea, carried out with much taste and elegance."—*Daily News.*

My Lady's Boudoir for 1874, containing numerous choice
gems of Art. 4to., cloth extra. 21s.

My Wife and I. *See* Mrs. Stowe.

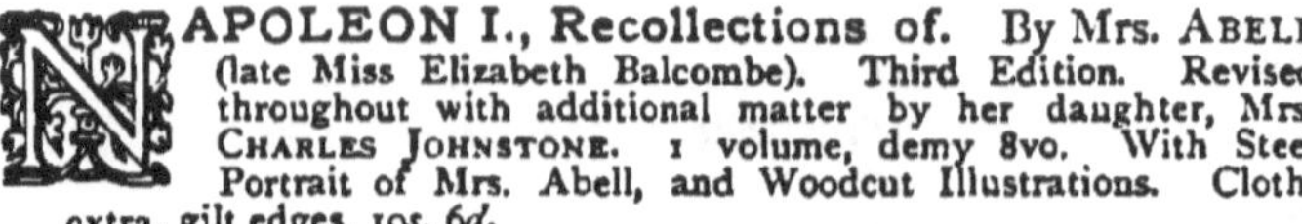

APOLEON I., Recollections of. By Mrs. ABELL
(late Miss Elizabeth Balcombe). Third Edition. Revised
throughout with additional matter by her daughter, Mrs.
CHARLES JOHNSTONE. 1 volume, demy 8vo. With Steel
Portrait of Mrs. Abell, and Woodcut Illustrations. Cloth,
extra, gilt edges, 10s. 6d.

Napoleon III. in Exile: The Posthumous Works and Unpublished Autographs. Collected and arranged by COUNT DE LA
CHAPELLE, Coadjutor in the last Works of the Emperor at Chislehurst.
1 volume, demy 8vo., cloth extra. 14s.

Narrative of Edward Crewe, The. Personal Adventures
and Experiences in New Zealand. Small post 8vo., cloth extra. 5s.

Never Again: a Novel. By Dr. MAYO, Author of "Kaloo-
lah." New and Cheaper Edition, in One Vol., small post 8vo. 6s.
Cheapest edition, fancy boards, 2s.
    "Puts its author at once into the very first rank of novelists."
—*The Athenæum.*

New Testament. The Authorized English Version ; with the
various Readings from the most celebrated Manuscripts, including the
Sinaitic, the Vatican, and the Alexandrian MSS., in English. With
Notes by the Editor, Dr. TISCHENDORF. The whole revised and carefully collected for the Thousandth Volume of Baron Tauchnitz's Collection. Cloth flexible, gilt edges, 2s. 6d. ; cheaper style, 2s. ; or sewed,
1s. 6d.

Noel (Hon. Roden) Livingstone in Africa; a Poem.
By the Hon. RODEN NOEL, Author of "Beatrice," &c. Post 8vo., limp
cloth extra, 2s. 6d.

Nordhoff (C.) California : for Health, Pleasure, and Residence. A Book for Travellers and Settlers. Numerous Illustrations,
8vo., cloth extra. 12s. 6d.

—— Northern California, Oregon, and the Sandwich
Islands. Square 8vo., cloth extra, price 12s.

Nothing to Wear, and Two Millions. By WILLIAM
ALLEN BUTLER. 1s.

Nystrom's Mechanic's Pocket Book. 12th edition. 18s.

CEAN to Ocean. Sandford Fleming's Expedition
through Canada in 1872. Being a Diary kept during a
Journey from the Atlantic to the Pacific with the Expedition
of the Engineer-in-Chief of the Canadian Pacific and Inter-
colonial Railways. By the Rev. GEORGE M. GRANT, of
Halifax, N.S., Secretary to the Expedition. With Sixty Illustrations.
Demy 8vo., cloth extra, pp. 372. 10s. 6d.

Old Fashioned Girl. See Alcott.

Oliphant (Mrs.) Innocent. A Tale of Modern Life. By Mrs. OLIPHANT, Author of "The Chronicles of Carlingford," &c., &c. With Eight full-page Illustrations. Small post 8vo., cloth extra. 6s.

One Only; A Novel. By Eleanor C. PRICE. 2 vols. Crown 8vo., cloth, 21s.

Only Eve. By Mrs. J. CALBRAITH LUNN, Three Vols. post 8vo. cloth. 31s. 6d.

Other Girls (The). See Whitney (Mrs.)

Our American Cousins at Home. By VERA, Author of "Under the Red Cross." Illustrated with Pen and Ink Sketches, by the Author, and several fine Photographs. Crown 8vo, cloth. 9s.

Our Little Ones in Heaven. Edited by Rev. H. ROBBINS. With Frontispiece after Sir JOSHUA REYNOLDS. Second Edition. Fcap. 3s. 6d.

PALLISER (Mrs.) A History of Lace, from the Earliest Period. A New and Revised Edition, with upwards of 100 Illustrations and coloured Designs. 1 vol. 8vo. 1l. 1s.

"One of the most readable books of the season; permanently valuable, always interesting, often amusing, and not inferior in all the essentials of a gift book."—*Times*.

———— **Historic Devices, Badges, and War Cries.** 8vo. 1l. 1s.

———— **The China Collector's Pocket Companion.** With upwards of 1,000 Illustrations of Marks and Monograms. Small post 8vo., limp cloth, 5s.

"We scarcely need add that a more trustworthy and convenient handbook does not exist, and that others besides ourselves will feel grateful to Mrs. Palliser for the care and skill she has bestowed upon it."—*Academy*.

Paper Manufacture. See Hofmann.

Parsons (T.) A Treatise on the Law of Marine Insurance and General Average. By Hon. THEOPHILUS PARSONS. 2 vols. 8vo. 3l. 3s.

———— **A Treatise on the Law of Shipping.** 2 vols. 8vo. 3l. 3s.

Parisian Family. From the French of Madame GUIZOT DE WITT; by Author of "John Halifax." Fcap. 5s.

Phelps (Miss) Gates Ajar. 32mo. 6d.; 4d.

———— **Men, Women, and Ghosts.** 12mo. Sewed, 1s. 6d. cloth, 2s.

———— **Hedged In.** 12mo. Sewed, 1s. 6d.; cloth, 2s.

———— **Silent Partner.** 5s.

———— **Trotty's Wedding Tour.** Small post 8vo. 3s. 6d.

———— **What to Wear.** Foolscap 8vo., fancy boards. 1s.

Phillips (L.) Dictionary of Biographical Reference. 8vo. 1*l.* 11*s.* 6*d.*

Phillips' Law of Insurance. 5th Edition, 2 vols. 3*l.* 3*s.*

Picture Gallery of British Art (The). Twenty beautiful and Permanent Photographs after the most celebrated English Painters. With Descriptive Letterpress. One Volume, demy 4to. cloth extra, gilt edges. 12*s.*

Picture Gallery Annual. 4to. cloth extra. 18*s.*

Picture Gallery of Sacred Art (The). Containing Twenty very fine Examples in Permanent Photography after the Old Masters. With Descriptive Letterpress. Demy 4to. cloth extra, gilt edges. 12*s.*

Pike (N.) Sub-Tropical Rambles in the Land of the Aphanapteryx. In 1 vol. demy 8vo. 18*s.* Profusely Illustrated from the Author's own Sketches, also with Maps and valuable Meteorological Charts.

Pilgrimage of the Tiber. *See* **Davies (Wm.).**

Plattner's Manual of Qualitative and Quantitative Analysis with the Blow-Pipe. From the last German Edition, revised and enlarged. By Prof. TH. RICHTER, of the Royal Saxon Mining Academy. Translated by Prof. H. B. CORNWALL, Assistant in the Columbia School of Mines, New York. Illustrated with 87 Woodcuts and 1 Lithographic Plate. Second Edition, revised and reduced in price. 8vo. cloth. 31*s.* 6*d.*

Plutarch's Lives. An Entirely New and Library Edition. Edited by A. H. CLOUGH, Esq. 5 vols. 8vo. 2*l.* 10*s.*

———— **Morals.** Uniform with Clough's Edition of "Lives of Plutarch." Edited by Professor GOODWIN. 5 vols. 8vo. 3*s.*

Poe (E. A.) The Works of. 4 vols. 2*l.* 2*s.*

Poems of the Inner Life. A New Edition, Revised, with many additional Poems, inserted by permission of the Authors. Small post 8vo., cloth. 5*s.*

Polar Expedition. *See* **Koldeway.**

Poor (H. V.) Manual of the Railroads of the United States for 1874-5; Showing their Mileage, Stocks, Bonds, Cost, Earnings, Expenses, and Organisations, with a Sketch of their Rise, &c. 1 vol. 8vo. 24*s.*

Portraits of Celebrated Women. By C. A. STE.-BEUVE. 12mo. 6*s.* 6*d.*

A Practical Treatise on the Manufacture of Colours for Painting. By MM. RIFFAULT, VERGNAUD and TOUSSAINT. Revised and Edited by M. F. MALEPEYRE. Translated from the French by A. A. FESQUET. Illustrated by 85 Engravings. 8vo. 31*s.* 6*d.*

Preces Veterum. Collegit et edidit Joannes F. France. Crown 8vo., cloth, red edges. 5*s.*

Preu (M. T.) German Primer. Square cloth. 2*s.* 6*d.*

Prime (I.) Fifteen Years of Prayer. Small post 8vo., cloth. 3s. 6d.

—— **(E. D. G.) Around the World.** Sketches of Travel through Many Lands and over Many Seas. 8vo., Illustrated. 14s.

—— **(W. C.) I go a-Fishing.** Small post 8vo., cloth. 5s.

Publishers' Circular (The), and General Record of British and Foreign Literature ; giving a transcript of the title-page of every work published in Great Britain, and every work of interest published abroad, with lists of all the publishing houses.
Published regularly on the 1st and 15th of every Month, and forwarded post free to all parts of the world on payment of 8s. per annum.

Queer Things of the Service. Crown 8vo., fancy boards. 2s. 6d.

ALSTON (W. R. S.) Early Russian History. Four Lectures delivered at Oxford by W. R. S. RALSTON, M.A. Crown 8vo, cloth extra, 5s.

Rasselas, Prince of Abyssinia. By Dr. JOHNSON. With Introduction by the Rev. WILLIAM WEST, Vicar of Nairn. (Bayard Series). 2s. 6d.

Red Cross Knight (The). *See* Spenser.

Reid (W.) After the War. Crown 8vo. 10s. 6d.

Reindeer, Dogs, &c. *See* Bush.

Reminiscences of America in 1869, by Two Englishmen. Crown 8vo. 7s. 6d.

Reynard the Fox. The Prose Translation by the late THOMAS ROSCOE. With about 100 exquisite Illustrations on Wood, after designs by A. J. ELWES. Imperial 16mo. cloth extra, 7s. 6d.
"Will yield to none either in the interest of its text or excellence of its engravings."—*Standard*.
"A capital Christmas book."—*Globe*.
"The designs are an ornament of a delightful text."—*Times*, Dec. 24.

Richardson (A. S.) Stories from Old English Poetry. Small post 8vo., cloth. 5s.

Riffault (MM.) A Practical Treatise on the Manufacture of Colours for Painting. Illustrated. 31s. 6d.

Rivington's (F.) Life of St. Paul. With map. 5s.

Rochefoucauld's Reflections. Flexible cloth extra. 2s. 6d. (Bayard Series.)

Rogers (S.) Pleasures of Memory. *See* "Choice Editions
  of Choice Books." 5*s.*

Rohlfs' (Dr. G.) Adventures in Morocco and Journeys
  through the Oases of Draa and Tafilet. By Dr. GERHARD ROHLFS,
  Gold Medallist of the Royal Geographical Society. Translated from
  the German. With an Introduction by WINWOOD READE. Demy 8vo.,
  Map, and Portrait of the Author, cloth extra, 12*s.*
    "He throws, indeed, quite a flood of light on the religious, political,
  and social life of the Moors."—*Graphic.*
    "Will have great and permanent value as a repository of facts."—
  The Scotsman.
    "As an explorer of the interior of the vast African continent, Gerhard
  Rohlfs stands next to Barth and Livingstone."—*Athenæum.*

ANDEAU (J.) *See* Sea-Gull Rock.

SANTO DOMINGO, Past and Present. *See*
  Hazard.

Sauzay (A.) Marvels of Glass Making. Numerous Illustrations. Demy 8vo. 12*s.* 6*d.*

Schiller's Lay of the Bell, translated by Lord Lytton. With
  42 illustrations after Retsch. Oblong 4to. 14*s.*

School Books. *See* Classified.

School Prizes. *See* Books.

Schweinfurth (Dr. G.) The Heart of Africa; or, Three
  Years' Travels and Adventures in the Unexplored Regions of the Centre
  of Africa. By Dr. GEORG SCHWEINFURTH. Translated by ELLEN E.
  FREWER. Two volumes, 8vo., upwards of 500 pages each, with 130
  Woodcuts from Drawings made by the Author, and 2 Maps. 42*s.*
                                                    [*Second Edition.*
  N.B.—The Text is translated from the Author's Unpublished Manuscript.
  *** For long reviews of this important work, see the *Athenæum* (two
  notices), *Saturday Review, Spectator* (three notices), *Illustrated News,
  Graphic, Pictorial World, Ocean Highways, Nature, Daily News, Tele-
  graph, Standard, Globe, Echo, Pall Mall Gazette, Literary World,* &c.
  *** A pamphlet containing the principal reviews will be forwarded gratui-
  tously on application.

Sea-Gull Rock. By Jules Sandeau, of the French Academy. Translated by ROBERT BLACK, M.A. With Seventy-nine
  very beautiful Woodcuts. Royal 16mo., cloth extra, gilt edges. 7*s.* 6*d.*
    "A story more fascinating, more replete with the most rollicking
  fun, the most harrowing scenes of suspense, distress, and hair-breadth
  escapes from danger, was seldom before written, published, or read."—
  Athenæum.
    "It deserves to please the new nation of boys to whom it is presented."
  —*Times.*
    "The very best French story for children we have ever seen."—
  Standard.
    "A delightful treat."—*Illustrated London News.*
    "Admirable, full of life, pathos, and fun. . . . . It is a striking and
  attractive book."—*Guardian.*
    "This story deserves to be a great favourite with English boys as well
  as with French."—*Saturday Review.*

Sedgwick, (T.) Treatise on the Measure of Damages. 8vo. 6th Edition. 2*l.* 5*s.*

Shadow of the Rock. *See* Bickersteth.

Silent Hour (The), Essays original and selected, by the author of "The Gentle Life." Second edition. 6*s.*

Silliman (Benjamin) Life of, by G. P. FISHER. 2 vols. crown 8vo. 1*l.* 4*s.*

Simson (W.) A History of the Gipsies, with specimens of the Gipsy Language. 10*s.* 6*d.*

Smith and Hamilton's French Dictionary. 2 vols. Cloth, 21*s.* : half roan, 22*s.*

Socrates. Memoirs, from Xenophon's Memorabilia. By E. LEVIEN. Flexible cloth. 2*s.* 6*d.* Bayard Series.

Spayth (Henry) The American Draught-Player. 2nd edition. 12mo. 12*s.* 6*d.*

Spray from the Water of Elisenbrunnen. By GODFREY MAYNARD. Small Post 8vo. Fancy Boards. 2*s.* 6*d.*

St. Cecilia, a modern tale of Real Life. 3 vols. post 8vo. 31*s.* 6*d.*

Stanley (H. M.) How I Found Livingstone. Crown 8vo., cloth extra, 7*s.* 6*d.* This Edition contains all the small Illustrations, and a long Introductory Chapter on the Death of Livingstone, with a brief Memoir and Extracts from Dr. Livingstone's last Correspondence with Mr. Stanley not yet published.

*** This Edition has been revised most carefully from beginning to end, and all matters of a personal or irrelevant character omitted. N.B.—Copies of the Original Edition, cloth extra, gilt edges, may be had, 10*s.* 6*d.*

—— **"My Kalulu," Prince, King, and Slave.** A Story from Central Africa. Crown 8vo., about 430 pp., with numerous graphic Illustrations, after Original Designs by the Author. Cloth, 7*s.* 6*d.*

—— **Coomassie and Magdala :** A Story of Two British Campaigns in Africa. Demy 8vo., with Maps and Illustrations, 16*s.* Second Edition.

"His new book, telling the story of two campaigns, will be almost as welcome as that which told of the finding of Livingstone."—*Daily News.*

"We are struck throughout his volume by the shrewdness of his surmises when he is guessing in the dark, and of the frequency with which his hurried judgments are confirmed."—*Times.*

"He fairly wins admiration by the frank and yet stern eloquence of his narrative."—*Telegraph.*

"Mr. Stanley writes in a brisk and characteristic style, full of picturesqueness and vivacity. . . . We commend it as a spirited and graphic story of an expedition which reflected credit on all who took part in it."—*Standard.*

Steele (Thos.) Under the Palms. A Volume of Verse. By THOMAS STEELE, translator of "An Eastern Love Story." Fcap. 8vo. Cloth, 5*s.*

Stewart (D.) Outlines of Moral Philosophy, by Dr. McCosh. New edition. 12mo. 3*s.* 6*d.*

Stone (J. B.) A Tour with Cook Through Spain. Illustrated by Photographs. Crown 8vo., cloth. 6*s.*

Stories of the Great Prairies, from the Novels of J. F. COOPER. With numerous illustrations. 5*s.*

Stories of the Woods, from J. F. COOPER. 5*s.*

——————— Sea, from J. F. COOPER. 5*s.*

Story without an End, from the German of Carové, by the late Mrs. SARAH T. AUSTIN, crown 4to. with 15 exquisite drawings by E. V. B., printed in colours in facsimile of the original water colours, and numerous other illustrations. New edition. 7*s.* 6*d.*

—————— square, with illustrations by HARVEY. 2*s.* 6*d.*

—————— of the Great March, a Diary of General Sherman's Campaign through Georgia and the Carolinas. Numerous illustrations. 12mo. cloth, 7*s.* 6*d.*

Stowe (Mrs. Beecher). Dred. Tauchnitz edition. 12mo. 3*s.* 6*d.*

—————— Geography, with 60 illustrations. Square cloth, 4*s.* 6*d.*

—————— House and Home Papers. 12mo. boards, 1*s.* ; cloth extra, 2*s.* 6*d.*

—————— Little Foxes. Cheap edition, 1*s.* ; library edition, 4*s.* 6*d.*

—————— Men of our Times, with portrait. 8vo. 12*s.* 6*d.*

—————— Minister's Wooing. 5*s.* ; copyright series, 1*s.* 6*d.* cloth, 2*s.*

—————— Old Town Folk. 6*s.* Cheap Edition, 2*s.* 6*d.*

—————— Old Town Fireside Stories. Cloth extra. 3*s.* 6*d.*

—————— My Wife and I; or, Harry Henderson's History. Small post 8vo, cloth extra. 6*s.*
"She has made a very pleasant book."—*Guardian.*
"From the first page to the last the book is vigorous, racy, and enjoyable."—*Daily Telegraph.*

—————— Pink and White Tyranny. Small post 8vo. 3*s.* 6*d.* Cheap Edition, 1*s.* 6*d.* and 2*s.*

—————— Queer Little People. 1*s.* ; cloth, 2*s.*

—————— Religious Poems ; with illustrations. 3*s.* 6*d.*

—————— Chimney Corner. 1*s.* ; cloth, 1*s.* 6*d.*

—————— The Pearl of Orr's Island. Crown 8vo. 5*s.*

—————— Little Pussey Willow. Fcap. 2*s.*

—————— (Professor Calvin E.) The Origin and History of the Books of the New Testament, Canonical and Apocryphal. 8vo. 8*s.* 6*d.*

—————— Woman in Sacred History. Illustrated with 15 chromo-lithographs and about 200 pages of letterpress, forming one of the most elegant and attractive volumes ever published. Demy 4to. cloth extra, gilt edges, price 1*l.* 5*s.*

STORY'S (JUSTICE) WORKS:

Commentaries on the Law of Agency, as a Branch of Commercial and Maritime Jurisprudence. 8th Edition. 8vo. 1*l.* 11*s.* 6*d.*

Commentaries on the Law of Bailments. 8th Edition. 8vo. 1*l.* 11*s.* 6*d.*

Commentaries on the Law of Bills of Exchange, Foreign and Inland, as administered in England and America. 4th Edition. 8vo. 1*l.* 11*s.* 6*d.*

Commentaries on the Conflict of Laws, Foreign and Domestic, in regard to Contracts, Rights, and Remedies, and especially in regard to Marriages, Divorces, Wills, Successions, and Judgments. 7th Edition. 8vo. 1*l.* 15*s.*

Commentaries on the Constitution of the United States ; with a Preliminary Review of the Constitutional History of the Colonies and States before the adoption of the Constitution. 4th Edition. 2 vols. 8vo. 3*l.* 3*s.*

Commentaries on the Law of Partnership as a branch of Commercial and Maritime Jurisprudence. 6th Edition. by E. H. BENNETT. 8vo. 1*l.* 11*s.* 6*d.*

Commentaries on the Law of Promissory Notes, and Guarantees of Notes and Cheques on Banks and Bankers. 6th Edition ; by E. H. BENNETT. 8vo. 1*l.* 11*s.* 6*d.*

Commentaries on Equity Pleadings and the Inci-dents relating thereto, according to the Practice of the Courts of Equity of England and America. 8th Edition. 8vo. 1*l.* 11*s.* 6*d.*

Commentaries on Equity Jurisprudence as admi-nistered in England and America. 11th Edition. 3*l.* 15*s.*

Treatise on the Law of Contracts. By WILLIAM W. STORY. 4th Edition, 2 vols. 8vo. 3*l.* 3*s.*

Treatise on the Law of Sales of Personal Property. 4th Edition, edited by Hon. J. C. PERKINS. 8vo. 1*l.* 11*s.* 6*d.*

Sub-Tropical Rambles. *See* Pike (N.)

Suburban Sketches, by the Author of "Venetian Life." Post 8vo. 6*s.*

Sullivan (G. C.) Dhow Chasing in Zanzibar Waters and on the Eastern Coast of Africa ; a Narrative of Five Years' Experiences in the suppression of the Slave Trade. With Illustrations from Photographs and Sketches taken on the spot by the Author. Demy 8vo, cloth extra. 16*s.* Second Edition.

Summer in Leslie Goldthwaite's Life, by the Author of "The Gayworthys," Illustrations. Fcap. 8vo. 3*s.* 6*d.*

Sweet not Lasting. A Novel, by ANNIE B. LEFURT. 1 vol. crown 8vo., cloth. 10*s*. 6*d*.

Swiss Family Robinson, 12mo. 3*s*. 6*d*.

TAUCHNITZ'S English Editions of German Authors. Each volume cloth flexible, 2*s*. ; or sewed, 1*s*. 6*d*. The following are now ready:—

On the Heights. By B. AUERBACH. 3 vols.

In the Year '13. By FRITZ REUTER. 1 vol.

Faust. By GOETHE. 1 vol

Undine, and other Tales. By Fouqué. 1 vol

L'Arrabiata. By PAUL HEYSE. 1 vol.

The Princess, and other Tales. By HEINRICH ZSCHOKKE. 1 vol.

Lessing's Nathan the Wise.

Hacklander's Behind the Counter, translated by MARY HOWITT.

Three Tales. By W. HAUFF.

Joachim v. Kamern; Diary of a Poor Young Lady. By M. NATHUSIUS.

Poems by Ferdinand Freiligrath. Edited by his daughter.

Gabriel. From the German of PAUL HEYSE. By ARTHUR MILMAN.

The Dead Lake, and other Tales. By P. HEYSE.

Through Night to Light. By GUTZKOW.

Flower, Fruit, and Thorn Pieces. By JEAN PAUL RICHTER.

The Princess of the Moor. By Miss MARLITT.

An Egyptian Princess. By G. EBERS. 2 vols.

Ekkehard. By J. V. SCHEFFEL.

Barbarossa and other Tales. By PAUL HEYSE. From the German. By L. C. S.

Tauchnitz (B.) German and English Dictionary, Paper, 1*s*. ; cloth, 1*s*. 6*d*. ; roan, 2*s*.

———————— French and English. Paper 1*s*. 6*d*. ; cloth, 2*s*. ; roan, 2*s*. 6*d*.

———————— Italian and English. Paper, 1*s*. 6*d*. ; cloth, 2*s*.; roan, 2*s*. 6*d*.

———————— Spanish and English. Paper, 1*s*. 6*d*. ; cloth, 2*s*.; roan, 2*s*. 6*d*.

——— New Testament. Cloth, 2*s*. ; gilt, 2*s*. 6*d*. *See* New Testament.

Tayler (C. B.) Sacred Records, &c., in Verse. Fcap. 8vo, cloth extra, 2s. 6d.

Taylor (Bayard) The Byeways of Europe; Visits by Unfrequented Routes to Remarkable Places. By BAYARD TAYLOR, author of "Views Afoot." 2 vols. post 8vo. 16s.

———— **Story of Kennett.** 2 vols. 16s.

———— **Hannah Thurston.** 3 vols. 1l. 4s.

———— **Travels in Greece and Russia.** Post 8vo. 7s. 6d.

———— **Northern Europe.** Post 8vo. Cloth, 8s. 6d.

———— **Egypt and Central Africa.**

———— **Beauty and the Beast.** Crown 8vo. 10s. 6d.

———— **A Summer in Colorado.** Post 8vo. 7s. 6d.

———— **Joseph and his Friend.** Post 8vo. 10s. 6d.

———— **Views Afoot.** Enamelled boards, 1s. 6d.; cloth, 2s. *See* Low's Copyright Edition.

Tennyson's May Queen; choicely Illustrated from designs by the Hon. Mrs. BOYLE. Crown 8vo. *See* Choice Series. 5s.

Thomson (J.) *See* Illustrations of China.

Thomson (Stephen). *See* Chefs-d'Œuvre of Art.

Thomson (W. M.) The Land and the Book. With 300 Illustrations. 2 vols. 1l. 1s.

Threshold of the Unknown Region. *See* Markham.

Timothy Titcomb's Letters to Young People, Single and Married. (Low's American Series). Vol. xxi. 1s. 6d. boards; 2s. cloth.

Tinne (J. E.) The Wonderland of the Antipodes: Sketches of Travel in the North Island of New Zealand. Illustrated with numerous Photographs. Demy 8vo., cloth extra. 16s.

Tischendorf (Dr.) The New Testament. *See* New Testament.

Tolhausen (A.) The Technological Dictionary in the French, English, and German Languages. Containing the Technical Terms used in the Arts, Manufactures, and Industrial Affairs generally. Revised and Augmented by M. Louis Tolhausen, French Consul at Leipzig. This Work will be completed in Three Parts.
The First Part, containing French-German-English, crown 8vo. 2 vols. sewed, 8s.; 1 vol. half roan, 9s.
The Second Part, containing English-German-French, crown 8vo. 2 vols. sewed, 8s.; 1 vol. bound, 9s.
A Third Part, containing German-English-French, is also in preparation.
*** The First Half of Part I. sewed. 4s.

Townsend (John) A Treatise on the Wrongs called
Slander and Libel, and on the remedy, by civil action, for these
wrongs. 8vo. Second Edition. 1*l.* 10*s.*

Tuckermann (C. K.) The Greeks of To-day.   Crown 8vo.
cloth. 7*s.* 6*d.*

Twenty Thousand Leagues Under the Sea.   *See* Verne.

Twenty Years Ago. (Forming Volume 3 of the John Halifax
Series of Girls' Books).   Small post 8vo.   4*s.*

Twining (Miss) Illustrations of the Natural Orders of
Plants, with Groups and Descriptions. By ELIZABETH TWINING.
Reduced from the folio edition, splendidly illustrated in colours from
nature. 2 vols. Royal 8vo. 5*l.* 5*s.*

Under Seal of Confession.   By AVERIL BEAUMONT,
Author of "Thornicroft's Model." 3 vols. crown 8vo., cloth. 31*s.* 6*d.*

Unprofessional Vagabond.   *See* Carlisle (T.)

ANDENHOFF'S (George), Clerical Assistant.
Fcap. 3*s.* 6*d.*

———— **Ladies' Reader (The). Fcap. 5*s.***

Varia ; Rare Readings from Scarce Books, by the author of
"The Gentle Life." Reprinted by permission from the "Saturday Review," "Spectator," &c. 6*s.*

Vaux (Calvert). Villas and Cottages, a new edition, with
300 designs. 8vo. 15*s.*

VERNE'S (JULES) WORKS.

Five Weeks in a Balloon. New Edition: Numerous
Illustrations, printed on Toned Paper, and uniformly with "Around
the World," &c. Square crown 8vo. 7*s.* 6*d.*

Meridiana : Adventures of Three Englishmen and
Three Russians in South Africa. Translated from the French.
With Numerous Illustrations. Royal 16mo., cloth extra, gilt
edges. 7*s.* 6*d.*

The Fur Country. Crown 8vo. With upwards of 80
Illustrations. Cloth extra. 10*s.* 6*d.*

Twenty Thousand Leagues Under the Sea. Trans-
lated and Edited by the Rev. L. P. MERCIER, M.A. With 113
very Graphic Woodcuts. Large post 8vo., cloth extra, gilt edges.
10*s.* 6*d.*

Around the World in Eighty Days. Numerous Illus-
trations. Square crown 8vo. 7*s.* 6*d.*

From the Earth to the Moon, and a Trip Round It.
Numerous Illustrations. Crown 8vo., cloth, gilt edges. 10*s.* 6*d.*
New Edition.

A Floating City and the Blockade Runners. Con-
taining about 50 very fine Full-page Illustrations. Square crown
8vo. Cloth, gilt edges. 7*s.* 6*d.*

Very Far West Indeed. *See* Johnson.

Viardot (L.) Wonders of Italian Art, numerous photographic and other illustrations. Demy 8vo. 12*s.* 6*d.*

———— Wonders of Painting, numerous photographs and other illustrations. Demy 8vo. 12*s.* 6*d.*

———— Wonders of Sculpture. Numerous Illustrations. Demy 8vo. 12*s.* 6*d.*

Vincent (F.) The Land of the White Elephant : Sights and Scenes in South-Eastern Asia. A Personal Narrative of Travel and Adventure in Farther India, embracing the countries of Burmah, Siam, Cambodia, and Cochin China, 1871-2. With Maps, Plans, and numerous Illustrations. 8vo. cloth extra. 18*s.*

AKE ROBIN ; a Book about Birds, by JOHN BURROUGHS. Crown 8vo. 5*s.*

Warner (C. D.) My Summer in a Garden. Boards, 1*s.* 6*d.* ; cloth, 2*s.* (Low's Copyright Series.)

———— Back-log Studies. Boards 1*s.* 6*d.*; cloth 2*s.* (Low's Copyright Series.)

We Girls. *See* Whitney.

Webster (Daniel) Life of, by GEO. T. CURTIS. 2 vols. 8vo. Cloth. 36*s.*

Werner (Carl), Nile Sketches, Painted from Nature during his travels through 'Egypt. Facsimiles of Water-colour Paintings executed by GUSTAV W. SEITZ; with Descriptive Text by Dr. E. A. BREHM and Dr. DUMICHEN. Imperial folio, in Cardboard Wrapper. 3*l.* 10*s.*

Three Series, each £3 10*s.*

Westminster Abbey and Palace. 40 Photographic Views with Letterpress, dedicated to Dean Stanley. 4to. Morocco extra, £5 5*s.*

Wheaton (Henry) Elements of International Law. New edition. *[In the press.*

When George the Third was King. 2 vols., post 8vo. 21*s.*

Where is the City ? 12mo. cloth. 6*s*

White (J.) Sketches from America. 8vo. 12*s.*

White (R. G.) Memoirs of the Life of William Shake-speare. Post 8vo. Cloth. 10s. 6d.

Whitney (Mrs. A. D. T.), The Gayworthys. Small post 8vo. 3s. 6d.

—— **Faith Gartney.** Small post 8vo. 3s. 6d. And in Low's Cheap Series, 1s. 6d. and 2s.

—— **Hitherto.** Small post 8vo. 3s. 6d. and 2s. 6d.

—— **Summer in Leslie Goldthwaite's Life.** Small post 8vo. 3s. 6d.

—— **The Other Girls.** Small post 8vo., cloth extra. 3s. 6d.

—— **We Girls.** Small post 8vo. 3s. 6d. Cheap Edition 1s. 6d. and 2s.

Whyte (J. W. H.) A Land Journey from Asia to Europe. Crown 8vo. 12s.

Wills, A Few Hints on Proving, without Professional Assistance. By a PROBATE COURT OFFICIAL. Fourth Edition, revised and considerably enlarged, with Forms of Wills, Residuary Accounts, &c. Fcap. 8vo, cloth limp. 1s.

Winter at the Italian Lakes. With Frontispiece View of Lake Como. Small post 8vo., cloth extra. 7s. 6d.

Woman's (A) Faith. A Novel. By the Author of " Ethel." 3 vols. Post 8vo. 31s. 6d.

Wonders of Sculpture. *See* Viardot.

Worcester's (Dr.), New and Greatly Enlarged Dictionary of the English Language. Adapted for Library or College Reference, comprising 40,000 Words more than Johnson's Dictionary. 4to. cloth, 1,834 pp. Price 31s. 6d. well bound ; ditto, half mor. 2l. 2s.

" The volumes before us show a vast amount of diligence ; but with Webster it is diligence in combination with fancifulness,—with Worcester in combination with good sense and judgment. Worcester's is the soberer and safer book, and may be pronounced the best existing English Lexicon."—*Athenæum.*

Words of Wellington, Maxims and Opinions, Sentences and Reflections of the Great Duke, gathered from his Despatches, Letters, and Speeches (Bayard Series). 2s. 6d.

Young (L.) Acts of Gallantry; giving a detail of every act for which the Silver Medal of the Royal Humane Society has been granted during the last Forty-one years. Crown 8vo., cloth. 7s. 6d.

CHISWICK PRESS :— PRINTED BY WHITTINGHAM AND WILKINS, TOOKS COURT, CHANCERY LANE.